Just Representations
A JAMES GOULD COZZENS READER

Just Representations
A
JAMES GOULD COZZENS
READER
Edited and with an Introduction
by Matthew J. Bruccoli

Southern Illinois University Press
CARBONDALE AND EDWARDSVILLE
and
Harcourt Brace Jovanovich
NEW YORK AND LONDON

Library of Congress Cataloging in Publication Data

Cozzens, James Gould, 1903–
    Just representations.
    I. Bruccoli, Matthew Joseph, 1931–
II. Title.
PS3505.099A6   1978   813'.5'2   78-9357
ISBN 0-8093-0886-X
ISBN 0-15-646611-2 (pbk.)

First edition
A   B   C   D   E   F   G   H   I   J

For Bernice Baumgarten
30 January 1978
J.G.C.
W.J.
M.J.B.

Nothing can please many, and please long, but just representations of general nature. Particular manners can be known to few, and therefore few only can judge how nearly they are copied. The irregular combinations of fanciful invention may delight a while, by that novelty of which the common satiety of life sends us all in quest; but the pleasures of sudden wonder are soon exhausted, and the mind can only repose on the stability of truth.

SAMUEL JOHNSON

Contents

VI

VII

VIII

IX

X

Introduction
By Matthew J. Bruccoli

James Gould Cozzens, the only child of Henry William and Bertha Wood Cozzens, was born on 19 August 1903. Reference books correctly note his birthplace as Chicago with the suggestion that he was a native son, but "the matter was of pure peradventure." Thirty-five years passed before Cozzens, to his conscious knowledge, saw Chicago. His father's family had settled in Newport, Rhode Island, in the seventeenth century; his mother's people were Connecticut Tories who went to Nova Scotia at the time of the Revolution. In 1906 Henry William Cozzens became an executive with a New York manufacturer of typesetting machines and moved his family to Staten Island, where Newport cousins of his had long been settled. Cozzens showed early ability as a writer, which his mother encouraged; but his father did not regard writing as a serious occupation. "At about the age of ten I decided definitely that I was going to be a writer, I imagine because I got praise and high marks in 'composition,' which I found no work at all, while most other school subjects were hard and uninteresting."[1] In 1915 Cozzens achieved his first appearance in print with "The Andes," a poem in the Staten Island Academy *Quill*.

Cozzens entered Kent, a Connecticut Episcopal Preparatory School, in 1916. Then hardly aware of it, Cozzens in retrospect recognizes the lasting influence on him of Kent's headmaster, Father Frederick Herbert Sill: "If there's work to be done and I get out of it, I feel extremely guilty. That's the attitude 'Pater' inculcated in us."[2] An uneven student (he had trouble with mathematics), Cozzens became something of an intellectual rebel at Kent; however, his first professional publication, "A Democratic School," in the March 1920 *Atlantic Monthly*, was a rejoinder to criticism of preparatory schools. In his sixth-form year Cozzens was editor of *The Kent Quarterly*.

Cozzens entered Harvard in 1922 and began writing a novel during his freshman year—at the same time that his fiction, verse, and reviews were appearing in *The Harvard Advocate*. At college his literary ambitions were

1. *Current Biography 1949*, ed. Anna Rothe (New York: Wilson, 1950), p. 125.
2. "The Hermit of Lambertville," *Time*, 70 (2 September 1957), 74.

encouraged by poet Robert Hillyer, a faculty member and Kent alumnus. *Confusion*, Cozzens's first novel, was published in Boston by B. J. Brimmer in February 1924. The nineteen-year-old sophomore became a local celebrity, attracting the attention of Lucius Beebe, then a Boston reporter, who pressed him to grant interviews and give readings. This experience ended Cozzens's interest in personal publicity. *Confusion* chronicles the brief life of Cerise D'Atree, a young French aristocrat whose elaborate education makes her superior to her society in America and unfulfilled by the opportunities it offers. Though over-written and perhaps pretentious, *Confusion* introduced the search for values or standards of conduct that would characterize all of Cozzens's work. At this time he announced that he was planning two novels, "Ignorant Armies" and "Cloud Trophy"—which were not published. In class-cutting academic difficulties, Cozzens took a leave of absence from Harvard in 1924 and never returned.

   Michael Scarlett was written in Nova Scotia during 1924–25 on a small advance from Brimmer. In 1925 Cozzens also edited *The Criticisms of John Keats on English Poetry* for Brimmer, but the firm went out of business before either work was published. Albert and Charles Boni published the novel in November 1925. His only historical novel, *Michael Scarlett* is set in the England of Elizabeth I—with a cast of characters that includes Shakespeare, Marlowe, Jonson, Nashe, and Donne. The hero, a young nobleman, is destroyed by the withholding of responsibilities commensurate with his training. *Michael Scarlett* showed what would be the mark of Cozzens's fiction: his ability to treat a subject with authority, for the novel manifests a knowledge of Elizabethan literature and society remarkable in a twenty-two-year-old Harvard drop-out.

   During 1925–26 Cozzens tutored the children of American employees at the Czarnikow-Rionda Central Tuinucu sugar mill in Santa Clara Province, Cuba, where he absorbed the material for his next two novels. The following year he travelled in Europe tutoring an American boy. Cozzens returned to America in 1927 and was librarian at the New York Athletic Club in the fall and winter of that year. On 31 December 1927 he married in New York literary agent Bernice Baumgarten, who was with Brandt & Kirkpatrick (later Brandt & Brandt). She continued her work, with her husband as one of her clients. The Cozzenses had no children.

   Cozzens's third novel, *Cock Pit*, was published by Morrow in September 1928. The heroine is an American girl who defeats the schemes of a Cuban sugar tycoon—which include murdering her father. Cozzens's first three novels developed superior young figures who need an occupation worthy of their abilities; however, *Cock Pit* was the first novel in which he used material he knew from experience and observation. It established what became the most notable quality of his major fiction: the authentic presentation of a profession and the society associated with it. This authenticity is something more than accuracy or realism. When Cozzens learned something, he really learned it and was able to use the information without appearing to be writing from research.

After three novels in which rebellious figures were treated sympathetically, Cozzens created a character who embodies disorder and destruction. Published by Morrow in August 1929, *The Son of Perdition* marked the end of Cozzens's apprenticeship in terms of his attitudes towards his characters. The novel examines the effect of an American drifter on a Cuban sugar-mill community. Oliver Findley, the outcast agent of disorder, cannot be redeemed, and society cannot accommodate him. *Son of Perdition* shows the need to impose at least the effect of stability on society, although Cozzens fully acknowledges the power of chance.

S.S. San Pedro is the first of his books that Cozzens now regards worth claiming. Planned as a longer work, it appeared in the 1930 *Scribner's Magazine* short novel competition and was published by Harcourt, Brace in August 1931. (With the exception of *Castaway*, the rest of Cozzens's trade books were published by Harcourt, Brace or Harcourt, Brace & World.) Based on the *Vestris* disaster, *S.S. San Pedro* details the unaccountable sinking of a ship; but the real subject of the novelette is the dissolution of authority. The captain, a sick man, cannot act; and none of the officers is willing to assume the captain's responsibility.

The Last Adam, published in January 1933, was the first of Cozzens's major "professional" novels, which examine a character in terms of his profession and its effect on his community. Set in the Kent area, it deals with a typhoid epidemic in a small Connecticut town. Dr. George Bull is a transitional figure in the development of the Cozzens hero. An old rebel against conventional behavior and a careless doctor, Bull is nonetheless a necessary member of the community—both an establishment figure and an outsider. *The Last Adam* is not a sentimental country-doctor novel. Indifferent to his patients, contemptuous of his townsmen, and in some ways incompetent, Dr. Bull nonetheless embodies the vitality of life. *The Last Adam* sold ten thousand copies in ten days after publication and was Cozzens's first Book-of-the-Month Club selection; it was also converted into a Will Rogers movie as *Dr. Bull*.

In 1933 the Cozzenses moved to a farm near Lambertville, New Jersey, at the Pennsylvania-New Jersey border, where he became increasingly inaccessible. He did not make public appearances, sign manifestoes, join committees, provide blurbs, or participate in what is supposed to be the literary life. During the depression he did not embrace proletarian causes. He stayed home and wrote. His hobby was gardening, especially growing roses; and he collected popular recordings from the Twenties. Cozzens developed a scholarly interest in Anglican and Roman Catholic theology; but his religious beliefs he thinks are best summarized in Somerset

Maugham's pronouncement that all sensible men are of the same religion though no sensible man ever says what it is. In a rare personal statement Cozzens has said:

> My social preference is to be left alone, and people have always seemed willing, even eager to gratify my inclination. I am more or less illiberal, and strongly antipathetic to all political and artistic movements. I was brought up an Episcopalian, and where I live the landed gentry are Republican. I do not understand music, I am little interested in art, and the theatre seems tiresome to me. My literary preferences are for writers who take the trouble to write well. This necessarily excludes some of my most lauded contemporaries and I think I would do well to skip the presumptuous business of listing the three or four who strike me as good. I like Shakespeare and Swift and Steele and Gibbon and Jane Austen and Hazlitt.[3]

Castaway, a novelette published by Random House in November 1934, is a sport in the Cozzens canon. His only allegorical work, it is admired by critics who resist the rest of Cozzens. A reversal of *Robinson Crusoe*, *Castaway* shows a man who is unable to survive alone in the abundance of a modern department store. The meanings of *Castaway* are not political. Cozzens's subject is the inadequacy of the modern individual and the deterioration of character.

During the Twenties and Thirties Cozzens sold twenty-four short stories to mass-circulation magazines such as *The Saturday Evening Post*, *Woman's Home Companion*, *Collier's*, *Atlantic*, *Scribner's*, *Redbook*, and *American*. (Two more stories—"One Hundred Ladies" and "*Candida* by Bernard Shaw"—were published in *The Saturday Evening Post* in 1964.) He has remarked that he stopped writing short stories when he no longer needed the money they brought, but his dismissal does not do them justice. "Farewell to Cuba," "The Way to Go Home," "Every Day's a Holiday," and "Total Stranger" are excellent. "Total Stranger" won the O. Henry Memorial Award for the best story of 1936, and "Farewell to Cuba" took the second prize in 1931. A series of stories about the Durham School—based on Kent—developed Cozzens's thinking about youth and experience. One of the recognitions in his later novels is that "youth's a kind of infirmity."[4]

Men and Brethren, published in January 1936, is the first full portrait of what can now be recognized as the Cozzens hero—the man of experience, education, and responsibility who serves his community and profession as a matter of duty. Ernest Cudlipp, an Episcopal priest who is vicar of a parish chapel in a New York slum, is the best depiction of a clergyman in American literature. *Men and Brethren* is significant in Cozzens's development toward tightly structured novels in which a multiplicity of events impinge

3. *Twentieth Century Authors*, ed. Stanley J. Kunitz and Howard Haycraft (New York: Wilson, 1942), p. 323.
4. *By Love Possessed* (New York: Harcourt, Brace, 1957), p. 6.

on the central character in a period of two or three days. The controlling point of view is Cudlipp's, and everything in the novel is filtered through his intelligence.

After *Men and Brethren* Cozzens began assembling material for a Civil War novel about the Army of the Potomac, but "was much disappointed to see it worn out as a book subject before I was ready to write it."[5] He would later reject this explanation: "Actually, I couldn't write it for a simpler reason: I wasn't there: I never saw it for myself."[6] In 1936 he commented, "I have no theories about literature and other people's irk me. With great difficulty and uncertainty and much lost motion I write whatever I find that I can. The view I have of writing is that a writer does well to write in a clear and unobtrusive way, trying not to be dull, and being careful to avoid obvious untruths and general nonsense."[7] At the urging of *Fortune* editor Russell Davenport, Cozzens tried out Henry Luce's plan of "interim" guest-editorships by established novelists, abandoning his seclusion in 1938 to work on the magazine for a year.[8] "Russell and Henry made the experience agreeable, but the finding was (as none of us could deny) that I'd never make a journalist."[9]

Ask Me Tomorrow, published in June 1940, interrupted the cycle of professional novels and is uncharacteristically personal, drawing on Cozzens's experiences as a tutor in Europe. This portrait of the writer as a young man is ironic and even satirical, for the tutor himself undergoes an educational process as he recognizes his vanities and learns to temper his pride. At the time *Ask Me Tomorrow* was published, Cozzens acknowledged that he was still learning his craft, noting his great difficulty in using language precisely and his distrust of rapid writing in which meanings "at least in my own case can be no more than barely approximated."[10]

The Just and the Unjust—Cozzens's most successful novel to that time in terms of reviews and sales—appeared in July 1942. The background is a murder trial in a small community in the northeast, during the course of which Abner Coates, an idealistic and naïve lawyer, comes to accept the realities of his profession—which are the realities of his life. The theme of the novel is limitations—a basic Cozzens theme: the limitations of the law as well as the limitations of human nature. *The Just and the Unjust* has been frequently called the most authentic American novel about the legal profession.

5. Fred B. Millett, *Contemporary American Authors* (New York: Harcourt, Brace, 1940), p. 304.
6. Letter to Matthew J. Bruccoli, 28 June 1977.
7. Millett, p. 304.
8. Most of Cozzens's *Fortune* articles underwent editorial rewriting, but "The Fuller Brush Co." (October 1938) appeared substantially as he wrote it.
9. Letter to Bruccoli, 28 June 1977.
10. Robert Van Gelder, "James Gould Cozzens at Work," *New York Times Book Review* (23 June 1940), 14.

In 1942—at thirty-nine—Cozzens joined the Air Force in the Training Aids Division, serving at the School of Applied Tactics in Orlando and briefly in New York City. By order of General H. H. Arnold he was reassigned to the Hq. AAF Pentagon staff and spent the last years of the war in various classified assignments. He was discharged with the rank of major in 1945. While serving with the Air Force Cozzens accepted election to the National Institute of Arts and Letters.

Guard of Honor, published in September 1948, is the best American novel of World War II and is generally regarded as Cozzens's finest achievement. It is a war novel that does not depict battle or heroics. Set at a Florida airbase, it examines the three-day proving of a young general in dealing with a problem of racial discrimination. The guiding intelligence in the novel, though, is an older man who is a judge in civilian life. Complexly structured, *Guard of Honor* shows the full development of Cozzens's concern with "the dramatic inner meaning that lies in the simultaneous occurrence of diverse things."[11] As he later wrote, "Whatever happens, happens because a lot of other things have happened already."[12] Although it won the Pulitzer Prize in 1949, the novel did not attract a large readership. Harvard awarded Cozzens an honorary Litt. D. in 1952.

Reacting to the reception of *Guard of Honor*, Bernard DeVoto wrote in 1949 that critics avoid Cozzens because his novels are so carefully written that "they leave criticism practically nothing to do."

> They contain no fog of confused thinking on which, as on a screen, criticism can project its diagrams of meanings which the novelist did not know were there. There is in them no mass of unshaped emotion, the novelist's emotion or the characters', from which criticism can dredge up significance that becomes portentous as the critic calls our attention, and the novelist's, to it. Worse still, they are written with such justness that criticism cannot get a toehold to tell him and us how they should have been written. Worst of all, the novelist's ego has been disciplined out of them, so criticism cannot chant its dirge about the dilemmas of the artist in our time. . . . He is not a literary man, he is a writer. There are a handful like him in every age. Later on it turns out that they were the ones who wrote that age's literature.[13]

By Love Possessed, Cozzens's twelfth novel, was published after a nine-year interval in August 1957. This novel covers forty-nine hours in the life of Arthur Winner, Jr., a middle-aged lawyer in an old community in the Pennsylvania-New Jersey region. Like all of Cozzens's canonical novels, *By Love Possessed* is unsentimental—really antisentimental—in its assessment of emotional responses to life. Even the most reasoning characters in this novel are love-motivated. The strongest lover in the novel is, para-

11. *Ask Me Tomorrow* (New York: Harcourt, Brace & World, 1940), p. 150.
12. *By Love Possessed*, p. 118.
13. "The Easy Chair," *Harper's Magazine*, 98 (February 1949), 72–73.

doxically, Winner's caustically rational partner, Julius Penrose, who scornfully dismissed the "rabble of professional friends of man, social-worker liberals, and practitioners of universal brotherhood—the whole national horde of nuts and queers."[14] While showing that reason and ripeness of experience are the surest guides for conduct, Cozzens recognizes that the over-riding factor in life is chance: "Always remember, son, to provide for the thing you think can't happen; because that's going to be what does happen."[15] That *By Love Possessed* dissects the limitations of reason while arraigning the follies of passion was not always perceived. Indeed, many of the misapprehensions about Cozzens's novels result from readers' inability to apprehend irony on the level he practices it—what Cozzens has called "the dangers and failures of irony." *By Love Possessed* is Cozzens's most thorough examination of moral complexity—not moral ambiguity. The epigraph to *The Just and the Unjust*—"Certainty is the Mother of Repose; therefore the Law aims at Certainty"—echoes through Cozzens's later work as it is shown that there are no certainties. At best there are choices in which emotion, experience, and imperfect reason respond to circumstances determined by chance and by what has already happened. Learning to recognize his limitations, the Cozzens hero makes his moral choices and does his best to maintain the stability of his world.

    By Love Possessed was a best-seller (*The Reader's Digest* bought condensation rights, and the movie rights went for the then-considerable price of $250,000), bringing him unsought notoriety. At the request of his friend Henry Luce he agreed to cooperate for a *Time* cover story, which he did not take the trouble to check, and "sees only himself to blame for the errors and misquotations which set out opinions not in his words and not in his meaning."[16] The *Time* article did include one accurate and "fairly to be called key Cozzens statement": "I have no thesis except that people get a very raw deal from life. To me, life is what life is."[17] The initial reception of *By Love Possessed* was strongly favorable. John Fischer, the editor of *Harper's*, wrote in "Nomination for a Nobel Prize": "If your great-grandchild should ever want to find out how Americans behaved and thought and felt in the mid-years of this century, Cozzens' major novels probably would be his most revealing source."[18] There was a prompt attack from critics who deplored Cozzens's social presentation. He was charged with bigotry and branded a reactionary. The popularity of *By Love Possessed* was attributed to its appeal to the complacency of the Eisenhower years. Cozzens did not debate with his detractors; but in a later reply to a questionnaire from *Contemporary Au-*

---

14. *By Love Possessed*, p. 217.
15. *By Love Possessed*, p. 536.
16. Letter to Bruccoli, 28 June 1977.
17. *Time*, 78.
18. *Harper's Magazine*, 215 (September 1957), 20.

thors he permitted himself a comment on the indictment that he not only defends the status quo but eagerly asserts his approval of it: "This is just plain crap. I don't defend anything. I don't eagerly assert anything."[19] The style of *By Love Possessed*, which is more elaborate than that of his previous novels, was parodied and ridiculed by critics who regarded it as a self-indulgence or involuntary aberration rather than as controlled technique to achieve precision of statement. In 1960 *By Love Possessed* received the William Dean Howells Medal for fiction, which is awarded every five years by the American Academy of Arts and Letters.

The Cozzenses moved from Lambertville to Williamstown, Massachusetts in 1958. *Children and Others*, his only volume of short stories, published in July 1964, assembled the seventeen stories that Cozzens regarded as worth preserving. *Morning Noon and Night*, Cozzens's latest novel, published in August 1968, had a poor reception. Reviewers were disrespectful, and some of Cozzens's admirers demonstrated remarkable opacity in "missing points no matter how clearly phrased and in misreading meanings one might think hard to mistake."[20] It is the Cozzens novel that most merits reappraisal. Less tightly structured than his other major novels, *Morning Noon and Night* is Cozzens's only first-person novel. The narrator, Henry Worthington, ruminates on his career as a highly successful business consultant and admits that luck has been the chief factor in his life. The characteristic Cozzens conclusion in this novel with its clear valedictory note of summation is that while recognizing the over-riding factor of chance, the responsible man acts responsibly. The subject of *Morning Noon and Night* is vocation, which is the dominant subject in Cozzens. Throughout his career Cozzens has been concerned with the interconnections between character and occupation. As Worthington explains, "what a man spends his time doing is what he is, and through what he is he sees things as he sees them."[21] In 1973 the Cozzenses moved to Stuart, Florida, where Bernice Cozzens died in January 1978.

II

James Gould Cozzens is the least-read and least-taught of the major American novelists. It cannot be said that his work has suffered from inadequate exposure; but not even six Book-of-the-Month Club selections have attracted a broad readership.[22] Except for *By Love Possessed*, no Cozzens

19. *Contemporary Authors*, 9–12 (Detroit: Gale, 1974), pp. 193–94.
20. Letter to Bruccoli, 28 June 1977.
21. *Morning Noon and Night* (New York:Harcourt, Brace & World, 1968), p. 38.
22. *The Last Adam*, *The Just and the Unjust*, *Guard of Honor*, *By Love Possessed*, *Children and Others*, *Morning Noon and Night*. The total hardcover sale for Cozzens's novels before *By Love Possessed* has been estimated at 140,000 copies.

novel has had a substantial mass-market paperback sale; and none has become a college classroom standard text. Although he has staunch admirers, one of the master American novelists is in some ways a cult-author. The resistance to Cozzens's work has been blamed on his refusal to make concessions to inattentive or unintelligent readers. Yet he is not difficult to read. His prose is precise; his meanings are clear; and, before *By Love Possessed*, his style is unembellished. The increasing dignity of style enforces Cozzens's objectivity. The "coldness" that critics have cited in Cozzens's observation of his characters is the stoical detachment of a writer trying to achieve "the stability of truth" in dealing with profound matters of human conduct. The periodic sentences and heavy subordination of *By Love Possessed* and *Morning Noon and Night* can intimidate only those who have not mastered the structure of the English sentence. The by-no-means overwhelming use of uncommon words achieves exactness of statement. Such words are intended to fix the reader's attention and, if necessary, send him to a dictionary. Cozzens's developed style is the natural expression for a highly literate writer with a traditionalist's respect for language. The complexity of sentence structure is appropriate to the complexity of his thinking. His use of open or concealed literary allusion in *Guard of Honor*, *By Love Possessed*, and *Morning Noon and Night* does not exclude the much-cherished general reader. The allusions are there for readers who recognize them; but the meanings of the books do not depend on that recognition. Cozzens is not a mandarin author; his work is far more accessible than that of many novelists currently in critical favor. He does not, in fact, make extraordinary demands on readers—beyond requiring them to pay attention.

The concept of vocation is central to Cozzens's representations of general nature, but he fully credits the determining factors in human conduct —education, social position, intelligence, training, luck, and what used to be called "character." The mark of Cozzens's people is that their values and behavior are developed in terms of their professions. You are what you do and how well you do it. This recognition may partly account for the denigration of his work among humanists who hold the job of teaching literature. Believing that success is a sign of corruption, they endeavor to persuade students that the real business of life is to live in accordance with one's feelings. Cozzens alarms proponents of the higher failure.

Cozzens has been called a conservative, an aristocrat, and a classicist. He rejects all of these identifications, insisting that he tries only to render life and people accurately as he sees them. He respects intelligence, moral firmness, and self-discipline. He rejects emotions as guides for conduct while recognizing the force of "Man's incurable wish to believe what he preferred to believe."[23] If it is too strong to attribute Johnsonian subordi-

23. *By Love Possessed*, p. 204.

nation to him, it is clear that Cozzens believes that responsibility will be
assumed by those whose natural ability and training qualify them for it. He
recognizes that some people will prove themselves abler than others and
sees no reason to aggrandize fools or to sentimentalize vice. That the ablest
people are often the ones who have had the advantages that go with money
or position is a fact that Cozzens neither bewails nor conceals. His conclusion that advantages entail responsibility—not guilt—offends egalitarian-
minded critics.

It is risky to categorize a writer who insists that "to me, life is what life
is." Nonetheless, *Morning Noon and Night* indicates that Cozzens would not
reject the claim that his view of human conduct is compatible with New
England Puritanism:

> In the Puritan tradition, what you took yourself to be superior to was not com-
> mon man as common man. What you looked down on were personal qualities or
> practices bad by your standards, not on any human being. . . . Individuals who
> exhibited those qualities or indulged in such practices were necessarily held low;
> yet your own not exhibiting them or not indulging in them never exalted you.
> You did little more than meet ordinary obligations (or, as at best the case must
> be, you met many of them much of the time) and from *that* you took no title to
> glory, laud, and honor. Indeed, in your justifiable looking-down-on, say, the
> feckless or the fornicators, you were obligated under the code to pause and
> earnestly pronounce: *There but for the Grace of God, go I.*[24]

An unfashionable doctrine. But Cozzens has scorned literary fashions and
literary politics for fifty-four years. He has declined to accommodate temporary concepts of relevance. He has refused to play the game of literary
success—"writing only to say as precisely as he can what by standards of
his own he judged worth saying."[25] At present his work is disparaged or
ignored by custodians of literary reputations. Weighing their standards,
Cozzens must assuredly want it no other way. If there is truth in the comforting promise that justice will be done to masterpieces, the novels of
James Gould Cozzens have a safe place of proper stature among the sound
achievements in American literature.

III

Just Representations: A James Gould Cozzens Reader has been planned as
an introduction for new readers of his works and an omnibus for the initi-
ated. It provides a complete novel, *Ask Me Tomorrow*—which was recommended by Mr. Cozzens—and excerpts from all of his post-apprenticeship
novels. Three short stories representing his work in the thirties and sixties

24. *Morning Noon and Night*, pp. 41–42.
25. Letter to Bruccoli, 28 June 1977.

are included. There are six previously uncollected essays by Cozzens—four of which (with the *fact* letter) form an autobiographical section for this private author. Of the six reviews and essays about Cozzens's work, those by George Garrett, Noel Perrin, and Frederick Bracher are published for the first time. These essays do not focus on a single novel, but address themselves to aspects of his craft. The selections from Cozzens's writings were made by the editor, with the author's consent.

Some Putative Facts of Hard Record
or He Commences Authour Aetatis Suae 19–20
Excerpts from 1923 MS Diary and a Few Notes
By James Gould Cozzens

AN INFORMAL APOLOGY
A Letter to Matthew J. Bruccoli

Dear Matt:

Herewith the help, and small I'm afraid it is, that I thought I *might* be able to give you, the material we discussed in connection with the 'bio' sketch and the few facts of record available anywhere—the how, when, where (and, possibly, why) of the first novel publication by which I came, in Doctor Johnson's phrase—just, if there ever was one—to commence Authour. I knew, as I said, that I was suffering at the time from the youthful selfconsciousness of keeping diaries. Whether, as the wisest course must surely be, I had, coming to grow up, destroyed them I wasn't certain. If anywhere they'd be packed away in the Princeton Library papers. I can't deny that, asking for a check of the many-page contents listing I'd not have minded if the report came negative. When it came: *Item: Ms Notebook Diary 1923*, my feelings could only be called mixed. When the text was made available and I got the long-ago writing deciphered, they were worse than that; they were closer to qualmish, an is-you-is-or-is-you-aint distress. We can put this point of toss-up behind, since, here evident, the fall the passage shown you and what comes after can matter a lot. I find I'll have to leave it so. I know I can't face, and neither you nor any reader ought to have to face, what is here page after crammed page of 'context,' the flow of juvenilia characterized by the too-kind poet as "long, long thoughts." Yes, the help is small but I can hope for the digging out lie some of the missing facts of how, when, where.

Remaining is that possible 'why.' No excerpted passages seem to mention it, but rereading them makes me feel (or fear?) the facts of *that* are also present, to the discerning more discernible than the young writer could have imagined. This youth commences author—for what? He labors long and hard—his chase had what beast in view? Let me elect to be as cryptic as I can. I call Doctor Johnson again. From Boswell we have it that the Doctor once observed: *No man but a blockhead ever wrote except for money*. When I read the line, about the time those diary pages were written, I put a quick check against it. No, I decided; I must dissent. Take my own case. Fond of money as the next person I assuredly was, but out of indolence and impracticality *I* had no will to do hard work for it.

Then consider those published, often well-known writers from Dickens down who wrote with more in mind than a payoff of frivolous entertainment. Though not in the present numbers of today's non-book literature with its commitment to 'relevance' in partisan causes economic or political, that times' world of letters had quite a few who made no secret of their writing aim to expose evils of bias or prejudice, to end inequalities and injustices, of working not for lucre but humanity's betterment. Recall too the stern point of high-minded taste established by the Victorian what's-his-name who pontificated: those who wrote for money didn't write for him. Now, what in the world did the Great Cham, as Smollet in our trade's common bond of good will chose to name him, conceive himself to be saying? I certainly couldn't see.

That was then. Time now the present. While of course I can't be sure, my drawn-out term in experience's dear school has been suggestive. I must ask myself if what the Great Cham (he found you an argument: he cannot find you an understanding) had done, plain and simple, in clear homeliness, in no Great Chamery, wasn't best put this way. He'd said a mouthful.

Jim

Thursday February 13, 1923 [30 Mt. Auburn Street, Cambridge]
The talk about writing made me think of having another try at the novel. I wrote steadily from four until quarter of twelve and satisfied myself that with a little more application I could finish it shortly. It is very long. I must have added 15 thousand words today and it will take me more than as much more to complete it. It had roughly thirty thousand already. I don't know how long an ordinary novel is but this seems likely to be about seventy thousand. Hillyer came in about eleven with a book for me and seeing what I was doing about the novel—the imposing chapters in a fat snap notebook were at my side and praised the idea strongly, liking the title, which I also like. I suppose it will do me no good but at any rate there would be satisfaction in getting it done. I shall try to finish it before the end of the week.

Friday February 14, 1923
. . . afterward I worked quite late on CONFUSION and got all tangled up over it—my footing's insecure, a phrase vague enough to fit the difficulty nicely. I suppose I must go on and prove Marcus Aurelius' point from which

I borrowed the title and the theme originally but I have such a conviction of pleasant futility in life—it isn't at all bitter, I just feel most of the so-called mainsprings of human action are rot—that I doubt whether I can prove it without betraying the fact I don't believe what I say. It developed a pretty problem and kept me frowning and fretting until three oclock.

Thursday February 22, 1923

. . . I can't restore my temporarily distracted attention to the novel so that hangs fire which it would probably do well to do world without end; but I feel a strange impulse to keep after it and see the last words written. Somehow my prose is quite rotten, I realize—it is either very incoherent or extraordinarily thin and concise as in *Remember the Rose*.[1] What I need is a couple of good composition courses and I can't get them until next year unfortunately.

Saturday February 24, 1923

I finished Confusion today and ended it not at all as I planned. It seemed to take itself out of my hands; and after futile objecting and side-stepping on my part made Cerise die, throwing my last year's moral to the winds and giving a queer ironic flavor to the epigraph quotation.[2] I liked it. She seemed to die with all the abruptness of death. I saw suddenly I had been paving the way up to the white inevitable door[3] for at least twenty thousand words—a decently offhand way of computing. That seemed to take a great deal out of me and other work was out of the question so rather disliking the idea of meeting anyone I knew I went up and ate supper at the Union.

Wednesday February 28, 1923

I thought it would do my incipient cold good to get a decent night's sleep so I cut all my classes with the brazenness I'm noted for and which will doubtless get me into trouble soon.[4] The afternoon went into a critical estimate of Confusion and its comparative chances of being good enough to publish. It seems better than I thought.

Tuesday March 13, 1923

Looking at the novel Ms today I don't feel, for all Hillyer's kind enough commendation, that my writing is any damn good; and if that isn't, why

1. "Remember the Rose," *Harvard Advocate*, 109 (1 June 1923), 395–97. Short story.
2. "Wipe off all idle fancies and say unto thyself incessantly; now if I will it is in my power to keep out of this my soul all wickedness and lust, all concupiscences, all trouble and Confusion."
3. "The white inevitable door": from Robert S. Hillyer's sonnet XXV, *The Collected Verse of Robert Hillyer* (New York: Knopf, 1934).
4. I did it. Dean Little put me on probation on the next week and I remained there for the rest of my freshman year. —J. G. C.

nothing is, and I may about as well help myself to the bichloride of mercury now as ever. That of course doesn't reflect my sentiment very exactly, though I feel a shade what the romanticist calls 'sick at heart' but what is better described as 'conscious of futility.' Hillyer's Egyptian book is out, and is very good, a neat little volume from Brimmer.[5]

Sunday March 18, 1923

I wish I could stock myself with knowledge enough to get something written which would be interesting and sell. It's all very fine to have Hillyer say I 'do extremely well' but I would like some more concrete testimony of it. It's really about time I did *do* something. Of course I've said that off and on for the last year but I can see easily enough why the stuff of a year ago was rotten. There may be a moral in that, but Hillyer's judgment fortifies me to hope, where it fails to console me in disappointment. Good God I shall publish this spring or know the reason why—more probably the latter.

Thursday March 22, 1923

God knows I've paused here before to observe there's something wrong with my writing but anyway I need to do it again, as every so often I realize the fact keenly and feel as if I ought to do something about it. The whole affair gets more and more distressing as I can no more stop writing than fly and the annoyance of writing badly will spoil even the nicest spring afternoon. . . . some of my boring complaint let out to him made Hillyer say he's not sure I wouldn't do well to stop writing for awhile and I had to point out it would be easier—and more economical—to stop eating.

Friday April 27, 1923

. . . Odd moments went into a debate about the rewriting of Confusion— the idea of taking the next summer off at Kent and spending it writing. It would give me three months of undisturbed calm, absolutely nothing to do but write as Grandmother[6] would be up and I would have to live away from the place. Then I considered the rottenness of my prose with disfavor which is deserved and concluded nothing.

Monday April 30, 1923

So I did about nothing and pored over Confusion with critical displeasure but a certain feeling of faint hope. I wish I could get something decent done.

Thursday June 7, 1923 [Lincoln, Mass.]

Back at Lincoln with a feeling I had the history exam business well in hand

5. *Coming Forth By Day*. Boston: B. J. Brimmer, 1923.
6. My mother's mother, widow of Joseph Eaton Wood of Wolfville, Nova Scotia, my mother's birthplace. —J. G. C.

which somehow enabled me to turn about and write quite a lot to go into Confusion. John heard it with approval and my hopes of getting it done next summer and published next fall are gradually getting the better of my doubts. I am awfully keen on it because I think the psychological lift would be good. Speaking of that, John seemed in a mood that evening, a sort of amazing decay-of-a-great-house mood, a strong family consciousness I suppose, looking back at his people, he might naturally have. His point; now they are all coming to nothing. My amazement was at what I had to see he meant. Certainly his own more or less rare spirit could never amount to anything politically and that's the family underlying one concept of 'decay.' [I seem to have got up to Kent Wednesday June 13 and note presently: "I got to work." Some similar phrase recurs quite often, but the wordy text is in the main about people, and books read, and swimming and tennis for a month—]

Friday July 13, 1923 [*Kent, Conn.*]
I could go to work with some cheerfulness today though parts of Confusion are giving me a great deal of trouble. I've rewritten Blair making love to Cerise three times and am not very well satisfied with the results. Evidently theory and practice don't go together enough to hurt.

Monday August 6, 1923
. . . I wrote at Confusion until quite late to attempt a final arrangement, a division into parts. I think it will fall into ten chapters, all except the last a little more than ten thousand words each and they'll be named and subdivided into sections, that being my final conclusion on easiest mechanical composition as far as a reader goes. If they find it makes them think and they see an unbroken stretch they quit.

Thursday August 23, 1923
. . . I have been working every available instant for days and will continue to do that for days more and all the while D. is not waiting in a sort of trance for me to come around and begin where I left off. It's a damn cinch to see I never ought to marry—I mean I have to forsee an existence wherein I'll want to do nothing but write—when no one, nothing will matter except that. I can see it reacting on Mother already and yet I haven't the will power to stay away from my desk for any longer than I can help. It doesn't seem to matter in the least whether this stuff ever gets published or not, anyway while I'm writing. I've tried asking myself how I'd feel if things go wrong and I can't find the prospect bothers me in the least. I feel an absurd confidence in my own ultimate success, in my own future ability to write what will be good beyond question, what *I* will find satisfying. So how about D?

As soon as I finish the work I somehow feel she'll again become extremely important. I shall finish by the 1st, I think. D. goes down the 31st and Heaven knows when I'll see her again.

Tuesday August 28, 1923
It's extraordinary how this summer has gone. I've hardly been conscious of the passage of time, it has melted away—remarkable considering the piffling doings on the filled pages back of this. What explains it but writing? I really don't desire anything in life outside similar opportunities to work, to make things like this, the swiftest and pleasantest summer I can remember. If only Confusion can justify it all will be well and I daresay will be well anyway, as so much work can't be wholly thrown away—after all I had the doing of the work. . . .

Thursday August 30, 1923
A note from Hillyer promises not so smooth going as far as Confusion is concerned for he will be too busy to go over it until almost November, or so I should judge from the list of new and unexpected activities he outlines. The fact I did not get all I planned done today combines with my probably having to wait to have H. take me to his publisher[7] to put me in low spirits for the first time in some days. I have to admit I did more or less count on getting published this fall. . . .

Sunday September 9, 1923 [Alexandria Bay, N.Y.]
(Note) I spent most of the morning reading Confusion to the patient Tom and Louisa. . . . an annoying cold which was helped very little by my swimming experiments yesterday rather pinned me down and Mrs Howard anxiously fed me cough medicine. . . . later they insisted that I go on with the reading so we did that until near midnight. In a way it fusses me—how patient can you expect people to get? I try to think; I'd certainly never ask them to listen, or offer to read; and honestly I don't know how they stand it when they don't in anyway have to, so I can tell myself they want to—yes; I see how that's a kind of kidding myself. . . .

Wednesday September 19, 1923 [22 Plimpton St., Cambridge]
[Note—down to college 15 Sept.] . . . For some reason I do not seem to get Confusion changes done—there's a matter of 20 pages of typing which refuses to seem immediately important—yes I think I really know why, so let's say no more.

7. William Stanley Braithwaite, president of Boston publisher B. J. Brimmer.

Saturday September 22, 1923
. . . I worked resolutely on Confusion all evening with an interest quickly and easily awakened. It now seems rather good, much better than I'd been slowly deciding during the last wasted week.

Wednesday October 3, 1923
. . . John and I rather specialize in late hours and we never seem to get anywhere before half past two or thereabouts and then its to bed. John sits pensive over his Fine Arts plates or mixes colors or experiments in design and I do my history reading or correct the book Ms which by the way I still detect myself stalling on and I daresay I *am* secretly afraid of submitting it to H's Braithwaite; so all the corrections I constantly find necessary mean nothing more than that. I try to make delay plausible by thinking certainly I'd hate to spoil my best chance by not having the thing wholly ready.

Wednesday October 10, 1923
I got the last touches on the book while a telephone man drilled and twisted wires all over the study. Having it in made me think I'd use it, so I called and brought the Ms in to Braithwaite at 384 Boylston.[8] He is a dark genial enough person who seemed much more anxious to know if I would stick by Brimmer in the event of the book's being published than what was in the book. He did however promise to let me know in ten days.

Friday October 12, 1923
Out to Wellesley in Frank's car and I found to my amazement a phone call for me. It proved to be Braithwaite who was flatteringly complimentary about the book and said Brimmer would publish it.

Wednesday October 18, 1923
About half past three I went in to see Braithwaite and he amply confirmed all his arrangements. The book will be set up at once and he thinks finished by December 1st though it will not be released until January. I saw amusing sketches of jackets and advertisements[9]—I am accused of reintroducing beauty to American fiction and such like rot. A sketch of a contract that binds me to them for nine years but which likewise binds them to publish without further consideration all the manuscripts I shall bring in. That relieves my mind about the Cloudy Trophy[10] which I started preliminary work on the other day and I think the danger of being sketchy and hasty is far too obvious to make that really a peril. All in all things look auspicious.

8. Hillyer had spoken to Braithwaite of my MS and arranged that I would call when I had it ready. — J. G. C.
9. The jacket finally used was the work of my roommate. — J. G. C.
10. This novel was never published.

Wednesday November 7, 1923

My desultory work on the outlining both on paper and in my head of plans to make up Cloudy Trophy which I trust (too sanguinely?) to get written in Nova Scotia next summer at once convince me of the writing value of these diaries I have kept and of the fact that I don't keep them the right way. It's too purely negative (I mean that feeling) giving me no solid suggestion as to how a writer's diary should be kept; and in certain matters such as the painfully faithful recording of my relations and emotions—if they may be so dignified—in regard to several girls I think I have done quite the best thing for my work. On the other hand I wander into much stuff which at best merely serves to cover pages. It may be I put in too many facts and too few ideas, but the transitory quality of most of the ideas, the surpassing difficulty of transcribing the ones that seem vital and pertinent, the poor showing that such as I *have* recorded make—all these factors interfere considerably. I want Cloudy Trophy to be an entire exposition of what I think about Women, as an instance. I blush to write a line so naive, and my inability to define myself less self-consciously doesn't aid in a fight against immature embarrassment in the least. I can get nowhere by trying to justify 'young' impulses and unjudged actions to any more experienced mind. I fear such reflections as these are that immaturity won't permit them to work the change needed.

Thursday November 15, 1923 [Lincoln, Mass.]

Cloudy Trophy goes well enough, growing and developing slowly in my mind, its outline being constantly revised and amplified. I trust it will— well, I'm going to have to see that it is a much better and more vital book than Confusion, which unquestionably retains a great deal of my affection, but not much else. I mean I already see it is not at all the book Braithwaite, say, kindly but I come to think in his case dumbly, tells me it is; but I've a notion that, absurdly, as the song says: I'll always adore it even though I mean to and I damn well will do many books of greater import and maybe real power.

Wednesday November 21, 1923 [22 Plimpton St.]

I spent the rest of the evening re-reading This Side of Paradise with attention, beginning mainly with the idea of seeing what I knew I wished to avoid in Cloudy Trophy; and then because in some way to find parts of it more effective or true than I remembered finishing it. I have plenty of doubts about CT, the principal being; can I really portray Harvard life fairly. That I can do it vividly I don't doubt; but whether or not every side of it has yet become clear to me is another and disturbing matter.

Saturday December 15, 1923 [Stillman Infirmary]

Most of the day sitting in the sunroom doing notes on a scheme of books I guess I owe to 'bed rest,' whereof both Confusion and Cloudy Trophy would come into place. The others would be: Ignorant Armies (Dover beach line) and Avalon (as ironic myth) and I plan privately in the four to cover the whole case of youth as it appears to me. If it all goes well I ought to get Ignorant Armies (to be second) done this summer; and all of them once in mind, the others should follow rapidly. Heaven alone knows when I can get out of here but I hope sometime next week, as I daresay I can go down when they let me loose.

Friday December 29, 1923 [Staten Island, N.Y.]

. . . The arrival of seven odd galleys of Confusion proof forwarded here today both by just arriving and looking all right on arrival encouraged me. I daresay the book will go well enough—everyone down here needlessly interested which is nonetheless pleasant because I can get out of idiot conversation by playing modest.

PLACES LISTED IN DIARY

30 Mt. Auburn Street, Cambridge, Mass. Harvard use at that time was assignment of admitted Freshmen to then new Brattle Street Dorms. Impossible in my case because of a 'condition'—my College Board algebra exam flunked; though oddly I'd passed geometry. Maybe because of that the Admissions Board directed me to report myself to their Dean Pennypacker in September as a special case. After a looking-over by him and what he himself described as a 'Dutch Uncle' talk about my scholastic unruliness; and also, from his glances at his file, what I think was a letter from my Headmaster; cautionary no doubt—he must regard the school's long reputation for turning out serious well-conducted students (on its arms: *Temperantia Fiducia Constantia*), not 'difficult' individualists—but also I feel sure more evenhanded than I had right to expect, I was passed in. However the dormitories had been filled. Robert Hillyer, Kent '13, then on the college English Dept. faculty, kindly found a room for me in the privately owned house where his apartment was.

Lincoln, Mass.; where John, to be my roommate in the fall, was allowed, even I believe, encouraged to bring his friends to his grandparents' large house.

Kent, Connecticut; where I had been at school and where my mother, when my father died in 1920, came and took part of a house in the village.

Alexandria Bay, N.Y. My indicated close college friend and his married sister were summering at a lodge belonging to their parents on a St. Lawrence River island.

22 Plimpton Street, Cambridge. A college-owned small house beside the *Crimson* building. Because so small it had no Proctor and so in effect no rules. Very desirable. In practice of those years the college's several such once private houses "belonged" in the sense of usually passing down to, when seniors moved into the Yard, certain particular New England schools' alumni. Kent's was generally Apthorp House. 22 Plimpton was Groton's where John had gone—an adding, you might say, to little anomalies of my college existence. Another; because of my never having lived in the Freshman Dorms, my really close friends, even including those from Kent, were all '25, not like me '26.

Stillman Infirmary where a mild 'jaundice' attack led college medical officers to send me.

Staten Island, N.Y. My mother and I were spending the holidays with people who had been neighbors of my parents when I was growing up there.

Just Representations
A JAMES GOULD COZZENS READER

I

Ask Me Tomorrow

or The Pleasant Comedy
of Young Fortunatus

ONE

On a day of early November in the mid-1920's Francis Ellery was leaving Florence. He and his mother had come down from Paris a week before to the Via Solferino hotel, good but of the second class, which old friends of hers in Florence recommended as an economical yet comfortable place to spend the winter. The hotel was made out of what once had been two quite grand private houses by informally interconnecting them, so most of its guest rooms were large-sized. In the room they had given Francis, his mother sat in a big armchair beyond the unmade bed looking at him. The window was behind her. Through it Francis could see the thin sunlight falling on the bare trees and the wet red tiles of the house across the street rising against a chilly pale blue sky. Francis closed his last bag. He set it with the others by the door and pressed the bell button three times. He looked at his watch and said, "I'd better keep moving."

His mother said, "It only takes a few minutes to the station. Victor knows you're going. He'll have a cab."

Francis sat on the edge of the bed and fished out a package of cigarettes. "Let me have one of those," his mother said. He brought it to her, standing by her chair while he struck and held a wax match for it. When the cigarette was lighted she took it from her mouth in her left hand, laid her right hand on Francis's arm and said, "Well, tonight you'll be in Milan. And tomorrow night in Montreux."

Francis said, "I don't know that I ought to go. You'll be all right, of course. But—" She had been very ill in Paris earlier in the fall, and Francis was obliged to see that, sitting there under the window, she looked ill now. The cigarette had not been what she wanted and she let it burn between her fingers. "I'm much stronger," she said. "I shan't mind it." She released his arm. "You might write me from Milan. Or, no. That's silly. Write me from Montreux Wednesday. You'll do that."

"Of course," Francis answered.

"Yes, I know you will. You've always been very good about letters. You know how I'll be depending on them."

There was a rap on the door and Francis yelled, *"Avanti!"* not sorry to interrupt, for the subject made him uncomfortable. He would have preferred to think that she hardly gave him a thought. Knowing the vain wish to be a real and deep one, he had to accuse himself of selfishness.

When the bags were out his mother said, "I suppose you'd better go. I won't come down. I wish you'd look out a little for Faith Robertson. She'll be on that train, and she's all alone. I told her mother you would."

"Well, I won't," Francis said. "She's perfectly capable of looking out for herself."

"I wish you could be pleasanter to people, darling. I think she was rather taken with you the other night."

"I wasn't much taken with her," Francis said, which was indeed the case, for she was a plain girl of a brisk and sensible type. Whatever his mother fancied about it, Francis had been well aware, on the few occasions of meeting Miss Robertson, that she thought, for reasons best known to herself, either not at all or very little of him. He said, "These musicians! They're all simply insufferable. Like actresses. There's always something wrong with a person who performs in public. If you have any sense you can't want to do it." He knew that dislike of the Robertson girl made him overpositive; yet he had seen enough of music and the stage to know that as a matter of course the people connected with them reached heights of conceit and pretentiousness that painters and writers, for instance, hardly dared dream of. He said, "She's perfectly able to get to Milan without any supervision from me."

"Well, darling, never mind. It doesn't matter. But some day you'll see that it's just easier to be pleasant." His mother stood up and came and kissed Francis. "Tell Mrs. Cunningham that I'm really very glad to have you with her." She let him go. "God bless you," she said.

"Fine," said Francis. "Take care of yourself, and for heaven's sake see that they keep you warm."

He went quickly downstairs, through the lower hall and out onto the pavement in the thin noon sunlight. He gave the porter a filthy five-lire note and was slammed into the cab. The wretched horse struggled and clashed his hoofs, the wheels ground sideways, scraping the thin muddy slime that covered the paving stones. They got around and went off with lively jolts. Not until the cab had gone a few blocks and was cutting through the Via Bernardo Rucellai did Francis remember that his mother had probably been watching from the window upstairs for him to wave.

The made-up train was moving in along the platform sheds when Francis went through the barrier. Though there was some sun on the edge of the paving, a bleak wind smelling of oil and steam and the lavatory traps blew hard down the moving cars. Tottering with his strapful of luggage over his back, the porter swung on a passing step while he held the door handle of a second-class compartment. Walking below to keep up with him, Francis turned to see how much of a crowd there was going to be. Not looking where he was going, he very nearly bumped into Faith Robertson.

She had on a spotted fur coat of what is called leopard skin. Skirts were short that year, so the coat did not come much lower than her knees and out from under it issued directly her big silk-covered legs. A green felt hat was pulled down on her blonde hair. Since she looked straight at Francis, he felt compelled to take his hat off, for he never had the courage of his distastes, or the simple composure to be frankly and openly rude. He stood embarrassed and bareheaded while Miss Robertson said, "Oh, hello. Where are you going?"

"Montreux," said Francis, "unless I get killed in the rush."

"There's never much of anyone on this train. I've taken it dozens of times. You'll have to change at Milan."

"So I've been told," Francis said, somewhat distantly, for if he were unwilling to look out a little for her, he was even more unwilling to have her look out for him. Although his tone, suggesting that she mind her own business, had no visible effect on Miss Robertson, the sound of it embarrassed Francis himself. He attempted to modify it by adding, "I'll have to stay over at Milan. I can't get a connection. It's very boring."

Her full, freckled face was turned toward him and she gave him a composed, critical look. "Why?" she asked.

"I think Milan's one of the most boring cities in the world," Francis answered. He realized at once that Miss Robertson, who spent most of her time there, might not, and in fact did not, like the disdainful reference to her city. She said sharply, "I always think it's one's own fault if one's bored. I wouldn't think you'd be. I mean, a writer—" Though this was an oblique acknowledgment that something about him was known to her and remembered, the tinge of chiding disapproval in her voice hinted that she found him not half the person someone had led her to suppose he was.

"Nevertheless, I think Milan boring," he said in tones intended to be dry. She paid no attention. Instead she jerked her green hat at the porter with Francis's luggage, who, as the brakes went on, snapped open the door and shouldered himself into the compartment. "Come on," she said. "We can make sure of the corner seats at any rate." From behind her she caught up a small suitcase and gave his arm a push.

"Let me have that," said Francis.

"I'm not a cripple," she said tolerantly. "There's nothing in it but a bathrobe and a pair of pajamas." She looked up at the porter, who was heaving Francis's bags onto the rack. "Sooner or later," she said, "you'll learn to travel with less luggage." She glanced at him. "I'll bet you couldn't change trains by yourself."

"Yes, I could," Francis said, a good deal nettled. "My mother pins my name and address on me and I go and show it to the *chef de gare*." She gave him a stare and then she reluctantly laughed. "Well, I couldn't," she said. Francis had taken out some money. He folded over a five-lire note. "Don't give him all that," she said. "It's silly. He doesn't expect it."

"Then I'll surprise him," said Francis, who habitually overtipped, feeling that money spent in averting the possibility of a row was well spent, even when he was very little able to afford it. Miss Robertson shrugged her leopard-skin shoulders. "*Prego!*" she said with an excellent accent to the porter, whose broad back blocked the door while he stood wiping his forehead elaborately. She stepped up with a strong clumsy movement, giving Francis a glimpse of her thick bare leg above the top of the rolled stocking. She elbowed the porter aside, swung her suitcase, which clearly held not more than she said it did, with one hand onto the rack and dropped into the corner by the window. Francis handed over the five-lire note, got a gratified look, and followed her. "Close the door," she said. "We'll probably have this to ourselves." She passed her eyes over Francis's luggage on the rack above. "What's that?" she asked. "A typewriter?"

"Yes," said Francis.

"Do you write right on a typewriter, or do you have to write it out first?"

"I write right on a typewriter," Francis said.

"I should think the noise would drive you crazy."

"Well, maybe it does," Francis said. "I've often wondered."

Outside, there were mournful cries passing down the platform. The carriage shook and began to move. This seemed to put a period to the conversation. At least, Miss Robertson automatically looked out the window and Francis was able to take a book from his overcoat pocket and open it. When, a few minutes later, the conductor slid back the corridor door, Francis, looking up, saw that Miss Robertson had been reclining with her eyes closed, as though trying to get some sleep. She produced her ticket from a small alligator pocketbook. When it was returned to her she settled her head and shut her eyes again. Francis handed over his own tickets in an American Express cover and waited while the conductor examined them all with interest. From his pocket he pulled a booklet, consulted it, and addressed Francis in Italian too fast for him to understand. *"Cosa dice?"* Francis said doubtfully.

Without opening her eyes, Miss Robertson said, "He says you won't be able to get a connection for Brigue tonight."

"Io lo conosco, grazie," Francis said to the conductor, flushing. "Much obliged," he said to Miss Robertson. She nodded, still not opening her eyes, and Francis began to read again. The book, a volume of Baudelaire, did not interest him much and soon he had begun to think about the half-completed manuscript of the book he was writing. In this way almost an hour passed. He glanced out the window and saw, surprised, the jumbled buildings of Pistoia surmounted disproportionately by the cathedral's great ruddy dome. The train passed into the shadows, jarred, and there was a sudden silence as it stood still.

Though he did not think Miss Robertson was really asleep, Francis got out as though trying not to waken her. He walked over to the buffet and drank a glass of vermouth, standing at the counter. This cheered him a little. When he got back, Miss Robertson was eating a huge roll with a slice of some sort of sausage that looked like soiled red leather in it. She had another lying on a bit of waxed paper in her lap. Her mouth was too full to talk, but sliding her hand under the waxed paper she held it out to Francis.

The gesture, cordial and casual, took him by surprise. He shook his head, smiling. "No thanks," he said, both because he was not hungry and because he could see, not far off, the vendor from whose basket she had bought them, and he was very dirty. "I couldn't possibly."

She managed to say, "You don't know what's good." And after a moment, "I really got it for you. You don't eat enough. You're thin as a rail."

"I eat all I can stand," Francis said. "Eating in Italy isn't any pleasure. Even drinking is pretty bad," he added, still tasting the vermouth.

"It's pretty bad for you," Miss Robertson said authoritatively. She seemed displeased because he had not taken the roll. "I suppose in Paris you sat around drinking all day."

"And most of the night," said Francis, nettled again.

Miss Robertson wiped her mouth with the waxed paper and began on the second roll. "Didn't you?" she asked.

"No," said Francis. "Not that I wouldn't have liked to, but it's too expensive." The train had begun to move and they came out of the shed into the sunshine. He opened his book again. Miss Robertson said with what appeared to be contempt, "You're awfully touchy, aren't you?"

"Yes," said Francis.

"Well, it's silly of you. I always say what I think and I expect other people to say what they think. It's the only way to get on."

"Not with touchy people," Francis said. "With them, you have to sit and say how wonderful they are. They like that."

"I should think you'd have got enough of it in Paris."

"I never get enough of it," said Francis. "And what is this business about Paris, anyway? I was only there a few months. My mother was ill at the American Hospital and I was living most of the time in a pension in Neuilly."

"Well, I was in Paris last week. It didn't sound as though you'd had too bad a time. I happened to meet someone who saw quite a little of you."

"Did you?" said Francis as casually as he could. Miss Robertson looked at him intently. She must have decided that his indifference was assumed. "Yes, I did," she said. "Lorna Higham told me all about you."

Francis looked out the window. Moving slowly and laboriously the train was beginning the climb to Corbezzi and the cold clear Tuscan plain was already spreading out behind. The tones of black and purple and olive in the thinly sunlit distance seemed sadder than anything in the world. "I didn't know you knew her," Francis said.

"She was one of my best friends at school."

"At Vassar?"

"I didn't go to college. If you sing you haven't time for any of that."

"I expect not," said Francis. He let his eye fall on his open book, reading at random: *Quelle est cette île triste et noire? C'est Cythère. . . .* Then he looked up again. Miss Robertson was still studying him, and he felt foolish to have shown so naïvely that he was not at ease. Miss Robertson said, "I don't know anything about writing, but I don't believe you'd have much time for anything else either, if it seemed important to you. I haven't read any of your books. How many have you published? Two?"

"Yes," said Francis, "and it does seem important to me. You see, I have to eat. I don't know any other way to go about providing for that."

Miss Robertson smiled coldly. "Why can't you be natural?" she asked. "Why do you bother to try to cut a figure?"

"I wasn't conscious of bothering," Francis said. He detested Miss Robertson.

Concluding that he had no better answer, Miss Robertson said, "What are you writing now? If you want to tell me, that is."

Even if he had liked her Francis would not have wanted to tell her. It gave him no pleasure to talk about his writing and he was never able to say what he meant about it in reasonable compass. Confused, fragmentary things he could say served only to reduce whatever idea he had in mind to its essential banality and the more he explained what he was planning to write, the sillier it seemed to bother to write it. "I'm not sure I'll get very far with it this year," he said. "You see, I had to take a job. It ought to give me some time, but I don't know how much."

"Lorna told me," Miss Robertson said. "I think you're making a mistake."

"Maybe I am," said Francis. Under the relentless, inquisitive fire of Miss Robertson's faultfinding he was too harried to make a stand, though surely no one had asked her for her opinion. Moreover, he did not want to talk about Lorna with her, so he said, "I don't like the idea a great deal. It wasn't any choice of mine. But I was lucky to find it."

The train, getting up into the hills, passed with a long anticipatory roar into a tunnel. Out of the total darkness Miss Robertson, raising her voice, said with derision, "It sounded like a pretty soft job to me." Through the windows, wreathed with smoke and steam, daylight appeared again.

"It isn't my idea of a soft job," Francis said. "They're nice people, and the kid's all right; but I don't fancy it." The roaring darkness enveloped them once more, continuing second after second. This, he found, was not a subject he wanted to discuss with her, either. "As a matter of fact," he said, "the book I'm trying to write is about an incident in the war between Chile and Peru in 1879. Do you know anything about it?"

"I never heard of it," said Miss Robertson.

"Well, it didn't amount to much as a war, and that's part of the point. The causes and so on don't matter a great deal. On 8th October, 1879, the Peruvian turret ship *Huascar*—it was the only ship they had that was any good—commanded by a Rear Admiral Grau who had previously had several small successes, was caught off Angamos—I want to call the book *Action off Angamos*. It was hopeless, but they put up such a fight as you wouldn't believe. Of course that's just the setting. On board the *Huascar* from 3:00 A.M. when they sighted the Chilean ironclads until eleven, when there was no one left to fight her any longer—"

Light was at last coming down the sides of the car, the shadow sweeping back. Clouds of smoke rolled and rose by the dirty glass. Francis could see a little stone hut close on the hillside and some sloping patches of tiny cultivated fields. The glass cleared, the hillside swung away, opening an enormous windy vista of purple receding hills. Sunlight fell on his lap. "It's hard to explain what I mean," he said. "The situation is ironic, but also heroic. I don't think I can explain. But at any rate, that's what the new book will be about—if I ever get it done."

Miss Robertson's plain freckled face was composed. "It sounds very exciting," she said.

Francis winced, for he had more in mind, even if he had not been able to say it, than that. "Well, we'll see," he said, wishing, as always, that he hadn't spoken of it. He lit a cigarette. After a short silence, Miss Robertson, leaning her head back, shut her eyes again.

At four o'clock the change in the afternoon, apparent as soon as they were across the high divide, in new pallor of sky and sicklier sunlight had become complete. Over Bologna more of the endless rain was imminent. While they drew out of the railroad yards the first slanting drops began to strike the dirty windows. It became immediately a downpour, as, moving much faster now, they headed up the great plain to Modena.

Near the end of the corridor, balanced to the rapid shake of the car, Francis stood depressed watching the driving rain. It hid the mountains in successive heavier veils. The autumn afternoon was turned to an early twilight, somber on the wet countryside—the ditches full of spattered water; the drenched fields and puddled lanes; the occasional rows of leafless dripping poplars. "The Aemilian Way," Francis said to himself. "The Via Aemilia. The great military road. M. Aemilius Lepidus (and who else?) being consuls—" He saw an old bust; a solid, square stone face with blank stone eyes, the stone toga folds thrown across the powerful shoulder. *"Et facere et pati fortia Romanum est—"* he said aloud. "I wouldn't have lasted a minute. They'd have given me one look—" Who knew what Marcus Lepidus, or any Roman republican like him would think seeing Francis twenty-one centuries after that consulship standing there looking out at the plain through a pane of rain-wet glass while he was moved along the line of the Aemilian Way, two days' forced march every hour? "God!" said Francis. "I wish I had a hundred thousand dollars."

But he could easily believe that he never would have. He would just go on to the end of his days never knowing where money for his next extravagance was coming from; yet never, probably, being quite destitute enough to have to give up thinking of extravagances. How many times at college would an extra fifty dollars have made all the difference between —between what? Between the peace of mind in which one could properly lose ten dollars at bridge, buy a few quarts of gin, and send a girl gardenias enough to cover her shoulder for the Hale House Ball; and that unquiet in which one lost the money anyway, accepted a little too often somebody else's gin (he could feel the hard shape of the silver flasks, taste, as he tipped them, the scald of the reclaimed alcohol and water, see the crooked ties and bulged stiff shirt fronts in the crowded subterranean glare of the men's room), and let his bills ride still another month.

His mind recoiled, humiliated; but at once Francis heard music . . . *one little kiss, and then we will whis*—(a dying fall. Oh, it came o'er my ear like—indeed, yes!)—*per good night. . . .* The wheel of movement shifted,

serenely turning in the variegated dusk below the ballroom balconies. Up
through the music . . . *stay at home, play at home, eight o'clock sleepy time*
. . . rose the murmur of hundreds of voices, the shift and scrape of innumerable feet. Francis breathed the sweet hot air; he smelled the dampened powder. Skirts, down that season far enough to cover the shins,
switched and swayed; the bare round arms lifted, the innocently rouged
faces kept turning up to talk. They bent their bodies back, balanced in a
lithe way from the hips. "Ah, you damned fool!" Francis said.

Yet it was hateful, he had sense enough to see, not because of its folly
or triviality. He hated it for the small wounds to pride, the private chagrins, the anxieties of living, because you felt that you had to, willfully
beyond your means, that distempered a pleasure, to everyone else he knew
apparently so pure. Of what he had left from all that now, Francis would
rather forget everything—just forget it, however; not change it to something more estimable, like solid work or the fruits of scholarship. The
drafty cold of the corridor was making itself felt, for he had learned at
school that it was indecent to wear woollen underwear and this truth still
seemed to him self-evident. He might as well go back to Miss Robertson.

Miss Robertson met him halfway. She was coming down from the
lavatory at the other end of the car. "Oh, don't look so downhearted," she
said with partly humorous impatience. "What have you got to worry
about?"

Francis made an effort. "Life," he said. "I worry about life. And
money. And love. I'm freezing to death." He slid the compartment door
back and she went in. "I don't know how you stand it in Italy."

"You get used to it," she said. She put her skirt straight with a jerk
and sat down. "Where are you going to stay tonight?"

"The Palace, I guess."

"It'll cost you fifty lire. I was going to suggest you come to my place.
I guess you don't worry about money much; just about life and love."

Whatever happened, Francis knew, he was not going to her place. He
said, "I never know where one begins and the other leaves off. What do
you pay?"

"Eighteen, pension. And it's plenty good enough. The wife of the
man I study with runs it. Of course, it's out by the Porta Vittoria, and I
don't say it would be fancy enough for you."

"I thought you studied at the conservatory," Francis said, feeling
that he had heard enough about himself.

She smiled. "The conservatory's just nonsense," she said. "You have
to be on the rolls, but studying there's just a way of getting a hearing.
If you're good, the director can do a lot for you—not musically. He's a
second-rate composer and the way you handle him is with an aria from an

awful opera he wrote. But he can get you on at La Scala if anyone can. And I'll say this for him. You don't have to trade him anything. Of course, if you're pretty, too, there are people who can save you time."

"Really?" said Francis, little interested, for he did not believe her. "I thought that was just something in a book."

"Well, it's not. God knows I'm not pretty, but I wear a skirt, so every now and then somebody in a position to help makes me a proposition."

"And what do you do?" asked Francis, tempted to see what she would say.

Miss Robertson shrugged. "A girl from England I got to know quite well last year had to sleep with five different men before she'd finished. She had a fairly good voice; but she wouldn't even have had a chance, otherwise."

Involuntarily Francis's eyes rested on Miss Robertson's body. He snapped them away, relieved to see, at the same time, that Miss Robertson had been looking out the window. "Well," he said, "they tell me it's really more fun than work." A disagreeable vision of Miss Robertson, in a state of beefy nature, grimly advancing her art on a bed with some wop whose amorous taste was catholic enough to include anything he could get, interrupted his pleasantry. "That would certainly be more work than fun," he said to himself.

"You think it's funny," Miss Robertson said. "You wouldn't if you were a woman. You're as likely as not to end up with syphilis. That's not so romantic."

"On the contrary," Francis said, "syphilis is extremely romantic. It's in the grand tradition. All the great men had it. What it's not is practical, or sensible, or good for you." He had been taken unprepared, for in talking to people like Miss Robertson he was accustomed to be the one who made harsh observations at the expense of romance and sentiment.

"What silly rot!" cried Miss Robertson. She was quite angry, Francis supposed, because her mood was solemn as she considered the hard life of the artist and the woes of women. She did not relish levity on sacred subjects. Francis would just as soon have annoyed her more by developing the theme; but he could not very logically, he saw, be ironic in so many different ways at once. The alternative was to declare in earnest for wholesomeness, virtue, and common sense. Those were things certain to be dear to Miss Robertson. Wholesomeness and common sense were what made her so hard to stand; and, as for virtue, if there were any truth at all in her implication, and if she actually had been obliged to sacrifice her virginity on the altar of her career, it wouldn't count in her own mind. She would retain her natural impatience with lapses occasioned by mere concupiscence, or by curiosity, or even by that muddle of indecision that at some unplanned and pleasureless moment made girls of less sound sense than Miss Robertson distraught principals in the second degree to the loss of their virtue.

"Yes, it is rot," Francis admitted, meaning to extricate himself. "I don't recommend it." But, perversely, he had to add, "Just the same, I wouldn't take your English friend's sufferings too seriously. This reluctant-maiden business is all right once, maybe. But the fifth time—it's like the song, 'Once again she lost 'er nyme. . . .'"

"You men!" said Miss Robertson. "Because you can only think of just one thing—"

The remark, with its air of knowing prudishness and affected propriety, stung Francis. It sounded like those amateur Central Square tarts who took their pay for wrestling with drunken sophomores in the form of automobile rides and tickets to burlesque shows. "And why not?" he said flatly. "What in God's name else is a woman supposed to make you think of? What else is she for, anyway?"

"You would say that!" said Miss Robertson. "You would! Because you happen to be good-looking, or think you are, I suppose you imagine every girl you see is just crazy to have you make a pass at her. You don't know a thing about women."

The startling news that Miss Robertson considered him good-looking, even if quickly qualified, brought Francis up. The instant's halt, in effect like counting ten before you say it, enabled him to speak good-naturedly. "I may not know as much about women as some men," he said, "but at least I know more about them than any woman does. A woman can't see herself any better than a man can see himself; but, in addition, she's psychologically incapable of seeing another woman objectively—with enough detachment to realize what a woman actually acts, looks, and sounds like—" Francis spoke fluently, for the statement, once he had stumbled into it, was one he had composed long ago in mental answer to a critic, a woman, who had printed, commenting on a piece of action in his last book, a similar accusation. Not yet insensible either to the pleasures or the pains of his trade, Francis could spend a good deal of time enjoying praise and taking blame to heart this way. "I don't expect you to believe me," Francis continued, feeling that the statement was getting too literary, that it too clearly answered the critic according to her folly, "because, of course, if you were able to believe me it wouldn't be true. What women don't credit themselves with and don't see in each other is the principal thing about them—a sort of vital, sustaining bitchiness. Did you ever keep a dog? Mrs. Cunningham has an old bull terrier called Rose with her—older than God and hardly able to walk. I was admiring it in

Paris. I don't think I'd ever noticed an old bitch before. They're still just like women. You wouldn't believe how much like an old woman that dog is—and, of course, vice versa—" He broke off, for Miss Robertson, standing up, turned and took her suitcase out of the rack.

"What on earth are you doing?" Francis asked.

"I'm going to sit somewhere else."

Francis began to laugh, the burden of disadvantage that Miss Robertson had managed to keep him at all afternoon dissolving. "What did I do? Insult you?"

"You don't insult me. You bore me."

"Don't be such an ass!" he said. "Put that back and sit down. You act like a two-year-old." He stood up himself, took the suitcase out of her hand and replaced it.

Miss Robertson cried, "Let me alone, please!" Apparently abandoning the bag, she gave him an angry, ineffective shove with her elbow, trying to get to the door.

Still laughing, Francis stepped that way, too, blocking her, so she drew back. "Don't be such an ass!" Francis repeated. He caught her by the forearms—through the supple layer of spotted fur her arms were firmly rounded, with big biceps, and it occurred to him that if she resisted in earnest he would have his hands full. "I said, sit down!" he told her. She was facing forward, so the motion of the train was against her. Easily enough, he controlled the rebellious indignant squirm by which she tried to get free and sat her down just where she had been before. Her attempt to rise again needed no more than a hand put hard on her shoulder to stop it. "Now that will do," Francis said, taking his hand away. "I'm sorry if you thought I called you a bitch. It's at least two-thirds a compliment. Besides, it's nothing to what you've been calling me." He sat down in his own corner and looked at her amiably.

Regarded with the indulgent eye of a victor, breathlessness and higher color had much improved Miss Robertson's appearance. It did not make her pretty, but her physical presence lost that forbidding quality that you associated with brisk, competent schoolteachers and strong dictatorial trained nurses. The warmth of her cheeks and her flustered manner gave her the absurd yet engaging air of a disgruntled schoolboy who had just, to his own surprise, got the worst of a tussle to which he had committed himself not quite so seriously as to leave him altogether humiliated, and yet seriously enough to make him wonder what the spectators were thinking and to feel that he ought to do something to show that he had been only fooling around.

"I didn't know you were so athletic," she said sarcastically, but the sarcasm itself was flustered, and sounded halfhearted—a last hitting-out of that alert disagreeableness, meant to show that, though defeated, she would scorn to court anyone's favorable opinion by losing with good grace; and that if she acquiesced, she didn't do it humbly, and no one need suspect her of complaisance.

Since Francis could not help liking people who amused him, he now felt well disposed toward her. "What kind of music do they give you in Milan?" he asked.

Music was not one of Francis's natural interests or pleasures, for he was practically tone-deaf; but the love of it is a mark of superior culture, and so he had heard a great deal of music while he was at college and supported with disciplined patience many concerts and evenings of opera rather than have his friends suppose he was in any respect their aesthetic inferior. Those days, no more than two years back, seemed long ago to Francis. He had begun to draw off. He was more and more ready to leave music to people who liked it; partly because, becoming a published writer, he felt that he had established his claim to intellectual distinction in a modest but sufficient way, and no longer needed to give examples of it in every field; and partly because he had come to observe that instead of making himself impressive, a person putting it on may make himself ridiculous. Francis had a sense of narrow escape. Two years ago he would have been as likely as not to try to impress Miss Robertson. He did not think she would be slow to grasp so glorious a chance to make a fool of him.

Since he took care to tell her right away that he knew nothing about music, Miss Robertson was, to start, grudging and reluctant. She spoke of the role she was getting up—it was the one Mary Garden had sung in *L'Amore dei Tre Re*. Soon she found that Francis had been too modest. His comment, though brief and diffident, showed her that he had heard—and after all he had; he had required himself to hear—practically everyone and everything and that he was capable of appreciating music's paramount place in human endeavor. Miss Robertson became more voluble and informative, making it unnecessary for Francis to comment at all. She took the trouble to tell him about ideas and feelings of her own which might make what she meant clearer. She repeated, self-deprecatory yet with the candid tone of one musician to another, some interesting compliments that had been paid her.

Smoking, Francis listened in much the same way that he used to listen at concerts, paying outward attention. Inconspicuously he sought the frequent relief of thinking of something else. He thought of the blind king strangling Mary Garden, who had worn a remarkable wig. He thought of this or that person at college with whom he had often attended the opera. As Miss Robertson talked more and more about herself and her prospects, he tried to decide whether or not he did believe that she was going to be a great singer. To do this, he had to project himself into the future and to imagine, as a sort of test, that she had come to be acclaimed universally as the greatest singer of her age; and how well he would remember that curious rainy afternoon on the Milan train; and would he or would he not be surprised, now that he thought it all over? He looked at her in a careful detached manner and thought that maybe he would not be surprised. After all, she had the physical vitality that plays so large a part in any sort of success, and she had it abundantly—at a tangent, Francis saw that this was something he had neglected to consider when in his mind he had marveled at the anonymous, if not imaginary, wop who had felt fancy enough for her to make a proposition. Though Miss Robertson's face and manner did not offer much of an invitation to love, that vital fleshiness might stir some experienced lecher who had long ago sated himself with delicate or pretty girls. In fact, though stocky and thickset, her figure might be thought good by someone who didn't find meaty heaviness distasteful.

As well as physical vitality, Miss Robertson showed an aggressive firm purpose. Supposing she had any voice at all, it would surely carry her further than she could ever get with the same voice, or even a better one, seconded less ably. Supposing she really did have, actually or potentially, a voice of the first rank, why shouldn't her triumph be inevitable—far more inevitable, Francis thought, than any notable success in writing would be for him? Whatever his natural talent (and he did not think too poorly of it) his purpose, though not changing, did not drive him so hard; and, as Miss Robertson pointed out in her disagreeable earlier mood, he was not ready to make wholesale sacrifices of his comfort and convenience. This reflection filled him with a foreboding, or uneasy dismay, lest he be throwing away, through supineness of will and undisciplined habit of mind and life, certain opportunities for greatness that might have been his, but, every day, perhaps every minute now, slipped by his own fault through his hands.

Several agitated resolves were hazily taking form in his mind when he realized that it had been a long while since he had let himself hear what Miss Robertson was saying. Returning with a start, he found that he was in the nick of time, for she had interrupted herself to say: "It's freezing in here. They've let that heat go off."

This was true, Francis realized, though he might have been a long while in noticing it. In Europe he was used to being always more or less cold. He said promptly: "Well, suppose I find the conductor and raise hell."

"It won't do you any good." Miss Robertson huddled her coat about her and shifting sideways brought her feet up on the seat, clasping her hands over the top of her insteps. She peered out the dripping window. "This is Parma," she said. "Maybe we'll get some heat when they put the lights on." Francis could see the sidetracks and switches, the crowded dull-colored backs of buildings in the rain-hazed dusk beyond. They were in practical darkness when the station shadows fell, and at once the lights did come on. Francis stood up and opened the door. "I'll see if I can get you some coffee or something," he said.

"You can't."

"I can try." He stepped down on the gritty paving and slammed the door behind him.

When he came back he carried a stack of paper cups, a bottle of mineral water with the cork drawn, and a flask of brandy. "It's probably poison," he said, drawing the door closed and setting these things on the window ledge, "but it's bound to be warm." He separated two cups, poured an inch of brandy into one and filled the other with mineral water. "Just take a deep breath and swallow that," he said holding them out to her. "You'll think it's summer."

"That's much too much," Miss Robertson said. Her fingers touched his as she took the cups. "You're the one who needs it," she said. "Your hands are like ice."

Shivering, Francis said, "And how!" He poured brandy in another cup and tasted it. "It's dreadful," he said truthfully, and swallowed it.

Miss Robertson, holding both cups, tilted the brandy and gingerly took a little. She screwed her face up and gulped the water. "I don't see how you do it," she gasped. She put the cups on the ledge, pulled a handkerchief from her sleeve and wiped her mouth hard.

Francis said, laughing, "Better drink the rest of it and get it over. It works. I can tell you that." He reached and took the paper cup and poured more mineral water in it.

"I will in a moment," she said. "If I take it all at once, it goes to my head."

Francis held up his own cup and looked at the bottom. "You have to watch it," he said. "Probably it will eat a hole through paper. I've seen so-called *fine* eat a hole through leather. Lorna Higham and Gwen Davis and a chap named Bancroft—do you know him?—and I went up to Amiens to look at the cathedral one day last fall. It was raining, of course, and we got soaked, so we tried some brandy in a disgusting little grogshop. Lorna spilled a drop on her bag and before she could wipe it off, it had definitely begun to eat through."

Miss Robertson raised the cup. Shuddering, she emptied it and seized the water. "It does help," she said when she could. She wiped her mouth again. "I never saw much in the cathedrals," she said. "I hear you know all about architecture."

"I don't know anything about architecture," Francis said, "but some of them are pretty good—just as things to look at."

"I always thought the cathedral in Milan was hideous."

"And so it is," Francis said. "Next time you're in France, go and see Bourges."

"I went to Chartres," she said. "I thought the glass was beautiful."

"Yes," said Francis, dismissing it, for after all Chartres was pretty well done to death, and you could hardly admire it without sounding like a Paris-in-seven-days tripper. "There's rather a curious cathedral at Angers," he said. "I happened to be driving back from Brittany up the Loire Valley last August and we stopped overnight there—"

"You certainly know a lot of France," Miss Robertson said. She spoke admiringly, without the least malice; but the way in which she had reduced to its simplest terms the idea conveyed by what he said made Francis pull up. The only 'rather curious'—a phrase from the college jargon of critical understatement meaning 'extremely interesting'—thing about the cathedral at Angers was that few people Francis talked to would ever have seen it. Ashamed of himself, he said: "I don't know France at all. The truth is, I hate these people who always know something perfectly wonderful somewhere out of the way where only a few rare spirits like themselves have ever been. I suppose that's what I sounded like."

"No, you didn't," Miss Robertson said. She raised a hand, grasped the edge of her hat and pulled it off. "Warm is right," she said. "I shouldn't have drunk that so fast."

Francis, about to make some inconsequential answer, stopped, almost staring, for he had never seen her bareheaded before. From the blonde bits of it showing around her hat brim he had formed an idea of what her hair would be like. As he had expected, there were great quantities of it, and it was slipshodly bundled up; but the released loose coils shone with metallic luster. You felt that, weighed in your hand, a braid of it would be as heavy as gold. It was so clearly operatic, fit for a Wagnerian heroine in stage armor, that, in itself, it seemed to show that her future was assured, already stamped on her.

Into his cup, shaking with the train's motion on the window ledge, Francis thoughtfully poured brandy. Examples of appearance as a form of destiny occurred to him and without waiting for the many, perhaps more, exceptions to present themselves, Francis began to apply it, wondering whether he already showed that he was bound to become a distinguished writer, or whether what he showed was that he never would be one. Since he had the matter at heart, he tried to dismiss such disquieting speculations; for where would he get the courage to hear the answer if someone in a position to see offered to tell him?

Miss Robertson said: "Lorna's pretty, isn't she?"

Brought sharply out of his preoccupation, Francis said, "She's charming." The word pretty was not a word he liked or used in that connection and he corrected it; but he did not know what to make of the sudden remark, or of the fervor with which Miss Robertson spoke. He could not see that she and Lorna had anything in common, and he had put down the acquaintanceship as one of those formed at school, and then accidentally maintained through the years in disregard of the fact that both the one-time friends have long been dead and gone, leaving only two, in all but name strangers, to share an unreal, embarrassing intimacy.

Miss Robertson said: "I hope you're going to be nice to her."

"You hope I'm going to be nice to her?" Francis repeated. He spoke blankly; but before he had said the last word, he got it. Limply, affecting continued incomprehension, he said, "Why shouldn't I be nice to her?"

His confusion—the implications of Miss Robertson's remark seemed to rise one after another and burst like rockets in his mind—let him do no more than go on gazing with a controlled blank expression at her. It occurred to him then that the stiff shot of brandy had made Miss Robertson, not used to drinking, drunk. His relief was enormous. He had met the shock of the idea that Lorna would talk to someone like Miss Robertson about him and been ready to accept it—as he had learned to accept and even expect all those rank offenses to dignity or reticence that women think nothing of, and must actually enjoy, since so many of them are able calmly and cold sober to make confidences to the first acquaintances they meet of things that a man, blurting them out drunk or beside himself, could not for years afterward remember saying without a convulsion of mind; but Francis passionately preferred to think that Lorna had said nothing to Miss Robertson. General conversation, or some chance comment of Gwen's, had given material for a romantic conclusion, the least little bit tipsy, of Miss Robertson's own.

Francis guessed that protests would only make her rally him the more intolerably. He smiled, and since it would let her have her sly idea, and yet might get her away from the present or immediate past, said with what seemed to him adroitness: "Tell me what she was like at school." He saw in imagination a thin, large-eyed adolescent girl, the same flush of color near her cheekbones, standing breathless in a middy blouse, bloomers, and hockey pads, on the playing field. She had the air of finding this game a silly one, yet she was jubilant with excitement and interest, even so. He could think of her in the morning, slight-breasted, in a sweater; her narrow legs crossed under a short serge skirt, biting the end of a pencil over an algebra paper to which, frowning, whispering figures, shaking back her fluffy hair, she added neatly and accurately fresh equations.

Recognizing fancy at mawkish work on these pictures, Francis discounted them. He forced himself to guess that, more likely, Lorna had been skinny and anaemic with a poor sallow complexion. Far from being youthfully engaging, or showing any resemblance to what she was today, her manner and ordinary temper had probably been sullen and moody. Good spirits and amiability—he told himself—were very much a physical thing. Physically, Lorna never could have been robust. If she were not robust there was a good chance that the menstrual function, establishing itself, had made her wretched and so for several years more or less hysterical. At fourteen or fifteen (a left-handed tenderness lay in thinking this way, that it was not really her fault, poor kid. Francis saw it, but perhaps because of her present charm for him, he did not reject it once he had put it in realistic terms) he was prepared to believe that she might have been as disagreeable and unattractive a girl as any fair-sized school could show.

Miss Robertson said, "Oh, she was frightfully clever. She was very quiet. In the lower school they used to call her the Dago." Miss Robertson's voice was gently bemused. While the brandy was no doubt having a genial effect on her memory it was possible that Miss Robertson had been—in fact, at the time; not in later sentimental retrospect—happier during those years at school, before her ambition got a grip on her, and before she felt the full melancholy effects of having so few of the qualities that would attract boys, than she had ever been since. "They took me out to study voice before I graduated," she said. "I used to see her during vacations. While she was at college I went to Europe. I just happened to meet her in Paris. We hadn't seen each other for years."

There was a long pause, either because Miss Robertson was feeling what she had drunk enough to be afraid that it would show in her voice; or because she felt pleasantly numb and talking seemed unnecessary. She sat gazing owlishly at the windowpane and after a while Francis helped himself to a little more brandy. He remembered coming back from the excursion to Amiens, rain running down the black glass like this, the cold arc-lighted caverns of the Gare de l'Est late at night. Although, actually, it could have been no more than six or seven weeks ago, it seemed hopelessly past, and regret consumed him. He could have wished the autumn to go on that way forever; and, from regret, his spirit sank to a mute and helpless resentment that refused comfort and despised hope.

After a long while the train began again to slow down. Miss Robertson said in a normal-sounding voice, "This is Piacenza. I think we're late." She opened her bag and looked at a cheap watch she had in it. "Half an hour," she said.

Francis roused himself. "Does it matter?" he asked.

"No, except I won't get any supper."

"Eat with me," he said, taking himself by surprise. "It would be a great kindness," he added, recovering; for even the company of Miss Robertson seemed, now he thought of it, a little to be preferred to this wet and dreary evening alone. "After all, it's my last day of freedom and I feel very low."

"I don't think I'd better. Signora will give me a couple of sandwiches."

"Doesn't she approve of your dining out with men?"

"She doesn't care what I do as long as I pay her every month. But why should you take me to dinner? I thought you were taking a job because you were broke."

"Not as broke as that," Francis said, "and beginning tomorrow night I have no more worries. I'm being kept."

"Well, we could get something in the station."

"Yes, but we're not going to. I feel bad enough anyway. We'll go across to the Palace and get a decent dinner, if they have one."

II

Rain drove against the high windows of the elegant, though old-fashioned and somewhat hearselike bus. Rain beat loudly on the roof while Francis and Miss Robertson, the only passengers, were carried in a sedate circle around the piazzale. Perhaps the driver had been told to make the most of this trifling trip from the Central Station steps to the doors of the hotel. Noticing the maneuver, Francis's impulse was to comment; to say that the conscience of the management could not be wholly dead since in exchange for the 'omnibus incl. luggage, 10 fr.' sure to appear on the bill, they were supplying as much travel as they possibly, short of approaching the hotel by way of Venice or Genoa, could.

He did not say it. His glumness or grumpiness following the bright feeling of the brandy as he regretted Paris and deplored his fortunes had been aggravated by difficulty in getting a porter; then, by the slowness of the hotel runner to appear; and, particularly, by the moving crowd. The Milan station was full of people who seemed to imagine that if they waited a moment the rain might stop. They crowded all the doors. When any mouth opened, out came a jabber of Italian that, for Francis, rarely contained an intelligible word. Those who crossed brusquely in front of him, or loitered senselessly so that he could not get by, in speaking Italian sounded as well as looked like even greater imbeciles—asses, apes, and dogs!—than the people who normally compose all crowds of strangers. Sunk in the shadows of the lumbering bus, cold and disgusted, Francis despaired of humanity. He could not see the use of saying anything.

Miss Robertson did not say anything, either. Indeed, it was too late to expect her to say just once more that she thought she'd better get home. She sat quiet on the narrow seat, her leopard-skin coat held close about her, her green hat and impassive face lit up now and then as light passed on the glittering windows. Francis wondered if he might say: "Look here, I know you're bored to death by this. I'll just leave my bags and get a taxi and run you home—" But he hesitated, not sure enough that he could say it with the right tone, and unwilling to risk the embarrassment of behaving—or, by a wrong tone, of letting Miss Robertson see that he was behaving—in a mannerless way. The bus at a crawl came around between the dark clumps of dripping shrubs and the flower beds full of withered stalks and dead plants. The runner snapped up a great umbrella and opened the door.

In the shelter of the glass roof of the portico Francis drew a breath. His eyes met the many slabs of marble affixed to the vestibule walls, each commemorating in gold letters an occasion on which some person of royal blood had been the hotel's guest. Francis's poor spirits involuntarily lifted. "How marvelous!" he thought. "How marvelous! The gracious monarch! The well-conducted hotel proprietor!"

It was like a sudden glimpse of that other sunny basking world before the war. Francis seemed to hear in solemn obbligato faint strains that proved to be the music of "Pomp and Circumstance." Up the cleared steps, with a measured affable inclination of the head toward twenty or more frock coats bent by simultaneous constantly repeated bows, clad maybe in the duster and goggles of an early motoring costume, came King Edward VII. Innumerable gray and white hairs spoiled his beard. Majestic dissipations had puffed and thickened his face to the tight, fat remoteness of a graven image. The dignity of his swollen abdomen acknowledged his long hard life of pleasure. Yet no ignoble consciousness of self showed in the matter-of-fact acceptance of respect due to his exalted station. The King did not give the least sign—held at a distance, an idle friendly rabble cried, *'Viva il Re! Viva l'Inghilterra!'*—that he understood the preposterousness, surely taught him by age and illness, of being a person whose stop at an hotel was event enough for bows, crowds, and cheers; and advertisement enough to be subsequently celebrated on a marble tablet.

The doors closed out the rainy night behind. Francis and Miss Robertson advanced into a warm silence, sparingly but snugly lighted. It smelled of old plush, of furniture polish, of pomade. The concierge in his decorated, gold-laced coat bowed. The man behind the desk inclined his gleaming head. Miss Robertson said, "Look, Francis. I really think I'd better go home. I'll just pick up a taxi—"

"Now, do we have to go through all that again?" Francis asked benevolently.

The waiter turned about and went.

"Wine is good for you," Francis said. "Drink it. Drink it. You're more trouble than any ten girls I ever met."

Miss Robertson said, "I'll be tight. I'll bet you'll be tight—" The first sound of her voice had been critical or reproving; but it wavered unexpectedly loud to something like a giggle.

"Nonsense," said Francis, but he looked at her attentively. Miss Robertson's forehead as well as her cheeks were suffused with a pleasing animated pink; but at the same time a relaxing of muscles subtly broadened her already too-broad face. She sat heavily in her chair. Her big square shoulders were a little bit stooped and she rested her elbows hard on the table, as though propping herself up. Francis said, "Don't drink it if you don't want it."

"It's that cocktail," Miss Robertson said. "Don't you feel it?"

Francis smiled, but he let his glance go off in a quick turn around the dining room. At a table thirty feet away a party of Germans or Swiss seemed engrossed in their food. No other people remained. "You underestimate me," he said; though in fact he had acquired a wonderful renewed sense of vivacity and well-being. Miss Robertson, going to wash her hands, had taken some time. Francis registered. He handed over his passport for the police. He spoke to the concierge about the luggage. He did his own washing. Miss Robertson still did not come, so he drank a Martini at the bar, had in a waiter from the dining room, and asked for a menu. He had drunk another Martini before Miss Robertson reappeared. Then he took one with her. Three cocktails were more than he needed; but, cursorily examining his present feeling, it seemed to him that he could truthfully say he did not feel it in the sense Miss Robertson meant. "You underestimate me," he repeated.

"Oh no I don't," Miss Robertson said. She set down her glass and made a little, to Francis somewhat alarming, motion with the fork she had been raising to her mouth. "I don't underestimate you at all," she said. "Don't think that. I wouldn't be here if I did."

"Could you make it a little clearer?" said Francis, grinning. "That has a sinister sound."

"I just mean I wouldn't waste my time with somebody who hadn't anything to him. I don't underestimate you at all. There are things about you that ought to be changed; but—how old are you? About twenty-three?"

"Yes," said Francis, "but I think I look older."

"I'm serious," she said. "You'll grow out of them." She gave a wise nod. Suddenly she laid her right hand on the table, palm up. "Do you see that?" she said, indicating a perpendicular line near the edge below the little finger. "You don't often see that. It's intuition. I can tell what's going to happen."

Francis looked at his own palm. There was certainly no such line to be seen on it. He laughed. "Chiromancy!" he said. "But if you really want to know what's going to happen you ought to try alectryomancy. Now, that really is something. You describe a circle on the ground and mark around it the letters of the alphabet. On each letter you drop a grain of corn. Then you tether a cock in the center and every time he eats a grain you write down the letter he took it off. I never make a major decision without—"

"You can laugh," said Miss Robertson. "Laughing's one of the things you'll get over when you get older."

"Don't I know it!" said Francis. "'The last stages of an infirm life are filthy roads. I find the further one goes from the capital, the more tedious the miles grow, and the more rough and disagreeable the way.' Lord Hervey wrote that in 1743 to Lady Mary Wortley Montagu. It's still true. I don't expect to find anything funny about it."

"That's another thing you do," said Miss Robertson portentously. "You're pretty fond of showing how much you know and how much you've read."

Francis had no trouble in laughing. "Drink some wine," he said. "I'll have to get your critical faculties dulled. All I did was try to amuse you with small talk. It's unkind to start again on my failings. People won't like you if you do things like that."

Miss Robertson said nothing for a moment. She stared fixedly at her plate. She put her fingers around the stem of her wineglass, started to raise it, and then decidedly put it down. "Forget it," she said. She made a short little angry gesture. "I have a mean disposition, I guess." Her words were laborious. "I say things—I don't know why. I wish I didn't."

"Ah, how we all wish we didn't!" said Francis.

The painful, harshly forced-out answer disconcerted him, but expressions of regret always filled him with the tenderest compunction. Even when he had been injured or was righteously angry, a word of this kind was enough. He was placated not so much because his heart was charitable, or because he loved concord, as because he felt, knowing himself, a moral vulnerability that the saints are not alone in feeling. Self-indulgent people may lack the temperament to sink under the awful conviction of sin, and they may not know the daily need to get right with God; but many of them sink daily under the awful conviction of unwisdom or short-sightedness. To Miss Robertson Francis said, "It was entirely my fault. I—" But before he could bring himself, even in his new state of grace, to make a gracious or respectful reference to the science of palmistry, Miss Robertson, having suffered all she could stand of whatever she did suffer when she apologized, interrupted him. Roughly she changed the subject. "Tell me about this boy, this Cunningham boy," she said. "Isn't there something wrong with him?"

"No," said Francis. "Well, he had infantile paralysis. One foot isn't so good. He has to wear a brace. But he gets around much better than you'd expect. He plays tennis. You have to feed your shots to him, but you'd have to anyway—it's what you're paid for, after all." That was not fair, he reflected at once. Walter, skipping, dragging his foot agilely, could move along the base line as fast as he needed to. He could even get up to the net for a return not cut hard. Walter never complained—or never had to Francis, on the one occasion Francis had played with him on an indoor court in Paris—either of balls he could not reach or of balls placed where he couldn't help reaching them. Francis said, "I think he also gets asthma. Maybe it's the same thing. I can only say he puts up with it all a damned sight better than I would."

"Well, what's he doing over here?"

"Oh, that's a sister of his, I think. She's having a year at one of those schools in Paris where they teach you *est-ce-que* French and cultivate you with performances of *Phèdre* and visits to the Louvre."

"Lorna knows her, doesn't she?"

"Yes, but Lorna's friend was an older sister. There are two older ones, I think, both married. They're quite nice people."

"So you said."

The words, with their effect of detached, gently sardonic comment on the incoherent or repetitious ramblings of a person amusingly unable to say what he means, surprised Francis; but he saw that Miss Robertson could not have meant them that way for she appeared hardly aware that she had said anything.

"So I did," Francis said. "I'm afraid I can't be very bright about it." He drank some wine. "It's a shocking thing to be rich," he said. "You hire somebody like me, which is very nice of you really; but do I like it? I do not; and so when your back is turned or you're out of earshot beyond the Alps—" He shook his head. "I didn't order anything else," he said. "I thought you might like to—"

"Oh, I couldn't eat another thing." Miss Robertson's voice was faint and far-off. Worried, Francis saw that her expression was very much like that indecisive stare, fixed inward, often appearing on the face of an unpracticed drinker who has, perhaps, topped off his whisky with a little gin and is beginning to wonder. "Look here," he said, "do you feel all right?"

Miss Robertson stirred in her chair. The expression that disquieted him was gone and almost absent-mindedly, but warmly, she smiled. "I feel marvelous," she said. "I didn't, for a while. But all the time you were talking I could sort of feel it—I must be really tight. I never felt like this before. It's very nice."

"Men beat their wives and starve their children for it," Francis said. "It ought to be good—" He broke off. A moment before he had been feeling what might fairly be called marvelous himself; but now all this changed for he was thinking about the things he had said about the Cunninghams. He not only did not like these things, but discussing the Cunninghams at all seemed in questionable taste. Inspecting himself, he did not think that he was drunk; yet he knew from experience that this reaction, deferred numbly until it had to emerge slow and irrelevant through a succeeding and different line of thought, this plummeting from exhilaration to distaste, this exaggerated intensity in scrutinizing himself, proved that he was not sober. "You've had about enough," he thought. "All another drink will get you is a head in the morning. You know that." Aloud, he said, "Shall we get out of here, then? We'll have some coffee outside."

In the hall, following Miss Robertson into the empty lounge, he was still intent on repairing his lapse. "Walter's really a very engaging kid," he said, "and his mother was as sweet as possible to me—over there," he said to the waiter. They sat down beyond a large palm in a pot. "Have some brandy?" he asked. Nothing seemed to him less likely than that Miss Robertson, after her afternoon's experience, would want brandy, so it was a question perfectly fair to his intention of not having any himself.

Plumping down under the palm Miss Robertson said: "Oh, I don't know. Do you think I'd better?"

"Well, you're the best judge of that," Francis said, smiling. To the irritated remonstrance of his own mind, he pointed out that he could not very well say, "No, I think you'd better not." On the other hand, he very carefully hadn't said, "Yes, you'd better." In acknowledgment he got only a knowing sneer. Vexed by the justice of it, he said aloud, "It ought to be fit to drink here."

"No, I know what I'll have," Miss Robertson said. "I'll have some crème de menthe. Don't you like that?"

"No," said Francis. "I'll have some brandy."

He sat silent and defiant while the waiter was out. Tomorrow morning, when this triumph over the plaints of his better judgment would sicken him with exasperation, was somehow receding. Tonight, though diminishing hour by hour, magically expanded. The barrier of time that it set between now and the oppressive forlornness, the whole hateful matter of getting to Montreux loomed paradoxically larger. Tomorrow, on the other side of it, could take care of itself.

The waiter had set out the cups and glasses. Miss Robertson said, looking at the green gleam of the crème de menthe, which had been brought frappéed, "I like this. That English girl I was telling you about used to like it. She used to keep a bottle up in her room, and days it rained we'd go up after lunch and have some. She called it our cold medicine. She was lots of fun." Miss Robertson bent forward and sucked at the small straw.

She did not, Francis reflected, sound any too funny. His brandy had come in a balloon glass and he raised it to his face, sniffing the acrid fumes, wondering who on earth this English girl was. "Oh," he said, "you mean the one who—"

"I guess I shouldn't have told you that," Miss Robertson said. "I don't know why I did."

"You gave it as an example," Francis said, abstracted. He thought how true it was that you ought to be careful what you told a person you did not know. You might get to know him better. But he was more interested by the discovery of obvious mistakes he had made in summing up Miss Robertson. Mixed with, even accounting for, the pity and indignation that she had expressed in giving him an example of the sacrifice, so many times repeated, for art, Francis had credited Miss Robertson with a native distaste, a severe censoriousness. If this English girl had been intimate with her, perhaps her best friend, Miss Robertson might have felt many things, but not that.

Francis let himself picture those rainy days—the monotonous studies and exercises through the raw morning; the unappetizing rapidly served food and empty polyglot gabble of a cheap pension luncheon table; Miss Robertson and the girl from England going upstairs to a constricted, uncomfortable bedroom where the mouthful of crème de menthe gave them who knew what illusion of zest or good spirits or even of gay sophistication, while they turned over magazines or musical scores that they had seen before, gossiped about their work, or gazed out on the hazed, wet street. Francis's thought went off the track, for the picture of the ghastly day crowded out, by its universality, its part in everyone's experience, Miss Robertson and her friend. Francis himself sat at the gloomy luncheon table, he climbed the stairs, he saw the room and the wet street and faced the afternoon.

He said: "You didn't tell me her name. I'm not ever likely to meet her. I wouldn't be likely to hold it against her. The truth is, I thought maybe you did hold it against her."

"Against her?"

"You can sometimes see that a thing is not a person's fault; but it does not always make you like it or him any better."

"I'd be a fine one to do that," said Miss Robertson. With the straw she poked at the mush of green ice in her glass. "Why should I? I don't blame anyone for anything. Don't imagine I haven't any feelings." She took up a package of American cigarettes which Francis had laid on the low table before them.

"Sorry," Francis said, "I didn't know you smoked."

"I don't often." She felt in the package. "Never mind," she said, "there aren't any."

Francis looked around. The lounge was empty. The waiter had withdrawn. "They ought to have a bell," he said. "I have a carton upstairs. We may as well use those. I doubt if I get them by the Swiss frontier."

"I don't really want one."

"Well, I do." He swallowed his brandy. "I'll only be a moment. Look, don't you want another of those?"

"No, I mustn't. It must be awfully late."

"It's barely half past ten," Francis said. He went out into the hall. The waiter who had served them put his head past the door jamb up by the bar. "Two more of those," Francis said to him. He looked at the number of his key and went up in the elevator.

A light had been left on in the large heavily furnished room. The red curtains were drawn and it was very warm, perhaps because it took European systems of central heating all day to get up steam and they began to function only when you no longer wanted heat. Putting the curtains aside, Francis jerked up the window a little, looking down at the piazzale and the station façade through the steadily falling rain. His luggage had been arranged against the wall by the door. Coming from the window, he stood a moment staring at the row of bags, for the heat, after the chilly breath of air, set his head swimming, though not unpleasantly. The cigarettes, he remembered, were in his small bag, and, moving toward it, he saw suddenly that the concierge had simply sent up all the luggage, Miss Robertson's black suitcase, too.

"Hell!" Francis said, picking it up to take down with him. Halfway to the door, he remembered the cigarettes. He went back and unlocked the bag. Taking out a couple of packages, he straightened up, the movement making his head swim again; and he waited a moment, breathing deep, steadying his vision on the big bed with the covers turned back. "Ellery," he said aloud, "you're pretty drunk—"

But it was impossible to put much reproach in the admonition. The immediate sense of pleasure, of being invulnerably committed to the principles of pleasure without fatigue, or disgust, made reproach absurd. It would be absurd, having stumbled into this rich state of enjoyment to want it changed, or to find fault with it, or to leave it any sooner than he had to. It occurred to him that going to Montreux tomorrow was not strictly necessary—at least, not until tomorrow night. Nothing was more easily missed than a train connection. The evening would simply extend itself through the next day; and suddenly he heard Miss Robertson's moody voice saying, "Don't imagine I haven't any feeling. I don't blame anyone—"

Francis stood still another moment. "Ah, what the hell? Why not?" he said.

He went out and closed the door. In a careful, controlled way he walked straight and quiet along the shadowed hall, and, not ringing for the elevator, down the two flights of stairs. In the lounge Miss Robertson sat where he had left her. He saw that the waiter had brought another glass of brandy and more of the crème de menthe. "There you are," said Francis, sitting down. He opened a package of cigarettes and offered them to her.

She took one. "I've really got to go," she said.

"I don't think that follows," said Francis.

"I really do. Signora won't know what became of me."

"I have it on good authority that as long as she gets her money she doesn't care what becomes of you."

This chitchat, Francis saw, sobered out of some of his warm immoderate confidence by the imminence of definite steps, of decisive things to say, was hesitancy on his part, a postponing. For an instant he contemplated, moved to take it, the ready relief he could get if, instead of going on with it, he abandoned the still desirable but somehow risky project. As though aware that his mind was no longer entirely made up, and that raised expectations might in another moment find themselves cheated, physical urgency flooded his body in a vast impatience, recommending to his mind the idea or image of Miss Robertson's female body. Its effort was intense enough to make Francis tremble a little; and blowing out the match he had lit for her, he tried to get himself in hand by being quick. "I'll tell you something," he said. "It's going to pain and surprise the management if you leave. What have they put upstairs with my luggage but your suitcase?"

"My suitcase?"

"Your suitcase. I wish I could—" Francis found his voice not entirely steady. The distress of jeopardy or riskiness was stronger than ever, and this was ridiculous, the infirmity of a schoolboy. He put himself in mind of a remark, thrown out once by a college friend who had seldom much to say about love but whose almost satyr-like successes spoke for him, that had frequently helped at such moments: *What are you fooling around for? You know what you want. Ask for it, ask for it! You'd be surprised. . . .* Francis repeated, trying for a lightness of tone, "I wish I could say it was by my subtle design—" It was not light enough. Whether through desire or nervousness, it did not ring quite true; but he could not quit now. "On the other hand, it seems to be fate. We can't struggle against fate, can we? It would be ungrateful and impious. The wise man always takes care to be on destiny's side—"

Francis stopped. By letting himself talk on, even in a way meant to be fluent and confident, for talking's sake, he did not show the right confidence. "So," he said, "with credit and good conscience, I think we ought to go to bed." He picked up her hand and raised it to his lips—his movements, he was pleased to see, were precise and easy. He took the cigarette from her mouth and dropped it on the floor. With a convenient movement, he put his arm around her. "As Doctor Donne so well wrote," he said, "Come, Madame, come, all rest my powers defy—"

His success appeared to be complete. Miss Robertson drew a curious long breath and seemed to let herself slump against his arm. Francis lifted his hand, took her hat by its short brim and twitched it off. "Oh, don't!" said Miss Robertson. She started to raise her own hand to her hair but Francis put a finger on the wrist and she let it fall back. "Never mind that," he said. "It's wonderful the way it is. You can fix it tomorrow, if you feel you must. Now, we're going upstairs."

"No," she said.

"It would be much better. Think how the waiter would feel if he came wandering in. Come. This is a very pressing matter."

"Oh, no," said Miss Robertson.

"Oh, yes," said Francis. "You'll see."

"No," she said again, straining away against his arm. "No. You don't give a damn about me. You know you don't. You—"

Francis knew. Hopeful, he must have been going on the hopeful assumption that Miss Robertson's experiences in Milan and the world of music had prepared her to do without all that—the jockeying for emotional position, the protestations of devotion, the tedious running of the unsmooth course of true love to the pale, musty O Promise Me flowering, associated by Francis with late-June-afternoon weddings, one or two of which he had assisted at as an usher for some college friend, among the well-to-do simple society of small upstate cities. He saw the marquee on the lawn joined by a canvas tunnel to the big old-fashioned house, the five hundred guests who had to be asked and the men who kept an eye on them as they filed through the improvised museum of wedding presents, the quick shots of rye in a bathroom or secluded library, the evening clothes in the still bright sunlight making you feel like a waiter—all the tiresome (something borrowed, something blue) elaboration of naïve or sentimental custom that went into a lovely wedding.

This is joy's bonfire, then—Francis thought; derisively, for the epithalamium ought to include some mention of those humorists of the college party slipping downstairs again into the bedlam. (After the orange blossoms and the Baptist or Methodist organ music it was hard to blame them; perhaps they were the true Elizabethans.) They had cunningly eluded the best man and made themselves a laughter-shaken opportunity to get at the groom's luggage and scissor out the front of all his pajama trousers. There was the jocular kissing of the bride; the caterer's expensive, hard-to-swallow food; the bouquet falling from the stairhead; the rice, the shoes—the sweetest story ever told.

The succession of quick, untoward pictures brought Francis within a jot of stopping to set Miss Robertson right on what was decent and what wasn't. He recovered himself in time. "Why should I ask you if I didn't give a damn?" he inquired. "I find you urgently attractive. Don't tempt me to demonstrate it here."

"You wouldn't say that if you weren't drunk," Miss Robertson said. Her tone of nervous accusation seemed to imply that he had protested undying devotion, and that was all very well, and she didn't find the possibility of its being genuine as fantastic as the possibility of genuine undying devotion to Miss Robertson appeared to Francis; but he owed it to her to make so important a declaration soberly.

"Possibly I wouldn't," Francis said. "Now, are you satisfied? Probably I'd be too depressed to say anything. That's one of the nice things about drink. It eases constraint. Come. You'll enjoy it."

Miss Robertson turned her head down and away. "I have to go," she said.

"Of course you don't have to go. You don't even want to go."

"Yes. Yes. You mustn't ask me. You mustn't—"

"Now, why do you want to go? It's raining hard. It's a nasty night. Consider it carefully."

"Please," said Miss Robertson, "please." She shook her head back and forth. "I wish you wouldn't. Why do you want to do this to me?"

"What on earth do you mean by 'this'?" said Francis. In the warmth of his mind a coldness toward Miss Robertson must, at some point, have begun a gradual unnoticed growth. He noticed it now. Looking at her with his face still set in an expression intended to present amiable amusement, he found that he really disliked her a good deal.

"I mean," said Miss Robertson, at last looking him in the eye, "why do you want to sleep with me?"

The effect of her solemn, rather lumpish gaze was to repel him further. Francis viewed this reaction with curiosity. To his senses she made no more actual appeal than a cow, but he heard himself saying: "Well, you see, it's part of nature's great plan. One of the few good parts. That explains everything, doesn't it? Now, come upstairs."

"No, no," said Miss Robertson. "Francis, it would be so silly. Tomorrow we'd both be sorry. It isn't worth it. You know it isn't."

She was right. It wasn't worth it. Francis had the ineluctable evidence of his own eyes. He had, too, the easily examined evidence of his imagination, which foretasted, half-appalled, remonstrative, the crude not-very-exciting stripping in the bedroom, the heavy sweaty mechanical exercise of the bed. He said, "Ah, but I know it is."

Miss Robertson moved her body desperately. Her big knee, shifting, hit the edge of the table. The crème de menthe glass rocked on its stem, went over and rolled, fell from the edge and broke on the floor. "Oh!" said Miss Robertson. The waiter appeared, hovering at the door.

"Very neat!" said Francis. Again he was surprised to hear himself, for he spoke savagely, in cold anger, as though some low trick had been played on him. One moment, he was conscious of his surprise at himself and at his unreasonableness—the interruption was obviously not fatal, nor even serious; the next, this surprising anger, like an incoming tide, reached his mind and poured into it. Immediately he was enraged by the very consciousness that rage was unreasonable, that he was letting it serve as a stupid and unfair excuse for the failure of a stupid and unfair attempt. His anger grew with his inability to control it, or to prevent senseless fresh angers from joining it. He was angry at Miss Robertson for being so unattractive, and yet having the damned impudence to resist. He was angry at himself for the crazy effort to get what was patently repulsive and not worth having. He was angry at his ineptitude for failing to get it, worth having or not. He snapped at the waiter, "Get out of here! See that somebody finds a cab for the signorina. *Subito!*" He broke off, checked, for he had been taught that he had no business to speak to a person in the waiter's position that way. He swallowed the brandy in his glass, got hold of himself, and stood up. "I'll have the elevator man bring down that bag of yours," he said with enforced calm. "I won't offer to see you home. I expect you've had enough of my company."

"I didn't do that on purpose," Miss Robertson said.

In the door the concierge had now appeared. Francis said to him, "That small black bag shouldn't have gone up. It belongs to the signorina. Please have someone bring it right down." To Miss Robertson he said, "As you say."

"You think I did, don't you?"

"Perhaps we'd better go out in the hall."

"Well, I didn't."

"Ah, hell!" said Francis, smiling, not able any longer to keep the plain fact that his lofty manner was ludicrous hidden from himself. "Of course you did. Don't you know that the reflexes have reasons that the heart knows not of? You do what you have to do. I do what I have to do. I'm sure we should all be as happy as kings—" He searched about in his

mind for some concluding phrase, something telling, philosophic, genially cynical, and likely to make her feel a little foolish.

It was a large order, and his mind's contents seemed inaccessible.
Fumbling with it, Francis grew conscious of a faint nauseated feeling, a
starting-out of sweat in the palms of his hands and on his forehead. "If
you'll excuse me, I'll say good night," he pronounced with some difficulty, for that sensation, he very well knew, ended in only one way.

TWO

Walter Cunningham said, "Well, I didn't get it all. I didn't get—"

"Let me hear what you did get," Francis said patiently. "I'll find out
about what you didn't get soon enough."

"Don't I know it!" murmured Walter. He twisted himself in his chair
and drew a deep breath. "It snowed at Caux last night," he said.

"I doubt if it snowed much," Francis said.

One of the narrow casement windows that allowed you to step out on
the little balcony stood ajar. The mild damp air was not warm, but neither
was it cold. The pall of clouds, low above the lake, was brightened by
approaching noon, and while Francis looked, across a mile or two of quiet
gray water one thin steeply slanting golden shaft broke through. Sunlight swept a narrow course along the precipitate dark lower slopes of the
Savoyard mountains and went off toward Evian. "The sun's out up at
Caux," Francis said. "Any snow they had last night is probably melted."

"The concierge said it snowed a lot. There was snow before that. He
said there'd be lugeing."

"Now, when did you see the concierge?" asked Francis. "You haven't
been downstairs this morning."

"He came up. Mother wanted to find a vet to take Rose to. He told
her somewhere, and she and Maggie went. I'd better see if they're back
yet. It must be pretty near half past twelve."

"No it isn't," Francis said. "It just seems that way."

"Let me see," said Walter, seizing Francis's hand to look at his wristwatch. It was five minutes of twelve. "It must have stopped," Walter
said, bending his ear down toward it.

"Sit up!" said Francis. "Line twenty. Get going."

"*His Caesar,*" said Walter with a burst of energy, "*ita respondit . . .*"

Wheeling inshore, the gulls floated and fell against the low gray clouds. Footsteps crushed the pebbles on the promenade under the bare lakeside willows. Somewhere a door opened downstairs, letting out the sharp voices of women, kitchen workers. Francis heard each word, distinct, known to him, yet in the quick ellipsis of the slang they spoke, hard to follow.

"*C'est un as!*" The voice had a blank, surprised sound. (An ace of what?)

"—*J'ai pesé en moins de deux*—" A door slammed, cutting off the scornful answer. Perhaps it meant, 'I sized him up—it didn't take me two minutes to get his number.' What matter it concerned, what circumstance of money or love, or politics; of tips; of triumph over the management; of contempt for some guest, or some fellow worker; of the man who wanted to marry the bitter speaker, or was married to her, or hadn't the faintest intention of marrying her, Francis would never know. Without preparation or warning he found himself saying silently: "Think and die! Think and die!" for that inward eye, that bliss of solitude, had presented Francis with a lively and scarifying re-enactment—no appalling detail, no horrible trifle obliterated by the weeks between—of Miss Robertson and himself under the palm in the hotel at Milan. Stringently revolted, his stomach folded up. His frantic mind backed away; but Francis could not stop seeing it. "Christ Jesus!" he said, soundless.

Walter's voice, which had been growing more and more uncertain, ceased. Walter's straight hair was that light, dusty-blond color that darkens later. Blankly, while his mind stirred in its numb and bruised obtundity as though wondering where it was, Francis considered this nearby head of hair. His silence probably alarmed Walter. Walter turned furtively, looking sidelong up through his lashes. He had his mother's eyes, which were close to the esteemed shade called violet by her generation.

"That child has the prettiest eyes—" Lorna had remarked. Francis could remember her saying it as they walked in the foggy dusk along the iron fence of the Tuileries garden. They had been having tea at the Cunninghams' hotel. "It's not fair," she said. "He ought to have been a girl." Francis could hear her heels on the pavement. Her arm was through his, her gloved hand laid on his wrist. Across her shoulders the fur of a silver fox trembled with a fine beading of moisture. White under the hazed glow of a lamp standard her face lifted as she spoke and shadows fell from the depressions at the temples past the evident high cheekbones. Light filled the delicate hollows under them and for an instant you could see that her eyes were blue. Francis took off his hat. Not stopping, he bent his head down and kissed her mouth. Taken by surprise, her breath caught, gasping. She got it again and laughed. "Why, my dear!" she said. "In public! I'm surprised at you—"

"Well," Walter said defensively, "I told you I didn't get one part."

Francis dropped his eyes and compelled them to focus on the printed lines. "Try thinking of it in direct discourse," he said.

While Walter affected this trial, Francis managed to read the passage himself, and then read it again. He went on: "Think what Divico would say if he were speaking. He'd say: *Helvetii instituti sunt*, wouldn't he? That gives you your tense. This is it, literally: 'Divico replied, thus the Helvetians by their forefathers to have been trained.'"

An expression of exaggerated anguish crossed Walter's face. "Now, pay attention!" Francis said. "Don't look at me. Look at the text. It's simple. Here is what their ancestors trained them to do—" He had to pause, for the words refused to make sense. He saw the shop windows glowing out of the fog through the arches of the arcade, the radiance in gilded columns shining up the wet asphalt. A gloved hand squeezed his wrist briefly.

"It's a result clause after *uti*," Francis said; and saw, relieved, that so it was. "The Romans thought differently, remember. *Ita uti*—'in such a way that as a result'—of the way they had been trained—hostages, *accipere*. What is it?"

Walter writhed in his chair. "Well, it means to suffer, doesn't it?"

"In a different use. You don't suffer hostages."

"Hostages," repeated Walter, bending his head down almost to the page and screwing his eyes closed, "*accipere*—uh, they killed them."

"Oh, God!" Francis said to himself. "Would you mind sitting up?" he asked.

Walter sat up. "Hostages," he began again, "*accipere*—"

"Yes, *accipere*! What does it look like? To accept, to take, receive. *Accipere non dare consuerint*. 'They were accustomed to take, not give, hostages.'"

"Oh. Well what's it mean?"

"It means that Divico is trying to get tough with Caesar. He goes on: *eius rei populum Romanum esse testem*. Literally—look at it!—'of the thing the Roman people to be a witness.' It's a wisecrack. He's saying: 'Listen, the Helvetians weren't brought up to give anybody hostages. They take them. You ought to know that.' He means that, in earlier times, the Romans of the province had to give the Helvetians hostages."

Since it was the end of the passage, Walter had allowed himself to relax again. He thrust out his left foot. There was a felt slipper on it, and in the mornings he did not wear his brace, so the trouser leg of the dark-gray flannels gave no sign of anything wrong. He cocked his head and eyed the slipper. "Wasn't Caesar sore?" he asked idly. He moved a hand with caution, pretending he thought Francis might not notice it, and touched back Francis's sleeve to see the wristwatch. Francis removed the hand and looked at the watch himself. "All right," he said, "we'll find out tomorrow."

"I can hardly wait," Walter murmured. Francis said to him, "What did you say?"

Walter giggled. "Nothing. I didn't say anything."

"One more like that, and we'll find out right now," Francis said, obliged to laugh himself. He closed his text. "Do what you can tonight with the next section," he said, reaching over and putting a pencil check beside it in Walter's copy. He piled his books together.

"Oh," said Walter. "I guess I'll go and ask the concierge where we can get some skis. Shall I get your mail?" He put a hand to his knee, stood up, and with a quick skip reached the connecting door. There was no answer to his knock and he opened it. "They're probably still down with Rose," he said.

"If Rose is sick," Francis said, "your mother may want to stay here this afternoon."

"Maggie can stay. Anyway, Mother doesn't have to go. If we're skiing she'd just be standing around. I'll tell her we're going up to Caux."

"We'll see what she thinks."

"She said to see what you thought."

"Well, I'll talk to her about it."

"Oh, it's all right," Walter said tolerantly. "The doctor said it was all right. I can do it."

"I wasn't thinking of that," Francis told him, disconcerted. He had no prepared explanation of what, if not that, he was thinking of. He said, frowning, "I don't know anything about skiing over here. It may be pretty dangerous. It certainly would be around Caux."

"Fellows from the English school at Glion ski there."

"We'll see," repeated Francis. "Are you going to get that mail, or aren't you?"

"Sorry," said Walter. "Can we have lunch right away?"

"We can't have lunch until your mother's ready to have lunch."

Francis went into the hall and down to his bedroom at the other end. Still constrained—when simply to ignore Walter's disability? When to acknowledge it as the most natural thing in the world? The occasion that brought up the matter of skiing he remembered very well. They had bicycled to Aigle one damp gray afternoon. Sitting on the bridge end, their bicycles leaning against the wall, they rested while Walter tossed pebbles into the rapid cold stream. An open truck heaped with skis and luges, probably going to some resort hotel, passed them. Francis could just as well, and not very untruthfully, have said that he didn't know how to ski; but that was during the first week with Walter, and Francis supposed that his impulse had been to make the most of any accomplishments he had with the idea of fostering a useful admiration. Walter asked at once if they could try it.

Francis might have answered simply and directly, "I don't think you'd be able to manage skis." He had not said it. His feeling about Walter's misfortune was too complicated. Trying to ignore it, he had been anxious to pretend that it did not exist. He was unwilling to refer to it. Sympathetically, he did not want to show that he ever noticed it; but his sympathy was mixed with other feelings. He felt an irrational embarrassment, as though he owed Walter an apology for the callous and cruel way in which he, Francis, walked around on two good legs; and to cover up this unfair difference, his impulse was to talk down or make little of the advantage he enjoyed, to imply that Walter could do anything he could—certainly not to imply, let alone directly say, that Walter mustn't hope, being partly crippled, to attempt the activities of happier, normal people. "There won't be enough snow," Francis had said to both Walter and himself, "for a long time yet. We'd better start back. I told your mother we'd be at Zürcher's before five. She was going to have tea with us."

Francis dumped the books on his bed. From a briefcase on the floor near the small writing table he took the file folders that held the manuscript of his book. Earlier in the morning he had thought of something that he meant to change, or see to. Though he could not now remember what it was—perhaps a word in Walter's spelling lesson that he recognized as the one he wanted in some particular passage—it had impressed him as an important improvement. He was still searching, hoping, if he hit on the part to be changed, it would recur to him, when he heard the uneven quick sound of Walter's footfalls coming up the hall from the lift. "Yes!" he said.

Walter slid into the room, laid the envelopes he held on the table. The bed squeaked as he dropped bouncing on it. Francis closed the folder. Deliberately, he lighted a cigarette and took up the envelopes. "Well, what about Caux?" he asked. He turned the first envelope over. It was from his mother in Florence.

"Look," said Walter, "could we go to Les Avants instead? They've been skiing there for a week. It's good there. The proprietor told me. He said he'd tell Mother. They have a funicular up to a place. Do you know where it is?"

"I expect we could find out," Francis said casually. He looked at the last envelope, shrugged, tapped them together and stood up.

"What's the matter?" Walter said.

"Nothing at all," Francis said, looking down at him. "Why?"

"Oh, you sounded kind of funny. Don't you want to go to Les Avants? The proprietor says it's swell. He says his regiment practices up there. On skis. Did you know that? They have soldiers who have skis."

"Yes, I knew it," Francis said. "They're very good troops, the Swiss. What's *accipere* mean?"

"Means to accept, receive, take—and to suffer, in another use. Fooled you."

"So you did," Francis said.

II

Ten minutes out of the Montreux station the Oberland-Bernois train, in an unhurried electric glide, climbing silent, hardly vibrating, reached the clouds. Mist closed in like a white tunnel. The long rising folds of land, the leafless stone-walled vineyards, the evenly planted, bare-branched orchards, all disappeared. Walter, his nose against the oblong of plate glass, said, "Look at the snow! Look at the snow!"

Through the white mist snow could be seen in a low pile along the bend of the track. A tall dark shape arose in the obscurity, became suddenly a clump of pines, the branches lightly whitened with snow. "My, my," said Maggie. "Isn't that pretty!" At once she added, "Oh, dear! Mrs. Cunningham, I've gone and—" Her lean face lengthened. Through her horn-rimmed spectacles she stared with dismay at the knitting she held. "I lost my count. I believe I should have begun narrowing." She unfolded the knitted strip and blinked at it. The ball of wool rolled from her lap, and Francis bent forward and picked it up. "Oh, dear—" Maggie said again. "I thank you very much, Mr. Ellery."

Mrs. Cunningham said, "Let me see it, Maggie. I don't think you ought to be narrowing." She drew the gloves from her small, prettily formed hands—quickly from the right hand, from the left with caution of habit, for she wore on it, next to her wide gold wedding ring, what had been her engagement ring; an inconveniently large diamond made more inconvenient by the old-fashioned mounting. She smoothed the gloves and laid them neatly in her lap. In the capacious embroidered bag beside her she had all sorts of things—a Tauchnitz novel, knitting of her own, smelling salts, a little round box of local chocolates, some cubeb cigarettes in case Walter had a touch of asthma, a gold fountain pen, a writing tablet whose sheets could be folded on themselves to make their own envelope. She felt these things over. Then she investigated the pockets of her Persian lamb coat; and then the pockets in the suit of violet tweed that she wore under it. From one of them she produced her glasses' case, giving Francis a fleeting sympathetic smile, as though she felt that her stupidity in not knowing where she had put the case must be painful to anyone watching her. She lifted her face a little, closed her eyes, and pushed the earpieces into the waved almost white hair covering her ears. Tapping the bridge into place on her nose, she opened her eyes and took the knitting from Maggie.

Francis looked at her with liking. Not too directly, he continued to watch her while she examined the knitted rows. Mrs. Cunningham looked no less than her fifty-two or three years. As the underlying tissue lost its tone, her cheeks had filled out and her skin showed loss of freshness and the signs of sagging. Though her ankles, crossed one on the other in thin wool stockings, were shapely, her figure was the necessary figure of fifty. The remarkable thing, Francis thought, was that though time had made so many changes and she looked no longer as she had looked when she was twenty, you could still see what, at twenty, Mrs. Cunningham had looked like. The girl's face remained close behind the relaxed cheeks and the wholesome but aging skin. The shape was strangely unaffected; just as her wide, well-placed eyes and candid brow were not themselves affected by the glasses, horn-rimmed like Maggie's, that she had imposed on them. Undoubtedly she had been beautiful.

Francis acknowledged it. He saw, too, that his acknowledgment might be an understatement. She had really been more than that—what, at the turn of the century, they called a raving beauty; and her husband had probably considered himself the luckiest man in the world—without, Francis guessed, finding subsequently that he was very much in the wrong, either. A photograph of the late Mr. Cunningham stood among the numerous photographs—of all three of the girls, of the husband of one of them, of Mrs. Cunningham's sister—that crowded in their folding leather frames Mrs. Cunningham's bureau top. The placid, intelligent face suggested sound principles and a financial acumen of the prudent sort fit not to make a fortune, but, more decently, to conserve one already made. Indeed, in the picture itself was proof enough of Mr. Cunningham's importance. That flowing mustache, that two-inch collar closed in front over a retiring ribbon of necktie, could only have been worn, when the comparatively recent photograph was taken, by an officer so high in a bank so old, rich, and powerful that direct contacts with the public and its changing fashions were for him unnecessary.

The ridiculous mustache, the ridiculous collar were obviously those worn by the bridegroom, or the young father of the late nineties, so they helped Francis to form a picture; yet the picture, being obscured by the gentle absurdities of a day too remote to be real, yet not remote enough to have accumulated the dignity of history, left unanswered most of the questions in Francis's mind. When young Mr. Cunningham, with his high collar and softly curved mustache, beheld in yon window niche his statue-like Psyche, fresh from regions which are holy land, what reverent agitation swelled his breast? For that matter, what of the other agitations, the visions somewhat less chastely classic, that, though not in those days mentionable, might be assumed to have received private consideration, and to have played some part in Mr. Cunningham's hope that she would consent to be his? And when this decorous young man with his sound principles and flowing mustache came to make her his, what scenes of frightened embarrassment, what palpitations of horrified innocence, surrounded the nuptial couch where, surely not helped much by the hyacinth hair, the classic face, the Naiad airs, a prompt impregnation was nonetheless achieved?

Tugging sharply, Walter took hold of Francis's arm. "The sun's coming out!" he said.

Beyond the windows the dense whiteness had brightened to a yellow shimmering haze. A curved white slope dimly marked with pines and a black mass of rocks showed through. Then abruptly sunlight itself poured on the snow. The interior of the carriage lit up. The mist-dewed glass shone like gold.

"How perfectly glorious!" Mrs. Cunningham said. She was folding up Maggie's knitting. Giving it back, she said, "It's the next row you begin to narrow in." She removed her spectacles, gazing with pleasure at the light and the golden window. She turned to Francis a smile of great sweetness, as though she were crediting him with being responsible for the blue sky, clear now behind the last shimmering wisps of cloud to the high horizon, the immaculate snow fields marked in the hollows with deep clean shadows and gilded on the sunny rises. Amid them and not far off, Francis could see the village roofs, the tiers of hotel windows, which, no doubt, was Les Avants.

Fretting at all delays, fidgeting even in the midst of the pleasures of picking out skis (as though he were so hemmed in that he did not know where to turn, and grudged time spent at any given enjoyment since it was just so much time taken from other enjoyments to come), Walter got off toward the funicular ahead of everyone else.

"Now, darling!" Mrs. Cunningham said.

"What?" said Walter passionately. "What, Mother?"

"You know," Mrs. Cunningham said. She slipped an arm around him, slowing him down firmly to walk with her. Walter made an excited motion to wriggle free, but she did not let him go and the strong pressure must have been significant to him. He submitted to it with an effort, his face pink, his eyes still sparkling, his rapid breath visible on the frigid mountain air.

Getting the skis together had delayed Francis a moment. He stood supporting them against his hip while he pulled on his gloves, gazing after Walter and his mother, who were already across the road approach-

ing the ticket window. He had heard their voices. Mrs. Cunningham's
arm about Walter, and Walter's self-imposed obedience touched him, and
Francis did not like to find himself touched. Working his fingers with
care and exactness into the gloves, he stood unseeing, his face blank, for
that particular sensation, described so well as a tug at the heartstrings,
put Francis unpleasantly in mind of the things as a rule tugged up, the
treasures of sensibility ancient and modern. Old fools remembered, they
remembered the house where they were born; horrible little boys asked
where Mama had gone away to; in more than fair exchange, a tear was
wiped at sight of the little toy dog covered with dust.

Francis wanted no part of it; but, want it or not, there it was. The
mingling of pity—like parting, such sweet sorrow; of pain, you could
hardly say what pain; of the sense of things gone, of the unfairness of fate,
of disappointment, of disillusion; perhaps, of the hour of death and the
day of judgment, all thrust toward the bowels of his compassion. They
were bowels not particularly easy to get at; but, on close inspection, were
they any different or any more decent than the man of sensibility's belly-
ful? Eviscerated, gushing freely out, all bowels looked alike, and Francis,
in revulsion, snapped himself up. Ill at ease, he had to realize that a painful moment of the same affecting sort might be to come if Walter, putting
on his skis full of hope, discovered that his brace wouldn't support him
under such novel and peculiar strains. Francis did not think Walter would
make a fuss, which was all you could ask of anyone and more than you
would get from most people. You could not ask Walter to decide at once,
if he found skiing impossible, that he had never wanted to ski anyway,
and, in the interests of sparing a spectator, not merely to act, but to feel
accordingly.

Skis on his shoulder, Francis had caught up with Maggie. Maggie was
still on this side of the road. She picked her distrustful way over the
packed soiled snow, which had been softened earlier when the sun was on
it, and now, in the shadow, was freezing again. A procession of sleds
carrying milk cans approached, and Francis stood still beside her. "Dear,
dear," Maggie said cautiously, "Walter's all flushed up. Mr. Ellery, it's
a thing I dread. For what it might lead to." Her lined face, wary and
apprehensive, twitched as she noticed, apparently for the first time, the
passing horses. She went back a step in case one of them should reach out
and try to bite her.

Francis knew nothing about asthma, but he said, judicious, "We'll
stop this pretty quick if he seems to be having trouble."

"Oh, Mr. Ellery," she said, "that's the worst of it. You can't tell until
afterward. With poor Rose being so sick and all, I wasn't watching him
this morning. He begins being excited, you know. As soon as he gets up.
About nothing, that is."

"He seemed all right this morning."

"Did he now? Well, I'm glad of that. Oh, the times we've been through! That he's alive at all seems a miracle. It's from the paralysis, you know. As a baby he was never sick a day, not one. He was delicate-looking, not so fleshy as the girls when they were little, but never sick—"

Francis had heard most of this recital before. No matter where she began Maggie would presently arrive at it, turning it over and over in sad, incredulous tones for as long as she had a listener. In Francis she had a good if unwilling one. Not knowing that Maggie expected, as a matter of course, that he would interrupt or cut her off without ceremony whenever he had the notion, Francis thought that he ought to wait for a conversational pause in order not to hurt her feelings by evident boredom or indifference. In Maggie's recount there never were any pauses, either for breath or for lack of material. With money so little object, Walter's medical history had been extensive. A dozen specialists were known to Maggie by name, and she remembered where and when each saw Walter, and in a general way she could sum up what each said or did. By their works she knew them, too; and she showed it in minute changes of tone. Some had helped Walter. Others might get themselves a reputation all over the country; they might put on airs and talk very wisely—you could imagine Maggie, inconspicuous in the background, probably not even noticed by the great man, seeing everything, hearing everything, thinking her own thoughts—but their knavish duplicity was proved by the event. They had pretended to know about poliomyelitis and then had not done a thing for Walter. Maggie would never in this world forgive them.

More than loyalty, you had to realize, this was love. A wish to please, even an attachment to duty, could be hired; and money would buy a convincing affectionateness and a very good show of interest but not that brooding concern that retained every trifle, relevant or irrelevant, that absorption, tragic yet tiresome, that could not stop thinking or talking about the sad, sad thing.

"Then this other doctor," Maggie said, "came from somewhere in the west. Perhaps you'd know of him, Mr. Ellery. He was very well known—" The sleds and their savage or dangerous horses had gone by, and Maggie, word following word in the hypnosis of her theme, perceived that the road was clear. She stepped out. Her overshoe descended on snow polished by the sled runners and she almost fell. She staggered sideways against Francis, who was close enough to catch her elbow, and had to break her narrative to apologize, gasping with embarrassment, for it took a moment to get her balance and she naturally seized hold of him. "Oh thank you, Mr. Ellery!" she said. "I'm so terrified of falling! There's this sister of mine, she's in a convent, who fell two years ago and fractured her hip. She isn't off her bed yet."

That Maggie had a sister who was a nun was news to Francis but not
surprising. Half hidden in mufflers, sweaters, and the collar of some un-
namable gray fur on Maggie's black cloth coat, she wore on her bony
breast a small gold cross entwined with gold thorns and roses. Under the
black cloth dress Francis knew that she wore, in addition, a number of
medals, for Walter had described them to him with interest. Presumably
Maggie was able to believe that a look at Saint Christopher would keep
her safe all day; and if it didn't, the valuable periapt of Saint Benedict
must, by its formidable initials, give the devil pause; and if the worst
came to worst, there was the scapula of some confraternity probably associated with whatever order this unfortunate sister of hers was professed in,
to cut a little shorter Maggie's detention under the pains of longing and
of material fire in purgatory. "That's too bad," Francis said sympathetically.

"Oh, it's terrible," said Maggie. "They may have to take her up to a
shrine in Canada, Saint Anne's, it's called, to be cured."

Francis nodded, sober and sympathetic still; but the marvelous, matter-of-fact statement filled him with delight. Why not? Why not? What
could be better—parmaceti for an inward bruise—than thaumaturgics for
a fractured pelvis? Why not take a train to Quebec and get some? The
heart swelled with glee. It shook with the silent peals, cruel but refreshing, of that genuine Homeric laughter—the mirth of the younger world.
By all means, the train to Quebec; and, borne by pious friends, in haste to
the half-rebuilt basilica! Saint Anne, seeing a sufferer earnestly venerating
pieces of her precious bones could not but be touched. God, listening
indulgently to His Grandmother, formed the awful thought: *I will: be
thou clean*, and there you were.

Francis was sure that he had not smiled; but he saw Maggie blinking
doubtfully at him. Recovering from the distraction of her alarm and embarrassment, Maggie deplored her incaution in mentioning to Francis
things that were not for him. Guiltily she pressed her lips together, as
though reminding them of the virtue of silence. Francis did not think his
sober air had deceived her. Just how exhilarating a jest he found her faith
she might not know, but she knew enough to be sure that it was a faith he
could not share, or take seriously. She was not offended. In this case,
silence was a privilege, not an imposition, and though she made most of
her life the property of the Cunninghams, there had to be things—her
religion one of them—that she kept for herself. She would have done anything for Walter, but Francis doubted if the idea of inducing Saint Anne
to take a hand in Walter's cure had ever so much as crossed her mind. In
the Episcopal church they did not have miracles or interceding saints—an
arresting example of the Divine Economy, perhaps; since relatively
speaking, the need was less acute. Maggie would not be likely to either

wish or pray for something so surely contrary to reason and what Mrs. Cunningham would like as Walter's conversion. In the end, on the last day, it would probably be all right. Anyone could see that committing a lady like Mrs. Cunningham to hell was out of the question.

Francis supported Maggie's elbow. He got her across the road. They went through the gate to the waiting funicular and he found a place to stack the skis. Walter, though sitting down with his mother, could not sit still. He had kept his ski poles and he balanced his hands on them. He jabbed the worn floor with their metal points. Supported this way, he swayed from side to side. His cheeks were still flushed and his eyes darted here and there, delighted with everything. He nudged Francis with his elbow. "Gosh," he breathed, swinging himself over close, "pipe the motorman's hats."

"Don't shout," Francis said. "They're English."

He had already observed the two young men Walter nodded at. Though he was seeing them worn for the first time, it had been apparent to Francis at once that those were the skiing costumes he and Walter ought to be wearing. The baggy trousered suits of blue-black flannel, the straight visored caps of the same material heavily stitched, contrasting with his own sweater and golf trousers, made Francis uncomfortable. If he were going to ski often he saw that he would have to do something about that.

Unabashed, Walter rolled his head around, taking in through his lowered lashes the other passengers. These were French, or possibly the gayer or more Gallic sort of Swiss from Geneva or Lucerne—two men with big pointed noses, long loose lips, and no color; and two young women. All four, like Walter, bubbled over with pleasure and excitement. They never stopped talking and laughing. One girl, whose curls were colored the unnatural yellow of egg yolk, constantly touched, patted, and held on to her escort. She looked at Francis and smiled. She looked at Walter and became suddenly grave, for she must have noticed his brace. Francis could not hear her, yet from the motion of her lips as she squeezed her companion's arm he was surprised to see how simply and surely the words *pauvre* and *petit* could be read. He looked indirectly at Walter; but Walter's whole attention was given to the other girl, who had a sleek bang of jet-black hair coming from under her beret down her forehead almost to her eyebrows. She kept her eyes on her young man's face. She held a lighted cigarette and with surprising skill was blowing smoke rings toward him. In the disturbed air most of them never arrived, but when one did, they both cried out with delight. "What's she trying to do?" Walter whispered.

"Convey her affectionate regards, I expect," Francis said. Forgetting a moment to whom he was talking, he went on, "It's like a picture in

Le Rire—" He had in mind one of those gayer, less anatomical jokes that lightheartedly demonstrated the conventional French proposition that, in life, the really important (but not serious) thing was love. Love was so amusing, so delightful, and fortunately to be found everywhere and all the time—in the black-haired girl's swelling breasts and blown smoke rings; in the yellow-haired girl's limber amiable mouth and kittenish hand-strokings. Just in time, Francis saw Walter's interested expression and checked the comment he had nearly made on the gay relationship. "We ought to start," he said.

This was enough to distract Walter. He twitched about, looking out at the man in uniform who stood holding what seemed to be an old-fashioned automobile horn. "Hey!" Walter said. *"Nous voulons partir!"*

"Walter!" Mrs. Cunningham said. Walter put his hand over his mouth. "Excuse it," he said. "Frank thought we were going."

The horn honked. Humming on the overhead wires they moved. They swung slowly out above the long slope of the snowy fields. "See?" said Walter. "See?"

The yellow-haired girl smiled again at Francis and then tenderly at Walter, but Francis looked away. Checking the remark that he had almost made had served to check, too, that love said to be felt by all the world for lovers. Francis considered coldly the ridiculous yellow dyed hair. He sized up the dark girl's stupid thick features under the coarse bang. Something from *Le Rire* was right! *Le Rire*'s advertisers spoke to you of love. What about the *pied-à-terre grand luxe* always open and the articles *d'hygiène en caoutchouc?* What about something for *les soins intimes (Que des larmes évitées!)*; and if that did not work, the *Sage-Femme 1ere classe discrétion absolue?* What about the disorders of the *voies urinaires*, the *pilules* and *pastilles* good for *impuissance, acte bref* and *frigidité féminine?* You couldn't say they hadn't told you!

"Ah!" said Francis, shaking his head. Below, the long road on the hill bent from left to right and back to left again in easy gradients. Directly underneath them moved the horse-drawn sleds with the milk cans, the same ones that had held him and Maggie up. The moment's audible jingle of metal made him think suddenly of the story about the sleigh ride. *Then I put my hand up all the way*, boasted the lewd little boy. *Well, what was that like? I don't know*, the simpleton confessed, *I had mittens on. . . .*

Francis suppressed indignantly the mind's idiotic quiver of laughter; but laughter startlingly filled his ears. The French party was convulsed. Francis dared say it was a joke of the same sort, for the blonde girl was blushing. She bit her lip, shaking her head in vehement protest, trying not to laugh; but with triumphant pleasure her companion pressed his advantage. Bending forward he dropped an emphatic hand on her leg, through her wool skirt frankly palming the inside of her thigh, and said something more. Everybody cried out again with laughter, the speaker himself loudest of all. In the transport of mirth his foot shifted and hit the end of the ski that the nearer of the two English youths had been sighting along critically to see whether it needed more wax.

The Frenchman turned his still-smiling face and instantly apologized. He got for it a short nod, a chilly withering glance. Drawing up his kicked ski, the English youth waited a bare moment, then moved six inches farther away. From his mouth he took an unlighted pipe, lifted his eyebrows, and said, perfectly audible to Francis, "Shan't be sorry when we get to Grindelwald."

"Quite," said his friend, removing for a moment a pipe of his own. Although naturally round and ingenuous, his plump boyish face stiffened in a demeanor much too old for it, a diverting expression of weary dignity. He passed his eye over Francis, not unobserving, but not interested, and looked away.

"Simple ass!" thought Francis, partly amused, since the two were several years younger than he was; yet partly annoyed. "These Britishers!" he said to himself. "It's really time they were put a stop to—" He shook his head, ruminating the joke of England in case the round-faced youth happened to look back. But the round-faced youth, looking back, if he happened to, would never dream of what was so amusing.

Francis's mind took itself disconsolately away, wishing not for any single thing, but for vague new states of things which would—*comfort and relieve him according to his several necessities!* He brightened a little, unable to see his so-called necessities without irony. He was comforted and relieved already by the ludicrous ending of a solemn obsecration in the wish to be more appropriately dressed for the occasion, so that, exchanging cool stares with Britishers, he need rest at no disadvantage.

That took care of that; but he had deeper discontents, and even they were not exactly necessities within the prayer book's meaning. Francis did not know why he got no letters from Lorna in Paris, and the worried mind could not expect much comfort or relief there. He did not dwell on it, because he could not endure to; but what about that detestable misbehavior of his in Milan? Rationally or irrationally, the inexpungeable suspicion of the anxious heart is that the gods may be just; that you reap what you sow; that the nature of things operates by an awful law, a sort of *lex talionis*, which, whether you revere or deride any given moral code, will take an eye for an eye and a tooth for a tooth, and complaining will not help you.

Formulation was, however, a defense; for the gloomy notion was most effective when half felt, when pushed away where the sharp eye of the mind saw its terrific shape in the dark, but not its cumbersome construction of who knew what remnants of taboo or bloodguilt, or tribal magic.

Put in words it sank to more or less imposing rodomontade. "Accuse not nature," Francis found himself declaiming—what a priceless old imbecile Milton was!—"she hath done her part—"

He stopped dead.

With a jolt Francis lost interest in old imbeciles. The head-filling recitation broke. "Lord God!" he said to himself. "She hasn't been in there, of course—"

Francis started to get up. He was indefinitely impelled to do something—stop the funicular, get out, rush off to—well, perhaps to telegraph. Hung on a cable halfway up a hill this was not practicable, so Francis did not complete the movement. He sat staring, at once frenzied and perfectly still; stabbed to the heart, yet thinking clearly; as, detail by obvious detail, the stupid, the ruinous reason why he had not heard from Lorna after that first letter demonstrated itself.

It might be weeks before she happened to go in to Morgan Harjes. Any fool could see that, for what would she expect to find? By now there couldn't be anyone who ever wrote to her who didn't know where she was staying. Had he thought she might be in for money? How could he think it? How could he? Had he lost his mind? He had been with her the day she cashed all the rest of her letter of credit—it was on George Bancroft's tip, got straight from someone on his paper, who got it straight from someone who must not be named in the Agence Havas, who got it straight from M. Poincaré's secret memorandum to the Governor of the Bank of France, that the franc was to be supported. Gwen Davis kept her traveler's checks on the off-chance that, despite George, the Agence Havas, and the secret memorandum, what the franc was really going to do was collapse entirely; but the tip had been good. They would not need money from the bank. They had it already in ten-thousand-franc notes deposited in the hotel office safe. You might ask what Francis could have been thinking of.

Francis could answer, though in despair, that he had been thinking of the mail brought up in the morning, with Gwen wandering in, drinking her chocolate, ripping open her own letters, probably reading aloud and commenting on what she read. In Florence two days after he got down, replying to Lorna's first—her only—letter, Francis had thought of it. Not that Gwen could possibly be in doubt about him and Lorna, nor that she had ever showed anything but friendliness; but, even so, when he came to address the envelope, he wrote 14 Place Vendôme. There it went; and three or four others after it; and there, presumably, it stayed.

"Lord God!" Francis said again.

When Lorna had remained silent he had found reasons. Understanding her it seemed to him so well, he could understand. With the letter gone, she regretted, too late, too late, the impulse that had made her write out her heart, an hour's painful pleasure, saying what would soon seem to her so much more than she was obliged to say, so much more than Francis needed to hear or know. *My dearest*, she wrote, *you can see that I'm not the same person who came to Paris in August so blissfully uncertain of what Fate had in store for her. . . .* In contrast to the careless rush of the wording was the fine, finished, vaguely runic script; the backhand 'P' of Paris driven like a little flag, the 'my' of my dearest one level line decisively ended by the struck-down tail, as like her in its controlled nervous grace as the ready-made phrases about blissful uncertainty and Fate were unlike her. To have their real meaning they must be read by someone moved as much as she was; and Francis could imagine her recalling them the day after and wishing she were dead. No matter how much his reply reassured her, she might normally wish so still, until enough of his letters had come to make it sure that he was the one who waited and wondered, not she.

"But as it happened," Francis said ponderously to himself, "she didn't get any answer. None at all."

Francis supposed that he could, as his first impulse had been, telegraph her that there were plenty of answers in a pigeonhole at Morgan Harjes; but even he could see that after so many weeks, his answers could be in hell for all the good they would ever do her, or him. "And that's that," he said aloud.

"What?" demanded Walter, swaying over against him.

"Nothing," Francis said. "I was just thinking."

The stubborn thick leather of the strap resisted his cold fingers. Francis said, "Hold still!"

"I'm sorry, Frank," said Walter. "Maybe it's busted."

"It's all right," Francis answered. He managed to force the buckle pin through the next hole, pressed it flat, and snapped over the metal catch that locked the harness around Walter's heel. "I'm just not very bright. I should have done that before you put your foot in." He heard his voice full of pettish exaggerated blame.

"Well, gosh, thanks very much," Walter said, plainly supposing that in some way not clear to him he had offended Francis.

Francis arose from the packed snow. "It's not your fault," he said. He smiled, the grimace stiff and arbitrary on his cold face. "How does it feel?"

"O.K.," said Walter. Francis had been warmed by his exertion with the straps but he saw that Walter, forced to stand still, was shaking with cold. "Move out into the sun, there," he said. "Don't try to pick your feet up. Just slide them." Walter shuffled cautiously a yard or so, out of the shadow. He turned then, looked up and waved a pole to the glass-enclosed porch of the little hotel, hardly more than a small chalet, at the head of the funicular. Mrs. Cunningham waved back. Maggie, in eloquent pantomime, went through gestures meaning tuck your muffler in.

Francis repeated his unreal smile. Kneeling again, he slid up one of his own skis and drove his toe in. His fingers were almost insensible, yet he could feel the skin catch and stick, freezing against the cold metal. Sharp hard bits of frozen snow dug into his bent knee and he winced, shifting it; but in his bitterness of mind the pain, like the pain of his bare aching hands, pleased him. He wished in anger that they hurt worse, that he could give himself, the stupid ape, something to remember. "Come on, come on," he thought; for the anger was asinine, too; you didn't get anywhere that way.

Past him up the road came the round-faced young Englishman sliding along quickly and easily. Reaching a low place beyond, he side-stepped up onto the deep snow. He kicked his heels about, gave himself a mighty shove with both poles, and shot away down the steep slope into the hollow behind. At a hundred feet, going fast, he swerved right, and then left, dodging a clump of small pines. With a snow burst like a small shell exploding he executed a neat stem turn and stood still, facing back up the hill. Francis straightened up painfully, getting his numb hands into his gloves.

"Gosh!" said Walter. He looked over his shoulder at Francis. "How does he do that?"

"It's a matter of practice," Francis said.

"Show me how."

"I couldn't do it," Francis said. "I'll show you another kind of turn. But not today." He pulled his poles from the nearby snow pile. "Head over that way," he said, gesturing to the dip, flooded with dazzling sunlight, where the road along the crest of the col went off west. "That will do to start on. All right?"

"Sure," Walter said. "It's a cinch." He pushed out vigorously, sliding ahead until he reached the imperceptible edge of the slope. The acceleration, once begun, threw him off balance.

"Bend your knees!" Francis called, rousing himself. "Bend forward! If you let your feet get ahead of you—" Before he could say it, Walter displayed it in a spasm of acrobatics, flinging his arms wildly. One pole, whose thong was broken, left his hand, spun over and over through the air, and landed a surprising distance down the slope. Walter went in a heap, his skis angling every way, and instantly covered himself from head to foot with snow.

Francis pushed off and overtook him. "Hurt yourself?" he asked.

His falling feeling of apprehension was really, he recognized, as much for himself as for Walter. He did not feel equal to it—to alarms and concerns, to saying or doing sensible, decisive things. He saw then that Walter was not hurt. Floundering, Walter began to laugh. "But how do I get up?" he asked.

"Get your skis straight," Francis said. "That's right. Now, catch hold." He pulled him to his feet, still prepared to see Walter stagger or fall when he put weight on his leg; but Walter, looking back at his tracks with admiration, said, "Say, all the way to here!"

"Now, wait a minute," Francis said. "I'll get that other pole." Turning to look for it, he saw that the round-faced English youth, side-stepping his way back up the hill, had already come on the pole. He stopped, looked to see whose it was, swung an arm down and pulled it out of the snow.

"Much obliged," Francis called. He turned his points that way and glided carefully down. The English youth had started climbing again. Rosy, breathing hard, he held the handle out to Francis. "First day?" he said.

"Yes," said Francis stiffly. "Thanks."

He took the pole, ready to return, for he neither wanted, nor wanted the Britisher to have the faintest reason for thinking he wanted, to strike up an acquaintanceship. It took him a moment to head around, and before he could move off the English youth said, "Been up here before?"

"No," said Francis.

"Better slope over beyond there."

"Thanks," Francis felt obliged to repeat. "I don't want anything too fast for him."

"No." The round face turned up to where Walter, high above them, stood against the bright-blue sky brushing off snow. "Crocked leg?" he asked. His voice had that note of schoolboy solemnity, of doing that duty of manly compunction that England expects every man, and particularly every boy of the upper middle class, to do when he is confronted with the dumbness of dogs and horses; and, by extension, with the plight of a handicapped human being.

"Infantile paralysis," Francis said.

"Plucky kid!" He looked back at Francis and said warmly, "Let me show you this place."

Francis hesitated. The round face, ruddy with the labor of climbing, softened by the spectacle of pluck, had the expression natural to it, the open look of ingenuous friendliness. The small brown eyes, narrowed in a squint against the sunlit snow, shone with good nature—the physical good nature of a person who likes food and gets all he wants of it; the mental good nature of a person, sturdy and well fed, whose idea of fun is so simple and wholesome that he can have it anywhere. Francis would not have expected to be cheered, and in a sense he was not cheered. Relieved or grateful, he simply seemed to find, in the forbidding circle of the world, one point not definitely hostile, not requiring any new resistance or defiance.

"Thanks," Francis said, aware that he had now said it three times. "If it isn't too far—"

"Oh, it's not far. Just over there. What's his name?"

Francis hesitated again. He saw the cordial intention to make friends with Walter, and certainly he could not see any harm in it. Yet having often watched, a little scornful, a little impressed, the characteristic start of wariness, the slight cool withdrawal of rich people—or at least of the few with whom he had been intimate—when someone they knew nothing about attempted what seemed to Francis perfectly natural and spontaneous advances, he was not certain that Mrs. Cunningham would approve if he made Walter some new friends this way. He did not want her to think him unsophisticated, and in the fraction of a second given him to decide, Francis tried to be judicious. He told himself that there was nothing about Walter or Mrs. Cunningham that advertised wealth on a scale likely to allure strangers with ulterior motives—even granting that Francis could be wrong about the friendly eye and adequate manner, and wrong about the accent and inflection, which sounded to Francis indistinguishable from that rarefied bleat, the mark he had been told, of Balliol, and so of all that in England was highest and best; but which might not seem so indistinguishable to an Englishman.

"His name is Walter," Francis said. "He'll have to take it pretty easy. If he gets too excited, he has asthma attacks."

                                        III

The station lamps were lit. Those great snow fields hung luminous in the dusk above the town. The wind had died in fragile silence and a few stars, a few infinitesimal points of light, were white yet brilliant in the darkening zenith of the pure cold sky. Francis, hardly knowing why, told himself that it was a remarkable moment. Years from now he might remember it; he would remember the last light on the snow, the white mountains, the indescribably fine motionless silence of the high air into which they stepped as they left the stuffy electric-lighted restaurant in a hotel otherwise closed for the season, and walked down the short street to the station.

The comfort of hot tea in his stomach soothed Francis. He liked the tiredness of his muscles and the tight warmth over his cheeks and forehead where the wind and glare had reddened the skin. Slow and quiescent, his thought went its way. He thought of Lorna in Paris without undue distress, for he had no active plans and hope did not trouble him. Sadly he thought that it might be as though she were dead; as though she had been dead ever since he left Paris. By now the mind accepted it; pain wore itself down. Death seemed all right, the necessary thing; perhaps, the very thing—a thought fairly familiar in poetry; but he had not, by merely reading it, grasped it clearly—that made youth and beauty mean what they meant; and there might be worse things than death—less peaceful. *Unarm, Eros*—grandiloquent, he seemed to feel that beautiful, mortal quiet—*the long day's task is done, and we must sleep*. . . . "Ah, well!" he said to himself. "Ah, well!"

With no warning sound of a locomotive, the Montreux train, as quiet as his thought, came rapidly around the bend against the dim high snow-banks, its windows lighted. They got in, and Francis sat in pensive silence until the train began to move. Walter roused him then. "Where is this Grindelwald anyway?" he asked.

"I don't know," Francis said. "Somewhere above Interlaken, I think."

"Is that far?"

"Quiet a distance. It would probably take all day."

Mrs. Cunningham had brought out her knitting, but she soon found the light not satisfactory. She rested her hands in her lap. Smiling, she said suddenly to Francis, "Don't you think Toby's a nice name for him?"

"Yes," said Francis, smiling back surprised; for, first hearing it, Toby Troop had seemed to him almost too good to be true.

"Tom's the best skier," Walter said.

"The better of two," Francis told him.

"What is this school of theirs?" said Mrs. Cunningham. "I don't seem to know it."

"Wellington? Oh, it's a public school. I think it's quite a good one."

"Isn't it a strange time for them to be having a vacation?"

"Oh, I think they're out," Francis said.

"Graduated?"

"I think Troop is. From something one of them said, I expect Best was superannuated, if they do that at Wellington."

"What is it?" demanded Walter.

"Well, if you don't get through by the time you're a certain age, they turn you out anyway. They do at Harrow, I know."

"You mean you don't have to pass anything?"

"I think not."

"That's where I'd better go," Walter said. "No more work for poor uncle—"

"Darling!" Mrs. Cunningham said. "You mustn't say that! Of course you can pass."

Walter shifted his shoulders against the seat back. "Of course I can't," he murmured. He smiled feebly.

"Darling!" said Mrs. Cunningham. She looked at him with pained reproof, and Walter pushed himself down farther in the corner. "Well," he said, ostentatiously reasonable, "we don't know that I can until I do, do we? We don't know I can even get in. Maybe I'm too dumb."

"Now you're being silly, dear," Mrs. Cunningham said. "Please sit up."

"That shows I'm dumb, being silly, doesn't it?" Walter sat up. He put his arm through Francis's, and rested his head against Francis's shoulder, transferring the question to him. "Doesn't it, Frank?" he said. "Doesn't it?"

"Now, Walter!" his mother said quite sharply.

"You're not dumb," said Francis. "You just do your work and we'll get you in all right." He spoke calmly, confidently, with what, he immediately told himself, derisively, was a note of manly cheer. Since manly cheer was not his real attitude toward the matter, he felt, though every word he said was true, deceitful. Walter was not dumb. If you just kept at him, Walter couldn't help knowing what he needed to. Mere tiresome repetition would din knowledge into Walter's head. He would know how to go about solving the inane cryptograms of certain short Latin sentences; he would remember that the product of the means was equal to the product of the extremes. He would be able to spell apparatus, say whether a clause was restrictive or non-restrictive, and write a few fairly coherent paragraphs about my favorite sport—accomplishments, after all, not to be laughed at. There was a point on the dolorous way of learning when arithmetical ratio and proportion might confound the mind as utterly as the quantum theory. Francis supposed that the fatuity of confounding a mind to so little ultimate purpose was what made him feel deceitful when he heartily recommended study to Walter and cheered him with the promise of success.

From the phantasmagoria of Francis's own experience—sound of voices and the meager smell of chalk in once boringly well-known classrooms; exact colors and shapes of textbooks not seen for years; the tick of the study-hall clock in progress through hours much longer and slower than the hour of today (yet not so long and slow that Francis couldn't conveniently idle them away and have half, or even none, of his work done when the bell rang); the occasional late lights under which, while most of the school slept, he tried with vain violence to make himself learn in haste what he had neglected at leisure—there emerged in the end the uncomfortable, apposite picture of that wide worn bulletin board in the main-building hall. It was pinned thick the last day of term with typed slips, every few hours a batch of new ones, as master after master finished marking his examinations.

Plane Geometry IV (Mr. Blackman's Section) . . . Stomach lifting toward

his mouth, on how many of those successive little doomsdays had Francis
crowded in to learn his fate. *Post II, 95; Upjohn, 92*—in fearful haste his
eye went down the column, to bring up, perhaps, with a ringing shock on
Ellery, 60, thank God! He was by, all right, safe among the saved. Or, at
least, sometimes he was by. It had been *Ellery, 50*, or *45*, often enough
(*Be not deceived, God is not mocked*—at least, not every time) for him to
know, better than the almost emetic spasm of relief, the slow queasy
leaden feeling that he could bring home with him; under the excitements
of the school going down, and the joy of release, waiting right there on
the eventual question and the obligatory answer. It was no good answering untruthfully, for the marks would be along from the school office in a
few days, sometimes reinforced by one of those letters in which the
Headmaster made it known that he had personally seen the enclosed
report and felt that the gravity of the situation ought not to escape Francis's father.

What expressions of grief and disappointment! What reproaches, curt
and disgusted, or sad and gentle! What serious talks and suggestions to
think things over pretty carefully! The gravity of the situation was duly
not allowed to escape; but that was hardly the half of it. There remained
those other considerations. Think how proud and happy the mother of a
boy like Post II must be! Wouldn't he, for her sake—Didn't he want her
to be proud of him—Everyone said that if he only wanted to, he could—
Francis groaned, in an evoked memory so real that he could almost feel
himself, with alarm, appalled at his wickedness, swallowing down the
fantastic shocking yell, the horrible honest answer that struggled toward
his lips—*I don't care! What do I care about Post II? Let me alone, why can't
you?*

"What I needed," Francis thought, "was a damned good licking, and
never mind who was proud of what." But of course that was now, when a
few long-ago beatings would seem well exchanged for the advantage and
convenience of having at his command habits of discipline and application that would make work of all kinds no trouble at all. Offered the
choice ten years ago he doubted if he would have reckoned the sufferings
of this present time not worthy to be compared with the glory which shall
be revealed. He might not have cared to insure the future at the immediate expense of his backside. Soundly thrashed, he might, far from turning
industrious and tractable, have sought solace all the oftener in the moody
comforts of reading in study periods and the nervous release of being idle
and impudent.

The implied contradiction—pity for the child consigned to such a
piddling yet effective hell, and contempt for the little whiner—would not
resolve itself. Francis felt both. He thought it was a shame that Walter
had to go through with it, if he did have to; and if he did have to, whose

fault would it be but Walter's? Francis said aloud, "And if you just go on doing your work after you're in, you'll never have any trouble."

Walter's look was patient. He looked resigned to having Francis inflicted on him; and if they had been alone this polite boredom might have moved Francis to some imprudent remark, an exasperated hint that he was by no means sure that it wasn't all bunk, too; but Mrs. Cunningham looked at him kindly. Francis saw her gratitude, and even, apparently, her admiration for his vigorous sayings and hearty good sense. Francis let it go. It was only to himself that his mind, sardonic, added: "And when you're dead you'll never have any trouble, either."

By the clock surmounting the grill above the reception desk it was quarter past seven. Mrs. Cunningham said, "Oh, how late it is!"

Though personally she moved without a trace of ostentation, Walter, Francis, and Maggie, making in effect a train or suite, turned her entrance and her progress toward the elevators into something of an event. All members of the staff within sight straightened up, bowed, smiled, made little gestures or movements indicating alertness or readiness to serve. The proprietor, a frowning stout man of military carriage, posted at a point which he often unobtrusively occupied when there was much coming or going, touched his mustache. He made a dignified inclination of his torso. He said, "Madame!"—not only with the deference due any guest who had extensive and expensive accommodations, but also with an unmistakable note of genuine respectful dislike. He must know by now that Mrs. Cunningham felt no uncertainty about what money ought to buy, or any embarrassment in seeing that it bought it. Probably, though paying plenty, she was paying not a Swiss franc more than what she received was worth. Mrs. Cunningham acknowledged his greeting with a gracious nod. She continued, "Are you starved, Francis? I know we're going to be down late."

Francis smiled and shook his head.

"And not even anything nice for tea. Would you like not to dress? Only you'll both want baths, won't you; so that wouldn't help any. Well, we'll try to be ready by quarter past eight."

From the reception desk the typist with the little pinched face who worked in the inside office called quietly, "Monsieur!"

Francis turned. She had her hands full of mail, and from the mass she detached an envelope. *"Voilà, Monsieur!"* She gave him a fatigued, mechanical smile.

The square blue envelope lay a moment on the counter where it had dropped while Francis, his knees weak, looked at it. Recovering the use of his hands, he picked it up and said with difficulty, *"Merci bien, Mademoiselle."*

Facing about, he found that no time had elapsed. Mrs. Cunningham was still not quite to the elevator; Walter, hanging on Maggie's arm, was still in the act of glancing over to see what the girl had wanted Francis for. Francis pocketed the letter. The gate slid shut. The elevator stirred and rose.

Snapping the light on in his room, Francis put the blue envelope on the table. His mind seemed strung to a pitch, ringing and reverberating with a deep tremble of agitation. It was hard to think, and he could not repress the continual little quiver of his hands. Opening the wardrobe, he took his dinner coat off its hanger and laid it on the bed. Opening a bureau drawer to get a shirt, he paused, noticing that he still had his overcoat on. He took it off and hung it up. He took off his tweed jacket and hung it on the back of a chair. He pulled his sweater off. Going back to the coat, he got a cigarette from the pocket, went to the table and tore the end from the envelope. In the pen tray lay a box, much worn and almost empty, of Italian wax matches which must have come forgotten in some pocket from Florence. Fumbling with the elastic that kept the lid closed, he extracted a match and lit it. Breathing smoke deeply, he tried to draw the enclosed sheet from the envelope, but the tissue paper lining caught it, so he ripped the envelope down the center. *Darling*—he saw the word numbly, more as if he heard it spoken than as if he were reading it—*I never regretted anything*—

Francis laid it down. He balanced the burning cigarette on the edge of the pen tray and took his shirt off. Picking up the letter again, he saw that the blind was not drawn, so he went and pulled it down. Standing by the window he read: *I never doubted anything. Why should you think that? Because I write so badly? I do. I know it. You couldn't imagine what that's like, trying to say something and then you can't, and so you don't write at all. You see, I am a very stupid person. Are you sure you know that?*

Francis moved away from the window. He put the letter down and finished undressing. He slipped on his bathrobe, put the letter in a pocket, picked up the cigarette, and went down to the bath. With the water on, he sat on the edge of the tub and read: *Paris has been horrible, a hell of rain. Do you remember Amiens? Like that, only much worse. And so cold. I wired this morning to ask Aunt Mabel to ask us to Cap d'Ail a week earlier because Gwen says she doesn't care, she is going to buy a fur coat if*—

The sentence broke off. Francis reached toward the water in the tub. It scalded his knuckles, and, whipping away, shaking the hand, he turned the cold water on and held his stinging fingers under it a moment. Half an inch down the page was written the word *Later*, twice underlined. The flat decorative script went on: *Just before lunch Aunt Mabel wired back we could come any time we wanted. Some people who were going to Africa had to leave. Gwen went right over to see her beau and she actually came back with a two-lits on the Blue Train tomorrow—*

Mechanically, Francis turned the page back, looking for the date. It was yesterday, he found. *Everything is supposed to be booked weeks ahead to Ventimiglia, but the head of his department has some sort of drag with the P.L.M. My dear, we'll just have to make Mrs. C. come down. I think we can, because you remember she did say something about Menton. This afternoon I dashed around to see Helen—*

Francis shut off the cold water and stood up. He could not see anywhere to throw the cigarette, so he continued to hold it, shifting his fingers gingerly on the hot end. *Mademoiselle almost ate her alive, poor child, because she caught us speaking English in the salon and that is a horrible crime. Helen's going to write her mother that she would like to go down for Christmas. So all you have to do now is tell Mrs. C. that you don't think Montreux is at all good for Walter. There is a nice hotel up the point, called the Eden—*

Unable to hold the cigarette any longer, Francis crushed it out on the window ledge. *My dear, I would be so blissfully happy if you would only come. So you must, mustn't you? Gwen sends her love. She says to tell you that Brentano's has copies of your book. They were English ones. Isn't this a stupid letter, but I am unsteady with joy about going south; and I love you—*

The searching, hardly-to-be-borne heat of the water enveloped Francis. In a plenitude of comfort, he breathed deeper, closing his eyes, feeling his muscles, gratefully warmed, relax. It might be twenty minutes to eight, he supposed, so at this instant Lorna and Gwen would be in a taxi bound for the station. The idea caused him a quick, unexpected pang. Thinking of them gone from the hotel on the Rue Jacob, he had a sense of dismay—as though, ten minutes ago, it would have been still possible to go back to Paris, walk down past Saint-Germain-des-Prés, turn the corner and find Lorna where he had left her. Now, he thought, now, it wouldn't do any good. There was nothing to go back to.

Sunk in the stone *quais* of the Gare de Lyon waited the sleek line of long buff-topped blue cars. Francis could hear the bump of luggage, the click of compartment doors opened and closed. Lights gleamed on the sheet steel enameled to look like marquetry; lights blazed in the little washrooms. Down the corridor passed a muffled sonorous voice calling the first service. The cars moved; the high *quais* went by. That was really the end, the end of Paris; the end of the summer. It gave him a second pang to know that Lorna would be jubilant—probably too happy to eat as she and Gwen faced each other across a table and saw, beyond the black glass, the suburban lights moving faster, growing fewer. Francis could see her sitting there, her face flushed, her fingers locked together, radiant in the glow of the small table lamps, while Gwen with practical calm ordered for herself and Lorna; and calmly, with appetite, ate what she had ordered.

Time passed. Hour after hour, down through the heart of France, the brass-bound locomotive, the long shining train drove through the night. Francis could see that, too—the high signal lights coming up, the endless starlit rails. The cars shook gently, jarred on their heavy springs, while, in the dark compartment Lorna lay asleep, half on her breast, her neat narrow hip outlined by the thin blanket, her knees bent, her dark hair in disorder against the pillow. From time to time she would stir as some alteration in the ceaseless noise brought her with a sigh close to consciousness.

Back in his room Francis found that it was eight o'clock. He did not think the Cunninghams would be ready at quarter past eight, but they might be ready at half past, and if he hoped to get down and have a drink first, he needed to hurry. He was hastily working studs through the stubborn starched buttonholes of his shirt when Walter's unmistakable limping step sounded in the hall. "Hell!" he said. "Come in!" He attached a collar and took up his tie.

Walter let himself around the door and closed it. Turning his head, Francis saw, surprised, that he had on a bathrobe. Walter cleared his throat. "Look, Frank," he said, "we won't be down to dinner."

"Feel all right, don't you?" Francis asked. Maggie's warning jumped to his mind; but, naturally, if Walter didn't feel all right, it would be Maggie who came to tell him.

"Oh, sure," said Walter. He swung the heavy tasseled cord of his bathrobe in a circle. "But, well, Rose died, that is. Maggie started to take her out, and she kind of keeled over—"

"You mean just now?" Francis asked. He spoke with concern, as though the point were very important, in an effort to arouse his mind from its far-off preoccupation, to find something sympathetic and suitable to say. "Has the vet seen her?"

Walter shook his head. "I guess Mother doesn't want him," he said. "Rose is dead, all right." He paused. "I guess she thinks he might want to take Rose away and do something to her—you know, cut her up." Francis admired the perception—or was it childishness, bored by explanations and qualifications, not yet much confused by reason?—with which Walter got at unexpressed feelings and things not said. "Very likely," he nodded. "Wait. I'll be along."

Francis thought slowly, the fact bearing in on him, "Poor Rose, poor dog—" Though his mind was still remote, the words set up a stir of probably superfluous pity for the dependent, useless old animal, to whom neither illness, nor age, nor death could be presented as intelligible, reasonable things; who got stiff, grew blind, until she had no pleasures left outside eating and being warm. She might expect to be allowed to

keep those, but her implacable tormentors came around again in a year or
so; she could not eat; weak and sick, she still tried to totter through her
daily round; so they knocked her down suddenly, poured into her an
ultimate, absolute cold; and that was the end of Rose.

"Say, pretty neat!" said Walter.

"What is?"

Walter made a gesture. "Tying the tie. Don't you even have to look in
the glass?"

"Yes," said Francis, looking in the glass. He straightened the tie a
little. "All right," he said. He slipped into his coat and tucked a handkerchief in the breast pocket.

Maggie was moving about carrying a laundry bag, as though she had
forgotten what she planned to do with it, or where she had put Walter's
shirts. Her gray hair was loosened, escaping from its ordinary complicated
tight pinning-up. Her spectacles were awry on her reddish nose. She
made a snuffling sound before she spoke. "Mrs. Cunningham is lying
down, Mr. Ellery," she said. She took a handkerchief out of the turned-
up sleeve of the sweater she still had on and blew her nose. Near the connecting door, which stood ajar, she said, "It's Mr. Ellery, M'am."

Francis looked at what he first took to be a pile of bath towels, part of
the half-collected laundry, on the sofa. He saw then that it was Rose, with
one towel over her and one towel under her. The towel on top did not
quite cover the worn pads of her hind paws.

From the room beyond Mrs. Cunningham said, "Oh, Francis. Do go
down and have your dinner. Something's being sent up for Walter and
Maggie."

The melancholy distress of her tone abashed Francis. His own unimpaired appetite seemed to him callous. He said, "I'm so sorry about Rose,
Mrs. Cunningham. Isn't there something I can do?"

"Well, Francis, have dinner. You must be awfully hungry." With an
affectation of composure she said, "I don't know why I should feel so upset. I really brought Rose over because I knew she wouldn't live long. I
didn't want her to die alone. I wish I hadn't left her alone this afternoon.
It seems a little sentimental, doesn't it?"

"I don't think so," Francis said. "One gets attached to a dog."

"We had her so many years," Mrs. Cunningham said in a wretched
voice. "We got her for Helen, when Helen was a baby."

In the sad atmosphere Walter was ill at ease. He avoided looking at
Francis. He sat down and then he got up again. He lifted a crystal bottle
of lavender-colored smelling salts from the table, drew the stopper, and
cautiously sniffed at it. Francis wondered if it had been brought out to try
on Rose. "Sure, she was older than I am," Walter murmured, plainly
impressed by the idea.

"Let that be, Walter," Maggie said, taking the bottle away from him. "It's your mother's."

"Whose did I think it was?" asked Walter.

Mrs. Cunningham said, "I don't know that Helen ever cared much about her. She was really my husband's. He was very fond of her." Francis thought of the photographed face, warm with private pleasure or affection; the ridiculous yet dignified droop of the mustache; the sedate stoop to pat Rose's lean white head, while the man gazed down and the devoted bitch gazed up, both well content. Mrs. Cunningham's voice continued, much troubled: "I don't know quite what to do about—I can't bear to just ask them to come and take her away. Don't you think she could be buried somewhere?"

"Yes," said Francis. "Leave it to me. I'll—"

"I wish she could be put in a box, or something. I mean—"

"Of course," Francis said. "I'll find one." He looked toward the sofa, measuring Rose's concealed form with his eye.

"Oh, Francis, I'd feel so much better if you would! I don't really trust any of these people. But not now. I want you to go and have dinner first."

"I could eat, myself," Walter observed.

"Darling, it will soon be up."

Maggie had moved over to the sofa. She must have noticed that Rose's feet showed, and shaking her head she gave the towel a little tug and covered them. From the floor she picked up the no-longer-required leather lead and began to coil it.

IV

And, of course, another means of decent disposal might be to weigh Rose with stones, and take her out and drop her in the lake—*and we commit her body to the deep in sure and certain hope* . . . Francis checked himself, ashamed to idle here over his coffee, making fun of the thing, while Mrs. Cunningham was trusting him to take care of it. He tossed his napkin on the table, nodded to his waiter, and walked out of the dining room to go over to the office.

In the *caisse*, the proprietor's nephew was counting money. "You look rich," Francis said. He was on friendly terms with the nephew and had several times drunk a glass of beer with him in the evening after the office had been turned over to the concierge.

"Not writing tonight?" the nephew said. He stroked back his thick black hair, stacked together a pile of German ten-mark notes, and tucked them in an envelope. Francis explained about the death of Rose. "I've got to find a place to bury her," he said. "Do you think your uncle would mind if we found a place in the garden?"

"I don't know," the nephew said. He lifted his shoulder a little, tipped his head back toward the closed door of the inner office. *"Fait du pétard,"* he whispered. *"Pan! Pan!* I wouldn't dare ask him tonight. Soon he's going to the drilling."

"Well, you let me ask him," Francis said. "I've got to do something about it right away."

"Better not," said the nephew, screwing his mouth up. He inclined his head slightly the other way, and Francis noticed that the typist was still working. She pored over some papers, from time to time touching down keys on an adding machine. "He sacked her," the nephew murmured.

"Do you think he's going to sack me?" Francis asked somewhat drily.

"Well, come in," the nephew said. "I'll see."

He went and opened the door to the left, admitting Francis. Then he went over to the door behind and tapped on it. The typist, lifting her tired homely face, showed that she had been crying. *"Soir, Monsieur,"* she said very faintly.

Trying to phrase some friendly remark to make to her—he would have had trouble thinking of one in English; in French he had more trouble—Francis did not hear what the nephew said, but his effort was interrupted by the proprietor's voice in response, a loud snort of annoyance: *"Eh bien! Quoi!"*

Through the open door Francis could see him sitting at a desk, his cropped head against the sepia still waters of a large framed photograph of the castle of Chillon. He was wearing a gray-green uniform with stars on the collar tabs. Looking up, he saw Francis looking at him, and he frowned. Then he barked out—in the corner of his eye Francis could see the typist wince at the sound—"I am very busy, Monsieur. I have an engagement shortly."

Francis stepped to the door. "I'm sorry to have to bother you," he said. "Mrs. Cunningham wanted me to make an inquiry."

Mrs. Cunningham's name had an effect. "Well, what is it?" the proprietor asked, still frowning.

The nephew had drawn aside to let Francis in. His uncle said to him, "Get back and finish! I am late enough already!" He turned to Francis again. "Well, Monsieur?"

There was no particular reason why the proprietor should get up; but on the other hand, Francis saw no reason why he shouldn't. He might be a reserve colonel of infantry; but he was also a hotel proprietor. Francis stared at him a moment to convey his surprise. Then he said, "Mrs. Cunningham's dog has died. Perhaps your nephew told you. She must be buried. Mrs. Cunningham has had her a good many years, and you'll understand how—"

At the word 'dog' the proprietor stiffened. "No," he said, "no, I do not understand. My nephew said nothing." His hard light-colored eyes fixed themselves on Francis with a menacing glint. His blond mustache bristled. "What does Madame wish? I cannot spare any more time——" As he looked at Francis the expression of the eyes, the lines of the full face, changed again—a sudden unmasking, a partly voluntary uncovering of more than annoyance or impatience. It was hate.

Neutral for an instant, Francis regarded this disclosure with surprised interest, asking himself what experiences with Americans, or perhaps only with English-speaking people, or perhaps only with hotel patrons, had made the proprietor feel like that; but his disinterested curiosity, a writer's instinctive inquisitiveness, did not engage Francis long. He felt then an emotion of his own rising to answer—the damned cocky little Swiss in his ridiculous uniform! Who did he think he was?

Francis's indignation enlarged itself. It swelled, as he asked himself the question, to a blaze of contempt for the whole monkey house of Europe and Europe's mostly undersized, jabbering, mostly not-quite-clean inhabitants. In this view, all was lumped together, a year's accumulation of passing annoyances and small disgusts—the shoddy posturing bombast of the new Italy (Francis had not forgotten those sallow blackshirts boarding, at Turin, the train when he came down from Paris with his mother. One of them looked at the book Francis was reading to see if it needed to be confiscated. So they thought they were soldiers, did they? They ought to study their disgraceful history!); La Belle France with its savage avarice and all-pervasive smell of urine; the belching, blockheaded Germans—why should anyone have any patience with any of them? The only demonstrable good reason for their existing was to satisfy the curiosity or serve the convenience of traveling Americans. Francis said, "Perhaps you don't understand because I haven't finished telling you."

"Well? Well?" the proprietor said. He pouted. He made a noise like a pig.

"What we need," Francis said, "is a piece of ground about a yard square. It ought not to be hard to find. Perhaps somewhere in the garden——"

"That is impossible! I have no place to bury dogs. It is unheard of!"

A growing brightness expanded at the back of Francis's skull. Against the heat and light, his conscious thought crossed the foreground in a sort of silhouette. "If you have no place to bury dogs, I advise you to look for one," Francis said. "Mrs. Cunningham wishes the dog to be buried. Now. This evening. Is that clear?"

The proprietor's heavy-seated posture seemed to get heavier. The impatient perked-up tenseness left him. He subsided, paralyzed. From collar

to hair roots a flood of dull red suffused his face; his lips shook; his eyes
protruded. The resulting appearance of dazed idiocy gave Francis pleasure.
Exhilarated, violently pleased, he said, more peremptory, as though he
had no time to spare either: "Well, can't you inquire? Call up! Send
someone out! Mrs. Cunningham is waiting."

Probably, in the noise of his own breathing, the proprietor did not
hear him. Finally, working his lips in and out, he managed to say in a
thick, husky voice: "You—you tell me—" he hit at his bulky chest, tight
under the tunic—"me to look for places to bury dogs?"

It was an object lesson in anger, and seeing before his eyes how anger
looked, Francis made an intense effort. "Mrs. Cunningham needs help,"
he said, forcing mildness and reason into his tone. "I'm doing what I can.
I expect you to do what you can."

Francis paused. The sound of battle must be carrying some distance,
he realized, for the nephew had reappeared, standing uncertainly in the
door. His uncle paid no attention to him; perhaps did not even see him.
"You expect—" he cried, choking. He made an effort to stand up. Francis
could see the polished black boots draw in, the fat knees bunch under the
straining gray-green cloth. The proprietor's trembling, grabbling hands
tried to clutch the chair arms. His voice mounted in a paroxysm of stammering: "You—you—what are you? A boy. A boy. You come to me with
dogs—"

The popping eyes, the face now really as red as blood, shocked Francis. He thought, aghast, "Good God, is he going to have a stroke?" He
turned, frightened, to the nephew, and said: "I'm sorry. I'm extremely
sorry. Is he all right? Is—" Yet, though Francis was sorry, and in the pre-
cipitant reversal of feeling, his pleasure and his anger were both gone, he
did not like backing down. He said, "He can't shout at me—"

The matter, he saw, was probably being made worse, not better.
Francis turned and went past the nephew, out through the office. The
typist was sitting terrified, her clenched fist pressed against her mouth,
and Francis tried to smile reassuringly at her. He went through the door,
crossed the lobby—the concierge, too, he saw, had heard something—
and walked upstairs.

There were two double pairs of stairs, so a minute or more must have
passed while Francis climbed them, but he was not conscious of the interval. Instantly he stood in the upper hall. At the pit of his stomach a sick
feeling of exhausted anger made it difficult to get hold of his thoughts;
and even his feelings—so many of them at once were without impelling
force. He did not know what to do. In one sense, he was angry still; but it
was a low, futile sort of anger—the remedyless anger that might fill you
when you missed a train, or dropped a watch and broke the crystal. He

felt tired, with a slight stiffness or soreness from the afternoon's skiing. He felt baffled and exasperated, wishing he could just forget about the whole business.

This wish was vain; for already he had begun to repeat to himself, searching for the exact words, things that the proprietor had said, and things that he had answered; things that might be said in defense or explanation. But defensive explanation was aside from the point. What exactly had been said, and why, did not matter. If he had involved Mrs. Cunningham—and how could he have failed to involve her—he had behaved like an ass. He asked her to leave it to him; and she left it to him; and he made of it a stupid occasion to quarrel. You could not get around that!

The apprehension, the self-disgust, the melancholy wish that he had done differently, brought back that uncomfortable vivid moment when, talking about Walter and his work, Francis had remembered those trips down from school, and how his heart had sunk to know so well that the news he brought was inexcusable, that doing so badly was his own grievous fault. Facing the awkwardness of having to report to Mrs. Cunningham that he had done worse than nothing for her, Francis resolved to postpone it. He might go out and talk to the man at the tobacco shop up the terrace; or perhaps the fellow who rented the bicycles could suggest something. He turned, but at the same instant he heard an elevator door clash closed downstairs. At once he had the plausible presentiment that this matter was by no means concluded; that the proprietor, in fury, was going to take it to Mrs. Cunningham. An instinct of ordinary precaution made Francis move quickly. He went down the hall and knocked on the door.

Walter called for him to come in. Walter was twisted up in an easy chair, legs hanging over one arm, his head against the other, his Caesar propped open against his knees. "We fixed it," he said, rolling his eyes up at Francis. "Martin's going to do it. The waiter. He lives in Villeneuve."

Mrs. Cunningham came from the room beyond. She smiled sadly, but with composure. "Oh, I hope you didn't hurry, Francis," she said. "The waiter took Rose. Martin, that nice one. His mother has a place under some pines where she buries her cats when they die. He's taking Rose home tonight and he's going to put her in a box. We can go up tomorrow and one of his brothers will bury her. Maggie and I will go. You and Walter won't have to upset your morning."

"Well, I'm glad," Francis said. He hesitated, steadying his voice, listening for the rising elevator. "Because I wasn't much of a help. In fact, I expect I put my foot in it." He looked at the palm of his hand and smiled slightly; for he meant to make it a sort of rueful joke, as though he regretted it, but, God help him, he could have done no other.

"The proprietor," he said, "appeared to think that the idea of burying Rose in the garden was insulting. He wasn't very pleasant. I'm afraid I spoke sharply to him."

He looked at Mrs. Cunningham, retaining his rueful expression. If she were to respond, "How stupid of you!" as she so justly might, a rueful expression was what he would need. He would say: "Yes, it was; wasn't it?" meek and deprecatory. The humiliation of not being free to make an ass of himself was something he might as well swallow—that, he realized, was the elevator; and he was in for it. He could hear the quick military tread in the hall.

The sound, if Mrs. Cunningham noticed it, of course meant nothing to her. "Oh, Francis," she said. "I'm so sorry. He's really a very disagreeable man. Was he rude to you? Sit down. Tell me about it."

The relief Francis felt was precarious. It waited on the tramp of boots, almost here now, and probably bringing with them something good for a high look and a proud heart; yet it was a relief so great that Francis could breathe again. "I'm the one who's sorry," he said. "I got rather angry. He has a way of speaking—"

On the door came the hard rap.

"*Entrez!*" called Walter, twisting his head to look.

The door opened briskly. The proprietor wheeled about and closed it. He clicked his heels together and bowed. His face had lost its solid apoplectic red; it was still swollen or congested, but the color had ebbed to patches and mottlings. "Madame," he said. He cleared his throat. "I have something that I regret I must see you about."

Mrs. Cunningham looked from his uniform to his face. "It is not entirely convenient for me to see you now," she said. "In the morning would be better."

The cool, even tones were what Francis had expected; but, to his astonishment, they did not have the expected effect. He had never succeeded in it himself, or seen anyone succeed in it, but Francis half credited the fiction that it was possible, by a dignity of presence (which was certainly Mrs. Cunningham's), or some other mysterious virtue of innate superiority, to abash any impertinent person; and, no matter what he had to say or how angry he was, with a word, to silence him. By no means silenced, the proprietor said truculently: "No, Madame. It would not be better."

Mrs. Cunningham gazed at him with utter astonishment. "What did you say?" she asked.

"I said that it would not be better. No, Madame."

Mrs. Cunningham stood speechless, and Francis, angered into defending what, he would have said, could never need a defense, cut in: "Don't speak that way to Mrs. Cunningham!"

Mrs. Cunningham extended an arm toward Francis and touched his sleeve. The proprietor paid no attention. He went on, "I wish to say to you that I will not be insulted!" Now he did glare at Francis. He gestured toward him with a shaking hand. "He breaks into my private office. He orders me about—"

The insanity of his procedure, supposing the proprietor had any idea of getting redress, of getting Francis into trouble, was manifest. Francis looked at him with unconcerned contempt. "Your nephew asked me to come in," he said.

"I do not speak to you!" cried the proprietor. "Be still, if you please!"

"You are speaking to me," Mrs. Cunningham said. "What is it that you are trying to say?"

"Yes. I am speaking to you, Madame. Good. I am saying to you that you must—"

"Why, really!" Mrs. Cunningham spoke with a sort of gasp. Though breathless, her voice nevertheless had a firmer sound. She must at last be beginning to believe her ears. "I think you forget yourself."

The proprietor, regardless, said, "I do not forget myself, Madame. I—"

"No, no," Mrs. Cunningham said decidedly. "That will be enough. You are very rude. Go and make out my bill. I shall want it by eight o'clock tomorrow morning. Good evening."

"Yes, Madame," said the proprietor. More than merely preparing for this eventuality, the proprietor showed that he had intentionally provoked it. He visibly savored the costly moment. The excitement of permitting himself in insolence made him shake. "That will be very well, Madame," he said. "I will not have him in my hotel."

"Maggie!" Mrs. Cunningham said.

Maggie had, at some point, appeared silently. Her gaze, full of indignation, rested on the proprietor. She tightened her lips and went and opened the door.

"That will be all," Mrs. Cunningham said.

"Yes, Madame," said the proprietor. "That is all. Good evening."

He marched triumphantly out the door, and Maggie closed it after him so fast that Francis, surprised at the old girl's spirit, guessed she wouldn't have minded if it had caught up with him before he got clear.

"Whee!" said Walter. He laughed. "Desperate Ambrose!" he said. "Where'll we go? Let's go—"

"You go and finish your work, darling."

"Well, why don't we go to Grindelwald?"

"Now, darling, get up. I want you to go to your room and get through. It's long after nine o'clock."

"Ah, heck!" said Walter, getting up. He directed an exaggerated

wink at Francis. "Grindelwald," he said. Maggie said, "Wouldn't I
better start some packing, Mrs. Cunningham?"

"Yes. Please do, Maggie. I'll come in a moment." She turned to Francis. "I think we'll move to that hotel by the *Kursaal*. I don't believe they
can be very full. That would do for a day or so. Will you see about it,
Francis? You know what we need. I hate to ask you to go out, but I don't
feel that I want to use the telephone."

"Of course," Francis said. It had been in his mind to say when they
were alone that he was sorry for having caused all this trouble; but the
matter-of-factness of Mrs. Cunningham's tone made him feel that he
would surprise her by reopening a subject already closed. If she had appeared a trifle less formidable than he had expected in the face of impertinence, she now showed herself more formidable—not with a grand
manner, but with an absoluteness above debate or argument, above explanation or excuse in her habit of not putting up with what did not suit
her. The proprietor had offended; the proprietor, as far as he concerned
her, was no more.

Francis remained silent, ready to be dismissed; but Mrs. Cunningham
said suddenly, "What would you think of Grindelwald?"

Taken by surprise, Francis answered, "I don't know, really."

The excitements that had crowded his mind, the regrets and fears,
still obscured for a moment the importance of the question. With alarm
he realized then that it was important. At noon Mrs. Cunningham had
no particular reason for leaving Montreux; but now, nine hours later, the
decision to move to another hotel, her melancholy over Rose, and Walter's
successful afternoon might make her just about ready to leave. Francis had
not a moment to spare if he meant to take a hand in forming her plans for
her. "It would depend on Walter," he said slowly.

Trying, uneasy with haste, to scheme intelligently, Francis did not
know where to begin. That letter of Helen's to her mother had probably
been mailed. It would be indeed a remarkable coincidence if Francis were,
tonight, to suggest the substance of a plan that her daughter would be
proposing, no doubt with some mention of Lorna, from Paris tomorrow or
the next day.

Mrs. Cunningham misunderstood his hesitation. "Is the skiing going
to be too hard?" she asked. She spoke directly and simply, looking at him
as though he were the one to decide, as though she were ready to believe
that his expert eye might have noted more than he had yet had occasion
to tell her.

Helen's impending letter prevented a mention of Cap d'Ail; it did not
prevent him from insinuating a disadvantage to Walter in Grindelwald. If
Francis could not press the plan he wanted, he ought at least to hold up
or block any plan that he did not want. He ought to answer regretfully,

yes. After all, Grindelwald was not Les Avants. Runs like the one down from Kleine Scheidegg, which Best, with rather vainglorious understatements, had described to Francis, could only be attempted by a skier of some seasons' experience. Francis didn't doubt that it would be too much for him, and if it were too much for him, how could Walter hope—the important yes, thus half-justified, and more than half, by Mrs. Cunningham's air of trusting consultation, invited, would not come. Francis waited a moment. If yes were more than he could say, hadn't he the dexterity to say something that would at least imply it, something that might make Mrs. Cunningham rule out Grindelwald herself?

But Mrs. Cunningham was waiting, too. Francis said, "No. It's not too hard. He was all right this afternoon." His mind, rocked by the unlooked-for, treacherous blow to the scheme it had been frantically framing for him, stood off with anger and anguish. Francis said, "But what about this asthma of his?"

"I wish we knew," Mrs. Cunningham said. "It's completely mystifying. He had an attack, not a very bad one, in Paris, during that awful week in October. It might have been the damp. But he has spent whole summers at the seashore without any."

Did Francis expect opportunity to go on knocking forever? He frowned and said, "Maybe altitude has something to do with it. At sea level—" The painfully acquired elements of the art of not making a fool of yourself, remembered in time, shut him up. He finished vaguely: "Perhaps he'd be better off somewhere milder. It might be good for him to get some tennis."

"That's true," Mrs. Cunningham said thoughtfully. "Some friends of ours are at Taormina. They think it would be very good for him there."

This danger could be easily handled, and Francis's hope of being adroit recovered tentatively. "I've heard it's lovely," he said. "But, of course, it's a long way from Paris."

"Yes, it is," Mrs. Cunningham said. "That's one advantage Grindelwald has. Helen could easily come for Christmas."

If he had only dared to mention it, here was a natural opening to bring up a coast, a milder climate, no farther from Paris than Grindelwald. Francis shrank with anxiety. Maybe if he said Menton, or even Rapallo—

Mrs. Cunningham said, "I liked those English boys. It was so nice of them to bother about Walter."

"Yes," said Francis. To cover his inner nervousness he smiled. "They were very decent." He had an idea then. "The truth is, that's one thing I can't help wondering about, as far as Grindelwald is concerned." Mothers being mothers, Mrs. Cunningham might easily find it probable that Troop and Best in Grindelwald would continue to have lots of time for Walter. "I don't think Walter ought to stop work." He frowned. "We have a good deal to do. I just wonder how well Grindelwald would mix with study." But that air of arch, honest doubt! That ripe pedagogical concern! Francis stopped, ashamed.

"I know that," Mrs. Cunningham said. She looked at Francis with one of her sudden charming smiles. She said, "Walter hasn't been very well prepared—" She glanced toward the door of Walter's room to assure herself that it was closed. "After all, he's only twelve. I don't know that I really expect him to pass those examinations this year. I don't want you to feel that you're responsible for that. I know it worries you." She paused.

"I've wanted to tell you how happy I've been about this arrangement," she said then. "You've been wonderful with Walter, Francis. There's never been anyone he liked so well; or anyone who was so good for him."

"I'm very glad," Francis said. He felt himself coloring. Mrs. Cunningham's more than kind, almost affectionately maternal candor spoke, as the show of candor always did, to an impulsive candor of his own. He understood that this was not a virtue. He did not—he was this minute demonstrating that he did not—lack the will to be devious; he simply lacked the skill and patience. How nasty, how damned stupid and tiresome all this ineffective plotting was! The resolution to do no more of it stirred in him; yet abruptly, with passionate distress, Francis felt it less a gesture toward decency or good conscience than a pusillanimous, a contemptible readiness to fail—still another choice of the less difficult, the meaner way.

Immediately he was possessed with the idea of Lorna. The mute entreaties, the expostulations of a yearning outside reason besieged him. He could hardly bear her absence; he could not bear to let a chance of seeing her go like that. He thought suddenly, standing strained and dry, *And for the peace of you I hold such strife. . . .* The brittle, bitter amusement of seeing that so he did filled him. The extravagant phrasing—as food to life, as showers—he had to laugh. In terrible silence, he did laugh; but the perfervid wish, the pain of sweetness, survived in things too simple to be touched by the scorn that laughed at extravagance or high-falutin' expressions—the way she sank down on a chair drawn out for her; the slight discoloration of nicotine, for she smoked too much, on her graceful emaciated fingers; the bruised undercircling of her eyes, periodically marked enough to show its cause—there was no sure limit to the things like those that, tenderly recalled, he did not find any obvious way to mock.

Still smiling, Mrs. Cunningham proceeded, "I know those boys wouldn't have much time for Walter, and I certainly wouldn't want him to be a nuisance. But they seemed so really interested I thought they might go on taking a little interest in him. I mean, he wouldn't be thrown absolutely on his own."

"I'm sure they would," Francis said apprehensively. He saw their irrelevant faces—Troop's, round and amiable; Best's, pink and white, perhaps conceited; but conceited in a way that would make him do at all costs the kind or decent things he would be admired for doing.

"Francis"—Mrs. Cunningham gave his arm a light, earnest touch— "wouldn't you like to go down to Florence and spend the holidays with your mother? I know you would. And this hasn't been very much fun for you. I'd like you to have a change. Would you go down over Christmas and New Year's? I want to pay your expenses. This is the tenth, isn't it? Suppose we go to Grindelwald at the end of the week. You go down the twenty-third and come back some time after the first. Would you like that?"

Francis looked at her. The sympathetic generosity of her gaze made him feel like a child. With a sort of despair, he said, "How kind you are."

THREE

Friday was a long day. Of course, it had been understood for several days that they were leaving for Grindelwald Friday; but Francis put off writing Lorna until Thursday night. He wrote that Mrs. Cunningham had unfortunately other plans; and how he felt about that: and how he felt about life; and how he felt about Lorna. The task was painful; but he had the writer's fond faith in the power of words; and by the time he had combined the best parts of two drafts in a third and final version two o'clock was past. He went to bed, tired, and if not happy, resigned. In the morning his letter seemed less good, but it was already posted. Francis shrank to think how sad and brave he had sounded; and anyway, what it boiled down to was that he wasn't a free agent (a fault not easily forgiven in love) and therefore was contenting himself with the hope that absence made the heart grow fonder. The hope was too silly to stand examination by daylight.

Meeting Francis's mood halfway, the whole Oberland was under clouds; and at four o'clock in the afternoon a light drizzle had just ceased falling on Interlaken. The open gravel platforms of the Bahnhof Ost were soaked. Mist hid the mountains. The surrounding fields stretched away damp and silent.

They walked across to the Hôtel du Lac by the narrow, canalized cold waters of the Aare between lines of miserable pollarded trees. Walter was tired. Maggie's general attitude, while not exactly disapproving, was that of hoping for the best—as though going to Grindelwald, wherever that might be, were a natural calamity not to be averted since it was Mrs. Cunningham's wish; but in facing it Maggie meant to exercise foresight so that as little harm as possible would come to Walter from the rash project of encouraging him to slide down mountains. Feeling the dead weight of her glum entourage, Mrs. Cunningham showed traces of exasperation. She spoke sharply to Walter, who had begun absent-mindedly to pick his nose while they waited for tea. With impatience she disposed of Maggie's notion that Walter ought to eat a nice egg. The moderate delay caused her to send Francis to find the maître d'hôtel, or manager, or whoever was in charge.

The train up the valley to Grindelwald did not leave until after dark. Somewhat heartened by the tea, Francis made an effort to keep Walter interested in a game of chess played inconveniently on a small folding pocket board whose men were slips of red and white celluloid and whose squares were slits in the leather. The train, which was cold, seemed to make no progress. They waited a long time above a brilliantly lighted hydroelectric plant. They waited even longer under the massive timbered shed of an avalanche gallery while the windows froze over.

Walter had been restlessly playing to lose the chess game; and in the end he succeeded. Relieved, he scraped clear a small space on the windowpane. They had stopped again and Walter was apparently able to see a station sign. "Burglauenen," he said. "Is that near? How much farther is it? Say, it's snowing."

Since no one could tell him how much farther it was he subsided and started to draw pictures with his fingernail in the white frosting. Eventually the train moved, began with infinite deliberation a jerking rack-and-pinion climb. After three-quarters of an hour they reached Grindelwald.

The vast barnlike bulk of the hotel, seen through the falling snow, rose above them as high as a cliff, with few lights. In the ill-lit lounge, a large glass-enclosed court beside the entrance, there were two people. One was a young woman, obviously English, with pale shining hair, brows arched in a permanent aspect of astonishment above blank wide-open eyes and the characteristic disdainful or ostentatiously fastidious lift of the upper lip. She wore an unbecoming green evening dress with stockings of the wrong shade on her well-formed but too long legs. She was drinking a cocktail and smoking a cigarette in a holder. Not far from her sat a pursy, choleric-looking elderly man, obviously English, too, who was still wearing his knickerbocker suit with boots and extra socks. For some surely remarkable reason he was reading a book.

Upstairs the long dark halls were empty. As they passed down them —the heavy tread of the porters with the luggage, Walter's limp, the murmur of the assistant manager's voice as he walked apologetically beside Mrs. Cunningham—they moved echoing through a profound silence that must show most of the building was empty. The lights turned on in the big warm rooms were low and feeble; but nothing could be done about this because some auxiliary system was supplying the electricity. The regular system would be working tomorrow. To the assistant manager, who was explaining, Mrs. Cunningham petulantly said, "This is very inconvenient—"

She left it unfinished, realizing suddenly that she was too tired to care, and wished only to be bothered no more about it. She said to Francis, "You'd better go with him and see your room. Be sure you're comfortable. At least it is warm enough. I didn't expect it to be." She sat down, and with a heroic effort, smiled. "Poor Francis!" she said. "Hasn't it been a dreadful day! We won't go down to dinner. I don't think we'd better try to have lessons tomorrow. We'll just get up when we feel like it. Good night. Perhaps it won't look so dismal in the morning."

Alone in his room at the end of the hall Francis looked at his luggage. He brooded a moment on the pleasures of a bath, but to get dressed, he would have to unpack. *"Why this is hell, nor am I out of it,"* he thought at random. He washed his hands at the basin. He snapped the light off and went downstairs to the bar. This was empty, except for the man behind it, who was drawn close to the low light reading a German newspaper. He made Francis a Martini. "Pretty quiet," Francis said.

"Yes, sir. We will not have many people until next week." He went back and took up his paper.

The Martini, painfully cold, tasted of varnish. "Let me have another," Francis said, though the effect of the first had been not to warm or cheer him, but to start above his eyes the faint throbbing of a headache. *How comes it then that thou art out of hell?* His mind mechanically returned the senseless lines. *Why this is hell, nor am I—* "Ah!" he said. With a cold quaking, a drawing-tight of his stomach, he remembered sitting in the bar at the hotel in Milan drinking Martinis. He saw Miss Robertson's big solemn face and sturdy legs. He could hear her saying, 'You mustn't ask me. You mustn't—' Francis could hardly swallow what was left in the glass. "God damn you!" he said to himself. He stood up and took out a billfold.

The dining room was empty, too; but beyond, in a large dim room that opened from it, there seemed to be a number of people. Francis could not immediately understand what they were doing; but the woman in the green dress, he realized, must be a sort of hostess connected with the hotel staff. She moved about with brisk artificial sprightliness directing or instigating whatever it was. Several times informal applause rose. While he ate, Francis could catch glimpses of the applauders, some dressed for dinner, some not. From one of these visible groups a girl of fourteen or fifteen, wearing the sort of frock a child would wear to dancing class, stood up and went forward out of his sight. Loud, and in a childish way firm and clear, with elaborate expressiveness, Francis heard her voice: "O what can ail thee, knight-at-arms. . . ."

Astounded, Francis realized that the people in there were listening to recitations by their own children and those of their fellow guests. He sat still, nursing his head by taking care not to move it abruptly, and lifted his eyes from time to time, looking past the open glass doors. The woman in the background, smiling a thin-lipped but loving smile, must be the young performer's mother. She had the strong features of a refined horse. Her hair was piled in great loose wads all over her head; and, as far as Francis could see, she had dressed herself for the evening by pulling around her an ample sheet of puce-colored silk, pinned together at various points to cover her undergarments or otherwise spare her modesty. She was surrounded by additional children and two grown-up girls. A marked similarity in the line of nose and eyebrow made it plain that the man beyond these girls was their father.

Unlike his wife, he was elegant, though in a manly way—narrow-headed, spare, and tall. His high forehead, his direct look, and the clean military cut of his graying hair gave him the *integer-vitae-scelerisque-purus* air that so becomes a person past his youth, and that, perhaps, can only come to those who have lived a life of gentility, made materially easy by money, but rigorously bounded on the public side by the decent duties of respectability, and on the private side by the ascetic exercise of cleaving to a conscientious wife, pure, you might feel certain, in thought, word, and deed.

Francis drank his coffee. These little studies of the people in the other room depressed him more than ever. It dispirited him, it added to his loneliness to consider the long English occupation of Switzerland implicit in the artless scene—a hundred years of university mountain climbers, of deans in mufti inspecting the wonderful works of God, of lovers of Alpine flowers wandering lonely as a cloud, of middle-aged walkers, out in stout boots for their constitutional, ascending (2¼ hrs. guide unnecessary) to this or that magnificent VIEW. The holidaying families, aloofly jostling each other, bringing their tea, ordering bottled water, discreetly ascertaining the whereabouts of the W.C., had—while they preserved its 'foreignness' just as game was preserved at home—made the country theirs.

Watching the ingenuous, indeed, the boring and stuffy means by which this home from home was set up, Francis felt excluded from them, the only human beings in sight. They would normally have a deep-rooted dislike or resentment of Americans; but, just as bad, Francis was excluded by his own instinct or unconscious opinion. Speaking to him, Englishmen were almost always kind enough to conceal their distaste for the not quite-quite; but how could Francis conceal from himself his feeling—his real feeling, ineradicably established in childhood, and no matter how he tried to correct it by reason or observation, still his—that England, in planting the American colonies, had served her purpose; that her blood and language, her literature and laws, were all in the hands of the rightful heirs? While one might feel a perfunctory gratitude for the long-ago gift, there were limits; and England, by her continuing pretensions, made herself tiresome and ridiculous. Not really unfriendly, but for this reason faintly impatient with the presuming English, what could Francis find to say to that vapid high-minded woman, to those grown-up gawkish girls —since Romney painted Lady Hamilton, had they, Francis wondered, had in England a girl anyone would particularly want? Behind the man's distinguished but fatuously stiff front there might lie interesting things; but where Francis's prejudice ended, the Englishman's began, and he would not be likely to share his interests with any callow young American, whose mere presence at a hotel where one had stopped for years was an example of the pushing transatlantic cheek that made all colonials so hard to bear.

Francis shrugged and prepared to leave. He found then that, seeing, he had not been unseen; and that he was right about English kindness. At least, the woman in the green dress was ready, in her official capacity, to include him. She must have had an eye on him and noticed that he was finishing his dinner. Taking advantage of the recitation's end, she sallied suddenly through the doors with plain purpose.

"Oh, God!" thought Francis, unable to move. Her intention of speaking to him could not be mistaken, and he knew that the very dreariness of her proposal, the intensity with which the prospect bored him, would work, not to make him refuse her, but to prick him with compunction for her; and, reluctantly, with bad grace, he would do what she wanted.

But, thus half resigned, he found himself delivered. A voice cried, "Oh, Miss Poulter! Miss Poulter!" The little reciter in her party dress darted in pursuit, probably not willing to stop showing off so soon. "Miss Poulter, could we—"

The woman in green turned, and Francis's compunction did not go to the quixotic point of missing such a chance. Furtively he sprang to his feet and was out of the room in an instant, and in an instant more safe in the lift.

The hasty escape had set his head throbbing. Francis walked down the hall to his room screwing his eyes up against the distracting low ache. He kept yawning while, with chilly fingers, he got things out of his bags. Partly unpacked, he sat down on the edge of the bed, trying to make up his mind about having a bath. He did not feel like it so soon after dinner, and the difficulties of looking up a bathroom, of waiting while the water ran, seemed enormous and exhausting. On the other hand, going to bed without taking a bath, not having a bath after traveling all day, seemed a dirty idea. Francis sat in wretched indecision, pondering as desperately as though he had to choose between his money and his life. He held his head.

But in the eighteenth century, surely the age of the most civilized human beings who ever lived, people rarely bathed. Instead, they powdered themselves with—the name of the perfumed powder used to mask the odor of sweat eluded him. Francis pressed his head harder—empasma! They employed an empasma.

"Oh God!" said Francis. "Oh God—"

He got undressed and put on his pajamas, and went and opened the ventilating device at the window. A scurry of snow, dimly illuminated, drove past the double panes. He put the light out and crawled into bed, shivering against the cold sheets, pressing his aching head into the pillows. He tried to think of nothing; but in his mind formed slowly the picture of an extravagantly tropical shore—the palms, the gardens to the water with marble balustrades and corniced pillars through which showed a sea of cobalt, of a poster-blue not of this world. Quiet surf creamed white where, far off, beyond the Mexique bay, the rocky headlands pushed into the ocean; and Francis surveyed the beautiful coast, calm and remote, as though from a great height. The mythical, the golden afternoon lay over it in enchanted stillness, a marvelous mild radiance. Cool, fitful airs stirred beneath the myrtles and olives where in the shade my love lies dreaming, her beauty beaming—

The picture dissolved and Francis found himself thinking of a girl he had known when he was at college, of walking with her happily in the sunny haze of a bright autumn afternoon through the colored woods beyond Wellesley. He remembered her crinkly blonde hair, the faintly husky tone of her voice, the tone of her skin, dusty, faintly freckled, about the same gold tone as her hair. With pain he thought, "I could have had her—"

The pain was not for lost enjoyment; but for the recollection of the person walking with her; the dolt, too ingenuous to make his own opportunities, too timid to take the ones she gave him, who besieged her so many months; the jackass with his affectations and posturings—the silly things he said; the awful, inexperienced things he did!

"Oh, God—" Francis murmured again; but he was drowsy, only indistinctly aware of his cold feet and his painful head; and suddenly he slept.

At Montreux most visitors come for the whole winter and, with several months to pass, they settle into a careful monotonous routine. The damp lake's edge, where an occasional rose blooms in December, is thought to have a salubrious climate. It attracts semi-invalids whose complaints are not too serious or too incapacitating, or who suffer from the general indisposition of old age. At any rate, Montreux's dank thin sunniness is a not inappropriate setting for invalids. Because they hope, if they do what the doctor ordered, to put off dying or being reduced to the last resort of spas and sanatoria, much of their attention centers on the close scrutiny of themselves.

Their symptoms and natural functions absorb them, and the resulting ups and downs of hope and fear give inward excitement enough, and more than enough, to lives apparently so humdrum. They go for short slow walks, looking at the lake, but listening to their fluctuating heartbeats. Some of them take a glass of wine for its medicinal properties with their meals, and some of them simply take medicine. They borrow novels from the English library and try to read them while they wonder what that pain during the night meant. Unwilling, worried scatologists, they find books in a chamberpot, sermons in bowel movements—something to ponder when, for consolation or distraction, they sit enjoying a little Offenbach at a *Kursaal* concert; or, in Sunday best, wait in their pews at Saint John's or Christ Church for morning prayer to commence. (O all ye Beasts and Cattle, bless ye the Lord. . . .)

Grindelwald is a different world.

The late dim-lit depressing arrival obscured it for the moment, but the difference came to Francis at once as soon as his eyes opened the next morning. Perhaps people laughing as they went downstairs or the mere animated rise of voices going by in the hall—things never heard at hotels in Montreux—reached Francis when the *valet de chambre* came in; perhaps from outdoors the noise of sleigh bells, a hearty shout, or the sound of someone whistling had nearly awakened him a moment before. The room was full of the lucid reflected glow of a clear cold day, and Francis even while half asleep could feel his heaviness of mind gone as completely as last night's headache, and, in its stead, a light joyful anticipation, as though he were a child and this were Christmas morning.

The tea was hot and good. Francis drank it sitting up in bed and ate his rolls. He got out of bed then, lit a cigarette and moving to the window beheld abruptly the gigantic mass of the piled-up mountains.

"My God!" he said, incredulous.

Closing the valley to the south, the solid wall of the Eiger, the immense Mettenberg, the Wetterhorn's vast elevated granite shoulder, stood over Grindelwald in a splendor of morning sunlight, in great bare precipices, in immeasurable sweeping scarps of snow. Far up there, across those exposed sky-high snow fields a tremendous wind must be blowing, for every minute or two puffs arose like a flutter of white flags, drew out, thinned to sparkling smoke, and were gone against the deep icy blue. Staring, standing motionless, Francis's heart beat harder with a quick exquisite festivity. It mounted, shining and immortal, in a world immortal and shining, too. Putting on his dressing gown, he went, exultant, along to the bathroom.

Downstairs everything looked cheerful. In the lounge those expanses of glass that served last night to let in the dark and to show the blind whirl of snow, let in now a blaze of sunlight. The high, ample corridors, then obscure and empty, now seemed bright and animated. With a burst of chatter a group of people came out the dining-room doors together and separated in purposeful haste to prepare for some expedition. A couple of young women, plain but pleasant in colored sweaters, their fur coats bulging over their arms, left the elevator and went by Francis with a whiff of carnations. They were followed presently by the father of that family Francis had watched during dinner last night. He looked less forbidding. He lounged along smiling and agreeable in good tweeds smoking a pipe from which a pleasant fragrance drifted after him.

Francis had paused, standing aside while he watched. He felt contentedly idle, and in any event, he could do nothing until the Cunninghams got down; but the possibility of Troop and Best appearing among the passers-by occurred to him. He would not want them to think that he had been standing around with the idea of not missing them. He crossed the hall and went down the double steps into the lounge, took up a two-day-old copy of the Paris *Herald* and seated himself in a concealed corner. The stale news was not interesting; but he kept the paper open because it gave him an occupied air, if anyone happened to look in. From time to time voices arose beyond the hall pillars.

Loud and hearty, someone said: "Good kit, that, Mrs.—"

"Oh. Thanks so much, Admiral! I—"

What on earth admirals were doing around here Francis could not imagine, but he pricked his ears up. The subject of his new book had led him to read a good deal of naval history and it would have interested him to talk to somebody who had been through an actual engagement—Jutland, perhaps. Not that there would be much resemblance between the *Huascar's* affairs in 1879 and Jutland, and not that any eyewitness except yourself ever noticed the right things—but on the battle cruisers they must have known, like Admiral Grau, that they were for it, and though Beatty's celebrated remark told you something, what men with less chance of being recorded for posterity thought and said might be worth hearing.

More people passed.

"But, good Lord, man, in that case—"

"—the blasted limit."

The speakers were gone and the sound of the door revolved for them arose.

A new voice said with emphasis and satisfaction, "—and that takes doing, let me tell you!"

Nobody denied it.

Coming up, someone said good morning, and two people answered together. There was a pause and the door went around. One of the answering voices then said clearly: "Who the devil was that?" A woman responded, "No idea." The door went around again with a stir of fresh air and the sound of horses stamping in the snow and shaking their bells.

"Morning, Miss Poulter."

"Good morning, Admiral. Curling today?"

"When those fellows have the snow off. Good kit, that. Most becoming—"

Looking past his paper Francis saw that the naval dispenser of compliments was the old boy who had been reading in the lounge last night. Though he was of the age—well past sixty—common in Montreux, he did not therefore spend all his time knowing his end or the number of his days. His ruddy, irascible face softened as it followed Miss Poulter, who was clad completely in white—a skating skirt, tights, and a brief braid-covered detachable cloak like a dolman, as though she were the daughter of a hussar regiment, or possibly of a circus. To the Admiral the effect was evidently piquant. He looked her up and down with relish, enjoying her show of long legs. "The old goat!" thought Francis, smiling; for the stout, frank display, the forthright, damn-your-eyes adultery going on in his heart was cheerful to see.

Through the glass, beyond the dazzling banks of snow, Miss Poulter came in sight again, passing down the drive and across to the rinks. In summer these were tennis courts, but they had been flooded and several men were now working with big pushers and shovels, still clearing snow from the far end. The posts supporting the backstops had been topped with gonfalons of colored bunting, lifting and flapping in the wind in a long gay line before the scattered façades of the open platz and, on the high side, the short spire and snow-burdened roof of the English church.

"Hello," said Walter. He propped himself on the arm of the chair and bent his head down to look where Francis was looking. Miss Poulter had appeared on the swept surface of the ice with a skinny black-clad man —probably a professional instructor, though it was apparent that Miss Poulter did not need instruction. The good kit was no doubt one of a number supplied her for advertising purposes by some dressmaking firm.

"Who are they?" said Walter. "Say, did you see the notice about the hockey team?"

"No," said Francis.

"It's over there. They're going to have one. I saw Tom and Toby down. Why don't you—"

"Nobody asked me," said Francis. "Besides, I haven't played since I left school. I doubt if I'd be good enough."

"Nobody has to ask you. You just write your name on the list. I'll write it for you, shall I?"

"You'll do nothing of the sort," Francis said.

"Ah, come on. Please, Frank."

"What is this, anyway?" said Francis; but he knew. With proprietary enthusiasm Walter, as soon as he saw the notice, put Francis mentally in the team, had him perform in dashing and applause-commanding ways; and envisoned, as a result, all kinds of triumphs in which, since Francis represented the emotional equivalent of our side, our team, they could share and share alike.

Sense of self-interest, even if its exact nature was not clear to him, made Walter apologetic. He said defensively: "Well, I know you played hockey. You said so. You—"

"We'll see," Francis said, fending it off.

"You did, didn't you?" Walter insisted, with what was either anxiety or suspicion.

"I did," said Francis shortly.

During those first days with Walter he knew that he had let drop plenty of offhand remarks from which a bright boy would hardly fail to deduce (and possibly even exaggerate) Francis's decent acquaintance with manly sports. Francis was abashed; both to think that he had done it and to think that Walter, with one of his ingenuous, unexpected flashes of penetration—a thing Francis never would have thought of then: the study of Walter was instructive—might have sized up silently the effort to impress him. "I'll play," Francis said, "if we have time and they need someone. And listen. Go easy on this Toby and Tom stuff. We've hardly met them, and we can't do the kind of skiing they want to do. I think maybe Troop won't mind giving you some pointers sometime; but don't ask him to."

"Gosh, I wasn't going to," said Walter. "I just saw their names. Why don't we find out about some skis?"

"Is your mother down yet?"

"Oh, she's in the office. They're trying to get Paris for her."

"Anything wrong?"

Walter shrugged. "Helen sent her a telegram about somebody going to Geneva or something. Heck."

"Now what?"

"She'll probably be coming tomorrow or the next day. We'll probably have to take her skiing."

"Why not?"

"Oh, it won't be any fun." He swayed back and forth on the chair arm. "She's too bossy."

"You're not very polite," said Francis, feeling that a rebuke should be administered, but not knowing just what, since Walter was very likely right, in the sense that holidays with Helen meant that, to his mother's and Maggie's solicitude, Helen's would be added.

"I know her," said Walter. "She wasn't coming until next week, but she's just sick of Paris. She wanted to go somewhere—I forget. She wrote mother. It's where Lorna Higham is. Do you know?"

Francis had forgotten that letter of Helen's. It dropped from his mind, since he had known before it came that it would be to no purpose; but of course it had duly come and Mrs. Cunningham had duly read it. He paused, considering what he wanted to say. He said then: "I think it's Cap d'Ail. It's near Monte-Carlo. It's very pleasant, I'm told."

Francis wished he knew what was in Helen's letter, but to get it out of Walter, supposing Walter knew, he would have to show an interest, by continuing the subject, that might strike Walter as odd. Trying to imagine what Helen would be likely to write was difficult, for Francis had seen little of her. That afternoon when he came to tea with Lorna she had been there; but she was unobtrusive—a tidy, quiet girl with hair somewhat lighter than Walter's. She wore it in a sedate way, smooth, with knots over her ears, and it gave her a quaint grown-up air at variance with her evident shyness. She sat with lowered eyes, speaking when she was spoken to, not looking at anyone—because, you might think, she feared that if she did she would find someone looking at her.

In the lighted dusk of the hotel sitting room, made more comfortable by the outside gloom of an October afternoon in Paris when it was, naturally, raining, Francis had found little time for anything but his own thoughts. Mrs. Cunningham had talked, asking pleasantly about his mother, keeping away from the real point, which was whether, if she stayed in Europe, Walter could be trusted to Francis. From her standpoint the matter was delicate, and her delicacy was so perfect as to be a little disconcerting. While this was new to Francis, Mrs. Cunningham had been all through it often before. Her kindness and consideration—she wanted to put him at ease, both for his sake and for the sake of seeing more than his best behavior—showed practice.

Thinking back, Francis now understood her position better. To find in Paris someone like Francis, who would be all right on a half-dozen counts, probably seemed a stroke of luck to Mrs. Cunningham; but she was practical, and wary for that very reason. If the arrangement were made, and then proved unsatisfactory, there would be complications. She might have to explain, for instance, to Francis's mother, which would be awkward. She could not let herself be hurried, and until she had reached a decision it was more convenient, in case the decision were no, to proceed as though he and Lorna had just dropped in to tea.

This really suited Francis very well. To show himself to advantage, to try to please not because he liked to be liked, but because he wanted a job, was (wasn't it?) unthinkable. He did not mind pretending that he was not doing it. He wished that he could not see Mrs. Cunningham's purpose as she led the conversation here and there. Surely politeness made him answer her—though with what humiliating self-consciousness!—more or less as she wished to be answered. Meanwhile Walter fidgeted; and poor old Rose lay on her side dozing and illustrating her pleasant dreams with faint eager whimpers and minute motions of running; and Helen looked down, diffident with an older sister's friend, and spoke shyly to Lorna; and Lorna was marvelous.

Lorna sat against the worn dark-yellow brocade of an empire settee, brass-mounted with stars and bees. The arms were swan-necked. It had been one of the moments when she seemed to Francis distractingly charming, and he was delighted with her—with the color of her eyes, and the infinitely appealing hollow-cheeked face and wide but beautiful mouth, with the dull shine of silk on her crossed legs, the supple use of her fine slender-boned hands in putting a teacup down or lighting a cigarette—but he had to give his attention to Mrs. Cunningham. He held himself ready to meet at any moment Mrs. Cunningham's eye, readiness or unreadiness to do which, he was fairly sure, Mrs. Cunningham would regard as one of the tests of virtue.

In confused discomfort, Francis tried to keep his wits about him—not knowing what impression he was making, wanting the job because he needed the money; detesting the necessity; thinking how pleasant Mrs. Cunningham was and what a bore with her questions. One half his mind hoped that his answers suited her. The other half entertained outrageous impulses to say that he had no interest in school requirements, no time for twelve-year-old brats, and no qualifications for the job since he had never learned any of his own lessons outside a few subjects he happened to like. As for his character, he had what might as well be called a marked taste for wine and women, he was self-seeking and self-centered, and she must be crazy if she didn't see that his only motive in taking such a position was to get his keep and a little spare cash while he finished the book he was writing.

When Mrs. Cunningham finally came to indicate that enough ground had been covered for today, the relief of his freedom to leave, of being about to have Lorna to himself, filled Francis with affectionate gratitude to everyone. He said that he would like very much to try some tennis with

Walter tomorrow, and noted an address on the Rue des Belles Feuilles. Through this arrangement Helen, who had jumped up prematurely, stood straight and stiff. She wore a grayish-brown skirt and a thin, closely knit pullover sweater, also brownish. About her round, still childish neck was a string of smooth dark beads like beans. Nothing made her conspicuous, unless it was a trick she had of doubling her right arm behind her back and clutching tensely her left elbow. Mrs. Cunningham disapproved of the pose, either for its juvenile awkwardness or for the unmaidenly way in which it brought out the breasts. Still talking to Francis, Mrs. Cunningham tapped the arm to make Helen stop. Helen let her elbow go, blushed, shook hands with Lorna; and offered her hand then to Francis. Francis took it and said good-bye. It was the only conversation he had had with her, and he did not see her again.

II

Francis wiped the undersides of his skis clean and stood them against the wall. "Got it?" he said to Walter, who sat on the bench by the door bent double while he worked at the harness straps.

"Sure," said Walter. He freed his other foot, moving his bad leg stiffly, and began to scrape the thick cakes of snow from the wool socks doubled down over his boot tops. "I'll bet we beat them by a mile," he said, peering up sideways.

"Now, don't get cocky," Francis said. "We started first and this way is a good deal shorter."

"Well, even so—say, you've got a swell tan! Have I?"

"Good enough," said Francis. "It was the glare up at Alpiglen yesterday. Does it bother your eyes?" The painted door beside him opened and a man with a napkin in his hand put a bald head out, blinking at the trampled snow of the road.

"*Mittagessen?*" Francis said.

"*Ja, mein Herr*—" He began at once to reel off what must be the menu. "What's he say?" demanded Walter. "I haven't the faintest idea," Francis said. He held his hand up. "*Jemand hier der Englisch spricht?*"

"*Nein, mein Herr.*"

"In a minute!" Francis said. "We're waiting for some others."

"*Ja, ja.*" The door closed.

"That's all the good German A ever did me," Francis said. "I can read it a little, but—"

"Never mind," Walter said. "If we meet any Romans you can always talk Latin to them."

"That will do from you!" said Francis, amused, but embarrassed, too,

by the 'never mind,' which seemed to touch unerringly the ruffled pride
that would wish, in smiling ease, to speak fluent German while Walter
and everyone else looked on with respect and admiration; and perhaps
touched, too, the self-consciousness that (through fear of causing smiles,
or of failing to be instantly intelligible) made him hesitate over the little
he did know. "All I could understand was something about an ox," he
said. "Or maybe it wasn't."

"Maybe it's boeuf à la mode. Ugh! Or just veal. I'll bet it's veal. Or
horse. Toby said he thought that stuff the other night was horse. You had
it. Remember? Say, what's the difference between an ox and a bull, anyway? Are they the same?"

"It's the same animal," Francis said.

"Well, isn't there any difference?"

"The difference is that oxen have certain glands removed. It tends to
make them fatter and heavier. Are you cold? We'd better go in if you are."

"I want to see them come down. It's not cold. It's swell in the sun."
Walter leaned back against the white wall, closed his eyes and smiled.

On Francis, too, the radiance fell. It lay keen and hot across his face;
hot, not on the skin, which tingled pleasantly to the freezing air, but
under it, permeating the web of muscles (were there thirty of them?),
warming the maxillae until the curving bone glowed with comfort, absorbing sun. The shining air had a quality like the clearness of cold water,
refreshing you at every breath.

Francis looked at Walter, whose eyes were still closed, his faintly
smiling face turned up. Expressed in the smile, Francis saw suddenly, was
all the pleasure, inexpressible in words, of being alive. For the moment
Walter was completely happy—and happy in a way, Francis would almost
have said, and to a degree that he might never reach again. The trouble
with this affecting thought, in theory so sound, was that in practice Francis did not find it true. In the rare shining air, lit by the golden snow,
sheltered by the warm wall, Francis, though taught by experience how to
worry, and by the elaboration of ideas and desires how to be discontented
at a moment's notice, was nevertheless completely happy, too—as happy
as he had ever been in his life, as happy as he would ever hope to be.

Francis had been looking up the steep rise to the fringes of the pine
wood. Abruptly, over the crest, down onto this dazzling expanse, flicked
the crouched dark figure of a skier coming like the wind. His poles angled
up behind him, the lengthening line of his track streaked a clean shadow
on the hanging slope. "Wake up!" Francis said to Walter. "There's Best."

Walter jerked himself erect, lifting a mitten to shield his eyes.
"Golly, look at him!" he said. He began to laugh.

Two other figures had appeared by the high edge of the pines. Screwing his eyes up, staring off under his hand, Walter laughed again. "Helen took a spill," he said. "Gosh, she's terrible!" He waved his arm vigorously.

Best, bareheaded, wearing dark goggles, his jacket tied about his waist, his shirt open on the loose folds of a scarf in his school colors about his neck, slewed with a flurry of spangled snow dust into the road above and headed down toward them.

—turned up Sunday, Francis wrote. *Mrs. C. asked at tea how you were and she said you were fine, she saw you just before you went south. I felt like yelling yes, yes, go on; but I said not a word and she immediately dropped it for the dreary topic of herself and her travels—mostly timetables and how she got from Geneva to Interlaken. Somebody was with her as far as Geneva, for I gather her Mademoiselles regarded such a trip by an unescorted seventeen-year-old girl as little short of épouvantable; and maybe Helen herself was not unimpressed by the potential perils and dangers of this night in a wagon-lit—enlivened, no doubt, by visions of suave and sinister Frenchmen with spade beards and boutonnières of the Legion of Honor making improper advances.*

Francis held his pen. "Anything for a laugh!" he said. He went on: *Actually I doubt if such thoughts crossed her mind, for she is a levelheaded little thing under her bashfulness. Our Britishers have been fairly attentive and Troop at least gives signs of being much smitten. We've been skiing with them twice, and she was around this afternoon for some time while I futilely tried to show a fantastic hockey team we are getting up which end of the stick you are supposed to hold—we're scheduled to have a game with a hotel up the road tomorrow. Troop, who was always falling down, would limp over and sit beside her to recover, very jolly and admiring; but I noticed that her reserve is great enough to keep matters at the Miss Cunningham stage. I think the hitch here may be that it is Best, whose looks are distinguished in the conventional young-blond-god manner, that takes her fancy, if fancy she is not too shy to have; and he, alas, is aloof—bored and rather hostile to us all, as well he might be, I suppose, since Troop came with him, not with us—*

Francis broke off. Then he laid his pen down, took the sheet and ripped it back and forth until he held a handful of fragments. He shot them into the wastepaper basket and drew out a fresh sheet. *The mountains,* he wrote, *go on being unspeakably grand—nobody could ever imagine anything like the Wetterhorn in the morning—but man is as vile as usual, and I am sick of these damned winter sports. Helen has arrived. Wretched child, she is oblivious to her good fortune in, hardly two weeks ago, having seen and talked to you. Wednesday I'm leaving for Florence to spend Christmas. These dreary festivals! I hope you don't have too merry a time, and as for the New Year, to hell with it. Many more months like these last will be the death of me. I must do some-*

thing about it and so must you. You might begin by writing to Florence that you love me madly. . . .

He sealed the envelope and addressed it—*Villa Apollon, Cap d'Ail, Alpes Maritimes, France.* "Suppose," he said to himself, "I simply went down there Wednesday?"

He sat quiet a moment, thinking of it with attention—probably there was some fairly short way to get over to Turin, to Genoa, and up the coast—as though good clear planning might make it feasible. But what nonsense! By the time he arrived he wouldn't have a cent, or the slenderest hope of getting a cent. Still, the fact was, he could do it; he was physically able to do it since he had money enough to pay for the tickets. If he went straight to a hotel and registered he could probably count on his clothes and luggage to give him a week at least before anybody began worrying about whether he could pay the bill—anybody except Francis himself. He would worry plenty.

The mere imagining of his plight made him shrink now—shrink not only from the inevitable, appalling showdown in which it would have to end, but also from the few days of grace he could expect, for he would not have even an ordinary amount of money to tide him over those—like that so-called 'beau' of Gwen's in Paris; an intense, hollow-eyed youth living on some miserable salary in French francs (for wasn't his bank giving him, free, experience in the foreign service and opportunity?), tied to long and dreary hours, who, if he bought Gwen a drink, paid for it with his meals next week. This surely was real devotion, a classic heroic passion that you might think a girl would be moved by. Gwen was moved, all right; she was almost distracted. "But I hardly know him!" she said with a sort of despair. "I met him once at a dance, and he was on the boat last spring. He can't afford to take me to dinner again. I know he can't. My God, what shall I do? I think he's sweet, but—"

Yes, but, but, but!

Francis stood up. He took off the dressing gown in which he had been sitting, straightened his waistcoat and put his coat on. Downstairs he dropped his letter in the box and went along to the bar. Miss Poulter, gowned in a color that must be the one meant by the term 'electric blue,' sat on a stool talking to the barkeep. "Hello, there!" she said cordially.

"Good evening," said Francis.

"Are you going out?"

"Not that I know of. I have some work to do."

"My dear man, you have indeed! Everyone under ninety seems to have gone on some razzle up the road. You can't possibly let me down. The orchestra's come and we're supposed to be having dancing."

"How about Troop and Best?"

"Oh, they went. They were in here toping until a few minutes ago."

In the mirror between the fancy bottles and pyramids of glasses Francis saw his face. The snow glare had burned his skin to a red-brown tone deep enough to make it hard to tell whether or not he had flushed. The barkeep set a cocktail glass in front of him and filled it.

He said, "Thanks, Karl," and took a swallow. Drily and carefully, with detachment, for he did not mean to give Miss Poulter an inkling of anything so absurd, so humiliatingly absurd, as the chagrin he felt to know that, though Troop and Best had been on the rinks with him most of the afternoon, he had not learned anything about this 'razzle' to which everyone else under ninety had gone, he said, "I'm afraid I will have to let you down. I have some work I've really got to do." He smiled indulgently. "I am a drudge by nature," he said. "My youth is behind me."

Francis drank the rest of the drink, nodded to her, and to the barkeep to indicate that he should write it down, and went out as though in haste. It was fifteen minutes before the Cunninghams appeared.

Helen's peach-colored dress must have been her best last spring in New York. Something new, made in Paris, had doubtless superseded it and, rescued by Maggie with exclamations of admiration from the crush of packed clothes, hung now upstairs ready for Christmas or New Year's Eve; but the peach taffeta, simple and good, looked like a party still. Helen herself had a gently flushed, beautifully washed look. Her smooth hair had been brushed until it shone and was arranged with a neatness in which Maggie or her mother must have had a hand. Almost indistinguishable, a scent of rose-geranium surrounded her. She wore a little string of suitably small real pearls. She was all dressed up, and since the chances were she had taken special pains because of Troop and Best, it seemed too bad. Mrs. Cunningham paused a moment at the desk to speak to the clerk, and Francis said, "What a charming dress."

"Thanks," said Helen, and added, "It's awfully old." She colored then and literally bit her lip, commemorating awkwardly the fact that once again she had remembered too late that grown-up women do not deprecate compliments, they just acknowledge them gracefully. She moved ahead with Walter, and Francis went into the dining room after them with Mrs. Cunningham.

Mrs. Cunningham, seated, gave Helen an affectionate critical glance. Satisfied with Helen's appearance, she looked at Walter, and at once said pleasantly, "People will think you haven't any handkerchief, darling."

Walter squirmed a little and investigated his breast pocket, producing a folded corner of linen. "That's better," she said. She looked, Francis thought, highly personable herself, as much a credit to her children as they were to her. The headwaiter stood at her side, and she smiled, gracious and agreeable, accepting a menu card. From a chain about her neck hung a collapsible lorgnette in thin white gold and she brought it up, opening it. "Francis, you must be famished after all that hockey," she said. "Do eat a great deal. I think we might have some wine. You choose it. Walter, dearest, look at the menu. You mustn't keep everyone waiting."

"Gosh!" said Walter. "Gray pearls of Volga. I want some of that."

"All they mean is caviare," said Francis.

Mrs. Cunningham said, "Do you suppose the chef is a poet? No, dear, you don't want any. It doesn't agree with you."

"O.K.," said Walter. To Francis he said, "Say, what does S period, A period, G period, mean?"

"Walter!"

"I'll have *potage* and *poule aux* what's-it."

"Very well."

"What does it mean, Frank?"

"I don't know. Where did you see it?"

"Maggie writes it on her letters and then puts the stamp over it."

"Oh," said Francis laughing, "that means Saint Anthony Guide. It's an old Catholic, or maybe Irish, custom. So the letter won't get lost."

Mrs. Cunningham gave up the menu, folded her glasses together and let them fall. "Francis," she said, "I think you're really remarkable. How do you know things like that?"

Francis smiled, not displeased, for by a natural sweetness of address Mrs. Cunningham did make it seem rather remarkable. Walter was craning his neck to look at the table in the corner where Troop and Best ate. "Where is everybody tonight?" he said. "Toby and Tom aren't there."

"I think they went out," Francis said.

Swaying over toward Helen, Walter raised his hand and whispered loudly behind it, "Tough luck!"

"Oh, you keep still!" said Helen, though with good enough temper.

"What did you say, dear?"

"Oh, he's being silly again."

"Walter, please don't sprawl on the table." Turning to Francis she observed (when gentlefolk meet, and the compliments have been exchanged, conversation on general topics of intelligent interest follows as a matter of course): "I was just looking at the paper. Did you see that the German Cabinet had resigned? Do you think anything serious is going to happen?"

"It's hard to tell," Francis said; but to answer so poorly was to shirk his social duty and put Mrs. Cunningham to the trouble of selecting another topic. "It's interesting about the Scheidemann business," he said.

"Who's he?" said Walter.

"He's the fellow who said in the Reichstag that Gessler and the Monarchists were secretly arming."

Helen volunteered abruptly, "Mademoiselle says there's going to be another war." She then subsided, abashed.

"Maybe she's right," Francis said. He looked from Helen to Walter to Mrs. Cunningham and they made together a pleasant sight, grouped in innocent calmness, and he was struck—he would have liked to write about it, if only he could grasp the dramatic inner meaning that lies in the simultaneous occurrence of diverse things—by the picture of them sitting here in the Alpine night in a flood of light and warmth contained by the shell of the hotel. While good and expensive food was put before them, while a waiter held in a napkin the bottle of Moselle Francis had ordered and twisted a corkscrew, while they waited quietly for the wine and for more food, they looked down from this high mountain on all the kingdoms of the world in a moment of time, and spoke of what they saw, or thought they saw.

Francis went on speaking about Germany, mentioning the names of men he had never seen and knew nothing about, repeating what he more or less correctly remembered reading in some newspaper, surveying Germany from the mountain as it lay out like a map in his mind, the million lights of Berlin in an incandescent vast pattern leagues to the north. The glibly mentioned Scheidemann, whoever he was, whatever he was trying to do, would be there somewhere—Francis tried to think of him as he must have looked when he finished speaking and the jumble of voices in pain and fury roared traitor, traitor. Francis would have joined any such roar, it seemed to him—at least he would unless, impelled by some awful necessity of conscience or ambition or self-expression, he had been the one to rise and speak, he had been the one roared at.

His eye went out, over Prussia, over the Vistula, over Tannenberg and the snowbound Masurian lakes. Far to the south stretched the incredible, still-feudal fiefs of the Polish counts; far to the east glowed Moscow; all one in the unity of the winter night of Europe, a unity of nightmare in distances, in mountains and rivers, in millions of men and millions of buildings—huts, palaces, fortifications, hospitals; in the intricate web of circumstance, of local condition, of complicated history, of incomprehensible language, of resulting ideas and efforts that Francis would never know enough about to understand.

Where, for instance, was Trotsky tonight? Francis tried to think of him, too; of the tailor's body like a dwarf in its Cossack's greatcoat, of the hope and fear, the love and hate, behind the screwed-up Jewish comedian's face, brooding (in ever deadlier personal peril as, his great services forgotten, enemies in his party worked to pull him down) on the havocs and ecstasies of the Soviet apocalypse—the Byzantine treachery, the torture chambers, the spies in the wall, the concealed revolvers, the monster parades, the waving red flags, the broken furniture, and the frozen plumbing. Like scenes from *Gulliver's Travels*, all day and all night a double column serried past the mummy of Lenin; and in the factories the moron mechanics sang as they ruined the new machines; and in the fields the peasants like Nebuchadnezzar ate grass; and in crowded halls a thousand commissars shouted speeches; and in a thousand frowsy committee rooms the illiterate architects of the future scratched for lice and made mistakes in arithmetic as they tinkered with their millennium. Meanwhile the wine was poured for Mrs. Cunningham and Helen and Francis, and a half a glass for Walter; and down the long bright room came Miss Poulter in her electric-blue gown.

Walter and Francis stood up while she paused by Mrs. Cunningham and said to them, "Oh, please don't move. Mrs. Cunningham, we're having a little dance this evening. I hope you'll all come in. . . ."

Helen was amiable by nature and she had been taught to dance well; but once out on the floor, which was far from crowded, she was half-paralyzed. She held her body as though she loathed it and wished she had left it upstairs. When the obligation to speak arose she spoke with a difficulty that made plain her fear that she was about to say something stupid. She was afraid, too, that Francis danced with her only because he had to; and this fear was so plausible that she must next be afraid that he might think she didn't realize it, and that she was such a fool that she actually imagined dancing with her was fun. Since he thought her a fool and a bore, he certainly didn't have to dance with her. She hadn't asked him to. She didn't really want to dance.

At this point her natural amiability, functioning as common sense, would probably point out to her that he couldn't help it; and that it was her mother's fault for bringing them in here. This was unfair, too; since her mother only wanted her to have a good time; and if, instead, she was having a simply ghastly time, why that was her own fault; for being her hateful self, and not like other girls, who always knew what to say and who danced with grace and ease so extraordinary that nobody could fail to enjoy dancing with them.

The struggle to control and conceal these feelings made them obvious to Francis and easy to follow. He regarded Helen with compunction (another thing she might fear he would regard her with); but helping her was uphill work. He asked about Paris and the school.

"Well, we do a lot of things, I suppose," she said. "I mean, we're always having classes and things."

"Do you like it?"

"Yes. I like it."

"Are any of the girls amusing?"

She gave him a guarded glance. Either it had never occurred to her that she was qualified to decide such a point, or her apprehensive mind, feeling acutely her own failure to be amusing, wildly wondered if he intended the question sarcastically.

"There's a Mexican girl," she said with a sort of anguish. "She doesn't speak very good English."

"I thought you weren't allowed to speak English."

"Well, we're not." Helen let her eyes go off toward the orchestra to see how much longer they were going to continue this interminable music. "But in the—well, everybody does when Mademoiselle isn't around."

"What happens if you get caught?"

"Well, you have to stop. I suppose we're there to learn French, so—" She gave a shamefaced little shrug. She missed a step and touched his foot with her slipper. "Oh, sorry," she said painfully. Her desperate eyes went toward the orchestra again, but she halted them halfway, ashamed of her bad behavior. To make amends, she began a question; but Francis, not expecting such a thing, had begun one, too. They both stopped, and she flushed deeply. "Sorry," said Francis, laughing. "What did you say?"

She swallowed, made an effort, and answered, "Nothing. I was just going to ask if you'd heard anything from Lorna."

"Not for some time," Francis said, reminded that Helen was, or had been, a fellow conspirator of his. It gave him shock, for you could as easily think of Helen, bashful and artless, simple and singlehearted, cast as Lady Macbeth and demanding the daggers. Being incapable of conspiracy Helen would have little taste for it, and he might as well ignore the (naturally) unsuccessful business and let her, if she would, suppose that Lorna had not told him of it.

"Oh. I thought you might have," Helen said.

Some fresh wave of awkwardness came over her—Francis recognized it by the now familiar increase of tension under his hand on her firmly formed back. To puzzle out what exactly she meant seemed useless, since there was so good a chance that she meant nothing at all; but her awkwardness could be explained by supposing that she suspected Francis and Lorna of being in love; and this fussed her, for she probably did not like love. Love, too, was a form of conspiracy, its pretty first stage of presents and kisses no more than means to an end. What this end was her mother would not have failed to impart fully and clearly, in the nicest possible way. However, few parents, or none, could keep in countenance through a full explanation without harping on the sacredness and beauty of the arrangement; and an adolescent girl was more likely to come away intimidated than reassured. The sacredness and beauty would not be very clear without the solicitations of strong feeling. If she knew nothing of these solicitations, they were not readily imaginable. If she had discovered their nature by herself, subsequent remorse and self-reproach were sure to have made them distressing and repellent. In either event she would try to think of 'all that' as little as might be; and in either event it was natural to view her sympathetically.

To make a diversion, Francis murmured: "Don't miss the Admiral."

At once he wondered if his diversion, picked at random, the first that occurred to him, had been fortunate. The Admiral, swelling with exertion, his eyes glinting in a foxy triumph of appetite over senescence, trotted rapidly in and out of the moving dancers, hugging Miss Poulter in time to the music; and, viewed squeamishly, the spectacle had its disgusting side. However, Helen, if squeamish, was not so squeamish as that. Magically, the stout bouncing old man must have restored for her a comfortable schoolgirl's-eye view of life. She gazed past Francis's shoulder a moment and giggled. Trailing out, falling to pieces with much pounding of his drums by the tall sunken-cheeked drummer, the music came to a halt. A dreary silence, broken by the sound of someone clapping and the scuff of feet as the dozen, mostly middle-aged, couples turned to leave the floor, descended.

Released, Helen stood an instant with the schoolgirl's repressed grin still lighting her face. She colored then, returning to her painful age. "Thanks very much," she said, precipitate and husky in renewed self consciousness. She moved quickly to get back to her mother.

Mrs. Cunningham said, "You look very nice on the floor, dearest." Sitting just behind, in the second of the two rows of folding chairs arranged around the walls, Maggie had appeared; and putting aside her knitting, she shook out a shawl. "You'll be catching cold," she said to Helen.

"I don't need it," Helen protested; but she let Maggie settle the folds of silk over her shoulders. "How lovely," Francis said, looking at the intricate burst of big embroidered flowers.

"You know, it used to be my mother's," Mrs. Cunningham said. "I was so pleased when they started wearing them again. Though I don't believe this ever was worn; I'm sure Mother thought it was too loud. A friend of hers, who was a missionary, brought it back from China. I always thought it a rather odd thing for a missionary to pick out."

"Was he the guy who wanted to marry her?" asked Walter.

"Well, darling, I don't know that he really did. And I don't know how you know anything about it."

"You were telling Edith when she said Helen could have it. I know. He's a bishop."

"Well, darling, he was a bishop. He died several years ago. His wanting to marry her was an old family joke your Great-Aunt Clara used to tease her about."

"Then there was all that lovely lace—from the Philippine Islands, I think," said Maggie. She half stood up and shifted the shawl a little on Helen's shoulders.

"Oh, please don't, Maggie," said Helen. "It's all right!"

"It was all falling down, dear," Maggie said, settling back again.

"Francis," said Mrs. Cunningham, "I think it would be an act of charity if you would go and dance with poor Miss Poulter. She was having a very hard time with her elderly admirer. Why don't you?"

"She's the queen of the village green," said Walter.

"What a silly thing to say, darling. Do go, Francis, before the music starts or she'll be caught again."

Francis arose and crossed the floor to Miss Poulter, who was standing down by the pine-trimmed bower which housed the orchestra, talking to the leader.

"Will I not!" she said to Francis. "Would you like a waltz? Everyone else would." Her hand dropped on his arm, holding it, and she spoke to the orchestra leader in German. Switching about, he faced his musicians, struck two sharp taps, and out of the bower, with a ponderously gay rocking-horse swing, the "Blue Danube" began to gush.

Miss Poulter, moving into Francis's embrace, proved to be peculiarly made. Her head rose to within an inch or two of his, but her neck was long enough to make her shoulders lower than you expected. On the contrary, her arms in proportion to her height were shorter than you would expect. Under the blue gown a kind of tight garment encased her and gave her high stomach a flat board-like front, from beneath which her long well-muscled thighs moved with vigor and precision. She smelled of clean sweat and some borated dusting powder with orris root in it.

Though nimble and light on her feet, Miss Poulter did not let herself be led easily, and Francis found that she required firm handling. This she resisted for a moment or two, covering her stubbornness in going her own way by a real or affected absorption in the review of her social charges. Then abruptly she gave in, let her boarded-up stomach come against Francis, tightened her fingers a moment on his left hand and said: "I was awfully angry at you before dinner."

This could only refer to his flight from the bar. To explain that, if he had been rude, he had been rude in revenge, because he was offended; and that he had been offended because a couple of kids neglected to ask him (he couldn't and wouldn't have accepted) to go out with them, would not

please her and would be painful to Francis. He feigned great surprise.
"You appall me!" he said.

"Why did you say you had to work?"

"Because I did have to. And I still do."

"Why don't you chuck it? I'm going out to skate later. There's a marvelous moon. Why don't you come?"

"It would be too embarrassing," said Francis. "I've seen you skate.
I'm not quite in your class."

"What rot! I saw you playing hockey this afternoon and you're frightfully good. You made our public-school men look a bit silly, didn't you?"

Francis thought with interest, "So that's how it is!" The acid emphasis, the not-altogether-convincing tone of amused disdain, could mean
only one thing. Making her way through the intricacies of the English
social system, Miss Poulter like the Ephraimites came down to Jordan
hoping to get over; but the public-school men, having heard her say one
or more of a hundred well-established shibboleths, killed her with a look;
and she would just have to make the best of the limbo where the lower
classes were lost. Francis dared say she was now, wounded and angry,
making the best of it. "Speaking of ice," Francis said, "would you mind
if I asked an idle question?"

"I don't see why. Should I?"

"How did you learn to skate like that? I didn't know ice had been
introduced into England yet."

"Oh, we have ice. Quite often. However, I didn't learn in England."
Her upper lip lifted a little in her fastidious expression. "As a matter of
fact, I was at school in Switzerland when I was a kiddy. My people were
in the Diplomatic Service."

Best or Troop, Francis reflected, would probably know that they were
like hell. At any rate, you could take it as proved that Miss Poulter had a
natural wish to represent herself as a person of quality; and the vanity of
so wishing could hardly be more apparent. Her present circumstances, she
meant him to know, were misleading; appearances were deceptive. Francis
found himself growing uncomfortable, for there had assuredly been times
in the past (and he did not know but what they continued into the present) when it had seemed desirable to him to make such a point on his
own behalf. The hard fact was, circumstances rarely misled, and appearances were always full of truth. Neither he nor Miss Poulter, by credible
or incredible claims on a more impressive background, would change the
fact that people of worldly consequence are not obliged to earn their living as professional hostesses at a hotel, or as private tutors. People who
are poor, while they may be estimable and virtuous, confess in the fact
of poverty an incapacity for mastering their environment; and what ex-

cuse or justification their incapacity may have interests only themselves.

Miss Poulter, with disconcerting aptness, said, "You're a writer, aren't you?"

"At the moment I am mostly a tutor," Francis answered, fresh from his lesson.

"I think the little lame lad is sweet. Is he nice?"

"Yes, he is," Francis said, feeling that in some ways it was an understatement. Walter's patience in his affliction, good temper, and politeness cost him, being expressions of a disposition, no special effort, and so perhaps deserved no special credit from the moral standpoint; but they were none the less ornaments to character.

"Is that his sister? I think she's frightfully attractive. Shy, isn't she?"

"Is she?" said Francis, repelled by a tone intent and predacious that seemed to pick over the Cunninghams rapidly with an eye eager for any little things it might be useful to know.

"Yes," said Miss Poulter. "But she rather fancies you."

Flabbergasted—the suggestion was put forward with such positiveness; annoyed—was she felicitating him as one freebooter to another on solid advantages bound to result from his shrewd imposition on a schoolgirl?—Francis began tartly: "As a matter of fact—" The habit of speaking first and thinking afterward had nearly made him say that if Helen fancied anyone she fancied the Best boy. He bit his lip and said, "You're mistaken, I think."

"My dear man, she never takes her eyes off you!"

"I must see about that," Francis said coldly. He pivoted Miss Poulter around and looked over toward the Cunninghams. Helen was talking to Walter, obviously in an argument. The effect of the beautiful flowered shawl was demure, like a dressed-up child. Though she sat with the straightness of good training, the argument made her wriggle with belligerence; and it would have been no great surprise if, finding herself scored on, she began to poke and pull Walter. "She seems to have lost interest," Francis said sarcastically.

"Are you offended?" Miss Poulter asked. In order to look at him, she backed off, becoming hard to lead again.

"Not in the least," said Francis. He tightened his arm brusquely, forcing her toward him. "Come back here!" he said with irritation, for she resisted him. "I'm running this."

"You *are* offended!" Miss Poulter said. She squeezed his hand. "Don't be." Docilely she moved close against him. Past his ear she murmured: "Of course you know we're the cynosure of all eyes."

"I should hope so," Francis said shortly. "Don't you like it?"

Miss Poulter was silent an instant. "What would you think if I said yes?" she asked finally.

"Say it and I'll see," said Francis baffled by the change in her voice.

"Can't you tell I do?" she said, speaking in a whisper. "Much too much." She squeezed his hand again. "Come skating, won't you?"

Francis almost let go of her. "Why, the simple bitch!" he thought. "Does she imagine—" The music sank rollicking into silence, and he did let her go, trying to compose his features. The sense of outrage had made him flush; but Miss Poulter scanned his face with a knowing, soft-eyed look that plainly credited his color to the emotional effects of his coy little courtship by friction, and to excitement over her hint of more, and more complete, satisfactions possibly to come later. "About eleven-thirty," she said, dismissing him as she turned to go up to the orchestra.

"Why, the simple bitch!" Francis repeated to himself. He was incapable of speaking; but Miss Poulter seemed not to have expected any response. He moved across the floor to the Cunninghams suffering surges of mortification. The low and vulgar intent she must have seen in his measures to get her close enough to be led, the insulting assumption that he had no better taste than to be attracted to her, kept him hot with anger; yet, at the same time, he could not close his ears entirely to the still small voice, like that of conscience in its punctual awakening and calm persistence (and in the incidental complacency of being right, not unlike that of conscience), which heeded his indignation very little and whispered: *You know, you could lay her if you wanted to. . . .*

Mrs. Cunningham welcomed him with a smile. "Francis, you waltz beautifully," she said.

Francis regarded her, surprised; for, though pleasing, the compliment discomposed him. It was one thing to dance well; it was another to be beautiful about it. He said lamely: "She's really very good." It sounded, to his chagrin, much like one of Helen's rejoinders, and to cover it up he added, "Have you seen her skate? She's marvelous."

"You know," Mrs. Cunningham said, "I think I saw her skating last night—very late. She seemed to be by herself. Where do you suppose she comes from? Do you think, from an agency, or something of that kind?"

"The cat brought her in," said Walter.

"Walter, I think you'll have to go upstairs in just a moment."

"Ah, heck, what did I do?"

"You're too fresh," said Helen.

"I don't want to have to speak to you about it again, Walter."

"I was only joking."

"Well, darling, it wasn't very funny. We'll stay for one more dance."

Helen, Francis felt sure, would much prefer not to dance again; but he saw that he would have to ask her. To his surprise, she got up with alacrity, not easy, but much easier than she had been before; and easier in some ways than Francis, who was not unaware when Miss Poulter, over the shoulder of a new partner who was too short for her, looked at him and Helen (very likely to see what licentious exercises he was practicing now). In annoyance he turned sharply away, making Helen miss a step.

"My fault," he said.

"No, it wasn't," said Helen. "I didn't follow." Though apologetic, she spoke without confusion; and Francis, with a start, amazed at his own denseness, saw why. Mrs. Cunningham had noticed Helen's discomfort during the first dance and taken the simple steps to relieve it. She told Helen that she looked well on the floor. She sent Francis to dance with Miss Poulter so that he would not just sit there patiently waiting for duty to call again. When Francis returned nominally she told him, but actually she told Helen, that he, too, danced well. And there it was. Helen, without knowing why, found herself composed, and even, from her own point of view, bold. "You're leaving Wednesday, aren't you?" she said.

Francis said that he was.

Since that had been all right, Helen drew a breath and went on recklessly. "Does it take more than a day to get to Florence from here?"

"I'll have to stay overnight at Milan," Francis said. Recollection of the last occasion of his staying over at Milan made him wince; but he could not help seeing that Helen was growing nervous. Her phenomenal feat of initiative had surprised her as much as it surprised Francis, and she was elated; but if she did not get any help, all Mrs. Cunningham's deft work would be undone. "When are you going back to Paris?" Francis asked quickly.

"After New Year's, I think," she said. "I suppose, when Mother leaves."

Disconcerted, for Mrs. Cunningham, though certainly she did not have to give him advance notice, had not mentioned leaving, Francis waited a moment. To ask when her mother was going, and where, would be to let Helen know that nothing had been said to him, and he was reluctant to do that. He said: "I think it's fine here for Walter. But we have a lot of work to get through."

"I don't think it's very good for him," Helen said. She blushed, nearly stammering over so positive a contradiction; but the female prerogative to warn, to comfort and command, supported her and she pressed on with severity. "He had some asthma the night before last. Maggie and Mother think it was something he ate. I think it's too much excitement." Her attention was attracted and she said, vindicated, "I guess Maggie's going to take him up now. Yes. She is. It's about time! It must be ten o'clock."

Turning his head to look for Mrs. Cunningham, Francis's eye came first on Miss Poulter. As she moved across the floor it could be seen from this angle that the shaved armpit disclosed by her lifted right arm could stand shaving again. Walter and Maggie were on their way to the door down the side, and Mrs. Cunningham sat alone, Helen's bright shawl hanging over the back of the chair beside her. Francis met her glance, and Mrs. Cunningham smiled and shook her head, reading his question.

Helen was preparing (you could feel the resolution rise in her) to make another remark, which would probably be something more about Walter, and so would get them even farther from the subject. Francis saw that he had better give up the credit of omniscience. He said: "Did your mother say where she thought of going?"

"Oh," said Helen. "Well, I thought probably you knew. I don't think she's told Walter. I think she's going to the Riviera. I thought maybe you'd heard from Lorna. I know she wrote Lorna's aunt about a hotel near there."

"I see," said Francis. He spoke weakly, conscious of the loudness of the music. He moved numbly, hardly knowing what to think, what to make of it, what it meant.

"That might be good for Walter," he said. The remark sounded strained and false to him, since, if it were good for anyone, he was the one for whom it was good, for whom it was wildly desirable. Either because his mind, trained to have no serious thought of seeing Lorna, refused to credit the simple statement; or because this way of hearing it, blurted out incidentally in a trivial conversation, somehow spoiled it, the thing Francis had so much wished for did not bring much satisfaction.

Still numb, his heart still beating heavily with shock, Francis was thinking then of Miss Poulter—the muscled legs, the flattened abdomen, the raised bare right arm. With slow incredulous recoil he knew, because now she wouldn't, that five minutes ago it had been as good as certain that when eleven-thirty came Miss Poulter would have found him waiting for her in the bar.

FOUR

The doors, decorated with crisscrossed greens bound by red ribbons closed behind them, and Francis came with his mother from the windy vestibule on to the Lung'Arno. Above the joined wings of the nearby Corsini palace, the sky, darkened by moving storm clouds and later afternoon, was one of those invented by Gustave Doré to emphasize important Biblical calamities. A colorless light filled the empty quay. Up toward the fine flattened spans of the Trinità bridge, cold little waves about the same color as the stone wrinkled the river. His mother took his arm and Francis said to her, "Do you really want to walk? It must be almost a mile."

"I think so," she answered. "Doctor Giglioli said I ought to walk more. If I feel tired there are usually cabs down by the Grand Hotel. You didn't have a very good time, did you?"

"No," said Francis. He felt the glum repletion that may be expected to follow a holiday dinner with several wines begun in the early afternoon.

"Still, I think it was kind of them to ask us."

"No doubt," said Francis. "Mrs. Jasper thought so, all right. This damned business of being poor!"

His mother said, "Sometimes I wish you didn't remind me so much of your Grandfather Ellery. That was his complaint, too. He always felt that he was entitled to live on a certain scale; and so he did, long after there was really no money left. For years before your father died, he was always paying the debts."

"Oh, Lord!" said Francis, exasperated both by the arbitrary *non sequitur* and by the justness of the resentment that had provoked her to it. She responded not to his words, but to a complaining tone; and Francis could hardly doubt that she was right. It was the tone of the selfish and conceited old man, the spoiled sexagenarian baby, who considered the part of a gentleman of leisure done when he had called attention to any straitening of his circumstances; who sulked majestically at criticism of his debts, since they were no fault of his—he hadn't chosen to incur them, and it was a humiliation to him that he owed any man a penny. What he did owe, he owed because the world at large had stopped, without right or reason, making him proper provision. When the world came to its senses and recognized that he, not it, was entitled to be the judge of his financial requirements he would set everything in order and meet every obligation fully and promptly. His creditors knew his name and knew him; and they had his word. What more did they want?

This foolish presumption and the stupid irresponsibility, the (to give it its right name) dishonesty, on which the presumption rested were not agreeable to think about, and, angrier, Francis said, "Am I supposed to like it when a couple of overstuffed old imbeciles like your Jaspers can go around being kind to us? Lord God, that dining room! Those stamped leather curtains. Those beautiful, beautiful oak carvings! Those gold inscriptions! All from Dante. Did you hear Sargent"—he let his voice mimic Mrs. Jasper addressing her husband—"tell how he came to pick them out? Fiorian Fiorenza; and how about the seven muses pointing Sargent, potbelly and all, to the Bear?"

"I think it was a great deal pleasanter than having Christmas dinner at the hotel. I suppose poor Sargent is a little dull. I remember that everyone was surprised when Carrie married him."

"Surprised?" said Francis. "I would have thought they were made for each other. Dullness with transport eyes the lively dunce!"

"Well, darling, let's drop it. They were friends of mine many years ago, and they've been kindness itself to me this winter. I wish you'd be able to talk a little more; you seemed so sullen; but I know it was hard for you." They came to the corner by the opening of the little Piazza Ponte Carraia and crossed over. "Faith Robertson's mother lives there," she said. "I've had tea with her once or twice. Did I write you? She told me that Faith said you were so nice to her, going to Milan."

"Did she?" said Francis.

"She said you had dinner with her. You never wrote me that. She's such a plain girl. I suppose men don't bother with her much. It shows you can be pleasant when you want to. I never understand why you don't want to."

"I don't understand, either," Francis said. "So let's drop that, too."

"Francis, another thing I never understand is why you are so rude to me. I don't like it."

"Sorry," Francis said. He walked in silence, feeling that it would not have hurt him to make a better apology (it was certainly not her fault that he had found her comment uncomfortable), yet unable to make it; just as, though recognizing them, he was helpless against the complicated, mostly misbecoming impulses that made him (the term was not too strong) rude to her. He heartily hoped, understanding why so well himself, that she never did understand. He could not excuse and he would not care to avow the plain fact that anger filled him when she courageously made the efforts she must make if, being ill and alone, she were to support her circumstances at all. He was ashamed to think that far from admiring as he should the patience she must show if she were to be liked by the after all agreeable and kindly people on whom she depended for any sort of society or companionship, he detested her patience as a humiliation in itself, a wound to pride reaching through her to him.

"Far enough?" he asked, trying by solicitude to show himself that he had some virtuous principles. He paused at the corner of the Piazza Manin, looking at the disturbed sky as though a weighty concern for her immediate well-being could count as a point in his favor. By the cramped front of Ognissanti were two cabs. "I think we'd better take one of those," he said. "It may rain in a minute, and I don't want you to get wet."

His mother said, "No, I'm not tired. It's a little shorter, I always think, to go over and up the Via Montebello." They walked on, and she added, for they were suddenly sheltered from the bitter river wind, "That's better. We should have done that before."

"Are you cold?" he said alertly. The effort of penitence was becoming successful, and he was really feeling the anxiety he wanted to feel.

"No. I'm very warmly dressed." She took his arm again and said, "You haven't told me much about Grindelwald."

"There's nothing to tell. Walter's in heaven. It almost seems a shame to take him away. But on the other hand, I suppose we wouldn't get much work done. He'll have all this week."

"What kind of a girl is Helen?"

"Harmless."

"Do you like her?"

"Yes."

"She's going back to Paris, isn't she?"

"Yes, as far as I know."

"Did you see a great deal of her?"

"Well, she was there. Why?"

"I wondered. You'll be seeing Lorna Higham when you go to the Riviera, won't you?"

"I imagine so. Mrs. Cunningham's planning to stay at a hotel at Cap d'Ail. She knows Lorna's aunt. I don't think very well."

"I suppose Lorna's going to be with her aunt for some time?"

"I really don't know."

"It would be rather a blow to you if she left as soon as you got there, wouldn't it?"

"I would be sorry. Why do you ask?"

"Well, darling, I thought you seemed rather fond of her in Paris."

"I like her," Francis said uncomfortably.

"I thought she was a pretty girl."

Preferring to take this as a comment needing no answer, Francis made none.

His mother said, "If you don't want to talk about her, I won't make you. You like her better than Helen, don't you?"

"Good God!" said Francis. "Why should I like Helen?"

"You said you liked her."

"What is this?" asked Francis. "A plot?" He laughed.

"What do you mean, dear?"

"It's a long story," Francis said. He laughed again, asserting, against his embarrassment, a great ease or good humor. "An English girl, a sort of hostess at the hotel, took it on herself to insist that Helen had a sentimental interest in me. It just isn't so; and I don't feel any in her, either."

"Don't be cross, dear. When we get back I have something rather amusing to tell you."

"I'm not cross. What is the amusing thing?"

"Wait. I'll feel more like telling you when I've had some tea."

They passed behind the Garibaldi monument in the gathering dusk and turned up the Via Solferino. A single weak light burned in the entrance hall of the hotel. Beyond, where a little sun parlor opened in summer on the garden, Francis saw the dark shape of a man huddled in an overcoat, sitting in one of the wicker chairs. Slumped down, he seemed to have been asleep, but their steps on the bare tiles roused him. He stirred, his face turning toward them. With enormous difficulty he got to his feet and stood not quite straight. He gave Francis's mother a shaky, infirm bow.

"Who in God's name is that?" Francis murmured.

"Sh!" said his mother. The man had begun to move out purposefully, looking up to see where they were and down to see where he was walking. Rising and falling in the poor light, his face, incredibly old and sick, was like the face of death. Francis's mother said: "I'm very glad to see you up again, Mr. Woodward. I hope you're feeling much better."

"Thank you," said the old man. "I feel pretty well. I wanted to wish you a merry Christmas, Mrs. Ellery. This is your son, I suppose." He swung his wasted face toward Francis and advanced a hand, bony and loose-skinned; and though dry, slippery to the touch and cold. Francis let it go and said, "How do you do, sir?"

"Merry Christmas to you, too," said the old man, beginning to move away. "I just sat down to rest a moment," he said, still moving. "I find I tire easily. Good night. Good night." Slowly and cautiously he went on into the darkness along the hall.

"Look into the dining room and see if you can find Victor, darling. I suppose you aren't hungry, but he might as well bring up some tea. Poor Mr. Woodward! I feel so sorry for him. I must tell you about him."

When Francis, following her upstairs a few moments later, reached her room she had taken her coat and hat off. "Light the fire," she said to him. "It's an extravagance. They really keep the house quite warm, but it's more cheerful. Faith Robertson's mother told me it was simply freezing where she is. I think Faith is in town, by the way."

Stooping over the grate Francis struck a match. "What about this Woodward man?"

"Oh," said his mother, arrested. "He's been very ill. His wife died a year or so ago. They'd been living here for a long time. I don't think he has anywhere else to go. He's so old and he has very little money—" Though distressed, as anyone would have to be, she spoke with animation, unconsciously laying to herself the grand solatium of the idea of people lonelier and worse off, much older than she was, and yet still living, or still not dead. Francis said, "I know. Montreux was full of them."

"I thought he might interest you. He used to be an editor of some quite good magazine. *The Century*, perhaps. He was the friend of a lot of people—George William Curtis and Frank L. Stockton, and Brander Matthews—"

"Lord!" said Francis.

"I know you don't think much of them as writers; but they were quite distinguished once. Before he was ill he asked me to lend him one of your books. He said he thought it was a very fine piece of work."

"What else could he say?" asked Francis. "Mother, I wish you wouldn't do that."

"Do what?" she said rather sharply.

"Well, force my damned books on people. No one's interested in them."

"He was very much interested."

"Does it seem likely?" said Francis. "In the first place I don't write books for friends of Brander Matthews. In the second place—"

"You sound so silly and self-conscious, Francis. I never mentioned you to him. Miss Wilson told him that you were a writer. He asked me if— yes! *Avanti!* Oh, thank you, Victor, I think we could have it here."

In the increasing light of the fire Francis stood silent while the tea things were disposed. When the door had closed his mother said, "Sit down and have some tea. We won't say any more about it. Though I wish you wouldn't act always as if you thought I were a complete fool. I'm really not, you know. Naturally I'm interested in your work."

"I don't think you're a fool. It's just that the books aren't good, and the less people see of them, the better." He sat down wearily, recognizing that (while he meant what he said and it was true) his real feeling was that what he wrote was his own. He did not want work of his pressed with maternal pride on other people, who, bored and perhaps privately derisive, would skip through it, tchick-tchicking with the satisfaction of superiority over faults that Francis was already aware of.

"Well, darling, I don't think they're bad. But of course you're going to do better. How do you like your new book?"

"That's lousy, too."

"Oh, darling!"

"Well, I don't know. At this rate I'll never get it done anyway—and maybe that would be just as well." He spoke sincerely, for, like most writers, he had begun to write before he had the judgment to see the al- most hopeless difficulties; and by the time he was old enough for judg- ment to begin to develop, it was too late; he liked to write. He drank some tea and said, "You were going to tell me something amusing."

"Yes. I was." She paused and the firelight on her face and carefully arranged gray hair seemed to flicker a little as she overcame a quiver of indecision. She said: "I had a letter from Mrs. Cunningham. Really a very nice letter."

"When was this?"

"Well, yesterday. I didn't know whether to speak to you about it or not."

Francis frowned. The hesitation, indicating some difficulty, surprised and disquieted him. His relationship with Mrs. Cunningham had become settled and easy, and he was confident of her liking for him; while her candor, as of one discerning person to another, gave him pleasant assurance of a good understanding with her. "Has she decided she wants to get rid of me?" he asked. "I can't say I'd blame her."

"Oh, no. I don't think so. Why wouldn't you blame her?"

"I don't think I'm entirely fitted for the position."

"Well, darling, she speaks very highly of you. I think she's more than satisfied that way. She said that Walter was devoted to you; and that you'd been most helpful to her. She seemed really touched by what you did when her dog died at Montreux."

"What I did was have a stupid row with the manager. That's why we left."

"What kind of a row?"

"Oh, he didn't want to bury the dog. Never mind that. What else did she say?"

"She said a number of nice things. About you and Walter. She said you told him so nicely about the difference between a bull and an ox."

"So I did," said Francis laughing. "He must have told her. Perhaps he didn't believe me. Let me see this letter."

"Well, darling, I didn't keep it. I'll answer it some time soon. But I knew that if I kept it, I would be so provoked every time I looked at it—"

"You couldn't have minded hearing of my delicacy about the bull." Planned as a bit of raillery to cover Francis's confusion while he cast about, trying to imagine the thing she might mind hearing of, it was a failure; but his mother, though she had heard him say something, could not have heard just what.

"No," she said slowly. "You remember I asked you about Helen."

Francis frowned again. "Perfectly," he said.

"Well, she wrote that Helen had arrived, and that you'd been together a good deal, and that she was rather concerned about it."

Francis sat stunned. "How extraordinary of her!" he said finally, flushing.

"Well, you see. I was a little put out, too."

"What were her exact words?"

"She said quite frankly that anything like that would upset her very much."

"Upset her?" said Francis. "And what about me? Why, she must be crazy!" He spoke spitefully, striking back in chagrin; for at a touch, the whole comfortable edifice in which he had been living seemed to go down, and he stood discomfited. "God damn her to hell!" he said to himself. "Does she think I'd want to marry her stupid brat! Why—"

But these venomous extravagances were no help; and in fact hurt him, since he could not miss the splenetic, hitting-the-air silliness of shouting, even if it were true, that you did not want what you had been told you could not have. He put out a hand, took up his teacup as steadily as he could and drank the cold slop remaining in it.

"Francis," said his mother, "don't be upset. I think it's possible that, whether you knew it or not, Helen was a little taken with—"

"What nonsense! Helen was fooling around with a couple of English kids. You would think that!"

"Now, please! You must not lost your temper, dearest. Mrs. Cunningham had, or thought she had, some reason for writing me about it. Either she thought that Helen was getting a little interested, or—"

"Or what?"

"Well, Francis, you won't like this, but you have a silly, cynical way of talking sometimes. She knows you haven't any money, and you always say that money's the only thing that matters. I suppose you only do it to shock people; but if Mrs. Cunningham were to hear you say something like that she might reasonably be a little worried."

Francis tightened his mouth. "And so," he said, "you wish I'd stop saying things like that so people like Mrs. Cunningham won't be a little worried."

"Yes, since you ask, I wish you would stop." They looked at each other eye to eye; and Francis saw that he might be like his Grandfather Ellery in some respects; but in some others he was not unlike her. She said, "It always has a very sophomoric sound."

"Thank you," said Francis bitterly. His ebbing anger was no longer high enough to support a quarrel in which, to his great and conscious discredit, he snapped at her because he could not reach anyone else. "Well," he went on, "I don't know whether I ought to go back or not." He said it sulkily, less as a serious question than as an experimental attitude to try on himself and see how it looked.

"I know how you feel," his mother said. She paused; and by an easy transference of thought Francis realized that she was putting from her mind the consideration, necessarily first, that not going back would mean among other problems, a financial one, unless he could get something else to do; and what could you get to do in Florence?

Tempted for a moment to point out that money was making its customary prompt appearance as the thing that mattered—would he go back for any reason but money? Would she want him to go back, leaving her alone here, for any other reason?—Francis opened his mouth; but he closed it again, for the truth was a mean and senseless sort of triumph, and, anyway, it was too true. She said, "I don't know that it's as serious as that. I wish I had saved the letter. So much of it was really very nice. Perhaps I oughtn't to have told you about Helen. I was so put out; but I really did think you might be amused."

"Of course you should have told me," Francis said. His irritation feebly revived. "Why else did she write it to you? She felt my ambition must be checked. Naturally I would like to tell her to go to hell; but—" But how could he? He thought, aghast at angry impulse's blindness, of Cap d'Ail for the first time, and, frightened, he let go any last notions of intransigence. "But I won't," he said. "It doesn't seem feasible."

"Francis," she said, laying a hand on his arm, "you don't have too bad a time. I can tell by your letters. I don't think any of us is ever entirely suited in this world. I think you're very fortunate, really."

"Yes, I am," Francis said, for the word, satisfying his unconscious want, telling him that he was enviable and a little out of the run of common men, aroused him from despondency. The virtue of the vice of pride was the impossibility of self-pity; and Francis's mind, when it went to work on the private picture of himself, to please him was obliged to show him always fortunate—with uncanny luck, attaining successes he had not stooped to deserve; in his failures, still fortunate, since reflection was never at loss to see ways in which the outcome might have been much worse. Gathering confidence, he took a little heart.

His mother said, "You're really very young, you know. You have everything before you. In a few years you'll feel differently about all this."

"Don't worry," Francis said, restless. "I'll live."

"Yes. Well I think it's nice that you're going to the Riviera. And I'm glad you're going to see Lorna."

To avoid answering, Francis said, "What are you doing about supper? I don't want any. I think I'll go out and walk for a while."

"Oh. Isn't it raining?"

"Not yet." He got up.

"Well, darling, if you really want to. Don't go out by the Fortezza. Several people have been robbed there."

"A hot lot they'd get off me," Francis said. "If I see anyone who looks rich I'll probably try a little robbery myself. If it rains, I'll be back soon enough."

He put on his coat, and went downstairs and out into the dark street. The air was raw with dampness and the dampness was aromatic with a blended odor, both revolting and agreeable, of sewer sludge, of rancid oil and cooking tomatoes, of crumbling mortar, and of what seemed an exhalation from church vaults sooted by incense smoke and the grease of burned candles. Francis buttoned up his coat and walked.

A half an hour later he was in the Via Strozzi, passing through the great two-story arch into the piazza. Cold and smoky, the café had only a few people in it. A quiet domino game with several spectators was going on in one corner. By himself among the empty tables sat a uniformed militiaman, his tunic belted tight over his fat little torso, the gold fasces pinned to the collar of his black shirt. His eyes fixed on Francis with the important, truculent air of one who watches for suspicious characters.

Francis returned the stare disdainfully—as though he gave a damn for a lot of absurd wops dressed up to frighten other wops!—but not too disdainfully. In Florence the Sicurezza never bothered much with passports, and Francis did not have a *Soggiorno degli Stranieri* receipt. One of these little rats, if he wanted to make Francis trouble, could probably get him a night in jail while the technicality was adjusted. The exchange of stares, continuing a second or two, began to make Francis uneasy, for the last thing he really wanted was trouble; and yet he could not bring himself to look away first, trouble or none.

Curiosity, probably never anything but idle, satisfied, the man did look down first. Spread on the table in front of him were the diapered backs of a pack of tarot cards arranged, as for a peculiar kind of solitaire, in rows under several of the trumps major turned face up. Francis could see the striking, crude-colored images: the moon, the wise man, the fool, the wheel of fortune, the card of judgment, the hanged man. Passing by, he seated himself against the wall not far off. After a while a waiter, who had been loitering, biting his nails, beneath the figure of King Gambrinus, came over. Some time later he brought Francis a glass of beer and writing materials.

The beer tasted both thick—as if a good deal of dirt had been dissolved in it; and thin—as if the keg were regularly watered. Francis had forgotten this unpleasant peculiarity of Italian beer. "Siren tears," he said to himself. "Distill'd from limbecks foul as hell within. . . ."

He began again: "What potions have I drunk of Siren tears"—seriously this time; for the iambics, falling in their double alignment of sound and meaning, amused his mind by that prestidigitation that kept everything—words and sentences; the metrical feet and the alternate rhymes—dancing in the air together, and for a moment at least made other thoughts unnecessary.

Once, with the wish to be a poet, and if possible an Elizabethan one, Francis had learned—a laborious course of instruction—the sonnets by heart; but that was four or five years ago, and much of what he had learned fell into disuse when, with pleasing simultaneousness, his own poetry and poetry in general began to dissatisfy him, and to seem too trivial for serious attention. Now he could not think of the third line. The pattern broke up and he let it go. The blackshirt, he realized, was not playing solitaire. Shuffling and shifting his cards, he was getting ready to see what they said —inviting fate, with furtive and awful absurdity, for a sign.

Francis shrugged. He lifted the pen that had been brought with the inkpot and looked at the sheets of flimsy lined paper on the blotter before him; but he did not dip the pen in ink. As though he, too, required a sign, and he, too, were asking reassurance, he waited. His idea had been to write a note to Lorna and so by a subterfuge to escape himself, for the person who wrote Lorna was naturally a character in fiction—not always the hero, but at least the protagonist of a continued story, the product of the important arts of selection and elimination.

To write, Francis had first to become this person; not as an act of deceit, but like a monologuist clapping on a cocked hat or turning up a collar to suggest an appearance that helped the part. Tonight the change would not come. Instead of that other lively and sardonic, witty, worldly-wise, and adventurous Francis Ellery like to the lark at break of day arising, he remained the glum one who sat with a half a glass of stale beer in a dreary café—he let his eyes go around, past the domino players, past the adenoidal waiter who was scratching himself in a way that seemed to indicate that he had piles, past the blackshirt fussing with his cards, and all the empty tables, to a range of wall mirrors framed in tarnished gilt where he found himself several times repeated in diminishing scale. His forehead was still brown, burned by the sun on the Swiss snows; and he remembered astonished that he was not much more than twenty-four hours in Florence. Tuesday night he had been in the Alps having dinner with the Cunninghams.

At the thought of that dinner on his last evening, Francis quailed. Mrs. Cunningham, who could not have appeared more gracious, had already written her letter; and, everything else aside, Francis was crestfallen to know how effectively, as far as any acumen of his went, her fears had been dissembled. He could not think without a qualm of how he must have looked, sitting there unsuspecting, prattling away, much of the time with the direct intention of interesting and amusing Helen—a piece of helpfulness he had resolved on following that night when they first had dancing, and one he thought Mrs. Cunningham would approve of and appreciate. In fact, all the while Mrs. Cunningham, though she sat imperturbable, patiently putting up with his fatuous intermeddling, must have been saying to herself that it would not be long now; that, dinner over, Francis could be dismissed to pack; and in the morning he would be gone hours before they were up.

To swallow the mortifying truth, Francis was obliged first to laugh, to show himself certain absurd things in his situation or his notions about it. Given his choice, he would perhaps have preferred Mrs. Cunningham to mistake him for a sinister and dangerous schemer, weaving, resourceful and unprincipled, his subtle web; and that was good for a laugh, because she never could have made that mistake. There was only one fool there, and Francis was it. He was dangerous not because of his resource, but because, as Solomon so justly observed, the instruction of a fool is folly, and Mrs. Cunningham had Helen to think of.

Without reaching, except in some strictly legal sense, the age of discretion, Helen had grown to the age of consent; and Mrs. Cunningham, alert, too wise to command, began to plan or arrange. If not necessarily best, mother indubitably knew better, for she could think, while Helen merely felt or thought she felt. "Poor kid!" Francis said with compunction. He seemed to himself an age, practically a generation, older than Helen, and beyond the touch of those special feelings, in the sense that they might distort his judgment; yet, open to them, in the sense that he could still take her part against the adult world, and be warmed by the compliment of a possible secret and innocent regard. The delicacy of this sentiment was so blameless that Francis no longer felt embarrassment in supposing that Helen might have found him attractive. Instead he began to feel superior to the distrust Mrs. Cunningham's treatment of him showed. If she had simply been frank, he thought, how much anxiety she might have spared herself!

He sat rolling a cigarette around between his fingers while, now in a solemn mood, he reminded himself of those extra and unnecessary distresses that the human mind adds to the regular distresses of living. He must admit to adding one when, full of the rancor of his hurt pride, he said of Mrs. Cunningham, God damn her. Helen added one (for they came in all sorts and sizes) when turning her mind on herself, she saw everything wrong. Mrs. Cunningham added one when she let herself in a crisis of nerves suppose that Francis—sweet Francis, kind Francis, true Francis, valiant Francis—needed to be schemed against.

Francis drank his beer.

Beyond the arcade falling rain swept the piazza, and he would have to see about getting a cab. He signaled to the waiter and counted out money for him. Passing the blackshirt's table, Francis was in time to see the man sit back, holding in his hand, crowned with dirty broken fingernails, the last card. Then, with a grand gesture, he turned it over. It was the Queen of Cups. Clasping it in both hands, he stared with an immobility that might be either joy or consternation. Francis silently wished him luck, for why hate the little rat? What had he ever done to Francis?

The cornices streamed water. Dimly lighted from all sides, Victor Emmanuel II sat his pawing charger, his pedestal pointing him up the storm. By the curb waited a cab hitched to a drenched, drooping horse.

As Francis looked at it, its driver started from the shelter of the arcade, gesticulating.

Francis called his address out, and got in. In the musty dark he sat silent, listening to the rain on the roof while the horse, beaten to a trot, went splashing through the muddy puddles. Francis felt old, charitable, and only slightly sad.

FIVE

The room was shadowed, but the large window framed a section of steep hillside. Pocked masses of rock rose from mounds of jagged debris, some of it gray, some of it brown, and much broken up by patches of vegetation. Cliffs showed through clumps of trees and the sweeps of stone rubble were overgrown with shrubs. Afternoon sunlight fell full on the hill and this light was reflected down into the room.

Sitting on the edge of the bed Francis held the telephone, looking at the deep pink façade of a house whose square shape was set about with umbrella pines halfway up the hill. Lower on the road behind, Francis could see the windows of a couple of shabby little detached stores. He had just been cut off, and from time to time he said, "Allo!" Eventually a voice broke out in French. *"Ecoutez, s'il vous plaît,"* he said, exasperated. *"Je—"* The voice was silenced with a crack. "Allo!" said Francis again.

English suddenly filtered through the receiver. "Isn't this annoying! You're Francis, then." There was a pause, and Francis realized that the speaker must be Miss Imbrie herself. "Yes," he said. "I'm so sorry to bother you—"

"I'm bothered to distraction," the voice replied. "But not by you. Are you alone?"

"Yes, I am."

"Well, come to dinner, do. I couldn't ask the Cunninghams. I don't know that we'll have any dinner. The truth is, I'm in the act of firing the cook. Do you speak French very well?"

"Abominably," said Francis. Looking at the high-up pink house he began to smile, pleased by the nasal, humorous voice. He had not known what Lorna's aunt was going to be like. "But often people find me intelligible," he said. "Can I help you?"

"Would you really like to? I always thought I spoke French myself; but I can't understand the monster; I warn you, it's the most formidable—"

"How do I get there?"

"Where are you? At the hotel? I can't send the car up. The girls and Eric went to Nice in it. Well, it's really not far. You go right down through the hotel gardens. There's a footbridge across the railway by the station that lands you on the road. Turn left—no, right, downhill around two rather long bends, down to the point. It has a long white wall. Rather pretentious-looking, with lions. They look like dogs. There's a gum tree in a kind of well. I may have it all done before you get here. She keeps saying she'll take me to a party. Would you have any idea what that means?"

"Well, yes," said Francis. "I think so. It's probably just talk. She may think she's going to sue you." He hesitated, asking himself if he would not be well advised to mind his own business, for the agreeable feeling of rushing to the rescue was dampened a little by a question of how effective he would be in a good rousing domestic altercation in French with fine points of law on the side.

"Oh, do come down at once!" she said. "Ought I to telephone for a lawyer? I know one. A nasty little man who got me the lease here."

"You might tell her you're going to."

"What would be a rather stern way of saying that?"

"I'd just say," said Francis, scowling in concentration, "*alors, faut en finir! Je vais*—er—*appeler un avocat*—no, *avoué, un avoué.*"

"What a comfort you are! Do come. She'd probably listen to a man. She frightens me to death."

"I'm on my way." Francis put down the telephone and paused a moment, for he was just off the Genoa train, his bags not even opened. He looked at himself in the mirror, straightened his necktie, and catching up his hat trotted downstairs, out through the long lofty hall onto the terrace where a few people reclined in the shade of striped umbrellas, reading; or in the sun asleep, or blinking out at the sea which extended under them burnished and metallic to a high horizon haze. All of them were well wrapped, for though the sun was fairly warm, the persistent breeze was cold.

Francis headed down the wide walk edged with low iron hoops through the thickets of the garden, now in sloping curves, now in little flights of steps. Across the railway he found a narrow macadam road between successive garden walls and hedges of sickly-looking geranium. It ran a long way to the right and then, obviously wasting ten minutes of his time, a long way back to the left. Beyond a second curve he could see the water much closer through an iron gate overhung by a couple of casuarinas trailing down stringy foliage toward him. A hundred yards ahead was what must be the gum tree, in a railed cement pit cut out of the sidewalk.

The white wall had begun, running on a slant before a house of whitened stone with a heavy tiled roof of bright green. Sure enough, at the break in the wall were two lions sitting on their haunches supporting blank shields. A flight of stone steps went down, crossing an areaway to a door whose little porch rested on twin caryatids. The door was plate glass behind an intricate bronze grill. Centered in a stone rose, one of a carved garland of flowers with which the architect had averted the threat of a plain stone casing, was a bell button.

Francis pushed it and stood looking at the door. Lorna had gone through it scores of times and he felt a stir of emotion to be standing here, able to touch the handle her hand had closed on, standing on the threshold her neatly shod, though not in fact very small, feet had often crossed. Behind the grill and the curtained glass a dim shape moved and the door swung heavily in. "Miss Imbrie?" he said, which was silly, since he saw at once that she could be no one else.

"It is, indeed," she said. She was rather tall, with a mobile, splay mouth and bobbed brown hair thickly threaded with gray. She was wearing a blouse with a great frilled jabot, over a short black skirt. "Are you admiring our grand luxe?" she said. "Come in, and I'll show you more. Francis—I shall have to call you that; it's Francis this and Francis that around here all the time—your plan worked like a charm. She's gone! Look in there. Isn't that absurd?"

She nodded toward a sort of atrium surrounded by a railed stone balcony opening on the second floor and topped by a skylight. In the floor was set a circular fishpond, ten or twelve feet across. On a stone in the center crouched the metal figure, life-size, of an extraordinarily nude woman who was tilting from an amphora a thin jet of water to splash in the pool. "That's Mrs. Sweeney," said Miss Imbrie. "Yes, she left. When I said it to her, she grew pale. I think she thought I was crazy. I've telephoned an Englishwoman in Monte who runs a kind of agency. She says she'll have somebody for me tomorrow. It's very awkward, though. I have a chauffeur called Raymond, and I think she was his mistress, so I suppose he'll leave. Oh, dear! Come into the kitchen. I'm trying to see if she's poisoned everything. You know, I liked your last book very much. Do you mind being told that?"

"I love being told that," Francis said.

Cocking her head at an alabaster clock on the drawing-room mantel, Miss Imbrie answered, "Why, it's after four. I don't think we can have any tea. I'm sure the fire's out. Wouldn't you rather have a drink? The girls said they'd be back by five; but of course they won't. Did you ever see a gold piano before? This place used to belong to a Greek, but he borrowed money on it, and lost it all at the Casino. Poor man, how happy he must have been here! I think the dining room's rather nice, looking out over the water that way. The thing you see down there is a swimming pool, but it has a special pump to bring up salt water. Raymond thought it didn't work well enough, so he took it apart, and now it doesn't work at all. The water's so low that if you ever got in you'd never get out. I was really just as pleased. Gwen went swimming Christmas and we had to put her to bed afterward. Will you drink whisky and soda?" She caught up a bottle of Scotch in the pantry and carried it with her.

Francis followed her into the kitchen. "I don't know what we were to have for dinner," she said, standing still. "I used to tell that camel what I wanted, but we almost never got anything but what she wanted. Do you cook, too? I've yet to find a man who didn't think he did. You don't know Eric, do you? Fortunately he's a very good cook, so we'll probably get something when the time comes. I know he won't let himself starve."

Since Francis had been about to say that he could make muffins, he was forced to smile. His pleasure in Miss Imbrie was great; but he began to feel a little uneasy, too. It was hard to see how anyone else ever got a word in edgewise; and entertaining responses are useless when the remarks they respond to are lost under several further remarks before you can open your mouth. Miss Imbrie extended a hand over various parts of the long range. "Cold," she said. "I'm sure she did it deliberately. Nobody can start it but Raymond, so heaven knows when we'll have dinner."

"Well, now, I think I could start it," Francis said.

"Oh, could you?"

"I don't see why not." Francis advanced and began lifting lids and looking in doors.

"Well, do fix yourself a drink first. Look, here's some Perrier water."

Downstairs in a cold whitewashed room Francis found some tidy French bundles of kindling, and briquets of coal wrapped in paper. Carrying them up, he heard Miss Imbrie, who had begun with unexpected efficiency to put things in order, whistling the Indian merchant's song from *Sadko*. As his step approached, she lifted her voice and sang: *"Les diamants chez nous sont innombrables. . . ."* She said, "Isn't that lovely? Eric says it must have been the Greek's slogan. Every time he passes the gold piano he sits down and plays it. Oh, Lord, there's the telephone!"

She darted out; and Francis set about shaking down the ashes. He had filled an empty coal scuttle with them and laid his fire before she returned. "That was Eric," she said while he washed his hands. "He thought they might stay and have dinner some place near Nice. I told him they would do no such thing, that he had dinner to get here."

Francis lit the fire, opened the draft, and stood up. "Would you mind telling me who Eric is?" he said.

"Oh, he's Eric McKellar. He's a sort of cousin of mine, poor lamb."
She looked at Francis with interest. Francis leaned on the edge of the table
and took a sip of whisky. "He lives in England. Like Henry James, rather." She paused, still looking at Francis. "He's fifty-four years old," she
said suddenly.

Francis set down his glass, aware that he had colored, for the super-
vening thought that had made her say it was easy to guess. "Thank you
very much," he said with conscious composure. "I sometimes wish I
were."

Miss Imbrie gave him a smile. "There," she said. "Would you mind if
I washed these dishes? There are so many of them. I was going to be
strong-minded and leave them, but I find I can't. I think the hot water
ought to be all right. It comes from a sort of furnace Raymond takes care
of. I haven't seen Martha Cunningham for years. How is she? When is she
coming?"

"Some time tomorrow, I think," Francis said.

"She used to be amazingly beautiful."

"Well, she still is, really."

"How tragic about the child!"

"Yes," Francis said. He took a dish towel from the rack.

"Oh, you don't want to do that!" she said.

"Yes, I do," Francis said.

"You're a very amiable young man," Miss Imbrie said. "I think they'll
be along pretty soon. I told them you were here."

At quarter to five Miss Imbrie said, "Doesn't it get dark early! Something to do with the sun, I suppose." She held up her dripping hands.
"Will you snap that light on?" In the resulting yellow glare Francis could
see that her eyes, like Lorna's, were actually dark blue, not brown.

The kitchen grew warm from the fire in the range. Distantly the
albaster clock struck five. Miss Imbrie did not stop talking for any length
of time, and Francis was interested in what she said, both because it was
often amusing and because out of it he was forming an idea of the life,
animated, busy, and purposeless, of the Villa Apollon; yet he was growing inattentive. At last Miss Imbrie emptied her dishpan and set to work
scrubbing the sink.

It was now half past five, but by a great effort Francis did not ask her
how long it took to come from Nice. "Shall I put these away?" he said.

"They go in the pantry," she answered. "You—"

Francis had already started to stack the plates with care, but the third
one he picked up slipped in his hand. On the floor it smashed to fragments. "I'm frightfully sorry," he said, crouching to get the pieces together.

Miss Imbrie, drying her hands, said, "Oh, break all you like." She began to laugh, hung up the towel, and reaching down, gave his shoulder a pat. "Let it be," she said. "You go in and put some lights on. They'll be here any minute. And have another drink. That will—"

In the pantry an electric bell rang.

"Get up," she said, tapping his shoulder again. "That's the front door. Open it. But please don't fall in the fishpond."

Francis got up. The sharp sound of the bell seemed to stay on, ringing through him while he felt something not readily distinguishable from anguish. He was swallowing down agitation, and it made the heart sick— not in the peevish way of hope deferred, but sick through and through with one of those suspenses that come at the end. He thought suddenly of that man in the café at Florence Christmas night, the card with the Queen of Cups on it turned up. There it was, and now he knew.

In distress, because he must look comic—fit to fall in the fishpond— Francis could only say, "All right. I'll try not to." His voice shook, and his hands, which also shook, he pushed, to conceal them, into his pockets, turning to go through the pantry.

"Light by the door!" said Miss Imbrie.

Francis got the door open and felt down the wall. A half a dozen crystal brackets sprang up glittering and he walked ahead. The barely supportable beating of his heart filled his chest so he could not get his breath in. Beyond the columned arch at the end of the drawing room he groped in the darkness, but he could find no switch.

"Hell!" he said, standing still, for this was ridiculous, and he forced air into his lungs and held it there hard. The bell rang again, and so he walked down toward the oblong of dimmed light broken by the shadow of the grill and the shadows of people behind it. He depressed the heavy door handle and stood back while the glass swung in and cold air poured on his face. Above, on the street, he saw the flood of headlights and the shining car. In front of him they stood together, darker than the light stone steps.

"Well, welcome, stranger!" said Gwen.

"Francis!" said Lorna. Both her gloved hands found one of his and closed together on it convulsively.

Francis said, "I can't seem to find any light here."

"Right here," said Gwen. She moved, and a bronze lamp suddenly poured down a glow on them.

"Francis!" said Lorna again, releasing his hand. Francis looked at her nervelessly, seeing with a new spasm of the heart the faint hollow of her cheeks and her lips twisted tight in a smile.

"You don't know Eric, do you?" Gwen said. "Mr. McKellar, Mr. Ellery." Francis took the hand held out to him. "The kitchen!" said

Gwen. "I saw the light! She isn't trying to cook, is she? For God's sake, let's stop her, Eric." She grasped Mr. McKellar by the sleeve of his overcoat, tugging him after her through the dark atrium.

The door closed with a solid click. Lorna let her hands drop. Hanging open on a plaid frock, she wore a straight dark-blue coat with a couple of gardenias pinned to the lapel. "Oh," she said, almost recoiling, "Raymond will—"

"To hell with Raymond," said Francis. Her slight, thin body came against him, her arms went up around his neck. "Ah, darling—" she said.

Francis could feel her lips move under his, and at the same time, the cold petals of the gardenias, lifted with the lapel, touching his cheek. Her hat slipped back and fell on the floor, releasing her dark hair in disorder. "Sorry," he murmured. The latch sounded, and he let her go. He stooped and snatched up her hat. The man in chauffeur's uniform, several boxes under one arm, came around the door, touched his cap, and passed them.

"Lipstick," Lorna said. Her eyelashes were shining wet. She pulled a folded handkerchief from her sleeve, waited while the man went through the door at the back, and applied it with hard unsteady strokes to Francis's mouth. "All right," she said. Her voice broke into laughter, but the tears in her eyelashes overflowed, running down her face. She took the hat out of his hand. "I'll have to go upstairs," she said. She went by him, running on the shallow steps.

"Lorna, darling," Gwen called.

Francis walked into the drawing room. "She went upstairs," he said.

Pulling her hat off, Gwen came through the room toward him. "Greetings," she said. "How are you?" She shrugged out of a coat of splotched calfskin, and Francis caught it.

"Thanks," she said. Her fresh-colored round face, while not unfriendly, had a cast of annoyance. She surveyed Francis with critical reserve, inspecting him for some sign that he acknowledged her service in removing herself and Mr. McKellar. She was grimly ready to despise his complacence if he showed it, and his ingratitude if he didn't.

"Have a good time in Switzerland?" she asked.

"No," said Francis.

"Poor you!" she said. She took the coat from him and went upstairs.

Fixing something to eat took so long that it was almost ten by the time they finished dinner. On the dining-room table stood a high silver candelabrum with six lighted candles in its branches. There were two cheeses, several plates of biscuits, coffee cups, a gold-inlaid port decanter and glasses to match it, a bottle of crème de cacao, some of which Miss Imbrie drank with cream, and a bottle of brandy, some of which Francis drank, though he did it circumspectly. Before dinner—Lorna was upstairs some time; then (it happened as soon as she came down) Lorna and Miss Imbrie and Raymond held one of those interminable conferences with proposals and counterproposals, ending finally in Raymond departing for Saint-Laurent to fetch an aunt of his who would assuredly wash the dishes, but might or might not accept a permanent position; and then, to keep Mr. McKellar company, they all sat around the kitchen watching the cooking—Francis, in the impatience of living through all these delays, all this confusion and chatter, had taken more cocktails than he meant to.

The dining room, large and airy—a little too airy for the cold night—was filled with shadows rising to the high white coffered ceiling and moving on the white curtains drawn in folds to cover the terrace doors. In this chilly serenity Francis sat dejected, his head swimming slightly, his heart sunk. Mr. McKellar's principal dish had been a sort of stew of sweetbreads with cream and mushrooms and wine. It was delicious. Its savor excited the mouth, and Francis's stomach, flushed by the repeated doses of cold gin and vermouth, was hollow with hunger; but between the two his tense throat seemed to rebel, choking him with agitation. He had to swallow by main force.

Mr. McKellar had begun to talk as soon as a full audience was gathered in the kitchen; and, though that must have been hours ago, he really had not stopped a moment. He talked while he cooked, he talked while the table was laid and the food brought in, he even managed to talk while he ate; or, at least, he managed not to let go of the conversation, by starting a sentence, suspending it while he took a mouthful, and finishing it as soon as his mouth was empty. He did not eat much, so he was through before anyone else. He pushed his plate away, poured himself a glass of port; and, like a river spreading out broad and full after a short passage of rapids, he talked on, raising and lowering his glass to admire the light through it.

Even Miss Imbrie was silenced. From the head of the table Mr. McKellar simply held forth, the candlelight bright on his large rugged features and mop of wiry gray hair worn just long enough to tuck behind his ears. His skin was weathered like a farmer's, with deep down-drawn lines about the mouth and a fine puckering of wrinkles at the corners of his eyes, which were big and dark brown beneath dense brows. It seemed that during the afternoon they had discovered an ostrich farm out the Route du Var.

Mr. McKellar told about it. "Unspeakably splendid creatures!" he said. "They have such pride, such assurance! All plum'd like estridges that wing the wind!" Starting, Francis thought: *I saw young Harry with his beaver on* . . . but the gratification of guessing that he, probably alone there, knew the quotation, was faint. His knowledgeableness could not be turned to any advantage, and Mr. McKellar was already off, impassioned, on a new tangent. With paeans and apostrophes he contrasted the state of creatures living as nature meant them to and man, living as a foul and flagitious civilization dictated. Spoken by Mr. McKellar, the English language died in extremity, was solemnly buried, and rose again having put on incorruption. It became more English, not in the imitative sense of resembling an Englishman's speech—until Mr. McKellar took up his residence there such an accent could hardly ever have been heard in England—but absolutely, in the sense of resembling a Platonic ideal, with 'a's so nobly broad and feats of synaeresis so extraordinary that the most supercilious don would have to go down, and Mr. McKellar bore the palm alone. If it did not abash, this way of speaking was likely to irritate people hearing it for the first time.

Francis had felt the irritation. He had even expressed it by listening with exaggerated politeness while he extended a conscious confident forbearance to this astonishing old freak. Presently out of patience, he dropped an ironic remark or two, meaning to demolish him. They sank without a ripple, and Francis began to swell with secret indignation.

That was long ago. Like irritation, like forbearance, like irony, indignation had been swallowed up in despair. Mr. McKellar was murdering time. The moving finger wrote and Mr. McKellar quoted D. H. Lawrence. Francis tightened his hands together and found them damp with sweat. He fixed on his face a smile intended to show reflective amusement; but Mr. McKellar gave a synopsis of one of E. M. Forster's works. He did not show the least sign of stopping and getting the hell out and taking Gwen and Miss Imbrie with him. Meanwhile, across the elaborate still life of cups and glasses, the cut cheeses, the assembled bottles, Lorna leaned on her elbows, her chin on her hands. Her face looked warm, drowsily flushed, for she, too, had drunk a number of cocktails and they were making her sleepy.

"Well, children," Miss Imbrie said at last, "let's move. Are you through, Gwen?"

"Completely," said Gwen.

"How right she is to contemn abstract discussion," Mr. McKellar said, standing up. "All young people are materialists! What good is it if you can't eat it? Well, be quick. Gather therefore the rose whilst yet is prime! Gather your self-indulgence while you may. When you're young it doesn't show; but when you get to be thirty you will find that you face a choice. After that it does show. You must decide what you want to be when you're fifty."

"Suppose I want to be dead?" said Gwen going into the drawing room.

"Nonsense, nonsense!" said Mr. McKellar. His great shadow aped him on the wall as he swallowed the last of his port. "No one wants to be dead. Ah, the conceit of youth! If you can't be ever young and fair you have the confounded cheek to think you won't play. You will. You'll insist on playing. It will be like trying to get Lorna home from the Casino when she knows that next time it just has to be *pair et rouge*. You don't arise from the table gracefully. No one does. Lucretius was an ass. What does he say? Well, now I have forgotten."

"*Cur non ut plenus vitae conviva recedis,*" Francis said distinctly—almost viciously, for he felt entitled to one triumph and what a wretched one this was! "*Aequo animoque capis securam, stulte, quietem.*"

"Bravo!" Mr. McKellar said, startled. He swept a bow to Francis. "I acknowledge my master! *Plenus*, indeed! You can always use a little more."

"She wouldn't leave because she was winning," Gwen said. "Tomorrow we'll go and win again."

"Just because you lost all your plaques!" Lorna said.

"Hold your tongues, sauceboxes!" Mr. McKellar assumed a ferocious mock scowl. Sirrahs, impudent saucy dear boxes! Propped up in bed in his nightgown, Jonathan Swift wrote—the unwieldy elephant to make them mirth—to Ireland to his young women, little dears both, tasking them to love poor Presto. Mr. McKellar was having a wonderful time. He bent his rugged profile on Gwen and said: "Tomorrow we're all going to Grasse; yes, so we are. Ellery and I will discourse on the Latin poets while you buy vile perfumes, grossly overpriced."

"Oh, let's!" said Lorna.

"Faith, and now we'll have music," Mr. McKellar said. He stalked to the gold piano and seated himself before it, sweeping his hands left and right across the keyboard.

"No, wait," said Gwen. "I must get my—oh, Lorna, darling! Your dress! We must show Aunt Mabel. Come up and put it on at once!"

"I won't," said Lorna. "It's a fright. It has roses as big as your face. It's black taffeta."

To Miss Imbrie Gwen said with enthusiasm, "It has two huge silver roses on what might as well be called the thigh. Such fun! We went into Rouff's, and—"

"Be gone!" said Mr. McKellar. "Get what you're going to get. You can describe the fascinating circumstances any time. I am about to execute 'The Twelve Days of Christmas.'" He began to play.

"No, wait, wait!" cried Gwen.

"Francis," Miss Imbrie said, "would you light that fire? It seems awfully cold."

Time passed. The alabaster clock struck eleven. The fire under the broken and irregular marble curves of the rococo mantel burned lower.

Mr. McKellar remained at the piano. Songs, mostly old English, occurred to him, and he sang them with humor or sentiment. He extemporized, he played Schumann; he did excerpts from *Iolanthe*, constituting himself, most amusingly, a whole company of players. Miss Imbrie and Gwen were both sewing; Miss Imbrie embroidering initials on the pocket of a blouse; Gwen, who sewed very well, replacing an ostrich-feather hem on a frock of pale-pink chiffon. Busy, they spoke infrequently.

"There!" said Gwen, biting off her thread. "The damn thing's done. Shall I try it on?"

"Yes," said Lorna.

"No," said Gwen. "You wouldn't try yours on. I'll have to wear it Thursday anyway." She stroked the hem. "You know, I thought they killed the ostriches, like egrets. But they don't. The man said they didn't, this afternoon. Isn't that nice?"

"Francis," said Miss Imbrie, "you'll go to this, won't you? You must. I'll tell Johnny we're bringing you. It's a dance some people near Menton are giving."

Lorna said, "Well, I wondered if I'd have to ask him myself." She, too, had spoken infrequently, lighting cigarettes and crushing out the ends marked with lipstick in a silver ashtray shaped like a scallop shell. Relaxed, her feet doubled up under her on the sofa, she now looked pale and tired, the skin dark under her eyes, the hollows in her cheeks more marked. She smiled at Francis, but the effect was wan.

"I don't know about taking Ellery," Mr. McKellar objected over his shoulder. "I have to have an exclusive supply of polka partners. I must start giving you lessons, both of you." He played a polka.

"You don't have to give me lessons," Lorna said. She pressed her knuckles to her lips. "I learned about a thousand years ago at dancing class. Eric, stop! It gives me a headache. You can't mean to say that people did that when you were young for pleasure. Play something soothing."

She did have a headache, Francis realized. He was filled with bitterness, as though it were somehow Mr. McKellar's fault. Thanks to this superannuated buffoon, it would soon be midnight. Lorna ought to be in bed and he ought to leave.

The superannuated buffoon, shifting his hands gently down the keyboard, caught on a tune. He began to sing: "There is a lady sweet and kind." He swayed his head, scattering a cascade of clear notes. "Was never face so pleased my mind—" Reduplicating the chords without hurry, he said: "Soothing, very soothing." He sighed, burlesquing regret or renunciation. "When I was young," he said.

The remark, delivered in Mr. McKellar's ordinary orotund manner, produced no impression on Francis for a moment. Then something in the words 'when I was young' made him look up. Mr. McKellar, jesting at scars, spoke lightly, but not lightly enough; and Francis saw, exultant, the secret wound. Invited once too often, at the eleventh hour Mr. McKellar got something for his pains in overriding Francis all evening, for his Age-of-Queen-Anne baby talk, for his learned lust for life, for his rugged, gallant glances that did not miss Lorna's legs doubled up on the sofa, or Gwen's small but well-defined breasts as she laid aside the chiffon frock.

Easy and slow, the notes moved on. The air unfolded. "I did but see her passing by, and yet—" Mr. McKellar's aloof accent hovered. Probably imagining that his chagrin had been secret, he put it down. To show his ease he decorated his performance with tones of tender wisdom. He reproached the inhumanity and imperception of youth. He extracted consolation from the thought of the things he understood that youth did not understand. In words and music he showed himself nonchalantly relishing the rarer spirit of the seventeenth century, with its innocent lusts, its passions profound but blameless, its perfect poetry. Deep and soft he concluded, "—I love her till I die."

Francis stood up contemptuously. "I must go," he said.

"Oh, don't go," said Miss Imbrie. "We sit here and yawn until all hours. It's the custom."

To hear her describe in calm terms his wasted evening stung Francis back to an awareness of his own hurts, not, after all, cured by the pleasure of seeing Mr. McKellar hurt, too. "I must," he said bitterly.

"Well, you'll go to Grasse tomorrow, won't you? We'll stop and pick you up."

Irresolute, wanting to go, but seeing an indignity in going as Mr. McKellar's guest on Mr. McKellar's excursion, he said, "I don't know when the Cunninghams are coming. When would we get back?"

"Not late," Mr. McKellar said. He faced about and gazed at Francis cordially.

"Well, I really don't know. Perhaps I could give you a ring in the morning." Did he imagine that by punishing himself he could punish Mr. McKellar? Francis said, "I'd love to go. They probably won't be here until tomorrow night."

"Good. We'll try to leave about nine."

Miss Imbrie said, "Oh, you haven't any coat! It will be freezing!"

"I'll be all right. It was so nice of you to take me in."

"Come any time," Miss Imbrie said.

Lorna sat up. "Can you get out?" she said.

"Yes," said Francis. Disconsolately he blamed her, too—for being so tired, for having a headache, for so surrounding herself with people. The agitation of yearning—she was offering in spite of everything to come to the door with him—shook him; but he thought: "If she wanted to, she would without asking. If she doesn't want to—" And could he blame her, if she recoiled, as he recoiled, from the intolerable advertisement to Miss Imbrie and Mr. McKellar and Gwen that he could not leave without fondling her for a while in the partial privacy of the hall? "Good night," he said, "good night."

Out of the room, he took his hat from the table, faltering in the hope that she might still come; repenting the lost chance, ready now not to give a damn what they thought. The awful evening grew too heavy for him. His anguish of disappointment that, after so long, it should have fallen out like this reduced the pride that required her to want to come. He set his teeth together, full of resolution too late for tonight, too early for tomorrow. The door jarred shut behind him and blindly he climbed the dark steps to the street.

He stopped then. Twenty yards to his right stood a lighted gas lamp, and stock-still, he gaped at it. Past the lighted panes of glass, like a thick veil, snow was falling. The damp pavement was beginning to whiten. Fine snow whirled and spun, dusting off the fronds of a palm raised above the garden wall.

Francis took a step and then another. With a crack like a dam breaking, floods of rage poured into him. He tasted salt in his mouth, he felt blood at his eyes in the torrential passion, small enough to make him kill, great enough to make him cry. The snow drove hard across his cheek, around his neck, a hundred times unkinder than man's ingratitude. Invulnerable, unanswerable, it derided him, careless of what he thought or what he did, executing its aimless joke on him, on the January flowers, on the whitening palms.

Francis got his breath in. He was shaking with cold, and turning up his collar he began to walk fast along the blank walls, up the endless empty street. From the bridge across the railroad he could see the colored signal lamps dim in the murk. On the sloping walks of the hotel gardens there was snow enough for him to leave clear black tracks behind him. A whistling, moaning blizzard swept down the terrace of the hotel, obscuring the line of palms in wooden tubs. He stamped up the steps and jerked open the big door. Into the still air with him whirled a flurry of snowflakes.

A chasseur in blue jacket and brass buttons started up, advancing on Francis with eager solicitude, a brush in his hand. From the recesses of the *vestiaire* another appeared, also with a brush, and possessed himself of Francis's snow-covered hat, exclaiming, uttering apologies, extending commiserations.

In proper dignity the concierge left this menial work to others.

"Telegram, Monsieur," he said. He put his hand up to the rack above his desk, produced the folded green sheet, and bore it grandly across the floor.

Francis took it. "That will do, thanks," he said to the brushers. A man in a striped apron had now appeared discreetly, and as Francis moved, he whisked out a mop and began to wipe up the tessellated paving. Francis unfolded the sheet. It was from Genoa at noon. *Arrive 19.09 please meet Cunningham.*

Francis stared a moment. The printed letters looked remote, the words inscrutable, the 19.09 senseless. A sort of meaning began to force its way toward his consciousness. He said uncertainly, "The fourth. That's Monday. Today, then."

"Yes, Monsieur. Directly after you departed."

"Mrs. Cunningham is here?" he said, incredulous.

"Yes, Monsieur. They are arrived. Several hours ago. Madame inquired for you. If you would come up, if you returned before ten." They both looked at the clock, which showed quarter to twelve, and the concierge's eyes came back to him.

"I see," said Francis, annoyed by something in the look that seemed to show that the concierge also thought he ought to have been here. "Well, that's too bad," he said lightly. "I wish I'd known. I'd better be called at eight."

"Bien entendu, Monsieur. Bon soir, Monsieur."

Folding the telegram blank absently into smaller squares, Francis stood silent while the elevator went up. "That was not so good," he said to himself.

The thought came to him that, whatever else he did, he would not go to Grasse tomorrow; but he put it by in infinite weariness, thinking that soon, thank God, he would be asleep.

II

The snow was gone. The morning was very fine. Into the blue sea Cap Ferrat, a lighter, grayer blue, extended far off against the west. The cloudless sky was a third blue, tender and pure, a dome of light above the stony mountains. Coming a hundred miles over the Gulf of Genoa the wind brought a moist feel and smell of spring. Everything shone with melted snow water. Water rippled sparkling down the paved walks into the breezy semitropical thickets of the garden.

Before Francis did anything else, he had to let them know at the villa that he could not go to Grasse. Harassed, afraid of calling too early, yet pressed to get it done before he presented himself (and he must not be late) to Mrs. Cunningham, Francis had picked up and set down the telephone several times while he was shaving and dressing. Probably he ought to ask to speak to Mr. McKellar, since it was Mr. McKellar's party, but he shrank from the idea. When he thought of the lofty expression on that rugged, intelligent face, and of his own furtive rudeness, his sulky silences, and the way he had gone off in what was doubtless seen to be a huff, leaving, you might guess, Mr. McKellar to exchange glances with Miss Imbrie, it put Francis out of countenance.

At quarter to nine he could not make his mind up. At ten minutes of nine, mind made up or not, he would have to call; and he did. Miss Imbrie answered the phone herself. "Oh, Francis!" she said. "You're all right, then? I suppose you must be. We thought we'd have to send the dogs out for you."

Francis said that he was all right, but that Mrs. Cunningham had arrived, and so—

"Well, Eric thought we'd better not go to Grasse," Miss Imbrie said. "It's quite high up and the roads may not be good. Well, do tell Mrs. Cunningham I shall come to call—" Francis held the telephone tight, relaxing with relief, for she spoke in a friendly way. After he had listened a reasonable time (it was five minutes to nine) he said, "Could I speak to Lorna a moment?"

"Oh, I don't think she's awake," Miss Imbrie said cheerfully. "Call later, won't you? Oh, she is awake—" Her voice faded, and she cried faintly, "Angel child! You'll catch your death of cold on those damned tiles! Take these. And put this around you. And here. It's Francis. I'll get you some coffee." He heard the telephone passed over and Lorna said, "Hello."

"Oh, God!" said Francis. "I woke you up?"

"It's all right. I'm only half awake."

"Is Miss Imbrie there?"

"She's getting me some coffee."

"And you have no slippers on?"

"I have hers on."

"Lorna."

"Yes."

"Ah, what am I going to do about you? Will I ever see you alone?"

"If you want to."

"What does that mean?"

"Nothing. I don't know. I haven't had any coffee. Why don't you come down later?"

"I can't. Mrs. Cunningham is here. Would you mind saying that you loved me?"

"I'm so cold."

"Then say it quickly."

"Gwen's making fun of me."

"Tell her I'll knock her block off," Francis said. Since it takes two to talk of love, he felt disconsolate and foolish; but the picture of Lorna stupid with sleep, shivering in pajamas, brought with it a deep ringing of nerves. "You're sweet," he said. "Good-bye."

It was nine o'clock. In the high corridor Francis walked quickly looking for the number of Mrs. Cunningham's sitting-room door—303, 307, 309, 3B. Francis had this first meeting all worked out. Christmas night he had shown himself why he ought not to be angry, and why Mrs. Cunningham's letter was more to be pitied than censured. During the next few days in Florence he kept pitying, at odd moments, her unnecessary anxiety; but soon his wounded feelings were near enough whole again for Mrs. Cunningham's plight to seem somewhat less pathetic. He began to show himself that her concern, though groundless, was reasonable— more to be respected than pitied. He did not blame her in the least for her vigilance. Authors were two for a nickel (by the contemptuous appraisal he took himself down a peg, of course; but, then, he took down the celebrated and successful several pegs and the exercise was not unpleasant); and though by some miracle your choice fell on a good author, art was long, the egotism inseparable from it tiring, and meanwhile everyone knew that two could and would live at least as cheaply and meanly as one. Mrs. Cunningham ought not to let Helen risk her happiness and welfare that way.

Nevertheless, Francis had his self-respect to think of. To forgive Mrs. Cunningham for worrying was one thing. To forget that in her worry she had let herself believe him capable of starting something like that was another thing. Francis decided that he would view his situation more strictly. He would be less familiar. He would think of himself as an employee; agreeable and efficient, but reserved; attentive to Mrs. Cunningham's interests and wishes, not because he had a friendly regard for her, but because he was conscientious. It seemed reasonable to hope that she would feel the difference. Without having presumed to reproach her, Francis would artfully bring her to reproach herself, and to be sorry that she had misjudged him.

To this end Francis had thought carefully of what to say and what to do. More than that, Mrs. Cunningham's part, too, was tentatively arranged for her, since Francis was prepared to meet various openings or attitudes with rehearsed exchanges in which he had taken pains to give her good lines, even if his own were, by and large, better. Unfortunately he had not prepared one to be begun by him with an apology for failing to do some of the duties whose perfect performance was to make her sorry. The conscientious employee had got off on the wrong foot. He was an expense to Mrs. Cunningham the minute he reached the hotel; and they were both agreed that she was not paying him to amuse himself; and he was afraid that they both would agree that he had no business to go away and stay away on the irresponsible assumption that she could not need him.

Standing at the door, Francis tried to summon up his forces, to gather head as far as conscious effort could do it, against the unreasonable feeling that everything was going wrong. He showed himself that this was not the case. His own impatience and ineptitude had made his position a little uncomfortable, a few trifles went wrong; but here he was with a kind of magic ease at Cap d'Ail. By no other exertion than wishing for what a month ago seemed the impossible, he was here; and that was the main point. That was the main point, all right; yet from the corner of his eye Francis kept scrutinizing the happy fact. He held himself above superstition, but he had not failed to observe that, as one thing follows another in life, patterns, often repeated, are formed. Viewed with detachment, a number of these patterns seem to be jokes. Francis stood apprehensive, with kind of pricking of the thumbs, wondering if it were not just possible that he had seen all this before; and if, though still inchoate, the pattern of a joke everybody knows might not be emerging. It begins with a man wishing; and then the man gets his wish and then (you could die laughing) he wishes he hadn't got it. Francis raised his hand and rapped on the paneled door.

The room glowed with sunlight. Whistling "Valencia" slowly and shrilly, Walter slouched in a chair, scowling at a jigsaw puzzle, half completed in the cover of a large white hat box in his lap. "Say, hello!" he said, breaking off his music. "Say, Frank, Tom and Toby and I went pretty near up to Salzegg. Gosh, you should have been there! It's much better—" He got up impulsively, let the box cover slip, and sent a hundred pieces of the puzzle rolling over the rug.

"Walter," said Mrs. Cunningham, "how careless you are!" Pen in hand, she sat at the writing desk, pressing flat a folder of traveler's checks to be countersigned. She wore a suit of brown knitted silk that Francis had not seen before, and a Victorian gold bar with large topazes and small pearls on her breast. She looked very handsome. She said, "How are you, Francis?" Turning, she gave him her hand and smiled while her voice, easy and pleasant, bore down on the 'are,' making her sound anxious to know.

Francis said, "I'm so frightfully sorry about—"

Walter was on the floor, sheepishly picking up his puzzle; and, stepping back, Francis bent to help him. Busily he picked up piece after piece, enlarging his apologies because he could not seem to stop. He accused himself with abandon.

Mrs. Cunningham took it in good part. When she came to answer, she did not say that his absence didn't matter; she simply told him, as though he would be (and he was) relieved to hear it, that she had been put to no serious inconvenience. She told him she had been afraid that he might not get her telegram because she wasn't certain when he was to arrive.

Francis then told her about Miss Imbrie and Miss Imbrie's cook— really an emergency. Nothing less would have tempted him to leave his post. All the pieces of the puzzle had been collected, so Francis straightened up.

"They were getting dinner themselves, so I stayed to help," he said, a little lamely, for the state of emergency that explained his going did not seem quite to cover his staying until eleven o'clock. Mrs. Cunningham asked how Miss Imbrie was, and how the girls were. She paused and added, "Helen was so pleased when Lorna came to see her in Paris."

The simple remark, or perhaps the minute pause that preceded it, threw Francis into confusion again. Taken at face value, the meaning was that Mrs. Cunningham, reminded of Lorna, was reminded that in Paris Lorna had taken the trouble to be pleasant to Helen, and Mrs. Cunningham thought that was a nice thing for Lorna to do. If, as Francis's strained alertness immediately suggested, more than that was meant, and Mrs. Cunningham had said it to see just how he would react to a mention of Helen, it was important that he respond easily, since he was, first, innocent, and second, unresentful. But Mrs. Cunningham might mean (conscious or would-be ironists see irony everywhere. They have their reward) that she knew all about Lorna's reasons for bothering with Helen; and that she thought Francis ought to realize that if he were in Cap d'Ail now it was not because of such attempted management.

"They seem very well," Francis said promptly, for he could keep his composure and prevent a change of color best when he was talking. In the nick of time, he caught himself, and undoubtedly he did color. He had almost told her, logically enough, that he had just been talking to Miss Imbrie, and Miss Imbrie had asked him to say that they would come to call.

But why had he just been talking to Miss Imbrie? If Mrs. Cunningham felt surprise to find him gone away Monday afternoon without waiting to hear from her, what would she feel to learn that he intended (another emergency, perhaps) to be away all day Tuesday, too, when he knew that she was virtually certain to arrive sometime? Francis had seen this danger well in advance. The danger he did not see until the last moment was one arising when, prudently practicing to deceive, he suppressed the projected trip to Grasse. He had been about to invite Mrs. Cunningham to wonder why he telephoned so early in the morning unless the villa were so much on his mind that everything else must wait. With a mental movement analogous to wiping his forehead, he dodged again. "Miss Imbrie asked me last night to say she was coming to call," he said.

This time it was too late. It would have to stand, complete with its exemplary blunder, its fine specimen of that folly that answers questions before they are asked. Did he have to say last night? He did not. He had not even sense enough to imply his falsehoods instead of telling them. Such trivial involvements, taken in their stride by intelligent liars and disposed of with easy precision, rattled Francis to distraction. He jumped from the frying pan into the fire and back again. In a frenzy of snap judgments, of stopgap answers, of quick unthinking, Francis covered a break here, snipped off a loose end there; but he had never yet failed to find himself, when the dust settled, left holding, sick with exertion, a masterpiece of botchery, fit only to be thrown away before somebody caught him with it and recognized him for what he looked like—one willing to deceive, but too talentless to succeed. It was Francis's unalterable conviction that honesty is the best policy.

Mrs. Cunningham made a conventional remark expressing pleasure at Miss Imbrie's suggestion—Francis did not hear just what; for he was intent on getting out of his mess the shortest way. He waited a painful instant or two and then said brightly to Walter, "Well, how do you feel? Pretty well rested?"

"Ah, heck!" said Walter. He smiled guiltily. He writhed with reluctance.

Francis looked at Mrs. Cunningham to let her see that though duty had pushed him to waste no more time, he now checked duty to defer to her wishes. "I really think," he said frowning, "that if it's convenient for you, we'd better—"

"Ah, heck!" said Walter.

"Yes, I think so," Mrs. Cunningham said. "Now, darling, let's not have any of that. You mustn't make it hard for Francis."

"You've been given quite a break," Francis said, kindly but firm. "And we have a lot of work to do. Are your books unpacked?" He spoke with unfeigned zeal, for the bad moment was over and with unfeigned zeal he (though in a different and humbler spirit than he had planned) introduced at last the conscientious employee.

"Heck. Maggie's got them," said Walter. "Hey, Maggie!"

"Now, Walter, go and get them yourself. Maggie has—"

The connecting door opened and Maggie brought the pile of books in. "Good morning," Francis said.

"How do you do, Mr. Ellery," said Maggie. "Good morning." Her tone was civil and obliging; but Francis heard it with a start. Maggie, he had observed before, was one to think her own thoughts; and last night she must have thought them when no Francis appeared; and now she was probably thinking a few of them. His sense of regenerated conscientiousness was impaired, for Maggie might be considered something of an expert on conscientious employees—or, at least, Maggie would know one when she saw one.

III

It was not exactly a matter of getting permission to go to the dance Thursday night. Walter's lessons took up the forenoon, and the afternoon went into Walter's exercise or amusement. They had tea about five and dinner about eight. When dinner was over Mrs. Cunningham said good night and took Walter upstairs. Francis did not see them again until nine o'clock the next morning. Usually—Mrs. Cunningham might suppose, always—Francis went upstairs, too, and worked on his manuscript until midnight; but Mrs. Cunningham had no way of knowing what he did and she never asked.

Just the same, Francis felt obligated to let her know that he was to be out Thursday night, and probably out late. To say nothing was impossible. Mrs. Cunningham would think it so odd of him—or so rude of him; and he himself would think it was so furtive of him. There was not even a remote chance of her having an objection; so, as a matter of form, what could be simpler than asking if she had any?

All Tuesday morning he was busy reviewing Walter's work. Walter had forgotten a good deal; and, in natural loathing of the things to be remembered, practiced an effective obstructionism by asking for longer and fuller explanations. By noon they were both worn out. Francis meant to speak of the dance at luncheon and get it over with, but no good opportunity presented itself, and he did not feel like making one, so he let it slide. On second thought, speaking of it at luncheon might be a little precipitate. It might seem to Mrs. Cunningham a kind of going-on-from-where-he-left-off, and an indication that Walter's lessons had interrupted his thoughts very little. Some simple opportunity would probably come before the afternoon was over.

After luncheon they went to Monte-Carlo to get tennis rackets, and Walter wanted to see the Casino. This took a long while, and though Francis was watchful for good openings, none that suited him appeared. He thought that a good time would be when they had tea. They had tea on the partly sheltered terrace of the Café de Paris, but it did not prove a good time, for Walter could not keep quiet. The Casino had knocked his eye out. Though he had been coached into taking some creditable first steps in the fine art of learning what not to admire, he derogated with a bang. The elegant columns and colored marbles in the floor enchanted

him. The crystal and red plush ravished his soul. Plainly he felt a holy
joy, like that of Lord Byron surveying the noble remnants of the Parthe-
non, or Walter Pater noticing that the Gioconda's eyelids were a little
weary. He lingered, peeping in at the empty theater; he kept taking out
his admission card and looking at it; he loitered down the Salle de Jeu
staring shyly at the tables half-filled with careful afternoon gamblers,
rolling his eyes to the fake Persian vaults and trappings. With guilty
glances—for it was clear that his mother and Francis did not share his
enthusiasm—he measured the chances of delaying their departure.

Finally dragged away, Walter began to rouse himself, to come down
to earth from the realms of romance as conceived by M. Blanc and splendor as constructed by M. Garnier. He reached a pitch of pleasure and
hilarity. By biting small pieces out of a brioche he tried to transform it
into a bust. He put a little butter in his chocolate. Reproved by his
mother, he ducked down as though to hide his head under the table. At
last abashed by her expression, he succeeded in sobering somewhat, and
plied Francis with questions about roulette, about the Prince of Monaco,
about how many people committed suicide. Mrs. Cunningham was both
displeased and concerned, and Francis felt that it would not be tactful to
introduce the subject of the dance. Perhaps it would be better, anyway, to
postpone the whole business until tomorrow.

Wednesday Francis did not see Mrs. Cunningham until noon. It
developed then that Miss Imbrie and Lorna and Gwen had come up about
eleven, while Walter's lessons were going on, and had sat for half an hour
with Mrs. Cunningham in the garden. Here was an opportunity of the
most convenient kind; but Francis could not take it. He was tongue-tied.
That they should have come and gone without his knowing stirred in him
a sense of injury—of that unwarrantable injury he regularly did himself
by tameness and submission. How intolerable to waste mornings upstairs
with Walter and schoolbooks! Who gave a good God damn whether
Walter ever learned anything? This whole preposterous farce—what was
he doing here, anyway, studying Mrs. Cunningham to see how she felt,
worrying about whether he could do this or that? Pettish, Francis let
himself imagine scenes of repudiation and declarations of independence.
"Mrs. Cunningham," he might say, "this really won't do. I'm not cut out
for this. In many ways it has been very pleasant; but it takes too much of
my time. I think, if you can possibly make some other arrangement, I
must ask you to do it. . . ."

But since Francis spoke nothing aloud, Mrs. Cunningham went on
with her luncheon, observing that she thought Lorna looked much better,
that she had really been concerned about her in Paris—she looked so
tired. It occurred to Francis that a mention of the dance might have been
made during the visit, and that Mrs. Cunningham, knowing of it, might

be expecting him to speak, was even inviting him to. In that event, Francis told himself, she could go right on expecting; for the idea renewed his sense of injury and aggravated his indignation. If she was waiting to see him do what she knew he was going to have to do, why, let her wait. She needn't worry; he would ask her; but he would ask her when he got ready, and she mustn't suppose that he felt any anxiety or much interest. Viewed this way, it was a minor triumph for him when Mrs. Cunningham changed the subject, and said that she had some shopping to do, and that she and Maggie would go to Nice after luncheon.

The afternoon went slowly. They had planned to play tennis after Walter had his nap; but at two o'clock the King of Sweden, an aged, animated beanpole of a man with frail-looking long legs encased in narrow cylinders of white duck turned up from somewhere to use the hotel tennis courts. To start another game while this was going on would be lese majesty in its modern meaning—a special sort of bad taste, a vulgar bumptiousness that saw in a simple and democratic monarch's loss of all practical powers a chance to treat him just like anybody else. The royal game was therefore the only one. As a further mark of deference it appeared proper for everybody to restrain his curiosity and to keep at a distance, so that the old man might play in peace.

Walter, coming down in flannels at half past two, was excited and interested by an actual king out on the courts hitting a ball around; but he was sensitive to the element of fantasy, almost of farce. From the glassed-in porch at the northeast end of the hotel, Walter gazed, shaking his head and grinning, at the distant tall figure. Walter's instinctive sense of values was nice. The king did not lack dignity, even when he ran or skipped; but it was dignity of the mild sort that would have suited a distinguished but senile preacher, or the president emeritus of a rich university. The royal entourage of three or four ordinary people who had descended with the king from a large but ordinary automobile left Walter unsatisfied. Whispers, hushed in good behavior, to look, that was the King of Sweden, struck him as funny. Maybe Julius Caesar or Napoleon would be along in a minute. He grew bored and restive. He murmured: "Hey, come on, King! Let's go!"

After an hour the King went, and Francis and Walter were able to have a short game. They had tea alone. Mrs. Cunningham got back a little after seven and sent word to Francis that she and Walter would not be down for dinner. Francis ate by himself, debating whether or not to call the villa. Calling must amount to asking them to ask him down, and he did not like it; but after dinner he did call. The man, Raymond, told him that they had all gone out to dine. Francis went upstairs, put on a bathrobe, and tried to get some writing done.

Thursday morning Mrs. Cunningham was there when he came for Walter's lessons; but she was merely waiting to say good morning to him, and Walter was ready to work, so it did not seem just the moment to mention the dance. However, he really would have to say something at luncheon. Finishing work at half past twelve, he stayed a moment to see if Mrs. Cunningham was upstairs and would come in. It was Maggie who came in. "Mr. Ellery," she said, "Mrs. Cunningham has had to go out. Some friends came unexpectedly—"

"Who are they?" said Walter.

"Well, a Mr. and Mrs. Peters. I don't think you'd remember them. They were friends of your father's."

"Gosh, are they here?" said Walter. "They're awful."

"Pipe down," said Francis.

"She'll be back before tea, Mrs. Cunningham said to tell you."

"Well, what are we going to do?" said Walter.

"What do we usually do?" said Francis. "We'll have lunch, and you'll lie down, and then we'll have some tennis."

"I thought you said we might go to La—what was it?"

"La Turbie," said Francis, "but we'll have to speak to your mother. Perhaps we can go tomorrow."

"Promise?" said Walter.

"How can I promise until I know what your mother's plans are?" Francis asked reasonably.

Beyond Beaulieu, above the headlands of Cap Ferrat, the sun was getting down. The extended shadow of the hotel covered the tennis courts. Francis kept an eye on the door, but he could not watch it all the time, so he missed seeing Mrs. Cunningham drive in. He had been delaying the end of the second set by taking five games and then letting Walter begin to win; for he wanted to be still playing, but able to finish quickly. Mrs. Cunningham would be fairly sure to come down to the court, and since they would have to wash before tea, he would have a chance, when Walter had been sent up, to get a moment alone with her. He had the eighth game at a deuce when she did appear. She settled on the bench under a striped canvas tilt at the courtside to watch. Walter, his hair blowing forward across his forehead, yelled passionately, but much winded: "We have to finish! We have to finish!"

Anyone could see that Walter was tired, so without wasting more time Francis tossed the red ball over his head. It mounted against the late sunlight on the rock masses of the Tête du Chien, he eyed it carefully, dropped his racket back and drove it hard to the inside corner of the service court. Walter, too far over, had to let it go. "Good!" he panted.

"Nice one!" But he hugged his racket in disappointment.

"Ad in," said Francis, hardening his heart. He held a hand up and the fat little ragamuffin of a ball boy bounced him two more.

"Say, set point!" said Walter. He changed courts with agility, acting out for his mother's benefit the importance of the moment. Francis fed him an easy one, and then put back Walter's return where he could not fail to get it. Pulling in the new return, Francis lobbed it to land well to Walter's left, where Walter was weak. With a dramatic frenzy of effort, Walter tied himself up and backhanded into the net. "Ah, gee!" he said. The ball came coasting slowly back to him and he stopped it with his foot.

"What's wrong with your backhand is that you don't hold your racket right," Francis said, coming around the net. Taking Walter's damp hand, he loosened the fingers, shifted them on the handle, and pressed them closed again. "Like that," he said. "You'll get it. Come on. Put a sweater on. It's cold." They came off the court toward Mrs. Cunningham.

"Say, how about some lemonade?" Walter said to her. "Gosh, I'm thirsty."

Mrs. Cunningham said, "All right, dear." She looked toward the enclosed end of the porch above. "We'll have tea there. I don't think they like people in the lounge in flannels. Maggie would probably like to come down. Will you tell her? And wash a little, darling. You look very warm."

Francis slipped on his jacket, turned a scarf about his neck and tucked the ends in. The persistent cold wind, blowing off the water, went through the wizened orange trees. Mrs. Cunningham was getting her things together silently, and Francis, waiting to take some of them, felt panic, for this was his moment to speak, he absolutely must; and yet he heard himself saying, "It's really quite cool, isn't it?"

"Yes," Mrs. Cunningham said. "It isn't as warm here as I hoped. I've noticed that it gets very cold about sunset."

In another moment they would reach the steps and go on to the glassed-in porch. Walter must be already upstairs; perhaps, his washing no more than a lick and a promise, already hurrying Maggie along to the elevator. Was he, Francis asked himself, or was he not going to say at once, this instant: *Mrs. Cunningham, I've been meaning to ask you . . .*

Hushed but insistent, someone said behind him, "*Hé. Tiens, Monsieur. Hé!*" The ball boy, running with the box of balls, had overtaken him, and Francis stopped in confusion, shifting the rackets under his arm and groping in his jacket pocket for some franc pieces. "*Fort bien,*" he said automatically, "*à demain.*"

But how did he know what Mrs. Cunningham had in mind for tomorrow? Taking the box, Francis nearly dropped it. He flushed and said to her, "Sorry. Had you other plans? He's always hanging around anyway."

"Well, Francis—" Mrs. Cunningham said. She appeared to hesitate. "I know it's hard for you when we don't keep to a regular schedule. You see, I didn't interrupt you this morning." She smiled and then looked seriously at him. "But tomorrow I do want these people—they're very old friends of ours—to see Walter. They're at Monte-Carlo, but they may be leaving soon. I thought we'd go over there to luncheon. If we left by twelve it would be time enough, so most of the morning wouldn't be disturbed. What do you think?"

"I think—" said Francis, and drew a breath. The note of consultation, the confident question, doing him if not the honor, at least the justice, of assuming his responsibility and real concern, seemed to bring them back in an instant to where they had been at Montreux. The difficulties he had labored under during the three days past resolved themselves, for they were difficulties of relationship or attitude, and could exist only if, feeling himself distrusted, he returned the distrust.

"I think," he repeated, smiling, "that it certainly wouldn't do any harm. I don't think it's good for Walter to feel that too much is going on around him. But going out to luncheon one day couldn't very well amount to too much. Speaking of that," he added—a little stiltedly, but without losing composure—"some people in Menton are giving a dance tonight. Miss Imbrie asked me if I'd care to go; but it occurs to me that when I'm making Walter toe the mark, it might be better if I didn't—"

"Oh, Francis," said Mrs. Cunningham. "I don't see that. You have Walter on your hands all day. There's no reason why you shouldn't go if you want to."

"Well," said Francis, nervous with delight, "I thought I'd wait a day or so and see how things shaped up." His sense of virtue was strong and pleasant—a little too strong, considering that the things he had waited to see shape up were mostly elements of self-interest. He said deprecatingly, "As a matter of fact, I did rather want to go."

"Then, do go!" Mrs. Cunningham said. Her charm of manner was never greater. "I'd really like you to."

SIX

The chill, noticed by Mrs. Cunningham, that fell at sunset was generally succeeded by a return of warmer air. You felt it about seven o'clock; and it continued through the evening. Moreover, Francis was warmed by his own high spirits; and he was sure that he would need no overcoat for the trip to Menton. He did not bring one downstairs, where he waited, with time to kill after Mrs. Cunningham and Walter went up, for the car to come.

Waiting, Francis thought of having a drink; but he remembered Monday night, and he thought it likely that Miss Imbrie might have observed that at supper he was not quite sober. It seemed better not to turn up now smelling of liquor; and in too fine fettle to want a drink anyway, he went instead into the empty billiard room. He took down a cue and set himself to knocking the balls around; missing easy ones; to his astonishment, accomplishing occasional shots much too hard for him.

While he moved about the table Francis hummed, and then under his breath he sang, and then he stopped and laughed; for he was singing: *Now the Queen of seasons bright, with the day of splendour . . .* and he saw, a little fussed by the unconscious mind's irremissible naïveté, the hymn's connection. At school, ranked years ago in chapel, they used to feel good to that tune, when the triumphant gladness of Our Lord's resurrection was given a compelling fillip by the thought of the impending Easter recess. Raising the strain at the top of their lungs, several hundred off-key singers in common celebration raised the roof. Francis was not sure that he liked these often-discovered proofs that, too young to have a say in the process, he had been marked for life; but, glancing to see that no one was near enough to hear him, he soon went on singing. Across the radiant green woollen broadcloth the running balls struck and broke apart like magic. Several times he laid his cue down and walked out on the terrace to test the temperature. Though not warm, the night seemed to him delightfully soft and mild. The truth was that neither of the two overcoats he had with him was entirely suitable for formal evening wear.

At half past nine the car came, and Francis went out to it. He was not halfway down the lighted steps when Miss Imbrie got the window beside her open a crack and called, "You can't go that way, Francis! It may turn very cold!"

"I'm quite hardy," Francis said, smiling.

In Florence the local bloods, the often-not-spurious Russian princes, the sporty Italians, cousins and cadets of noble houses whose grand cinquecento names embellished the evening, achieved (whether because they were inured to the climate, whether because they had not the price of an overcoat) an effect indubitably dashing and continental when they arrived, even on bitter nights, bearing in their left hands a pair of folded gloves, a dress scarf of black or white silk, and a soft black felt hat. Francis lifted his left hand, showing Miss Imbrie these objects. He laughed and turned his face up to the stars above the mountains. "I don't think it's going to snow again."

"Well, then you'll have to come in here."

"Not at all," said Francis, realizing that to avoid crowding it had been planned to seat him in front with Raymond. Raymond stood waiting for the final word; and Francis stepped past him, opened the front door, and got in. "Perfectly all right," he said through the pushed-back glass.

Out of the depths Mr. McKellar said, "I might offer to change places with you, Ellery, were I but now the lord of such hot youth as when brave Gaunt—but I'm not. I prefer to be lapped in women and luxury." At patriarchal ease, one elegant thin leg thrown over the other, his patent-leather slipper winking in the light, Mr. McKellar occupied the back seat with Lorna and Miss Imbrie. An opera cloak shrouded his shoulders. He was bareheaded, but he held his collapsed hat in his white-gloved hands. Francis guessed that he was costumed with precious care exactly as he used to be a generation ago in his polka-dancing prime.

Francis laughed again, for everything, even Mr. McKellar, appeared agreeable to him. Wonderful old ass! "Please don't worry about me," he said. Impatiently he was preparing to look at Lorna. She was folded in a wrap of dully shimmering gold cloth with a scarf bound over her head. Her lips opened in the shadow and she said, "Hello."

"Hello," said Francis.

He could hardly speak the word. His heart enclosed her. Without the use of hands, his heart cupped up her face and held it. Her bound head, her shadowed eyes, her smiling, twisted lips possessed, as much as his mind, his pumping blood—not by beauty, for the instant was one of those when he noted (and admitted; for what did he care? What difference did it make?) that her face, at other times so enchanting, could seem plain, even ugly. He looked at her face, and hunger, the wild imperative wish consumed him. He wanted her; and not merely in terms of coverture and access. He wanted all that, and he looked at her body, distracted because he could not even touch it; but in his mind he saw the sexual connection as a step, means to a vital emotional end. It was the entering wedge to be pushed home until, sooner or later rendered by pleasure beside herself, she let all go, convulsively gave up to him the something more, he did not know what, that, over and above her body, have from her he must.

He thought he must. In that longing, while it lasted, there was no choice; and in that helplessness, Francis saw with surprise (it was naturally not the first time; but he often forgot or made fun of it) that all the self-devotion and all the obscenity of love in literature or in court records was comprehensible. He understood. Men who could not stop their longings did crazy things. Through ardent temperament or extreme constancy of mind, or, perhaps usually, through a thickheadedness that formed few thoughts and so did not easily replace one with another, some wretches remarkable for their grossness or their delicacy loved their women night and day. Frantic all the time, what would you stop at? She could despise or cheat you and that would be all right. She could be a nun or a motion-picture actress and you would be fool enough to love her. She could be married to Simone de' Bardi; she could be a dirty old worn-out tart; she could be dead; while you, *lacrimans*—the word was sniveling, Francis remembered; and he recoiled—*exclusus amator*, groveled through the hopeless days or years, still loving, still locked out. Shaken, Francis thought: "To hell with that!"

He turned his head. On the *strapontin* in front of Miss Imbrie, Gwen, her hair bound up, too, faced him. She was close to the window, and Francis found that he need not have worried about that drink he didn't have, for the scent of brandy hung pleasantly on her breath. "You smell like a barroom," he said, still trying to steady himself. "I wish I'd been along."

"'Twas a balmy summer evening and a goodly crowd was there," said Gwen. She stuck her tongue out at him. "Now would you just as soon close that glass and freeze by yourself?"

Francis smiled and closed the glass. His shocking thoughts had become suddenly silly, a neurotic's-eye view of what was in practice not like that; a parade of images about as lifelike as the procession of the passions in the *Faerie Queene*—Gluttony on a swine in vine leaves, Lechery on a goat with a burning heart in his hand. He thought at random that Gwen probably lived a happy life, unfanciful, orderly, humorous without the tension of great attempts at wit, progressing gravely and intelligently from a neat happy child to a neat amiable young woman, to the neat comfortable marriage whose reasonable affections would operate to make her the mother of more neat happy children.

The cold air blew in on Francis. He put his hat on and began to dig for a cigarette case that was in one of his waistcoat pockets, glancing about to see where they were. Up through the dark, past bits of wall and infrequent houses, past overhung olive trees, the headlights lifted steadily along the rising paving stones and the white retaining ramps of the long traverses.

"Grande Corniche?" he said to Raymond.

"*En chemin.* Yes, sir," Raymond said. "*Regardez à droite*— down."

Francis turned. Over the moving door frame, over the near parapet edge paralleling it, the tremendous void fell away. A lacework of lights was stretched out, hanging from the mountain, sunk in crumpled folds about the bays and crooked headlands of the coast below. Linked by festoons of gold points, the towns beyond Cap Ferrat showed like far-off rakings of embers. On the right above Monte-Carlo glowed a hazed radiance, a pleasure dome of light. Francis swung back his hand and rapped on the glass behind him. "Look down!" he said, pointing. "Look down there." He was shivering a little, but more from festivity or excitement than from cold.

"This way is the quicker," Raymond observed. "We go to Roquebrune and down a little. The other way, we go to Menton and far around and up a lot." He nodded his head with that peculiar Gallic satisfaction, that perpetual *soyons-sérieux*, by which foreigners and even other Frenchmen are persuaded that the evidence of their senses is in error, and that to live in France is to live by reason. Francis wondered where Raymond had learned his English.

II

"Lord Bardo," said Mr. McKellar, "allow me to present Mr. Ellery."

Having heard his host named only once, several days ago, and then as Johnny, Francis could not wholly suppress his surprise and interest. He was not in the habit of being presented to British peers; but he composed himself and inclined his head with the polite reserved look copied by close observation from the bearing of those who seemed to show to best advantage when meeting, along with Francis and a good many other people, a bishop, a senator, or the president of the university.

As in some of those encounters, Francis's first sensation was of being let down. If he acknowledged a duty of politeness to defer to his civil or social superiors, they surely owed it to him, or at any rate to themselves, to look as though they ought to be deferred to. Lord Bardo was not as tall as Francis. Spare, small, somewhere between forty and sixty, he had a shrewd pointed face, not much hair, and a pleasant leathery tone of skin. His manner was that of a shy man who wishes people would leave him alone, yet realizes that they mean no harm, and so shrinks from offending them by suggesting it. When Mr. McKellar caught him, he stopped, stood harassed, making ingratiating grimaces, but glancing aside with twitches of consternation that seemed to say that all this—the massive fantasy on a Pompeian villa surrounding him; the movement of guests down the cross-vistas, one terminated by a long linen-draped table set with punch bowls and clusters of bottles, the other by a band obviously French playing behind a breastwork of flowers *"I want to go where you go"*—had nothing in particular to do with him and he was a stranger here himself.

Disregarding, or not noticing, Francis's bishop technique, he thrust out a hand shortly, looked up to a point just past Francis's shoulder and said, "Of course, of course. How-do-do. Glad you could come."

Hastily Francis took the hand, hoping he had not been convicted of some notable gaucherie by his failure to realize that Lord Bardo would expect to shake hands. Mr. McKellar, however, seeing somebody he knew, had turned away with a flourish to speak to him. Lord Bardo stood at obvious loss. He looked covertly past Francis again. He cleared his throat and said suddenly, "Here for long?"

"I've just come up from Florence," Francis said; and realized then that, for no reason he could think of, he had mistaken the question.

"Florence, eh?" said Lord Bardo. He brooded a moment on the remarkable circumstance. "Know a number of Americans there. D'you know the Robertsons?"

"I'm afraid not," Francis said.

"Girl's a singer. Good one. Sang for my wife once."

"Oh," said Francis. "Well, yes. I didn't—Mrs. Robertson's a friend of my mother's. I don't know them very well."

"Let me introduce you to a charming young lady," Lord Bardo said in answer. He gave Francis's arm a quick, directing tap.

"Thanks awfully," said Francis, "but I'm waiting for Miss Imbrie to come down."

"Just as you like," Lord Bardo said. "Make yourself at home." He nodded, his manner more harassed than ever, and went away, skirting the loiterers at the foot of the great stairs, and slipped along the red wall painted in classic rectangles with griffins, baskets with thyrsi, and branches of herbs.

"Johnny," said Mr. McKellar, swinging about, "I—"

"He got away," said Francis.

"Interesting fellow, Johnny," Mr. McKellar said, perceiving that it was true. "Lady Bardo's an American. Old friend of Mabel's. Bardo's the celebrated yachtsman and ichthyologist."

Francis smiled at him, but Mr. McKellar did not appear to see anything funny in the twin avocations; and Francis guessed he was right; there wasn't. Down the noble staircase Miss Imbrie and Gwen and Lorna were coming at last with a number of other women. "That's Lady Bardo, talking to Mabel," Mr. McKellar said. "Delightful person. You must meet her."

Francis looked up at a stocky, hearty woman in old-rose satin under row after row of short crystal-bead fringes. On her head grew amazing fluffed-out, towy hair that looked like (though doubtless it was not) the result of a bad accident with some dye or restorative. Her expression was lively and intelligent. She might very well be, as Mr. McKellar said, a delightful person; just as Miss Imbrie was excellent company, esteemed by all who knew her; but, descending the pseudo-Roman stairs in step together, dressed with the idea of looking pretty, nodding together with affectionate animation, chattering away, the cruel touch of caricature was on them. They were old.

Francis marked it and was given pause. He had the writer's laboriously cultivated, unnatural habit of mind and eye. Like the froward and odious child, overadmired in the fairy tale, this habit of eye sees, along with most other people, that the emperor hasn't any clothes on. There is then no holding this habit of mind. It hastens to tell everyone.

Past the adipose, coarsely rounded flesh of Lady Bardo's bare arm Francis saw Lorna's arms and shoulders, slight and white against the bodice of the black dress. Lorna's freshly painted lips were a vivid sullen red. Her face, perhaps partly because of the lipstick and the black taffeta, looked pale and tense, but that was nothing. The line of her cheek and chin, not unlike Miss Imbrie's, and close enough to compare with it, was delicate and charming. For skin, Miss Imbrie had a sort of tough tegument, well scrubbed, suitably rouged, well powdered; but who would want to touch it? Lorna moved with a limber unconscious ease just behind the older women, the joints of whose thighs were certainly no longer like jewels. On Lorna's thigh, close to the dipping waistline, those two big silver rosettes that she and Gwen had exclaimed over shifted and fell.

To meet them, Francis and Mr. McKellar advanced onto the central paving circled by Ionic columns, walking across a mosaic of a mighty wheel of fortune with numerals and signs of the zodiac. Other people had come up, some just arriving, some leaving the dance floor, to speak to their hostess.

Hanging back, Francis moved near Lorna. "Here," she said. Putting out her hand she slid a gold compact into his coat pocket. Standing closer in the press, she let her hand fall, held his a moment.

"—and Mr. Ellery," Miss Imbrie said waving an arm toward him. Francis bowed to Lady Bardo. Somebody stepped in front of him, and groping quickly, he caught Lorna's hand again. "Run along, children," Miss Imbrie said.

"But I don't care to meet anyone else," Francis said. "I don't want to dance with anyone else. If I do, I'll dance with Mr. McKellar. I've met him."

Lorna choked with laughter. Swaying back against his arm, she turned her distorted face up. "You're such a fool!" she said. "Do you know something? Ever since you left Paris, I—oh, I'm so glad you're here. We're going to have fun, aren't we? But, look, darling. Quick. Someone's coming to cut in. He's an artist named Goodwin Kirkland, from California. His sister's a friend of mine, and I—"

"You have more damn friends," said Francis. He felt a moment's pang, his sense of possession affronted, the inconvenience of his situation emphasized, for he knew no one here, and the way his days were arranged made it unlikely that he would come to know anyone. The high spirit of his happiness faltered; and, spiteful and reasonable, his mind invited him to go on, to look at the fact that he was in a poor position if he hoped to keep Lorna for himself; and then to look at several more facts like it. What did he mean, 'keep Lorna for himself'? Did he think he was going to marry her? That was certainly interesting. What would he use for money? Did he, perhaps, think he was going to have her without marrying her? That might present a few difficulties, too. Then, what was he doing? What did he have the half-wittedness to feel so good about?

Francis did not know. The questions were unanswerable. He looked at them steadily, and he could not offer a suggestion or indicate any possible plan; and this stubborn muteness which would not rise to insults, or offer objections, or answer arguments became suddenly his best defense. The vindictive mind, in its turn, seemed to falter. A kind of silence fell, prolonging itself; and Francis, still not answering, simply thinking, thought: *I don't know and I don't care.* He looked at Lorna and found her just lifting her eyes to look at him—all of it could hardly have lasted a second, for she was looking to see what he meant. He took a breath and holding her eyes he said, "Well, don't get gay with any California artists, or I'll break your neck."

The effort of deliberate compulsion to hold her gaze was unnecessary, he discovered, for she did not try to look away. "All right," she said. "I won't. But I'm not. I—"

"I believe you," Francis said.

The expected hand touched his elbow. Before this, Francis had observed that on the Pacific Coast a new race was being bred, or at any rate a marked mutation, larger, handsomer, and not much stupider than the pre-existing Eastern types. Francis, with his shoes off, lacked nearly half an inch of being six feet tall. The evolving Californians were always three or even four inches more than six feet. Francis glanced at this specimen, this grinning lumbering cub, with tolerant approval—Napoleon pinching his guardsman's cheek. He relinquished Lorna and turned away.

Crossing the hall to go along and get himself a drink he met Miss Imbrie face to face. With presence of mind, he said, "Will you dance with me?"

"You are very kind," Miss Imbrie said. "But, no thank you, I won't. I am not much of a dancer, and you can dismiss me from your mind. We have a couple of tables of bridge in the library, and I shall stay until I lose all my money. Then I shall probably go home at a reasonable hour."

"How long does this affair last?" Francis asked.

"Indefinitely. Till morning, I suppose."

Francis had turned to walk along the passage with her, and she continued, "I shall slip away when the time comes. It has nothing to do with the rest of you."

Whatever happened, whenever it was over, Francis remembered that he would have Walter's lessons at nine o'clock. "Do you think I could go down with you?" he said.

"Oh, you don't want to do that."

"I don't want to. But, alas—"

"Well, I shall be in here. If you're really serious I'll try to let you know." Through the tall open door Francis could see walls of books behind glass and wire grills so lofty that the top shelves were accessible only from the rungs of a mahogany ladder. In the corner a bust of Edward Gibbon stood on a pedestal. A huge varnished terrestrial globe stood beside a desk covered with silver-framed photographs. One of them, signed with several lines, was of the King of Italy. There were also two bridge tables, a couple of champagne buckets, and a half-dozen people standing laughing together. A woman who was talking to Lady Bardo wore the only diamond stomacher Francis had ever actually seen. Turning on the threshold, Miss Imbrie said, "Stay and have a good time. I would if I were you."

Her look was one of liking. The grave lift of her eyes and the humorous line of her long mouth offered nothing so definite and solid as advice, which she would neither presume nor trouble to give; but, for a whim, she seemed to be intending a hint, based on some casual hunch, that he was free to take or leave.

"Very likely I will," said Francis, smiling. Of course there was nothing Miss Imbrie could, or, for that matter, would, do for him; but from her expression he had the pleasure of being able to guess that she found him not bad at all, and that, strictly aloof, amused, even ironic, she would at least not hinder any proper or reasonable designs he might have on her niece. Asking her to dance had been a good idea; and, pleased with her and feeling better about himself, Francis found his way to the buffet, where a footman served him with brandy and soda.

He stood aside, holding the glass and watching the crowd, listening to the music beat up to the caissoned Roman vault beyond the hall. Though not much good to dance to, it was that French music, hilarious to hear, whose master tune is called le jazz, or le fox trot. The drums and horns, no matter what they were supposed to be playing, abandoned it after the first bars and furiously struck up something that might or might not be the *"Sambre et Meuse,"* while the strings and piano set faintly against it American tunes of last year. Swallowing his drink, Francis set down the glass, and went with decision to cut back on Lorna.

At half past twelve supper was served in a sort of conservatory, a large room with a glass roof that seemed to be Lord Bardo's aquarium. The walls were lined with lighted tanks full of swimming fish, some unremarkable except perhaps to an ichthyologist, some extraordinary and

highly colored. The effect, for there was no direct light, was the disconcerting but beautiful one of thirty tables at the bottom of the sea. They
were arranged around a piscina, lit from below the water. Aquatic plants
and immense lily pads filled it, and there was nothing to keep the inattentive person from falling in. Francis wondered how soon someone would—
if not a guest, then perhaps a footman serving, or the young man who had
detached himself from the orchestra and, strolling around with a concertina, entertained them with songs.

By half past one nobody had fallen in. It was in fact apparent that the
party was fairly serious. The Prefect of the Department was present, and
officials of the municipality of Menton in what must be a body, and a
number of important-looking Monégasques, almost all wearing the
ribbon of the Order of Saint Charles. Francis had seen very few of them
dancing, but they had been sitting around all evening on the edges,
patronizing the buffet and greeting each other with dignity and satisfaction. They remained now with their cigars, their decorations, and their
dressed-up wives in the submarine glow below the fish tanks. Though the
orchestra was playing again, the singer with the concertina remained, too.
So did Francis and Gwen.

The young man from California, who seemed to be known as Goody
to his friends, had sat down to supper with them. He brought along a girl
named Emily, who was married, though not to him. She was large and
well made, with dark-reddish hair and the rounded, somewhat pasty
features and heavy eyelids that often go with such hair. Her voice sounded
as if she had laryngitis. At the sound, most men would prick up their
ears; and at sight of her, to most men various impure or improper
thoughts, whether welcome or unwelcome, would occur. It was plain that
she was not sober, and also plain that she either was, or would soon be, a
confirmed alcoholic, for she showed the characteristic stuporous amiability
that comes from adding a great deal of fresh alcohol to a system more or
less permanently saturated with it. Tomorrow morning or afternoon she
would wake up with no idea, or only the haziest, of where she had spent
the evening. From certain small indications—a swelling of his face when
he looked at her, and an unconscious shifting in his chair—the Californian
left little doubt that he was nowadays the man she frequently found in her
bed when she did wake up.

He—this Kirkland—though drinking plenty was not at all drunk.
Heated by an inadvertent thought or glance, he would forget himself,
look popeyed an instant at Emily and move his big frame in the guile-
lessly indecent squirm. Then he would recover, be ingenuously worried
about what Emily might take it into her head to say or do next. He was
friendly to Francis, polite to Gwen and Lorna, and, in a manly, frank,

western way, respectful to Mr. McKellar, and to Miss Imbrie, who had joined them soon after they sat down.

Kirkland must be rich; he was assuredly simple, for this seductively rounded slob Emily obviously looked exotic and exciting to him—the kind of passionate and tragic fatal woman found drunk in France in one or two recent novels. What his art was like Francis couldn't guess; but he had the diffidence sometimes seen in a big man brought up as an athlete—it seemed that he had rowed a year or two ago in one of the great University of California crews—who discovers or thinks he discovers (and it is almost always too late) that his real interests are intellectual or artistic. He sat around humbly regretting the sane and wholesome way he had wasted his youth.

All this amused and interested Francis, and he was not offended by Kirkland's show of regard for him as a genuine author; but he could easily have done without him and his girl; and he did not like it when, the orchestra having begun to play again, and some man having come up to dance with Emily—she rose in a kind of sagging trance, just not slumping against him—Kirkland asked Lorna to dance. Mr. McKellar said, "Well, Mabel, shall we tread a measure?"

"Part of one, perhaps," Miss Imbrie said, and they arose, too.

Subduing his annoyance, which he had no right to feel—this was only the second time Kirkland had danced with Lorna—Francis said to Gwen, "I guess I'm stuck with you."

"And how!" Gwen said. He made to rise, but she clapped a hand on his wrist. "Sit still!" she said in a loud whisper. "Give a girl a break! If you must know, I've just got my shoes off. Oh, why did I buy those damned things! They looked so sweet. I'll probably have to go home barefoot. All right, laugh. I wish you had them on. Give me a cigarette."

Francis gave her one. "Look," he said, "just as a matter of curiosity, who is this pie-eyed Emily, and why?"

"Her name is Hartpence," Gwen said. "Mrs. Hartpence. She goes around with Goody. There's a very big important scandal about her. D'you think she's good-looking? I don't. Though I will say her clothes are gorgeous."

"Goody!" said Francis. "It's true, then. Do you have to call him that?"

"Oh, do I?" said Gwen. She rolled her eyes. "That could be my man. Beautiful blond beast." She drank some champagne. "Oh, my poor feet! Do you think anyone would mind if I went and sat with them in the pool?"

"I think everyone would mind," Francis said. "That's the Chief of Police, right over there. He—"

"Oh, he's going to sing again!" Gwen cried. She clapped her hands hard and the man with the concertina inclined his head toward her.

"Sh!" said Francis. "Do you want to wake up in Buenos Aires? I'll have to take that glass away from you."

"I wish you would. Think how my head is going to ache tomorrow! No, please, please! I want it."

"Reason subdues the appetites, as usual—" Francis began.

"No, I want to listen! I want to learn the words!" She clenched her hands and shook them in front of her. "Oh, he sings so fast!" She seized Francis's arm. "What was it after that? What was that?"

"Modesty," Francis said, "forbids—"

"Oh, I'll bet you didn't get it, either! What did she have—*petons?*"

"Feet," said Francis. "You know, like yours. Itsy-bitsy ones. Then, well, she had also *tout petits tétons, que*—"

"*Tétons?*"

"Let it suffice," Francis said, "that most women do have them. In moments, I suppose more or less intimate, he says he was in the habit of —well, *que je tâtais à tâtons*. Didn't they teach you any French at college? It's the language of art, diplomacy, and the passions."

"What's this about passions?" Mr. McKellar said. He let himself grandly down in the next chair. "I have been deserted," he said. "Tell me about passions."

"They are a closed book to me," Francis said. "I was just trying to spare Gwen's modesty while still giving her some idea of what he's singing."

"My dear Ellery," said Mr. McKellar. He shook his head. "Have you yet to learn that women know no modesty? Well, I can't pretend that I found it out any quicker. You presume to imagine that you can spare Gwen's modesty? Never believe it. Of course, it's you that makes her blush—"

"On the contrary," said Francis, who did not feel in the mood for an oration, "she practically made me blush."

"In a word, in a word!" said McKellar, and he saw that he was going to get the oration anyway. "Being male, you suffer from false modesty, and of course there is no other kind. You make her blush. If she likes you, she knows enough about men to know that she will have to blush to oblige you. If she doesn't like you, she blushes because a blush serves to bring up your own fatuous notions about modesty, and so may keep you from being a nuisance. At heart Gwen never blushed in her life. Do not confuse it with chastity. Chastity is innocent of affectation. Hamlet says to Ophelia: 'Lady, shall I lie in your lap?' She answers: 'No, my lord.' He says: 'I mean, my head in your lap.' She says: 'Ay, my lord.' 'Do you think,' says he, 'I meant country matters?' She says: 'I think nothing, my lord.' How exquisitely right! Like Gwen's, her chastity is as clear as day."

"I am as modest as anything," Gwen said. "And if you have to talk about chastity, would you just as soon not talk about mine? It makes me feel like one of those articles on should a bride confess, or that last lecture in freshman hygiene."

"My dear child," said Mr. McKellar, "I apologize!" Fondly, he patted her hand. "I was carried away on the high tide of allocution. When I meet a young man of wit and sense, like Ellery, I feel a great obligation to hand on my hard-won store of wisdom and experience. From my faltering hand, may he catch the torch—"

That was right, Francis realized. Mr. McKellar had been a little carried away; and not altogether by allocution or any other intellectual disturbance. Francis drank the rest of the champagne in his glass. His mind, which seemed gradually to have taken on the same gold tone as the wine, moved distinct and lucid. Poor old man, he thought, for in his genial comprehension or understanding a mellow mild pity, without disgust at others or distress to himself, ruffled the moment's smiling surface. Mr. McKellar ought to pay more attention to Lucretius. *Conviva recedis. . . .* Here Mr. McKellar sat at the table, the litter of the supper on it, half the people gone, and bent his cavernous eyes on Gwen. "Now, come and dance with me," he said.

"Eric, I can't," Gwen said. "My damned pink slippers are killing me." She wailed. "There. They're on," she said to Francis. "But it's no use. I won't be able to endure it. Do you know, I'm going to have to go home with Aunt Mabel."

"Well, maybe we ought all to cut along," Francis said. "The truth is, I've got to be on the job tomorrow morning."

"Nonsense, nonsense!" cried Mr. McKellar. "Let her go down and get more slippers and come back. Any girl worth her salt danced out six pairs an evening in the good old days."

It was, Francis told himself, as though the Ancient Mariner, instead of detaining pleasure-seekers for an edifying homily, were, at sound of the loud bassoon, to cut a caper; and, far from preferring a walk to the kirk, made tracks for the merry din where he only hoped they wouldn't go home until morning. Francis hesitated.

"More champagne!" said Gwen.

"You little drunkard!" said Francis. He pulled the bottle out of the pail and poured her some. Abstracted, he was still hesitating, trying to weigh his own desires, so he poured himself some. He did not want to stay up all night, especially with no chance of outstaying Mr. McKellar, and certainly no chance here of getting Lorna to himself. The thought

held him up; as though something in all this, going contrary to his experience, did not make sense; and then he recognized it. Did he really suppose Lorna so lacking in resource that, if she wanted him to get her alone,
she would not easily arrange it? Turning the stem of the glass slowly
around in his fingers, watching the fine bubbles come up, he began to
think how little Lorna here was like Lorna as she had been in Paris.

For one thing, she did not sound the same; indeed, she said almost
nothing—what, after all, could she say, since he himself (if not because of
Mr. McKellar or Miss Imbrie or Gwen; then because of the racket of dance
music or the expectation that someone would cut in on him) had certainly
said little. "I've got to do something about this," he thought suddenly.
"All this damned nonsense—" One thing he could do was let Gwen and
Miss Imbrie go, wait an hour or so for them to get to bed and asleep,
dodge Mr. McKellar, and see if Raymond, who would probably be sent
back for them, wouldn't in consideration of a hundred francs run them
down and go back again for Mr. McKellar. Mr. McKellar might not like
it, but Francis had had enough of Mr. McKellar anyway. "Well," he said
aloud, "I know better; but I've never done it yet."

"Bravo!" said Mr. McKellar. "Youth at the helm and pleasure at the
prow!"

At half past two Miss Imbrie and Gwen left, but not without putting
a hitch in Francis's plan. He came out to the portico with Mr. McKellar
to see them off, and Miss Imbrie said: "Eric, I believe I'll let Raymond go
to bed. Telephone to that place in Monte and get them to send for you
when you want to go, will you? I know they're open all night."

Re-entering the great hall with Mr. McKellar, Francis saw that he
would have to discover where this place in Monte-Carlo was, and do some
telephoning of his own. Kirkland would be very likely to know. Francis
found him having a drink by the buffet.

"Well, old boy," he said to Francis rather boisterously. "How is it?"
He clapped him with warmth on the shoulder.

Francis did not know just when they had got to be such good friends;
but it was after all complimentary, and if Kirkland liked him as much as
that, Francis in return found the circumstances a reason for liking Kirkland. He took a drink, too, and asked him if he had any idea where this
place in Monte-Carlo was.

"Why, hell!" Kirkland said. He began to feel in his pockets. He produced some keys. "Got a car outside there," he said. "Take the damn
thing, why don't you? Red Renault. The chasseur will get it for you."

"Thanks a lot," Francis said, evading this happy-go-lucky generosity, "but I want to go home. I hear there's some place in—" God alone
knew what it would cost him, and he wondered if Kirkland wouldn't be

just as ready to lend him, instead of a car, five hundred francs, which would be enough to put him on the safe side.

Kirkland still held out the keys. "No, look, Francis," he said. "Take it. I wish you would. Emily's got a car up here. She's putting some of us up."

"No, honestly," Francis said. "I don't have a *permis de conduire*."

"You don't need one. Nobody ever bothers you. If they do, mine's in the side pocket. Take it. I don't want to leave it here. Where are you staying? Cap d'Ail? I'm near Eze. Run the girls up for a cocktail tomorrow afternoon—they know where it is—and I'll drive you back. How's that?"

"I—" began Francis, for this was insane. He couldn't possibly go to Eze tomorrow afternoon—unless, of course, having the car he used it first to take Walter up to show him the Ligurian trophy at La Turbie—after all, an educational thing to do. Lorna and Gwen might go along, too. Afterward they could run over to Eze and deliver the car. Walter would be enchanted.

"All right," Francis said. "Much obliged. I'll take care of it." He slid the keys into his waistcoat pocket.

III

Slowly, with caution, Francis turned the Renault up the long cypress avenue. He knew how the gearshift worked, for he had driven one a few times in Brittany the summer before; but this was probably a later model, and the clutch action was different—or he was nervous, for he had trouble getting it out of neutral. He had given the chasseur ten francs for acting as though the infernal, embarrassing screeches he evoked were perfectly natural and due to the wickedness of the machine and not to Francis. In the dark he said to Lorna, "If this were my car, I'm damned if I'd let myself drive it." But that might alarm her, and he added, "I've got it now. It was just a battle of wills. It is gentle as a lamb." He glanced aside, saw far below the wink of the pharos on the Menton breakwater. "Left," he said. "That's right. We'll pick up the Corniche at Roquebrune. Raymond gave me a lecture on geography coming up. Are you going to be warm enough?"

"I'm all right. You ought to have a coat."

"Over here I would have died long ago if exposure could kill me. Though as a matter of fact, this is about the same latitude as Portland, Maine; and I don't think they go driving there on January nights in open cars."

"Is it?" said Lorna.

"Look here," said Francis, "do you feel cold?"

"I'm all right. I think we should have told Eric."

"Your friend Goody will tell him when he needs to know. I simply didn't dare tell him. He'd probably come along. You aren't seriously worried about that, are you? He's old enough to go home by himself—" He made a turn and said, "Now this ought to be Roquebrune. It is. *Sens Unique*. It would be. We'll try through here. Do you suppose everyone is dead? Look, see that? The iron balconies. Isn't that charming?"

He was shivering a little. January night in the latitude of Portland, Maine, was right! "Ah," he said, "there's the Corniche. That's pretty good, if I do say so." Bending his head he brushed her cold cheek with his lips.

"You don't have to do that," she said.

"Did you say," said Francis, letting the car slow down, "that I didn't have to do that?"

"Yes."

"Would you just as soon tell me what you mean?"

"It seems perfectly clear. You don't have to. And I wish you wouldn't."

Francis cast his eyes around. Up came a neat sign, *Défense de Stationner*. "To hell with them!" he said. "No, wait."

The curve of an observation point bent out in the starlight and he turned the car sharp, jerked it up with the headlight shafting over the parapet into space. Cutting the engine and the lights, he took her angrily in his arms.

"No, please," said Lorna. "I want to go home. No, Francis. I don't want you to."

"What is this nonsense?" said Francis. Angrier still, he kissed her with indignation, repeatedly and hard. "You're hurting me," she said between her teeth.

"You must have been reading a book," Francis said. "I'm not hurting you."

"Oh, Francis. Please. It's so stupid. What's the good of kissing me?"

"None," said Francis shortly, letting her go. "If you feel that way."

"It isn't the way I feel. That doesn't matter. I won't tell you about that. It would just be so much easier if you'd—"

"If I'd what?"

"If you'd let me alone, drop it. I would like to know one thing. Why did you go to so damned much trouble with me? Was it for fun?"

Speechless, Francis searched for cigarettes. When he found them, he lit one, held it out to her, and lit another. "Now, let's get this straight," he said slowly. "What's to be let alone? What was so damned much trouble? What was fun?"

He paused, his effort to be reasonable wilting a little in the face of the phrase 'just for fun.' He knew what that was. That was something from the fantastic female world of the emotions, with its usually low romantic taste, its unpredictable fancies, its folklore of pursuit and marriage by capture, its cherished fairy tales of Cinderella, of Beauty and the Beast. The never-quite-adult habit of a woman's thought—no doubt actually believed that, just for fun, just for a practical joke on a trusting little girl, men went to so damned much trouble—checked him. She ought to have been exempt from nonsense. The wonderfully clear intelligent cast of her blue eyes ought to have meant a clearness of sight that recognized the world as it was, not—*The hours I spent with thee, dear heart, are as a string of pearls to me*—as it was sung. "It's a hard thing to phrase," he said. "It's so ridiculous. But are you trying to tell me that I am tired of you, or something like that? That"—he couldn't resist the temptation—"I forgot to remember?"

Instantly Francis regretted it, penitent, even frightened; for the cheap strains of that music might be taken with reason as a mortal insult. He did not know, unless it was the injury of an obscure insult offered him, how he had been driven to say it. Francis opened his mouth to cry out that he never meant that; but she said first, with what would have to be described as a little laugh, "That's about it, I guess."

"So you think that's about it." He sat appalled, looking at her. He looked at the beautiful hollow face, the gold wrap and the tied scarf. For a moment there seemed to be nothing he could say. Trembling a little, he felt the sharp cold of the air. Then slowly he said: "It's not true." For it was not. Ah, she could have it her way, on her terms! "You will have to tell me why you thought it was."

"What is there to tell?" she said. "When I wrote you from Paris, the day you went to Italy—you see, it was very serious to me. I didn't want— I'm trying to say, I suppose, that I'm a kind of coward. I don't want to be hurt. If I hadn't thought that—" She stopped. "What's the use?"

"If you hadn't thought that what?" said Francis, putting the cigarette to his lips. By holding his arms close against him he felt the cold less.

"I don't know. Paris was marvelous. It was the happiest time I ever had in my life." She drew a breath. "I suppose nothing would ever be like that again. You see, it meant more to me—well, I decided long ago I wasn't going to care about anyone. It's not worth it."

"I see," said Francis. He looked at his cigarette end with a kind of anguish. The remark, so silly, so fatuous even, cut him with terrible tenderness, a sort of quick killing of any scorn or derision. It must be love, for how would mere liking ever survive the blow of getting to know these things a person really thought?

She said, "I loved your letters. They were so sweet and funny. I was in heaven when I knew you really were coming down. I suppose I expected something. Well—"

"I see," repeated Francis. Reaching out, he took her hand. "Sweet and funny." A contraction of pain or nervousness nearly made him laugh. "And when I got here I was only funny," he said.

"Yes," she said steadily. "The other kind of funny. You were so funny Monday night. And then I didn't see you for days. When you got into the car you gave me a kind of stare, and then you began to laugh and tease Gwen."

"Do you know what I was thinking then?" said Francis. "Do you know why I—"

"No, I want to tell you. When we came downstairs I thought perhaps I was being silly. And when we danced, you said that about Goody. You see, I haven't any sense. I didn't know how it was done. You'd dance with me now and then, and laugh and go away—"

"When somebody cuts in, what else can you do?" said Francis. "Knock him down? If you want to know, I damn near did knock down that spick—"

"And then at supper," she said, "you did nothing but talk to Gwen. And stayed there with her afterward—"

"Good God!" said Francis. "I thought you liked Gwen."

"I adore her."

"So I supposed," he said. "And the only reason I paid her any attention was because she was your friend." The way he heard himself saying it, in tones of self-justification, of having an explanation for everything, was futile and depressing—not sweet and funny, it wasn't even fair to Gwen. Attending Gwen was no chore. If it came to being sweet and funny (or was he just paying back the vexation of being told that he had changed for the worse?) Lorna could not be called, since he had been at Cap d'Ail, very sweet and funny herself. Gwen had been ten times as entertaining, if you wanted entertainment. Only he didn't love Gwen, and that very fact— "I can believe that you don't know how it's done," Francis said. "I can only tell you it isn't that way. You can't have been jilted very often. I can only tell you that I am serious, that this is serious. You don't know how serious. You must learn about that—"

But did he think the matter could be explained in a short lecture, that she would learn by precept? One more asseveration and the girl is mine? He put an arm around her and she made no resistance. He kissed her, and she rested passive a moment, as though measuring her own reaction. She drew a breath then, returned the kiss with a quick firm air of stopping him, of giving him what he wanted as a matter of policy to forestall any possible use of force. "We'd better go home," she said.

"Not yet," said Francis. "I don't think I can leave it like this." His tone was dispirited. Despite his anxiety, he was tremulous with cold, and tired.

"It's late. It must be five o'clock."

"I don't care what time it is."

Meant to show masterful ardor it was plainly so poor an imitation that she shook her head. "Please," she said. "I get to a certain stage where things don't seem real to me." She spoke with nervous weariness. "It isn't I, any more. I might say something I'd be sorry for. Do let's go home."

"All right," Francis said.

He did not know whether he was making a mistake or not. She could be, herself, mistaken. She might only think that she wanted to be taken home and left alone. To his past faults of failing to amuse her, of leaving her last fall in Paris, of not seeing her since Monday night, he might be adding now the inexpiable one of doing nothing, of letting her have her way.

"All right," he repeated. Though this generally understood danger filled him with still more anxiety, no answering resolve arose to meet it. What he felt, looking at her dim face, was not desire but an extreme painful dejection; and he was so cold that he could not think carefully about it. He jabbed the switch on. The awakened engine roared up, and he craned back over his shoulder. A solitary pair of headlights was coming up fast, so he waited in silence to let them go by.

Near La Turbie he picked the wrong turn, for they came presently into steep vacant streets and faced an octroi sign: *Principauté de Monaco*. "God damn it to hell!" Francis said. He swung right, but the next curve began to turn him uphill, and he went right again. The cobblestones dropped off as steep as the roof of a house, and he slammed his brakes on, got into low, and crawled down with a great racket between echoing close-packed house fronts. What they reached seemed to be a sort of high viaduct. Below at a distance he could see the pattern of occasional lights around the mass of the castle beyond La Condamine, so at least he wasn't too far west yet.

"I know where we are," Lorna said. "Just keep going. You'll see a church in a minute. Yes, down there."

But she was wrong, for they ran into a sort of park. "I'm sorry," she said. "I shouldn't interfere. I just thought that looked like—"

"Well, this is the tramline," Francis said. "It runs behind the hotel sooner or later. You were pretty nearly right. There's the corner."

The exchange of listless, formal sentences echoed in his head. He put out a hand and laid it on her leg. "It's all right," he said. "You'll be in bed in a minute." He took his hand back quickly, afraid that she would mistake the touch's meaning.

They went down past the long curved garden walls. "There you are," he said at last. He saw the street lamp that he remembered as the one he had seen snow falling past Monday night. A light shone in the elaborate door and he halted the car. "Key?" he said.

She felt in her evening bag and gave it to him. Stepping out on the curb, Francis saw that it was starting to get light; the darkness was dimmer; the heavy roof of the house was darker than the sky. "It's morning," he said. He slid the key into the lock and turned it.

"I'm sorry about tonight," Lorna said. "Francis."

"Yes." He looked at her in the gloom of the overhanging entry, and then he kissed her. The lipsticked lips were cold; but she smiled, tightening them with pain or tiredness. "Good night," she said. "Ah, darling, don't let me be that way!"

SEVEN

It was half past six when Francis got to bed. He was called at eight o'clock; but to his surprise he did not feel particularly sleepy. He was no sooner awake than his thoughts were animated with a nervous cheerfulness. The temporary possession of Kirkland's car enlivened his mind with plans and schemes. He had left it in the drive, and when he had dressed he went down with a certain importance to speak to the concierge. "I brought that Renault in last night," he said. "I'll give you the keys if you want to have it moved somewhere else. I won't be using it until this afternoon."

Punctually at nine o'clock he knocked on the door of Mrs. Cunningham's sitting room with that active sense, a little distorted by fatigue, of successfully managing many arrangements.

"Wild party?" said Walter.

"Not very," Francis said.

"Good morning, Francis," Mrs. Cunningham said. "Did you have a nice time?"

"Very pleasant," Francis said. "But as a result I am stuck with a car. It belongs to a California fellow who was going home with some other people. He asked me if I'd take it for him. It's rather awkward because I can't get rid of it until this afternoon late. I drove"—he found that he did not want to say simply Lorna, so he said—"the girls down, and I had to bring it up here. Though as a matter of fact, I thought it might be handy. If you hadn't any other plans, I thought I might run Walter up to La Turbie this afternoon. He ought to see the monument. We could go over to Eze then, where this fellow lives. He'd drive us back and drop us."

"Who is he?" said Mrs. Cunningham.

"Well, actually, I have no idea," Francis said. "He's a friend of Miss Imbrie's. I hardly knew what to say when he asked me if I'd take the car. It's down in the drive and—"

"Let's see it!" said Walter.

"No," Francis said, "we have some work to do now."

"Well, Francis, if you're sure it's quite safe. Aren't you afraid something will happen to it?"

"Well, no, I'm really not," Francis said. "I drove one like it a good deal last summer. I think it's just possible that it's safer with me than it is with him." He smiled to show that any sound of self-esteem his remark might have was not serious, but that she need feel no uneasiness about Walter.

"Hurray!" said Walter.

"You wouldn't be very late, would you?"

"Oh, no. I explained to him. The girls were going up there to tea, and I said we'd run them up, but we'd have to come down." He felt at ease, and spoke easily, but Francis could not help experiencing a moment's hesitation, since he had now, in effect, uncovered his hand; and the various harmless half-truths or evasions of choice that he had used in proposing the expedition might, some or all, be plain to her.

"Well, I think that would be all right," Mrs. Cunningham said. "As it happens, Mr. and Mrs. Peters are coming to dinner here, instead of our going there to luncheon. I wouldn't want Walter to be late." With discomfort Francis saw that, at least in a small way, he had put his foot in it, for the matter of the Peterses had slipped his mind altogether, and Mrs. Cunningham must naturally see that it had. She said, "When were you picking up the girls?"

"I thought when we started," Francis said, no longer easy. That had been very stupid of him, and there was no possible way to repair it now. "It won't hurt them to go to La Turbie," he said as casually as he could, "and that would save time."

"Yes. Walter should have his nap, I think. That would give you time to go down and pick them up." She paused thoughtfully, and Francis wondered, with some alarm, if she were going to observe, surely with asperity, that, since he was in this situation with the car that wasn't his, and had engaged himself the way he had described, it might be simpler if he didn't take Walter. However, she said, "All right, darling" to Walter, gathered up some letters and went from the room.

At the shop door hung a wire rack of picture postcards. Glancing at them, Francis lifted one out and gave it to Walter. It was divided vertically. One half showed the Ligurian trophy in conjectured restoration, a vast polygonal pile, tier on tier of columns and bas-reliefs, friezes and mold-ings, and on the top platform, the crowning colossal statue of Augustus. The other half contained the lines of the inscription pieced out from the discovered fragments and Pliny's text. "There you are," he said.

Walter looked at it. Then he looked across the road to the battered part of a tower rising on the sunny dilapidated mound of broken brick and stone, with an enclosure around it and the roofs of mean houses clos-ing up one side. "Gosh!" he said. He held it out politely to Lorna. "It's Latin," he said.

"So I see," said Lorna. "Can you read it?"

"Gosh, no," Walter said sheepishly.

"Oh, yes you could," said Francis. "It begins with the titles of the Emperor, and then the list of the conquered tribes. One or two of them are old friends of yours—well, we'll let you off this time."

Walter returned it to the rack hastily. To Lorna, he said, "Did you have to learn Latin?"

"As a matter of fact, I did," Lorna said. "I even used to act in Latin plays at college. So did Gwen."

"You mean a real play? I'll bet it sounded crazy."

"It did at that," said Gwen. "How young we were then!" They were walking on, and she added, "How young I'd be still if I hadn't clothed myself from head to foot with the apparent idea that we were bound for Baffin Bay. I don't mind saying it is hot."

Below the escaping tendrils of sandy hair a delicate sweat shone on her forehead. "It seems to me," Francis said, "that every time I meet you you are complaining about what you have on. I've read somewhere that the poor workman quarrels with his tools."

"Oh, you have, have you? How would you like to have your shins kicked?" She slid a hand inside her jacket experimentally. "Oh, dear," she said. "I can't take it off."

"Why not?" said Francis. "You seem to have an adequate undercov-ering."

"Because," she said, "it was impressed on me as a child that nice girls do not sweat. I do. I am. Look at Lorna. There is how a nice girl ought to look."

Francis looked at Lorna. She was walking slowly ahead with Walter, who limped along pursuing the incredible but interesting subject of the Latin plays. "You mean nobody says anything except in Latin?" he asked. Lorna wore white, a white silk jumper and pleated skirt with a white coat over her shoulders. It was something she must have got with the notion that it was really warm here. For the moment, in the full afternoon sun, it made her look as it was meant to, wonderfully fresh and cool.

"Come on," said Francis, realizing that he was again, no matter how casually or indifferently, laughing and teasing Gwen. "We'll give you a good airing." They approached the car.

"In Switzerland," Walter was saying, "they have soldiers who go on skis."

"And they speak Latin," Francis said, compelled to laugh by the process of association that made Walter return for one fantastic circumstance another one.

"Ah," said Walter, "they speak French. Or German." He began to giggle. "You ought to hear Frank speak German," he observed.

"Yes, you ought to," Francis said. "You let Lorna sit in front with me. She'll have to show me how we go. Tell Gwen about coming down from Alpiglen. She feels warm, and she's one of the best female skiers in Europe."

"Say, are you?" cried Walter.

"I am not," Gwen said. "I couldn't ski a foot."

"I'll bet you could," Walter said encouragingly. "Gosh, you know Helen, my sister? She could even ski. It's easy. We met these English fellows—"

Francis smiled, feeling his heavy eyelids stick a little. The sunlight lay in a haze over the mountain slopes. In Monte-Carlo below the glistening blocks of the big hotels, the clear white shape of the Casino with its towers, the patches of park, the wide but short asphalt strips of palm-lined boulevards, though small in perspective, looked closer, and he saw that the majestic sweep of lights last night was only an illusion.

Francis stood an instant, staring, bemused. His muscles with no rest to speak of for thirty-two or -three hours took what they could now by making him postpone slightly every movement. Vague sad thoughts of this coast, covered, below the then resplendent trophy, with villas two thousand years ago, much as it was covered now, weighed down his mind. He felt about two thousand years old himself.

Gwen said to Walter, "You and Goody must get together. He knows a place back of Nice somewhere where they have skiing."

"Is it far?" said Walter. "Is it—"

Close to Lorna as he opened the door for her, Francis murmured: "You look enchanting." Surprised, for he had not planned to say it, he saw that she was surprised, too. An instant tinge of color showed on her cheekbones. "My dear," she said, "thank you."

Simultaneously their eyes made a move to see whether his remark had reached Walter or Gwen; but it had not, and so they both laughed. "Why couldn't we go there?" said Walter. "Gosh, I wish we—could I ask him?"

"I don't see why not," Gwen said.

Francis started the car.

"He's sweet, isn't he?" Lorna said under the mounting sound of the motor. "Don't you think his mother would let him?"

The damp dark stone stairs came down into a big low vaulted room, perhaps a couple of cellars made into one. There was a cavernous overhung fireplace with the embers of a fire in one part of it. On the whitewashed stone hung paintings of various sizes, probably by Kirkland, in cheap wood frames. A great scarlet cope was spread out on one wall. To Lorna, Francis murmured, "They must have shot a bishop last week and skinned him."

She did not hear.

Kirkland introduced a man named Frost, who by his speech was a Southerner, and who seemed to be living there, too. Francis guessed that Frost was another artist and that they rented the farmhouse together.

Whatever had happened since three o'clock this morning Kirkland was a good deal the worse for. His blunt strong frank face was puffed and tumid, his blue eyes bloodshot; but he seemed to remember that he and Francis were old friends. He kept cordially taking him by the arm, and through him including the girls and Walter in haphazard introductions to people already there. "Mrs. Farr," he said to a fat woman, "Miss Higham. You and Gwen know each other, don't you? And Mr. Ellery. And Mr.—er—Cunningham—" Dazed, but plainly delighted by this description, Walter was very polite. "Justin Gourbeyre," Kirkland said with the conscious accenting of syllables that showed the names were supposed to be important, well-known ones, "and Fred Armingeat—"

As far as Francis went, the names meant nothing, and the immediately observable fact was that they were a couple of French fairies. Kirkland closed his hand on Francis's arm again and said, "You've met Emily—Mrs. Hartpence."

"Yes," said Francis.

She smiled at him in a friendly, abandoned way. Finding it, as usual, hard to dislike anyone who smiled at him, Francis moved off, resisting, too, the irritating difficulty, really, the impossibility, of looking at Mrs. Hartpence for more than a moment without thoughts of her undressed or in bed. "Some drinks are coming," Kirkland said.

Mrs. Farr cried out, "Now, Goody, I want my tea. Young Mr. Cunningham must come and sit by me, and we'll have tea like civilized human beings." Her voice was shrill and her ruddled cheeks repellent; but Walter was gratified. He limped over and sat down with shy covert glances around him. Mrs. Farr said something to him and he turned civilly and answered, blushing a little, but composed.

At the end of the room, doors stood open on a terrace under a pergola supporting the branches of an enormous bare grapevine. The worn stone blocks of the paving were littered with many old leaves. An empty stone conduit ran along to an open cistern half full of stagnant water. You could look right across at Eze, the compact round of walls and roofs crowning the little summit, lit with sunset against the distant low hills and long narrow harbor of Villefranche in diaphanous shadow a few miles away and a thousand feet below. "Look at that," Francis said to Lorna.

She stepped out the door with him and they stood near the parapet. In the air was a faint smell of smoke and a faint keen chill, like the end of a fine October day. Closing his hand over hers, Francis said at last, "You don't want to stay very long, do you? Walter and I will have to get down. It's quarter to five."

He stopped. Tightening his fingers on her hand, he said, "At quarter to five this morning we were having a discussion up on the hill, you may remember. There hasn't been a chance to say anything to you about that. What I am going to say now is this. I don't want to hear any more nonsense." He spoke peremptorily, out of a numbness of fatigue that simplified everything by leaving him no patience or energy to waste on doubts or alternatives. "I am going to take care of you. I have not decided exactly how; but never mind that. I am. And you are to be a good girl, and behave yourself, and not make a lot of difficulties. Do you understand?"

"Yes," she said, looking at Eze.

"Yes, what?" said Francis.

She switched her head sharply, looking at him. She began to laugh. "Yes, please," she said. Her eyes glinted with an abrupt crowding-up of tears. Twisting in his, her hand turned over, clutching his fingers. "Ah, Francis! Nobody was ever so sweet to—"

"Now, now!" Francis said. "Come along." His tiredness gave him the sensation of being partly disembodied, in buoyant tranquillity, in clear, happy lightheadedness. "I must keep an eye on Walter. God knows what he's making of that obscene tramp Emily, and that pair of *tapettes* in the corner. And more important, what he'll tell his mother."

Inside, several big candles had been lighted and there was a new log flaming on the embers. Thin disturbed veils of cigarette smoke floated toward the arched ceiling. Mrs. Farr, Francis saw, had been successful in getting her tea; and Walter, still very polite, nursed a hot cup. The taller of the two fairies was telling Gwen something in French. Kirkland was nowhere around, but the Frost man came up at once. "Now, Lorna," he said, "what you need is a great many Martinis right away." The fairies, Francis decided, must be friends of his. "Mr. Ellery, what will you have? There's brandy, Scotch—"

"Is Goody around somewhere?" Francis said. "I'm afraid we'll have to go pretty soon, thanks."

"Oh, but do have a drink. As a matter of fact, Goody ran Fred Armingeat down to their place to get a bottle of absinth. Emily wanted some. I'm sure he won't be long."

Francis found it on the tip of his tongue to say, though as a joke only, for he felt remote, beyond annoyance: "Aren't you jealous?" He managed not to. Turning to a refectory table under the big candles, Frost poured out a cocktail and gave it to Lorna. "Darling," said Gwen, "Monsieur Gourbeyre says that—"

"I'll have some Scotch, if I may," said Francis.

At quarter to six Kirkland had not returned. To get down to the hotel would probably take less than half an hour, so if they left at six, it would be time enough. If they left much later than six— Francis said to Lorna, "If he doesn't show up pretty soon, I'm going to be in a jam. Mrs. Cunningham is having people to dinner." Frost was passing, and Francis said to him, "You don't know when Goody's getting back, do you?"

"Why, I'm sure he said he'd be back. I'll ask Emily again." Mrs. Hartpence was leaning against the wall by the scarlet cope, holding a glass and looking up at a thickset dark man who stared with absorption down the front of her dress as he talked. When Frost spoke to her she shrugged, closed her eyes a moment, and said clearly, "I don't know where the son of a bitch is!"

Walter, eating a cookie, started; for it was unlikely that he had ever heard a lady use the expression before. To Lorna, Francis said, "I wish Mrs. Hartpence would be a little less forthright. With one thing and another, Walter is getting an earful. For all I know, that aged harridan is telling him dirty stories. I'd better see, I guess." He stood up and went over there; but Mrs. Farr proved to be telling Walter, to his vast interest, about the training of dogs, Saint Bernards and Great Pyrenees, that were company mascots in some of the Chasseurs Alpins regiments. They were making a great hit with each other. As soon as Walter saw him, he said, "Frank, I found out where it is. Mrs. Farr knows."

Mrs. Farr showed Francis a haggard smile. "He wants to go to Peira Cava," she said. "I know Goody's been up. It's a *petite station de sports d'hiver*—" Her accent was very French. "One of the Chasseur regiments has a big barracks there. I was just telling him about their wonderful dogs."

"Well, that's very kind of Mrs. Farr," Francis said to Walter. "We'll have to see what your mother thinks—" Though the Scotch he had drunk proved, as far as exhilarating him went, about as effective as so much water, and it was impossible to doubt that he was cold sober, Francis found slight embarrassing difficulties in enunciation. Exhaustion alone, or alcohol alone, would not do it; but against both of them together, the effort to speak clearly was trying. "We must run along in a moment," he said. "The trouble is that Mr. Kirkland isn't here. He was going to drive us down. I think I'd better see if I can telephone." He went back to Lorna, and Frost, who stood talking to her. "Emily doesn't seem to know," Frost said to him. "I—"

"So I heard," Francis said. "You don't happen to have a telephone, do you?"

"I'm afraid we don't. It's really quite primitive." He laughed. "I'm awfully sorry."

"Well, damn it all," said Francis ungraciously, "I don't know what to do. I've got to get down by half past six."

"Oh, well, it's only five or ten minutes of. I'm sure he'll be back. It doesn't take any time to get to Cap d'Ail."

"What is all the trouble?" said Mrs. Hartpence. She wandered up with her glass in her hand. By now she had drunk enough to be approaching what must be normal for her. "You want to get down? It's really too bad of Goody. They probably met some people. Take my car."

"Oh, God!" said Francis. "I mean, that's awfully good of you; but I can't take any more cars. I've just brought Goody's back." He sounded so ridiculous, the next thing to hysterical, that he had to laugh.

"There, there," Mrs. Hartpence said. Probably she supposed he was a little drunk. "Of course you can. If you just turned it loose it would come home by itself. Anyway, Pink can drive you down. Can't you, Pinckney darling?"

"Well, yes, I could," Frost said. "If you really must go."

"I hate to upset everything," Francis said. "But I have to get Walter home. I'd appreciate it very much if you'd come down with me and bring the car back."

Mrs. Hartpence regarded her glass a moment. With a casual underhand flip she shied it into the fireplace where it smashed loudly on the stone. Heads turned, and Walter, who had jumped, gaped at her. "Think nothing of it," she said. "I'll drive you down. And, Pink, just tell Goody he can go—" She apparently noticed Walter gaping, and stopped. "Come along," she said, and presented her back to them crossing the room.

To Frost, Francis said, staggered, "Well, I don't know. Can she drive?"

"Probably," said Frost. "But tell her you'll drive. Everybody does. She's very tiresome. I'm awfully sorry about all this. I hope you will come up again. It isn't this way all the time."

In the dark court Mrs. Hartpence had the engine started in an Italian car. Francis walked up and said firmly, "I'll drive." Without comment, Mrs. Hartpence slid herself over on the front seat. In the light of an iron lantern, Lorna gave him a smile. "All right, Walter?" Gwen said.

Francis made a gingerly experiment with the problem of what gear-shift this was going to be. For once at least, it worked right. The car moved and swung slowly out the arch. "Good!" said Francis. He turned to smile at Mrs. Hartpence, feeling that after all she was being a great help. The clock on the long glittering dashboard said quarter past six, which was all right. "This is awfully kind of you," he started to say; but Mrs. Hartpence, slumped down in a light-colored camel's-hair coat, was weeping. Her bruised-looking mouth worked in spasmodic twitches. The tears squeezed out her swollen eyes. With difficulty she said again: "Think nothing of it." Francis felt along the board until he found the light switch and snapped it out. "Thanks," she said.

In back, Walter said, "I found out where. It's Peira something. We're going to see if—"

Francis drove in silence. There must be a short cut straight down, but he did not want to risk looking for it, and if he went up to the Grande Corniche, he knew now where the Cap d'Ail road cut in toward La Turbie. Once he reached that he would have no trouble.

In the darkness Mrs. Hartpence continued to cry, shaking slowly with a succession of weak quiet sobs. Perhaps ten minutes had passed when the smooth fast flight of the car broke on a jolt, immediately succeeded by more and harder jolts. Startled, Francis threw out his clutch and got his brakes on. "Oh, what's that?" said Mrs. Hartpence faintly.

For any intelligence to convey itself into Francis's head took several seconds. The car came to a halt then, and he said, "Well, that's what's called a flat tire."

There were two spare wheels locked one on the other behind, but neither of them had enough air in it to support the car. Francis did not find this out until, having groveled underneath, got the jack placed and raised, and the flat tire exchanged for the first spare, he let the jack down, and the new tire, getting the car's weight on it, immediately flattened to the rim.

Francis, on his knees, with the loose handle of the jack in his hand, looked at it. The car was equipped—a piece of good fortune with which he had tried to tell himself he ought to be satisfied, for how would he like working in the dark, or by lighted matches, or a briquet flame?—with a spotlight, really a small searchlight, mounted on a nickeled post on the running board. In this glare, moistening his lips, which tasted of grease, he regarded the folded side of the heavy shoe. He trembled with anger. He shook in the demented fury with which the sentient mind encounters the cogent It-is, so much like hate or malice, of insentient things. With the jack handle in his hand he would have liked to beat the collapsed tire to death.

"Ah, gee!" cried Walter. "Say," he said to Mrs. Hartpence, "you haven't got any air in it!" The sound of his own indignant voice committing what he had been assured was the mortal sin of impoliteness to a lady scared him, and he amended it. "I guess they forgot to test it at the garage."

"Oh, God, how ghastly," said Mrs. Hartpence. She had been obliged to get out when he removed the tools and she leaned against the low stone wall, her tear-stained face lit by the glare, a cigarette between her lips. "How really awful!"

Francis could not bring himself to speak to her. It was just what you would expect in a car kept by a drunken moron. He could feel the weary slugging of his heart. The sweat ran down his chest and back. "Oh, Francis!" Lorna said. "I'm so sorry. Isn't there something we can do?"

"No, thanks," Francis said. "We'll try the other."

Getting up, he went and lifted it with difficulty from its position. Walter had taken the hub wrench and was attempting to apply it. "Wait," said Francis. "It isn't on the jack. And better let me do it. First, let's see what we have here."

Holding the wheel as high as he could, he let it drop on its tread. It bounced; but the casing was heavy, so that really told him nothing. "Hang on," he said. "Who's got a hairpin?"

Lorna lifted a hand to her head and held one out to him. It was a fortunate idea, for when he had depressed the valve, the contained air showed so little pressure that this, too, would certainly have collapsed.

Francis got up again.

"Has someone a cigarette?" he asked. He held up his blackened hands to show that he could not get at his own. "Here," said Lorna. Sliding one from her case she put it between his lips. "And here," said Gwen. She sheltered a flame for him.

Bending his head forward, Francis got the cigarette lit. "How gratifying!" he said. "Men must work and women must weep—" He laughed; but he was a little giddy and he shook his head to clear it. "Well, now I'll have to see if I can't get some help. There was a driveway into a place back there. It looked fairly fancy, so they'd probably have a telephone. I'm afraid there's nothing for it but to settle down and wait."

The clock on the dashboard said ten minutes to seven. He looked at his watch, and that said five minutes to. "I guess I'll go with you," Walter said.

"Better not," said Francis, "I—" He had nearly said, "—will have to keep moving." With the unsteady sense of catching it on the fly, he said, "I don't want to leave the girls alone here."

It was hard to believe that Walter could accept the idea that he was going to protect them; but seemingly he could and did. "O.K.," he said seriously. "That's right."

Francis found himself shaken by a light high silent hilarity, touched by Walter's tone, touched, too, by his own patience and good temper. Clearly, he surpassed himself. He stood off with astonishment and looked at himself with wonder.

The heavens were brilliant with clear stars, and the cold wind was pleasant on his face. Francis threw the cigarette away and walked faster, looking for a light.

"Francis," Mrs. Cunningham said, "I have been frantic with worry." She was quite white. "How could you not let me know?"

"Ah, Mother," said Walter, "it wasn't our fault. Frank had to walk about a hundred miles—" He had managed to get several smears of grease on his face, and one arm of his overcoat was covered with dust.

"Maggie," said Mrs. Cunningham. Francis had not noticed Maggie before. Mrs. Cunningham had come out of the lounge dressed for dinner, and Francis could see the people she had left, these Peterses, a stout important-looking old man and a soft stout woman, attempting politely to maintain some small talk with each other over the empty cocktail glasses on the stand before them while Mrs. Cunningham—Martha—handled this awkward misadventure in her own way. Maggie must have come down and been sitting inconspicuously in the passage, frantic, too, no doubt. Mrs. Cunningham said, "Take Walter upstairs, please."

"Mrs. Cunningham," Francis said, "I'm frightfully sorry. I really did all I could. I finally found a place where I could get a car. They didn't have a telephone, and since we could get home in fifteen minutes, it seemed a waste of time to stop anywhere."

"Oh, Francis," she said. "Why did you do it? You must have known when you left this place that—it's quarter past eight."

Francis shook his head. "We left at six o'clock," he said. "We had this flat tire, and there was no air in the spares—"

"Francis, I can't talk to you about it. My guests are here and I can't keep them waiting for dinner. I think you'd better go to bed. Did you get any sleep last night?"

"Oh, yes," Francis said, "I—"

"Well, we really will have to talk about it in the morning. I'm sorry to say it now, but you know I feel quite free to terminate this arrangement whenever it doesn't seem to be serving its purpose."

"Of course," said Francis.

"Well, go along now." Perhaps she found his appearance pitiable, for she said equably enough, "Good night."

"Good night," said Francis. "I'm really very sorry."

In his room he put the light on and began to pull off his clothes. His hands and, in the mirror he saw, his face, were very dirty. Stripped to his undershirt, he ran a basin full of hot water and began to lather his cheeks and neck. He would have to get a bath; but if he wanted anything to eat, he'd better arrange for it to be sent up before eight-thirty. With the dirt off, he discovered that he had skinned the knuckles of one hand. Feeling in his toilet case, he found a small bottle of iodine and painted them.

The exquisite sharp stinging made him wince, and clasping his wrist, he sat down on the bed. After a moment he got up, put on his bathrobe, and stood looking at the telephone. It did not seem worth the trouble. Wrapping the bathrobe around him, Francis snapped the light out, went and lay down on the bed. No special thought came to him, but he seemed to see, against the darkness, bloated and disfigured, Mrs. Hartpence's foolish face shining with her alcoholic tears.

"The unspeakable bitch!" he pronounced, and immediately he was asleep.

II

Hiding the hillside, a dense white mist hung in the still air. On the calm, subdued morning a few sounds—the clatter and low grind of a hidden tram; the soft bang and bump of movement somewhere down the hall —made the essential silence seem greater. It closed in sad and heavy like the damp gray air. Shaving by electric light, Francis paused from time to time, his heart failing him, looking himself in the eye with a settled anxiety, but no settled resolve.

He could go back to Florence, and there were reasons why he ought to. He could really work on his book, get it done—maybe in a couple of months. He made an effort to see himself industriously writing away all day and most of the night (like Balzac), to feel in anticipation the powerful satisfactions that a writer can count on occasionally feeling; but in fact Francis had already done enough writing to know that the writer feels most of the time something quite different, something no humane man would want his worst enemy to feel. To be in that hellhole Florence, without money of his own, without any hope—

He unfolded a clean shirt and pulled it on. He would go to Paris. It was not impossible to pick up a job on one of the English-language papers, for their staffs were always changing; and on one he knew a man who had been at school with him (where they had not liked each other particularly; but after all that was long ago, and during the summer Francis had run into him once or twice, and they had got on well enough). He did not say the chance was any less than desperate; but, if not desperate, what were his circumstances?

And if as desperate as that, why be so moderate?

Francis's heart began to beat more heavily. If he threw out so much of caution and common sense, why try to keep any of it? He stood still with a necktie in his hand. Why not marry Lorna and take her to Paris?

Francis tied the necktie carefully. Why not? Why not? He would go down to the villa and, conveniently finding Lorna alone, say: "Hurry up. Get some things together. We have an engagement at the Mairie; and then we are going to Paris. Now, don't argue. Hurry——" Partly fright at what, if he did this, he would find that he had done; partly the trembling of the senses that jumped past successive pictures to one of her in the dark in his arms, the agitation Francis felt grew so great that he began to walk up and down. At that instant, shocking him as if he had been shot, the telephone rang.

Snatching at it, Francis knocked it over. "Allo!" he said.

"Mr. Ellery"—it was Maggie—"Mrs. Cunningham went down to the office. She will be in the writing room in a few minutes, and she wants will you please go down there before you come up here?"

"Yes," said Francis. "I will."

He set the telephone down. From a hanger in the wardrobe he took a coat and put it on. With Maggie's words, he had felt for an instant the queasiness that used to come when, fairly often, word, solemnly conveyed, reached him to report to the Headmaster's study at once; but this was absurd, for he was no longer a schoolboy. The flight to Paris, he saw, now that the terrible and exciting story he had been telling himself was interrupted, was just as much a survival—one of those well-circumstanced dramas, passionately envisioned but never played, that, while he expected the dreadful summons or while he went to answer it, he used to make up for himself. Francis went downstairs through the empty lounge to the door of the writing room.

In the gloom of the mist outside Mrs. Cunningham sat at the far end writing a note. She held her pen an instant and said, though without smiling, "Good morning, Francis. Come and sit down. Excuse me just a moment." She wrote another line, blotted and folded the sheet. Putting it in an envelope, she said, "Francis, I really don't know what to do." She looked around her. "I don't think we'll be disturbed here. Walter told me about the accident. I can see that it wasn't your fault, and that once it had happened, you couldn't have done anything except what you did do. There's nothing more to be said about that. What I must speak to you about is your whole attitude."

Though there was not yet anything to say, the indictment, larger and more general than Francis had expected (and, in discouraging truth, not new to him. Through the years, how many people had found themselves, as time went on, less and less pleased with Francis, and so, sooner or later, had felt, often for Francis's own good, that they must speak to him about his whole attitude!), made it hard to keep still. Francis shifted a little in his chair and Mrs. Cunningham continued: "It isn't responsible enough, Francis. You see, above everything else, I must feel your definite responsibility."

"I don't know what to say," Francis said. "I had hoped you did feel that."

"Francis, I think you mean to be responsible. But it is so much a matter of judgment. I must depend upon your judgment so much. I think you are impulsive; and sometimes I think you look at things from your own standpoint a little too much. I don't think you have the habit of looking at things from other possible standpoints—from mine, for instance. Unless you can put yourself in the place of the person to whom you feel responsible, I don't think you can be very successful in satisfying that person. I have to have someone who can do it. On one or two occasions before this I have been a little worried—" She broke off.

Since the phrase brought instantly to mind that letter to his mother, Francis could not help flushing. In defense he reminded himself that he was not always alone in lacking judgment. Mrs. Cunningham herself was not right every time, so he need not, at least in his own mind, take this lying down. He said, "I wish that on those occasions you had told me. I wish you would tell me now."

"Well, Francis," she said, "I don't think it's fair to bring up, long after they happened, things that weren't after all of enough consequence for me to speak of them at the time."

"If you don't mind my saying so," Francis said with as much of a smile as he could manage, "I think that letting me wonder is—well, hard on me." Automatically he had taken out a package of cigarettes; but, noticing it, he put them away again.

Mrs. Cunningham noticed, too. "Yes, do smoke, if you want, Francis," she said. "Perhaps you're right. As an instance, I had in mind that trouble at Montreux when the hotel proprietor was so unpleasant about Rose. I could see that it was partly because you were upset, because, I suppose, you saw that I was upset. Which touched me very much, Francis. But at the same time I felt—and unless I was greatly mistaken, you really felt yourself, didn't you?—that it could have been handled differently."

"I did," said Francis. "I lost my temper."

"Francis, you have excellent judgment in many ways. I think you handle Walter extraordinarily well." Her fear of not being fair was speaking again; and Francis listened, disquieted. When she said it would not be fair of her to rake up what was past, he had not understood what she meant. His own instinct was to dismiss the past because discussing the past was futile. Mrs. Cunningham did not care to discuss it because she must be afraid of its cumulative effect. A heady tide of resentment mounted in her as, woman-like, she thought back over the carefully kept account of displeasures felt, or wrongs done her.

The remarkable thing, Francis told himself, was that, notwithstanding, she recognized and valued fairness, and applied a concept, wholly unreal and alien to most women, to check that mounting indignation. Her voice had sharpened at the mention of Montreux; there was a tremor in it when she put, very carefully and mildly, the question to him. When he answered yes, it must have needed self-restraint to proceed directly to points in his favor. Francis did not doubt that she stated them by an act of will, against her impulse; and now that she had made herself be just, she would be free to go on with more and more bitter things she must say on the subject of responsibility. It was like the second commandment. The passionate and jealous god of her maternal love spake these words: Francis must not make unto himself any graven image. He was here to watch out for Walter.

After the briefest pause, what Mrs. Cunningham said was: "You know, I had a note from Lorna this morning."

Astonished, Francis said, "Did you?"

"Yes, I did," said Mrs. Cunningham. "Francis, did you ask her to write it?"

Francis could feel a stiffness, an involuntary tightening, tingling a little at the nostrils, spread over his cheeks. "Now, for God's sake!" he begged himself. He touched his tongue to the inside of his lips, and looked an instant at his cigarette. "Mrs. Cunningham," he said, "I don't know anything about this note—" Could Lorna, knowing that Mrs. Cunningham might be annoyed, have taken it on herself to try to excuse him? She surely could not! "Anything," Francis said, "that I wanted told you or explained to you, I would tell you or explain to you." He looked across the ringing air. "You seem to be under some misapprehension about me; and so I—"

"Francis!" said Mrs. Cunningham. "Now, really—"

"Yes. I'm sorry," Francis said. He held his breath a moment. "Would you mind telling me what the note said?"

"She wrote, very nicely, suggesting that a party might be got up tomorrow, when Walter wouldn't have any lessons, to go to a place in the mountains where they have skiing."

"Yes," said Francis. "I know of the place. Some people at Eze yesterday knew about it. I told Walter that we would have to find out more, and see what you thought. If any plans were made, nobody mentioned them to me.

I didn't know that Lorna felt any interest in it. She and Gwen must have decided after they got home last night that it would be fun for Walter."

"Well, Francis, do you see what I thought?"

"Not entirely," Francis said. "I don't see how you could think that I would make plans without consulting you."

"Well, Francis, I think you have sometimes made plans first and consulted me afterward. I came to Cap d'Ail for several reasons, but one really was that I hoped it would be pleasant for you. I really had thought of going to Taormina. I thought it would be nice for you to see some friends. Perhaps I ought to examine my own judgment—" She smiled for the first time. "One thing I didn't think of was that they would have friends, and that you would naturally meet them and that it might be quite hard for you, when they were running around all the time, to be so tied down. Much harder, perhaps, than if you were somewhere else."

"Yes, I see," said Francis.

Though not, maybe, in the exact way she wanted, it seemed to him that he could put himself in her place well enough. The honesty of mind that made her, without any pause to consider, say 'for several reasons' impressed him. It was not merely a form of speech. Moreover, if the decision to bring him down here, instead of to Taormina, to let him see a few, as she said, 'friends' was also part of the fantastic strategy to protect Helen, she had not denied it. Her regard for truth was not (like many people's; like his own?) regard for the benefit or credit of a reputation for being truthful, but for the thing itself. Whatever happened, she would not tell a lie; and, abashed, Francis wished that, whatever happened, he would not.

Mrs. Cunningham said, "I told you that I wanted you to go to the dance Thursday. And I did. Perhaps I didn't really consider that it was likely to last all night, and that even if you wanted to—which would be a good deal to expect—it would be inconvenient for you to leave before the others. At any rate, it did last all night, and it was fairly plain that you weren't in any condition to take Walter's lessons yesterday morning. Then there was the matter of this man's car. I didn't like that, Francis."

"I didn't like it much myself—" Francis began. But didn't he? If truth interested him, hadn't he, yesterday morning, liked it very well?

"You see," Mrs. Cunningham said, "I don't know whether you were conscious of it or not; but it looked so much as though by telling yourself that you would use it to take Walter driving, you had arranged to more or less continue the party."

"No," said Francis, "I didn't plan that. It all came out of trying to get away a little early. I was going to see if I could get a taxi or something. He insisted that I take it."

"That, of course, is different. But you see there had already been that slip-up Monday night when we arrived. And then, the first time you had an opportunity to go out with your friends again—it upset me very much. I was upset this morning, when Lorna's note came up. I thought that you had arranged that, too."

And justly, Francis reflected. This time he hadn't; but how about other schemes, other times, when he had? He said, "I knew nothing about it. I had nothing to do with it."

Mrs. Cunningham looked at him intently. "Francis," she said, "when you told me a little while ago that I seemed to be under some misapprehension about you, I think you were right. I'm very sorry."

But suppose Lorna had, by some chance, mentioned the plan to him? Would a plan to spend Sunday with her have seemed to him a good idea or not? Francis found himself unable to say anything.

Mrs. Cunningham said, "I'll be glad to have Walter go tomorrow. I think the skiing is good for him. It helps him to feel that he can get around like anyone else. When it doesn't interfere with his work, I'd like him to go off with other people as much as possible—really, to get away from me and Maggie."

Taking the envelope that held the note she had written, she tore it up. "You see what it is that I must be sure of, Francis. That I can count on you, that nothing else is more on your mind than Walter is. I simply have to know that when he's with you, I needn't worry."

"You can know that," Francis said.

EIGHT

"Gee, what do you want?" said Walter. He was halfway down the steps. "They're coming. That's the car."

"Put these in your overcoat pocket," Maggie said. "It's some dry socks, so if your feet get wet. You had your other sweater, and your extra scarf—"

"I know, I know," Walter said. "Gosh, I'll be all right."

"I'll see that he changes," Francis said.

"Yes, he oughtn't to drive back when it may be cold with his feet damp. Mr. Ellery, I hope you'll make him take his shoes off and let you feel. Sometimes he doesn't realize—"

"I will," Francis said.

Out now in the sun, Maggie said, "My, isn't it a beautiful day! It seems very warm. I think he'll be warm enough." Lifting a hand, she shaded her eyes to look at the car coming up the drive. "He oughtn't to have veal for luncheon, Mr. Ellery. Some nice chicken, perhaps—"

"Oh, Maggie!" Walter cried.

"Now, Walter, you know what happened—"

The good that Mrs. Cunningham might see in releasing Walter from his bondage to women would not be so apparent to Maggie. She came down the steps hesitantly, rubbing her hands, drawing back to efface herself, peering forward to find out where they were going to put Walter. "Hello, Maggie," Lorna said.

"Good morning, Miss Higham." Maggie came down another step. The little confidence she had in Francis, or in men, was clear, for to Lorna she said appealingly, "Walter has all his things if he's just made to put them on, if he needs them."

Lorna said, "Don't you worry, Maggie. I'll remind him."

"We'll take care of him," Kirkland said. "You hop in here with me, Walter. We'll put Francis with the girls."

"And away we go," said Gwen. "Oh, my," she said, looking at Walter's skiing trousers. "If I had a pair of those I might even try it myself."

"Say, aren't you going to?"

"You just want to have a good laugh," Gwen said. "Lorna has a motion-picture camera. We'll take pictures of you."

"All set?" said Kirkland. The car began to move. "Walter!" Maggie cried. "Put your gloves on!"

"Sure, sure," Walter said, but he was out of Maggie's reach now, so he made no move to. "Say, it's pretty hot!" he said to Kirkland. "I hope it isn't melting up there. I hope it's good and high." From his pocket he pulled a small can. "If it's sticky, you have to have a lot of wax," he said. "I thought I'd better bring some along. Is the snow deep?"

"Couple of feet," Kirkland said. "It's way up."

"How long does it take? About when will we get there?"

"Well, we go to Nice; and it's about two hours from there."

"Gosh," said Walter. "I hope we don't have a flat tire or anything. We had one Friday night with Mrs. Hartpence's car. Frank and I tried to fix it. Gee, it took two hours. Did she tell you?"

"As a matter of fact, I haven't seen her," Kirkland said.

Raising his eyebrows, Francis looked at Lorna. She shrugged and shook her head. "And damned good riddance!" Francis murmured.

Gwen gave a snort. "This story only goes to show," she said, "that there ain't no good in men."

"I'll be the judge of that," Francis said, keeping his voice low. "What happened?"

"If I knew, I wouldn't tell you." Behind the more or less friendly gibing tone, Gwen's voice rang with indignation—as though Mrs. Hartpence were her best friend, as though Gwen hadn't been happy to disparage her Thursday night; and Francis gaped.

"Yes, you!" Gwen said. She screwed her face up comically. When she was younger she must have been in the habit of playing the clown to cover these seizures of strong feeling, coming with no warning, and on so little provocation that she shrank from letting anyone see what the provoking trifle was. In this case Francis could see that when he said good riddance she read into it some smug maleness. She looked at him; and if cats thought, a cat might look at a dog that way—the gross, clumsy, noisy animal; despised, but feared, too; disdained because you could so easily make a fool of it (in a pinch, a cat could, if spitting and arching the back failed, run up a tree, which no dog could do), yet deferred to (for if no tree were handy and the angry dog caught you in the open, he would finish you).

"How disagreeable you are!" Francis said. "I didn't do a thing." But he was glad to turn to Lorna. She, paying no attention to the exchange, was listening to what she could hear of the conversation in the front seat. Putting a hand on Francis's arm, she pressed it for his attention. "That's the beginning of a beautiful friendship," she said, nodding toward it.

Walter was saying: "It's a pretty fast run, believe me. They have some wands in for you on the long fall; but, gosh, if you miss one, you could kill yourself. We had Helen, my sister, along, so we couldn't make such good time—"

"He does all right," Francis said. "You'd be surprised."

"Did Helen go on all this?"

"She did while I was there. The Britishers gave her a big time."

"And how about you?"

Francis could feel himself flinch. Helen had proved to be no joke, or if a joke, a painful one, a joke on him, and he didn't want to hear any banter about that. What disturbed him more was that Lorna could lightly make the remark. At best, taken as a conventional bit of coquetry, he did not like it, because it was not like her. At worst—he did not know how to put it; but what he felt for her was something he would not care to joke about; not —the galled jade duly winced; but still, it was not—a fatuitous game he played with every female he met, and so must regard lightly, and so would not mind her regarding lightly. He said, "Oh, they were mad about me. They gave me a big time, too."

Lorna laughed. "Fool!" she said. "Darling, let's have a lovely day!"

The shadow of her hat brim was on her face. The artificial but pure red tint of her lips stood out from the white skin. Her eyes in this light were the deepest imaginable blue. Oddly moved by the decorative effect, Francis almost said: "You look like the French flag"; but he bit his lip, no longer believing (and wishing he never had believed) that such original humors, such gay capricious turns of thought, by their spontaneity and whimsical suddenness set him apart from commonplace people and in general did him proud. "Why not?" he said. "Why not?"

In the streets of Nice there was a vacant Sunday-morning calm, and they went through quickly; but outside, toward La Trinité-Victor, they kept meeting or overtaking cartloads of people dressed up in black to go to Mass. This held them back, and as the rocky, windy valley bottom extended, Francis saw that Kirkland was mistaken about his couple of hours. At half past eleven they got to Lucéram, but the real climb was only beginning. They stopped in the frosty sunlight of the mean steep square while a waiter from the hole-in-the-wall café brought chocolate for Walter and coffee with rum in it for the rest of them.

Kirkland, leaving his engine turning over, got out and raised the hood to look at it, so Walter got out, too. He walked up and down on the cobbles impatiently, knowing that it was getting late, but too consciously polite to complain. "It's all right, isn't it?" he said to Kirkland.

"Just changing the carburetor adjustment a little. It's a pretty hard pull from here."

"How far?"

"Oh, twelve or thirteen miles."

"And I wouldn't mind arriving," said Gwen, giving Francis her empty glass. "Emancipating myself as well as I can from what Eric calls false modesty, I feel sure they do not have one here, and I would be glad to see a ladies' room."

Up the slow successive hairpin curves of the military road they came presently to the snow—melting patches in the shadows, then a thin crust over the frozen ground, then snow deep and unbroken through the hanging pine groves. It was one o'clock before, leveling off, coming slowly through the hazed shadows and vertical shafts of sunshine, past sledges loaded with logs and big horses breathing steam, they reached the first houses, the flimsy chalets in the woods; *Mon Rêve, Mon Repos. . . .* They drove along the great weathered wall of the barracks, past the arch of the gate and drew up in a line of cars and several buses across the road from the small hotel.

"Thank God!" said Gwen, stepping out on the packed snow. "Come along, darling."

"You know," Francis said to Kirkland, "I think I'd better see if I can get a call through to Cap d'Ail. It's a little longer than I thought. I think I'd better tell Walter's mother we may be a little late."

"Say, tell her we just got here!" said Walter.

"Good idea," Kirkland said. "I'll see if we can scare up some food."

The hotel was unpretentious and cheap. The cramped hall, paneled in varnished pitch pine, and the public rooms opening out of it were crowded

—officers from the barracks with their visiting families; French excursionists from Nice in inexpensive, not-smart sports clothes. At the desk Francis asked for a telephone.

"*Occupé, Monsieur. Prière d'attendre.*"

"How about a small drink?" said Kirkland.

"Well, maybe I'd better find out where we get skis," Walter said.

"Well, maybe you'd better wash first," Francis said. "We'll have lunch right away."

However, on inquiry, it proved that the dining room was full, and they would have to wait with the people who were already waiting. Persuaded that the French would do anything for money, Francis showed the maître d'hôtel, a loutish unprofessional youth in a threadbare dinner coat, fifty francs. With a spasm of obligingness the maître d'hôtel discovered the possibility of serving them in the family dining room. He went himself and brought them vermouth and cassis.

"Once Walter finds out where the skis are, there'll be no holding him," Francis said. "Look, Goody, order any damned thing, except no veal for Walter, and let's start getting the girls fed. I'll have another try at the telephone." Lorna and Gwen came downstairs. "We're going to eat in back," Francis said to them, "more or less secretly, because there are a lot of people ahead of us." Touching toward her the glass in his hand, Lorna bent her head and took a swallow from it. "Preserve thy body and soul," Francis said, "unto—"

"You shock me!" Gwen said. "And why can't we have some of our own?"

"You may," said Francis. "Order me anything. I'm trying to call Mrs. Cunningham." He could see most of the waiting people looking at them. Whether because some understood English, and they had heard enough to know that in spite of justice and reason the Americans were going to be served first; whether because the short army officers bridled to see Kirkland, who if big in America, in France was a giant, holding the center of the floor, eclipsing their virility and bewitching their women, the looks were all cold and irritable.

Francis went back to the *caisse*. This time the man let him through. The telephone was in a little room behind and Francis sat on the edge of a table waiting for his call to get through. Smudging the rim of his glass, Lorna had left a trace of lipstick, and the perfume was distinct from the aromatic smell of the vermouth. "The blood of Our Lord Jesus Christ," he thought again, though the wit, if any, in that comment had been obscure, and showed a silly taste, surely not his, "which was shed for thee. Preserve thy body—" The fine wording made him think of the Anglican doctors, the seventeenth-century nest of singing divines, serene in chaos—George Herbert tuning his viol to set as a pastime an anthem to his dear Jesus;

Robert Sanderson facing in patience the Covenanters who tore his prayer book. Today, Francis told himself, men were not half the men they had been. "Allo," he said, "allo, allo . . ." But there was no response. On the table lay a mussed, some-days-old copy of the *Eclaireur de Nice* and he started to read a column describing a process for the amelioration of the oils of olive of the middle grades. After fifteen minutes Mrs. Cunningham answered.

Francis said, "No, everything's fine. Walter's having a grand time. But it took longer than we expected. We haven't had lunch yet. I was afraid we might be a little late getting down."

She said, "Oh, well, Francis, I won't worry if you're late. Don't try to get here for dinner, if it's too hard. I'm going out with the Peterses. We thought we'd go to the evening service at the English Church in Monte-Carlo, and get something to eat afterward. I'll be in very early. By nine, I should think. You won't be later than that, will you?"

"Oh, I don't believe so," Francis said. "We ought to be down by eight."

"Is it nice there?"

"The hotel is dreadful," Francis said, "but it's marvelous and clear, and there's lots of snow, and wonderful pine woods. It looks like the top of the world."

"How lovely! Have a good time, all of you— Oh. Yes. I will, Maggie. Maggie's afraid Walter will forget the socks in his overcoat pocket. Remind him, won't you?"

"I will."

"And if anything should delay you, you'll try to let me know, won't you?"

"I will. And I'll try to see that nothing does." To Francis's left was a window, and looking out at the soiled sunny snow of the road he saw a car appear, swing slowly, and head in to park across the way. It was an Italian car, like Mrs. Hartpence's. "Good-bye," he answered, smiling, put the receiver down and stood up.

"Hell!" said Francis then; for the car was not merely like Mrs. Hartpence's, it was hers; and she was getting out of it.

The family dining room was small, with a round table. It had a bright south window half filled with potted plants. On the vilely papered walls hung religious pictures—the Sacred Heart frilled with flames; Saint Vincent de Paul surrounded by the poor. It was warm, and smelled, unless you liked the smell, unpleasantly of anisette.

"Get her?" said Walter. His mouth was full, and he was eating furiously.

"Yes," said Francis. "Now, take it easy! We have lots of time."

He sat down and the maître d'hôtel entered by the other door from the kitchen and put before him a plate thinly arranged with a soggy collection of hors d'oeuvres. "Thanks," said Francis.

He did not know what to say about Mrs. Hartpence. If he had left the telephone a minute sooner, he would not have seen her; so perhaps it would be simplest to pretend that he hadn't, to mind his own business and say nothing. On the other hand, though Kirkland might have known she was coming, Francis did not think he did. Kirkland, it seemed, was trying to shake her; and she was resisting the attempt; and God knew what tipsy or hysterical scene was in preparation. Not to warn him was a betrayal of those decent principles of male solidarity, so important if any peace or trust were to exist in a society overrun by women—in short, a dirty trick on Francis's part. Francis said, "By the way, Emily Hartpence's car just came in."

"That so?" said Kirkland casually, but he acknowledged the important tip-off by adding at once, "Who's she with?"

"I didn't see anyone."

"Oh," said Kirkland. Forewarned, he was forearming. On his face appeared the progress of his thought, and he was sick and tired of Emily. A woman—Emily herself, Gwen, any woman—might see it in affecting terms *(she was in love, and he she lov'd prov'd mad, and did forsake her . . .)*; but what Kirkland saw was that she he loved had swindled him. He had taken her with the understanding that she was romantic and desirable. She had as good as promised him ineffable pleasures in private, and the admiring envy of all his friends in public; but what did she give him? In private she was a disgusting maudlin nuisance; in public she made a fool of him. The bitch had misrepresented herself. Of course, it was mostly his own fault for not seeing that she was a bitch. Kirkland admitted that; and if she would decently accept the fact that the game was up, and go about her business, he wouldn't wish her any hard luck. But, by God, if she were going to—

Kirkland said, "Well, maybe I—" He pushed back his plate, arose, crumpled his napkin and dropped it on the table. Not finishing the remark, he went out the door and closed it after him.

Walter, who had watched with interest, said, "Hot dog!"

He ought to be reproved; but if Francis were to ask him censoriously what he meant by that senseless exclamation, the chances were good that Walter would further embarrass matters by defending his meaning, after all made amply clear by his voice. The connection between Mr. Kirkland and Mrs. Hartpence he had easily identified as a sentimental one, and he knew what that always meant. Suddenly abandoning everything that they said or implied to Walter or the world about their dignity and reasonableness, adults, seized by love, went into a sort of vaudeville act, side-splitting at first, but much too long; holding hands, kissing, bandying pet names; until, for no ascertainable reason beyond their own silliness, they fell to fighting and yelling, and the women, at least, to crying.

Walter surveyed these antics cynically, sometimes hiding a smile behind his hand, sometimes risking a guarded jeer. It did not seem feasible
to say to him: "Don't laugh. Mrs. Hartpence is a fool and drinks too much;
but she is probably in great pain. Mr. Kirkland's behavior is not to his
credit; but he is in a jam, and you will be lucky if you get to be his age without ever finding yourself in one like it. . . ." And anyway, though perhaps
not a bad speech, it was aside from the point. All Walter maintained was
that love looked funny; and who could deny that from the first infatuated
ogles and formal beatings-about-the-bush to the last ridiculous position
and brief pleasure, it did, it did? Walter hardly knew the half of it! On consideration, Francis decided that this was not the moment for reproof. He
said, "How about the skis?"

"Gee, they're terrible, mostly!" Walter said, ready enough to return to
the world of common sense. "I found some pretty good pairs for us. But I
don't know about Mr. Kirkland. It's pretty hard to find him any."

"Why is it pretty hard?" Lorna said brightly. Francis glanced at her
with gratitude.

"Oh," said Walter, "you see, he's so tall. He'd need awfully long ones.
The way you tell is, you stand them up, and if you reach your hand over
your head, you ought to just touch the tip—"

Francis looked over to Gwen. "I wouldn't tell you, even if I knew," he
said. "How do you feel? Better?"

"I believe you think you're smart," Gwen said. "Here. Have some
wine. It's ghastly."

What to do about a woman, your mistress, who would not take her
dismissal, and who was rich, so that you weren't able to free yourself by the
simple expedient of leaving her stranded somewhere (or if you could not
quite do that, of buying her off), Francis did not know; but two general
plans of action suggested themselves.

The first, and undoubtedly the better, for it was the method almost
invariably used by men experienced in getting and in getting rid of women,
was to be resolute, to persevere. A number of insults and indignities had
failed; but, never say die! Insults could be made more open, indignities
more brutal; and both could be better aimed, at tenderer points of pride
(there were always a few) and the more cherished fragments (no one could
lose them all and live) of self-respect. A lucky hit, one stroke dealt with no
squeamishness, might pull it off; and it ought not to take long.

However, not everybody was capable of simple directness, and the
other method, whose outstanding disadvantage was the practical certainty
that it wouldn't work, was to reason, to explain that you could not love her
so much were it not for the fact that you loved honor more—in short, to
make her see that it was no good, but in a way that spared her and gave

yourself the treat of trying to act like a gentleman. This must take longer —anything from an hour to a hundred years—and, when twenty minutes passed without Kirkland coming back, it seemed probable that this was the method that he was using. Francis felt a certain relief. . . .

Walter, finished long ago, had been restlessly entertaining Lorna with more of his exploits at Grindelwald; but as soon as he saw that Francis, who had started so much later, was through, too, he said, "Well, I guess I'd better go down and see that nobody took those skis."

"All right," Francis said. "Run along. But don't start off until we get there. If you see the maître d'hôtel—he's probably in the dining room— you might ask him to bring me a bill."

When he was gone, Lorna said, "This is my party." She reached for her pocketbook under her coat on the chair behind her.

Francis said, "Mrs. Cunningham gave me very particular instructions to do what I could to pay our way. I think she felt that since you had arranged the transportation—"

"Gwen did it," said Lorna. "And arranged is the word. It was the next thing to blackmail. After we got home Friday night, Goody called up. So sorry and all that. So Gwen invited us to drive up here in his car."

"I did not!" said Gwen. "I told him Raymond was going to drive us up, and—"

"Darling, I was only fooling," Lorna said reproachfully.

"I know you were," said Gwen. "Don't mind me. I am a great one for knowing what everybody ought to do, and for not seeing why they can't behave themselves; and when they don't, I get a little bit cantankerous. Now, I must either shut up or start what I believe is called backbiting. Let's go and see Walter ski. I expect Goody can find us, if he wants to."

A waiter had come in with the bill. Taking it, Francis glanced down the line of figures, not really expecting an overcharge, since the maître d'hôtel was fifty francs ahead to start with; but it was there, all right, a little matter of twenty-three francs. *"Voyons, voyons!"* he said indignantly. *"Cent dix-huit et onze—"* But it was not likely to be the waiter's work. "I'm damned if I'll let them get away with it!" He said, "If you'll excuse me, I'll just carry the battle out to the *caisse.*"

"Well, we might as well see where Walter is." Gwen dropped the end of her cigarette in her coffee cup and stood up. "Come, darling. Put your galoshes on, and we'll go for a nice long tramp in the woods."

Through a labyrinth of little passages Francis reached the front hall. The rush was over. The people waiting had all been admitted to the dining room. In the *caisse* was one of those formidable, high-bosomed French-women, on a few million of whom the economy of France appears to pivot. Francis supposed that she was the wife of the proprietor, the mother of the maître d'hôtel, and the calculating author of the slight slip in arithmetic.

Peremptorily she took the bill, shooting at Francis a look of suspicion and contempt. Swift and efficient, she added it, and then added it again. Pulling a pencil out of her pile of glossy black-dyed hair, she corrected a figure or two. *"Voilà!"* she said, triumphantly solving his stupid difficulty for him.

Francis thanked her and paid. The larcenous old gorgon delighted him, and, gathering up his change, he turned away smiling. He found himself looking into the shabby lounge at Mrs. Hartpence, who sat alone in the early-afternoon shadows with a half-empty glass of brandy and soda on a stand beside her.

"Oh, hello," she said.

"Hello," said Francis, recoiling.

He lifted his hand in embarrassment, meaning to give her a casual wave and get out of here. She sat slumped down, one knee over the other, her wool skirt rucked up a little, so that a person standing where Francis stood could see, above the tight stocking top, against the light-colored silk of a slip, much of her bare thigh. Francis shifted his eyes, outraged by his incontinent stir of interest; but before he could move, she said, "Going skiing?"

"Yes," said Francis, acutely uncomfortable. "I was just straightening up a little misunderstanding about the bill." He gave a laugh that sounded foolish to him. "I'm looking for Walter. I'll have to—"

"Goody went down with him to see about some skis."

"Oh," said Francis. Hearing her say Goody, it was impossible to shut out of the mind Kirkland's relation to her. Francis held his eyes rigidly on her face; but certain thoughts, though always spurned away, kept coming back; and not alone. As the saints, beseeching women to be virtuous, knew to their trial, as the fastidious often find to their disgust, the knowledge of a woman's looseness persists, through every revulsion of hate or anger, through every chaste resolve, in steadfastly promising (just in case you happen to change your mind) that what men have done, man can do. Francis said with another laugh, "Well, we'll all break our necks, probably."

"May I come along?"

"Why—" Francis began in consternation; for how could you answer no? "Well, of course; but I don't know where we're going, exactly. This is more or less Goody's show."

"Are Lorna and Gwen going?"

"They're not skiing. I think they thought they'd watch a while. I expect it's rather dull unless you—"

"Well, maybe I could go with them."

"Yes," said Francis in confusion. "Why not? I don't really know what they're planning to—"

"Oh, go to hell!" said Mrs. Hartpence. Dropping her face forward, she brought her hands up shakily, pressed them over her eyes, and broke into sobs.

It was not Francis's fault if Kirkland made Mrs. Hartpence unhappy. It was not his fault if, putting him in an impossible position by a request she had no right to make, his answers failed to satisfy her. She had no right to have hysterics in public—there were people in the dining room beyond; there was that loutish maître d'hôtel snooping around; there was the superb extortionist in the *caisse*; and some or all of them would soon hear, stare, ask themselves what Francis had done to her.

"Look, Emily," Francis said. "You must stop that! Please. I'm so sorry—"

But she was not going to stop. The crowding tears wet her hands; in spasms of anguish her shoulders heaved and jerked; the inconsolable sobs grew deeper. In what was practically an anguish of his own, Francis said: "Look. Wait here a minute. I'll get one of the girls to come up and—"

Downstairs, outside an open door ending the passage in which skis were stored, Walter and Kirkland, their skis already on, stood waiting while Lorna, holding her camera, moving to keep the sun behind her, frowned; shielding the finder and trying to get them in focus. Gwen stood in the door. Francis approached her from behind, and tapped her shoulder. "Come in here," he said. "I have a little job for you. It's Mrs. Hartpence. We'll have to do something about her."

"What's wrong?"

"She's up in the lounge bawling. She caught me when I came back from getting the bill fixed. I cannot cope with it."

"I don't know that I can, either."

"Well, you come right up and try. Get her out of there and make her wash her face or something. You must know what to do. What do females generally do to each other?"

"What happened? What did she say?"

"She didn't say anything. She asked if she could come along with you and Lorna, and I said yes. What else could I say? Then she began to cry. I don't know what went on with Kirkland. I suppose he just told her to go home, and then walked out—"

"I could kill him!" said Gwen. "Come on. Where is she?"

When Francis came downstairs again, Lorna was waiting alone at the end of the deserted passage. She set her hands on her hips, tilted her head to one side, and with an exasperation not entirely humorous, said, "Where have you been? Walter and Goody started off, and Gwen has disappeared somewhere—"

Francis glanced behind him, touched up her chin, and, though she tried with the same half-humorous exasperation to draw her head back, kissed her. "None of that!" he said. "We have our hands full. It's this damned Emily. Gwen is up giving her a sister's care. You know. Still for all slips of hers, one of Eve's family. It's pretty as a picture."

"Oh, Lord!" said Lorna. She slipped the strap of the camera case off her shoulder and held it out to him. "Take this. I'd better go up."

"I don't see why," said Francis.

"I can't leave Gwen to—"

"Well, damn your friend Kirkland to hell! He has the most ineffable brass! You know, it's a gift, this leaving somebody else to pick up the pieces. I wish you'd tell me sometime what you see in him."

"Francis, I told you that I know his sister. She wrote him that we were down here, and so he looked us up. Now, will you please stop, every chance you get, implying—"

"You know I didn't mean to imply anything; though if he isn't a friend of yours, what is he?"

"Oh, Francis! Why will you go on and on—"

"I'm sorry," Francis said. "I'm simply fed up with these bums and their hell-raising. They're all part of the same bunch of stupid drunks that lies around Paris pretending to be artists or writers or the lost generation— good God, I mean!"

"Francis, will you please go and ski? They went over to some hill some- where below the barracks. We'll come down later."

"Well, all I mean is—"

"Will you please not say any more about what you mean or don't mean? It doesn't matter—"

"On the contrary," said Francis, "it—"

"Francis, this isn't a joke. Will you—"

"Now, listen," Francis said. "What I mean does matter. What I mean is that Kirkland is a cheap bastard; and she is a vulgar slob; and I don't want you mixed up with any of it."

"You needn't worry about me."

"Damn it, I worry myself sick about you!" He took her by the arms.

"Francis, if you do not let me go—" She was white with anger, and her angry face, which he had never seen before, was like the face of every angry woman, spiteful and furious. Confronted with it, a man's right instinct was to beat the little hellcat until pain and fear brought back her senses (and, at the same time, brought back his; because her fright or injuries would rearouse tender feelings); but nowadays this was seldom done, and Francis let her go. Jerking away, she turned and went upstairs.

Since she had left her camera with him, and he could not put it down anywhere, or ski if he carried it with him, Francis, who did not feel much like skiing anyway, went out the door, climbed the packed snow of the path and walked along the road past the barrack gates to look for this hill.

It was not by any means the first time that, angry or resentful, he had, for little reason and that not good, said what it was stupid to say and done what it was foolish to do; so he understood very well that there was no remedy for the resulting dismay, except to try to stop thinking about it.

II

The hill where they skied proved to be no more than a sharp short fall in an open glade in the pine woods, a quarter of a mile along the road. Thirty or forty people were coasting down it or climbing up it, shouting cheerfully in the sun; but it would not be Walter's idea of skiing at all; and, in fact, Francis found him standing by himself watching a squad of young soldiers, probably new conscripts, in a line on skis being shown by a tough fat sergeant how to stand up.

Seeing Francis, Walter said, "Gee, it's not so hot. Aren't you going to try it?"

"I thought I'd see what it was like. Where's Mr. Kirkland?"

"He's down at the bottom. He's having a terrible time. His skis aren't any good." Considering the disappointment Walter must be feeling, it seemed to Francis that he was bearing up very well. He leaned, subdued, on his poles and nodded toward the sergeant and his squad. "Gosh, you ought to hear him swear at them!" he said. "They're terrible. Where is everyone? Lorna said she was going to come and take some more pictures."

"Mrs. Hartpence wasn't feeling well," Francis said. "They're staying a minute to see about her."

"Oh. Well, I guess I'll go and sit down awhile."

"What's the trouble?" Francis said, rousing himself sharply.

"Oh, nothing. I was kind of winded. It feels a little tight in my chest." He tapped his breastbone with his mittened hand.

"You mean, like asthma?"

"No, you don't get that in the afternoon. You only get that at night, usually. It will go away in a minute, I guess."

Francis pulled off his jacket and laid it on the snow. "Sit on that," he said. It seemed to him that Walter was perceptibly paler. Walter stood a moment looking at Francis's jacket; and then he said slowly, "Well, maybe I'd better go back to the hotel for a while."

Because Walter must know how unlike him it was to suggest such a thing, his tone was defensive. The expression in his eyes was withdrawn, turned intently on the sensations in his chest. It was plain to Francis that, just as adversity is said to make a man a philosopher, ailments like Walter's could serve to make you a rudimentary but sound psychologist. Walter did not let himself become frightened, for he must have discovered that a little fright sometimes turned what was only a threat into the thing itself. Furthermore, if he did not want to be frightened, he must not frighten other people; because frightened people around him, by their aghast expressions and their panicky movements, could infect him with their fright.

The thing to do, then, was at all costs to remain calm; to look at Walter's peculiar leaden pallor without surprise, to treat the whole thing as a trivial mishap—something to be attended to; but to be attended to merely as a matter of everyday prudence, like a cut finger or a bump on the head. "Think you'd better take your skis off?" Francis said.

"Yes. Would you do it? I don't want to bend down." From the nice balance of definite urgency against simulated unconcern, Francis judged that Walter's sensations, while no worse, were no better, either; and that this must be unusual; that Walter, keeping a tight grip on himself, tightened it to meet the insidious suggestions of a deeper fear—not the fear that this was the same old terrifying thing coming back, but the fear that it wasn't.

"All right," Francis said. "Step out. I think you started too soon after lunch. I think it's indigestion. Do you feel sick?"

Walter shook his head. "I think it feels better," he said. "It will go away, I think, if I sit down awhile."

"Well, we'll get you back to the hotel."

This was all very well, Francis reminded himself; but if Walter was going to have an attack, Francis had no idea of what ought to be done. He must find out at once. "If you feel that way, what does Maggie do for you?" he asked casually.

"Oh, she has a kind of vapor lamp she likes to try. Sometimes I smoke one of those cigarettes. I have some. If it gets bad, there's some stuff they give me. They inject it—" He gave a sort of yawn, and Francis could see that unplanned act must be a suggestive symptom, for the expression of anxiety in his eyes increased. "Better take it easy," said Francis, picking up the skis.

"Hey!" said Kirkland.

His shadow sloped across the snow before them. He came to an ungainly stop by driving in the point of one pole and running, like a Roman on his sword, against it. "Uh!" he said as it hit him in the ribs, and laughed. He was flushed and warm; his eyes sparkled like a child's. Skiing was new to him, but he was fitted for any kind of sport, and with the confidence of a person who knows he will get the hang of it, and in high spirits and for fun, he threw in a few buffooneries—the comic technique of the float, the boathouse, and the training table.

Francis, whose mind had been set against him almost with malignancy for the damage he did, was unwillingly disarmed. Far from being vicious, or, in the meaning of the word when it applies to a man, brutal, Kirkland was full of genial impulses. If he was selfish, the selfishness was a boy's, coming not from calculation but from urgent appetites, a sort of exuberant grabbing of what he wanted, a sort of truancy or skipping out on what was tiresome or hard, in no case deterred by the stick-in-the-mud reflection of what would happen if everybody did that.

Francis said, "I think Walter'd better rest awhile. I think he ate too fast and got out too soon." He did not know whether it was a help to Walter to have this theory insisted on, or not. Walter looked at Kirkland with a faint, sheepish smile. "Gosh, go ahead and ski," he said. "I'll be back—" He yawned again, and clearly he didn't like it at all. The anxiety in his eyes went a little farther along the contested line; and though he stopped somewhat short of the point where it would get out of hand, he turned, and began to walk, not too fast and not too slow, toward the road.

"Is he all right?" Kirkland whispered.

"I wish I knew," Francis said, unable to be cold and distant. "I'm afraid he isn't. I'll get him back and see—"

"Go on," said Kirkland. "I'll be along as soon as I can get these things off my feet."

Francis opened his mouth to say that this would not be necessary; but he recognized it as a silly last impulse of his anger or indignation. He might say, don't bother; but he didn't mean to save Kirkland trouble; he meant to tell him (speaking of childishness!) to go on, to do something else for Francis to despise, to show how right Francis was to think of him with contempt. Francis nodded, and overtook Walter. "How is it?" he said.

"Gee, don't worry," Walter said. He spoke with an effort, as much to himself as to Francis. He limped along doggedly, but he glanced frequently ahead to see how far it was now.

"Take it easy," said Francis, as lightly as he could. He was thinking that Walter would probably weigh sixty-five or seventy pounds, and he could not help measuring the distance himself.

From the staff projecting over the gate arch of the barracks, the hanging tricolour stirred, bloused, lifted up and down softly. The sun on the weathered old wall was soft and mellow, splashed here and there by water from icicles melting at the high eaves. Back and forth across the shadowed entrance the sentries passed each other, pivoted at the end of the beat, advanced and repassed. Francis observed the scarlet collar tabs and hunting-horn insignia. Upright, their bayonets, polished like silver, flashed on the turn. The pale shifting shadow of the flag lifted and fell away; and from the great court within arose the succinct but softly struck roll of one or more military drums, broken off soon, and then begun again, as though in practice, or at the directions of an instructor.

The afternoon was so fine, clear, and peaceful, bright with sun, bright with snow, that Francis began to take a kind of reassurance from it. It was not the setting in which anything serious (he resisted a closer defining of his doubt) could happen. Walter's face was definitely less pale. He seemed, in fact, to be gaining a good color.

Kirkland caught up with them, and they reached the hotel together, standing the skis up at the door. Inside safely, Francis looked at Walter with relief. "How about some water?" he said. "I'll get you a bottle of Evian. Do you think you ought to lie down?"

"I don't know," Walter said. He stood perfectly still; and then, turning abruptly, he let himself sink on a bench. "I—" He broke off. His hands came up and he pressed his crossed wrists to his chest. "Frank!" he said. "Look. I'd better go somewhere. I—"

"Goody!" Francis said. "Tell that hag we've got to have a room. Right away— Can you walk?" he said to Walter.

Walter could not answer. "I mustn't lie down," he managed to whisper. That good color was flushing his face crimson in the shadow. "Can't breathe—"

"Walter!" said Francis. He dropped on the bench. "Can you stand? Do you want to be picked up?"

"Here!" said Kirkland. "Give him to me." He encircled Walter's shoulders with his big arm, bent and slid the other under Walter's knees and lifted him with no difficulty. "Upstairs," he said to Francis, nodding toward the back.

Halfway up Francis could see the spread, sateen-covered rump of the woman from the *caisse* bobbing ahead in haste. "Goody," he said, "I'll have to telephone. I'll have to put a call in. I'll have to get Maggie. His mother was going out. We'll have to find out what to do. Ask Madame if there's a doctor anywhere. They must have one at the barracks—"

"Go on. Go ahead," Kirkland said. "We'll take care of him." He was steady and calm. His voice was unruffled, firm, and reassuring. "All right, old-timer?" he said to Walter. "We'll get you fixed in a minute." That lack of imagination, making him at other times such a dolt, now made him invaluable. There was no way through to his nerves. He knew only what he saw, and he saw only what was put in front of him. For never tasting death but once, it was as good as valiancy—it was really better, because what might happen to other people it feared no more than what might happen to itself.

A waiter, the one who had brought the bill, popped in, stood gazing around in surprise, his hands hanging; and Francis, distracted (if he stayed here, he could not know what was happening upstairs; if he went upstairs, he could not put in a call), saw a way to handle it. He said to the waiter,

"Ring up the Eden Hotel at Cap d'Ail. Ask for the manager. Let me know at once when you get him. I'll be upstairs." Francis stared at him, astounded, for the waiter's face relaxed in an uneasy deprecatory smile. Not moving, he began to shake his head.

"Hurry up!" Francis cried in agitation. "Don't stand there! What's the matter with you—" With a jar, he saw then what the matter was. *"Pardon!"* he said. *"Alors, vite, vite—"* but he had to stop, not able to complete the mental shift that would let him think in French. No words came.

"Francis!" said Lorna. "What happened?"

She stood three feet away, her hands clasped together.

"I don't know what to do," Francis said. "I must telephone. It will take forever to get a connection. He had an asthma attack or something like it. Maggie knows what to do—"

"Go up," she said. "I'll get it for you."

"No. I'll have to talk to her myself. I—"

"You can't talk to her until she's on the line. Go on." Moving up, she pushed his shoulder. "Here," she said, catching the strap of the camera case, "you aren't going to need that."

In a room just beyond the head of the stairs Kirkland had put Walter on the bed. "Better lie down, old boy," he was saying.

"No, don't," said Francis. "The trouble is he can't breathe. He has to keep his head up. Get some pillows behind him." To the woman, he said, "We need more pillows, Madame—*encore des oreillers.*"

She cried, *"Tiens, tiens!"* snapping her fingers in the face of a little old man wearing a black apron. There was also a chambermaid, who stood fascinated, both her reddened hands, as she heard the wheezing struggle of Walter's breathing, brought up to squeeze her own throat.

"We'll have to get a doctor," Francis said. "Lorna's downstairs putting through the call for me. Look, Walter," he said, grasping his arm, "would one of those cigarettes be any good? Do you want one? Can you manage it? Try in his coat pocket, Goody."

Walter's face looked choked-up, half-asphyxiated. Francis had seen him working hard—climbing a slope on skis, pedaling a bicycle along a rising path—but long before he reached such a state as this Francis would have made him stop and rest. Under Francis's hand, the muscles in Walter's arm knotted tight, for the work of breathing—*easy as breathing*, Francis thought with horror—seemed to involve his whole body. He made his utmost effort and, wheezing and whistling, forced in a little of the desperately awaited air. After he got it in, he had then to get it out. Merely to watch was exhausting; you asked yourself how long that could be kept up, how many such struggles a moderate—really, with the harm done by paralysis, an impaired—physique like Walter's could be good for.

He was not the only one asking that question. In Walter's dusky flushed face the pupils of his eyes, starting wide, were almost black. Wild and mute, they were full of terror, for the struggle, if horrifying to watch and hear, must stab the frenziedly engaged heart with unspeakable fear. Locked up there to fight it out single-handed, Walter could look from the nightmare and see people, and they could see him; but he could not reach them, and they could not reach him to help him. Kirkland pushed a small box into Francis's free hand. "Where is Madame?" said Francis. "We must get a doctor—"

"She's gone to do it. Here. Steady on! Give me that." Kirkland took back the box and picked a cigarette from it. Holding up a match he snapped his fingernail over the head, shielded the flame, and lit the cigarette. Taking a puff, he grimaced at the taste. "Now, let's see. Walter?" He brought it down to Walter's lips. "Want to try? Atta boy!"

"*Monsieur,*" said the waiter in the door, "*en bas, s'il vous plaît.*"

"Yes," said Francis, his eyes fixed on Walter. Walter was willing to try; but though he could close his lips and fill his mouth with smoke, he could not breathe it in any better than he could breathe in air. Francis turned and ran downstairs.

"All right, here he is," said Lorna.

Someone had fetched a chair for her and she sat on the edge of it, her legs twisted together, the toe of her left foot doubled behind her right ankle. Clapping her hand over the mouthpiece she held it out to him. "It's Maggie," she said. "But Mrs. Cunningham hasn't left yet. They're sending downstairs to stop her. I said Walter wasn't feeling well and you—is he all right?"

"No," said Francis.

He took the telephone and put his back against the wall. Maggie's voice rang faintly. "Oh, Mr. Ellery! What is it? What—"

From her pocketbook laid with the camera case on the table, Lorna slid out a cigarette case. "Shall I go up?" she said. Francis waved a hand at her. "No," he said, "you can't do anything. Stay away. Yes, Maggie. Yes— well, just a moment. Did that woman come down to see about a doctor?"

"They sent someone for the medical officer."

"We're getting one," Francis said into the telephone. "Yes. I understand. He's not to be moved. Oh. Yes, Mrs. Cunningham—" His hand was shaking, and so, he realized, was his voice; and that would never do; "I think we're going to have one in a minute." To Lorna, he said, "Listen! I want to be sure about this! Yes. No morphine unless the doctor thinks it's absolutely necessary. And not more than a quarter-grain. That was a quarter, one-fourth of one grain. Yes. And ask if he ever tried adrenalin. Yes. I understand. If he never has, he'd better not—"

From her pocketbook Lorna pulled an envelope, uncapped a lipstick, and marked on it the quarter-grain of morphine. "Yes," Francis said. "Yes, I will. I will see that it is. Yes." Slowly he dropped the telephone into its cradle. "She's coming up," he said.

"Here—" said Lorna. She pushed the envelope over to him. "Not more than one-quarter grain." She opened the cigarette case and slid that over, too.

"I must go up," Francis said.

"Francis," she said, laying a hand on his sleeve. "It may not be as bad as you think. He's had them before."

"It couldn't be worse," said Francis. "This isn't like the others. He would not be so frightened if— I ought to take that back about Kirkland," he said. "He's a good deal more good than I am." He meant it, but in the still, darkening room, his words had a sorry, stilted sound, as though much too late in the day, he were trying to call attention to the fact that he was just, and humble, too; yet what was he really but afraid? He took up the envelope and looked at the rude, but clear enough red markings. They ran across the torn flap where, written under them in a round feminine script, was a return address.

Francis read: *F. Robertson Pensione Vittoria Via Stella Milano Italia*. The reaction of surprise was to make him feel physically sick. He stared at it, revolted; though certainly Miss Robertson had a perfect right to correspond with her dear old school friend if she wanted to. "I must get back up there," he said.

"Hadn't I better come?"

"There's nothing to be done. Better wait for the doctor."

Of the state in France of medical science Francis was uninformed. If you had to go anywhere, the American Hospital at Neuilly was the only thinkable place. Francis had never been inside a French hospital; but the phrase called up pictures of a Hogarthian pesthouse or bedlam where the dead lay in their soiled beds because nobody got around to removing them; and the dying, *munis des conforts de notre sainte religion*, but otherwise unrelieved, went on dying *(Que voulez-vous? C'est la vie)*. In harmony with such harrowing squalor would be the doctors, men who could be bought by American advertisers to say that phenol was good for women and yeast was good for everyone; men like Madame Bovary's husband, or, if you read best sellers, like the physician in *La Garçonne* who had naturally taken the unexampled opportunity of a gynaecological examination to have a try at raping the heroine.

Francis wanted a doctor badly enough, any doctor; but with the news that one was coming he enjoyed only an instant of relief. He wondered if one from the army, presumably callous and cynical, with a short way with malingerers and a way not much longer—salvarsan for fifty, calomel for a hundred; and if they weren't better tomorrow, why what the devil!—with the indisputably sick, would not be less use than nothing.

Meanwhile in the room upstairs the afternoon sun fell in a slanting oblong, partly on the floor, partly on the wall. The old man had brought more pillows; and Walter, sitting nearly straight, rested against them stiffly. The sharp thin smoke of burned belladonna hung in the air; but Walter was breathing with no less difficulty. Instead of being flushed, he was now growing pale again, and a clammy gleam of sweat had appeared on his forehead.

Francis tightened his mouth. The pallor and the sweat hit him with a new impact of shock. It did not shock the eyes; it hit something deeper, maybe the cerebral cortex, a heavy and a shaking blow. The human face should not be gray. It did not sweat for nothing. Francis looked at Walter; and at Kirkland, big, not fat but full-fed and hearty. Kirkland was sober and concerned; but not shaken by any blows. His heavy frame (he must weigh more than two hundred pounds), sagging the edge of the bed as he sat on it, was in calm repose. Francis looked at the sunlight on the floor and wall; and because he could not help it, he admitted the waiting thought. Preposterously, in violation of the ordinary probabilities, in defiance of the things you had to trust and must count on—the narrow plain room, the usual midafternoon sunlight, the setting out from Cap d'Ail on a fine morning in Kirkland's car—there was notwithstanding no law, human or divine, against Walter, in an hour or less, being dead. Walter could get grayer; the ghastly sweat could get colder; and if he could not breathe Walter would not live.

That this was too awful, that nobody dreamed of such a thing, that, if it happened, Francis would have to go out and meet Mrs. Cunningham getting out of a car sometime after nightfall and tell her were not exactly reasons why not. To or about the course of events you could say what you liked; but events never stopped to argue with you. If Francis wanted to think that it couldn't really be he who would have to do that, Francis could go right on thinking it. If Francis liked, he could continue to show himself how absurd such fancies were—it couldn't happen; it was utterly unheard of; and how unlikely it was that a child born years ago halfway around the world (what was he doing here?) and at noon perfectly well would (why today, out of the possible thousands of days?) at three or four o'clock die in this bleak but sun-filled bedroom in a cheap hotel in Peira-Cava (who ever heard of such a place?). For years Walter's mother, and Maggie, and innumerable doctors had watched over him, and how could that all go for nothing, leaving him on this last day with no one near but Francis, whom he did not know six months ago, and Kirkland, whom he did not know three days ago, and Kirkland's sluttish mistress—where was she, anyway? Gwen must be doing something with her—and Lorna downstairs, and God knew what kind of French quack or degenerate for a doctor—

But, of course, it all could, maybe it all always did, go for nothing; and if you asked how, why, this was how. It was perfectly simple. One rainy afternoon last fall in Paris Mrs. Cunningham made up her mind about engaging Francis, and after that it was only a matter of time, while they moved closer and closer—from Grindelwald to Cap d'Ail; and Thursday night Francis met Kirkland. It was getting really close now. On Friday, for the first time, someone (Gwen, Francis guessed) dropped the fatal name, Peira-Cava. On Saturday Walter talked of nothing else. On Sunday, with a can of ski wax and his extra socks in his pocket, he went there; and—

"All right," Francis said to himself, for with the piling up against him of the odds or omens *(I look'd toward Birnam and anon methought the wood began to move . . .)* the heart resisted, the mind struck back in anger, "all right. Even so. Even so, God damn it, I will do something. I will make this doctor—"

In the silence there was no response, no help, no reassurance; but he expected none; and, though Walter's labored wheezes sounded in his ear, Francis began to breathe with deliberate measure. He heard the slam of the closed door below; and, starting up to step into the hall, Lorna's voice speaking French.

Upstairs came a short man in a captain's uniform. Behind him a sergeant, his oversized beret drooping on his forehead, carried his case.

"Par ici, Monsieur," said Francis.

"Yes, good day," said the captain. "I speak English." His face was oval and brown, with a cropped mustache. He smiled soberly, showing white even teeth. His eyes, which were alert and intelligent, went to Walter on the bed.

"Ah, just so!" he said.

Kirkland drew back and the captain sat down, taking his place. Silent a moment, he looked at Walter carefully. "You can't inspire, eh?" he said.

"Yes, I know. I have had it. It is not pleasant."

With precise movements he stripped off a pair of tight black gloves and laid the back of his hand against Walter's cheek. "How long now?" he said to Francis. "An hour, or more?"

"Yes," said Francis, "I think so." He looked at his watch. "An hour and a half," he said, surprised. The woman from the *caisse* was close beside him, her monumental features warm with sympathy, but with a natural ghoulish hunger of interest, too. The old man with the apron looked sad and frightened. Lorna had come up. She stood tensely, her hands, terrible

and expressive, twisted together, near Kirkland. She had taken her hat off
—as though, Francis thought, she lived here; and what a surprise that
would be, like finding something beautiful or valuable in a rubbish heap.

"*Bon courage, mon petit,*" the captain said to Walter. "Be tranquil." He
put his hand on Walter's stomach. "Very hard," he said. "They strain so
hard. Well, we will not lose time." He gestured to the sergeant, who
opened and brought up beside him his case. "I will give him a little injection."

"You aren't in the habit of using adrenalin?" Francis said.

"No, Monsieur. Morphine sulphate."

"I see," said Francis. "I must tell you that he won't tolerate more than
a quarter-grain."

"In that case, we will not give him more than a quarter of a grain." He
drew a glass syringe from its case and fitted a needle to it. Looking at Walter attentively, he said, "You will not mind this. It will not be painful.
You will be easier very soon." He held up a glass vial and passed the needle
through the rubber cap. "Let us see, now. There. The forearm will do. We
will not disturb him to take his coat off. Now, we will wipe it with this,
and—there! It's in. Did you feel that?"

He laid the syringe aside and with the bit of cotton went on rubbing
the lump down. "Soon it will be easier," he said. "You are up here for the
skiing, eh? Yes, that's right. Try to breathe. Now, quietly, again. The first
time I took skis, you would have laughed. I was not very proficient—"
Talking on, he put his things away methodically, closed the case, and mo-
tioned to the sergeant to take it.

"There," he said. He dropped a hand over Walter's wrist and clasped it.
He said, "I cannot often get out for a run. It requires much practice, skiing.
Yes. Breathe in. Slowly, slowly. That was a little bit better, wasn't it?
No? Well, soon now it will be."

He was silent for a moment, studying Walter. "Soon it will be a little
better," he said again. "Do you speak French? Some, eh? We have a saying:
petit à petit, l'oiseau fait son nid. Do you understand that?"

The silence fell again for a moment. Then Walter's face contorted,
and gasping, he said, "It's about a bird."

"Ah!" said the captain. He raised his left hand and gently pinched Walter's cheek. "You see now?"

He held Walter's wrist a moment longer and then he laid it down.
"Now, it begins to stop. Yes, that is how the bird builds the nest. There,
that was good! It feels good, eh? Soon you will breathe all you want. You
can lie down then and take a little sleep. Is that better?"

"Yes, gosh," said Walter. He spoke feebly, wheezing still, but with an
ecstasy of relief.

"Yes. We will wait. Soon you will feel a little sleepy. That will be good. I do not think we need so many people here. You see, all your friends have been worried. Now, we have nothing to worry about. One will be enough, I think."

"Yes. I'll stay," Francis said. "His mother is on the way up. We telephoned her."

"That is good. I think he must remain here until tomorrow. It is a piece of work, one like this. We will make him easy and he will fall asleep. If he does not wake up until morning, that will be good." Extending his hand, the captain drew down one of Walter's eyelids. "Yes, we are over the bad part," he said. He patted Walter's cheek. "Your friend will be here; and I will be within reach; but you are not going to have any trouble."

From where he sat Francis could see the cold shadowed mountains, the darkening tone of the nearer mounds of pine tops, and a roof or two covered with a thick crusted layer of snow. On the wall the block of sunshine had moved up, deepening from yellow to dull orange, a winter glow reflecting less and less light through the room.

Huddled under a blanket, Walter was asleep, his head pushed into the pillow. From time to time he stirred, sighed, or getting his face too far down, snored lightly for a moment. The first time Francis started up, alarmed; but at the sound Walter unconsciously moved, breathed easy and even again, and Francis sat down. The sunlight on the wall disappeared and an early dusk filled the room. Over the pine tops and the snowy roofs extended a limitless, frigid, thinly turquoise sky, made infinitely remote by the long perspective of the now obscured mountains. Across it moved shoals of small clouds that were nearly pink.

Francis sat exhausted. One like this, he told himself, was a piece of work, all right. The final great relief took in its way as much out of you as the anguish of doubt—perhaps more, for a certain amount of anguish kept you from reflection. Once it was over the spent mind was left at loose ends, and shifted at random, looking with a discouraged eye at everything.

The possibility that he had not known how he could face, the possibility of having horrible news for, Mrs. Cunningham was gone; but she would still want to know how it happened. Francis did not know himself how it had happened, because whatever he had done afterward (and though done agitatedly, he could look at it now and see that it had been fairly prompt and sensible) he had not done the one thing he promised her he would do. He had let himself be otherwise engaged, he had not kept an eye on Walter; and in short the whole thing was a mess, and he might as well drop it.

Dropping it with disgust, his disgusted mind wandered on its ugly and

futile way. He thought of the doctor, in his manner with Walter, his sympathy and intelligence, so different from what Francis had wildly expected;
and yet (how mean and petty to think of it; how impossible not to notice it)
the collar or neckband, or whatever it was, of the shirt worn under his tunic
could be seen inside the uniform collar, and it was greasy with dirt. Recoiling in disgust from human beings, you had to recoil, in another disgust,
from your own recoiling; and so it went; and after years of distaste, with
little done and nothing not somehow spoiled, you could look forward to
the appropriate rewarding of patience or effort. You would be old—like
Mr. McKellar, with everything going, so that wit began to labor, ele-
gances grew grotesque or sinister, zest for life creaked at the joints—nearly
a joke. And then, perhaps, you could hope to grow into an outright joke,
like the Admiral at Grindelwald, with everyone secretly laughing; and then
(far past a joke, a horror) you might enjoy the longevity of that old man,
what was his name, his mother's acquaintance, the friend of George William Curtis, in Florence. Mr. Woodward—

There was a tap at the door, and quickly, to prevent a second louder
one that might disturb Walter, Francis sprang up and opened it. Light
shone from below up the staircase, and though there was no light in the
hall, a last dusk came from the end where through a window you could see
snow and the fading colors of the sky. Lorna was standing there. She whispered, "How is he?"

Francis drew the door closed. "All right," he said. "He's sleeping."

"Don't you want to go down and get some tea? I'll sit with him."

"Not if Emily is there. I have seen enough of her." He got out a package
of cigarettes. "I'm sorry," he said. "I seem to go on and on, don't I?"

"What—" She stopped. "Francis, I'm sorry I lost my temper. Let's
forget it, shall we?"

Francis looked at her dim face. "Yes, let's," he said. He lit a cigarette
for her, and then he lighted his own. He filled his lungs with smoke and
let his shoulders touch the wall behind him. She said, "You must be worn
out."

"In some ways. You'll be going down tonight, won't you? There's no
reason for you to stay."

"Well, we'll certainly stay until Mrs. Cunningham comes. I think
Emily's going pretty soon. There seems to have been a slight *rapproche-
ment*."

"Isn't that nice," said Francis. "I like everyone to be happy. You
wouldn't care to marry me tomorrow and go to Paris, would you?"

Taken by surprise, she gave in the gloom a marked start. "I—" she
began, and stopped; though with her lips left parted in some commotion
of feeling. For an instant it appeared that she might be nerving herself to

say yes. Her lips came together then, contracted in a strained smile, and she shook her head. "No," she said.

"Why not?" said Francis.

"Well—because you don't really want me to, for one thing."

"I will pass that over," Francis said. "I thought I would ask you. I'll probably be leaving Cap d'Ail tomorrow."

"Why?"

"Because Mrs. Cunningham is not going to require my services any longer."

"You mean, because of this? Why, how absurd! How could you help it? You were wonderful."

"The answer to that is, something happened to Walter; and nothing is supposed to happen to him while I am there. It's all in order."

"It's too unreasonable. She couldn't do that!"

"If she can and does, will you come to Paris with me?"

"No." She began to shake her head again.

Francis looked at his cigarette end. "I can't make you," he said. "What, if anything, you could see in me isn't clear. Of course I am trying to take advantage of you. Of course it isn't prudent, and so you are afraid. That's why you keep saying that I don't really want you. I think you'd better come. You see, I think you want to."

"Francis, I don't know," she said. "You could be right. Sometimes with all my heart I—would you do me a favor? I mean, really. It's rather a rotten trick, and I know it; but this has been a hell of a day. I can't think. I just don't know. Ask me tomorrow—I mean, if you still want to." She drew a breath and added: "That's not very fair, is it?"

"If you do it, it must be," Francis said.

"My dear—" She lifted a hand and laid it on his cheek. "Did you mean that; or were you being—"

"I meant it." Taking her wrist, he brought her hand over and kissed the fingers.

"Yes. Do mean it," she said. "I implore you—" She began to laugh. "I sound absurd, don't I? Of course it really isn't fair. I mean, what have I promised you?"

"Nothing," said Francis.

"And you don't mind?"

"I mind. But what can I do?"

"Ah, darling, I wish—"

"So do I," said Francis. He dropped her wrist. "Now, go downstairs like a good girl. I've got to keep an eye on Walter."

"Don't you want some tea?"

"No," he said. "Oddly enough, I don't." He stepped into the dark room, closed the door after him, and sat down on the chair again. In the sky beyond the darker pattern of the window sash the stars were coming out.

III

The door was open and a light had been put on.

Blinking, Francis saw Maggie, her face pinched with cold, wearing her coat and hat still. "Oh, poor Francis!" said Mrs. Cunningham.

"I'm afraid I was asleep," Francis said. He stood up with twinges of stiffness. Walter, disturbed, but not quite to the point of waking, moved on the bed.

"I'm sorry," Francis said. "I meant to get downstairs to tell you—" Lights were on in the hall outside, too, and there was a bustle of people coming and going—proof enough that Mrs. Cunningham had arrived. Beyond the door, Madame from the *caisse* gesticulated, the little old man scurried by, the chambermaid passed and repassed. Thousands at her bidding speed, Francis thought in the dazed levity of uncollected wits, and post o'er land and ocean without rest—

He said, "The doctor thinks he ought to sleep through. He did give him an injection. He seemed very intelligent, so I just told him about the quarter-grain, and let him."

"You were quite right," Mrs. Cunningham said. "I think we'll move him to another room, with two beds, so that Maggie can sleep there. It's being got ready now. Maggie, would you go and see how they're getting on?" Bending over the bed, Mrs. Cunningham put her hand on Walter's forehead. "He's not the least bit feverish," she said. Straightening up, she repeated, "Poor Francis! I felt dreadfully when I saw you asleep on that hard little chair. I could imagine how exhausted you were."

"I must have been," said Francis, embarrassed. "Though I don't know what I did, really. I don't know how it happened. Walter was all right at luncheon. Out on the hill he began to feel queer—"

"Lorna and Mr. Kirkland told me. Francis, I think you managed it wonderfully. They said you thought of everything. I blame myself a great deal for never having explained it to you. You see, it comes on at night, usually—"

"Walter told me," said Francis. "The truth is, if anyone was wonderful, Walter was. And Kirkland. He got Walter upstairs while—"

"Yes, he seems to be a nice young man. He and the girls are waiting downstairs. They mustn't wait. It's going to be a very long cold drive for them. Won't you go and tell them? Tell them I'm deeply grateful for everything they've done. It's such a shame that it turned out this way! You haven't had anything to eat, have you?"

"No," said Francis, "I—" Looking at his watch he discovered that it was eight o'clock.

"Lorna told me you wouldn't have any tea because you didn't want to leave Walter. I'll come down as soon as we have him settled, and we'll see if we can get some supper. I had Maggie pack a few things for you. I imagined we'd have to stay, and I thought you'd be more comfortable. I suppose you can use this room. I'll have them put in here."

"How are you going to move Walter?" Francis said.

"Oh, Maggie and I can do it. It's quite easy. Do go now and see that they get off. I really feel worried about that long drive in the dark."

"They won't have any trouble," Francis said. "Kirkland's very good with a car."

Downstairs in the lounge, Gwen was sitting alone. Seeing Francis, she said, "How's the patient?"

"All right," Francis said. Deserved or undeserved, Mrs. Cunningham's expressed approval had made his spirits lighter. "How's yours?" he said.

"You mean Emily? She went hours ago."

The touchiness in her tone was a great temptation, and Francis said, "Yes, I meant Emily. Did you dry those tears? Did she tell you the story of her life?"

"Oh, you!" said Gwen. The jerk of her head showed mixed feelings; grudging amusement, for maybe Emily had done just that and Gwen must confess the hit; indignation at his unfeeling phrases. "Men are such pigs!" she said. "I've never, never seen one yet who gave a damn, a single solitary damn, for anything but himself."

"You must mean Mr. Kirkland," said Francis. "I'm not like that."

"Oh, aren't you?" said Gwen. "You're one of the worst. I suppose it comes from being a writer, too. As if they weren't conceited and selfish enough without that." She made the sound and movement of tasting something nasty. "I could kill them all—sometimes." Reluctantly, she grinned; but you could see that she was not far from meaning it. Men were a great trial; and, often, paraphrasing Posthumus, she probably asked herself, is there no way for women to be, but men must be half-workers? It was not that Gwen disliked men; just, sometimes, she felt like killing them. It was not that they didn't attract her; they did; and no doubt the conflict of her feeling came out of the subconscious—its archetype perhaps in childhood memories of being happy playing some intricate, orderly game with other little girls; and, at the best moment, having it broken up noisily and stupidly, for no reason, by horrid boys—all the horrider, since she might have been wishing that boys would come, see, admire, and play nicely, too.

Francis stood looking down at her, entertained by the explosion, but also a little disturbed; for he began to see where he came in. Gwen opposed disorder, all kinds of disorder; and Francis would certainly bear watching. Out of affection for Lorna, Gwen had been friendly to him; but now, still out of affection for Lorna, she listened to the messages of that extra sense, no doubt telling her that this had begun to go too far; that more of the man-made disorder, actual and impending, lay in what he was doing with Lorna. Gwen believed in love, all right—but not sentimentality, which would never be sensible; and not passion, which staggered and smashed things.

Gwen kept her eye on the main point. As well as a girl who had a right to something called romance, not quite so frenzied as in *Romeo and Juliet*, not quite so fatuous as in a new musical comedy, Lorna was a valuable investment. She was a work of reason and order, the finished product of invested money, a good deal of it, well spent to feed and clothe and educate her; of invested time, twenty-odd years of patient shaping by precept and example to fit her with special skills and accomplishments to keep house and raise children, not any old way, but in the style to which the sort of man she was meant to meet and marry would be accustomed. This fortunate man had conditions to fulfill; and one of them—not, to Gwen, mercenary at all, not snobbish at all, just orderly and reasonable—was to lay on the line the cash to take up this investment. Then it would be time enough for him and Lorna to begin worrying about whether it was the nightingale and not the lark. Gwen might allow that love laughed at locksmiths; but at common sense love would laugh over Gwen's dead body.

The thought was sobering, one of those thoughts he tried to put aside, but Francis began lightly: "Now, as writers go, I am a very nice one, and—" He saw Lorna coming through the hall then. He said to her: "Mrs. Cunningham is worried about you. She asked me to see that you got started. She sends her regrets and thanks, and so on—"

Gwen said, "Goody went to get the car." She stood up and crossed over to the door and looked out of it.

"How is he?" Lorna said.

"All right."

"What did she say?"

"Oh, that," said Francis. "It seems that she got very good reports of me. As far as I know, I am still in her employ. I am afraid it eases your mind."

"All right," Gwen called. "Here he is."

"Francis, it really would have been mad."

"You must get started. You probably won't be home until midnight."

"Well, call me when you get down."

"Yes." He stepped out the door and stood on the hard snow by the car. Reaching to unlatch the door, Kirkland said, "How's Walter?"

"All right," said Francis. "It's a good thing you were here. I'd have been in a jam—"

"Bunk, old boy. You were the hero of the occasion." To Gwen he said, "Pile in. Both of you get in front. We can make it. It'll help keep you warm."

In the starlight Francis felt the biting air, and he pushed his hands into his pockets. Encountering something in one of them, he drew it out. "Here," he said to Lorna, "I forgot." He gave her the envelope with the lipstick scribbling on it.

She turned it over. "Oh. Thanks. It isn't anything."

"I didn't know. It felt as though there were a letter in it."

"It's just a note from a girl I know in Milan. She's coming to stay with us next week."

"Is she?" said Francis.

"Yes. She's studying at Milan. She has a marvelous voice."

"I know," said Francis.

"Darling," said Gwen. "Get in!"

"Faith Robertson? Do you know her?"

"I have met her."

"Darling, Francis is freezing. Do you want him to get his death of—"

"All right!" Lorna said. She got in and Francis closed the door. "Go inside this minute!"

"Be seeing you," said Kirkland. The car began to move.

"Good-bye," Francis said.

The grateful warmth of the lobby enclosed him. Mrs. Cunningham was coming downstairs, and mechanically Francis went to meet her. She smiled and said, "Did they get off all right?"

"Yes."

"Good. I've arranged to have some supper brought up for Maggie. They'll give us something in the dining room whenever we want it. Do you suppose they'd have a possible sherry? I feel as though I'd like some. You'd like a cocktail or something, wouldn't you?"

"Very much," said Francis.

"Poor Francis," said Mrs. Cunningham. "I should think you would. Shall we sit in here?" She led him into the empty lounge. "If you'll excuse me," Francis said, "I'll get something ordered, and wash. I haven't had time to—"

"Yes. Of course."

After he had found the maître d'hôtel, Francis went to the small wash-room under the stairs. There was no soap and the towel that hung on the wall had been in use for a week; but Francis did what he could without soap, and stood waving his hands in the air to dry them. He thought how astonished Mrs. Cunningham would be if, when he returned, he were to say to her: "The reason I look so queer is that something has just happened that upset me. You see, I care a great deal about Lorna. I even thought of marrying her and going to Paris tomorrow; but, of course, I'd have trouble supporting her, so I was only going to do that if you fired me—" (At this point, Mrs. Cunningham could hardly fail to think he had lost his senses, so he would have to get on with it quickly.)

"Well," he might say, "that's water over the dam. I seem to be staying on here with you; so that's all right. Or, at least it would be, except that, when I was coming up to join you at Montreux, I happened to try to seduce a girl I didn't like very much at Milan. I was feeling depressed, and we'd had a couple of drinks, and she was there, and you know how it is—" A painful nervous laughter shook him. His hands were still wet, so he took out a handkerchief and finished drying them. "Well, at any rate," he could go on, "she—this girl—knows Lorna. I don't mean that I think she'd say anything about my making a pass at her; but she's coming for a visit next week; and somehow I find the idea of seeing her again a little awkward. In fact, I can't do it. Not with Lorna around. What would you do, if you were I?"

What, indeed? What advice from Mrs. Cunningham to the lovelorn? You could not easily imagine telling Mrs. Cunningham such a story; but you could imagine easily enough what she, what any woman, would say to the problem presented: *It serves you right!* My advice is; it serves you right. Francis opened the door and crossed the lobby. A bottle of sherry, two glasses, and a plate of biscuits had been brought in and set before Mrs. Cunningham. Francis would have preferred something a little stronger; but he had not cared to make a point of the preference.

He sat down; and Mrs. Cunningham sipped her sherry, and he sipped his. She was tired, too, he saw; she, too, had had no tea; she, too, had had her anxieties; and in spite of his ironic reflections in the washroom, he looked at her with respect; just as, in spite of his distressing quandary, he felt a sort of ease, as though, like her, he had been through a lot and earned a rest. She smiled when he came in; but for several moments she said nothing.

"I have been thinking a little about plans," she said at last. "You remember I've mentioned some friends of ours who are at Taormina. I wonder if it might not be a little warmer there—" She was looking at him, and perhaps she saw some change in his face; for she said, "I wasn't thinking of going at once. Perhaps next month. Of course, I know we mustn't keep moving around. I know it upsets Walter's work. What do you think?"

My advice, Francis thought, is: it serves you right. They put the question to you fair: woul't weep? woul't fight? woul't fast? woul't tear thyself? woul't drink up eisel? And what did you say? You said: I loved her very much, her face was charming. There was something about her I wanted. Maybe it was her soul; maybe it has a coarse name. But, on the whole, no. I will not weep, fight, fast, tear myself, nor drink up eisel.

Francis said, "It would be better for Walter, wouldn't it?"

"Well, I think it might."

Francis faltered; yet his faltering, like that change in his face, ought not to be dismay; for what could suit him better? All places that the eye of heaven visits are to the wise man ports and happy havens! He said, "It seems to me that if there is any chance that it would be better, we ought to go to Taormina." Habit made him pause cautiously; but this time, what was there to worry about? It cost him a pang to have to want it; but this time what he wanted was also what (How fortunate! How fortunate he always was!) Mrs. Cunningham wanted. He smiled and said, "I think we should go as soon as possible. This week, if it can be arranged."

Mrs. Cunningham had not, perhaps, expected so cordial an agreement. She looked at him with mild inquiry. She said, "You don't mind leaving so soon, Francis?"

The considerateness that used a form of asking ought to be acknowledged. "That's very kind of you," Francis said warmly. "But no, I would be glad to go."

Out of the dining room came the maître d'hôtel, bustling and important in his shabby dress clothes. He proclaimed: *"Madame est servie!"* With a clumsy but respectful flourish, he bowed, putting his hand on his heart.

II

Whatever Wishful Thinking May Wish: The Example of James Gould Cozzens
By George Garrett

Like many, maybe most of the American writers of my generation, I earn a large part of my keep by teaching reading and writing to college students who have a limited experience of both. One of the most crippling things they suffer from, as readers and writers, is a diminishing number and variety of exemplary normative models. There are times when you might well imagine that all the known possibilities of and for prose fiction are to be found somewhere between the graceful fidgets of Donald Barthelme and the salad-talk of Thomas Pynchon. Too bad, they (and I include Pynchon and Barthelme among them) could all learn a great deal from the example of James Gould Cozzens, looking at what he has done (his art) and what has become of it (his career).

Rereading Cozzens's work this time, I am struck most by the variety of it, the wide range of what he can do, therefore the choices he is able to make and has made. (A writer who writes only one kind of book is either obsessive and can't help himself or a hypocrite and the hustler of a single brand name.) Choice is the burden and the privilege of freedom. Freedom, as I understand it and within the limits of heredity, environment, and necessity, is something the artist celebrates, aspires to, hopes for. To dance, as graceful as can be, in chains. Absence of models for the student and apprentice means a corresponding absence of choices. Meaning, then, that in art as in life, we are learning to live and work within dwindling and ever more strictly limited freedom.

Of course I can understand why Cozzens is not taught much, if at all, these days in the colleges. In academic circles, especially in the last twenty-five or thirty years during which the study and the teaching of contemporary literature has become eminently respectable, he has never been likely to have or to gain much support. There are lots of reasons. One: the briefly captive "youth audience" is not really capable of dealing, not ready to deal with the materials, both form and content, of the major Cozzens novels. These works—like, for example, those of Joyce Cary or Wright Morris—are far from easy to teach or talk about in the classroom. The best literary works, for teaching purposes, are those with obvious and interesting or entertaining secondary or decorative characteristics. It is much more satisfactory for everyone to discuss style and imagery and structure, for example, than to test the tense and subtle relationship between the characters in the world of a fiction and the people, as we perceive them, in Real Life. Teachers are not interested in embracing difficulty. The teacher is primarily interested in developing himself as a performer. He, or she, looks for the literary work which can offer the greatest occasion for recognizable pedagogical virtuosity. Sometimes it is a work of quality and character. Sometimes it is not.

It is exactly for this reason that a great many highly regarded contemporary American writers (themselves products of the self-same academic system and destined to serve it in flesh and fact) have adopted the reasonable strategy of ignoring those elements of fiction that were once considered primary and have instead cultivated a fiction almost entirely composed of secondary and decorative effects. It could be argued that many of our most highly regarded serious writers have, perhaps wisely, chosen to exploit the superficial characteristics of fiction and to assume a retrogressive stance and pose of deliberate immaturity. Aiming to speak to a special group of the young, who are in this era as innocent and inexperienced in reading as they are of the lives of grown men and women, some of our best and brightest writers have come to depend upon tricks and pyrotechnical effects to capture and hold limited attention spans. And they have come to affect a rhetorical sensibility which lies somewhere between the infantile and the retarded. This combination of a sophisticated technique with a simplistic authorial sensibility has generated some of the most breathtakingly trivial literature since the great rash of sonnet sequences in the final years of the sixteenth century.

In any event, none of Cozzens's books was written for the academy or to make critics and teachers feel and look good. Since the New Academics (direct descendants of the New Critics) depend for their very survival on the celebration of the trivial, there is bound not to be much place for the work of Cozzens in their scheme. And there are other causes of and opportunities for conflict. Professors are more or less professionals and might be expected to have some sympathy and understanding at least for the main line of Cozzens's "professional" novels. But professors are not nearly so well paid as doctors, lawyers, and even the military. (I exclude the clergy.) Most professors hate the professionals. Moreover, for a very long time and dominantly so since World War II, in politics the Academy has been a sort of sacred grove, strongly dedicated to the Left. For many reasons—not the least of them being his techniques of story telling which are, at least superficially, highly objective and dramatic—I cannot honestly gauge or infer the politics of James Gould Cozzens. I can tell more or less where the characters stand. His central characters, whether liberal or conservative, among the American professionals are not revolutionaries or even Marxists. For some time in America (unless you happened to be lucky enough to be a Southerner and thus mostly outside of conventional labels and indices, beyond the pale, as it were) it has been dangerous for the career and reputation of any writer not to be a clearly identified member-in-good-standing of the Left. Even though he was southern, William Faulkner's career suffered more than once because of this. So, for a time, did Hemingway's and Fitzgerald's and O'Hara's and Dos Passos's. Cozzens has suffered too. Using the thoughts and feelings of some of his characters as evidence, together with some vaguely recalled scraps from the celebrated distortions of the *Time* magazine cover story of almost twenty years ago concerning *By Love Possessed*, critics have conveniently labelled Cozzens as a rigid reactionary. Therefore, in the thinking of at least some academics, since the Constitution appears to prohibit the outright suppression of annoying literature, truth and social justice require that his work should be ignored.

II

Although on rereading I found Cozzens's fiction must more various than I had remembered, still I can justify the memory because the main line of his mature work seems to be centered in the "professional" novels: *The Last Adam* (1933), *Men and Brethren* (1936), *The Just and the Unjust* (1942), *Guard of Honor* (1948), *By Love Possessed* (1957), and *Morning Noon and Night* (1968). There is always some overlapping in these novels, if only because the professionals inevitably deal with and relate to each other. But essentially we have a fiction built upon and around the lives of characters who are twentieth-century American professionals in the areas of law, medicine, the church, and the military. The central characters are (mostly) mature men of various ages who believe in their disciplines and who are, in fact, the men whose work has the power to shape and direct the quality of life in this country. No other serious American writer, except John O'Hara with whom Cozzens shares some concerns, but whose purpose was always somewhat different, has succeeded in dealing so effectively and seriously with this class and group of people. Which seems to me important for a number of reasons. First of all, because it is these people, the professionals, who have in fact and for better and worse most profoundly influenced American life in this century. Judging by most of our fiction, you might assume that the United States is chiefly populated by criminals, anti-heroes, wise children, schizophrenics, clowns, and, of course, plenty of professors and artists. It would be easy enough, on the strength of most serious and recent American fiction, to assume that nobody much puts in a day's work in the U. S. A., and certainly nobody does anything that might be called honorable or interesting. You might infer that the few among us who are sane are to be found trout fishing in Idaho or running from the bulls in Pamplona or white water canoeing in north Georgia. The so-called middle-class American in the workaday setting has often engaged the attention of popular writers, but the more prestigious, literary writers have simply avoided the problem, its challenges, and risks.

Which is strange. Because if we are even to try to understand what has been happening in America in this century, we have to understand the professionals. Witness both the heroes and the villains of Watergate. It is also a simple fact that almost all of the actual and potential "reading public" in America, throughout this century and no less now than earlier, is composed of mature men and women of the professional class. They are the only ones who have either time or interest or money for reading. There is no real "youth audience" for books of any kind (including paperbacks) outside of the briefly bookish and limited context of American higher education. In fiction and in poetry the heroes of college students are, almost exclusively, *assigned* heroes. It is no wonder that these heroes have brief lives in the light. Remember *Lord of the Flies? The Catcher in the Rye?* Renown and repute are gifts coming from an extremely self-centered group with a very short memory. Otherwise, aside from the captive audience of students, none of the other groups, which have been cultivated for purposes of exploitation by American publishers, has existed as a reading public except in the wishful thinking of the aforesaid publishers. The simple and statistical truth is that, so far in this century, Blacks don't read books, Chicanos don't read books, Native Americans don't read books. Ethnics don't read books. (The one great exception is the Jewish minority. Jews read lots of books and are a real audience.) Even Liberated Women, it seems, don't read books outside of the academic context. If there is going to be any audience at all for books by or about Blacks, Chicanos, Native Americans, Orientals, Ethnics (pure or impure), Liberated or Total Women, or even students, it is to be found in the standard "reading public" of America. Which is to say it will be middle-aged, upper middle class, professional in orientation, and predominantly female. The plain fact is that for all of this century in America the people who buy and read the books have been and still are mostly the wives of professional men. It is a small audience and appears to be dwindling.

The relationship of Cozzens to this audience should be interesting and instructive. His first novel was published in 1924, so he has had an active professional career of more than fifty years. Of course, we have to admit first and then keep in mind something that is not generally accepted by the critics and historians of modern American literature—that whatever else may be said about the present state of letters in this country, the workshop and the marketplace of it, it is radically different from that of the earlier generation of American masters. For the first generation of twentieth-century American writers, which has to include Cozzens as a younger member, it may or may not have been respectable to be a novelist, but it evidently seemed a reasonable thing for a grown-up to do, even though the odds were bad and the required sacrifices were considerable. At this stage it is no longer a rational ambition to wish to be a serious novelist. I have said elsewhere, and still maintain, that it makes about as much sense today to write a novel as to set out to be a professional kite flyer. So, when we look to the writers of the earlier generation for instruction and example, it's best to remember that, at least in the beginning, they were clearly saner than we are.

Having lived and worked long and well into our own times, Cozzens seems to have kept up with the times. And, as it happens, he has something recent and direct and explicit to say on the subject of success. It is something which he wrote to go along with his biographical sketch in the 1976–77 Bicentennial Edition of *Who's Who In America*. As an innovation for this special edition, the editors solicited statements from biographees, "statements of those principles, ideas, goals and standards of conduct that have helped them achieve success and high regard." Cozzens complied with the editorial request, though not, I'd guess, in precisely the terms they had in mind. His statement sounds more than a little bit like the words and thoughts of his own Henry Worthington in *Morning Noon and Night*. Cozzens wrote: "The longer I watch men and life, the surer I get that success whenever more than minor comes of luck alone. By comparison, no principles, ideas, goals, and standards of conduct matter much in an achieving of it."

Notice that he ignores the other most ambiguous part of the query— "high regard."

Coming from a certifiably successful American, that statement reads like what the theologians call a hard saying. Certainly if success (and consequently failure as well) come "of luck alone," then neither praise nor blame can attach to either condition. It follows, then, that only a fool would hope for the justice of more than minor reward or greatly fear the risk of failure. It follows that success and failure, in the terms of *Who's Who*, are meaningless.

Cozzens should know something about both success and failure. In his time he has had more than one best seller, and he has won important prizes. At one time and another he has been praised by many of the best-known critics and reviewers. By the same token he has also been subjected to the most outrageous (bordering on the purely malicious) kind of personal and artistic attacks. He has made the complete circuit with Fortune's wheel, seen both sides of the rainbow. It follows that his views on good luck and bad are to be taken seriously.

Luck (in the separate senses of both Fortune and Providence) plays an important part in all of Cozzens's fiction. In *Morning Noon and Night*, Henry Worthington thinks and talks a good deal about luck, and in one place he has some comments on the part it plays in the literary situation in America. Here is what Worthington has to say on the subject:

> The publisher who has unprofitably published a book, like the writer who wrote it, is taught nothing. The lesson they learn is only that they are out of luck. I used the word advisedly, for adducible figures from our publishing studies seem to show beyond doubt that neither merit as a piece of writing nor excellence, by literary standards of the moment, as a creative work is the determining factor in making a book a best seller. Indeed, as far as merit goes, so many books of no merit (that is, subsequently conceded to be without any) have had very large sales that, considering these alone, the hypothesis that badness does the trick— you find it proposed by almost every failed-writer-turned-critic in the literary-circle jungle—may seem tenable. It is not tenable because, whatever wishful thinking may wish, there are other figures to show that books of much and evident merit (that is, by subsequent critical consensus held so to be) often sell equally well.

Anybody lost in "the literary-circle jungle" today would be well advised to read Cozzens and to listen to Worthington. Perhaps with some regularity. Also with the understanding that in one small respect the advice and counsel are out of date. With few enough exceptions to make the rule seem iron-clad, no serious fiction sells well in this final quarter of our century. That is (and I like to think both Cozzens and Worthington might appreciate the irony of this), the difference between "success" and "failure" is so small that these very terms are virtually without meaning. Just so, the most "successful" novels published today would, in a relative sense (and I am as sure as Worthington that figures would bear me out), have to be called "failures" when compared with the most successful fiction of the previous generation. Yet even that fact, as Cozzens has shown us, is irrelevant.

III

Take this, if you will, as it intends to be, informal and personal, one working writer's brief attempt to express gratitude to and admiration for an influential writer of another generation. In that sense it has to be about "influence." Which is, I suppose, a word for teaching outside the classroom. In addition to the pleasure and instruction available for all readers of the fiction of James Gould Cozzens, there are special lessons for the writer. At a bad time for the art of writing, one of our most productive craftsmen has much to teach the rest of us. He offers a superior example of the integrity of the craft, of the daring refinement of language, of the creation of fully realized characters who matter, of structures and patterns of experience which seem, in the major novels, to shadow the complex patterns of Fortune and

Providence in our lives. Technically he can do it all and without seeming effort or wasted motion. It may not be possible, or even particularly useful, to use Cozzens as a specific model or to deal in the same way with the same kinds of subjects and materials; but every writer, certainly every apprentice and journeyman, can learn almost all that is worth knowing about technique from studying his work.

More important than that, however, is the example of the man and artist. Not the private man, who is, in spite of attention, unknown; but rather the man in the public light, bearing with equal grace his good luck and his bad. A cliché among the writers of my own generation, offered up when exchanging complaints, is: "Oh well, no matter what happens it can't be as bad as it was for Herman Melville." True enough. . . . It also can't be any better or any worse than it has been for Cozzens. That the best and the worst can be gracefully borne is as much a challenge as a consolation. That neither success nor failure need be a crippling condition, that it remains always possible freely to choose to do honestly and to do well without regard to what Cozzens calls luck, seems to me one of the most important lessons I can hope to pass on to my students whether they learn to read and write or not. Of course, it would help if they did learn to read. Because then they could find it for themselves in the novels of James Gould Cozzens.

Dr. Bull
[from *The Last Adam*]

New Winton lay there, but George Bull could not see it. The crest of the Cobble, now far below, concealed the village. He could see fields just west of it; the red brick, extensive slate roofs and cupola with golden top of the new village school; and part of the Episcopal cemetery. Beyond that, the fringe of bare trees marked the edge of the frozen river. He could even make out a small truck moving down the road to the heavy-beamed steel arc of the bridge.

Looking down more directly, between the slope of the hill he stood on and the low bump of the Cobble on which a thin screen or scruff of trees had been left, there was the round spot of the reservoir, adequately isolated. Two brooks, which joined with a now sunken spring to feed it, could be traced by their rocky courses some distance up and back through the irregular hillside. North, were the roofs of Joel Parry's house and barns. Seen from here, it looked very much as though Joel's barnyard would drain into the reservoir. George Bull wished that such a thing could be suspected. Then, as Health Officer, he could have Joel's whole place condemned and make him a lot of trouble. As a matter of fact, Joel's land was on a lower level, sloping into the gentle depression widening on, north, between Cold Hill and the northern point of the Cobble. Following this funnel-shaped falling away, one could see, well north, clear through the naked trees, the French provincial outlines of the house Norman Hoyt's cover-designing for a popular weekly had financed. It looked very pleasant this snowy morning. Thin blue smoke mounted, it seemed as much as fifty yards, straight up from the chimney at the end.

Out the small gap where the bridge road went west through the hills to Truro came the newest feature of the valley. George Bull hadn't seen the Interstate Light & Power Company's high tension transmission line with all the steel up before. It was said to be the most considerable yet erected in the East and George Bull could believe it. Even at this height the towers marched in tremendous parade. Gray skeleton galvanized steel, they crossed the narrow river, the flat fields, and, high above a special wire guard, US6W. They were hard to overlook; they were to carry 220,000 volts and it was deemed expedient to lift up such a thunderbolt on towers ninety-seven feet tall where there was any chance of people moving around and under them. Once across the valley, they shortened to get over the wooded rise which turned the railroad and US6W into two separate south-bound channels. The line took, in effect, four relatively squat steps up hill and across the summit. Now the great towers were resumed again, three of them standing at thousand-foot intervals between the south slope of the Cobble and the north end of a marshy sheet of water close to the railroad track, called Bull's Pond.

Through a denuded swath in the succeeding second-growth woods, the line stepped up the eastern valley wall. It straddled the roofs of the con-struction camp, lying southeast, behind and above the round spot of the reservoir. By turning, staring that way through the haze and shine of sun on snow and the blur of white bottomed woods, George Bull could see the tower tops in unbroken sequence, departing majestically to the hazed hori-zon. It couldn't be said to add much to the rural beauty, but it was some-thing to see. George Bull laughed, for Mrs. Banning had made an awful fuss about it—as it happened, belatedly, when the right of way had been quietly secured and the concrete footings for the towers were being put in.

He supposed it was quite an outrage to Mrs. Banning's proprietary feel-ing about New Winton. Looking back to the extreme high end of the Cob-ble, he could see a part of the aged, almost orange brick of the Cardmaker house set in its great trees, and he laughed again, for Mrs. Banning had had trouble there too. Four or five years ago Janet Cardmaker and her house had thrown New Winton into a turmoil of the sort which George Bull most enjoyed.

The Cardmaker house was the fourth of four houses actually dating from the eighteenth century. Of course, it was a close thing; it had been built in 1790. Levi Cardmaker, who happened to have lost his ears in En-gland, was doing better in America. About the middle of the century he had shrewdly possessed himself of what was then regarded as an iron mine, a few miles west of Truro. By the river he had built and owned New Winton Furnace. In 1777 New Winton Furnace cast fifty cannon for the Continen-tal Army, and they were paid for, gold in advance; a fortunate turn for Mr. Cardmaker, for the Continental Army never got them. When, in April, the patriots ran from the Ridgefield barricade, allowing the British to escape from burned Danbury, these cannon, unmounted and cradled for ship-ment, made the choicest item of the spoils. Mr. Cardmaker had better luck in keeping his gold. The house he built when he judged (even in his timo-rous old age) it was safe to build houses was much the finest and most elabo-rate in that whole corner of the state.

At any rate, New Winton had been taking this fine house calmly enough for rather more than a hundred years. Since it was not down on the green, it was as good as forgotten when a Mr. Rosenthal happened on it. Mr. Rosenthal was excited. Janet herself said that she thought he was going to have a stroke when she told him anything he wanted was for sale.

Recovering, Mr. Rosenthal had wanted a good part of the furniture in the front rooms. Plainly he would have liked the whole house, but since that was impractical, he took mantelpieces and paneling. Carefully and expertly, men he brought up for the purpose removed the long curved stair rail in the hall. They took the semicircular porch with four thin white columns; door, lintel, fanlight, and the beautiful scrolled iron work done by a blind German at the long-gone New Winton Furnace forge. Mr. Rosenthal gladly had his carpenters build Janet a new door at no expense to her. The truth was, he paid very well for what he took.

Now, led of course by Mrs. Banning, came the uproar. No possibility of doing it remained, but warm talk turned on the advisability of buying so fine and historic a mansion. A queer creature like Miss Cardmaker actually had no right to it; it belonged to posterity. Most of the uproar necessarily subsided when Mr. Rosenthal, personally supervising every operation, departed for New York, shepherding a truckful of spoils. The victory was his, if one excepted the spectacular triumph of Henry Harris, then a Justice of the Peace.

No one in the village was too humble, or too indifferent to resent (once told of what it consisted) this brigandage; but only Mr. Harris could find effective expression for the feeling. After consulting the town records he was able to announce that if Mr. Rosenthal was so keen on antiques, here was another for him. It was an ordinance passed in 1803. It provided a fine of twenty-five dollars for trespassing on the village green by a non-resident without written permission from a selectman. Once it had served to keep itinerant peddlers from camping there. Henry Harris guessed that it would apply just as much to Mr. Rosenthal, seen to be impudently walking around the old Congregational church which stood on this public land. Mr. Harris sent for Lester Dunn, one of the constables, and Lester went and arrested Mr. Rosenthal, who was examining the edifice with painstaking appreciation. Mr. Harris read him the regulation. If Mr. Rosenthal didn't think it applied to him, he'd better send for his lawyers and let them show Mr. Harris why not. Mr. Rosenthal paid. There were, he remarked, somewhat redder in the face but quiet and patient, many quaint and interesting things to be found in the old records.

Mrs. Banning, Doctor Bull guessed, was having quite a time, since in natural operation the course of events went against her. She got there late in the process. In 1774, nine hundred more people lived in New Winton than lived there now. They must have lived in houses; but only three of the houses they could have lived in were left—what they would have called the new Cardmaker house was almost twenty years in the future as they saw it. Changes and accidents which had reduced the count of eighteenth-century houses to four, would naturally proceed until there were none. The Bannings had two of them—that was, their own large house had been developed out of one and then restored back as far as practicable, and they owned the little Allen house, which figured in all books on the subject, across the way. George Bull knew that they coveted the Bull house; but their hostility to him personally kept them from making an offer. If Mrs. Cole—Aunt Myra—died, he wouldn't mind selling it—he supposed it would have to be to the Bannings; but, he reflected, grinning, not before he'd made an effort to find a wealthy Jew who might like to buy it—to live in, that was, not to take away. Mrs. Banning, bristling with upper middle-class New England abhorrence of New York Jews, would do some squirming then. That would really get her. He could imagine her saying: "Some dreadful people named Oppenheimer have that fine old house. They're the most odious and pushing sort of Jews. But what can you do? They simply force their way in everywhere. . . ."

George Bull's laugh boomed out unabashed by solitude. Suddenly remembering what he had come for; that he had at least a dozen of those damn brats to vaccinate, he took his bag. Walking around the bleak, unpainted corner of the barn, he swung open a gate and so approached the back door of the Crowe house.

It was after three o'clock when George Bull, down from Cold Hill, drove into Janet Cardmaker's road. He had just gone through the shadows lying along behind the Cobble, past the white, restored Colonial of the Lincoln place, past the Hoyts'. He was later than he had meant to be. The Crowes had given him dinner after he finished with the children—great quantities of tasteless scalding food and tumblers full of hard cider. He felt very cheerful. When, just past the Hoyts', he encountered Virginia Banning, driving a new Ford coupé, he roared, "All right. Wait a minute." With some difficulty he backed a hundred feet to a point where she could pass. She said, curt, unsmiling: "Thank you."

George Bull didn't resent the attitude, copied from her mother, for he guessed that Virginia was a longer thorn than he was when it came to pricking Mrs. Banning. "Got a bit of old Paul in her," he decided, remembering Mr. Banning's father. He liked her frail, still adolescent face; the cheeks a little hollowed; her sulky small mouth. Virginia Banning's blue eyes had a defiant gleam, as though she would like to tell every one to go to hell. There was, too, a wiry rebelliousness about her narrow, fleshless buttocks —he could picture her best walking down to the post office, the wind tightening her skirt around a frank, limber stride; a short, fur-collared leather jacket buttoned across her practically breastless chest. Only one of the lot with any guts, he always thought; and that amused him, for he guessed if she had been born fifteen years later, a hell-bent for science fellow like Doctor Verney at Sansbury would have changed her altogether. Irradiated ergosterol might have done the trick. Verney would tell you all about it— a trifling deficiency of the antirachitic vitamin D, with a consequent shortage of actually assimilated lime and phosphorus. That accounted for the constriction of the jawbones, giving her face that fragile, determined shape; a flattening of the chest cavity; a narrow, somewhat rachitic pelvis. Normal parturition would probably kill her; but fellows like Verney considered the course of nature undignified and poorly planned anyway. All that waiting around and mess, when a nice little Caesarian section—

He laughed, thinking: "I guess I needn't figure how to get it out until she finds somebody to put it in"; and then he laughed again, with relish, for he could imagine Mrs. Banning probably having a stroke at the impropriety of such gross speculations. He blinked into the golden sun and brought his car to a halt. Stepping out on the snow, beaten hard, stained with horse dung, polished in spots by the runners of a big sled, he went and banged on the kitchen door.

There was no answer. Turning, he saw yellow electric light in the small square windows piercing the concrete foundations of the big barn. Janet might be down there.

As he pressed his bulk through it, the narrow opening left in the wagon doors was forced wider. His boots resounded on the planking while he walked familiarly to the stairs in the corner. Down their dark turnings the cobwebs came off on his swinging fur. He shoved the door at the bottom open with his foot and stepped out.

"Hello, George," Janet nodded. "I could tell you a mile off. Harold thought it was an elephant upstairs."

Harold Rogers, her farmer, sallow, unshaven, in overalls and a black leather coat, grinned. "'Lo, Doc," he said. "One of those little Devons is kind of sick. Don't know what's wrong with her."

Janet Cardmaker wore a garment which she had made herself—eight or ten red fox skins sewed over an old cloth coat. Though the cows filled the long cement stable with a humid, ammoniacal warmth, she hadn't bothered to unbutton this. A round cap, also of fox skin, was crammed casually down on her head. The big bones of her face made her look gaunt, but she was, in fact, very solid; stronger than most men; almost as tall as George Bull, and fully a head taller than Harold Rogers. From under the circular rim of the cap's yellow fox fur some of her dark hair escaped, disordered. Her black eyes rested contemptuously a moment on Harold. She said: "Look at her, will you, George? She's an awful sick cow."

Harold said: "Might be a kind of milk fever, Doc. I—"

"Let's see," answered George Bull. "Oh. Down there."

He walked along the row of placid rumps; the cows, their necks in hangers, patient, incurious. On the cement, the last of the line had collapsed. Released from the hanger, she lay on her side, her lean, bony head against the feeding trough. In her terrible prostration, her ribs rose like a hill. Her great eyes were fixed in a stupor, hopeless and helpless; her legs inertly pointing.

George Bull stooped, put out a gloved finger and poked her udder.

"Milk fever, hell!" he said. "And listen to her breathe!"

Stepping over the stiff out-thrust of the hind legs, he pulled off his glove. Stooping again, he felt along the stretched neck until his big fingers discovered the artery in the lower throat. Compressing it, he looked at his watch. After a moment he announced, "That's better than one hundred." Unbuttoning his coat, he pulled a clinical thermometer case from his pocket, extracted the thermometer. "Good as any other," he said. He shook it, pushed it between the folds of skin where the hind leg lay half over the udder. "Bet you it's a hundred and five," he said. He looked at Harold. "Kind of milk fever, huh? Don't you even know what pneumonia looks like?"

He recovered the thermometer. "Hundred and four and a half," he observed. "Probably really more. Do you want to try to save her? Devons aren't much use to you anyway."

"They cost money," answered Janet. "It's not your cow."

"All right, get together about an acre of mustard plaster. Harold can beat it down to Anderson's pharmacy—" he fumbled until he found a notebook. Tearing out a sheet and taking a pencil, he began to write, reading aloud: "Twenty drops of aconite and one ounce of acetate of ammonia in— oh, say, a half-pint of water. Every two hours or so. Get a blanket and cover her up. In the morning, she ought to be dead, so you needn't bother to telephone Torrington for a vet. Harold can fix it."

"Fix it, Harold," Janet agreed. "Come on up to the house, George."

The front rooms of the Cardmaker house were as Mr. Rosenthal had left them, stripped of furniture, the stairs with no rail. The new front door was never used. Janet lived in the kitchen wing, principally in the enormous kitchen, sleeping in a small bedroom up the back stairs. A Mrs. Foster came every day in summer, but in winter, when walking was harder, only twice a week, to do what washing and cleaning was done. Janet, when alone, fed herself. Harold Rogers lived with his wife in a cottage on the slope beyond the barn. This Belle Rogers was one of a locally recurring pale, wan, blond type, descended probably from a single, pale, wan, but prolific individual five or six generations back. Janet ignored Belle's existence and George Bull didn't doubt that Belle tried to pay Janet back by spreading the continually resowed crop of scandalous rumors about his own intimacy with Janet. It was the sort of pale, wan, reprisal you'd expect from Belle; such rumors were an old story and Belle could hardly animate them into interest. George Bull didn't care in the least, remarking to Janet: "Somebody's started them chewing on the same old stuff. By God, I'm sixty-seven years old! They ought to get up a delegation to congratulate me."

Janet made no comment beyond shrugging her shoulders. Her indifference to talk in the village was so complete that George Bull doubted if she ever felt any of the pleasure he had in disregarding what was said. At moments like that he could understand Janet best. In her despoiled house, her grotesque clothes, her solitary existence, she was entirely free from the ceaseless obligations of maintaining whatever appearance you pretended to. Many people soothed themselves by saying that Miss Cardmaker was crazy; but George Bull guessed, when you thought it over, that they were the crazy ones. Other people—it would be the Bannings—thought that it was terrible. They meant that James Cardmaker's daughter had no business to live in a kitchen, eat her own cooking, care for her own cows. Her father, they said, would turn in his grave if he—

George Bull could remember Mr. James Cardmaker perfectly. Janet was about eighteen when her father finally died. She had been away for a year or so at some women's college, and it was Mr. Cardmaker's grave illness that brought her home. George Bull used to come up once or twice a week. The complaint had been, or had appeared to be, a multiple neuritis. Though Mr. Cardmaker was no drinker, his affliction showed many of the symptoms of an alcoholically induced one. George Bull couldn't help him; all he could do was charge for his visits.

Janet was around, of course; receiving his orders and instructions, of which Doctor Bull gave a good many, making up—he'd been younger then himself—learnedly for his actual helplessness in the case. Janet he'd known —in the sense that it is possible to know a child—for years. Meanwhile she had grown into a big, plain, dark girl. His head was as active as most men's on the subject, but George Bull was sure that the idea of seducing Janet had never entered it. Being Janet Cardmaker, she could be expected to order her life on the accepted lines of a dreary, drily educated, consciously high-thinking, virtue. Everything agreed with it—her plainness; her father's intellectual and moral tastes; her going away to college. George Bull certainly hadn't been prepared, that afternoon—well, he guessed it was twenty-eight years ago.

About this time of year, too; for he could remember Janet—the indelibly fixed details of great surprise assured that—standing by the window at the end of the upper hall, looking out at snow on the ground and the bare limbs of the maples. He had just left Mr. Cardmaker. Hearing him, she turned, coming down toward him, and he paused halfway, meeting her, ready to give her some needless directions. She said: "This is my room. Come in a minute."

"What do you want?"

It wasn't, even in this, her so startlingly arranged initial experience, at all an emotional matter with her. George Bull was free to enjoy, at least, the great relief of not having to pretend that it was with him. Janet simply said: "Go on. Go ahead." Even her own ignorant awkwardness did not disconcert her. She frankly expected him to instruct her. It was his problem, not hers; and to the solutions he found, she assented with a violent inexpert willingness.

The old man procrastinated. He considered himself a genealogical authority, because the Boston *Transcript* had frequently published letters of his about Connecticut families on its Saturday page. The hobby gave him something to do, or try to do, through the miserable tedium of dying. He took notes which he did not appear to recognize as the almost letterless scrawls his drooping hands made them. At least once Doctor Bull found him puzzling, in a bewilderment more grim, or even ghastly, than comic, over pages of books held upside down. Like his pendent wrists, his skin-covered face without flesh, his shoulders humped to his little round head, this confusion of aimless, vaguely human activity suggested one thing only. When you saw him shaking and shifting the book held upside down, you saw, too, what James Cardmaker—his notes in the *Transcript*, his historic house and name, his college-educated daughter, aside—really was. Not merely evolved from, or like an ape, Mr. Cardmaker was an ape. The only important dissimilarities would be his relative hairlessness and inefficient teeth.

George Bull came twice a week to look at this phenomenon. Janet, adroitly arranging occupations for the servants, would follow him upstairs and go into her room to wait until he had seen as much as the collection of his fee required of Mr. Cardmaker's inane persistence in living.

This was all right, so long as the old man did manage to live. In the village everybody knew how sick Mr. Cardmaker was. Doctor Bull's willingness to go up so often was, if anything, a credit to him. Going up after Mr. Cardmaker was dead would be different. George Bull planned, as a matter of fact, to end the affair with Janet altogether. He expected to be tired of her; not realizing that mere beauty was what custom staled. Until a man withered into impotence he would not tire of Janet's vital, almost electric sensuality.

It was the summer of 1903 that Mr. Cardmaker died. George Bull could remember the very warm, very clear and beautiful day of his funeral. The doors of St. Matthias's Church were standing open on the sunlit green and the hot wind in the trees. Afterwards, they went out to the cemetery behind and stood in the sun. Several women put up parasols. He could remember the strong south wind shuffling the pages of Doctor Hall's prayer book. The cast-up earth of the hole was dried to a crumbling yellow.

There, then, around that grave, George Bull had been able to see New Winton—every person who could be said to matter, with many who did not. They stood sweltering together, formally seeing the last of James Card-maker. Here were the ones he had to think of; old Paul and Mathilda Banning; Joseph Allen and his two elderly sisters; Samuel, his wife Sarah, and his brother, Daniel, Coulthard; the Herrings from Banning's Bridge; Micah Little from Truro—not one of those was left alive now. Perhaps thirty other adults, important only in so far as their talk might bring a matter to the superior handful's attention, and a scattering of restless, unwilling children raised the total attendance to sixty or seventy. Because of these people, he could not, plainly, continue to visit Janet Cardmaker.

In the early nineteen hundreds it hadn't occurred to George Bull that he could go anywhere, with or without proper reason, as often as he pleased; and if New Winton—that was, the Bannings, Allens, Coulthards, Herrings, Littles—noticed the improper conduct of two, by birth of their own small number; why, let them notice! Let them notice until they burst! George Bull thought that he would need to be above suspicion if he wanted New Winton as a place to live and practice in. He dared say that he had been right, then. Times had changed as much as he had, since; like himself, the age seemed to grow in experience. The naive sharp edge of shock and social outrage was gone from all the simpler improprieties.

Even in 1903 he had soon modified his view. What he needed to be was no more than careful. That meant some weeks when he could contrive neither to visit nor to meet Janet at all. Many of the meetings were marked by inconvenience of time or place which he had to laugh to remember. "By God," he thought, "we were pretty keen about it in those days."

In the kitchen, his fur coat off, George Bull sat down at the table. He could see one of those electric clocks on the shelf, its third hand a slim gilt needle crawling the steady circle without relief or rhythm. From it you got a glimpse of time as it must be, not as man measured it. It was all one, no beginning, no middle part, no end. He remained absorbed in it a moment while Janet took off her things. She was wearing a flannel shirt, so deep blue as to look black, and corduroy breeches. Her shapeless waterproof boots were laced to her knees. Leaving him, she disappeared into the pantry. When she came out she carried a gallon glass jug three-quarters full of hard cider.

"Have a drink, George," she said. "It's all I've got."

Knowing that she did not like cider, he finally found the booklet of government prescription blanks, unscrewed a fountain pen. "There you are," he said, "and take it to Sansbury. Anderson has in some new whisky so bad a bootlegger wouldn't sell it." He balanced the jug lightly. "I don't mind this stuff," he said.

The cooking stove had been removed from the kitchen, and where it had been, out from the sealed chimney, stood a Franklin stove, taken from Mr. Cardmaker's one-time study. Janet did her cooking, or had it done when Mrs. Foster came, on a gleaming, extensive electric range set against the east wall, out of the way. Bent, busy at the basin in the other corner, soaping her hands, she said: "How's Mrs. Cole?"

"Oh, Aunt Myra's a little vague, now and then," George Bull answered. He filled his glass half full of cider and drank it off thoughtfully. "She's quite a girl, when you think that she was born in 1846. I overhauled her last week, just for fun. There really isn't anything wrong with her; I mean, nothing you could put your finger on. She's spry as you please; got all her teeth. I don't see anything to stop her. I wouldn't be surprised if she lived to be a lot over a hundred. Every now and then she takes to calling me Kenneth for a few days—that was her son. Died of typhoid at Tampa in the Spanish-American war. But she does practically all the housework—you can hear her dropping dishes in the kitchen and telling the little Andrews girl to let things be, she'll do them. She gets to Sansbury twice a week to the movies. Won't bother to go down to the station for the bus. She just goes out to the road and waves at the driver, so now he stops for her. The Bulls are pretty hard to kill."

"What's all this I hear about a row in town meeting last week?"

George Bull roared. "Row is right! I guess you could have heard me having moral indignation all the way up here."

"Well, go on."

"What do I have to go on about? I just told Banning the Board of Health was going to fine him fifty dollars for letting Larry use the river bank for a dump. I told him I'd make it my business to see that water the children of New Winton used to swim in wasn't polluted. What did he think of that?"

"I heard Mrs. Banning wrote some letters to the County Health Officer."

"School Board stuff. I hadn't had a chance to vaccinate the brats at Cold Hill until today. She'll have to do better than that. Lefferts sent me the letter. He just took a pencil and wrote on the corner: 'Dear Bull: Here's your prize belly-acher again.'"

"What did you do?"

"I just told you. I got Lester Dunn to scout around until he found where Larry had dumped a lot of junk up the river. Then I fined Banning fifty dollars."

"Quite a coincidence."

"Banning didn't seem to see it; but I'll bet Mrs. B. guessed. It's just the sort of thing she'd do herself, the bitch. Well, one good turn deserves at least two others. I told Mrs. Talbot—and for all I know, it's true—that she ought to have more sense than to let Mamie live at the Bannings'. Mrs. Banning would feed her what the dogs didn't want and put her up in the back garret with no heat. Of course she gets pneumonia. I hear all over town now that Mrs. Banning practically fed her pneumonia with a spoon."

"George, you're a confirmed old devil, aren't you!"

Janet's amused voice was almost as deep as his. From talking mainly to men, her tones had taken on something male. Hearing that plain accent, that ruminative inflection given to words sober, positive, well-considered, you could see best not Janet, but out of a strangely vanished past, certain composed, farm-weathered faces; the men of an older Connecticut standing quiet, their grave eyes in direct regard, their opinions simply and unhesitatingly spoken—for they were as good as you were; a reticent, unpolished courtesy made them willing, for the moment, to assume that they were no better than you were.

Moved by these authentic, almost stilled tones, George Bull, who belonged here by blood, found himself regretful. When, after his father's death and his Uncle Amos's, he came East there had seemed to him to be something here which he liked and wanted. Part of the feeling might have been mere relief, to have his father dead, Michigan so far away, the hard, cheerless business of his youth there definitely done. Perhaps all of it was that. It was on Memorial Day, 1889, that he first saw New Winton. He got off the morning train and heard a band playing—*land where my fathers died, land of the Pilgrim's pride*—blaring distantly down the green. They were, it happened, that day unveiling the little Civil War soldier to the somewhat belated memory of those brave men who fought for liberty and union. Half a company of the men in question could still assemble, wearing the dark blue of the Grand Army. Every one for miles around was listening to the remarks of one of Connecticut's own generals. Everything looked festive—bunting sagged from elm to elm at that end of the green. The people in their best clothes looked well-to-do; the town looked well-kept and prosperous—even, with this crowd, populous. Almost at once somebody had said to him: "You Eph Bull's boy, may I ask?" The speaker could, it developed, recall the Reverend Ephraim Bull when he was a child in New Winton, and had never thought either of the ministry or of Michigan.

Remembering that holiday morning, it was possible to deduce from it and mourn a lost comfort, a lost ease and peace in the intimacy of small valley, small farms, small towns with a couple of church steeples, small hills and ponds; rivers passed by insecure covered bridges. George Bull wasn't sure that such a land had ever actually existed, except on some summer or early fall days for an hour, or an afternoon. In the same fanciful way, life here seemed to him kind and friendly; the men were simple, but honest and happy, to a point not known in Michigan. Of course, the truth was that men were always the same everywhere; Michigan had been full of his own terrors and chagrins. He hadn't, for instance, wanted to be a doctor particularly; but what he wanted was not important to his father. The Reverend Ephraim Bull thought in vague stern terms of humanity. Some form of the urge he had felt to preach to the Michigan backwoods, he expected to find in George. There were not enough doctors out there.

Made miserable by poverty and poor preparation, George Bull was certainly not promising. The exacting Doctor Vaughan soon advised him to leave Ann Arbor, where the new university medical school was beginning to get on its feet. Bull had mistaken his calling. George Bull couldn't leave; he had been afraid to go home. His father, getting older, got blinder, as though he had seen the glory of God to his permanent hurt. The old man went groping around, his hands out warily, and though George Bull could have broken him in half, the terrible voice, hoarsened and resonant, shouting as from a pulpit, paralyzed him; the blind, uncertain hands seemed sure to catch him. With desperation in his efforts, he did better; Doctor Vaughan, pleased, let him stay.

"That was pretty long ago," he said, and grinned, seeing Janet looking at him. "Thinking," he explained. "I'm getting a little vague, like Aunt Myra. Well, Banning paid his fifty dollars all right."

"I guess he can afford it."

George Bull laughed. "He can. But he's lost a lot of money. They figured it out in the post office that he got no less than seven notices of passed dividends last quarter—intelligent girl, that Helen Upjohn. What she doesn't know or can't find out from smelling the mail isn't worth knowing. Well, I'll have some more of this hog-wash, and then I ought to be going. I want to see Mamie Talbot."

"Is she very sick?"

"No. She'll get by. Not as bad as your cow. Sort of puny, like her mother, though. I ought to take an interest just for the looks of it. Mamie insisted on going home when she felt bad, so she kind of got out of the Bannings' hands. Mrs. Banning wanted Verney to come up—for a consultation. He wouldn't do it. Said it was my case. Damn delicate of him."

"How do you get on with him?"

"We're pretty polite. All he wants anyway is a little professional chit-chat about how slick he is. He sort of fancies himself as a surgeon. Sometime I'll beat him to it. I'll tell him about those orchidectomies I performed on your calves. 'What you say is very true, my dear Doctor, but, in my limited experience, I find that I get the most satisfactory results—this was the technique I found so effective when I was attending the King of Iceland; you may have heard—by grasping the balls firmly—'"

"Now, listen," said Janet, "if you think you're out behind the barn talking to—"

"Slip of the tongue," said George Bull, refilling his glass. "Good thing Verney didn't hear me. He'd have a piece in the State *Journal* about the dangerous abuse of the Basle Anatomical Nomenclature in rural counties— well, hallelujah, I think I'm tight! Let me try that again. Basle Anatomical Nomencla—"

"You must have had a drink or two up Cold Hill."

"I did, for a fact. You ought to see Crowe, that pot-bellied little rat, put it away."

"Well, don't fall in the fire. I've got to get over and help Harold. When he hasn't some one working for him, he never gets the stripping done."

"What happened to that Truro boy—Donald Maxwell? Didn't you have him?"

"Harold thought he was fooling around with Belle. Not that it was the first time. It was just the first time Harold thought of it."

"So what?"

"Harold came to me and said he wanted me to fire Donald."

"And you did?"

"Well, Donald's always been the village satyr, and so he probably wouldn't be able to stop. I was afraid Harold might mention the matter to him and get half killed. Donald said to me: 'Ain't I a good worker, Miss Cardmaker?' I told him he'd better ask Belle about that. He said: 'Miss Cardmaker, you don't mean to say you think there was anything wrong between me and Mrs. Rogers?' Since pretty nearly every morning, when Harold took the milk down, I'd see him walk up to the cottage and then somebody would pull down the shade in the bedroom, I thought he had plenty of brass. 'Listen, Donald,' I said, 'what do you want with that half-dead little slut? Why don't you go marry yourself a real woman and stop taking candy from kids like Harold?'"

"You must have scared him to death."

"I guess it gave him quite a shock. He said he would, he knew a girl in Torrington; only he hadn't any money. I took his note for five hundred dollars. Since it wasn't any good anyway, I told him I'd tear it up when his first son was born."

"Get it out and start tearing," said George Bull. "I helped a girl have his first son up to North Truro about five years ago."

"Yes, I know. But I told him no monkey business this time. Last Thursday he mailed me a clerk's copy of a marriage certificate from Torrington."

"Well, I'm damned," said George Bull. "You're quite a moral influence. But that doesn't help you milk the cows, does it?"

"Time was," Janet said, "when I could milk every cow in the barn with my two hands. With a machine to do all the real work, Harold can't even strip them."

"Well, of course," George Bull said, "you only have about twenty more cows now. That might make a difference. Let me know how my patient is."

Left alone in the warm kitchen, George Bull went and turned on the radio in the corner beside Janet's desk. Almost immediately—this was a much better set than the one he had got for Aunt Myra at home—a voice said: "WTIC, the Travelers, Hartford, Connecticut." With the suddenness of a switch swung closed, dance music of great volume and elaboration burst out, filling the room.

George Bull stood quiet a moment. Outside it had somehow got dark and he looked at the clock with the relentlessly turning gilt needle. It was practically six, and he decided that he could see Mamie Talbot in the morning just as well. The blurred glow of alcohol filled his big frame. It gave the music in his ears an unearthly sweetness, rich, intricate, and gay. Presently his pleasure in it had reached such a point that he felt impelled to dance; and so he did, after a fashion; performing a careless and exuberant two-step around the room.

After a time, the door opened; but he saw that it was Janet and did not stop. She looked at him and laughed. "George," she promised, "you'll be on your ear in a minute."

"Go milk your cows," he roared. "I'm fine."

"Harold brought Pete Foster up with him."

"Fine. How's my patient?"

"She looks pretty near dead."

"Fine. Best thing could happen to her."

"Want some supper?"

"Hell, no!"

"Well, I'll go up and change my clothes."

"Fine. I'll help you."

"You'd better stay down here, George."

"Sure, I'd better."

"Listen, George, it's cold as a barn. I left all the windows open. Wait until—"

"Wouldn't be the first barn we'd been in."

"I guess it wouldn't, at that," she admitted. "Come on, then."

Henry Harris
[from *The Last Adam*]

Henry Harris had been the smartest boy in the New Winton school. His father, Jacob Harris, rewarded him with the begrudged gift of his parental permission; the School Committee arranged about his railroad fares; and Henry Harris became the smartest boy in the then-new High School at Sansbury. He was a feather in New Winton's rustic cap.

Whether or not Henry Harris would have been the smartest young man at Yale was never determined. Jacob Harris thought that this had gone far enough. In his so thinking, an undoubted part had been played by the fact that Paul Banning's boy was at Yale. Like Jacob Harris, Paul Banning called himself a farmer, but in his case, other men did the farming. Paul Banning's personal approach to the soil was on the trotting tracks of the big eastern fairs. He had bred at least two pacers famous enough for the immortality of those sporting lithographs found in country hotel lobbies and the harness rooms of city stables. He was, of course, a rich man; and so had his father been. Even his grandfather, while he did his own farming, had done it with a simple, patriarchal authority, directing many laborers on the best and biggest farm in New Winton. Jacob Harris was a real farmer, a poor one. Yale was obviously a place for rich men's sons. By this Jacob Harris did not mean to be ordering himself lowly and reverently to all his betters; in his opinion, his betters did not exist. He meant that college was suitable only for such inconsiderable creatures as young Herbert Banning. He didn't believe Herbert Banning could load so much as one hay wagon without dropping dead.

Like many smart people, Henry Harris had always been a realist. The qualities of plainness, poverty unashamed, had their value mainly in his father's mind. Few people, able to be disinterested, saw them as the fine things Jacob Harris said they were. Henry Harris saw better the Banning stables—they had not burned down until after old Paul's death in 1908—stretched beside the green. The building was as long as three barns; and to prove it, carried three graceful cupolas, each vaned with a small gold horse trotting up the wind. A strip of sward as carefully kept as a lawn separated the permanently closed east doors from the road along the green. It was the biggest and, to the small Henry Harris, passing it every day on his way to school, the most beautiful thing in New Winton.

If he were smart enough to see, by some such symbol, how poor was prowess in loading a hay wagon compared to the money to hire all the good loaders you wanted who worked while you sat at ease, he was also smart enough to see, after a while, that Yale was less important to him than Yale had appeared in his hopes and first harsh disappointment. Of course, it was impossible not to feel an envious pang when Herbert Banning came home from college with a boating straw banded in Yale colors on his head; wearing a pale gray suit with narrow trousers and a double-breasted coat elegantly ample and padded on the shoulders; smoking a pipe with a curved stem and Y '04 inlaid in silver on the bowl; but all that took money. Henry Harris guessed that, poor as he would have been at Yale, he would not profit, except perhaps academically. The intelligence that made him a good scholar showed him too that scholarship was rarely of any importance in this world. The adjustment did not mean that he forgave his father or Herbert Banning—the one for thwarting, like the stubborn old jackass he was, the first major ambition of Henry's life; the other, for enjoying as a matter of course what Henry had wanted so passionately and in vain. Here were two accounts to be settled. For the moment he could not pay anything on them, and he did not waste time trying to or wishing that he could. Perhaps one of them was settled when Jacob Harris died without ever enjoying the ease which the prospering Henry, for appearance's sake, would soon have been forced to provide for him. Henry Harris let it go at that; all his energies were given to the problem of making money.

To make money, most young men might have thought it necessary to leave New Winton, where a dollar was seen in its true light—the certificate exchanged for a man's work all day—and where there existed no loose surplus for the gaining or wasting. Such a step is often praised as showing the vision and courage which brings success. Henry Harris had something better than that. He took what was nearest to hand and compelled it to serve him. He answered an advertisement about raising turkeys for profit. Raising them, he made money, exactly as the advertisement said that he would. When he had made a thousand dollars, he persuaded Isaac Quimby to let him buy into Quimby's feed, grain, and coal business. Once in, he began to consume Quimby by insisting on his privilege to reinvest his profits. Eventually they were large enough for him to stop that and begin to take a hand in Sansbury real estate.

This is perfectly simple to see and tell about; but most men, trying it, meet with every possible ill chance. Turkeys can pine and die. Mr. Quimby would have fleeced some presumptuous youths. Others would have plunged ignorantly in Sansbury building lots and lost everything. Doubtless luck is the chief factor, but, dispassionately considered, almost every financially unlucky person is a plain fool to start with. Henry Harris had that clever- ness which is the very touch of Midas. He knew how to fatten on other people's efforts. The general method he used could be seen when he first entered village politics. He threw in his lot with the helpless and disor- ganized Democratic minority.

At the time it was not possible for Democrats to win locally. Henry Harris never expected them to. He meant to live on the Republicans. Other candidates worked hard and worried for the small offices; but not Henry Harris. He was a Democrat. It was considered good policy to let the Demo- crats have one job. Republican voters might or might not elect this or that Republican candidate, but Henry Harris, the leading Democrat, was al- ways elected.

The next step in this old American story is transferal to a larger town, to a city; to state, then national politics. More than once it has ended only when some Henry Harris became President of the United States. Henry Harris would not be blind to the glitter of the chance, nor deaf to the thun- der of opportunity awakening Democrats about 1910. He had all the quali- fications. As well as a native, half-knavish wit, his was that careful mean shrewdness by which alone a man can climb, not too visibly soiled, through the sewer-like lower labyrinth of American politics. Henry Harris had, too, the bland, impregnable assurance required to rule on top.

Close-mouthed, sitting smiling on the steps of Bates's store in his old clothes, it might seem that sloth had stopped Henry Harris; but he was a thoughtful man and never an idle one. He might have reflected that here his time was his own, his money already ample to buy him everything he saw any reason to want. Out of what life has, Henry Harris lacked, in fact, only fame. Sensible though he might be to the violent pleasures found in overtaking and enjoying her, the whore, Fame, he did not follow. Musing, farsighted and reflective, owing no explanation to any one, he was apt enough at analogy. Like the girls at Maggie's in Bridgeport, Fame was at the end of a trip, inconvenient, tedious, fraught with expense and anxiety. He had given up Bridgeport, for he could see a bargain; and the short satis- faction of lewd dalliance, exchanged for a considerable expenditure of time and money, and a week of waiting to see if he had got gonorrhoea, made no bargain. National politics might be much like a trip to Maggie's.

Henry Harris was smiling now, watching Lester fold the ten-dollar bills into a pocket book. Henry Harris's face, saturnine, almost morose in abstraction, changed altogether when he smiled. Seen carelessly, it was a smile of rare, intelligent warmth. Attracted by it, many people would nev- er notice or understand the gleam of a puckish, merry spite, an indulgent malevolence in Henry Harris's dark eyes. The warmth was genuine. It was the inner warmth he felt while he surveyed the good order of his plans and resources. Reticent, dangerously smiling, he had taken loving pains with them. Each little plan was a work of art. He had perfected it; he had subjected it in the privacy of his mind to every sort of test and condition. He would get no surprises when it went into action.

Other people were the surprised ones. As much as success—and here perhaps lay a clue to the compensations of his simple, satisfactory life— Henry Harris could relish that familiar start of first blank surmise, the following quick or slow realization in his victims. Calm, steadily smiling out his unassailable relish, enjoying the belated twistings and fatally late quick-thinkings, he received objections, threats and insults as so much tribute. Knowing it, Henry Harris was modest about it; he never tried to make the fact that he was the smarter man appear in casual conversation. Any one could talk. Most people, if they kept trying, could score small triumphs of repartee. Henry Harris, rarely rejoining, could wait, foretasting the fine jovial day when his enemies themselves would, by their own confounding, speak, even roar, the proofs of his wit.

He said, "Hand me down that last volume of the Connecticut Code, Lester. I'll show you something. I'm fixing up a little surprise for Matthew Herring. He takes such good care of the town money, he probably won't like it, but I doubt if he can help himself."

"Say, what are you going to do?"

"I'm going to try an old Fairfield County dodge, Lester. I don't claim the credit. Down there, they've been doing it for years. They thought it up for the mill town Polacks. Lot of those people don't read English very well, so they never know when taxes are due. When are taxes due in New Winton, Lester?"

"Why, I guess, about March fifteenth."

"Smart lad! And if you haven't paid up on or before that date what happens?"

"Nothing I ever heard of, so long as the town knows you and you pay pretty soon."

Henry Harris fingered the pages of the open volume. "Yes," he said. "That's true. We've been kind of shiftless." He shook his head. "Well, it's never too late to reform. I read here that it happens to be the duty of the Collector of Taxes to swear out warrants promptly for all delinquents. There's a two-dollar fee for him; there's a five-dollar fee for the constable serving the warrant. How many people do you think we might catch napping the morning of March sixteenth?"

"Oh, come to papa!" groaned Lester, falling back in the easy chair. "I knew I was a sucker! But, Henry, I'll have to hand it to you. Why, I bet we could catch a hundred!"

"About what I figured," Henry Harris agreed. "I—" He stopped short, his face stiffening. On the panel of the closed door heavy knuckles had struck suddenly. Lester started with such violence that he stood on his feet while the door swung open.

"Good morning, Henry," said Doctor Bull. "Thought perhaps Clarence was over here. I have a certificate for him. How's tricks, Lester?" His blue eyes, twinkling a little, turned back on Henry Harris. "You don't look too well, Henry. Heart ever bother you? Palpitations?" He put out his hand, closed it over Henry Harris's wrist, his finger tips shutting down on the radial artery while he felt for his watch.

Henry Harris jerked his hand away; the corners of his mouth grew firm; he began to smile. "You move pretty quiet for a man your size, George. Is it hard?"

"Professional training, Henry. We try not to go banging around a sick room. Come in sometime and I'll look you over. You're not as young as you were, you know. Little things like a knock on the door shouldn't shake you up."

"I'll probably live."

"Sure, you will. But a time comes when we aren't so spry. Can't do all the things we used to do, Henry."

"Maybe not. Seems like I'm getting a little deaf, sometimes."

"Often happens. It hasn't affected me yet; but I always did have pretty keen hearing. Well, I'll have to see if I can get hold of Clarence. So long."

They could hear his heavy steps in the hall and the brisk thud of his descent on the stairs.

Town Meeting
[from *The Last Adam*]

George Bull stood still. "Somebody knows why I'm late," he said. "Who cut the tires on my car last night? He's here, all right. Is he man enough to stand up and say he did it? Well! I'm waiting!"

"Yeah," cried a voice, suddenly revived, "and where was your car when he cut 'em? You've been chasing around here long enough—"

"I'll take care of my business. I'll take care of where I go and what I do. Who doesn't like it?"

There was a stir now of general recovery, and, jumping to answer the challenge, a low growling murmur. "What are you going to do, George? Lick the whole town?" Robert Newell had faced about in his chair, grinning.

"Mr. Chairman," Matthew Herring said, "I think Doctor Bull is out of order."

"Sit down, Herring! First thing you know, you'll be out of order for a month."

"I have the floor at present, Doctor. I suggest that you sit down until you're recognized by the chair—"

"Do you want me to come and sit you down?"

Matthew Herring looked at him, unmoved. "You don't impress me with your threats, Doctor Bull. If you have anything to say, we are ready to listen to it; but I would advise you not to begin by attempting to bully the meeting. We have been patient for a long time; but I think the moment for a reckoning has finally come. You won't help yourself by—"

"So that's how you stand, is it? All right, Walter. Let me have this floor he's so worried about, and I'll tell you how I stand. I don't know who's doing all this grunting and groaning I hear, but let 'em keep still—" The murmur rose louder and he roared out: "I came here to try to make you half-wits see sense. Are you going to let me try or aren't you?"

"Throw him out!"

"Well, well, Joel!" He wheeled about. "I'll be seeing you afterwards. Unless you think you'd better start running now—"

Walter Bates began to hammer again on the table, but the hubbub had risen beyond that. The roar had a sharp edge, angry, chattering, a score of voices shouting their separate answers together. "So you don't want to hear, huh? Well, you'll hear this, you jabbering baboons! I can shout louder than the lot of you!" George Bull's tremendous voice went up in thunder; and he was right, he could. "What I have to say to you is, you and Mat Herring's meeting can go to blazes. I'll see you all in hell before I'll oblige you by resigning! If you can get me out, if you have any case, and the sense to handle it, why, God damn you, do it!"

Turning, he went down the aisle, with people recoiling before him, people, outraged, yelling after him. At the closed door, he put a hand on Grant Williams's shoulder, spun him aside. The sunlight poured dazzling in, his great shadow dropped down the aisle, and he cut it off, closing the door behind him so that all the windows shook.

* *

Henry Harris, standing up, said: "A man who loses his temper in a matter like this never makes a very favorable impression. Instead of helping, he hurts himself. When he cusses out his listeners, they resent it. They get all hot and start shouting back, and there you are. It's a pity."

He paused, letting his gaze move about. "Putting all that down for the *Times*, Miss Kimball?" he asked. "I hope you mention my name." He grinned at her a moment, and raising his voice a little, clear and sharp, said: "I've heard tell that they who draw the sword, shall perish by the sword. That means it's a risky thing to start a fight, because, once fighting's in the air, you can't tell where it'll stop. No, sir! Anything might happen. Well, I'll have to say what's on my mind anyway. Suppose Doc Bull's not perfect? Who is? Well, I don't want to start an argument now, Matthew, so I'll say I guess you're pretty near perfect. And Herbert Banning's perfect, of course. I'm not denying it. But you two aside, most of us just do the best we can, and usually it's not so good.

"You saw George Bull go out of here pretty mad. A lot of enthusiasts yelled him down. They don't want him to get a hearing. Those who are setting them on may be scared that, if they could hear George, they might get mixed up and think he wasn't so bad after all—

"You've heard people tell you he ought to have done this. He ought to have done that. Sure, he should. Sure, we all should have done God knows how many things we never did do. I can see now that I ought never to have let that camp site to the Interstate Company without making sure about the drainage first. I didn't bother. All I wanted was the rent money. Now, let me ask you, which one of you knows all about the drainage of any piece of land he might own back in the hills? Which one of you gives a damn?

Which one of you wouldn't try to realize some money on it first chance he got without fooling around trying to make all kinds of crazy investigations?"

A voice called out, "We ain't blaming you, Henry. You can sit down now."

"Now, let me say my say, if you will. I'm going to sit down in a minute. Who here thinks when he goes to get a drink whether the water with which he's filling a glass from the faucet is pure water? He ought to know by this time that the only way to be sure is boil it. Does he take that ordinary common-sense precaution? He does not. He thinks it's probably all right the way it is; it always has been all right. Well, what do you suppose Doc Bull thought about the reservoir? He hadn't seen any reason to worry. Who had? Who didn't know that there was this construction camp up there? Who worried about that? Who cared?

"Most every one with any sense realizes that living from day to day is taking a pretty big chance. I was thinking about that this morning. A while ago, I invested a hundred and fifty dollars in a little proposition which looked fool-proof to me. I didn't see how I could lose. Well, I find now that I'm just out that money. I didn't see any reason to worry, but it so happens that my agent in the matter took sick at the critical moment. It's hard luck, but will I get anywhere by raising a howl? I took my chance on that, even if at the time I didn't happen to reflect that I was taking such a chance. I don't know what you think of a person who is willing to take a chance, hoping he'll win or be all right; yet, when he finds he's lost, lies down and yells. I know what I think of him—

"Are things bad enough, or aren't they? Seems to me with the Evarts place full of patients, and Doc Bull working his head off for the sick, we could shut up about who's to blame and help him. If we can't, it must be because somebody won't let us. Who won't let us? Well, I hate to suggest what I haven't documentary proof of—there's been quite a little of that so far this morning and we don't need any more—but this I know. Banning— or Mrs. Banning; she wears that pair of pants—has been working for a long time to get Doc Bull. They don't think he's cultured enough; he can't be, when he don't appreciate that they're worth ten times as much worry and care as plain ordinary people. Maybe the idea of the Bannings not getting enough respect makes you mad, but before you try to fix it for them, you ought to reflect some."

In one sense, Henry Harris had been talking against time, holding the floor to prevent the interruption of a process of reaction begun the minute the door slammed after Doctor Bull. The effect was a good deal like going out with a light gun to hunt a rabbit, and suddenly turning up a bear. The fact that the bear retired couldn't altogether erase the first ringing shock of the face to face encounter. The more you reflected, the nearer supper time it seemed, the less advisable to hunt further here today. A certain withdrawal would go on all around the obstinate and courageous few who meant to have some skin, whether bear or rabbit, on the barn door.

Henry Harris could feel the warm slow spread inside him of the amusement which generally blossomed in his matchless mocking smile. He did not smile now. He went on: "I say to you, for near forty years Doc Bull has had the health of this town, the life and death of the people in it, in his charge. For that matter, I wonder just how many people in this room came out of their mother's wombs with Doc Bull standing by. Winter and summer he's been on the job without a break. He's spent practically his whole life working to relieve the bodily ailments of our people. Some paid him and some didn't, but he never worried over that. Now, what about it?"

He held up a paper. "Those hostile to him have been telling you how everybody knew this, and this was generally understood, and in their opinion, it would certainly seem—I guess you recognize it. It's the way people talk when they don't happen to have the facts, or maybe have them, and find they won't do. Well, here they are. Here are the figures they weren't so anxious to give you. In the vital statistics of this state, over a period of twenty years, the death rate per thousand in New Winton has never in any year ranked poorer than tenth lowest, out of one hundred and sixty-nine Connecticut towns listed. That means that you could name at least one hundred and fifty-nine places in this state every year for the last twenty years where life and health was less secure than here. One year could be an accident, but twenty consecutive years? How'll you square that with Doc Bull being as bad a doctor and as careless of public health as I've heard some tell you he is? This is a letter from the State Health Department, Matthew. Maybe you'd like to make sure it isn't a forgery. Maybe you'd like a copy of it for your newspaper piece, Miss Kimball."

His quick glance showed him at once that he had scored. He could see Howard Upjohn's face, surprised and gratified. Mrs. Vogel and Mrs. Ely exchanged glances; Emma Bates had a blank, jolted expression. He went on: "That's what I thought you ought to know. That's the record behind the present emergency. To my mind, right feeling, human justice, are against kicking a man down through no demonstrable fault of his; and the simple, plain, printed facts nobody can laugh off don't give much of a foothold to those who like logic better than sentiment. In fact about everything seems to be against what you're asked to do.

"I can speak my mind, because I happen to be in the minority party— or what has been the minority; next fall the people of this town may decide different. I don't have to toe any line, or keep in right with any one. So I'll say I think this is nothing but a political plot, engineered to work off a well-known grudge, by certain parties who've always tried to hold control of this town and run it to suit themselves. I'll speak plainer. I see Mr. Banning isn't present. I don't blame him. Why should he come and do his own

dirty work when plenty of people just jump at the chance to associate themselves with him by doing it for him—yes, Miss Kimball, I guess you're
one of them; but let me finish. Those of you who think that money and influence aren't everything in this world; those of you who believe in fair play
and the right of a man to be given the facts, and from them, freely to decide
what's right and do it, probably won't feel so anxious to fall in line. Mine's
one name will never be on their petition of town officers. I hope no friend
of mine has a vote for them. I'm through."

From the anonymous rear a voice or two cried, "That's telling them,
Henry!" But in the hesitant silence, Matthew Herring, erecting his tall
figure above the seated rows, said: "Mr. Chairman! Now that Mr. Harris
seems to have finished his misrepresentations, may I suggest that we proceed with the business of the meeting. I don't think there's any need to
waste time pointing out to intelligent people the irrelevance of such points
as Mr. Harris could be said to have made. His interpretation of the vital
statistics won't stand up a moment when you recall that this has always
been a prosperous and isolated agricultural community in one of the health-
iest sections of the state. No one here has denied that it is human to make
mistakes; Mr. Harris appears to feel that it is also divine and ought to be
encouraged. His attack on a person not present, and on the motives of those
who are, can only be called contemptible and, I am sure, has been recognized as only that. May we get on, Mr. Chairman?"

"Yes, I guess so," Walter Bates said. He hit the table with the mallet.
"Please don't make so much noise back there. Now the proposition, I mean,
the resolution offered is—I got it written down here somewhere. Just a
moment—"

This small inadvertency—Walter Bates's flustered search for his paper
—was plainly fatal.

"Ah!" said Robert Newell. There was a hard click of his boot heels
striking the floor as he stood up, and he stopped, staring about him, for he
could feel the crowded hall in psychological crisis. He had meant only to
say that he was going home, but aware now of the delicate balance, his
violent, destructive instinct was to bring it down. He shouted again, "Ah,
to hell with it! Never mind that paper! We know who wrote it! This meeting's been nothing but a lot of foolishness and a waste of busy men's time.
Harris said the things most of us probably believe—"

A quick mounting roar, which might be protest, but which had an
indubitable note of cheering made him pause.

"Mr. Chairman!" came Matthew Herring's voice, edged and distinct.

Walter Bates lifted his mallet, but Robert Newell put a foot on the
chair seat, stood on it, rising that much higher than Herring. He shouted:
"If you ask me, I think Doc Bull's all right, and I know more about it than
some. During the average summer, he probably is up to my camp a dozen

times. He's never killed anybody yet. I've never seen a guest who wasn't satisfied with the treatment given him. Now, let's adjourn and get out of here. We don't want any resolution; we aren't going to sign anything—"

Mrs. Bates had got up, livid in an inarticulate fury. "Just let every one who feels that way go," she said. "I believe there are enough decent and responsible people here to—"

"Sure," agreed Newell, "let the hens stay and scratch until they're tired! Good place for 'em. Who's chairman here, Walter, you or your wife? How long is this gang of yowling females going to run this town, anyway?"

In the back they were shouting, delighted, "Move we adjourn. Second it! Hell, I third it! You can't do that. Sure I can, I just did—"

Harry Weems cupped his hands and yelled, "Say, how about a vote of confidence in Doc Bull? All in favor—"

Miss Kimball, standing up, cried, "Shame! Shame!—" The stir and confusion of voices drowned them both out; so Harry called, "All right, let's go!" Some one opened the doors, and they began to move.

"Will every one please take his seat?" began Matthew Herring, but it was plain that very few were going to. "Let them go," Miss Kimball said. "They won't think so well of themselves when they see it in print. That much I'm sure of—"

"You don't mean to tell me," said Henry Harris, "that the *Times* would print it all?"

"I certainly do, and—"

Over the disordered front rows, over empty chairs, Matthew Herring said, "Henry, you're quite a speaker! You've beaten me. But I don't think you can beat truth and decency. Not every time, at any rate."

"Why, Matthew," Henry Harris answered, turning his delighted grin from Miss Kimball and her notebook. "I never have any quarrel with intangibles."

Unhurried, he went out, crossed slowly over to the station and stepped into a telephone booth. When his dropped coin got him Doris Clark, he said, "Doris, I want Sansbury one-six-two."

Smiling, leaning against the closed door, he reflected that matters could have been worse. Of course, it was too bad that Lester had to get sick and as he'd said—he grinned again, relishing the circumstances of his saying it—he'd never see his hundred and fifty dollars again; but after all, Matthew Herring couldn't have been any madder, or in any less doubt about who cooked his goose.

"Hello," he said. "Sansbury *Times*? Mr. Marden in? Yes. Oh, Marden. Harris. Listen, will you do me a favor? No, you don't. You don't have to do anything; I'm just asking if you will. I think it would be a good idea to kill the New Winton correspondent's story this week. Well, we've had a kind of hot town meeting, and she hasn't much judgment. No sense in spreading our troubles all over the state. Sure, that's all. No, after that, it'll be all right. She knows her business when she doesn't get excited. Fine. Much obliged. I'll do something for you sometime."

Emerging, he crossed the open space, saluting with a casual lift of hand various drivers of cars starting and backing. Reaching Gosselin Brothers' store, he went in. "Give me a dozen of those big Florida oranges you have that poetry about pasted on the front window," he said. "It is poetry, isn't it? I tell you what, put them in a bag and send them down to the Evarts place for Mr. Dunn, will you?"

Bending down, Mr. Banning brushed the thin crust of mud from the wooden tag, read the words: *Mevrouw Van Gendt*. Remembering at once the long pointed buds, the flowers in salmon shading out of yellow and pink, he applied his pruning shears. That was the last of the four beds, leaving him only the narrow strip of old-fashioned remontants in a curve beyond the sundial—*General McArthur, Jonkheer Mock, Mrs. John Laing*. They were varieties his mother had favored for a rose jar—he could even remember the jar, three quarters full of curled petals in a pungent, arrested decay. It was hard to think of anything more useless.

Straightening up, he pulled off his loose yellow horsehide gloves, laid them with the pruning shears on the sundial while he looked at his watch. It was half-past ten, and, refilling his pipe slowly, he wondered how the town meeting was getting on. He meant, more particularly, how his absence and Lucile's would be interpreted, supposing it was noticed at all in the excitement.

The truth was that he couldn't quite make up his mind, which always proved a great help in taking the easier course. Not regarding the business with any warm approval, he none the less wouldn't object to Matthew's success. The resulting picture of himself didn't please him. It had a complacently passive quality. When other men had got the unpleasantness over, he would be content to join them in what resulting profit there was. The one frank and correct course would probably be for him to oppose the whole scheme; not vaguely and half-heartedly in private, but publicly: *"I do not think any good or just purpose will be served—"*

That was, of course, impossible. Lucile would consider it too outrageous of him. If she thought about them at all, she probably made some distinctively feminine allowance for opinions he might express which were not hers. She didn't mind if it amused him to say what no one expected him to in casual conversation; but when it came to matters she considered serious, she would see it as a wanton betrayal of things which she couldn't help believing they both stood for. Matthew would naturally see it the same way; he would be deeply astonished, unable or perhaps unwilling to explain so irresponsible an attitude.

Sighing unconsciously, he roused himself, struck a match and laid the flame to the packed tobacco. A thick privet hedge sheltered him from the north wind and it was almost warm. He could feel the vehemence of the March sun on the turf, the spaced rose beds, the flagged path; he could even feel it through the suède jacket on his back, and it cheered him with the promise of an eventual peaceful summer, all this business somehow settled and largely forgotten. Taking up the shears and his gloves, he uncovered the swash letter script encircling the old dial plate: *It is later than you think*.

He was reminded again of his mother, who had placed the sundial and done, by fits and starts, a little general flower-growing around it. The inscription had, to her, he knew, a religious value. You were to think how little time remained to prepare to face your Maker, not how little time remained in which to be happy. Of course, having thought of it, that was enough. She would not expect that any person in her garden would be in the vulgar need of reforming his life. Gentlefolk meeting had no reason to exchange admonitions: Do not commit adultery. Do not kill. Do not steal. Do not bear false witness. Defraud not. Honor thy father and mother. Propriety would take ample care of the commandments. Manners and morals all fitted together, all made for the placid positiveness with which his mother accepted life.

So sure of it all, she was much less devoted to church work than Lucile. Her religious relationship was to God, not to the Rector. Only a very rude person would suggest it, but the Church, in its sense of the Episcopal parishes, undoubtedly meant more to Lucile than religion did. She thought of the Church with a comfortable sense of its formal beauty and dignity. In this particular fellowship in Christ, all was easy; the people everywhere would be approximately her own kind; their attitudes and interests would be comprehensible to her and in keeping with an ecclesiastical tradition of means, breeding, and education.

That was all very well, Mr. Banning could see, but it was not static any more. It would not be the end. Virginia, in a next generation of Banning women, would undoubtedly have no religion, nor any interest in a surviving tradition. At Virginia's age, he could feel intuitively his parents' sober, perhaps smug, acceptance. What Virginia felt would be his unspoken indifference; and little better, Lucile's preoccupation with the formal aspects. Presumably his parents would have taken disciplinary measures if he had failed in a sober, godly, and righteous attitude. Lucile, by doing nothing, acknowledged her failure. If Virginia went to church, it was distinctly as a favor to her mother and tacitly recognized as that. As far as Virginia was concerned, there was no sense in it. For her to go alone—that was, without any reason—would be unthinkable. Churchgoing was simply a form—fortunately growing milder as she got older—of that adult tyranny to which she submitted because she must. Lucile really would not dare speak to her about God or the teachings of Jesus. It would be safer not to bring up the issue of Virginia's real thoughts and sentiments.

What those were, he couldn't presume to know. Virginia didn't consider him or her mother suitable people to confide in. Probably she expected nothing from them but interference. What, she might reasonably argue, was the point in their declarations of love and interest when most of their time was spent in forbidding her to do what she wanted to do, or finding means to punish her when she did it anyway? Possibly she distrusted her mother more than him—sometimes he could see a skittish, wary approach to frankness or affection; but it never really got there. Prematurely, she would be emboldened to hope, would risk one more of her unpredictable requests; and, necessarily refused, draw back to nurse her new hurts.

There was nothing to be done about it, he knew now. His instincts, from the first to help her, defend her, cherish her—she was not like Guy, who never from the time he could walk and begin to speak was anything but the competent, reasonable, and assured master of his world—got him nowhere. Probably, as in other things, his inability to express himself, except in the most stiff and formal terms, hampered him. Perhaps, in any event, there could have been no explaining to Virginia. She did not care about explanations. If he answered indirectly, she would wait only until she was sure that the answer was going to be no. The light of her unquenched hope, the wild impossible appeal, went out. Wordless, she went away at once; or, if required to stay, stayed not really listening, never agreeing or assenting; as though she could not imagine why he found it necessary to talk so much when he had already said all that mattered.

Sighing again, he pulled his gloves on, for he could see that never would that difficulty resolve. The time was coming, perhaps was almost here, when saying no could not stop her; when, probably angry and bitter, she would do what she wanted without having to ask anybody. Common sense foresaw the disgraces and disasters almost certain to attend her when life, having no words, corrected her viciously with results. He stood still, looking at the sundial, for he had never been able to defend her, or help her, or save her. Perhaps the most he could expect would be the chance to comfort her when she had hurt herself beyond hope. Unhappy, he could see the fine cut script; *It is later than you think.*

"Mrs. Cole!"

"Now, my goodness, who's that? Who's there?"

"It's me."

Aunt Myra came out into the kitchen. The back door was open and she could see Mabel Baxter on the verge of entering. "Well," she said, "what time is this for you to come? Now, don't you let it happen again. You come here before school, and I told you you could have your breakfast."

"Well, I was here before. There isn't any school today; it's Saturday, Mrs. Cole."

"Oh, I forgot. Well, there probably will be next week. You march right up afterwards. If I'm not here, the key's always under the mat, so don't make that an excuse. Now, I'm sure I don't know what you can do this morning. I've done everything myself."

"Well, I just wanted to come back and tell you my father said it would be all right."

"I should hope so! I'm paying you as much as I paid Susie, who'd been here three years. You tell him that if he'd work sometimes himself he wouldn't have to worry so much about what his children were paid."

"Well, it wasn't that—"

"What wasn't what?"

"Oh, well. I mean, all right. Can I do anything now?"

"No, there's no need. I'm going to Sansbury at one o'clock. I won't be back until supper time. You come tomorrow at half-past seven."

II

On Tuesday, March seventeenth, the sun came up a poor yellow in the gray east. Soon it could not be seen at all. A gradual overcasting deepened evenly; the sky was a seamless cold gray; there was no wind.

Henry Harris, going out to sit on the steps with his paper, presently came in, went back to the round stove and settled down there.

"Get some snow this afternoon," he said contentedly to Walter Bates.

Unfolding his paper, propping his feet on the curved fender, he saw Matthew Herring enter, proceed in silence to the post office and start twisting the dial on his lock box. When he had drawn the mail out and clicked the door closed, he came across to the counter and said, "Walter, let me have a tin of cocoa, will you?"

With sober cordiality, Henry Harris said: "Good morning, Matthew. Looks as if we'd have some snow."

Half turning, Matthew Herring answered: "I should think it very likely."

Henry Harris grinned a little more. "Cold," he agreed. "Seems to be getting kind of cold in here, too. Well, we can't expect everything, can we? No, sir! We ought to be content with what we have." Rattling the paper, he got his chair to a more comfortable angle and began to read.

Numb in a weariness not really of work, but of prolonged strain and nerves exhausted, Miss Stanley, at the window, had her brooding vacant watch disturbed by a gradual change of tone in the afternoon. Starting a little, she gave it her attention, and saw that a hazy thin fall of snow had begun. Stronger, whiter, it was drawing a curtain of fine flakes down the light wind, spinning over the gray hills.

Doctor Verney, by the bed, made a movement, the chair shifting; and at once Miss Stanley was aware, her own heart seemingly louder, that the long interval was stretching too long. Turning sharply, she saw Doctor Verney start too, as though the same lull of weariness had half stupefied him. His hand went out to the table, drew the waiting hypodermic from the fold of sterilized cloth.

Miss Stanley, instantly beside him, clasped one hand tight over the other, and she could feel the color leaving her face, her cheeks stiffening, her eyes fixing in distraction, for it was going to be a near thing. Unprofessionally, she could experience at once a despair and a kind of desperation, oppressed, consumed with a sense of the great unfairness of this whole struggle. The child started with nothing; there was no flesh to sustain her —not an ounce in the narrow buttocks, nothing on the slight molded arms; on her narrow chest those piteous flat breasts. You would think she lived on nothing but the breath painfully passed out through the cracked, parted lips and the small, dull, stained teeth. Her hair was dragged back, tangled, as though the last thing she had known was that it was too hot. Miss Stanley could see the exposed ear, and stunned by the newness of something often seen but never noticed, she was aware for the first time of the remarkable delicacy of its structure, the astonishing frail beauty of its proportions.

While second went to stuporous second, they stood together, their breaths held, their minds pressing on the familiar physiological progression. Now, the hasty diffusion in the veins, the sudden indescribable biochemics of the absorbed adrenalin; now, the lash laid on, the cardiac muscle shocked alive, the arterioles in tumultuous contraction, the almost stilled blood resurging. Now, now, must come, caught back, quick still, rough from the shades, the gasp in of air; life at once extended a little, letting them breathe again too.

Slowly, first he, then she, did breathe. He looked at her, and she, blankly, back at him.

"Well, it's all up," he said. He dropped Virginia's wrist.

Yet they still waited a moment, facing each other in pointless expectation. Doctor Verney said: "Can you reach the stethoscope on the table there, Miss Stanley?"

Pocketing it finally, while Miss Stanley stood watching, he turned and walked to the door. In the hall, he called quietly: "Mr. Banning. May I speak to you a minute?"

Here in the heavy gloom of the stormy afternoon he waited, close to the door he had closed, while Mr. Banning came out of the upstairs sitting room and approached him. Doctor Verney lowered his voice. He said: "You will know best how to handle it with Mrs. Banning. I have to tell you that Virginia has just passed away."

Mr. Banning had, of course, known it already. Probably he had known it since noon, had not been at all deceived. "Yes," he said, "that was to be expected."

Silent a moment, he then added hastily, as though to make up for his strange way of speaking, his voice low, too: "I see, Doctor. Thank you. Lucile is asleep. I don't think I'll wake her."

Now they were both silent, and then both started uncertainly to speak together. Doctor Verney stopped and Mr. Banning went on. "I only want to say that I know that you've done everything humanly possible. I want you to know what a comfort it has been to be able to feel—"

"It came very quietly," Doctor Verney said. "Of course, she never recovered consciousness. There doesn't seem to be any way for me to—"

"Of course not. We mustn't—I mean, that it will be very difficult for Lucile. She seems to be sleeping quite soundly. Last night—you know. I think that it would be best if I saw that Guy was notified."

Turning, he went to the stairs and down them. There was still enough gray light in the library for him to find the telephone, and holding it, he waited, looking out at the whirl of snow, thinking. After a moment, he was distracted by the sight of Mary in a black coat or cloak making her way from the back toward the stables. In each hand she held a pan and now, dim and boisterous, arose the deep barking of the dogs. Galloping through the haze of falling flakes, they came to meet their suppers halfway.

Mr. Banning lifted the receiver and said: "May I have Western Union in Sansbury, please?"

"I'm sorry," May said. "He seems to have left the Evarts place. Just a moment and I'll try him at home."

She plugged in 11, twitched the key, waiting.

After a while she pulled it, let it snap back. "I'm sorry," she said, "Doctor Bull does not answer."

Another lamp lit, and whipping out the new plug, she slipped it in, thumbed over the key and heard Mr. Banning say, "—Western Union in Sansbury, please—"

Her right hand went out; the number six toll line lamp turned golden.

"Western Union, please," she said to the Sansbury operator.

After a moment a clear voice responded: "Western Union."

May said: "Here's your party, Mr. Banning."

She let go the key, sitting in the twilight, gazing out at the snow whirled over the green, blown around the iron soldier on his stone. This was like winter beginning all over again; but she felt strong enough to stand it; for sooner or later it had to be spring; and Joe would be well.

Content, she began to read, holding up the book to the light, filling herself again with the great harmony of lines which, perhaps at first passed over, you lived to see radiant:

His servants he, with new acquist
Of true experience from this great event
With peace and consolation hath dismissed,
And calm of mind . . .

Automatically she thrust out a hand, pushed back the key to see if her line were still busy.

Into her ear jumped the clear voice in Sansbury saying: "I will repeat the paid telegram to Mr. Guy Banning—" May let go, silence cutting in. Suddenly she thought: "But why does he telegraph instead of telephoning?"

She drew the key back—"Yale College, New Haven, Connecticut. Virginia died at half-past five today. Please come at once. Signed, Father. That name is, V as in victor, I as—"

From the kitchen Janet Cardmaker heard the blare of flames softly growing in the Franklin stove, the click and slide of the big chunks of cannel coal, now splitting hot.

Beyond the window the recently begun snow was thickening fast, a whirl of weightless, thin flakes in the early twilight. It hurried unseasonable through the lilac buds. It drove blindly down the sloping meadow. She took the whisky bottle by the neck in one hand. Between the fingers of the other she caught up two of her great-great-grandfather's fine crystal wine glasses.

In the kitchen George Bull sat back, quiet as the room. Janet could just see him, sidelong through the pantry door. Firelight shone across the solid slope of his cheek, making a shadow up from the arrogant hedge of eyebrow. He watched the flames with that bold, calm stare-away, his blue eyes steady. Now he moved, rousing himself, stretching his big legs, grunting in the comfortable heat. Casual, but sonorous and effortlessly true, she could hear him humming to himself.

There was an immortality about him, she thought; her regard fixed and critical. Something unkillable. Something here when the first men walked erect; here now. The last man would twitch with it when the earth expired. A good greedy vitality, surely the very vitality of the world and the flesh, it survived all blunders and injuries, all attacks and misfortunes, never quite fed full. She shook her head a little, the smile half derisive in contemptuous affection. Her lips parted enough to say: "The old bastard!"

III

The Opening Up of Windows
By Jerome Weidman

In the spring of 1937, shortly after I had published my first novel, the then editor in chief at Simon & Schuster, Mr. Quincy Howe, told me that he felt a young man embarking on a writing career ought to have a literary agent, and he asked me to lunch with him and Miss Bernice Baumgarten of the Brandt & Brandt office.

We met in the bar of the Murray Hill Hotel on Park Avenue, now gone, and had a cocktail. No, we had two cocktails. At any rate, *I* did. The number is important because, until that moment in my twenty-second year, the only alcoholic beverage I had ever consumed was the thimbleful of sacramental wine my father doled out once a year at Passover. What I drank at the Murray Hill tasted different: Mr. Howe called it a martini and, as I left the bar after my second, I was pleased to note that I had lost much of my nervous apprehension.

During the small, pleasant fuss over the menus, I heard myself saying to Mr. Howe, "You are the editor of one of America's most important publishing houses. Have you ever heard of a writer named James Gould Cozzens?" Only those who have known Quincy intimately, and have therefore learned to cherish him, will quite understand the charm of the confused look through which he mumbled, "Cozzens? Cozzens? No, I'm afraid I haven't." Flushed with what I learned later was alcohol, but at the moment I believed was triumph, I turned to the third member of our party. "And you, Miss Baumgarten?" I said, "You are one of America's most distinguished literary agents. Have you ever heard of James Gould Cozzens?"

Miss Baumgarten gave me the sort of look that Victor Hugo's illustrators always paint onto the face of Javert, and she made the gesture that women always make just before they sink the harpoon; she touched the invisible bun at the back of her head. "As a matter of fact, I have," said Miss Baumgarten dryly. "You see, I happen to be married to Mr. Cozzens."

Review of *Children and Others* by James Gould Cozzens, *Life* (as "Raise the Banner for Cozzens"), Vol. 57, No. 6 (Aug. 7, 1964), pp. 9, 12. Copyright © 1964 by Jerome Weidman. Reprinted by permission.

Ninety minutes later in her office I became a Brandt & Brandt client, which I still am, and I began to understand that my enthusiasm for the work of James Gould Cozzens did not exactly set me apart. There were quite a few of us. It was very satisfying, on meeting another member of the cult, to stop his "You know that scene in *S.S. San Pedro* where . . . ?" with a disdainful: "Oh, sure, but do *you* know the part in *Men and Brethren* when Ernest Cudlipp goes into the drugstore and . . . ?"

It was very satisfying until 1957, when Mr. Cozzens published *By Love Possessed*. Suddenly the members of the cult found themselves, somewhat irritably, part of a herd.

Their resentment cried out for a spokesman, and they hadn't far to look. One of their noisier and more voluble Liberal Intellectual critics leaped into the breach, and from the pages of *Commentary* he sent out to the sulking faithful a 9,000-word attack. The Spokesman had two basic objections to *By Love Possessed*: 1) most reviewers had praised the novel highly, and 2) Mr. Cozzens's syntax was on occasion almost as complex as the Spokesman's own. Perhaps because the attack lacked conviction, or few people who like novels ever read *Commentary* or its type of book criticism, Mr. Cozzens survived.

This is not surprising. A man who has published steadily for forty years—the first of Mr. Cozzens's twelve novels, *Confusion*, appeared in 1924—has something that we are constantly told by people like Mr. Macdonald that many American novelists lack: staying power.

This quality is evident in Mr. Cozzens's new book, *Children and Others*, his first volume of short stories. Even though some go back as far as 1930, it is difficult to tell which stories were written when. They range in subject from a nine-year-old's first confused and shattering contacts with adult passion, to astonishingly vivid recreations of the Civil War; but all seventeen of these superb pieces have one thing in common: the indelible imprint of the Cozzens intelligence.

It can be felt almost physically. The printed Cozzens page looks muscular. The reader immediately feels he is in the presence of an architect. Here are none of those easy rhythms behind which many writers conceal their inadequate grasp of their material. The Cozzens sentence is put together with the precision of a Swiss watch movement. Every word has been chosen to carry its weight toward clarity. The reader's mind is jolted into careful attention and Cozzens proceeds to say what only great writers of fiction can tell us: this is the way life is, not the way we would like it to be.

The Cozzens hero is rarely heroic. Even more rarely does he resemble that convenience of the Tape Recorder School of writers: the "average" or "common" man. Cozzens clearly subscribes to the important truth embedded in Franklin P. Adams's sardonic observation: "The average man is not so average."

The Cozzens hero is nearly always an acutely intelligent man born into a middle-class eastern family of tradition and a comfortable amount of worldly goods. He has gone to a good prep school and an Ivy League college. He spends his life in the professions considered appropriate for men of this background and breeding: medicine, the law, the church. When war comes, the Cozzens hero enlists and is, of course, commissioned.

Raised to believe that he is "better" than the common run, the Cozzens hero is constantly surprised to find that he is not *really* "better." Out of this repeated discovery, and the repeated adjustments the discovery entails, is fashioned the Cozzens drama.

A Cozzens drama is quiet-spoken. An Episcopalian minister, arranging an abortion as the only way out for a trapped parishioner, does not, quite naturally, shout his plans from the housetops. The son of a judge, who discovers at Harvard Law School that there are students smarter than himself, does not punch the smarter man in the nose. All he does is learn. And while we watch him learn, we learn. It can be an unpleasant process, not only for the hero, but for us, because Cozzens sheds light in areas that we always unconsciously assumed were adequately illuminated.

It comes as a shock, for instance, to a reader steeped in liberal clichés about race relations to discover that a highly intelligent Negro verger in an otherwise all-white Episcopalian church will voluntarily arrange to take Communion last, so as not to embarrass a member of the ruling race by forcing him to take to his lips a cup from which the Negro had drunk first. The shock is followed at once by a stab of pity: an artist has opened up for us a secret window in a human heart; he has shown us how one man worked out a way to get through his twenty-four hours in a world he never made.

Children and Others closes with a story called "Eyes To See" in which we do see through the eyes of a fifteen-year-old boy absorbing every detail of his mother's funeral, the death of innocence. We are led step by step through a genteel world, from the moment at school when the boy receives word of his mother's death to the moment after the funeral, in the home full of assembled relatives, when an act of self-abuse leaves us shaken by a new vision of the clay from which the human animal is fashioned.

The opening up of windows is a rare art, and nobody in my time has practiced it with more dedicated brilliance than James Gould Cozzens.

The Way to Go Home
[short story]

Meade Pons allowed always half an hour to drive himself from Calle H in Vedado to downtown Havana, to the offices and showrooms of the agency on Calle San Ignacio. It took him so long because the car he drove was, as a matter of advertisement, invariably brand-new. Resplendent in scratchless light enamel and glittering glass and metal, it passed, impressive and unhurried, along the Malecon, turned out of its way, up the Prado, around the Park, and through the difficult press of Obispo Street. Meade Pons did it as nearly as possible at the same hour every morning. It was a method of taking space more arresting to the contemplative Latin consciousness than any sold in newspapers. Meade Pons knew this business: and, indeed, he ought to, for he had been sixteen years in it. The general agency for Cuba was worth having, even in times of ruinous sugar prices and depression very widespread.

The latest, and surely the showiest, car of a long, distinguished line stood in the drive now, and Meade Pons was fifteen minutes late, still at the breakfast table, listening. It seemed to him that Luis took an inordinate time leaving. Ten minutes of nine. He thought, irritated, that Richard and Judith would, must, be late for school. Confirming him, he heard Judith's voice, penetrating, passing up the steps, through the shadowed, marble-floored hall, informing Luis of the fact. Meade was startled, as he always was, to hear her speak Spanish so naturally, like a native. She was eleven years old, and Spanish seemed something of an accomplishment. Richard, who was nine, shared it, but that never surprised Meade so much. Even at nine, Richard showed traits of reasonableness; Richard was earnest, thorough, somewhat conservative. Richard was, in truth, boring, Meade admitted: without thereby declaring any preference for Judith. He found them always, as he found them now, a mild annoyance—unnecessary. They were making him wait, for he wished to be sure that they were gone before he went up to speak to Alice. Alice could use their presence, without compunction, as a kind of club. They were entitled to an endless consideration and homage: because, presumably, they had neither the sense nor the strength to get on without it.

He heard the rising sound of a motor, then its fading, and the needless hoot of Luis's horn. He arose immediately, went out and upstairs. The door of his wife's room was open. She was still in bed, her breakfast tray on her lap; opened mail making a litter to one side. She said, "Take this away, Meade." Her appearance, considering her position, the hour, and the dominant fact of her forty-one years, was adequate. She did what she called "tidy" herself to say good morning and good-by to the children. Meade supposed that it was a point in her favor, since many women, especially when relaxed by this alien climate, would not bother. He came and took the tray, putting it on her dressing table. "No, not there," she said; "on the bureau. And ring for Pepita to take it away."

If Pepita were to be rung for, it surely mattered very little where he put it in the brief interval. Automatically he made the change, almost rang, when he remembered that Pepita's appearance would be undesirable for the moment.

He turned and said, "Johnny Cowden is getting in this morning."

He saw her face shutting up instantly; there was no pause for reflection. Her memory was often inefficient, but not here. She jumped eight years without the slightest effort.

She said, "Are you going to see him?"

"Naturally," said Meade. "I'm having luncheon with him." His voice was sufficiently casual. He looked at her directly and steadily. He meant to wait, perfectly calm, for her to say whatever she might have to say. Consequently, it was a sort of defeat when he added mildly, "Why? Do you mind?"

The question was idiotic. Alice had an infinite capacity for "minding," in that sense. You didn't catch her napping. Her elaborate and far-flung watch and ward missed nothing. The remotest threat to the state of things as she wanted them brought her to arms. Since no defense compares in effectiveness with an attack, she said at once, her eyes narrowing, the line of her chin aging instantly in its new tautness, "I suppose that means I needn't expect you home for a week."

Aiming at some cold irony of disinterested contempt, she went wide. She achieved a venomous irritation, but for the moment she saw herself, ludicrously, in the role of her intention—cold, superior. "I hope you'll try to keep out of jail," she said. It was terrible, Meade Pons recognized, for two people to know each other so well. Even were Alice suddenly to face a mirror, she could survive, cherish still the illusion of freezing dignity—a great lady. There are no defenses when two people know each what the other imagines himself to be. He thought, deliberately, removing his mind from the meaning of her words: "She wants her way; so do I. Only, her way in-cludes me. I must suit her. On the other hand, I don't want her to do, or not do, anything."

She interrupted him, reaching for the club that Luis had taken off to school. "And don't you dare turn up here until you're fit to be seen. I won't have the children—"

"Aren't you getting rather worked up?" he asked. He meant to be calm, but his anger jumped through. Before he could catch it, shut it up again, he had added: "Or are you trying to give me ideas? Honestly, Alice—" he said, speaking quick, intent on covering it; but that was too late. He had no right to irony; irony was hers. He would be punished for attempting it, and submission would be better than evoking the clamor of contradicted righteousness. Not yet angered beyond thinking himself, he was resigned; but he was aghast, too, as no man in his simplicity can ever help being, to see the claws, the sharp-toothed worm in every woman's heart.

"Do you expect me," she said, "to be pleased to hear that you're plan-ning a week's debauch with that drunken bum?"

"You seem to be planning for me," he protested. "I merely said I was having luncheon with him."

"Do you think I don't know what that means?"

"That's exactly what I think," said Meade. "I don't say I won't go out with him. I certainly intend to. But—" It was, after all, impossible to appeal to reason. Reason was the faculty which assured her that what she wanted could not help being right. It had, for the feminine mind, no other uses. If he were to say, "There's a difference between going on a party, and going on what you call a week's debauch," she would consider it irrelevant. Either went against her wishes, was equally damned. He might just as well turn and go now, but he wasn't angry enough. He was still looking at her with his incurable male incredulity, unable to believe that he couldn't still explain, making her understand. Understand what?

He was at an additional disadvantage, for he saw that he didn't know. He said, instead, "Johnny's pretty far from a drunken bum. He likes a good time, but that doesn't mean he's a fool. He's a pretty important man, as a matter of fact." He was, he realized, still laboring to be reasonable, judicial.

Alice, naturally, understood nothing but superlatives. "Nonsense!" she answered flatly. "You just think he is. He never was any good. I'm sure he's no good now. And what's more, Meade"—she paused, not because she was conscious of striking at a tangent, but for emphasis, her eyes deadly—"this time it may be pretty serious. I'm about through. I advise you to be careful. I'm not dependent on you."

She always produced that fact as though it were something new, some-thing he didn't know about. She had, as it happened, a comfortable income of her own. She could perfectly well take the children and do what she pleased. The difficulty, he saw at once, was that she didn't want to. She was, he thought suddenly, like the monkey in the fable who thrust his paw into the nut jar. When he had grabbed all he could, he found that his paw wouldn't come out. Neither could he bring himself to drop anything he held. Distressed, the monkey would sit there a long while. Struck by the image, he laughed, incautious. At once he saw the worm's face in hers, contorted like a mask, and white: heard the sound of her intaken breath. That did it. He could have killed it; he wouldn't have it around.

"Johnny Cowden is the best friend I ever had," he said, "and to hell with you!"

He was tingling a little with hard, warm rage as he got into the car, started it. "This," he said, "is a hot way to live." He almost rammed Luis, bringing home the other car, and made a few appropriate remarks in Spanish. "Just for that," he said, turning along the road in from Marianao, "we will have a party! We'll take the roof off!" It amazed him to think how much Alice did get her way. As long as Johnny Cowden had been in Havana, things had broken somewhat more evenly. That is, he had occasionally done what he pleased. Johnny had actually been an object lesson. Johnny was living proof that it was possible to do what you pleased, that you did not have to go home, that revelry was within your reach. Johnny had lived in a small hotel which he as good as owned; nobody would question his right to song and laughter at dawn. People went out on incredible errands; people came in humorously woebegone with hang-overs. You could hear cocktails being shaken at almost any hour. Scattered through Johnny's whole floor of connecting rooms, everyone you ever knew could probably be found. There were two China boys who tried to clear up, broke ice, eased people incapable of movement philosophically onto beds. They never, apparently, slept themselves. Alice, of course, knew about it. She had even been there on several occasions, tried consciously to be what she called a good sport. Those were afternoon cocktail parties, and perfectly orderly, but she sensed, as one did, an atmosphere. Her expression, at once interested and resentful, betrayed her conviction that evening parties were not so orderly, but she never made any comment. Johnny was too well established an evil. She said nothing against him until he was gone.

The car went fast by the prone guns ruined by sea water, the looped chains and the white shaft of the Maine Memorial. Meade Pons couldn't, he must confess, blame Alice. He attempted, intent on his driving, to calculate, to compute the sum. What it meant to her. Of course it annoyed her. The ordinary routine could not go on. She was legitimately offended when he didn't arrive as expected. He was, too, her husband. Rumors of behavior, outrageous, irresponsible, drifting quickly over the Vedado, could sting her pride. It reflected at once on her attractiveness—since he did not come when she called—and on her good judgment—why had she ever married such a creature? Around him the Latins ordered such things better—not, he insisted, merely better for the men. Well, that was aside from the point. The point, he decided—he was so late that he went past the end of the Prado, past the Palace of Justice, along the Avenida de Las Palmas—was that he didn't want to be sober, responsible, privileged to please Alice and be an example to what the *Times of Cuba* had just last month photographed and titled "her two charming children"—both of them stared, self-engrossed and petulant, at the camera; while Alice, her face considerably retouched with no protest from her, looked on them in a way Meade supposed was loving. He wished, in fact, that it was eight, ten, twelve years ago instead of now, in his forty-fifth year; that none of it— Alice, children, the place on Calle H, even the general agency for Cuba— had ever happened.

A policeman's raised glove halted him. He kept his foot on the clutch, remembering not to change gears—this year's model picked up in high from a halt, according to its literature. He was at the corner where he could see, cool across the heat of the green square, the façade of what had been Johnny's place. It would never be exactly like that again, perhaps, but Johnny was back, at least—must this minute be ashore. The hand fell, the motor picked up as advertised, and Meade swept around the double corner, his horn throwing out a musical note. He twisted expertly into San Ignacio. He ran the car with gingerly precision across the pavement into the cool cavern of the service garage.

"Lino!" he called through the door, open into the offices. "Get the Granada and ask if Mr. Cowden is registered yet."

As he came in, Lino, putting his hand over the mouthpiece of the telephone on his desk, said, "No, Mr. Pons. Not there."

"Ask when he's expected," said Meade. His secretary had stacked opened mail on his desk. He could see it through the door of his private office. There would be nothing of the slightest importance.

"He isn't expected, sir," said Lino; "they haven't a reservation."

"Say, that's funny." Meade frowned. He paused and out of him ran some sustaining warmth and cheerfulness. He felt the heat suddenly: he saw in prospect an intolerable day, beginning there in the letters on his desk and stretched out lifeless to improbably distant sundown.

"They think, sir," said Lino, "it might be the Alhambra." He made a conventional, elaborately courteous acknowledgment in Spanish, hung up.

"Get the Alhambra," said Meade.

"Mr. Cowden checked in an hour ago," Lino announced a moment later.

"Right!" said Meade. He jerked a hand toward his office door. "Take care of that stuff. I'll try to get around this afternoon or telephone you. If Camaguey calls, tell them—well, tell them they can have a couple of stock cars; or else they can keep their shirts on. We can't send what we haven't got."

"The shipment got in last night, Mr. Pons. The brokers have it. If you could get a moment to go down, we might make tonight's train."

"Send Max down."

"They want you, sir," said Lino.

"Let 'em stew a while," said Meade. "I've got to run."

The taxi dropped him in the shadowed side street at the wide doors of the Alhambra. He trotted up the steps. Once, when it was first built, he used to come here a lot. He had even taken Alice dancing on the roof—that couldn't have been more than seven or eight years ago. Johnny was either still in town, or had recently left, and Alice felt less secure in the saddle. She gave him a little rein, valorously feigning a taste for gayety herself. It hadn't been very convincing, he remembered; and she would not be long in thinking of the children. The fault, he saw, was probably his. What must have made a deep impression on him—for the atmosphere of the pale-colored, wicker-furnished lobby here brought it back complete—was that everyone else was either talking or drinking. Alice never drank much, and, naturally, there was little left to talk about. The essence of agreeable conversation is describing the many fascinating things about oneself to a person ignorant of them—a person who may, indeed, be able to credit statements which are little more than exhilarating wishes as facts.

Alice knew everything that was true about him, and could tell instantly what wasn't. Their comment must be mainly scraps elicited by people around them, with silences. Soon enough Alice would become restive, calculating with mute protest how much he was drinking. Her trained eye was alert for the inevitable signs of its effect. "We don't want another bottle," she would say; and he was pressed by her anxious assumption to agreement. Only he did want another bottle; he had no desire to get home.

The foregone futility of attempting to increase, or even to preserve, the moment's radiant content seemed to him aside from the point. He was perfectly prepared to exchange a bad head tomorrow for more of now. Now was what he wanted. It was not what Alice wanted. She was jumpy with irritation and distaste. She was at mortal war with the entrancing liberty which he gave signs of attaining. She must get hold of him quickly, make him do what she wanted; or, presently, he would be beyond her reach, doing what he wanted.

At the desk he said, "Mr. Cowden?"

"Room 1017," said the clerk promptly. "Oh! One moment, sir. Mr. Cowden just went out. He'll return shortly. Are you Mr. Durland?"

"No," said Meade.

The clerk had started to reach for an envelope in a mailbox. "Sorry, sir," he nodded. "Mr. Cowden left a message for Mr. Durland."

That was dumb, thought Meade. He should have had Lino put the call through, instead of dropping it and running over. Durland; he thought. No one he knew in Havana. An idea came to him, and he grinned, going around to a telephone booth, but he was wrong, he found. "Well, I think maybe he will," Meade told Lino. "If he does come in, tell him I'm up here at the Alhambra."

"Yes, sir," said Lino. "Oh, Mr. Pons. Camaguey has called. They are rather upset, but I told them. And a man has been up from the brokers. He wanted you to come down. He says your supervision is necessary if the shipments are to be delivered today."

"He can go to hell," said Meade, recognizing with impotent annoyance the conventional form of a threat, a promise of what he would find if he did not show a little more alacrity. He was not going to devote half this day to that dirty wrangle. Lino's pause of anxiety came to him—a subservient, phraseless exhortation not to neglect the firm's interests. It made him angrier. No real interest of his was remotely concerned with automobile shipments, the red tape of customs brokers, the qualms of a subordinate, the problems of the Camaguey branch over filling an order or two, probably on time payments and to be defaulted anyway. He added, sharp with this resentment, "That's all?" and hung up. Passing the desk, he said, "If you see Mr. Cowden and I don't, tell him Mr. Pons is in the bar."

He crossed the lobby, went through the door. Two elderly men in tight white flannels striped with black—obvious tourists—were sitting over bottles of Tropical in the corner. Otherwise that side of the room held only morning shadows. Against the mirrors leaned a patient barkeep, his few thin brown hairs laid level on his shining skull.

"Hello, Paul," Meade nodded.

The man's eyes went over to him, flickered an instant. "Why, Mr. Pons!" he said. "Haven't seen you for a long time! Just get back?"

Meade overlooked the implications. "You'll see a lot of me," he said. "You remember Mr. Cowden?"

"Yes, indeed, sir!"

"Well, he's stopping upstairs here. You better take on a couple of extra hands." He slid onto a stool and selected a potato chip.

"What'll it be, Mr. Pons?" said Paul.

"I'm waiting for Mr. Cowden," Meade said, "but since you mention it, it will be a daiquiri. Have something?"

Paul lifted his eyebrows slightly toward the old men in the corner. "If they get out," he murmured. "It's fine to see you back, Mr. Pons."

The daiquiri stood presently in front of him and Meade moistened his lips with it. Paul said, "I heard Mr. Cowden inherited quite a little money when his father died."

"I guess he did," Meade said, "and he's been doing mighty well on his own, by all accounts. He's about as smart as they make 'em." He raised the glass and returned it half empty to the dark wood.

"Mr. Cowden certainly used to give wonderful parties," said Paul. "I can remember one or two when he had me down to mix the drinks."

That was a fact that Meade had forgotten. Paul would be in a white coat behind an improvised bar. Often there would also be three or four men with homely stringed instruments, the pebble-filled gourds which marked out the sweet, melancholy measures of the *danzón*, not then revised for the elaborate orchestras nurtured to jazz. He saw faces, heard voices, long out of mind.

"It's not the same," Paul said, shaking his head. "Nothing like it any more. I never see any of those people. Not since I don't know when. Remember Mr. Delano? I heard he's dead."

"No!" said Meade, shocked, though he hadn't thought of Freddy Delano for years. "He was a fine fellow."

"People settle down or go away," said Paul. "There'll be a mob in here at noon, but I doubt if you'd see anyone you used to know."

"Fix me another of these," said Meade; "I want to see if Mr. Cowden came in."

The process of that general change absorbed him. If he wondered what had become of this man or that, some of them had no doubt wondered what had become of Meade Pons. Since he knew that, he knew what became of them all. You reached a point where peace seemed more important than gayety; there was nothing more to celebrate, only things to fear. Most of those good fellows had finally to see that they would never be rich, nor greatly successful, nor the free masters of their happy lives. Their aspirations, going out unfounded, came home empty; they must learn to be satisfied with the monotony of mere existence. They must keep their money, guard their health, employ their time to please the people who let them live at all. Apprehensive; with ambitions small enough to be plausible; with pleasures kept small, quiet, unexceptionable; they were said to have settled down. It was spoken of as a virtue, with an approving inflection, but the word, he saw, did not more than give a shoddy gilding to necessity. He had, for instance, in his own experience to get rid of his Cienfuegos manager. That man didn't settle down. He was a good fellow; he had very little time for business. The figures were eloquent, and Meade, in self-defense, had to fire him, get somebody who thought that selling automobiles was joy enough; somebody born to plod, or soundly scared into acquiescence. Burke had been that man's name. Meade never knew whether he learned wisdom, got virtue, or not. At any rate, Burke had roistered himself out of a position whose level he would be a long time regaining.

No, they said at the desk, Mr. Cowden hadn't come in.

Meade was still thinking of this Burke as he went back to the bar. Burke had been very much of his own sort, he knew; they had always got on well together. It might easily, in the realm of probabilities, have been himself who was fired at Cienfuegos, instead of Burke. That it wasn't, could, in one way, be laid precisely to Alice's credit. Her money had made it possible for him to stay on in Havana, refusing the deceptive advance of a branch managership. The ceaseless pressure of her opposition had made him seem sober, careful, hard-working—the sort of man who satisfied his lords in Detroit with the promise he gave of making money for them. He owed a lot to Alice—all the things about him which she liked, which they liked in Detroit. Perhaps he ought not to grumble because no one of those things happened to be what he himself liked.

The old gentlemen in the corner had gone; Paul had stepped out a moment. Meade slid onto the stool, sitting alone, his solitary drink before him. It seemed unpleasantly symbolic; everyone was gone, everyone was engaged in whatever way circumstances had taught him he would better be; Meade, startled, recognized the sensation. Infinitely long ago he had felt that same dismay, that growing loneliness; and he grinned a little, for he placed it on one bright morning of his childhood. He had left for school, but, unexpectedly moved, had not gone; he simply went his own way, amazed at the simplicity of thus obtaining freedom. The morning grew less bright; his own pleasure had faded with it before an hour ended. It was no good without companions. He had been, he recalled, spanked; promised more spanking if it happened again. And he remembered, it hadn't happened again, though he had always been ready to risk punishment in a good cause. He raised the glass, drinking slowly, and as he drank, his eye caught a movement at the door. Turning, he saw Johnny Cowden.

"Meade!" said Johnny, and his voice was just as Meade remembered it. "You old rounder! What are you up to now?"

His happiness was so sudden and so strong that Meade Pons found he literally could not speak. He got off the stool and, still trying to find words, took Johnny's hand.

The wrinkles were deeper around Johnny's eyes. Johnny's hair was thinned, definitely gray at the sides, but in his linen suit he looked as big, as red-brown-faced as ever. Meade saw then that he was not alone.

"Mr. Durland," he said, "meet Mr. Pons." His hand fell affectionately on Meade's shoulder. "Pete and I are going down to Oriente to look at some mines," he said, "but I guess we could have a drink." Paul had come through a door behind the bar. "Hello, Paul," nodded Johnny.

"Why, Mr. Cowden!" said Paul. "Haven't seen you for a long time!"

"Take a good look," said Johnny. "I'm going down the island tonight."

"What'll it be, sir?"

"Make it a bottle of Tropical," said Johnny. "How about you, Pete?"

"Not for me," said Mr. Durland. "Fix me up a lemonade."

"You don't want beer, Johnny," protested Meade. "Have a daiquiri. I'm going to."

"Wish I could," said Johnny, "but they won't let me drink cocktails. Sit down, Meade. Let's hear about everything. How are Alice and the kids?"

"All right," said Meade.

"Johnny tells me you're in the automobile business," said Mr. Durland. "How is it here?"

"So-so," answered Meade. "It could be worse, though I don't know how."

"What line do you handle?"

Meade told him. "I guess they're having pretty hard sledding," said Mr. Durland. "One of my best friends is connected with an automobile concern, and he told me—"

Meade waited until he had finished, and then he said, "Listen, Johnny; what do you have to go away tonight for? Boy, you just got here—"

"Johnny and I have got to be in Santiago tomorrow," said Mr. Durland. "A lot may depend on it."

Johnny said regretfully, "I hate to have to do it, but it's a chance we can't miss. I'd certainly like to look around here again, but not this trip, I'm afraid." He put out a hand and grasped Meade's shoulder. "It's good to see you," he said. "Believe me, I've thought of you a lot! We used to have pretty good times here eight or nine years back," he told Mr. Durland. "You'd be surprised. Wouldn't he, Meade?"

"Best time I ever had was in Paris," said Mr. Durland. "I was over on business, and I guess I'd have better sense now, but it was some show while it lasted."

"I guess that's when I first met you," said Johnny.

"That's right," agreed Mr. Durland. "Do you remember the night—"

Meade sat silent. The drinks had been brought and he took the daiquiri, tasted it, and set it down. He didn't want to hear what they did in Paris, but he couldn't very well help it, and it was, he saw, pretty stupid.

"I guess we could eat after this," said Johnny. "Where'll we go?"

Meade spoke suddenly:

"Johnny, it can't be done. I didn't know you were going out. I wanted to come over and fix up something for tonight. Got a man I simply have to see at lunch."

"Say, isn't that rotten?" Johnny said. "I certainly wanted to have a good talk. What about this afternoon? Got any time?"

"I haven't, Johnny," Meade said. "Got a shipment, and those lazy devils who do our customs brokerage want me to do all the work for them." Meade managed a bleak smile. "So I've got to run," he said. "Johnny, it's fine to have seen you. Next time—" He left it. "Pleased to meet you, Mr. Durland."

"Gosh, it's a shame!" said Johnny. They shook hands. "Well, take care of yourself, boy. Don't let water get in the gin."

Meade stopped at the bar, dropping money on it. "Say, this is on me!" called Johnny.

"Thanks, Paul," Meade said. "Not much," he called back. "It's on me."

Lino and Max went down at five o'clock to see that the cars for Camaguey got off. The porter was shutting up, and Meade, easing the brilliant car across the curblike sidewalk of San Ignacio, said good night to him. He worked his way up Obispo Street, slid around the Park and down the Prado. Along the Malecon the sea was marvelous, immeasurable deep blue. He turned west, the rich sun flashing off his windshield. He drove at ease. He had made the customs brokers play ball.

He turned into his own drive finally, ran the car straight back to its place in the garage. Now that the direct sun was gone, Luis, in his gardening capacity, was sprinkling a flower bed. Alice, he saw, was standing in the path, watching the operation, and he walked down. She had, of course, seen him come in, but she ignored his approach until he was within a couple of yards. She turned then, looked at him in acute appraisal.

She said, "Oh, I didn't expect you." She looked at him again. "What's the trouble? Didn't Johnny get here?"

"Yes, I saw him," Meade answered. "He's on his way to Santiago."

"Well, I suppose you expect me to thank you for managing to stay sober."

"Now," he said placatingly, "it's a long time since I've been on a bat."

"Oh, I know you," she answered.

Though she kept it in hand, spoke with grudging scorn, she was gratified; crediting herself with an accomplishment. This morning it would have been true; she knew him then. He was different now. At the end of the path Judith and Richard appeared, quarreling about something. He had those, and Alice, to see that he behaved himself, and today he had saved the company five hundred dollars at least. Many men at forty-five had less, could not do so well. He was lucky, he guessed, that he had anyone or anything, for this road was one way—not back—and had one end. In spite of everything, he liked now, the present, better than he would like that end; it was a progression, hopeless and natural. He would never meet the bunch at Johnny's again, nor Johnny himself, probably; but he had still a roof over his head, and he would better be careful, for soon enough he'd have only earth there.

Every Day's a Holiday
[short story]

From the front veranda Mr. Jamison called angrily, "Emily! You, Emily!"

"Oh, God!" she said. She slung the can opener into the sink, dumped the contents of the can of peas into a saucepan. "Howard! Get that liquor out of your car and make Father a drink. Make yourself one. Take them out and talk to him. He's going to run me crazy." She looked toward the door, noticing her father's chauffeur standing idle with a cigarette. "Mike, chop some ice."

Howard Hoyt had been sitting on the kitchen table, lax, in a sort of sad, dumb absorption. He stirred and stood up, removing his eyes from the stretched yellow linen of Emily's frock, the taut lines of her legs under it. Her feet were planted apart, stockingless, in ruined satin slippers which had once been gold-colored.

Mike said, "Where is the ice, Mrs. Brennan?"

"What would you think of looking in the icebox?" she asked. "And don't call me Mrs. Brennan. If you can't call me Emily, call me You. Do you think I like to be reminded of that bum?" She struck back her curly, dark-red hair, glancing the other way over her shoulder. "Howard, did you hear me?" Seeing his face, she turned quickly about. "Now, look here," she said, "if you're going to act like that, you can go home. Right this minute. Go on, get out of here! I won't stand for it. Those Peters people were down last night, and I forget who the night before, and they drank every drop of that other liquor. Now go and get what you brought and shut up!"

The screen door slammed gently after him. "Honestly," she said, "sometimes that man makes me want to scream. If he thinks he can be like that after we're married—put the ice there, Mike. Listen, is Father going to send you to the inn in the village? You can't sleep anywhere here unless you want to try the hammock on the porch. I told him Howard was coming. You didn't hear him say how long he was planning to stay?"

"No, I didn't, Mrs. Brennan."

"Listen, you aren't my chauffeur. I told you not to call me that. It kills me. If I liked to hear it, all I had to do was stay married to Brennan." She went to the door and yelled, "Phyl!" Her sister's muffled response came down to her. "Lord, she's still giving little Emily her bath. Do you know how to lay a table? Well, go and lay it. We'll never get supper."

Mike moved away with a creak of his black leather leggings, wiping his wet hands on his whipcord breeches. The screen door swung, admitting Howard, who lugged a case of bottles.

"Open one," Emily said, "open one! Father will be howling again in a minute." She whipped about and cried, "Phyl! Phyl! Look at little Emily! That child's down here without a stitch on! Honey, don't you know you can't walk around with a lot of men that way? Get upstairs and let Aunt Phyl put some clothes on you—" She dissolved in laughter. "She's just a slut at heart, like her mother. That's right, Howard. There's the ice. There are the glasses. Wait a minute. How about me?" She picked up a coffee cup. "Give me half an inch. And don't be such such a lemon. I'm warning you."

In a few minutes her sister appeared calmly. "Your daughter is dressed, Emily. You're welcome."

"Where's Keith?"

"I was going to tell you. I think he's upset. I told him to go to bed."

"And I told him if he ate any more cake at Mrs. Miller's I'd tan the hide off him. She just gets the little simpleton up there to try to pump him. God, these farmers!"

"He was there, all right."

"I know it. You can't do anything with him. He's just like Brennan."

"Emily, you jackass! If Father ever heard you say that—"

"Well, what's he want? I was married to the rat for three years, wasn't I? I should think that would fix it up."

"It'll never fix up the fact you weren't married to him when Keith was born; you were still married to Sheldrick. Or have you forgotten that?"

"It's one of the things you don't forget. Lord, I'll be crazy if I try it again with Howard."

"Well, why do you?"

"I have to live. Brennan will never pay any more alimony. He hasn't sense enough to make any money. He's probably pie-eyed from morning to night. What can I do? Put him in jail? That doesn't pay any bills."

"I'll speak to Father. That's what I mean about Keith, you little fool. He'd simply disown you."

"Lord, Phyl, how dumb is dumb?"

"He isn't so dumb. But you don't have to prove it to him. And you be careful about Howard."

"Don't you worry. Howard started to go funny on all that liquor the Peters drank and what else. He's going to lie down and play dead this week-

end. I've given him too darn much of a break. Father can have my bed and
I'll sleep with you. We'll put Howard down on the couch in the living
room. Maybe Mike can sleep on the porch. There's a dumb boy."

"I don't doubt it."

"Where did Father get him?"

"How do I know? Probably from an agency. Is there any reason why he
should be brilliant? And listen, I heard you tell him to call you Emily. I
suppose you think Father would love that?"

"He can't call me Mrs. Brennan and get away with it. I'll have to stay
and watch the steaks. Or, you stay and watch them. I'd better look at Keith
a minute. Where's little Emily?"

"On the porch with Father and Howard."

"That must be quite a party. See you in a minute."

After a while there was a sound at the door and Phyllis glanced that way.

"I finished laying the table, Miss Jamison," Mike said. "What should
I do now?"

"Nothing. Take a rest. If you want a drink, help yourself."

"Thank you, ma'am."

"I see what Emily means," Phyllis nodded. "Listen, my lad, you're
going to have to eat with us. Mrs. Brennan and I do what little serving is
done. Don't feel you have to be fresh; but we can't stand on too much ceremony. Adapt yourself. Relax. We're all one happy family on a holiday."

"All right."

"That's better. If you've got a real shirt on under that coat, you can take
the coat off. It's a pretty warm evening."

"All right." In his shirt sleeves, he sat on the edge of the chair. "Pretty
country up here," he ventured.

"Nice for the kiddies," she said briefly. "We're living here this summer
because we're good and poor. Or Mrs. Brennan is, and you can see how
devoted I am to her. Does that explain everything?"

"I hope Mrs. Brennan isn't mad at me, Miss Jamison."

"You hope, do you? O.K., Irish. Just keep hoping."

His stout form was sunk morosely in the sagging wicker chair on the
veranda. Mr. Jamison raised the glass to his cropped white mustache, tilted
it shortly, drinking, set it on the wicker table by the rail. He made a sound
half a snort, half a cough. From the pocket of his tweed jacket he drew a
huge silk handkerchief and wiped the knee of his white flannel trousers.
Then he wiped his mustache and thrust the handkerchief back. Without
more warning he addressed Howard, who had been sitting silent on the top
step clasping his glass and gazing out across the meadow and river.

"Where does all this liquor come from?" Mr. Jamison said.

Recovering, Howard said, "Why, I brought it up from town, sir. It ought to be—"

"Well, now, I wish you wouldn't do it," Mr. Jamison said. "There's too much drinking going on around here. If you didn't bring it up, they'd probably never miss it."

Howard looked at him, confused; but apparently no answer was expected, for Mr. Jamison continued more sharply. "Where's Emily?"

"She's getting supper, sir."

"Humph. I called her."

"She'll come as soon as she can, sir. Is there anything I can do?"

"No, no." He turned his heavy head abruptly. "Emily! Where are you going?"

"Upstairs," she called back.

"What for?"

"You'd only be embarrassed if I told you."

"Emily!"

"Oh, keep still, Father. Everything's all right. Keith isn't feeling well."

"What's wrong with the child?" Mr. Jamison asked Howard.

"I don't know, sir. I saw him running around half an hour ago."

"I don't think he gets proper food."

"Emily takes wonderful care of the children, Mr. Jamison. They couldn't get any better care."

"Well, I suppose she has nowhere to gad about to up here. In town, she behaved like a hooligan. What business are you in, Mr. Boyd?"

"My name is Hoyt, sir," Howard said, awkward. "Why, I'm in real estate."

Keith, flushed and bright-eyed in the early shadows, was not very sick, Emily saw. "Well, just for that you don't get any supper," she said, and laughed. "That's a break for you," she added. "You don't want any, anyway, do you?"

"No, Mummy. I don't want any."

"How much of that Miller garbage did you eat? Two pieces, I'll bet. Tell Mother what Mrs. Miller asked you."

"She asked me where my Daddy was."

"What did you say?"

"I said he was away."

"That's all right. What else?"

"She asked me what he was. I said he was a bum."

"Oh, my God! You would! What else?"

"I don't remember, Mummy."

"Yes, you do. Now, think hard."

"Well, she said didn't a lot of men come to stay at night here—"

"I knew it. The snooping old—Keith, honey, Mother's simply going to wale the life out of you if you ever go up there again. Honestly, I'd do it right this minute if you weren't sick."

"I feel like I wanted to throw up—"

"You and me both!" she groaned. "Get up! Get up! Get in the bathroom. Don't you dare throw up in here!"

"I thought so," said Phyllis. "This shack is wonderful that way. You don't miss a thing. Does he feel better?"

"He'll be all right. More ice, Mike, more ice. How about those steaks?"

"About five minutes. You stay here. I heard you telling Father to shut up. I'd better go out and smooth him down."

"Call little Emily, will you? She isn't out there. Father was riding Howard about bringing liquor up. You tell him to mind his own business. I notice he drinks it, all right. Lord, I meant to get a bath and put some clothes on. This is sticking to me."

She picked up the glass, tipped her head back and drank half of it without pausing, set it aside, and took a bread knife and a loaf of bread.

While she sliced swift and even, Mike, leaning against the far wall, his empty glass tilting forgotten in his large hand, looked at her. He said nothing and Emily sliced in silence until the whole loaf had been divided. Knocking off the ends of crust, she set up the pile of slices, cut it in half from top to bottom, shifted the result to a plate. She took the nearby glass and drained it, gave her hair a quick toss. Mike was still looking at her and, turning, she easily surprised his absorbed gaze. "Ah, there!" she said. "Thinking about your best girl, I'll bet!"

Starting, he reddened; began to smile sheepishly.

"Bring your glass here, Good-looking. We'll have another drink. One more stiff one and I may be tight enough to stand supper with Father." She looked toward the door. "Come on, Howard," she said. "You need another drink, too."

"Father, please don't be silly," Phyllis said. "Emily has supper to get for seven people. In this madhouse anyone else would collapse completely. I don't know how she stands it. Howard, get Father and you another drink."

"No, no. I don't care for another drink. There's too much—"

"Get them, Howard."

When he had gone, Mr. Jamison said, "Who is that fellow, anyway? When did Emily meet him?"

"Oh, he's the one who sold the Larchmont house for her. He's a nice boy."

"What's he come up here for?"

"He comes up here because he's trying to get Emily to marry him."

"What's he want to do that for? Who wants to marry a woman with two children who's been divorced twice?"

"Now, Father, don't be childish. He's been divorced himself and he's old enough to know his own mind."

"I won't have Emily marrying another drunken wastrel. I told him not to bring any more liquor." He pulled his mustache. "If he had any regard for her reputation he'd know better than to be staying here every weekend."

"Howard is the soberest man alive, Father. You needn't worry about him. Furthermore, I don't think you have any right to interfere with Emily."

"You don't, don't you!"

"My very words. You treat her like a dog. You always have. If Mother hadn't died, do you think Emily ever would have run off from school with Sheldrick that way? Maybe you've forgotten how you used to roar around the house."

"You leave your mother out of this! I can only be thankful, truly thankful, that she isn't here. The disgrace of it would kill her."

"Father, are you trying to fight with me, too?"

"I'm not going to have you being impertinent and speaking disrespectfully of your mother."

"You heard exactly what I said about Mother. Now, aren't you ashamed of yourself?"

Tugging his mustache again, he glared at her a moment. Grunting a little, he looked away then. "As soon as Emily can show me she's ready to live a quiet, sober life and bring up her children properly and decently, I'll see she has the means. That's what I've always stood ready to do. Meanwhile, she can live on that Brennan pup's alimony."

"He hasn't paid her any for months. As a matter of fact, we've been living, and are right this minute, on what money I can spare."

"Well, you shouldn't do it. She made her bed. Let her lie in it. She had no business to get herself into a mess like this. How old is she? Twenty-seven! Think of it! At twenty-seven she's been divorced twice. Like a lot of Broadway riffraff! I'm not going to make her an allowance. Not a cent. I don't want to hear any more about it."

"You won't. We'll get along. But don't you let me hear any more about what Emily ought to do, or ought not to. And if she wants to marry Howard, that's her business."

He had begun to grumble restlessly before she finished, and, pouting under his mustache, he could be heard saying now: "—thinks of nothing but pleasure. Other people have to work for a living. Decent and responsible attitude. Too much to ask, I suppose. Well, I won't make her any allowance. I'll give you a check before I go. Do what you want with it. But

don't ask me to—" She reached out and patted his hand. "There's your
grandchild," she said, indicating little Emily, who had appeared silently
at the bottom of the steps. "You might ask her where she's been and generally make yourself agreeable. I'd better see what I can do in the kitchen."

In the shadows of the hall she encountered Howard, who had a glass in
each hand. Nodding back toward the porch, she said, "The dust's settled a
little out there. He's a trial; but if you talk to him nicely he'll mellow down.
Do your best."

He nodded, looking at her. Then he said hesitantly, "Phyl, I don't
think Emily ought to drink any more. She's pretty tight. I mean, I don't
think your father would like it—"

"All right. I'll get her in hand."

In the kitchen there was a haze of grease smoke and a fierce crackle and
hiss of broiling steaks. Mike was sitting in the broken chair by the table.
Emily was on her knees before the oven, jabbing the steaks with a fork. The
intense jets of blue flame in the broiler shone on her flushed face. She was
singing, with a certain husky sweetness which showed Phyllis that Howard
was not wrong:

> "Why do I love you?
> Why do you love me—"

Glancing up at her sister, she said, "They're about done." She steadied
herself with her palm on Phyllis's hip. "I'm woozy. Give me a hand up,
darling. I'll never make it alone. Want another drink, Mike?"

"But not for you," Phyllis said, bringing her to her feet. "I've just finished repairing the damage and I want you to behave. I can keep these hot
a while. You haven't time for a bath, but beat it up and get under a cold
shower for a couple of minutes. Hurry!"

"I'm all right, darling. Honestly—"

"You are not. Hurry up. And come down decently dressed. I mean,
with something on under it. You know Father."

Mike put his glass on the table. "I guess I'd better not have any more,
Miss Jamison," he said. "Mrs. Brennan told me I should drive her in to the
village afterwards and get some groceries for breakfast. That's pretty strong
stuff. I wouldn't want to be driving a car if I had any more."

"Well, now, maybe we'd better have Howard drive her in."

"Why, Miss Jamison," he said reproachfully, "I'm sober as a judge.
Honest, I know where to stop."

"That's a wonderful thing to know," she said. "You might go out on the
porch and tell Father and Howard that supper will be ready in five minutes."

Emily had on a frock much like the yellow one, but clean; a pale-green
linen. "I certainly threw away a wonderful edge then," she sighed.

"Thanks, darling. Do I look refined? I swiped a brassière of yours." She slid her narrow tanned hand under Phyllis's arm, drew her close, their cheeks touching. Turning her head sharply she kissed her.

"O.K., brat," Phyllis said. "Get going. They're all in there."

From the dining room she could hear Emily asking presently, "Won't you say grace, Father?"

"Don't be blasphemous!" Mr. Jamison roared.

Catching up the steak platter, Phyllis came to the rescue. "That'll do from you, Red," she said. "Go and get little Emily's cereal. There's a carving knife, Father."

Later, when she came out to the kitchen to help Emily with the raspberries, Phyllis said, "If you've got to go up to the village, let Howard drive you. You've been treating him pretty rough."

"And it's only the beginning," Emily said. She filled a pitcher with cream. "He makes me sick. He sticks to me. He sits around, like a dog who wants something, looking sorrowful. I know he told you in the hall I was tight. The rat! My being tight has given him a lot of damn good breaks. He wouldn't be any treat to a sober girl, I can tell you that."

"All right, all right! Don't yell, darling. Father can hear too."

"He shouldn't mind. He didn't seem exactly glad to see Howard. He's so afraid I might have a good time, he wouldn't even let Howard by."

"He'll learn to like Howard better."

From the dining room Mr. Jamison roared suddenly, "What are you two whispering about in there? Come out! Get on with supper!"

There was a continuous wink of fireflies in the dusk across the meadow to the river. Beyond the river, the white fence of the valley highway rounded the bend. Preceded by their pale shafted lights, occasional cars appeared swift, small and silent in the distance. Resuming his seat on the veranda, Mr. Jamison offered a cigar to Howard. When they had them lighted, Phyllis said, "Father, let Mike drive Emily up to the village. We need some stuff for breakfast."

"All right. Don't get any liquor. She was drunk at supper."

"Oh, no, she wasn't, Father. She can't get any liquor in the village anyway."

"She can get it anywhere, and does."

Howard, turning his face quickly in the dusk, said, "I can drive her up, Phyl. I'll—"

"No, no," Mr. Jamison said. "Let this fellow of mine do something. He never gets half enough work."

Embarrassed, Howard looked wretchedly at him. Mr. Jamison drew on the cigar, regarded the end of it a moment and said, "I'm sorry to sound short. I don't mean it that way, I simply don't want Emily to get herself a reputation—humph! I mean people in a small community like this mis-understand. Would you care to tell me a little about yourself, Mr. Hoyt?"

"There isn't much to tell, sir."

"Well, what I meant, frankly—humph! That is, I had been given to understand that you entertained—I mean, in regard to Emily—"

"Yes, sir. I hope you wouldn't have any objections, if she were willing, to our being married."

"Yes. I see." He puffed a moment at the cigar. "Perhaps you'd care to tell me something about your financial—qualifications—" He turned his head. "Phyl gone?"

"She went out to the kitchen, sir. Did you want her?"

"No, no. I don't think the matter is one we need to discuss in her hear-ing, that's all. I mean, are you in a position to—"

In the kitchen Phyllis said, "Now, take that slow and easy."

"Caught again," Emily nodded. She set the glass down. "Come on, Mike. You don't have to put the coat on."

"Listen, Red."

"Yes, darling."

"Don't you be too long."

"Quick as a flash," Emily said. "I'll do all tomorrow's dishes, Phyl. Get little Emily to help you. She won't have to go to bed for half an hour."

"See you get back to put her to bed."

In the dusky sky over the eastern hills appeared the great edge of the rising moon.

"Beautiful night," said Mr. Jamison.

It was, in fact, practically night. Only a last radiance of sunset or twi-light remained on the pale dusty surface of the dirt road at the bottom of the short lawn. There was no wind, but the river and meadow and massing of big treetops about the wooden bridge across the small brook breathed a distinct coolness in the dark, now coming alive with the many sounds of summer evening.

Mr. Jamison said, "Are you a college man, Mr. Hoyt?"

Rousing himself, Howard answered. "Well, sir, I was at Lafayette for a little over a year. I didn't graduate. I couldn't afford it. I had to come home and work."

"I'm not a college man, myself," Mr. Jamison said. "They seem to make more of it nowadays, but I often think it's just a waste of a boy's time. More to your credit to have been able and ready to pitch in and help your family. You seem to have done well. I'm glad."

"Yes, sir."

Mr. Jamison removed the cigar from his mouth and looked first at it and then at Howard. He coughed and said, "I think Emily will settle down.

She's not been in a good environment. Those fellows she was married to weren't any good. If she could get away from all that into a wholesome atmosphere, she'd be different. I hope so for both your sakes."

"I wouldn't want to make Emily do anything she didn't want to do, sir. I'd want her to be happy. To have a good time."

"Of course. Of course. But that isn't all of life. Every day's not a holiday. Emily thinks it is."

Howard moved a little on the top step. Turning his wrist inconspicuously he managed to bring into view the luminous dial of his wrist watch.

From the door behind, Phyllis asked, "Are you all right, Father? I'm going to put little Emily to bed."

"Yes. It's high time. The child shouldn't be up as late as this. Emily should have seen to it before she went."

Left alone, Howard and Mr. Jamison were both silent. The sound of a motor reached them after a minute and they both turned to look. Headlights were descending the slope through the trees to the little bridge.

"That ought to be Emily and the car," Mr. Jamison said. "She had no right to go off like that and leave Phyllis with all the work to do. She could just as well have given that fellow of mine a list to take up."

There was a rumble of the coming car on the bridge. The headlights mounted the slope on this side. After a moment it was apparent that the car was a Ford. It went on past toward the Millers' farmhouse.

The moon, whiter, well clear of the low wooded hilltops, shone exactly mirrored, swaying a little with the slow current but unbroken, on the river. Howard had long ago finished his cigar. He lighted another cigarette. Finally Phyllis came downstairs and out into the shadows quietly. She dropped into the chair behind Howard. "Peace at last," she sighed. "Let me have one of those."

"What's keeping Emily?" Mr. Jamison said. "She ought to have been back long ago."

Howard had got up to give Phyllis the cigarette. He lit it now for her. She could see his disturbed face in the small glow and putting out a hand patted his arm twice. "Thanks," she said. "Emily had a lot of things to get, Father."

"Call up that store and see if they know anything about her."

"Father, don't be absurd. They'll be back in a minute."

"There's nothing absurd about it. She's been gone an hour and a half. It shouldn't take her twenty minutes. I want to know if she's been there, or if she's running around looking for liquor."

"Well, I'm not going to call up."

"If she isn't back in ten minutes, I'll call myself."

"That wouldn't do you any good. The store closes at nine."

"Humph! Exactly as I thought! She's trying to find a bootlegger. You don't expect me to believe she's riding around looking at the moonlight."

"Why not?" said Phyllis. "She's been cooped up here all day."

"She has no business to stay away. She has a child sick upstairs, and—"

"Keith's been asleep for hours. He's perfectly all right."

"She doesn't know it."

"Lord," said Phyl, "let's have a drink."

"No. I don't care for one."

"Well, I do. How about you, Howard?"

"I guess so." Belatedly he added, "Could I help you, Phyl?"

"No, sit still."

Busy with ice and glasses in the kitchen, Phyllis heard presently the fast hollow rumble of a heavy car on the bridge down in the trees. A moment later headlights wheeled, flashed along the side of the house. A motor was shut off. From in front Mr. Jamison called loudly, "Emily! You, Emily! Come here."

Phyllis held the whiskey bottle motionless, listening. Emily laughed clearly. "In a minute," she said. "I want to put these things in the kitchen."

"Emily!" Apparently it was a failure, for he roared, "Mike! I want to speak to you."

"Yes, Mr. Jamison. Be right there."

Phyllis set down the bottle, went and pushed the screen door open. "Hurry up," she said.

Emily, her arms full of packages, slid in. She dumped them on the table. "Darling," she said, breathless. "Am I all right?" She smoothed the dress, fluffed back her hair with both hands.

"Yes," said Phyllis. "You're all right. Go on out there."

"We weren't long, were we?"

"Hours. I ought to kill you, Red. Go on, before I do."

"Phyl."

"Yes, you bum!"

"Father?"

"No. He thinks you were trying to get some liquor."

"Thanks, darling."

On the porch Emily said, "I'm sorry, Father. We had to wait around for the proprietor at the Inn so we could get a room for Mike. He can't sleep down here. He can go back now."

"Is that true, Mike?"

"Yes, Mr. Jamison."

"Is there any liquor in the car?"

"No, sir."

"Well, all right. I'll telephone when I want you tomorrow."

"Yes, sir. Good night, sir." He looked at Emily and said, diffident, "Good night, Mrs. Brennan." He turned quickly toward the car.

"O.K., Irish," she said.

Mr. Jamison looked at her. He said: "What do you mean by talking to him that way?"

Phyllis had come out.

"Well, now," she said, "don't start a war. He is Irish, isn't he?"

One Hundred Ladies
[short story]

Elation was the proper word for what he felt. Owen Fulton felt it with an urgent, unreasonable completeness as soon as he got into the depot at Washington and saw the special train for Fredericksburg. Every car was elaborately swathed in fresh, vivid, red-white-and-blue bunting. The bunting made long formal festoons gathered at the center under plaques of painted and gilded wood. The plaques bore alternately from car to car the old First Corps disk, and the combined First and Fifth Corps badges of the last Virginia campaign.

Owen Fulton's simple pleasure assured him that, after all, he had been right to come. Hattie was wrong for once. It would do him good, just as Alfred promised. In the great crowd he looked around, not recognizing anyone, but glad to see that something was left of the army, that many people still remembered. As a rule he disliked and avoided crowds—that was what Hattie knew and meant when she told him he was foolish—but he liked this one. He had avoided it, if anything, too long. He had been letting himself forget that, whatever might be said about the present, he had once been a soldier.

The May day was very warm. A rumor that President Arthur was to join the group of guests from the Senate and House probably kept people out of the cars. Anticipating inconvenience with his leg in the last-minute rush sure to result, Owen Fulton clutched his bag tight and pushed on cheerfully. It would hardly be possible to find Alfred Bostwick before the train started.

Choosing steps at random, Owen displayed his Society of the First Corps card. He lifted his bag and threw it onto the car platform, preparing with complicated agility to follow it. On level ground his injured leg gave him practically no trouble. He knew how to manage it. But stairs he had to take sideways, keeping the knee straight while he stepped patiently up with his right foot. After all these years he could do it so expertly that, unless the stairs were long, he would be up before anyone could help him—supposing there was anyone who would think of troubling.

One of those who would have troubled was the conductor who had asked to see his card. Like everyone else, the conductor was watching for President Arthur, but he turned belatedly and cried, "Here, Captain! Wait. I'll—"

Panting on top, Owen answered, "Thank you, but I'm handy at it."

The conductor, perhaps conscious of his railroad uniform, said, "I'm an old First Corps man, myself, Captain. Eighth Pennsylvania Reserves. Magilton's brigade."

Owen looked down, surprised, at the full mild face. Those, he remembered, were Meade's Third Division men who broke Jackson's line, almost won the battle before it began. When no one was ordered to their support, they had in turn been broken. Remembering that bad December morning well enough, Owen could recall vividly the Pennsylvanians' alarming, unexpected reappearance about noon. They were falling back from the railroad through the brush and smoke in little groups—one or two behind stopping to fire, though surely at nothing visible. Others, showing the rough spite of defeat, herded ahead varying small numbers of ragged Rebel prisoners.

With that liberty of opinion which distinguished the volunteers, they felt that they had been senselessly sacrificed. They greeted the line with jeers and curses. "What were you waiting for, Dummy? Carriages to take you up?" some small-respecter of shoulder straps had roared in Owen Fulton's face.

Not knowing for what he was waiting, nor what was coming next, Owen Fulton, a second lieutenant at the time, let the company left in his charge get out of hand several times during the next half hour. Their panicky bursts of firing must have killed some men of Meade's, who had missed the first order to fall back, or been hampered by wounds. Down on one knee, staring in agony of attention, Owen would shout to stop it as soon as he could be sure. Even, rising, he would race down the line, flailing backs and buttocks of absorbed shooters with his sword flat—

This enlivening of memories, complete with all small sights and sounds, with tensions and anxieties as fresh as ever, certified the past to him, and Owen valued it as a foretaste of what he might expect when he saw Fredericksburg, saw the positions of the Left Grand Division. He found himself shaken by the mingling of regret and joy and pride. Holding the rail, he answered, "I was in the Ninety-seventh New York, the Second Division. It's twenty years since I've seen Fredericksburg—"

With a quick, overwhelming crash, a band which Owen had not noticed before broke into "Dixie"—*old times there are not forgotten.* . . . Paralyzed by the fine blare and bray of horns and bugles, the matchless roll of military drums in expert hands, Owen Fulton could feel the blood come up in his face, tightening his cheeks, tingling at the roots of his mustache. The locomotive blew its whistle. Plainly President Arthur was not, and probably never had been, coming. Owen raised his hand in a quick wave to the conductor. Limping in his haste to get out of the way, he entered the car, dropped down in the nearest seat.

A few people were in uniform. Owen noticed a hardy little old man with a forage cap set on the back of his head. He noticed him because the crown of the cap still carried a Corps badge in the faded color of Owen's own division. Sergeant's stripes had turned almost white on the ancient sleeve. Down the aisle went also a distinct perfume of whiskey, and Owen hoped that there would not be too much of that, especially by men who had elected to wear a uniform which would unmistakably identify them with the First Corps. Alfred had told him that the committee and the officers of the Society had suggested civilian clothes. You would not expect Fredericksburg to be exactly delighted by the old associations. Furthermore, General Longstreet was to be present as a speaker. He would not be likely to appear in a Confederate uniform.

Though the car, in rapid shaking motion now, was greatly overcrowded, no one had made a move to take the seat by Owen. The aisle was full of men standing. Forming boisterous circles, others perched on the arms, hung over the backs of seats. Left alone, Owen did not feel out of it. He could not really expect anyone to pick him out and greet him. The truth was that during the first years after the war he had been unable to find either the time or the money to attend army reunions. Later it had seemed to him too late. Some of the soldiers' organizations had begun to take on a pension-seeking political aspect with which he would have been ashamed to associate himself. Then, too, his wife exercised an adverse influence. Hattie's disapproval was certainly not based on unpleasant political aspects. To the best of Owen's knowledge, it was not even based on any appropriately feminine abhorrence of war and slaughter. Once or twice he had marched in Memorial Day parades in Brooklyn. He might even, Owen admitted, have liked to march in more, to talk about old days over a glass or two in some uniform-crowded saloon after the speeches. Like most women, Hattie was instinctively against this. She did not oppose him in words, or show bad temper; but she could adeptly make him realize, at first, that she would be left alone for most of one of his few holidays; and then, the desirability of taking the chance for a quiet outing with the children. She had even expressed anxiety over his joining, as this year, at Alfred Bostwick's insistence, he had, the Society of the First Corps.

"Mr. Bostwick," she said—it was perhaps significant that in fifteen years' acquaintance she had never thought of calling him Alfred—"I do hope that this won't be something with long conventions Owen has to attend. I'm sure it would be very tiring for him. It wears him out so when he has to travel on business."

Alfred, who arrogated to himself the brusque privileges of a long bachelorhood, grunted, "You should have seen Owen in the old days, Mrs. Fulton. He's pretty well domesticated now, but he used to march the farthest traveling company in the division."

Hattie didn't miss obvious opportunities. "Yes," she said. "It might be different if it weren't for his wound. You aren't likely to forget the army, are you, Owen?" She went out then, for Alfred liked a glass of bourbon with his cigar and wouldn't hesitate an instant to drink the one and smoke the other regardless of her presence. He considered her place to be in the parlor.

"Hattie just hates to have you where she can't run you," he said, grasping resentfully at his bushy, still-handsome auburn side whiskers. "That's all right. Or at any rate, it's a woman's nature. Only you oughtn't to let yourself get to like it—" He went on blowing and grunting for some time, doubtless appalled by the narrowness of certain of his own escapes from matrimony.

In co-operation with a Sixth Corps man named Hunter, who had settled in Fredericksburg after the war and done well in the foundry business, Colonel Bostwick was even then scheming about this visit to the battlefield. His friend Hunter had just financed the building of an opera house, perhaps only moderately grand, but suitable for a big banquet. Alfred had interested General Doubleday. He had written to General Longstreet and received an agreeable reply, which he showed to Owen.

Alfred had assumed right along that Owen was going; but, up to this point, Owen hadn't planned to. He was reasonably certain that Hattie would find the trip unwise, or inconvenient, or both. By not mentioning it to Hattie, he had left, he found, a loophole. Unaware of the matter, Hattie had not been given the opportunity to settle it once and for all in the negative. When he saw Longstreet's letter accepting the First Corps' invitation, Owen Fulton was curiously stirred. It was astonishing to hold in your hand a note with conventional salutation and subscription, amblingly courteous, the ordinary cordial phrases scrawled in an even, unnotable handwriting—and this was Longstreet! A name at once remote and thunderous; the formidable direction behind battle lines which, too often impregnable to assault, were always impregnable to the imagination. Owen discovered that he had a desire to see Longstreet—perhaps, shake hands with him. None of this could very well be explained to Hattie. She could not be expected to see why a glimpse of General Longstreet in the flesh would be worth something to him, or what would be gained if he saw again the actual spot where he had stood that December day, on the left, at Hamilton's Crossing. It would be very impolitic and ill-advised if he told her that he would like somehow to get in touch again with a time of his life when he was more important—yes, more noble; a man playing a man's part in the trying and dangerous realities of the fighting which had ended by preserving the Union. She would certainly presume that he meant to criticize her, to imply that she was not of any importance or interest to him—

Least of all would Hattie think it natural for him to wish to visit Fredericksburg again. He ought to remember it painfully. A hostile town, overflowing in heat and dust; one vast hospital, to which the wounded came up by the thousand from the lines of Spottsylvania to join those thousands from the Wilderness not yet evacuated. Owen Fulton had spent the whole month of June there in '64, expected, and expecting, to die. They told him he could not possibly live unless his leg was taken off. Perfectly pictured in his mind still was the face gleaming with sweat, the big red beard (his apron often bloody from beard to knees) of some regimental surgeon appearing about every ten minutes (or so it seemed) day and night saying: "Now, Captain, you're going to be reasonable about this, aren't you? You ought to think of me. Do I want your death on my conscience? You're committing suicide as wantonly as if you put a pistol to your head—"

Owen Fulton, raving, yelled: "Just give me a pistol and see what I use it for, you damned butcher!"

Afterward, when it became apparent that he was going to live, and that his leg, which they had wasted not a minute on, was finding some slow and incredible way of repairing itself, Owen was moved out to a tent in the garden. The tent stood close to a brick building which had been the slave quarters of the big house. Here the ladies of the family had established themselves. Lying on his back under the partly lifted canvas flies, Owen saw them frequently, frequently overheard their conversation. By degrees (it was all he had to do) he could identify them by voice; then, by sight. Mama was easy enough. So was Olivia, with her distinctively young tones. Sarah Ann and Lou he was less sure of—which was which he couldn't say, for he was never given a chance to assign the voice directly to the face. They spoke only when, imagining they could not be heard, they were indoors. When they came out, they passed down the path frigidly silent, looking neither right nor left. The part Mama had chosen for them to play was the preposterous, necessarily self-conscious one of being unaware of the tent in the garden, of their house from which they had been expelled to make room for Yankee wounded, of the wagons and artillery often passing on Princess Anne Street—even, of the sentries who, amused, were accustomed to present arms when they went through the gate.

The conversation indoors, usually quite clear, troubled Owen at first. Not only because it sometimes concerned intimate matters unsuitable for him to hear, but because listening at all was ungentlemanly and could not be defended. However, he did listen and he came to mind these aspects of it less. His leg was almost constantly painful and he could find a certain distraction in adding bit by bit to his acquaintance with the speakers. He corrected his impressions of them. He engaged silently his sympathy in their private concerns. He waited with interest to hear the outcome of the trivial plans or projects discussed.

In the end he knew them very well. Perhaps sometime he would marry some girl; but it was strange to think he would know far less about any girl he married than he knew about Olivia, who was engaged to a Rebel major in Ewell's Corps. Olivia, despite some charms of manner and speech, was selfish and irritable—like everyone else. Seeing these bad qualities in their right relation to her private life, Owen believed that he could condone and understand them better, and so perhaps evoke them less often. Less often than her major ever would be able to, when their appearance in a character presented to him as only amiable surprised and irritated him.

Able to see in Olivia's impersonal good looks the humanizing traces of her weaknesses and shortcomings, Owen was filled with a deep compassion and tenderness for her. Love, he knew, was reputed to overcome all obstacles. If not at the time, at least through the years since, an understanding between a Yankee officer and a southern girl had been shown in many books and plays to be the completest commonplace of romance. In his case it did not work like that. The uselessness of attempting to make Olivia notice him, or of hoping to exchange even a word with her, kept Owen from so much as considering it. When they came to move him to be sent north, she certainly did not feel sad to see him go, for she had never known that he was there. That would be twenty years ago, next month; but, very likely, if he cared to, Owen Fulton could today look at that house and garden again, find them little changed.

"I guess you wouldn't remember me, Captain."

The statement, close to him, broke through Owen Fulton's preoccupation. With it came again the scent of whiskey and he turned his head, startled. The little man with the forage cap and sergeant's stripes had wandered back from wherever he had been going. On the corner of the seat he put a shocking hand. The very old injury was smoothly healed, but he had only two fingers. Jolted, Owen Fulton looked from it to the face. This was familiar enough. Everyone knew it. It had the thick bending nose and knobby chin of a ruddy, aged little Punch; but Owen could not connect it with any person of his acquaintance. Embarrassed, he said, "I hope you'll excuse me, Sergeant. I've a poor memory for faces."

The little man said, "That's all right, Captain. I guess we've all changed some. I just saw your head there by the window turned a certain way, and I said, 'Lord, that's Captain Fulton!'" He grinned and nodded a few times, plainly hoping that Owen might suddenly remember him. Finally he said, "My name's Mintern."

"Mintern," said Owen, perplexed; for he had certainly heard the name before.

The little man laughed. "That's what it all comes to in the end," he said. "Lord, Captain, once I spent three whole days trying to get up nerve enough to shoot you. You had me reduced to the ranks going on to Mine Run. Me and Corporal Howard. We were out skirmishing with a keg of corn and we happened to find a horse belonging to General Warren's staff. Only trouble was, a man was sitting on the horse, so we took the man off. I remember Howard saying three was too many for one horse; it wasn't right to the horse. We borrowed his sword and pistol, and Howard happened to sell them to a sutler. I can still remember riding in, the two of us on the horse, staff blanket and all. Then the fireworks began."

They certainly had begun. In the rush of recollection, Owen Fulton saw it all again. General Warren himself came blazing over to brigade head-quarters with his abused officer to have the regiment paraded. Corporal Howard had been sent to military prison for larceny.

"I remember," Owen said. He found himself laughing, glad to remember. "It made us a lot of trouble. But I don't know what you wanted to shoot me for. It was all I could do to keep you from going with Howard."

Sergeant Mintern cackled cheerfully. "Captain, I wouldn't know myself, now. It just seemed pretty hard. Just a little joke like that, with nobody hurt and Howard offering to pay the officer the money he got for the sidearms. Well, they gave me back my stripes at Petersburg, where I lost my fingers. Of course, I know now I really owed you a lot. If it hadn't been for what you called my distinguished services at Gettysburg—Lord, do you remember getting the boys back through town that first day?"

Owen remembered. It was one of those things you don't forget. "You were a good man in an engagement," he said. "By Mine Run, we were beginning to get the scum and I hated to lose a good man." He was silent a moment, recalling the consternation, really the despair, which a line officer had to feel when he saw the consignments of human rubbish sent down by the fantastic state bounties and the draft to replace the volunteers, the veterans of the Peninsula.

Mintern said at once, "You were another good man, Captain. Everybody knew that. Even when I was thinking of gunning for you, I never thought different." He shook his head sadly. "Well, there was a lot of good men in the original First Corps. I've never seen or heard of better men than crossed the river down here in 'sixty-two." He made a melancholy sucking sound. "The ones we left here were like teeth pulled. No more coming. I thought when I read how old Burny died a year or so ago, he'd been here like a young fellow running through a fortune. And not his fortune, at that. Ever after, we kept losing tricks because those that would have taken them were stopped for good at Fredericksburg—" He cocked his eye upward and got to his feet. "Why, hello, Colonel Bostwick. How are you?"

Alfred Bostwick said, "I'm well enough, Mintern. Don't you let yourself get too high, this trip. Captain Fulton will have you on the chines. Come along, Owen, I want you to meet General Doubleday."

"See you again, Captain," Sergeant Mintern said.

Proceeding down the aisle with a hand under Owen's elbow, Alfred Bostwick grunted: "He'll see you again all right when he runs out of cash and has to touch someone for a drink. Regular pest. Never been to an army meeting of any kind yet where he didn't turn up in that uniform. He's got a pension for his hand, so he can get around. Makes a business of it. I'm told he was even seen out west somewhere at a Fifteenth Corps reunion, passing himself off as an old Army of the Tennessee man. He did so well, they say he managed to borrow five dollars from General Sherman. You have to admire his confounded impudence."

"He was the best sergeant Company D ever had," Owen answered uncomfortably, raising his voice above the noise of the train. "I suppose he hasn't known what to do with himself since the war—"

"Humph!" said Alfred. "You'd better look and see if you've still got your watch and wallet. Those are the sort of things he does know what to do with."

From the high bridge across the Rappahannock, Owen could see the shimmer of sun, gold on the water, a finer gold in the hazy air around the same church steeples. There was, naturally, a new Hanover Street bridge; but in the brief glimpse it seemed to him he could see the long repaired scars of shellfire on the riverside buildings.

Pouched eyes screwing up, still-curly, coarse gray mustache drawing down in an amiable grimace, General Doubleday said, "Here it is, Slocum. Little less trouble getting over this time."

Major General Slocum agreed. "Why, I understand from Alfred here that a hundred ladies have kindly consented to greet us at the banquet. It seems to me it was Barksdale's Mississippi boys in the cellars on the bank there who did the greeting when Burnside came to town." Their laughter, the hoarse perfunctory laughter of old men, reached Owen. He had been introduced to both of them. They were both, they said, very pleased to meet any friend of Alfred's; but they soon saw that Owen was of little interest and no importance, and took up their previous conversation. Owen did not blame them and certainly expected no attention from them. It meant much more to him to meet someone like Mintern.

The train had run past the station, for they were to go down to Hamilton's without stopping. Looking sharp through the window to his right, Owen marked the gradual fall away of ground, the abrupt tree-covered rise of hill. At the top, three parts hidden, he could see the wink of white columns of the portico of a house—Marye's, of course! Here, then, was the scene of Summer's and Hooker's repulse on the right. Owen's eyes, going lower, stopped suddenly on a distant, hardly noticeable section of over-grown stone wall. Up his back went a kind of quiver as the train, with a pro-longed sad whistle, began to veer away. Bushes, trees, houses intervened, left him the sharp brief picture of the neglected back lots, the gardens and outhouses, the obscure low line of stones in the sunlight. He heard Sergeant Mintern saying, *like a young fellow running through a fortune*.

On December 13, 1862, at one o'clock the Second Corps moved out from the streets of Fredericksburg across the old canal—brigade front, intervals of two hundred paces! Owen supposed that, had it been the First Corps on this wing, instead of the Second, he would somehow have man-aged to make himself do it. With the aid of good men like Mintern, the company could doubtless have been made to do it with him. Hancock's division lost more than two thousand, a hundred and fifty-six of them offi-cers. French, succeeding him, lost twelve hundred; Howard, almost nine hundred. After an hour and a half, the Second Corps, ruined, gave way to divisions of the Fifth Corps—it hurt Owen even to think of it; but, shaken, he was very proud, too. It might be horrible, it might even be stupid; but it was an honor to belong to the same race, the same army as those men—

He realized that the train had stopped. Alfred was standing up with his customary agreeable assurance and he called out, "Gentlemen! If I may have your attention a moment!"

Conversation fell away, and Alfred continued, "We are now at Hamil-ton's, on the old First Corps battlefield. It is half past eleven o'clock. Re-member that General Longstreet is to make an address which I am sure you all want to hear, in front of the Marye mansion at two o'clock. Those who care to, may easily walk back, following the lines. The distance is about four miles. Those who do not care to may take the train back. Assembly will be blown when it is to leave. At half past three o'clock, the mayor and city council, assisted by many ladies of Fredericksburg, will receive us at the new opera house. The banquet begins promptly at four. Members of the Society, and our distinguished guests, will spare the committee sorrow and confusion if they will please be punctual—"

The woods, the field, the road down from the Crossing toward the hid-den river were full of men straggling here and there, moving in groups in the clear hot sunshine. Forced to limp by this uneven ground, Owen paused to rest his leg, breathe, and wipe his hot face. Looking back, he could see the massed bunting of the long train, the crowd by the big refreshment tent at the road. Once or twice he had thought that his surroundings looked vague-ly familiar, but he saw now that he was not yet nearly far enough from the railroad. Men were too plainly visible on the higher ground behind the tracks, moving through the trees along what had been Jackson's line.

Coming at last upon a large log, Owen sat down and fanned himself with his hat. Many men were making the effort—he could hear their loud argumentative voices across the fields—but he knew that no regiment's position would ever really be found. The growth of twenty summers changed all small features of bush and tree and field. There were new fences, probably new roads.

Owen sat still, discouraged, gazing at the low rain-worn rise of bare earth to his right. He might have been in any open, sparsely brush-covered field, anywhere. Then, curious, he got up, walked a few steps and managed to stoop awkwardly. From the red gravel he picked up a thin oval of metal. Brushing it off, he made out the big faint lettering U.S.—a belt buckle. The heat of the sun impressed itself on him now. Owen replaced his hat and, pocketing his little trophy, limped slowly back toward the train.

Sergeant Mintern said, "I was looking for you, Captain. It don't take long to see all there is left, does it?" He had, however, seen a bottle or two in the refreshment tent. That was apparent.

Owen, sitting alone in the shadows of the hot, empty car, realized that he must have been drowsing. A bad night in the Washington hotel, the early start, the heat and exertion of his vain little journey over the fields had exhausted him. It was just as Hattie said; he ought to conserve his energy. He wasn't fitted for Alfred's easy bustle and cheerful activity—Alfred, he supposed, would be in the refreshment tent having a drink with people of importance. Out of the pleasant meeting would come more meetings, more honors and benefits for Alfred in an ever-expanding future. Owen must see that his own life was the antithesis of that. He survived, like a sort of stump, blighted at Spottsylvania. He had only the past. Like Mintern, all he had to his credit was in the past.

Probably able to feel in the short silence Owen's sympathy for him, Mintern said, "Come and take a drink, Captain. What they have at the tent isn't bad."

Owen thanked him and said that he was sorry. "I never drink spirits during the day. It upsets my stomach. I had to give it up." That was quite true. Except for a glass with Alfred on evenings when Alfred dropped in, Owen had practically ceased to drink. As Hattie pointed out, he felt better for it.

That was too bad, Mintern told him. "But come and have a good cold glass of lemonade," he urged. "They have it."

"Thanks, I'm not thirsty," Owen said. Long unaccustomed to such throngs of talking, expansively cheerful men, he knew that he would only be ill at ease—a conscious specter at their feast; the very man they talked and laughed and drank to keep from being.

Owen saw now that he had unconsciously forestalled Mintern in Mintern's ordinary method of approach. Checked, Mintern was not routed,

however. He was not even abashed by the exposure of a real intention behind the roundabout tactic. "Captain," he said, "I wonder if you'd care to
do me a favor? Could you lend me a V note until we get back to Washington? I went into a little game with some of the boys, and—"

"Certainly, Sergeant." Owen unbuttoned his back pocket and took out
his wallet. At least, he reflected, he was in General Sherman's distinguished
company.

Mintern took the bill, beaming, the little Punch's face rosier still. "I
surely appreciate that, Captain," he said. Heat of triumph seemed to rouse
the fumes of alcohol, for he became instantly much drunker. "I always said
you're a good man, Captain. I always said Company D was the best company and had the best Captain—"

With Mintern so far past shame, Owen had to be ashamed for him. He
was also ashamed for himself, and angry. Alfred, if for any contemptuously
tolerant reason Alfred decided to give Mintern the money, would have done
it in such a way that Mintern could not consider him a simpleton. Catching
Owen still wordless in vexation the sudden clear notes of a bugle sounding
assembly somewhere ahead stiffened him in automatic response. Mintern,
taken unawares, started, too. Caught thus in so eloquent a demonstration
of their common past, Owen said, "Get along, Mintern! You have what
you came for."

"Lord, Captain," Sergeant Mintern said with amiable reproach, "you
wouldn't be sore at me, would you?"

Owen delayed, as usual, to let those who moved more quickly go first.
The train had dropped them at the curve of the railroad, and it was necessary to pass along the narrow dirt road behind the fatal stone wall before
turning up the slope to the Marye house. Dust still hung in the air from the
passage of the crowd before him. Countless footprints flattened the whole
soft surface. It was like trying to overtake his regiment in a marching
brigade column—Owen could almost expect to hear around the bend of the
road the monotonous harsh calls through a thicker dust haze: "Close up,
men; close up!"

Reaching finally the top of the low rise, and turning in under the trees
toward the house, Owen found the crowd so extensive that he stopped.
There was a good chance that Alfred would be holding a seat for him in the
few rows of folding chairs arranged directly before the portico, but he felt
too tired and out of breath to attempt to push his way through. Peering between the nearer heads and over the ranks of farther ones, he supported himself against a tree trunk, trying to catch what the speaker under the big
white pillars was saying.

It was not possible to hear well. The men around him had discovered
that and ceased to pay attention, conversing among themselves. Owen
caught several ringing, but remote and incomplete, references to a united

nation, the healing of old wounds. He did not know the speaker—probably some politician introducing General Longstreet, but unable to let pass an opportunity for extensive remarks of his own. Prolonged applause broke out, partly because the sentiments expressed were proper and popular, partly because what must be Longstreet showed himself. He stood erect, his full, neat beard moving on his linen and cravat, as he inclined his broad, finely formed forehead repeatedly in acknowledgment of his reception.

Owen had wished to see Longstreet, and now he could see him well enough—a handsome, elderly gentleman with humorous eloquent eyes and a straight nose. It was not possible to be disappointed in him, for he had a face and manner which would be liked everywhere on sight. One look told you why Longstreet, of all the former Confederate generals, had been most successful in obtaining posts and honors in the government against which he had rebelled. Not disappointed, Owen could still feel let down, dissatisfied, for he had expected—he did not know what; maybe, something grimmer; something more like a soldier. A more formidable face; a presence which would command respect rather than invite cordiality.

What he had come for was eluding Owen once more. The others, even those who could hear no better than he could, seemed to be getting what they came for. They were obviously content, glad they had come. They were satisfied with the present, with their holiday. Owen reflected that it would be necessary to walk into Fredericksburg when this was over, and it occurred to him that he might as well start now. If he got there much before the others, he could go along Princess Anne Street and try to find the house and garden where he had spent that month wounded.

It was not really a great distance, but Owen's leg was throbbing before he reached the outskirts of the town. He dragged slowly down Princess Anne Street, not, for a moment, sure about the big house. Undoubtedly the brick had been red when he was there. Now it was a pale yellow, or cream. A long veranda in modern style had been added to the side, relieving somewhat the plainness common to houses built long ago, as likely as not before the Revolution. Moving along the shoulder-high brick wall, alternately in the midafternoon sun and the shadows cast by the trees across the street, Owen saw the old slave quarters. Those, too, were changed. The lower part had been given double doors and made into a carriage house. The little back gate at which the sentries had solemnly presented arms for Mama and the girls was gone. Instead there was the necessary wide opening for the drive, with an iron lamppost on each side.

Resting his elbows on the wall top, Owen looked at the old Negro in frock coat and worn silk hat who was absorbed in adjusting some buckle, ducking about an indifferent pair of bay geldings hitched to a sort of surrey with an oblong fringed canopy. Right behind there would be the spot where he had lain in the tent. The Negro finished whatever he was doing, straightened up, and turned. Owen Fulton found himself saying, "Would you be able to tell me if Mrs. Ferris lives here?"

The Negro gazed at him a moment and said, "There ain't no Mr. Ferris, sir. Unless you mean Colonel Ferris. The colonel visits here sometimes, but this is Mrs. Baylor's house. Mrs. Baylor and Miss Lou live here. Colonel Ferris ain't here now."

"I see," Owen answered, embarrassed by the difficulties of proceeding further. Obviously Olivia had married her major and sometimes came to visit. "I was inquiring about Mrs. Ferris, the colonel's wife."

The Negro looked at him with a reticent, not disrespectful suspicion. "The colonel never had no wife, sir. He's an unmarried gentleman."

Finally Owen said, "I was here, wounded, during the war. I remember that then Miss Olivia Baylor was to marry a Major Ferris."

"She surely was, sir," said the Negro, astonished. "You wouldn't know, then, Miss Olivia died the year the war was over?"

"No, I didn't know," Owen said.

After a moment he realized that the Negro was speaking to him. He said, "Excuse me, I didn't hear you."

"I say, would you like I should take your name in to Miss Lou, sir?"

Owen shook his head. "She wouldn't know me. I was a Yankee."

The old Negro smiled. "Oh, I know you was a Yankee, all right, sir. Mrs. Baylor wouldn't have dealings with you; but Miss Lou don't feel that way. I have this team out here now to take her to the big entertainment. She'd be happy to see any friend of Miss Olivia's."

"Thank you," Owen said, "I wasn't a friend of Miss Olivia's." He turned quickly, limping away, leaving the Negro staring after him.

Owen passed slowly back up the street. A distant band must have begun playing some time ago. Becoming aware of it, Owen was also aware of torpor and silence in the dusty, sunny street. Leaves moved in the wind. An odor of wisteria reached him. Out a gate ahead stepped three ladies with parasols and, not wishing to overtake them, Owen limped still slower.

Soon the ladies were gone around a corner and Owen could hear the band again, gay and brave, but remote, as though it played back across the years. Sadly, sentimentally, he could think of it attempting to muster in, not this handful of First Corps veterans, but all the innumerable dead of the Army of the Potomac who lay not far beyond earshot, west and north and south, from Wilderness Run to Spottsylvania, to the Massaponax, scattered who knew where in one great uncared-for, unmarked, unordered cemetery.

Thinking of that, Owen thought suddenly that he could probably find Olivia's grave if he liked, and read her name on the stone. Yet he knew he would not bother. The fine melancholy afternoon light made everything seem long over, of little importance. Several carriages had passed him, and wondering how late it was, Owen began feeling for his watch. Finally he stood still, felt in other pockets.

How Mintern, tipsy as he was, had managed it, you couldn't guess, but Mintern had, all right—doubtless while Owen was dozing. Alfred was, as always, right.

Two more carriages filled with the light colors of ladies' dresses went by. The watch was a gold hunter, an expensive one. It had, too, a sentimental value. Hattie, on the occasion of a legacy from an aunt of hers, had given it to him. In the back cover under a small oval of glass, it contained an ingeniously plaited lock of Hattie's hair. Mintern might have found a way to dispose of it here in Fredericksburg; but, on the other hand, drinking more, he might have neglected to.

Being always right, Alfred in these circumstances, wouldn't wait a minute. He would denounce Mintern, have him arrested and searched. If it were not on Mintern's person, Alfred would shrewdly follow up every possible avenue of disposal until the watch was recovered and Mintern's guilt established. In his own case, Owen had even more reason to take these steps. Hattie, displeased about the trip anyway, would find the loss of his fine watch the last straw. It would be just what she had expected and he would be a long time hearing the last of it. She would say that it seemed a high price to pay for a silly and expensive trip which had worn him out. If he had listened to her, or cared at all for her opinion, he would have stayed home and still had his watch.

Distressed and doubtful, Owen turned the corner. Before the opera house were many carriages, a crowd of people, and the band whose music he had heard. A big, red-faced, cheery man with a paper in his hand was calling out something. It proved to be: "Now, Baxter's brigade, gentlemen! Anyone from Baxter's brigade? Any members of the Twelfth Massachusetts Regiment? Table number five, please. Anyone from the Eighty-third and Ninety-seventh New York Regiments—"

Owen started to answer, to raise his hand; but the words did not come. He let his hand fall. In the foyer he caught a glimpse of Alfred with General Doubleday and General Longstreet. They were being introduced to some ladies. Jostled, he looked the other way in time to see the old Negro, the bay geldings, and the surrey which had been in the Baylors' yard come to the curb. Someone pushed through the press and very courteously assisted two flustered but smiling old women to alight. One of them must be Miss Lou, Owen realized, suddenly reminded of her and Sarah Ann, of Mama and Olivia, prim and frigid, going down the garden path. Both of these women were now older than Mama had been then. Who could doubt the war was all over; and, as the speaker on the hill had said, how glorious, how inspiring to see North and South one again!

Anxiously, the man on the steps was still calling, "Now, please, gentlemen! The Eighty-third New York Regiment! The Ninety-seventh New York Regiment! Isn't there anyone from—"

"No, no," thought Owen, "no one—" A movement in the crowd gave him a last sight of the simpering old faces of the two ladies. It was wrong, it was even wicked of him to think it, but in indignation, he had to think of three hundred and fifty thousand Union dead; of Longstreet reduced in the end to speeches and funny stories; of the First Corps persisting only as a crowd of fatuous jolly banqueters; in the place of the Army of Northern Virginia, one hundred ladies of Fredericksburg—

Owen turned away. The man on the steps had given up the Ninety-seventh New York. As he limped down the street, Owen could hear him, fainter and fainter, as though in parody of the Army of the Potomac's roll, calling the names of other regiments. At the station he learned that there would be a train, though not a fast one, for Washington in an hour.

Recovering his bag from the guard in charge of them, Owen carried it painfully back along the siding where the bright cars of the morning stood deserted. The platform of the station was empty. Owen sat down on a bench to wait and the wonderful comfort of being off his feet, able to rest, filled him slowly with a kind of content. The shadows lengthened. Musing, yawning, he reflected that things might be worse. By leaving this way, without waiting for the tour of the Spottsylvania and Chancellorsville battlefields, he would be home a day, perhaps two days, early. This would please Hattie so much that he felt sure she wouldn't make too great a fuss about the lost watch.

IV

The Good Dukes
By Noel Perrin

The dominant theme in James Gould Cozzens's novels is that of order imposed on a meaningless world—or, rather, that of order being maintained, and even occasionally extended. It is not the individual order of the philosopher who "makes sense" out of the world, nor of the artist who makes a private design out of it. It is the order of a whole society. The society has created that order through millions of small acts which, meaningless in themselves, acquire meaning through being repeated and remembered—that is to say, through custom and tradition.

But such order is always precarious, at least in the America of Cozzens's novels. It tends to dissipate even as it is created. Men forget their traditions; they break them through greed or lust; they are unable to adapt them to present circumstances, through stupidity. It is always a comparative handful of men whom Cozzens shows as holding society together and keeping it orderly: the few adults of his novels, as opposed to the many children.

The best and smartest of these grown-ups operate somewhat the way Shakespeare's dukes do in the late comedies. That is, they are the centers of their societies, and not merely in some social sense, but truly in the middle, so that most information passes through them, and most connections are made by them. Occasionally both the real dukes in Shakespeare and the ducal characters in Cozzens are central as the puppeteer is central to his puppets—not merely maintaining order on the stage, but directly causing the action. Such manipulation, no matter how intelligent or high-minded, tends to seem offensive in a democracy; and Cozzens's obvious approval of it has done almost as much as his antiromanticism to hurt his reputation. Shakespeare we can readily enough forgive because he's not writing about *us*; but if we accept Cozzens, we must look warily at our own heels to see what strings are attached and where they lead.

I do not mean to overstress the parallel between Cozzens's heroes and Shakespeare's dukes. It is far from complete. On the most obvious level, no Cozzens hero has magic to help him, as Prospero does. (Though through mere use of intelligence, many of them are able to produce what seem to lesser men like magical results—a fact they are well aware of, and utilize.) No one of them, not even General Nichols in *Guard of Honor*, has the kind of personal authority that makes manipulation so easy for Duke Vincentio in *Measure for Measure*. More important, Shakespeare presents his dukes and their worlds as charming fantasies, Cozzens his heroes and theirs as descriptions of reality. But I think the case remains that a man like Judge Ross or Arthur Winner is usefully compared to Duke Vincentio, is ducal himself, and is part of a pattern that runs through much of Cozzens's work.

Much. Not all. The ordering character does not appear in the early novels that Cozzens later disavowed, nor even in all of the nine novels he does acknowledge. *Castaway* is a psychological novel rather than a social one, *Ask Me Tomorrow* a *bildungsroman*, and *S.S. San Pedro* a faintly Gothic novella. All three ignore the ordering character, except insofar as the ship's captain in *S.S. San Pedro* should have been one because of his position.

But the remaining six of Cozzens's novels all have such characters, and the two greatest are wholly dominated by them. One can trace the growth of the ducal type in Cozzens's earlier work, the hard-won but triumphant mastery of a town or an army base in the great novels, and the final defeat in *Morning Noon and Night*. (Not at the hands of society, which the ducal character can still in large part manipulate, but partly through the aging of his own body, and partly through the late-adult awareness that his world is not quite worth ruling.)

The type first appears in *The Last Adam*, not as a duke but a duchess. Mrs. Banning is the upholder of stability and order in New Winton, Connecticut, as her son Guy will be after her. (Though probably not in New Winton. Probably in Hartford or New York.) What is surprising when one looks at the whole sweep of ordering characters in Cozzens is that both Mrs. Banning and Guy are viewed satirically. Or, at least, more satirically than not. Cozzens is far too complex and realistic a writer to deny them their genuine power and worth. But Mrs. Banning in particular tends to appear as an absurd if occasionally heroic meddler. The New England tradition she upholds is presented as both outworn and rather petty. Her son, Guy, though a natural leader, is mainly out for Guy. Neither has much insight.

Mrs. Banning *does* have one characteristic that foreshadows the later ducal characters. She is able to hold a good many thoughts in her mind at once, without getting muddled and without losing the power to act. "She could, almost simultaneously, be anxious about Virginia; regret Guy's violence when annoyed; remember to speak to Mary about the mint sauce. From the afternoon's meeting of the School Committee, she kept her resolve to do something—perhaps appeal to Hartford—about Doctor Bull's utter neglect of his duties."[1] This is a trivialized and faintly comic version of what Colonel Ross does throughout *Guard of Honor*—but even in Mrs. Ban-

1. *The Last Adam* (New York: Harcourt, Brace, 1933), p. 67.

ning it does not lack impressiveness. Most people in New Winton can barely handle one thought at a time.

Cozzens reserves his sympathy in *The Last Adam* for three quite different sorts of characters. The first, exemplified in Mr. Banning, is the person who has simply opted out, who attempts to order nothing more intractable than a flower garden. The reader is invited to feel a certain scorn for Mr. Banning's weakness (he is not a true man—read duke—as his father had been) but a good deal more sympathy for his insight, even when it cripples his power to act. He is the powerless perceiver, like Francis Ellery in *Ask Me Tomorrow*. Hereafter he appears seldom in Cozzens.

The second type is represented by three important characters in the book: Mrs. Banning's daughter Virginia; Dr. Bull, the last Adam of the title; and Miss Janet Cardmaker, Dr. Bull's mistress. (His cow, one is tempted to say. Unfortunately, that word now connotes something soft and large-breasted merely, not the horned, earthy power that it should.) All three are members of New Winton's small upper class, and all three feel contempt for the orderly and ordering life of that class, as seen in Mrs. Banning and in such minor characters as Matthew Herring. All three are, in fact, centers of disorder. Virginia might be a young Sartoris out of Faulkner, roaring about the countryside in her brother's enormous sports car, a menace to all other traffic. (She takes the car without his consent, and gets away with it.)

Virginia is sixteen and foolish, but George Bull and Janet Cardmaker are sixty-seven and forty-six. Neither is in a phase to be grown out of; their disorder is their final state. Cozzens asks you to admire them for it. Why? Principally because New Winton's tradition is an exhausted puritanism turned to sexual prurience, and New Winton's people are an enfeebled stock not worth maintaining. "They make me sick. The whole lot of them," Janet Cardmaker says at a time when Dr. Bull is being accused by rumor of having let a patient die through negligence. "Kill all you want, George" (p. 174).

It can also be suggested, though not proved, that Cozzens's own age was a factor. He was thirty when *The Last Adam* appeared and apparently by no means in his own final state. At any rate, it is certain that the book is (for Cozzens) rather romantic and that Dr. Bull and Janet are both a little larger than life. If Virginia Banning is Cozzens's Sartoris, Dr. Bull is his Gatsby. Symbolically, it is apt enough that Virginia dies at sixteen, and that Dr. Bull and Janet leave no descendants—are each the last of their families.

Finally, there is a third type, the most interesting of all from the point of view of this study. Its main representatives are May Tupping, a twenty-two-year-old phone operator in New Winton, and Henry Harris, the local boy who made good. (He is no boy now; he is a contemporary of Mr. Banning's.) These two are embryonic ducal types, though very different ones.

Henry Harris is by far the most richly drawn minor character in the book. A kind of *eminence grise* in New Winton, he seems to get his greatest pleasure from secret manipulation of the town. For example, he owns the local newspaper (published a few miles away in Sansbury); and he keeps his ownership so quiet that even the New Winton correspondent has no idea that he is her boss. She is thus as baffled as everyone else in town when, after a particularly noisy and even savage town meeting, no word appears in the Sansbury *Times*.

Henry Harris is presumably based in part on Cozzens's observation of what self-made New Englanders are really like—at least when they live in and wield their power in small towns. Such men and women often do affect a life-long guise of being ordinary. That is, they conceal both their wealth and their power as much as they can. In a small town, that can be simple self-defense.

But there is another aspect of Harris which I think comes entirely from Cozzens's interest in modes of rule. Harris is amoral. He is not a bad man, but he almost entirely lacks human sympathy. He enjoys playing with his fellow townsmen, cat-and-mouse style. He is a duke or a semiduke tinged with cruelty. (His cruelty, of course, fits with Janet Cardmaker's indifference and Dr. Bull's hearty contempt; all three reflect the book's view of the relation between superior men and the rest of humanity.)

Harris was an experiment. His type vanishes, along with the Bulls and the Bannings. The full Cozzens dukes, when they appear, will be almost his opposites, except in ability.

May Tupping, on the other hand, is a very faint sketch of the good dukes who will dominate the later books. Intelligent and responsible, May is literally the center of communication in New Winton; she plugs the town in to itself. She also, with Cozzens's approval, listens in on a good many calls and knows almost everything that goes on in town. She is able to influence some events, and when she can, she does, invariably to the benefit of New Winton.

May had once hoped to learn everything that goes on or ever went on in the world, as he who proposes to help order the world should, ideally. Put less dramatically, she once hoped to go on a scholarship to Mt. Holyoke. During her year of hope, she had raptly studied the catalogue, noting the three courses in Provençal literature, the fourteen in physics, and so on. "Seeing really nothing that she did not long to know all about, she would have done anything to go there" (p. 201). Not able to, she has turned to an immense set of books "said to contain everything ever written with which an educated person should be familiar" (p. 6). At the time the novel begins, she is midway in volume 16. The persistence and the will to know are equally ducal.

May is, at twenty-two, too naive and too powerless to be more than a sketch of what a full Cozzens ordering character will become. She perhaps also starts from too low a social position. But she is clearly already an adult in Cozzens's terms. She sees the world without illusion, or without much, and she nevertheless accepts it. It and her duty to help keep it functioning. It is within her mind that Cozzens first formulates ducal awareness and duty. The context is her pondering why things are as they are in New Winton. She concludes that there is no reason at all. "This immense mindlessness [the universe] knew no reasons, had no schemes; there was no cause for it. . . . There was even an error in personifying the universe as It, saying: How could It either plan or prevent Mrs. Talbot's misfortunes? How could It care? 'Only, I care,' May thought" (p. 202).

In *Men and Brethren*, published three years later, the characteristics that May and Mrs. Banning possess only embryonically or comically appear at close to full force. Ernest Cudlipp is the first of Cozzens's major ordering characters. The vicar of an Episcopal mission church in New York City, Ernest is a highly educated man in his middle forties and the undisputed ruler of his little world. That world includes his two assistant ministers, half a dozen other employees of the parish, and a variety of parishioners and friends, most of them in trouble. It is Ernest's job, of course, to get them out of trouble. In most cases he does.

Cozzens first uses in *Men and Brethren* what is going to be his favorite and most successful narrative structure. Using his central character as a batter, he throws pitch after pitch, sending them at steadily shorter intervals, until there seem to be a dozen in the air at once. Or to put it more abstractly, he presents the mounting tension, over a brief period, of more and more almost insoluble problems coming at the central character (and the reader) faster and faster until it seems impossible for him to deal with them all. If he does not, they are not going to be dealt with, and a series of disasters will result. Several do result. Then, almost at the end, summoning his full ability to deal with many things simultaneously, the central character gets control of the whole situation; and the society around him returns, if not to a state of grace, at least to order.

The problems that come at Ernest are much less interrelated than those that will later come at Colonel Ross and Arthur Winner, but they are as numerous. The book covers a period of just under twenty-four hours, from early Friday evening to late Saturday afternoon of a summer weekend, about the year 1935. During that period Ernest prevents a suicide, delays (and possibly prevents) a divorce between two of his oldest friends, arranges for an abortion, compels a Catholic colleague to administer extreme unction, succors and returns to his monastery an apostate and homosexual Episcopal monk.[2]

2. Most of these disaster victims, and a good many other people, physically arrive at the vicarage during the course of Friday evening and have to be stowed in different rooms and made to entertain each other. The cumulative effect has something in common

In the same brief period Ernest also twice nearly resigns his post; reads proof on the hundredth anniversary report of the parish of which his mission church is a part; deals with two serious employee problems; takes an old friend to dinner at what he considers the one really good restaurant in Manhattan; and still has time for quite a lot of theological discussion, a little of it in Greek.

Such a pace would be intolerable to most people, and even Ernest finds it exhausting. "I don't know why everything happens at once," he says late Friday evening to Wilber Quinn, the more competent of his two assistants. "Lord, what an evening!"

But actually, if you are the center of a society, such evenings are to be expected. "It looks about as usual to me," Wilber answers.[3] Furthermore, Ernest in fact thrives on such fare—a duke is most himself when ruling—and when he is compelling Father Maloney, the reluctant Catholic priest, to come and give extreme unction to Mrs. Hawley, and for a moment losing his temper, it acts as a tonic. He thinks briefly he ought to be ashamed for getting angry. "But he felt very well. He felt that alert exhilaration always provoked in him by difficulty or opposition" (p. 201). Two minutes later he is squelching Mr. Hawley as one would an unruly child.

In accomplishing all this, Ernest gets remarkably little help from the people around him. One of his two assistant ministers is an elderly fool; the young one, Wilber Quinn, is bright and eager, but in judgment still a child and likely to remain so. It is his naïveté that leads to the death of one of the people Ernest is trying to save. From there one descends rapidly to the mere infantilism of Lulu Merrick, or Lee Breen, or Bill Jennings, or Carl Willever, the apostate monk. But Ernest is not the only adult in the book, and not even the only ducal character. There is also Dr. Lamb.

Dr. Lamb (who does not fit his name the way Dr. Bull does his) is interesting in two ways. He is the rector of the immensely wealthy parish to which Ernest's mission belongs, a smart man, and Ernest's boss. In that hierarchical sense he *is* the duke, the Old Duke, and Ernest merely a kind of heir apparent or subruler. It fits with the place of *Men and Brethren* in the progression I am tracing that Ernest should be shown not quite in full power yet, but still operating under the tutelage of a man a generation older.

Furthermore, though Dr. Lamb is quite a minor character in the book, and not a fully sympathetic one, he quickly shows himself to be the Old Duke not just in position but in genuine ordering ability. Like Mrs. Banning, like Ernest himself, he can deal with several matters simultaneously, as he proves during his Friday night call at the vicarage. More important,

with Restoration comedy. I take that to be intended. Cozzens can develop the humor of a situation in a minor key, without in the least disturbing his overriding serious intention. Not many novelists have that gift.

3. *Men and Brethren* (New York: Harcourt, Brace, 1936), p. 139.

at least once in the book he shows himself to be well ahead of Ernest in thinking out the consequences of a well-meant action—in fact, he saves Ernest from an impulsive mistake, just as Ernest so often has to save other people. He thus faintly foreshadows the background adults in *Guard of Honor* and *By Love Possessed*. Just when a character in a Cozzens novel begins to think that he alone can hold the world together, he is likely to discover that not only is he not alone in this ability, but that from time to time there is someone holding *him* together. Dr. Lamb does not clearly play this role in *Men and Brethren*, but he suggests it.

Finally, as there is an adult in the generation behind Ernest, there is also, if not an adult, at least a potential one in the generation ahead. Ernest's greatest success is the saving of a young woman named Geraldine Binney. She has left her rich Cincinnati husband and has been having an affair in New York. The book begins with her phoning him in despair, and it ends with them talking in her hospital room just after she has had an abortion. In the interim, with an intuitive flash of intelligence that seems to other people like magic, Ernest has gone to her just in time to prevent her committing suicide, arranged the abortion, and persuaded her to go back to Cincinnati and her life.

From the start, Ernest has realized that she is a good, an intelligent, and a responsible person—a bearer of tradition and order, in short. She will probably never be a duchess, but she will be at least a lady in waiting. She just needs to stop yearning after "fulfillment" and reenter her society. At the end she is prepared to. In the last two pages of the book, Ernest explains to her why he is a minister. "A great obligation has been laid on me to do or be whatever good thing I have learned I ought to be, or know I can do." And after a minute he adds, "One like it is laid on you. You know your obligation, Geraldine" (p. 281).

Never again will Cozzens put it this overtly. And certainly not with a divine sanction behind it. Even here, very little sense of God or of an ultimate purpose in things is present. If Ernest lost his faith, he might leave the ministry, but his sense of the duty laid on intelligent and responsible men in this world would remain identical. Ernest is a stoic who happens also to be a Christian minister. Presumably what led Cozzens to invent him was an interest in the traditions and social dynamics of the Episcopal church and an even greater interest in the natural ordering roles played by ministers, not any new awareness of a transcendental It.

The Just and the Unjust, though published six years later than *Men and Brethren*, is a step backward in the presentation of the ducal character. (The book itself is no step backward.) Ernest Cudlipp long ago accepted his obligation; what we watch is how he fulfills it. But Abner Coates in *The Just and the Unjust*, though he comes of a ducal family, decides only at the very end of the book to accept his. What we watch is the process by which a nice young man finds himself forced to give up his scruples and his privacy and become an adult.

Between these two ducal novels, Cozzens wrote *Ask Me Tomorrow*. This may explain some of the step backward. At first *The Just and the Unjust* seems to be a successor to *Ask Me Tomorrow*, at least regarding the sensibility of its protagonist. Francis Ellery, the central character of the earlier book, is much too preoccupied with himself to order anyone else's life; he can't even order his own. Francis is prickly, easily offended, the sensitive young man in a world of vulgar events. Abner Coates, though he holds public office as the assistant district attorney in an unnamed county of what is presumably Pennsylvania, is very much like him. Abner is more concerned with his own feelings than with any external reality. In fact, he finds reality, in the shape of other people, mostly a strain. Over a short period in one afternoon, for example, he suffers three times in a row. He finds it "taxing" to be polite (to "simulate cordiality," as he sees it) to the Republican county chairman, who is about to invite him to run for district attorney.[4] He goes home to change his clothes before picking up his fiancée for the evening, and he sneaks into the house because he doesn't feel equal to saying hello to his father, at the moment housebound after a stroke. Arriving at his fiancée's house, he tries to avoid going inside so that he won't have to talk to her mother (a cousin, whom he has known all his life). One can hardly order a society one is trying to duck.

There is a perceptible moment in the book, however, when Abner opens himself to outside reality. It comes during a later conversation with Jesse Gearhart, the county chairman. For the first time in his life Ab sees Jesse as he is, and even a little as he must seem to himself, not just as he has happened to impinge on Ab's prickly sensibility.

This awareness (which, having stumbled on it, he soon finds himself able to extend to other people) gives Ab a kind of strength he has never had before. He is able to forgive Jesse for being a politician and even, in a limited way, is able to work with him. He is able to govern himself—the necessary precondition (in Cozzens) for governing others. For example, when he is being deliberately baited by his old friend, Harry Wurts, on the most sensitive possible subject, he feels a strong impulse to punch Harry in the mouth. But he now is able to look at Harry as well as at his own feelings, and he realizes with a shock that Harry is half-consciously trying to make him throw a punch. Despite his anger, this awareness gives him the self-control to answer calmly and even to one-up Harry in the matter of using quotations. Cozzens adds, "Since they were looking each other in the eye, Harry probably realized that Abner had grasped his intention. He looked sheepish" (p. 306). No wonder. He has just made a fool of himself in front of the new duke.

4. *The Just and the Unjust* (New York: Harcourt, Brace, 1942), p. 193.

Because it is so near the end of the book that Ab finally decides to run for district attorney—and, of course, beyond the end of the book that he actually takes office—we see him in only one ducal action. That one is major, however. Ab will have the right to appoint his assistant, as his predecessor appointed him. A few pages before the book ends, he offers the job to an able young lawyer named George Stacey, who for a variety of reasons is having a hard time in private practice. Having done so, he gains one more insight.

> He was unexpectedly made aware of the pleasure of patronage. It was, he saw, a fairly pure pleasure. If it made him feel good to be able to give what was plainly so much wanted, the good feeling was at least in part the good feeling of being able to adjust the fallings-out of a too impersonal and regardless chance so that the deserving got some of their deserts. It would be a pleasure that Jesse Gearhart had felt often; the one real pleasure, when all was said and done, of power. (p. 423)

Duke Vincentio, in *Measure for Measure*, might not agree that it is the one real pleasure a ruler has; but it is certainly the one that play concerns itself with. At the end he gives the deserving their deserts—including, near the end of a long list, the case analogous to George Stacey, the Provost singled out for promotion and a greater role in the government of Vienna. What May Tupping would like to do, Vincentio and Abner can do.

To discuss *The Just and the Unjust* solely in terms of Abner Coates's growth is, of course, to give a very meager account of the book. There are other ordering characters besides Abner. And there are other ideas besides that of the power to reward. The ducal theories of Judge Irwin and of Judge Philander Coates, Abner's father, are both worth attention. But since *The Just and the Unjust*, despite its own independent virtues, is a kind of trial run for or miniature version of *By Love Possessed* (one can show Childerstown, almost point by point, to be a scaled-down Brocton), other things can wait.

One way to describe *Guard of Honor* is as the search for a duke. In the context of a novel nearly all of whose characters belong to the U. S. Army Air Force, "duke" means someone worthy to command an Air Force base or a substantial military unit.

For most of the book, there seem to be no such people—at least not among those with sufficient rank to be given command. It is naturally the regulars who have most of the rank: Colonel Woodman, the paranoid fool who commands Sellers Field; Major General Beal, the nice, boyish flier who commands Ocanara Air Force Base; Colonel Mowbray, his child-like executive officer; Colonel Coulthard, his not-too-smart Chief of Special Projects, and so on.

In contrast to these high-ranking children (several of them in their fifties and gray-haired) are the low-ranking civilian adults who have joined the Air Force for the duration and who must now obey the children. The extreme case is Staff Sergeant McCabe, an artist of major stature. But there are many: Captain Hicks, the recently powerful magazine editor now reduced to working on foolish training manuals because foolish colonels and generals tell him to, Captain Duchemin, Captain Collins, Lieutenant Wertheimer . . . the list is a long one.

Linking the two groups is, of course, Colonel Norman Ross, the central character of the novel. Judge Ross is a civilian adult of high rank, the only one in the book. Though a civilian, he understands the military mind, having served in the Air Force during World War One and then for a good many years in the Reserve. He himself would be the one logical duke—except that he is not a regular; he has never been a flier; and his job as Air Inspector in theory completely separates him from command functions.

The search for a duke is not carried on by any of the characters in the book, but by the reader. The stupider characters are unaware that there needs to be any search, because for them rank and worthiness to command are identical (or almost identical—some of them make a separation in the case of Colonel Woodman). Since General Beal is two ranks higher than anyone else at Ocanara, he is automatically their duke. The smarter characters have already decided before the book begins that the search is useless. No one of ducal caliber is available. Not only not at Ocanara, but perhaps not in the Air Force itself.

Judge Ross is one of those who have come to that conclusion; and being the ranking adult at Ocanara, his response is silently to take charge so that the base won't fall apart. This would not have been possible if he were not a colonel. It is not easy, even so. He is not only not in the chain of command at Ocanara, he isn't even in the Air Force. He is an Army Service Forces colonel permanently assigned to Air Force duty. He must always work in General Beal's name, and he does. For the first three-quarters of the novel, this outsider in effect commands the 20,000 troops at Ocanara. The implication is clear. The Air Force cannot run itself. It requires a benevolent but usurping duke from outside. A civilian.

During this first three-quarters of the book, the reader watches two things. One is the failure of regular after regular to deal with the problems of leadership (when they are more complex than drilling a company or leading a wing of bombers). These regulars not only fail to maintain order, but through sheer stupidity, they create disorder. The other is Judge Ross's dazzling ability to clean up the messes the regulars create. The reader is confirmed in his civilian sense of superiority. He almost forgets, in his enjoyment of Ross's extraordinary skill, the Air Force's need to have a true duke.

Judge Ross is the culmination of the development that began back with May Tupping. He is a full ordering character at the height of his powers—

caught just at the moment before the weariness of old age begins to topple him. Like May, he perceives a universe without meaning. But she, at twenty-two, can only wish it were otherwise. Judge Ross, at fifty-nine, can make it otherwise. At least while his strength lasts. In a famous passage he reflects, "If mind failed you, seeing no pattern; and heart failed you, seeing no point, the stout, stubborn will must be up and doing. A pattern should be found; a point should be imposed."[5] The pattern, of course, is justice; and the point, despite the book's title, is not so much to guard honor as it is to maintain and, if necessary, to invent human dignity. To put it another way, the point is to make human life worth taking seriously.

Like Abner Coates, but far more dramatically, Judge Ross has the power to give the deserving their deserts. The most striking case in the book is his instant promotion of Captain Collins. Collins, six months in grade as a captain, is the public relations officer at Ocanara. His job is largely a futile one, and he perceives it so, but he nevertheless does it well. Colonel Ross, the second time he encounters Collins, realizes that here is a fellow adult and invites him on the spot to help run Ocanara. Three hours later the orders are cut that transfer him to Ross's office. Ten minutes after that he is coping with an angry regular colonel, keeping him from making a little fresh disorder. Next week he will be a major, despite his lack of time in grade. The reader is impressed by this incisive display of power, and so is Collins. "Looking from below, Captain Collins saw him [Ross] in his kingly state" (p. 368).

Unlike Abner Coates, Judge Ross has done this sort of thing many times before; and though he still gets pleasure from extending the pattern of justice, there is nothing like Abner's sense of euphoria. "The warm feeling . . . lasted him, Colonel Ross supposed, half a minute" (p. 370).

In the final quarter of the book, Cozzens makes one of his customary reversals. The reader's half-forgotten search is rewarded, but in an unexpected way. He has already met one adult in the regular Air Force: Brigadier General Nichols, down briefly from Washington. Now he discovers (as Colonel Ross does, too) that there was one at Ocanara all along. General Beal, having almost resigned his command, having almost lost control of both his base and himself, regains his control and takes back the command that he had tacitly handed over to Ross. He is the true duke, after all, the man of action who will win the war. What the reader has experienced is what any civilian must experience during his first year or two in military service. In the beginning, he is amazed at the amount of stupidity and childishness in the way things are run. But gradually he perceives that things are not that bad. The stupidity and childishness are genuine, but they are offset by intelligence and virtues that at first he couldn't see because they are different from the ones he was used to in civilian life. *Guard of*

5. *Guard of Honor* (New York: Harcourt, Brace, 1948), p. 534.

Honor is a novel of acceptance, at the opposite remove from, say, *Catch-22*, where first impressions remain permanent. It is also probably the best war novel of the twentieth century.

As for Colonel Ross, his role at the end is suggested in the book's epigraph, which is from *The Tempest*. It is Ariel's speech beginning "I and my fellows / Are ministers of Fate." Colonel Ross, in the kind of chastening Cozzens loves to end with, learns that his actual role is Ariel to his general's Prospero.

When he wrote *Guard of Honor*, forty-five-year-old Mr. Cozzens could only guess what it would feel like to be fifty-nine, like Colonel Ross. A much younger Cozzens had guessed what it would feel like to be old Doc Bull, or middle-aged Ernest Cudlipp. The young man had guessed it would not be too bad. Never a Browningite optimist about the effects of age, young Cozzens nevertheless saw mental gains to equal bodily losses. He saw the stout, stubborn will in fact gaining impressive victories.

In *By Love Possessed*, Cozzens knows what it feels like. The fifty-four-year-old author has fifty-four-year-old Arthur Winner as his hero. Neither man much likes being fifty-four, though both are at the height of their powers. What they perceive that appalls them is just how temporary are the patterns and the point one can impose on life. *By Love Possessed*, among its many richnesses, contains a study of the aging and death of dukes. (*How dies the wise man? As the fool!*)[6]

There are at least five parts to this study. One is Arthur Winner's father, The Man of Reason, the man of all Cozzens characters who had the closest to total control over his own life—but who, nevertheless, lost humor, courage, and reason itself, as his body progressively failed him. One is Arthur Winner's father-in-law, old Noah Tuttle. Noah, the fourth duke of his line, has been a central, and even in some ways the central, figure in Brocton for many years.[7] His passion for order has been so great that in the smash of the Brocton Rapid Transit Company he secretly sacrificed both his own fortune and his legal rectitude to keep things going, to keep much of Brocton from being dragged down with the failing company. But now he is himself ruined by age. His own one-time junior law partner, Fred Dealey, now a judge, is about to rule against him in a case where Noah has simply gotten confused. Judge Dealey dislikes the idea of having to expose old Noah as incompetent. To his forty-year-old mind, the shame would be intolerable. But Arthur Winner says to him, "Things I've seen make me doubt if anyone but an old man can really put himself in an old man's place. Values seem to be different—I suppose; less and less matters to you" (pp. 440–41). So much for the stout, stubborn will.

6. *By Love Possessed* (New York: Harcourt, Brace, 1957), p. 366.
7. Ibid., p. 312. Noah's father, the third duke, was chosen by his father-in-law as "the only *man* in the whole lot of visible heirs."

The third part of the study is a black duke, the only one in Cozzens.[8]
Alfred Revere is the head of the extensive Revere family in Brocton, steward
of the Union League Club, and sexton of Christ Church—both jobs being
hereditary in his family. To some extent Alfred plays the role of the comic
servant, mirroring the upper-class action, as in a Mozart opera—or as in
Fenimore Cooper's novels. But like Natty Bumppo, who began as servant
and became something much more because Cooper took him seriously,
Alfred transcends the role. Cozzens presents him as a true ducal character.
Alfred has had a heart attack and been told he must give up his two jobs:
in one he "owns" Christ Church; in the other he rules the Union League
Club (p. 359). That is, he must resign his small dukedom. He does so with
dignity. He gets ready to make such intelligent, sensible steps as drawing
up a will that will minimize his taxes . . . and none of that helps much.
What Arthur Winner sees as they discuss, with dignity, his probably
prompt death, is "the blankness of a mind nauseated by animal despair"
(p. 364).

Then there is Arthur Winner's Aunt Maud, very much a Mrs. Banning,
a woman accustomed to giving orders and to mattering. But now she is
superannuated, reduced to endless games of solitaire. She copes by consciously acting the part of the tough old dowager, lest she seem pitiable.
But in moments of stress she cannot sustain it. She *is* pitiable, and Arthur
Winner must pity her.

Finally, and most lightly sketched, there is Colonel Minton, USA Retired, who copes by getting drunk every day, though never before noon and
never messily. In his own way he maintains control and order; he is a duke
whose dukedom has shrunk to no more than his own clothing and the precision of his drinking habits.

Some such diminished future is what Arthur Winner has to look forward to.

Meanwhile, he is a reigning duke: the most fully drawn, the most admirable, and the most believable that Cozzens created.[9] He is the culmination of the development I have been tracing. But at the same time he is in
two ways quite different from any earlier duke.

8. Second Lieutenant Stanley Willis in *Guard of Honor* is a future black duke, and one
whose dukedom will be much more visible on white maps. But in the book he functions ducally only in one paragraph.
9. Julius Penrose, it can be argued, is more admirable still. But he doesn't fully count.
His primary function in the novel is to be part of the education of Arthur Winner. He
is a fellow duke, but not a reigning one; he is a static character, not a changing one.
Julius is educative in two ways. First, because of his being crippled, he is an example
of the diminished *present*. (One can be simply cut off in one's prime like George
Detwiler and Tom Henderson. Or one can be arbitrarily stricken in mid-career, like
Julius.) Second, he both represents and helps to produce that state of final unillusion
that Arthur Winner reaches at the end of the book.

He is like the others in his possession of simultaneity. For example, questioning Veronica Kovacs, he sets himself what Cozzens calls a "double effort"; he can and does do a second thing while she supposes him wholly engaged with the first (p. 144). He possesses the apparent ability to read minds. Questioning Ralph Detwiler, he almost stuns that youth by the accuracy of his guess about the things Ralph has been trying to conceal. "With a look startled and fearful, as though the simple guess had struck Ralph as a miracle of second sight, the exercise of a divining power that nothing could escape, Ralph said . . ." (p. 166). Furthermore, he cares as much about tradition as any earlier character, perhaps more. He serves as a vestryman at Christ Church—though privately very doubtful that God exists at all—because he wants to help preserve the "sacred fiction" of his race (p. 351). It *is* a fiction, but it is one that helps to maintain the human community, and he sees it as his duty to help uphold it as long as it is up-holdable. (The time may come, of course, when it isn't, and then he will calmly adjust. Just as, on a smaller scale, old Judge Lowe calmly adjusts to—in fact, plans—the dissolution of the Union League Club in Brocton.)

But then there are the two ways in which Arthur differs from earlier dukes. One is that he sees much less prospect of using his power to reward merit or extend justice than they did. There is no scene in *By Love Possessed* comparable to the one in which Abner Coates chooses his assistant, or Colonel Ross plucks Captain Collins from the public relations office. Or, rather, there *is* such a scene, but it stands in sober contrast. This time a not altogether meritorious person comes to Arthur and asks to be chosen. Jerry Brophy, the down-county politician, wants the new judgeship. He is currently the district attorney.

Concluding that Brophy's obsession with proving himself equal to Coateses and Winners will drive him to become a good judge, Arthur does in fact support him. But it is a far cry from the happy ducal selection in earlier books. As if to underline the change, Cozzens gives considerable attention to Brophy's assistant, a young lawyer named Garret Hughes. He is the man of integrity that Abner Coates also was. There is no hint that he may become the new district attorney if Brophy gets the judgeship. Instead, Cozzens reminds the reader several times that Garret abandoned a bright future when he left (because it offended his integrity) a slightly sleazy law firm and became the assistant district attorney. Virtue—and a large salary cut—are virtue's rewards.

The other difference is that Arthur Winner neither holds nor aspires to office. He avoids it. In the somewhat loose sense that I am using the term "duke," it is possible to be one as a private citizen. But both in Cozzens's novels and in real American life, office, power, and responsibility are so intimately allied that actually to refuse office comes close to declining the ducal role.

Earlier Cozzens heroes never declined it. Back in the beginning, Dr. Bull was both Medical Examiner and Health Officer in New Winton. After the typhoid epidemic, a group of town leaders call a public meeting at which they intend to force him out. Bull walks in on the meeting. "I'll see you all in hell before I'll oblige you by resigning!" he says.[10] And he does in fact stay triumphantly in office. Ernest Cudlipp may consider resigning as Vicar of St. Ambrose, but he never does—and there is every reason to think that when Dr. Lamb becomes a bishop he will offer and Ernest will accept a higher office. Abner Coates, swallowing his dislike of politics, accepts the nomination for district attorney. It is fair to assume that one day he will become a judge, like his father and grandfather. Colonel Ross both runs the base at Ocanara and is a judge in civilian life.

But Arthur Winner, before *By Love Possessed* ever began, turned down the judgeship that Fred Dealey accepted. In the book, he is offered the new fourth judgeship, and he turns that down, too. As Cozzens puts it (reflecting how it must seem to Jerry Brophy), he "puts the crown by" (p. 298).

Cozzens leaves no doubt that Arthur Winner is fully worthy of the crown. The whole book is a statement of that. In addition, there are symbolic details at the beginning and end of the book to drive it home. At the beginning, Winner is seen driving up to the courthouse and parking in the space marked "President Judge." Four pages from the end, walking up Federal Street in Brocton, he passes two state troopers who literally salute him. Why, then, does he refuse? He is a complex character in a complex book, and there are many reasons. But the most important is his age. On the literal level, he simply considers himself a little too old. As he tells Brophy, "I don't think a man should be in his fifties when he starts" (p. 297). On a more important level, Arthur Winner and James Gould Cozzens, being both fifty-four, have lost the illusion that power really matters.

Morning Noon and Night is radically different from any of the other novels discussed. Indeed, it is arguably not a novel at all. Cozzens himself calls it all sorts of things: "scenes from an old play," a "tale of a thousand and one nights," and (twice) mere "notes."[11] He is right to. The book is a melange. And though comparatively short, it has room for a large number of digressions: little essays on Sacco and Vanzetti, on the sinking of the *Titanic*, on military railroad management in the Civil War, on the futility of writers' conferences. In the whole book there is precisely one action in present time.

But novel or not, the book completes Cozzens's study of dukes. *Morning Noon and Night* is a denunciation of ducal characters, by one.

The duke who attacks his class is old Henry Worthington, a man of

10. *The Last Adam*, p. 279.
11. *Morning Noon and Night* (New York: Harcourt, Brace & World, 1968), pp. 37, 92, 134, 336.

sixty-five, like his creator. Our Hank, he usually calls himself. He is the central character, the man whose loose and baggy autobiography the book purports to be. He is as ducal as human beings come. The son of a distinguished college president, he himself is the leading management consultant in the country. That is, he is a specialist in restoring order—a sort of duke for hire. Where he goes, order follows. He is even more the Prospero than Arthur Winner or Norman Ross. Though he never lets us see him at his work, he tells us about it, and what he tells us is that his clients, top executives of major corporations, find him "downright amazing," and his remedies "simply uncanny" (pp. 20–21). There is self-mockery in this phrasing, of course; and yet it is clear that the clients really do see him as touched with magic.

And more than any earlier figure, Henry consciously sees himself as a duke. Speaking in the same mocking-but-serious tone as above (and also playing on Shakespeare's Sonnet 94, which serves as an epigraph for the book), he describes himself in regal terms:

> I rule and dispose; others, whether members of my devotedly subservient, even admiringly worshipful, large staff, or selected clients of distinction respectfully waiting a word from me about what to do, are all of them but stewards of this my excellence, my profit, pleasure, and even pomp. (p. 353)

In Sonnet 94 those who rule and dispose are "They that have power to hurt and will do none." They alone are "the Lords and owners of their faces." All others are but stewards. With such lords Henry Worthington firmly places himself.

But such lords are not, Henry says, very nice people. Seen from without, yes, they look regal. They look like a Dr. Lamb or a General Nichols. Seen from within, they have every human vice. Himself he describes early on as having been, from time to time, a "liar, sneak, coward, cheap bastard, even monster" (pp. 13–14). Most of the novelistic part of the book is devoted to showing scenes where Henry has acted these unattractive parts—though it is fair to add that the one action in present time is a true ducal one in which Henry brings his about-to-be-a-third-time-divorced daughter, Elaine, to a catharsis.

Even the great, Henry insists, are not very nice when seen from the inside. He was high enough on the staff of the Commanding General of the U. S. Air Force during World War Two to get a true glimpse or two of the rulers of nations, and what he saw in each case was an ugly fraud: "the deviously arrived opportunistic trimming politician that a Roosevelt, a Churchill, a Stalin, a de Gaulle seen with inside knowledge had the alarming look of being" (p. 383).

Dukes are especially likely not to be nice people, Henry says, because they have power. Ernest Cudlipp and Norman Ross and the others had power, and used it to do good. Arthur Winner came to doubt that you could do much good with power, and his doubt was strong enough to keep him out of office. The lightning striking the ducal oak out at the lake is a symbol of that doubt. But as a private lawyer in Brocton, he continues endlessly to solve social problems and to work at keeping his society intact. (The oak survives, though damaged.) He sees no other rational option.

Like the Shakespeare of Sonnet 94, Henry Worthington views power primarily as the capacity to injure other people. And, taking issue with the sonnet, he says he has never seen a man with that capacity who didn't use it. "Power (the pleasure of the prince) simply by being in-being unfailingly brings hurt to someone, and never can do none" (p. 355).

If that is true, there is an end to the heroic figure of the duke; we are left only with the duke-as-bully. In fact, if we follow the strict logic of the sonnet, it is an end of dukes altogether, because there are no more "Lords and owners of their faces," only a race of stewards.

Henry does not go quite that far. He is clear that there will always be men of power, and he allows them one honorable quality. Yes, they will hurt people; he, Duke Hank, has often hurt people himself. But they will not do it for the sheer pleasure of hurting, only because it is necessary to hurt other people to achieve any goal. It is the base stewards who, when they get a chance, hurt for hurting's sake.

But the main function of dukes—to do good by creating order—is gone. The longing may still be there. "My mind is so constituted that in its everyday exercises it likes, even craves, order," Henry says (p. 61). But order is what it cannot justly have. To order things in the real world is to hurt people, and to order them in fiction (for example, in writing *Guard of Honor* and *By Love Possessed*) is to tell lies. In explaining at the very end of *Morning Noon and Night* why he made it a collection of notes rather than a coherent story, our Hank says he finds it dishonest to impose a "design of intention" on "the until now unarranged or designless" (pp. 400–401).

The stout, stubborn will, in short, has abdicated. And the novelist, James Gould Cozzens, has closed his career with a non-novel.

Back in the beginning, it was the lords of disorder—Dr. Bull, Janet Cardmaker, Virginia Banning—who left no heirs, while May Tupping and Guy Banning are sure to. Now it is the last duke whose line runs out. Henry Worthington has one daughter. She had two children, who died pointlessly in a plane crash, and she is not able to bear more children. There will be no more dukes.

But though Cozzens in effect disavows his own earlier novels and their ducal heroes, the reader is not obligated to. *Guard of Honor* and *By Love Possessed* have passed from their creator's control. Norman Ross and Arthur Winner exist in their own right as two of the great ordering characters of twentieth-century literature.

Ernest Cudlipp
[from *Men and Brethren*]

Ernest returned to the taxi. "All right," he said. "Start uptown. I'll think of the address in a minute."

He propped his feet against the back of the folded-down seat in front of him, reclining with closed eyes to the light sway and jolt. For a moment he thought of Geraldine, and his impression of her was not full or clear. In May or early June she had been twice to dinner at the Vicarage. She had come down to a number of services—he could recall, in the course of more than one sermon, observing her with surprise seated in back with John. Her clothes—Alice was right; he didn't notice or know anything about women's clothes, really—were simple and severe. He ought to pay more attention, for he could see that there might be useful trifles of information in knowing how good or expensive they were, or how smart. It seemed to him that she had worn white to dinner; to church, a dark blue with some white at the throat. Or, very likely, she hadn't. That might be merely the general effect of whatever she had worn on his inattention. She was somewhat blonde, her hair more brown than yellow; her eyes dark, her nose short and straight. He hadn't thought of it before, but the person she resembled was Wilber Quinn. She shared, and in a way not especially feminine, Wilber's boyish, clean and well-groomed tone of skin and hair, his frank, direct expression, his air of amiable receptiveness, rather than intelligence. She would be good with children, competent and comforting.

Time enough to deal with Geraldine's difficulties when he found out what they really were! Ernest relaxed more in the shadows, consciously loosening each muscle, blanking his mind, focusing his eyes on the inside of his eyelids, forcing on himself a poised, vacant quiescence—the brain resting, and, for the time of a moment, disengaged, held still.

He made no voluntary movement. He thought of nothing. He could measure the inflow of physical refreshment like coolness in the night and he began with firm tranquillity to let his mind form words: *O send out thy light and thy truth that they may lead me, and bring me unto thy holy hill, and to thy dwelling.* Unhurried, the phrases occupied his whole mind. The words returned, of themselves, with unforced deliberation, over and over. Soon he was aware, without the distraction or the interruption of taking an interest in it, of the automatically increasing depth of his breathing, the modulation of his heart beat.

Set, by the familiar practice of his will, on the deceptive threshold over which some people stepped to a supposed spiritual apprehension—where the senses, starved of nervous energy, were narcotized, kept no more check on actuality; where reason, deprived of ideas to work with, abdicated, impotent; where Grace might very well appear, as Calvin supposed, irresistible—Ernest released himself. Somewhat rested, he struck a match and lit a cigarette. The taxi driver said: "Far enough uptown?"

"How far are we?"

"Ninety-third Street."

"Too far. Go over and turn down Park Avenue. It's Eighty-first. I'll show you."

"I thought you was asleep."

"You thought wrong."

Ernest was reviewing as well as he could the shelves of books covering the walls of his bedroom in idle search of some likely source of light on John Calvin's personal religious experience. Nothing at all appeared to him. He used to have—and surely had still, since who on earth would borrow it?— an edition of the *Institutes of the Christian Religion* translated and laboriously annotated by an old-style Princeton Seminary supralapsarian—what a marvelous word, by the way! The Presbyterians, overturned in a doctrinal rout, with the liberals persecuting the conservatives, must now be altogether— didn't they call it, infralapsarian? Calvin would spit on them! They were no better than Lutherans. Genuine Calvinists, who didn't blench at a little sound logic, who really considered the fall of man inhumanly preordained by God's eternal decrees of reprobation, must have grown as rare as great auks. It might be interesting to try to determine the true nature of the changes—why the Calvinists had once accepted easily teaching so stern and awful; why now they were rushing to exchange it for a flaccid Arminianism, a mess of Methodist pottage.

His reflection was restless. Ernest recognized it, concerned; for ordinarily, presented with such a topic, he began to work with interest, gathering materials in his head, considering and classifying them in relation to each other until he had isolated the point or points he must look up sometime.

Brought to a pause, he glanced at his watch, struck his hand sharply to the side of his face. "Cudlipp," he said, "I think you are insane!" He started forward on the seat. "Quick!" he said to the taxi driver. "Get down

to Eighty-first Street! I'm hours late! Go on! Turn over there—don't stop
for the light—"

The taxi swerved on the corner, went roaring west. It darted south on
the changed light, across the traffic starting north. Four blocks down they
swung into Eighty-first Street and Ernest called, "Right there! Pull over!"
He jumped onto the pavement. To a doorman in white linen he said,
"Quick! Get in and ring Mrs. Roger Binney. The Reverend Mr. Cudlipp
calling."

"Yes, sir."

"At once, at once, please!"

The taxi driver looked at them both, the doorman propelling himself
across the wide pavement to the lighted alcove of the switchboard beyond
the big doors; Ernest, standing alert and troubled, digging silver from his
change pocket.

"So you think I'm crazy, do you?" Ernest said. "Sometimes I do myself;
but I have a strong premonition. There you are. And there's fifty cents for
getting here. Good night."

The elevator man had the switchboard phone to his ear. He and the
doorman turned and stared at Ernest. "I didn't see Mrs. Binney go out, sir,"
the doorman said, "but she doesn't seem to be in."

"Is there a pass key? Get it. We'll go up."

The elevator man, gaping, closed his mouth suddenly, opened it again,
and blurted in the mouthpiece: "Reverend Mr. Collins, Ma'am . . ."

"Cudlipp, Cudlipp," Ernest said. He stepped into the elevator, stood
leaning against the wall. By his wrist watch he was hardly more than twenty
minutes late; but only a simpleton would be late at all. The circumstances,
considered with any intelligence, shouted it to him. Unless she was really
desperate, a young woman like Mrs. Binney would never telephone him.
Any idiot would have sense enough to know that. Only at her literal wit's
end would she be able to make herself presume on an acquaintanceship altogether nominal. Her air of intimacy was unreal, no more than an imitation
of John's intimacy.

"To your right, sir," the elevator man said.

In the hall, Ernest thrust his thumb against the bell button. The door
immediately swung back. Unable to see, he walked forward through the
dark entry toward a light beyond. Over his shoulder he said, "Don't ever
think of doing that, Geraldine. Besides being vulgar and nasty, it wouldn't
be forgiven you, either in this world, or in the next. There are too many
people involved. How do you think they'd feel?"

The door clicked closed. "How do you think I feel?" she asked faintly.

He turned. "You know, it just suddenly came to me," he said. He
laughed. "What you'd do, I mean. Not the sort of thing I'd expect from

you." He put his hands hard on her shoulders, and held her while she wavered a little, regarding her steadily in the deep shadow. "You feel like hell," he said, "to the approximate degree of your aversion to God and your conversion to creatures. Go. Fix your hair. Wash your face. I don't want to see you this way."

He dug the fingers into her shoulders until, wincing, she tried to free herself. "That's better. You see, you easily can, if you want to. If you let go that way, I can't do anything with you. If you help me, I can do everything that needs to be done."

He released her and she put up a hand, rubbing her shoulder slowly. "No, you can't do anything," she said; but her voice was composed. "No one can do anything. I realize that. When I telephoned you I don't know what I thought. I'd just got in. It seemed so horrible—everything—that, well, I don't know. When you didn't come, I saw how silly I was—what could you do? What—"

"You're feeling better already," he answered. "Do as I say."

He went in toward the light. The living room was large, and looked even larger than it was, for it had almost no furniture—two chairs, a card table under the shaded glow of a floor lamp whose short cord stretched away taut to a baseboard plug. A handsome, heavy secretary desk had been pushed carelessly into a corner. The floor was bare, the quartered oak dusty, littered with small rubbish. The wide windows, open on the summer night, had neither curtains nor shades, only the empty brackets which must have suspended Venetian blinds. John had mentioned—or maybe she had —that she was moving. Probably she hadn't intended to be in town at all.

Ernest stood a moment at the windows, watching the city—the heavy dark masses, the far-flung direct lights of the great avenues, the indirect flares and glows. A breeze was perceptible up here, steady and persistent, but tepid. "We'll get a thunder storm," he said aloud.

He turned back. On the bridge table lay Geraldine's bag and hat, a pair of twisted white gloves, a bottle of sherry and a glass, a box of biscuits torn open. He picked up the bag thoughtfully, snapped the catches. Inside were a number of crumpled bills, a handkerchief, damp and soiled, a cigarette case in black enamel with small gold initials, a matching lighter; a compact, a lipstick, several keys; an envelope postmarked Cincinnati, addressed to Mrs. Roger Binney, 2nd; and, as he expected, a small straight glass vial with one dozen veronal tablets.

Ernest shook his head. What amazed you was the uniformity, the uncontrolled, not intentionally directed, but inevitable, sameness with which people proceeded to act out—though with real enough agony or desperation—the unreal, conventional emotional part. *When lovely woman stoops to folly*—the remedy, supposing of course that she knew she was stooping and could recognize folly, was classic. In a high-strung, ugly way, it was almost comic—at least, to the moment of swallowing the veronal. The veronal was as real as the anguish which had brought on the whole essential false and artificial gesture. It would redeem—in the sense of make serious—both the folly that recommended it and the folly that swallowed it. It was entirely realistic and straightforward. He heard Geraldine's footsteps coming through the empty apartment. Laying down the bag, he held the glass tube up. "I took the liberty of looking for this," he said. "At the moment, it isn't possible to treat you as a responsible person. Sit down and drink some of the sherry. Where did you get these tablets?"

"The man at the drug store told me I could buy them in New Jersey."

"He must be a man of very little sense. So you went to New Jersey and bought them! I don't like that, Geraldine. That's not impulsive, that's deliberate. Do you wonder that I can't treat you as a responsible person? How did you ever get yourself mixed up in anything like this? What's wrong with your husband?"

"There's nothing wrong with him. I can't stand him, that's all."

"That's never all. You must have been able to stand him when you decided to marry him. How long ago was that?"

"I don't know—well, seven years, about."

"How old are you?"

"Twenty-eight, or I will be next month."

"Then you weren't a child when you married. Now tell me what it is that makes you feel you can't stand him."

"I don't want to talk about him, Ernie. You'll have to believe that I can't, I really can't, stand him. He's repugnant to me. I can't live with him. I—"

"All right. We'll come back to that later. How about your children? Are you tired of them, too?"

"Ernie, how can you say such a thing to me? Can't you see that I'm almost crazy? Can't you—"

"I can see it, my dear. Now, I want to know about John. He's been sleeping with you, hasn't he?"

"Of course. Do you have to ask?"

"How else am I to know? You don't imagine it's a subject I'd discuss with John, do you?"

"I don't know," she said. "Sometimes I think anything's possible. I thought it was pretty obvious to you."

"It was. But in matters of this kind, Christian practice is to give people benefit of the doubt. However obvious it might be that you were infatuated with him, it might still be possible for you to feel some respect for your moral and social obligations."

"If you mean Roger, I don't feel any obligations toward him, Ernie. I never loved him. I—"

"Your obligations are toward yourself. You were the one who engaged yourself to abide by a contract as solemn as possible. If your word is good only so long as it is comfortable and agreeable for you to keep it, then clearly you have no regard for your obligations."

"Ernie, what's the use? I thought I wanted to marry Roger, of course. But how could I really know what I wanted? Hardly any men were interested in me. I'm not pretty and I never was. At Vassar I did my work, instead of going to dances and on weekends. I could have. I have a sister who's really attractive, and she quite often made people invite me. Only I didn't want to—" She fixed her eyes on him in desperation, as though he might doubt it. "I know it sounds as if I were miserable; but I was awfully happy. I didn't have time for all that. I was almost always on the honor list. I had lots of friends. I was treasurer of my class, and, oh, lots of things like that that sound silly now—" She had begun quietly to weep, her elbow on the table, her face bent against her wrist.

"Just so." Ernest lit the cigarette he had been turning between his fingers. "By temperament and training you were a nice girl."

She caught her breath spasmodically two or three times. "No, I wasn't," she said. "I don't think I was, really. I—"

"I didn't suggest that you were perfect. Doubtless you can remember failings in charity or chastity. It would be strange if you couldn't. You met John in Paris last year, didn't you? Was that the first time?"

"Yes."

"How did it happen?"

She took the handkerchief from the bag. "I went over with my sister. John had a place with her brother-in-law—quite a good deal younger than her husband. I mean, John's friend was the brother of my sister's husband—"

"Yes. I understand. Go on."

"Well, he and John had been at college together, and they had an apartment. They were both so sweet to us—we had such a lovely time. Going places and doing crazy things, I mean."

"But there was nothing between you and John then. You hadn't thought of such a thing. The four of you simply went dancing and drinking, and out to Chartres. And you all liked each other a lot."

"Yes. How did you know?"

"How could I help knowing?" Ernest asked patiently. "I know what you're like. I know what Paris is like. I lived there for some time after the war. There are several sorts of pretty well standardized American behavior. I've seen them all."

He leaned back in the chair, the cigarette smoking steadily in the corner of his lips, his eyes narrow and thoughtful. Allowing himself a moment's release from the disagreeable, overeasy task of badgering Geraldine, he nonetheless watched her gravely and steadily. As well as he could, he made himself see her freshly, for the first time; disassociated from John, or from any particulars of her history or character which came from meeting her previously and hearing her talk.

Certainly he knew what she was like. It was there to be seen, for everyone was in fact exactly what he looked like, provided that you had the experience to know what you saw. As he had said, she was a nice girl. Not in the casual trifling sense of a complimentary generalization; but deeply and definitely; in a way whose vitality and importance was nowadays generally overlooked or disparaged. She would represent well enough what he had to regard as the one convincing possibility of steadiness, of virtue and integrity, in the dissolving turmoil of an unlimited transition.

Her appearance advertised a breed or stock which, succeeding by its strength, was invigorated and encouraged by its success. Ernest didn't doubt that, finding all right with itself, it was too ready to find all right with the world; but at least no doubts hampered its initiative. It had nothing to live down. If, relatively, it had been fortunate; relatively, too, it had been superior in intelligence, in capability, in perseverance. No one had ever been in a position to humiliate it. The only contempt it faced was from people out of its sight, beyond its understanding, beneath its own contempt.

This seen, everything was seen—facts of her background and training spoke through her—her father would be perhaps a banker, locally trusted and respected in southern Ohio; or perhaps a doctor well known in Cincinnati; or a conservative, by his lights, earnestly just judge—something of the sort.

Born into a home perhaps architecturally tasteless, but comfortable and carefully maintained; sent to a simple sufficiently good school; nurtured in an entirely unemotional, fairly Low Church faith—old Bishop Vincent might have confirmed her; dispatched to a women's college in the East where not impossibly her mother had gone before her— Ernest sat up sharply.

"Geraldine," he said, "in my work I've had a great deal of experience with cheap people. I don't expect much of them. As far as I'm given grace to, I try to love them, since in God's sight they are precious. I do what I can for them. It isn't much, because there is usually little to work on." He leaned forward, pointing the cigarette at her. "Many of them seem to be simply bad stock, bad blood—just what those things really are doesn't matter. Whatever they are, I have seen what they mean. The matter is practical, not theoretical. They have no chance because they are no good. Why they are no good is another matter, not relevant at this point—" He drew a breath. "Just as they have what has been put in them, you have what has been put in you. You were born with almost every good thing. There is invested in you the hope and faith of a decent, dutiful people for a future of decency and duty. Take care of that! You've got the thing worth having, if only you won't throw it away before you find out what it is."

"Yes, I know," she said. "It sounds all right, Ernie; but it isn't like that. I can't think what I ought to, unless I do. It wasn't like that. I suppose you have to think that it was wrong when John seduced me. Only I know it wasn't. I knew it was all right for him to have me. I could feel it was all right—"

Ernest snapped the end of his cigarette out the open window. He rubbed the top of his head. "Lord help me," he said. "What can I do to make you use your intelligence? Well, first. You don't honestly imagine that John seduced you, do you? Can't you see the meaning of the things you've told me? You thought John was wonderful. What do you think John thought, except that you were a sensible girl to see it? You seduced him, of course."

She pressed the handkerchief to her eyes. "I didn't," she said. "How could you believe it? I suppose you think I'm so ugly and common that—"

Gazing at her, Ernest did not answer. She lowered the handkerchief at last. "I didn't," she repeated. "It happened because I couldn't stop him—" She colored a little. "I mean—"

"That's what you mean," Ernest said. "It doesn't need any change. Of course you couldn't, because you didn't want to stop him. I suppose you'd both been drinking—but even so, you'd have to let him see that it was a pushover before he'd make any serious advances. The only way it can be that is for you to want it to be."

"I didn't! I—"

"Of course you did, my dear. John isn't overwhelming. He's just a young man with an ordinary itch. Undoubtedly he liked you. As soon as he saw that he could have you—you know you'd have to be definitely repulsive for him to pull up at that point."

"Ernie—" she said, strangled.

"My dear, how little we'd disagree, if you'd let yourself see things as they are—or were. Evil can't be done in a nice way. In violating your morals you'll certainly outrage your sensibilities. No, you're not ugly and common. That's why you won't look at it. This great-love business takes two. As far as John's concerned, you can see what it amounts to. He's sick of it. I daresay he has been for a long while. He couldn't have the experience to know what he was letting himself in for. I'm sure you've taught him a lot. Another time—"

She put both hands over her face, dropped her head down to the table. "Come, come!" Ernest said. "Sit up. I won't allow you to start that. You had your emotional spree this afternoon. I don't condemn you, Geraldine;

but don't imagine I'm here to condole with you. I want you contrite, not bawling over lost candy. You don't mean to tell me that you don't know how John finally got out from under?"

She sat up; she brought her hands down. With her eyes still shut, she said, "I know. I just couldn't seem to believe it. I knew the last night he was up here. Oh, God, Ernie, it was so awful. I knew he wasn't just tight. He kept saying: 'This is terrible. This is terrible!' But he wouldn't tell me what. He'd say— Who is she? What's she like?"

"I don't know. I've only seen her once, at a distance."

"He hasn't been having an affair with her, has he? He couldn't be! He couldn't—"

Ernest sighed. "I don't know that he is; but of course he could. If he isn't, it's because she won't let him. You don't support the finer feelings long when you do without principles. He's a sentimentalist, so he probably finds it all very sad and moving—and unpleasant. But he doesn't stop it. None of them does. That's enough of that. Worry about your own behavior, not his. Where are the children?"

"At my sister's."

"Telephone her and tell her you're coming there. I haven't any idea what the exact situation is with your husband. What does he think you've been doing—or does he know?"

"He's in Cincinnati. I told him I didn't think I was coming back to him, he'd have to let me alone while I—"

"Then write him. Tell him that now you think you are. If he will start again and try to make a go of it, you will."

"I can't."

"You can. Get out of this mess. Go back home and behave yourself. That's easy enough. There isn't anything here for you." He held up the vial of veronal. "When all you can think of is this, what do you call it? Peace and pleasure?"

"Ernie, I would if I could. Why don't you believe me? I can't!"

"Geraldine, what is this nonsense?" He looked at the veronal tablets a moment, speculative. "Haven't you been frank with me? I asked you what was wrong with your husband. When you answer, nothing, I assume that you are telling the truth. This isn't the moment for reticences of that kind. What is he? Habitually unfaithful? Diseased? Impotent? Perverted?"

"Oh," she said. "No! No!" She looked at him a moment, her eyes wide, blank and despairing. "I suppose I have to tell you," she said. "It seems so silly. You see, I couldn't, I really couldn't. Ernie, I'm a couple of months pregnant."

Ernest dropped his hands and looked back at her. "Geraldine," he said, shaking his head, "Geraldine. Why did you let that happen?"

"It's silly, isn't it? That's just what I did. I suppose I didn't care. I loved John. I—"

Ernest pressed his palms to his forehead, slid them up, over his thin brown hair. "Were you insane, my dear?" he asked. "I suppose you were! You didn't care. You loved John. And so you thought you'd have a child. Geraldine, a child is a human being. Merciful God, must I tell a sensible woman that? When you undertake to have one, you embark on a business of the greatest seriousness and importance, lasting perhaps twenty years. What on earth am I going to do with you?"

He found a new cigarette slowly, lit it, slouched back in the chair. He put a hand over his eyes and said, "I'll have to think. I'll have to think."

At last he said, "No. Definitely no!" He dropped his hand, crushed the barely begun cigarette out in the ashtray on the table. "Now, let me see what we can do. How about your sister? Would she know— Wait. We can do better than that. Where is the telephone?"

In the darkness of the entry he put his back to the wall. "Lily?" he said. "Mr. Cudlipp. I want to speak to Mrs. Breen, the lady upstairs. Tell her she can take it on that telephone in the back room."

There was a prolonged pause and Lily said suddenly: "She's playing on the piano, Mr. Cudlipp. She don't hear me."

"Now, Lily, go upstairs at once and make her hear you. If those stairs are getting too hard for you to climb, do you know what I'm going to have to do? I'm going to have to get a new housekeeper."

"I'm going, Mr. Cudlipp, as fast as I can—"

After a while a receiver clicked and Alice said, "Ernie, don't you dare tell me you can't get back."

"I'll be along. Listen carefully. Do you know of a decent and capable doctor who will take a case for me?"

"What kind of a case?"

"Try not to be dense, my dear. When I ask you for such information, what kind of a case would you imagine?"

"Oh! Yes. Of course, Ernie. I know a very good one."

"Well, please call him right away and make sure he's in town. I want an appointment for tomorrow."

"She, darling. She. I know she's in town. I was there this afternoon. Not the same thing, though. A funny old man put his head in while I was playing the piano, started to say something, and then ran away as fast as he could. Do you suppose he was a burglar?"

"I suppose he was Mr. Johnston. He's a clergyman who assists me."

"Oh. I'd thought he might be the janitor. Lily's more remarkable than ever, isn't she? I expect I'd fire her."

"She is an extremely good cook."

"Well, it wouldn't hurt her to dust some, sometime. Lee called up, fine and drunk. I think he wanted to apologize to you for missing dinner; but when he found it was I, all he did was accuse you of having designs on me. I told him no such luck and to go to hell. Good-by, darling."

Ernest went back into the bare living room. He took the veronal tablets from his pocket, broke the seal, and shook out two of them. "Do you ever take this stuff?" he asked.

Geraldine shook her head. He put one table back and laid the other on the table. "Take it now," he said, "and go to bed. Everything's arranged. I'll call you about it in the morning."

"All right. I don't like it, Ernie. I don't think I ought to do it. I know it's silly to feel that way, but—"

"You ought not to have to do it," he said, "if that is what you mean. You have no right to put yourself in a position where you can only choose between evils, instead of between good and evil. But you cannot continue in any course which involves persistent violation of the rights of others." He fixed his steady brown eyes on her and said, "Come here, Geraldine. You've got into this over your head; but we won't let you drown. Kneel down."

She came automatically, knelt awkwardly, her dress catching tight under her knees, and he put a hand on her shoulder to steady her.

When he had occasion to use one, the long Roman absolution came first to Ernest's mind. It was a relic of seminary days. Spikes like Vincent McNamara and Carl Willever naturally championed it—though there had been a prolonged, enjoyable squabble over the admissibility of the deprecatory form. Thoughtful, Ernest began: "May Almighty God have mercy—"

But it was, he decided, too thick, in view of what Rome would have to say about his directions to her. He turned it into the words of the Prayer Book: "—upon you," he continued, "pardon and deliver you from all your sins, confirm and strengthen you in all goodness, and bring you to everlasting life; through Jesus Christ our Lord . . .

"Swallow that tablet," he said.

She put it in her mouth, her face contracting bitterly, and gulped the sherry left in the glass.

"That will take care of you," he said. "Good night, my dear. You're all right. You will be all right."

*   *

It was a narrow, white-fronted building, neat and quiet on the neat and quiet street. Ernest moved along the stream of sunlight falling up the pavement. A woman was walking two spaniels. Out an area-way came a delivery boy, whistling, and started off with his push-cart. Ernest went in.

The small, white, circular lobby, indirectly lighted, was empty; and he stood a moment, absorbed in his thoughts, feeling the artificially cooled air on his face. "There's a good chance," he told himself, "that she won't want to see me. Well, I'll have to see her anyway—"

A door in the circular wall opened and a small, sharp-featured woman in white, wearing a nurse's cap, came out. Seeing Ernest, she stopped by the small desk at the end, looking at his clerical clothes with stony surprise. When he had told her who he was and what he wanted, she sat down behind the desk, saying, "I'll have to telephone Doctor Stevens before I can let you go upstairs." She asked him for his name again and wrote it on a slip of paper.

"I don't like this place," Ernest thought, able suddenly to guess a good deal about it. He heard the woman saying ". . . a man, a minister, who says he has an appointment . . . very well." She slid a finger under the edge of her desk and pressed a button.

After a while the door in the curved wall, opposite the one she had come out, opened from the inside, disclosing a long deep elevator. "Six, William. Miss Perkins," the woman said.

The operator was a grave, watchful, no longer young, but stolid and powerful man. He confirmed Ernest in his guess. The simple, expensive fittings, the impregnable silence—mounting, the elevator made not a sound; there was not a sound as they passed the floor doors—were portentous. Ernest knew all about it. There would be only a few patients—men of prominence whose addiction to cocaine must be broken without anyone ever suspecting that they had used it; women of position or celebrity whose attempted suicide must not be dreamed of while they were recovering from what they had done to themselves—the shame, the folly, the fatuity of their desperate evasion hung over them.

When the elevator reached the sixth floor, the operator fastened back the gate and came into the hall with Ernest. He said nothing at all, simply walking ahead until he reached the door he wanted. He knocked on it. When he was told to come in, he opened it.

The room was a large one, furnished as little like a hospital as possible. Although the windows, closed against the outside noise and heat, faced south and were in shadow, they were so wide that the room was full of clear light. On the broad bed Geraldine lay flat on her back, a low pillow hardly raising her head. A magazine was open on the sheet near her extended hand, but she lay still, her eyes closed. It was apparent that she had been expecting, from the knock, a nurse or some attendant. The elevator operator, just behind him, waited a moment while Ernest said, "Geraldine."

Her eyes opened. "Oh," she said, recoiling a little, "Ernie—"

The door was drawn closed, and Ernest went up to the bed. He took the hand lying by the open magazine, patted it. At once she drew it away. She said stiffly: "Thank you for the flowers."

They were on the dressing table. Now that he saw them, he could smell them, mingling with a slight scent of cologne on the cool, quiet air. Without irony, simply thoughtful, he was obliged to remember Mrs. Hawley's room that hot morning. He said, "Are you all right, my dear?"

"I'm all right." She spoke with husky abruptness. "It's all right. I don't like it here much."

"Neither do I," said Ernest. "I know what you don't like. But they'll take good care of you, I think. You'll forget about it."

She had closed her eyes again and he stood gazing at her. Her face was almost wax-colored—he supposed, from the anesthetic used in the morning. Shut, her eyes looked deeply circled, bruised. The dark lids shone as though rubbed with vaseline. She lay perfectly still, but he could see the rapid rise and fall of her breast under the crossed flaps of a silk bed jacket, and while he watched, she parted her lips a little to breathe faster. Then she tightened her eyes, turned her head aside, and immediately he could see the much clearer shine of tears between the lids.

"No, no," he said. "It really is all right."

He walked around the foot of the bed and stood by the windows, looking at the afternoon light laid over the roof tops, at the fine dust and city smoke in a far-off shining horizon haze. Out of it lifted the hot blue, deeper and cleaner as he looked higher. He could hear her begin to sob quietly, with a rough, wincing restraint, as though it hurt her. "I hate him," she said. "I hate him! It's so awful here—"

He turned around and she said, "Oh, God, Ernie, won't you go away?"

"That wouldn't make it any better." He sat down in the armchair and found himself a cigarette. "Geraldine," he said, "there's no reason for me to go away. It isn't likely that you'll ever see me again. Of course I know all about it. But I know it as a priest, my dear. Not as a man, not as an acquaintance you will have to go on facing. So you don't have to feel that way."

She brought a hand up to her breast and pressed it while she made an effort to catch her breath. She said indistinctly, "Yes, I have to. I know someone knows—" Her face twisted and she turned it the other way. She put her knuckles to her mouth. "No, I couldn't ever see you again. I couldn't see anyone. I'm such a damned rotten little fool—"

"You know it," Ernest said. "I know it. God knows it. On me it doesn't make much impression. Lord, the things I've known in my time! I think I've forgotten most of them. I try to. Usually they signify very little about a person. It's more important to know what he does every day. This business isn't like you at all. Very soon we'll both forget it. We're taught that God forgives it."

"What good is that?" she said. "I couldn't forgive myself. I couldn't. I won't ever feel the same again. I can't think of myself the same way—" Her hand searched blindly until it closed on a handkerchief under the corner of the pillow. She lifted it and brushed it across her eyes. She opened them and looked at Ernest. "I can't stand it, Ernie. I could kill him! I could kill myself—"

"That's why I'm sitting here," Ernest said. "Because you can stand it. You're not going to kill anyone, or want to." He smiled. "You can't forgive yourself because you're not entitled to forgive yourself. The good of God is that, if you approach with a pure heart and humble voice, forgiveness will be given you." He looked at the cigarette end between his fingers. "I don't think the way you thought of yourself could have been a way worth keeping. If, from time to time, you find yourself remembering this, it won't hurt you—well, I'll risk the pure heart. I want to hear the humble voice."

"I suppose he couldn't help it," she said. "I suppose it was my fault. Maybe I won't think about it often. I couldn't ever feel that way again. There's that, I suppose. It was like a tearing, Ernie—" She looked at him, surprised, arrested. "You wouldn't ever know," she said. "It's really like having a child—something like it, more like it. You don't believe me, do you?"

"Easily," said Ernest. "I've suffered from ambition, from shame, from despair. You have to describe it in terms of your experience. Unless you keep silent."

She looked at him with an intense, frowning attention and suddenly she said, "Why are you in the Church? Why did you go into it?"

Ernest returned her look a moment. He answered at last. "There are so many reasons. I was temperamentally fitted for it. There was a priest I greatly admired who influenced me. Though not intentionally. I don't think he regarded me as promising. I did many things that were good for me because I hoped to change his mind. There were any number of influences."

"Tell me."

"My father was a severe man—and not at all religious, by the way. I mean, he was unyielding. I think it must have been a great surprise and pleasure to me when I discovered that most people were pliable, that I could work on them. I think I must have felt very sure that I could and would. Not because I could then. I couldn't. I wasn't at all a natural leader. I was just proud and incompetent. I didn't shine at school. I wasn't happy at home. I was too light and small to be good at sports. My father was principal of a high school and had an exaggerated sense of his position and dignity. I daresay I shared it. It was important, because it made him live beyond his means. So I never had any pocket money and, although my mother was a good Churchwoman, that was the real reason I sang in the choir at All Saints'. We were paid twenty cents a week. It led me naturally, when I was old enough, into the Acolytes' Guild. I found I could shine there. In short, the Church gave me an opening. I saw it."

"You mean," she said doubtfully, "that that was all?"

"Isn't it enough?" Ernest asked. He smiled. "It seems to me to be. It's

the best way to tell it. It can be understood by people who are satisfied with
chance as a sufficient cause. To those who have faith in the miraculous, and
believe that there is a purpose in the world, it is just as purposeful and
miraculous as the conversion of Saint Paul."

"You mean, it just happened?"

"Can you conceive of that?" he asked. "A year ago could you have
dreamed where you would be today? A year ago, was there one chance in a
million that I would ever exchange a word with you? Only in God's omniscience. Here you are. Here am I."

She continued to look at him. "You do mean, then," she said, "that
really you believe God meant you to be a priest?"

"Just as He means everything to be, that is."

She looked at him, troubled. She hesitated a moment and said, "Even
this—I mean, about—"

In the room the shadow was deepening. Over the unlimited acres of
roofs the descending sunlight shone a stronger yellow. At the horizon the
haze was toned with a faint violet.

Ernest thought: "As sure as night. When it is shown me, I see. And
how little ahead of her I am!" He said, "This is the answer. A great obligation has been laid on me to do or be whatever good thing I have learned I
ought to be, or know I can do. I can't excuse myself from it. I dare not bury
it or throw it away." He was silent a moment. "One like it is laid on you.
You know your obligation, Geraldine. It has always been, to go home and
do what your life has prepared you to do. It is all right. Now, you can.
Take your talent and employ it—"

He was silent again for a moment, thinking of that terrible twenty-fifth
chapter of Saint Matthew's gospel—the untrimmed lamps, the unprofitable servant, the Shepherd enthroned. She looked at him, silent, absorbed,
and he began to repeat: "For the kingdom of heaven is as a man traveling
into a far country—"

He could hear his voice, calm and clear in the twilight, see her quieted
eyes on him "—who called his own servants," he went on, "and delivered
unto them his goods. . . ."

V

Notes on a Difficulty of Law
by One Unlearned in It.
[essay]

As an admiring lay observer, I have always considered that W. S. Gilbert's Lord Chancellor, when he declared that the law is the true embodiment of everything that's excellent, stated no more than the truth. If it has a single fault or flaw, I lay that to the unfortunate intrusion of the human element —a fallibility and unreasonableness of mankind that enters to disturb the law's own august order of right and reason. This, I think, the law itself feels. In its accumulated wisdom, work of the best minds of many centuries, the law moves—and not without resource and dexterity—to minimize the damage men can do its processes by being men. Yet the law does not, I think, get rid of the problem; and what the law does do seems often to involve contradictions.

Among these contradictions, none is more noticeable to the amateur than the dual status of those indispensable intruders, the members of the jury. One view that the law takes of them appears in an excerpt from the notes of testimony in a case in this Court (Commonwealth vs. Stout: No. 22, December Sessions, 1949) heard before Hon. Hiram H. Keller, P.J., and a jury.

The District Attorney, Mr. Curtin, has produced and is examining in chief a Commonwealth witness. This witness is the sister of a young woman who has charged the defendant with raping her. The alleged attack took place late at night in an automobile in an out of the way place. When defendant brought the young woman back to where she lived, a boarding house, she saw no one to whom she could complain; so she made no complaint until the next morning. She then telephoned her sister. Mr. Curtin is questioning the sister about the telephone call. Abridged to the relevant questions and answers, this exchange ensued:

BY MR. CURTIN:

Q. You say she phoned about 8:30?

A. Oh, about that time.

Q. What did she say?
> MR. KAPLAN (of the New Jersey Bar, admitted Pro Hac Vice; de-
> fense counsel): Now, I object to that, if your Honor please.
> THE COURT: Yes. Objection sustained.

BY MR. CURTIN:

Q. She related an occurrence that happened to her the night before?
A. She said she couldn't tell me over the phone like that, she said she
    didn't like to go through it, she was so excited.
Q. Now, don't answer the next question until Mr. Kaplan has an oppor-
    tunity to object. Give us your full telephone conversation.
> MR. KAPLAN: I surely object to that.
> THE COURT: Objection sustained.

BY MR. CURTIN:

Q. Did you see your sister after this telephone call?
A. Yes.
Q. And did you and she have a conversation?
A. Well, she was very excited; yes.
Q. She was very excited. Now, did she or did she not at that time relate the
    affair that had occurred the night before; just yes or no.
A. Yes.
Q. Now, again don't answer until Mr. Kaplan has an opportunity to ob-
    ject. What did she tell you at that time?
> MR. KAPLAN: I object again, Your Honor.
> THE COURT: Objection sustained.

BY MR. CURTIN:

Q. Now, as a result of that conversation, did you go anywhere with your
    sister, or did you leave her?
A. Well, we talked there awhile and tried to think up, you know—well,
    she was excited and she wanted to know what to do, so I said—
Q. Well, you cannot give us what you told her to do. As a result of your
    suggestion to your sister, did she leave you, or did you go somewhere
    with her?
A. No, I told her I wanted to go to work. I went to work.
Q. But you and she had decided on something she was going to do, is that
    correct?
A. Yes.

What is going on here, though to the jury, we may be sure, so baffling,
is both plain and of considerable interest to those learned in the law. The
District Attorney, with elaborate care not to let his witness give ground for
a motion to withdraw a juror, is mooting a nice point. The conversation
with her sister was prosecutrix's first real chance to complain of the attack
she said she suffered. Will the Court be willing to hold this complaint part
of the res gestae of the occurrence? There is a citable Pennsylvania case in

which it was ruled proper for a witness to testify to a woman's explanation of her injuries, though it was some hours after she received them.

The Court is seen to think that *that* is different. The Court may be presumed to feel that a conversation the next morning cannot come within that exception to the hearsay rule toward which the District Attorney is reaching. Elapsed time is the point. The truth of prosecutrix's declarations is no longer guarded, as the exception seems to see it guarded, by spontaneity —or, bluntly; prosecutrix has had long enough to make up a story. Any person who heard her cry out: *that man running away there just raped me* may testify to it. It may not be testified that she said (unless, of course, she said it in defendant's hearing, and so makes it admissible on another ground): *that man raped me last night.*

Points like these are pleasures of the law; yet who can doubt that the bewildered jurors are wondering if someone isn't crazy. They have been solemnly impaneled and sworn in order that they may determine whether this offense charged actually occurred. They will gladly listen to everyone who can, or who he thinks he can, shed light on it. Why are they not to hear what prosecutrix told her sister? They are permitted to know that something was said; and they can guess, in general, what. But why should they have to guess? Why, if the witness blurts any of it out, must the Court order a new trial?

For the Court's peace and dignity it is doubtless just as well that the jury should be left to wonder. The law's view of them at this juncture is barely obscured. All these good men and women who have been summoned, and who must alas be used, are of less than average intelligence. They are flighty creatures of feeling, incapable of reason. All they hear, they believe. Fooling them is child's play. To a juror, what somebody says somebody told him is substantive evidence as good as what a man saw with his own eyes. In the present instance, the law does not feel that such simpletons ought to be trusted to hear the witness repeat her sister's complaint. It might be effectively pathetic. Could you expect their weak heads to discount emotion, to remember that this was a sister; and, anyway, that she was reporting not what she knew, but what she was told? Would they be capable of resisting a conviction that might be carried when they saw that the witness undoubtedly herself believed the story?

The average juror, incensed to understand that he was looked on this way, might well conclude that the law is an ass. Perhaps he would be comforted to know that the law manages at the same time to hold quite another view of him. The very nature of the duty he is told to do makes that much clear. When rules of evidence are in question, it may seem that judgment is the thing the law thinks he has little or none of; but the law can and does take also the more complimentary view that he is fit to say the last word. The law thinks he has quite sense enough to determine whether his peer, the defendant, shall go free; or shall be mulcted, imprisoned, or even executed. Court and counsel meekly stand down; facts are for the sovereign jury, and on a jury's wisdom our justice is held to rest safely.

For Pennsylvania at least this kinder opinion seems now to be much in the ascendency. Analyzing (99 U. of Pennsylvania Law Review 6; pp. 814–826) reviews of death sentences by the Pennsylvania Supreme Court during the last four years, an anonymous writer points out that the high court shows signs of not doubting that conviction by a jury below is in itself conclusive evidence of guilt. The desirability or propriety of this attitude in a court of last appeal we need not go into here; we note only the respectful reluctance to reverse. To avoid reversing, the court has much extended the range of 'harmless error'. Dispassionately examined, the rule as it is now, both in flat statement and in implication, seems a far cry from that historic lower-court view of the juror as boob. Indeed, the high court seems to esteem him as not incapable of superhuman feats of discrimination and distinction and unprejudiced reasoning.

Simplified, the thinking now seems to be that errors in the record must be proved to have so far harmed appellant that as the specific result of them his trial was unfair. If this can't be proved, errors, no matter what, are harmless. When defendant from the notes of testimony appears to be guilty as hell to the high court, and particularly when the offense charged is 'atrocious' justice should not be impeded by technicalities; the trial is correct if the jury found the fact the court now finds (362 Pa. 507). And, of course, all errors that the trial court gets around to 'curing' itself are well cured. If it can be shown that the jurors were instructed to disregard some definite slip, the high court concludes that, on the word, their disciplined minds expunged all memory of it, and so, any possible hurtful impression it might have made. Indeed, the court goes further. If physical exhibits of a 'prejudicial' (i.e. horrifying) nature are offered, fairness to defendant is assured when the trial judge directs jurors not to let their feelings be aroused (366 Pa. 182, 186). If the complaint is that His Honor neglected to charge on certain points of law, let it be shown, before the Commonwealth is put to the tediums, vexations, and expenses of a new trial, that the native good sense of jury could not have been guide to them enough (357 Pa. 391). If His Honor used hot expressions reflecting on the truthfulness of defense witnesses or on the adequacy of defendant's case, let it be considered whether intelligent jurors would not have been bound to form the same unfavorable opinion even if they had not heard his (361 Pa. 391, 397).

To the lay observer, these successive, and more and more forthright, displays of firm faith in juries are heartening. At least, to a point. Inopportunely, the lay observer here writing finds himself put in mind of another case recently heard in this Court—and in its circumstances not uncommon. Defendant was charged with molesting a child—a sexual offense. When the

evidence had been heard, the jury, no doubt taking to heart its instruction
on reasonable doubt and on defendant's presumptive innocence, acquitted
him. What was known to the Commonwealth all along—that the man had
been convicted of previous offenses of the same sort—became known to the
jurors afterward. Indignation, though vain, was high and vocal. If someone
had only told them—

Yet they were there to try one issue: whether the child who made the
charge, or the man who denied it, was telling the truth. The statements of
those two were the sum of the real evidence presented. They had heard all
that their office required them to hear. Now, let us suppose that defendant,
even though guilty on earlier occasions had, as well as serving his sentences,
long ago conquered his irregular impulses. This time he is as innocent in
actual fact as the jury found him. The child's charge was (as it could be)
pure invention, brought into definite form by prompting and coaching of
alarmed and angry parents. If it lets the Commonwealth put previous convictions on the record, côuld the law reasonably expect any juror—even me;
even you—to refrain from vehemently suspecting that the man who did
that before has done it again? Is the law an ass when it does not trust us, as
reasonable human beings, to regard nothing but the facts in evidence in the
case now trying? Would the innocent defendant have been safe with us?

Pondering points like these, I recollect with pleasure that I am merely
an amateur in the law. With what respect and with what relief I find myself
saying: let learned counsel expound; let the Honorable the Judges rule!

The Courtroom
[from *The Just and the Unjust*]

In the morning a cool wind blew over the hill of Childerstown, but the cloudless sky and the splendor of the sunlight meant that it was going to be hot soon. When Abner walked up with Bunting from Bunting's office to the courthouse the wind was dying. He could feel the blaze of sun on his cheek and bare head as they crossed by the county administration building from the shade on the east side of Broad Street to the shade of the trees around the courthouse steps. When court opened, the cavernous chamber seemed a little warmer than what had been the fresh morning outside. Now, an hour later, the air inside began to be cooler than the air outside. On the southeast windows the folding walnut shutters were drawn together, shadowing the round of benches, today only partly filled. The windows on the other side had been open, the colored glass top-sashes drawn down, the lower sashes drawn up. Judge Vredenburgh sent the tipstaffs to close them. He said that those jurors who wished to do so might remove their coats. From the way the black silk of his robe clung to his shoulders it was plain that the Judge himself wore nothing under it but a shirt.

Mrs. Zollicoffer, recalled, was on the stand; and this was a wearisome business. Last night Mrs. Zollicoffer must have taken something to make her sleep, and taken so much of it that she was still numb. After half a dozen questions Bunting abandoned his examination abruptly and handed her over to Harry Wurts. He said to Abner, "She doesn't know whether she's coming or going." Abner supposed that Marty had made one of his quick and usually correct decisions, and was ready to write her off, figuring that she could do his case no good answering that way, and though she might answer Harry unguardedly, her stupid stubbornness about what she pretended she didn't know would be increased if anything by the feeling she probably had that everything around her was remote and unreal.

Harry, cross-examining, was not quite himself, either. He was alert enough, and aggressive enough; but his manner was jerky and it could be seen that Mrs. Zollicoffer's sluggishness worked, as perhaps Bunting hoped it would, on his nerves, while the efforts he made to work on hers, because of the sluggishness, got nowhere. He kept moving around. He fired his questions at her from all directions. He asked her whether she wore glasses to read with; and when she said she did, he asked her whether she had received any communication from her husband during the day preceding the alleged kidnapping. When she said no, he walked away toward the Commonwealth's table, turned and snapped suddenly, "Did you ever see a can of opium?"

Mrs. Zollicoffer said dazedly, "I beg your pardon?"

"You heard my question!" Harry said.

Mrs. Zollicoffer looked distractedly at Bunting who said, "Did you hear Mr. Wurts' question?"

Mrs. Zollicoffer said, "I don't know what the gentleman means. I didn't hear it."

Harry said, "Simply tell the jury what a can of opium looks like. Describe it. How big is it? Has it a label?"

"I don't know the meaning of it. I'm sorry."

Harry looked at her with every sign of amazement. "You don't know the meaning? You can't describe the way opium is packed?"

"No," said Mrs. Zollicoffer. "I wouldn't know what that was."

Nearly shouting, Harry said, "You never heard of opium? You don't know what it is?"

"No, sir."

"Ah—!" said Harry. "Madam, you are under oath?"

"Yes, sir."

Harry pressed a hand across his no doubt painful forehead and closed his eyes a moment. "Where were you living when you first married Frederick Zollicoffer?"

"Several places," Mrs. Zollicoffer said woodenly.

"Where?"

Bunting half lifted his hand and said, "Objected to as immaterial."

Judge Vredenburgh nodded. "It is immaterial."

Looking to the bench, Harry said, "It goes to the credibility of the witness, your Honor."

"What does?" said Judge Vredenburgh. "Where she lived?"

"Or when she was married?" Bunting asked, standing up. Judge Vredenburgh moved his head from side to side. "No," he said.

"That is my ground, sir," said Harry Wurts, "for asking my question, subject, to be sure, to your Honor's infallible ruling."

Judge Vredenburgh, his hand over his mouth, thumb against one cheek, forefinger against the other, gave him a short dangerous stare. Harry must be feeling terrible if he were going to try being funny with Vreden-

burgh. "I will sustain the Commonwealth's objection," Judge Vredenburgh said. "You may except if you want to."

To Mrs. Zollicoffer Harry said, "Well, what was your late husband's
business?"

"Salesman, I guess," said Mrs. Zollicoffer.

"You guess!" said Harry contemptuously. "You would! Where did he
have his office?"

"Somewheres in town."

"Where in town?"

"I don't exactly know that."

Harry lifted his shoulders and threw up his hands. "What was he
selling?"

"Some kind of a brand of whiskey, or something like that." Harry was
at last succeeding to the point of annoying her. The woman scorned was
reacting.

"Something like that!" said Harry with increased contempt. "Was he
working for a distillery?"

"Perhaps."

"Perhaps! You mean he was bootlegging?"

"No, I don't!" said Mrs. Zollicoffer.

Bunting drew a breath and came to his feet. "Just a minute, now!" he
said. "I object to that as not being cross-examination. We have been very
patient with Mr Wurts. This witness was recalled on matters which we
went into in chief."

"I think this may be material," Judge Vredenburgh said. "Overruled."

Harry said, "Well, did he ever bring any samples of this some kind of
brand of whiskey home?"

"No, he didn't."

"Just a simple 'no' will do, Madam. Wasn't your husband also engaged
in selling opium and narcotics?"

Bunting said, "I don't know how far your Honor wants to permit this
to go. I object to it as not being cross-examination, or if it is, as an immaterial line."

Judge Vredenburgh said, "We will continue to overrule you."

"Again," said Harry, "I must direct your attention, Madam, to the fact
that you are under oath."

"You don't need to do that all the time," said Bunting. "She knows it."

"I don't know whether she does or not," Harry said. "Will you answer
the question?"

"No. He wasn't."

"He wasn't engaged in the sale of narcotics, if you know what the term
means?"

"Not that I know of."

"You mean, not that you want to know of! Your husband was in a low and criminal business, which you had to pretend to yourself you didn't know about. Wasn't he? Wasn't he?"

"Your Honor," said Bunting, "that I do object to. He—"

"Mr. Wurts is within his rights in asking if that were the case. There can be no objection to describing dope peddling as low and criminal. I think you'd better let your witness stand on her own feet, Mr. District Attorney."

Whatever Mrs. Zollicoffer might, a moment ago, have been stung or goaded into saying, she was able to say now, "Not that I know of."

Harry had wandered back to the defense's table. He spoke to George Stacey and looked at a memorandum. He made a gesture as though to dismiss the witness, and Mrs. Zollicoffer visibly relaxed. "In short," said Harry, looking at her with a smile, "you want the jury to believe that your late husband was a salesman, or something like that—" He mimicked her voice genially. "Only a cheap whiskey salesman, and nothing else. Not that we know of." His tone was now the very opposite of that harsh or brutal tone which he had risked for a moment, and which a jury so resents when it is used to a woman; but Harry nonetheless managed to insinuate derision, to invite her and everyone else to join him in contempt for the deceased. Harry had seen where and how to wound her without doing himself any damage; and, caught unguarded, Mrs. Zollicoffer burst out, "That doesn't say those people ought to kill him, regardless what he did! That—"

"That's all, Madam," Harry Wurts said. He bent his head to listen to something Howell was saying.

"Cheap but good," Bunting said to Abner. "Shall we—oh, let her go!" He stood up and said, "You may step down, Mrs. Zollicoffer."

Harry left the defense's table and went up to the bench. Sitting back, the Judge said, "There will be a five minute recess. The defendant Howell may be taken out."

Everitt Weitzel came limping across to the Commonwealth's table and said, "Your office called, Mr. Bunting. When you had time."

"All right," Bunting said.

Harry Wurts went into the Attorneys Room, and Joe Jackman stood up and followed him. Abner took out a package of cigarettes and went after Joe.

"Not much of a house, this morning," Joe said, yawning. He held a match for Abner and they stood together by the screened windows. Below them sounded a splash of water in the little cast iron fountain under the trees. Occasionally figures, coatless men, girls in thin dresses, moved slowly on the diagonal cement walks under the trees. "Going to be a hot day," Joe said. "I'll bet it's ninety right now."

"What happened to Harry?"

"In there," Joe said, indicating the lavatory. "He is taking a little some-thing for that miserable morning-after feeling, or over-indulgence in stimulants. You missed it, last night. Dick Nyce made a pass at Annette; and there was quite a row down at the landing. Dotty didn't like it. I think everybody's had about enough of those barge parties."

The lavatory door opened and Harry came out. "A much-needed pause!" he said. "Well, Ab, what did you think of your witness? She don't know nothing no time."

"I don't think she had anything to do with his dope business. She doesn't have to tell you what she thinks."

Joe said, "What's the trouble with that little boy blue of yours, Wurts? Got the trots?"

"Jackman," said Harry, "if you had ever been spread over a table and given a good kidney massage, an idea not wholly repugnant to me, you would suffer from certain disorders for some time afterward."

"Did he forget to suffer from them yesterday, or did you forget to re-mind him?"

"I don't blame you," Harry said, "you see the Commonwealth putting on these tear-jerking acts, that poor dear little widow-woman and all; and so you think everything's like that—"

The courtroom door opened and Nick Dowdy came in. "About ready," he said. "Judge Irwin's just come on the bench, too."

"Well, what the hell does he want?" said Harry. "Why didn't you tell him that it isn't the function of this court to gratify the vulgar curiosity of typical sensation-mongers?" Harry was reviving. "Just let me ask you," he said, backing Nick against the wall of buckram-bound reports, "has his Honor, the President Judge, read Mr. Wurts' concise and brilliant three thousand page brief submitted in the matter of Mat Moot, Max Moot, Manny Moot Junior, Mary Moot Moot, Mike Moot, Maurice Moot, and Muriel Moot by her next friend and brother Moe Moot, versus Moot and Moot, a corporation, action in assumpsit? I doubt it! I sincerely doubt it! Well, what's he idling around here for?"

Joe Jackman said to Abner, "He's certainly feeling smart this morning. I don't know why the Judge didn't slap his ears down in there—"

"Now, you fellows," Nick said, escaping from Harry. "Defendant's back, I think. Judge Vredenburgh was looking around—"

Joe Jackman went out, and Harry said, "What's he riding me for? Not that I wouldn't ride him, if I could; but it's hard riding only half a horse."

The answer, Abner thought was that Harry still held, just as he had years ago on the occasion of their difference at law school, that one of the perquisites of being Harry Wurts was making fun of people, so no reason-able person ought to object; while, of course, Harry had every right to resent the manifest usurpation when one of his ordinary victims took to answering affront with affront. Harry would have to content himself with the fact that one of his affronts was usually equal in effectiveness to several of most other people's.

In the courtroom, Bunting stood at the bar, his elbow on the edge of Judge Vredenburgh's desk, while they talked. Abner stepped up beside him, and Judge Irwin nodded. Abner said, "Good morning, sir."

Bunting had already called Walter Cohen, who waited awkwardly in the witness stand, the swart skin of his round, big-nosed face shining, his right hand with a diamond ring on it, suspended, while Nick Dowdy withheld the Bible on which he was to swear, pending the outcome of Bunting's discussion. Judge Irwin whispered to Abner, "How's your father?"

"Pretty well this morning, sir," Abner said.

Judge Irwin nodded with a little nervous, smiling grimace. His nature was reserved and aloof—unless, perhaps, you were a member of his own generation—and it was difficult to imagine being familiar with him. Judge Irwin's attitude was strict; but, by the simple if uncommon practice of disciplining himself just as strictly as he disciplined other people, he aroused, even in a heavily sentenced prisoner, no special resentment. His air of virtue, instead of being hateful, had in it an austere sweetness. Judge Vredenburgh sat calm, full-blooded, the intelligent sensual man, irascible about what struck him as wrong or unfair, astute about the failings of human beings, dealing with facts and things as they were, with no special interest in why. Judge Irwin thought constantly of why.

They were about the same age, in their early sixties; but Judge Irwin looked a good deal older than Judge Vredenburgh. He had little flesh on his face, and his finely formed, entirely bare skull was fringed with an inch or two of gray hair along the base from ear to ear. On the bench, he sat intense and earnest, tightening and relaxing his lips, clearing his throat, sometimes plucking with his thin long hand at his chin. To see him and Judge Vredenburgh sitting together when, for instance, they both doubted a witness, marked the contrast. Judge Vredenburgh cocked a hard, incredulous eye, pouting slightly, sometimes even giving his head faint annoyed shakes; Judge Irwin bent his angular, anxious gaze on the witness as though he hoped, because he wished so hard that men would not deliberately perjure themselves, to make this man stop.

It would not be fair to say that Judge Irwin was less attentive to the facts than Judge Vredenburgh, for he ended by acting on them with precision, abstractly balancing the offense against what the statutes provided; but in a way he hated the facts. He hated them as symptoms of a disease of folly and unreason pandemic in the world, and constantly infecting and reinfecting his fellow men. A good example was Judge Irwin's notorious antipathy to liquor. He understood no better than Cassio why men should put an enemy in their mouths to steal away their brains; but it was that pandemic folly and unreason that he blamed, rather than the individual. He did not even favor trying to abolish liquor by law, since that proposed the absurdity of blaming the liquor and enhanced the principle, false among free men, of preventing a choice instead of punishing an abuse.

What Judge Irwin knew was what everyone with his experience knew: that if there were no such thing as liquor, half or even three quarters of the work in each term of court would be eliminated. He was not fanatical about it; he did not suppose that a man who took a drink now and then, or even one who got drunk now and then, was a criminal. Undoubtedly he knew that his son liked a drink; and though he probably hoped that Mark never got as drunk as Mark had been last night, Judge Irwin would not be enraged if he found out—only, discouraged by the imprudence, the shortsightedness that defied common sense and invited danger in seeking so brief and miserable a pleasure.

Judge Vredenburgh sat back, and Bunting said to Nick Dowdy, "All right, swear him."

As they turned, Harry Wurts stood up and called out, "Just a moment, please, your Honor! I'm going to ask for an offer of proof here with Cohen."

"I thought so!" Bunting said to Abner. "All right, Mr. Wurts. At side bar?"

"I don't care," Harry said.

"Well, certainly I don't, either," said Bunting. "We expect to prove by this witness that on the night of April seventeenth he met a person outside a saloon near Milltown and talked with him. That he turned over to this person the sum of eight thousand dollars in bills of various denominations."

Judge Vredenburgh said, "Mr. Wurts, you stated that you did not care whether the offer was made in the presence of the jury or not. Do you want the whole offer to be made?"

"Well, no." Harry scratched his head. If he's going to make a complete offer, I would ask that it be made at side bar. What I want is for the Commonwealth to show how this man Cohen's testimony can be material. Of course, if to show that, he has to trot out all the—"

"I can't be expected to guess what you mean," Bunting said. "I supposed you wanted—"

Judge Vredenburgh said, "Yes; the offer should be sufficient to show the relation. Come up, Mr. Wurts. Come up, Mr. Stacey. This concerns you, too."

Abner came up with Bunting and they stood close together under the bench. Bunting continued, "This money was brought for the purpose of securing the release of Frederick Zollicoffer. To be followed by further evidence that on that same night Robert Basso, one of these defendants, brought into the presence of Roy Leming, the defendant not now on trial, but to be called as Commonwealth's witness, the sum of eight thousand

dollars; which money Basso, at that time and later, stated to Commonwealth's witness was obtained by him and Howell from Cohen, now on the
stand, who was paying it for the release of his associate and business partner,
Fred Zollicoffer. To be followed by further testimony corroborative in admissions by the defendant, Stanley Howell."

"Yes," said Harry. "Well, for the defendant, Howell, I object to the
offer." He turned to the bench. "Your Honors will understand—"

Judge Irwin said with his thin, pleasant smile, "I'm not sitting, Mr.
Wurts. I am present, but I am not participating."

"Nonetheless," said Harry, incling his head, "I think the point will be
as apparent to your Honor, as to his Honor, Judge Vredenburgh. The offer
is immaterial and irrelevant as to the offense charged here; namely, that of
murder. All this is evidence of a separate and distinct offense; namely kidnapping, holding for ransom."

Judge Vredenburgh said, "Is this evidence to show that the money had
anything to do with the kidnapping?"

"Yes," said Bunting, "naturally, your Honor. The Commonwealth offers to prove that this identical money was divided among the kidnappers."

Judge Vredenburgh said, "Mr. Wurts seems to want to know whether
your offer relates the kidnapping to the murder for which the defendants
are on trial."

"Oh, yes," Bunting said. "We intend to prove that the killing was
carried out as an integral part of the kidnapping, in the course of the perpetration of it."

"Well," said George Stacey, "in that respect there's no averment in
the indictment."

George had made the discovery—Abner remembered making it himself—that a natural impulse to defer to the impressive, seemingly never-to-
be-equaled experience of his elders, like Bunting and Harry Wurts, while
often politic in a younger man, was not always necessary. George said, "The
indictment merely charges an unlawful and felonious killing amounting to
murder in the first degree. It does not set forth that the killing was in perpetration of any other felony."

"It doesn't need to," Abner said, smiling. "Any killing in perpetration
of the felony of kidnapping is unlawful and felonious and amounts to murder in the first degree."

Bunting said, "I think you'd better give his Honor some authority for
your statement, Mr. Stacey."

With all eyes on him, George said, "I am familiar with the law that
holds an indictment sufficient that simply charges a defendant with first
degree murder." Abner could see that George had still to learn not to be
afraid that, if he did not say everything, people would think that he did not
know everything. The measure of his inexperience was in his error of antici-

pating objections. George said, "It is true that such indictments need not set forth as to the manner, or means, or instrumentality with which the crime was committed; but the law can certainly not be so elastic as to include other crimes, other felonies; and if these defendants are going to be charged with committing a different felony—" He threw out a hand. "Well, I don't think Mr. Bunting can do that."

"That's the whole point, your Honor," said Harry Wurts. "We object to this offer because the kidnapping was over, completed, finished, with the payment of the ransom money. As Mr. Stacey so well said, this isn't the crime these defendants are on trial for. It was not in perpetration of a felony that this killing was done. That was all over."

Judge Vredenburgh turned his head and spoke to Judge Irwin. "No," he said, turning back. "We will overrule you. You may have your exceptions. Let's get on with it."

Abner went back to his seat. Walter Cohen ought not to take very long; and Abner doubted if Harry would cross-examine, when Harry discovered (as he was bound to, if he didn't know already) that Cohen was going to lie out of helping the Commonwealth. Cohen was very willing to testify about handing over the sum of money for Frederick Zollicoffer's release; and he expressed himself as eager to see Fred's assassins pay for their crime, but he was full of nice scruples. He explained in Bunting's office, and again (to Bunting's helpless annoyance) before the grand jury, that he meant, of course, the actual assassins. He could not positively identify the person to whom he handed the money.

This was as ridiculous as Mrs. Zollicoffer's claim that she did not know her husband's business; and, in fact, both lies were probably Walter Cohen's. Probably he had told Marguerite to say nothing about Fred's business, no matter what happened. From Leming, and from Howell's confession, Bunting knew that it was Basso who received the money, and Basso himself had told Leming that he knew Walter Cohen recognized him. Walter Cohen would know that Bunting knew; but he had doubtless also made sure that Bunting could not or would not do anything about it. Probably Cohen judged accurately the importance to the Commonwealth's case of his identifying Basso. Bunting could show that money, to the same amount as Cohen paid a mysterious stranger, had been brought on the same evening to the bungalow and divided by the kidnappers. Bunting had all he really needed. No jury was going to suppose that by a coincidence other people had gone out that night carrying bundles of bills to pay ransoms at the same spot; and there, by a mistake, met one or more other kidnappers coming to get it, with the result that Cohen gave his money to the wrong person, not Basso; while Basso took his money from the wrong person, not Cohen. All the circumstances identified Basso; and Cohen could rightly conclude that Bunting would not bother to make any determined or dangerous attack on his own witness—compelling Cohen to identify Basso was not worth it. Cohen was left free to play his own game, moved by who-knew-what anfractuousities of honor among thieves, or fears of a man who could never call the police, or hopes of keeping the confidence of his business associates. Since Harry and George did not want the identification made, either, Harry had no reason to ask questions.

The Commonwealth's next witness would be Roy Leming, and Abner laid out the folders. This was important; and Abner would have liked it better if Bunting were going to handle Leming. Probably Bunting would have liked it better, too; but Leming, a nervous man, was more afraid of Bunting than Abner. Perhaps because Abner was younger than Leming, Leming shook and stammered less when he could address himself to Abner. Though Bunting seemed to feel no misgivings about leaving the most important witness to his assistant, and this both pleased and (as it might have been meant to) heartened Abner, Abner could not say that he felt no misgivings of his own.

For one thing, Mr. Servadei was present. Servadei was an insignificant little gray-haired man, and his part in the proceedings appeared only that of an interested observer. Nevertheless, Abner wished that when the matter of Leming's turning state's evidence was settled, Servadei had seen fit to withdraw and go about his business. From his firm's standpoint Servadei's time must be valuable; and Abner could not help wondering just what figure went down in Servadei's day book for each hour spent here doing absolutely nothing.

Of course, Servadei's waiting might be innocently explained. Servadei might want to see Harry handle this tough case so as to get a line, for his firm's information and possible future need, on a criminal lawyer in this county. The chances of such a need arising were not likely to be great, or not great enough to make such a purpose certain and shut out entirely the possibility that Servadei was there to preside over the pulling of a fast one. Once started in that direction, disquieting thoughts multiplied. The business of Servadei's firm was getting criminals off. Why should they advise a client of theirs to give testimony that would probably get two criminals electrocuted?

Without Leming's testimony the Commonwealth could hardly hope to convict Basso, and might not convict Howell; and there sat Servadei; and how easily he could slip Leming a word, a threat from those hidden parts of Leming's criminal past, a promise to help him in ways that the Commonwealth could not anticipate. Such a plan might even tie up with Basso's standing mute; and though Abner did not see how, it was always possible that he and Bunting would find out how in good time. Abner shrank to imagine the upset—Bunting's sudden angry realization as he arose to interrupt Abner and request permission to cross-examine; Bunting's biting, but if Leming lied firmly, vain attack; the eventual ignominious entry of a nolle prosequi, or the Court's necessary charge that there was no evidence against Basso. Servadei, finding Abner's eye on him, bowed civilly; and Abner, obliged to nod back, looked away in confusion and gave his attention to the witness on the stand.

Bunting said to Walter Cohen, "Does either of them look like the man you saw?"

"I object to the cross-examination of this witness," Harry Wurts said.

The tactic of constant obstruction was a boring one to Harry, whose type of mind was the type that demurs, that admits all you claim, and in a flash, taking a new direction where you are entirely unprepared, shows that for one reason or another there is no case. He tilted back in his chair, smiling at Bunting, and added, "The witness has said with the utmost positiveness that they don't look like the man he saw."

Judge Vredenburgh shook his head. "Exception noted," he said.

Bunting said, "Does either of them look like the man you saw that night?" Abner saw that he was venting his annoyance—a thing Bunting sometimes did when it could not make much difference to his case. Bunting was grimly going to force Cohen to anatomize his lie.

"I can't say they do," Cohen answered. He was probably not altogether easy. The careful way in which he was being obliged to perjure himself might make him wonder if, all unknowing, he was putting his foot in it. He gave Bunting a placatory, almost entreating look. He tried a rueful smile, as though to say that he only wished he could help.

Bunting said, dry and grim, "I ask you to look particularly at the defendant, Robert Basso."

Crossing and uncrossing his legs, joining his fleshy hands together, Cohen said, "I don't know that particular gentleman, sir."

"Just a moment!" Abner could see Bunting's silent ejaculation: *You damned liar!* "Did you ever know him?"

"No, sir."

"I ask you whether or not—" Bunting turned to the defense's table. "Do you mind having Basso stand up?"

George Stacey looked at Harry, and Harry said, "No. Stand up, Basso!"

For a moment it seemed doubtful if Basso would obey. Maybe he saw then that he could do the Commonwealth more despite by agreeing than by refusing. He got slowly to his feet and turned his black, rarely blinking eyes on Cohen in the stand.

Bunting said, "I ask you whether or not the man that you saw was about the size and weight—height and weight, of Robert Basso, this defendant."

Cohen went through his excruciating dumb-show of anxiety to please.

He tilted his head. He looked critically at Basso. He narrowed his eyes to weigh and measure him. Then he shook his head and said regretfully to Bunting, "To the best of my recollection, you understand, he may have been a slight bit taller and a slight bit heavier. I say about one hundred seventy-five pounds—"

Abner let his eyes go around. Beyond Servadei and Leming, Hugh Erskine sat in the raised chair at the end of the row. His slight elevation let him overlook his charges and Hugh from time to time gave them a glance. He then subsided, his solid slab-cheeked face in dignified repose, his long lipped big mouth shut in a firm line. Brown hair was thinning on the crown of his big head. Hugh's deep-set mild brown eyes encountered Abner's gaze, and he closed one in a slow amiable wink. On Hugh's broad chest, pinned to the left suspender strap, Abner could see, shining in the shadow of the coat hanging open, the silver, eagle-crowned high sheriff's badge.

Right under Hugh sat Dewey Smith. Dewey had been a sort of hanger-on and general handyman around the Rock Creek Road bungalow where Frederick Zollicoffer had been held prisoner. Dewey was frail, and sensitive-faced, with an alert manner that concealed from a casual glance the fact that he was a low grade moron. Abner had seen his record, which covered eight states and included over forty arrests, though always for minor offenses. Dewey would not have the nerve to plan anything serious on his own; and those who did have the nerve to plan something serious would not be likely to risk giving Dewey a real part in it. Bunting did not much care what disposal was made of him; but meanwhile Dewey might have a use. It depended on whether or not Susie Smalley decided to plead guilty to the charge of being an accessory.

For the purpose of defense, Susie was represented as Howell's so-called common law wife. Old John Clark from Watertown was her lawyer; and nothing could have been more surprising than his appearance for her. Mr. Clark would not have taken the case to get a fee—he had plenty of money; and, anyway, Susie had none. Leaving out Susie's person and character, it was not likely to be for love, since Mr. Clark was considerably over seventy. Abner, himself, guessed that Mr. Clark was appearing for no reason at all but an old man's vagarious impulse to show somebody or other that he could and would decide for himself what he was going to do; and if it were something unexpected, all the better. The position Mr. Clark had found for Susie was that a common law wife could not be prosecuted as an accessory; and this had been upheld more than once. The Commonwealth's only apparent chance was to destroy Susie's status. This ought to be possible, for Bunting believed it a factitious one; but unfortunately for Bunting, there was no evidence of the kind he wanted except Dewey Smith's.

Put baldly (though not so baldly as Dewey himself put it) Dewey's story was that Susie Smalley had relations with Bailey often and with Basso and Leming occasionally. If this were true, and could be shown, Bunting thought he might be able to explode Mr. Clark's common law wife theory —it would be a nice point, and would take some looking-up. The hitch, of course, was Dewey as a witness. Dewey had told his story with good circumstantial detail, and probably he would be able to repeat it on the stand; but, cross-examined, Dewey must soon show that he was a moron; and cross-examination would be bound to bring out, too, many things about him that were better kept in the district attorney's office than presented to a jury. It was simplest to describe Dewey as not normal; and investigating in open court the intricacies of his abnormality did not seem to Bunting in the public interest.

Bunting, though perhaps he would not have put it that way, meant to use Dewey (if he could) as a threat to persuade Susie or Mr. Clark to plead guilty. The complicating truth was that, good circumstantial detail or not, Bunting rejected Dewey's story, or at least the extension of it (Basso and Leming as well as Bailey) that would be most useful for his purpose. The district attorney's office had reason to know that a group of men might patronize the same prostitute, all friends together; a group of men might take a girl out and successively rape her; but they did not do things like this —have one of them bring his girl, and then all live together, all having coitus with her. It was not impossible; and looking at Susie, a jury might very well believe it. They might find her guilty of having a wide, smudged-looking, dissolute face, dead and shabby hair with streaks of fake blonde, and a debauched body under the tight green dress—doubly guilty because of the disproportionate, grotesquely prominent breasts. In Bunting's place, Abner did not know what he would do.

He saw Harry Wurts shake his head, and realized that Bunting had finished with Walter Cohen. Cohen came down, directing little bows to everyone—the Judges, the jury, Bunting, Abner, Harry, George, and the defendants. Bunting, approaching the table, shot Cohen a look, and said to Abner, "If you ever want any nice fresh narcotics, give him a ring. Deliveries at all hours."

Abner laughed. "Leming?" he said.

Bunting looked at the clock. "Yes," he said. "We can get some done before lunch. All set?"

"Sure," said Abner, "but look, Marty. I think Harry's going to kick about the severance right away, and I'd better leave that to you, hadn't I? And of course, if Leming starts to balk, you'd better take it over, because I won't know what you want to do."

"Let him try!" said Bunting. "I don't know what Servadei may think he's going to do; but just remember we can always bring Leming to trial for murder. If that wasn't what he was more afraid of than anything else, he wouldn't be testifying for us. Don't worry about it. Keep his story moving, and we'll be all right. Ready?"

"O.K.," said Abner, palming the card on which he had his notes written.

"Roy Leming," said Bunting, "take the stand, please!"

While asking Leming where he lived and how long he had lived there, and how old he was—Leming said he was thirty-eight: a significant admission, for in crime, as in athletics and war, youth counted; and Leming was past his prime, fit only for jobs of secondary importance—Abner, by his tone and manner, made what play he could for Leming's good will. It was not an effort that Abner enjoyed making, nor one that seemed on the face of it likely to succeed. Just the same, as Bunting said, if Leming had the idea that the assistant district attorney, as contrasted with his boss, was friendly or a nice fellow, it was clearly worth encouraging him. Abner knew that it was a mistake to assume that everything that seemed false or unreal to you, offending your sensibilities and insulting your intelligence, must necessarily seem so to everyone else.

Leming was nervous. He smoothed his thin blonde hair, shifted the knot of his necktie, tried, by shrugging his shoulders and pulling his sleeves to make his worn blue serge suit sit better. However, his voice was clear and pleasant. He was humble and obliging and the jury looked at him with glances that made their surprise plain. Leming was not their idea of a case-hardened criminal and dope addict. His air of being their humble servant was just right—they did not want him to fawn on them, only to look up to them, and this Leming seemed to do.

Abner said, "You are one of the defendants named in this bill of indictment, are you not?"

"Yes, sir."

Abner looked at Harry, who was busily scribbling on a slip of paper. Abner said to Leming, "Do you know one of these other defendants, Robert Basso?"

"All right," said Harry, holding up his hand. "If your Honor please, we object to this witness. We submit that under the law a joint defendant cannot be a witness either for or against those indicted with him until his own indictment is disposed of by trial, and, as the case may be, acquittal, conviction, or a nolle prosequi. That is not the condition of this record in this case."

Abner went back to the Commonwealth's table and Bunting stood up; but Judge Vredenburgh said, "Do you have any authority for that, Mr. Wurts?"

"Yes, sir," said Harry, holding up his slip. "I cite Wharton's *Criminal Evidence*, volume one, paragraph four thirty-nine; and Bishop's *Criminal Procedure*, sections ten twenty, eleven thirty-six, and the cases thereunder, which I would like to submit to your Honor." He turned, lifted the open books from the table beside him and brought them up to the bar. Nick Dowdy took them and laid them before the Judge. Judge Irwin, approaching his bald head to Vredenburgh's ear, said something. Judge Vredenburgh nodded, stared briefly first at one volume and then at the other. "Objection overruled," he said, delivering the books back to Nick Dowdy. "You may have your exceptions."

Leming looked politely at the Judge, and then at Harry, and then at Abner. Bunting said, "That puts the cork in there." He crumpled up the paper on which he had noted his opposing authorities. Abner went back to face the jury; and Leming said, "Yes, sir. I do."

"And do you know the other defendant, Stanley Howell?"

"Yes, sir."

"How long have you known Robert Basso?"

Leming had known him for some time. The story of how they met was naturally not relevant, and anyway Abner had no wish to remind the jury that Leming was not so harmless as he looked. Leming, an old hand, had met Basso in jail. Basso was relatively new, just out of reform school, and Leming, by being older, by his boasting, by showing, as he surely could, that he knew the ropes, probably induced Basso to work with him after they got out. Basso, young, vicious, and without the experience to see danger, was just what an older man like Leming wanted. Basso could do the risky and strenuous dirty work in schemes that Leming could think up.

Leming was guarded about speaking of such matters. He freely admitted as much of his criminal record as he knew would be forwarded as soon as Bunting broadcast a request for it; but the list of Leming's arrests and convictions were his failures. He had not always failed. In telling his story Leming picked his way from fact to established fact. He did not want to let out anything that Bunting might recognize as likely to interest the police in certain cities. His fear and dislike of Bunting were partly due to his early realization that Bunting was no fool and would catch any slips.

Though some of Leming's track was thus covered by silence and omission, it could be followed—a sort of tour of that everyday, routine world of professional crime. It did not differ as much as the imagination might suggest from the everyday world of those who were not professional criminals. In one, as in the other, the principal problem was how to make a living; and criminals who made good ones were as rare as millionaires. The rank and file could count on little but drudgery and economic insecurity; and for the same reason that most men in lawful pursuits could count on little else. They had no natural abilities, and lacked the will and intelligence to develop any.

Leming spent most of his time job hunting. He did not mean quite what the law-abiding incompetent meant by the dreary phrase; but the results, in their high proportion of disappointment and dissatisfaction, were almost identical; and in fact Leming's motions were those of the ordinary shiftless man looking for work. If you asked him what work, he answered with exemplary earnestness, any work at all. In search of employment, he would appear briefly taking a train here or there, getting a lift in somebody's car, disappearing into the poorer streets of the eastern cities. Often he could name jobs that he had obtained. Probably he could have named others, but thought it better not to, because, either while he held them, or directly afterward, there were pilferings, or even payroll robberies, not yet cleared up.

Several years before Leming met Robert Basso he had got to know Stanley Howell. Very likely it was an acquaintanceship resulting from the habit Leming had contracted of taking drugs, which Stanley Howell distributed. This was just a guess; plausible, because it would explain Howell's knowing so much about Frederick Zollicoffer—his habits, where he lived, the likelihood of being able to extort money from him. Perhaps Howell was once part of a little sales organization Zollicoffer had worked up; and Zollicoffer might have, for one reason or another, got rid of Howell, refused to use him any more. At any rate, Leming, coming and going on those searches for work of his, treated Howell's place as a base. When he and Basso got out of jail, Leming took Basso there, no doubt with the hope of making him useful.

It was unlikely that being useful to Leming had ever been part of Basso's idea. He meant to use Leming; and when he met Howell, Howell. Since they were two to one, he probably disguised his intention for a week or so, listening to their talk, sizing up the prospects—poor, he probably concluded, as long as a doper like Leming and a gutless wonder like Howell had charge. Perhaps the Zollicoffer idea looked good to him; and so one day he brought around a friend of his who also brought a friend.

Basso's friend was Mike Bailey, and Bailey's friend was Dewey Smith. In neither case was the word "friend" exact. Basso feared and respected Bailey; Dewey Smith was less than nothing, a half-wit who did what Bailey said; but now there were three against two, and one of the three, Bailey, was formidable. Abner had seen the rogue's gallery pictures of Bailey—a pup-eyed young man with a prominent Adam's apple and large irregular features. He did not look formidable; but few men do with a number hung around their necks, floodlights on the face, and the head against a wall-scale showing in feet and inches the subject's height. Formidable looking or not, Bailey proceeded to take over. Within a week they were all doing what Bailey told them to do. He had Basso steal a car; he had Leming plan out a route to Zollicoffer's house; he had Howell rent a bungalow out on the Rock Creek Road; and, if Dewey Smith were to be believed, he had Susie, whether through love or fear, sharing his bed.

While he continued with his questions, Abner tried to keep in mind as much of this knowledge of the general situation as he could. He needed it to check against Leming's replies. He was watching sharply, half expecting the first contradictions, a hesitancy, a little sticking or resistance, that might mean funny business; but Leming, though he avoided looking in the direction of Basso and Howell, was answering properly. He said that it was about a week after Bailey came that he heard the plan.

"What did you hear?" Abner asked.

"This about snatching Zolly, that we would do it."

"Kidnapping Zollicoffer," Abner said. "And what exactly did they say?"

George Stacey said, "If your Honor please, I think this witness should be pinned down to which of these men made the statement."

"Or, at least," Judge Vredenburgh nodded, "which ones were present when the statement was made. Yes."

Abner said, "Were Basso, Bailey, and Howell all present?"

"Yes, sir. All of them."

"Now, just state what you heard these three men say."

"Why, they were talking about the best time at night to go out and get hold of him. I just can't tell you exactly word by word what they said."

"Well, give the substance," said Abner.

"They decided the best time to get out to his house was about eleven at night, I believe, so they asked me would I show them the way; and I told them, no." Leming paused; but only for the reason that he doubtless needed an instant to consider implications; and, if necessary, not to invent or falsify the facts, but to edit them. "I had told them I was going over to New York, and they told me not to go to New York; and I told them I had to go; and so they asked me when I would be back. And I told them the following afternoon, late; so I got over to New York, and I was stuck there a couple of days."

The trip, Abner knew, had been to get dope. The trouble with asking a witness to give the substance was that the pressure of your questions, if not leading, certainly directing, was removed. There was no reason to help Harry put emphasis on Leming's former habits. Ignoring the concerted gaze of the jury, whose innocent instinct would be, regardless of relevancy, to ask: Why did you go to New York? Why did you have to? What do you mean, you got stuck there? Abner said, "Well, when you returned, did you have any further conversations?"

"Yes," said Leming. "So when I go up there, they were pretty sore about it, about me staying over; so they bawled me out pretty good about it; and I told them I had to stay over, the occasion called for it."

"After that, what, if anything, did they say to you?"

"So, finally," Leming said, "Bailey came to me and he said, 'Listen . . .'"

"Were the other two there?"

"Yes, sir. Right there."

"All right. What did he say?"

"He told me, he said, 'We were out there to grab Zolly the other night, and we got lost, and we want you to take us tonight.' I said, 'No, I am not going to take you. I told you before I would not take you.' And Bailey said, 'If you know what is healthy for you, you will take us out there to-night.'"

The formal, artificial-sounding phrasing served Leming's purpose—to show that he was threatened and felt fear—very well. Bailey might or might not have expressed himself so stiltedly; but the sinister quality of the conversation, by an unconscious onomatopoeia that picked words to fit the serious sense, was increased if anything when reported this way. "All right," said Abner. "Then what was said?"

"So, finally, I told them, I says, 'I will take you as far as Parkside'—that is the name where the road goes out to Zolly's. So we come to an agreement. They said, 'That is all right. Parkside is all right.' So I asked them what they are sore about. Well, it appears the night I left, there was this machine pulled down the street with the lights out, with two men in it, and they got out."

"Now, this is what they told you, is it?" Abner said. It was a curious little story, both for the light shed on relations between the kidnappers; and for the possibility, not to be ruled out, that Leming did, in fact, know more about "this machine" than he admitted. "Yes," said Leming, "so Bailey spoke up; and he said, 'It looks pretty funny as soon as you leave, this car comes right down. It didn't look so good to us.' And they claimed the whole three of them went out to see what these men were looking for; and they followed them, while these men were striking matches, looking at the different houses; and finally after fifteen or twenty minutes they went away. So I spoke up, and I says, 'It looks like you trust me pretty good, then.' And Basso says, 'What would it look like to you?' As much as to say—"

"Well, I object!" said Harry Wurts.

"All right," Abner said. "Never mind the 'as much as to say.' Basso said, 'What would it look like to you?' Now, will you state whether, on this night of your return, you did go to Parkside?"

"Yes, sir."

"Well, just tell us what you did, and what happened."

While Leming explained about the trip—he in one car, leading the way; the other three in another, Abner could not help wondering whether the real reason that Bailey assented to an "agreement" which gave Leming no active part, wasn't that Bailey had decided that Leming, with his drugs, would be worthless or worse. It would be interesting to know why Bailey trusted him at all, in that event—and the answer probably was that, in spite of all appearances of planning and strategy, Bailey acted mostly on impulse, and so never could think far ahead.

"Very well," said Abner. "And when you saw the other car come back, what?"

"Well, I saw they stopped; so Howell got out of the car, and I got out, and I came over."

"What, if anything, did Stanley Howell say to you?"

"He was laughing," Leming said. "He says, 'We got Zolly in here.'"

"Did Stanley Howell say anything else?"

"He told me they had to bust his head open pretty good, and said he was bleeding like a pig."

"Yes. Anything else?"

"Well, he told me they snatched Zolly, and had to bust his head, and he put up a pretty good fight with them. He said when they first grabbed him, Zolly thought they were the cops. He pulled out a can with some opium, and about fifty or sixty dollars, and said, 'Here is the money,' as much as to say, leave him go for it—"

The jury stirred. They were ready to go off the track again; for, of course, into every mind jumped the meaning. Down there, policemen could be bribed. This man thought it was the police—and why; unless the police did come sometimes; and then for fifty or sixty dollars, let him go. They sat up sharply. Left to themselves, the jurors would have dropped everything and haled in those corrupt policemen, and dealt with them. Abner felt like telling them that the detail, for what it was worth, had been brought to the attention of the district attorney's office in that county; and this was all they could do; and all that would be done, too. It was one thing to learn of irregularities on third-hand evidence; it was another to prove that they ever took place.

"This is what Stanley Howell told you?" Abner said.

"Yes."

The jury looked almost mutinous, and perhaps Harry Wurts thought it would do no harm to give them a little time to mull over the wickedness and hypocrisy of those who enforced the law. He said, "If your Honor please—" He got up and came to the bar.

"All right," Judge Vredenburgh said, "if it is necessary." Max Eich marched over to Howell and they went out the door together. "This is a five minute recess," Judge Vredenburgh said, "but I don't want everyone going out. Too long getting back."

Abner sat down beside Bunting, who said, "What's this about Pete Wiener and some accident last night?"

"Gosh!" said Abner. "Forgot about it! Pete called after I got home. One driver was killed. Pete had the other for manslaughter. He ought to be up in jail here. I told Pete to help him get a habeas from Judge Irwin this morning."

"I sent for the police report. It may be over at the office, but I haven't seen it. Was this fellow drunk or anything?"

"I don't believe so," Abner said. "Pete seemed to think it wasn't his fault. He called up because he wanted to know if he could take bail. All I know is, the other driver was killed. Pete could give you the details. He said it happened right out there on route sixteen."

"Jesse Gearhart called the office about it," Bunting said. "He told Theda he wanted to find out about it. It's the son of a friend of his, or someone he knows, who called him from New York. Name's Mason."

"Well, that's too bad," Abner said. "Maybe somebody ought to tell Jesse his friend's son isn't back in New York now."

"Look, Ab," Bunting said. He paused. "If you don't mind, I'll give you a little advice. You seem to be afraid someone won't know that you don't like Jesse. Don't worry! Everybody knows; and that includes Jesse. Now, just ask yourself sometime what you're trying to do. I can tell you Jesse is wondering. You haven't quite done it yet; but keep on, and you can make yourself a pretty serious enemy there."

"Well!" said Abner. "How long since Jesse's been your dear old pal? As for what I'm trying to do, I don't happen to like the way Jesse horns in on things. I think he has a hell of a nerve to call you up and—"

"Yes; and what?" said Bunting. "What do you think he's going to do? Slip me a hundred dollars to let this fellow off? Has he ever made you a proposition?"

"If you mean, did he ever try to give me a can of opium and fifty or sixty dollars, no," Abner said. He laughed a little uncomfortably.

Bunting—he was angry in his controlled way; and that was understandable. Abner wouldn't have liked his own attitude in someone else—said, "Did he ever make you any kind of a proposition? Did he ever offer to do anything for you if you'd—to influence your official action? If you have any evidence we'll slap an indictment on him for corrupt solicitation of a public officer and ask Irwin to recall the grand jury this evening. Now, how about it?"

"Ah, be yourself, Marty!" Abner said, smiling. In other walks of life a man who showed signs of temper was often about to go off the handle; but in the law, with its special training in altercation, signs of temper usually meant that a man was prepared to make peace. When you noticed them, he was himself apprised; and his instinct set him to get hold of it, to avoid at all costs that fatal error. Abner said, "If you think Jesse would ever give anyone any evidence, you think he's more of a sap than I do. But you know what I mean; and that's what makes you sore. If you can honestly say that isn't what makes you sore, I apologize."

"You're what makes me sore, Ab," Bunting said. He was already over his annoyance. He turned his pointed nose and sharp dry gaze on Abner, his tight lips shadowed with a smile. "You don't do it often; but when you get high and mighty it gripes me. I'm older than you are, and I know a damned sight more about these things than you do. There's no reason why you can't get on with Jesse if you stop acting like a young squirt."

"I don't mind whether I get on with him or not. I'm not just saying that, Marty."

"I know you're not," Bunting said. "And that's the squirt in you! The reason you're in office is because I appointed you; and the reason I'm in office is because for twenty years Jesse has been seeing that our ticket was better; and then doing the hard work of getting people out to vote for it. You may not like the way he wears his hair; but I think most people, because he's shown sense and had experience, would rather take Jesse's advice than yours. So, don't forget it. Here's Howell."

"You still haven't told me what you want to do about the boy in jail," Abner said, getting up.

"We'll see," Bunting said.

Patient on the stand, Leming straightened himself with a look of relief at Abner's approach. Abner said, "Now, if you'll just continue, please. After the conversation with Howell, did you get back in the cars?"

"Yes, sir. We went to Rock Creek Road, and they brought Zolly in the house, and put him in this room upstairs. That's where they kept him all week—"

Abner thought to himself: I'll bet Marty's resigning! That would explain a good deal—why Marty was sore. Jesse had probably told him within the past week or so about the new jobs Judge Coates had mentioned in the Attorney General's office, and that one of them was his if Marty wanted it. In that event, they would need to decide soon who would run for district attorney here in the fall. This, then, was the moment; and though Abner had taken care never to show that he expected the job, or that he saw what everyone could see—that he was the logical choice; it would be idle to pretend to himself that he did not expect the nomination. Since he had been consciously preparing for it, and as far as it was modest or prudent, counting on it, for the last three years, it would be absurd to tell himself now that he did not want it. He tried to control, and he hoped, succeeded in concealing, that moderate yet essentially jealous ambition, that egotism of confidence in one's ability and one's resulting right, which can never be shown safely, since it intrenches on every other man's ego. This could be damped

down by a sense of proportion, by the ludicrousness of great passions directed at small ends—to be district attorney of a county whose importance
was well declared when the legislature put it in class five—but when he
finished such exercises, the job was not any less what Abner wanted. In fact,
Abner could see that his dislike of Jesse was not so frivolous—annoyance
at some blundering compliments, or various unprovable suspicions about
Jesse's integrity—as he might want to believe; but, short and simple, resentment at a power, without regular authority or justification in law, that
allowed Jesse to interpose between Abner and Abner's long standing aims
and (he might as well say it) deserts, the impertinency of Jesse's pleasure
or displeasure. Abner brought himself up short, and said, "All right. Now
who was there at the bungalow during the time Frederick Zollicoffer was
held prisoner?"

"All of us. Bailey and Basso and Howell."

"How about Dewey Smith?"

"No, he didn't live there. He came in to bring the groceries and
things."

"And Susie Smalley?"

"They had her there one day, a couple of nights, only. Not regular."

Abner hesitated, wondering if a sudden question might help Bunting
by putting on the record something useful about how Susie employed her
nights; but Bunting did not expect him to open that up, so he'd better let
it lie. He said, "And Frederick Zollicoffer was there. Did you see him every
day?"

"Not every day, I didn't. He was upstairs and they didn't leave me go
there. I heard him. I knew he was there. But I think only once I actually
saw him. On the fourth or fifth day."

"What was he doing on that occasion?"

"Well, Bailey was dictating, Zolly was writing a letter, and Bailey was
dictating what he is to put in that letter. One of the letters of Walter
Cohen."

"Now, do you recall hearing any reference in conversation between the
three men about what was to be done with Frederick Zollicoffer?"

"Oh, yes," said Leming. "I came in one night and heard them discussing about it—"

"Who was 'them'?"

"Howell and Bailey and Basso. They had been out, and they crossed
this creek—"

"Fosher's Creek?"

"Yes, sir. They come across that bridge, and they got out and looked
at it—"

"I object to this," Harry Wurts said wearily.

"All right, Mr. Wurts," Abner said. "Leming, is this what somebody told you?"

"Well, I heard them saying it."

"Who?"

"Bailey and Basso."

"They were in your presence?"

"Yes, sir. They said they found a good place to throw him."

"Anything else?"

"They said they looked at this bridge, and the water looked pretty deep to them; and this is where they were going to throw him."

Harry Wurts said, "I want to know whether that's a conversation or a conclusion."

"Isn't it clear, Mr. Wurts?" said Abner. "All right, all right! Is that what they said in your presence, Leming?"

"Yes."

"That that was where they were going to throw him in?"

"Yes, sir."

"Do you remember which one said that: Bailey, or Basso, or Howell?"

"Well, all of them said it."

George Stacey arose and said, "We want to get this clear, if we may, your Honor. Now, is that a conversation between these men, Leming, or a conversation with you?"

"Well," said Leming, spreading his hands, "they were talking amongst themselves; and I was in their presence then. Did I answer what you mean, sir?"

"Did he?" said Abner, facing George.

Abner's eye took in the shadowed ranges of seats rising in semi-circles behind the defense's table, the sloping aisle and Everitt Weitzel's bent, blue-coated figure at the top. Just beyond Everitt, he was astonished to see Bonnie and Inez Ormsbee. No doubt they had been downtown shopping together, and one of them had said: Have you been to the trial? Let's go in a minute, if it isn't too crowded. Abner unexpectedly found that he would like to think the suggestion had been Bonnie's—perhaps because she generally showed little interest (no more than she, or most people, felt) in what went on in court. In slight ways, mortifyingly silly, not-to-be-given-into, Abner had often felt this disappointment. He was not so unreasonable as to require everyone to find the routine of the law interesting—just unreasonable enough to be aware of the wish that Bonnie would, or would pretend to, take an interest; not because it was interesting, but because it was what he did.

Abner looked up at them a moment, his eyes narrowed against the high light of the pointed windows. He could see Bonnie's bare graceful arms, her face clear against the big brim of a straw hat. She was wearing a blue checked frock, and Inez (they must have got them from the same shop) was wearing a red checked one. They looked cool and pretty. Abner could not tell at this distance whether they were looking at him, too, or not. He smiled, in case they were, and turned back to Leming.

The evening of April seventeenth had been busy. At Bailey's direction, Basso arranged, in Leming's phrase, "to make a meet" for ten o'clock with Walter Cohen. Howell was to drive him over, but not to show himself; pretty clearly indicating that Howell could identify Walter Cohen for Basso, but must keep under cover because Cohen would know him if he saw him. However, something went wrong; and an hour later Howell called back to Bailey at the bungalow and said that Walter Cohen—they called him Buck—had not showed up. Bailey thereon ordered Leming to telephone Mrs. Zollicoffer.

"And did you?" said Abner.

"Yes. Bailey tells me ask for Buck when I called up, in case he was there. So when I called, Mrs. Zollicoffer got on the phone. I says, 'Is Buck around?' She said, 'No.' So I said, 'What is the matter with Buck wasn't there?' She said, 'He just called up a few minutes ago, and he has been waiting there.'"

"You reported this to Bailey, did you?"

"Yes, sir. When I came back, I said, 'That man is still over there.' They was waiting in this pay booth; so Bailey calls back; and they wanted to talk to me. It appears something don't look right to Howell; and he got scared, so he balks. He wouldn't stop the car. He said it looked like cops or somebody there. Bailey is beside me and he could hear this, so he takes the phone and says, 'Well, if you are afraid—' and he bawled him out pretty good. He says, 'You are not worth the sweat off my—'" Leming paused in embarrassment, and coughed. "He says, 'You aren't worth anything—' To Howell. He says, 'Maybe I am coming over there; and Bob and I will get it; and maybe we will give you something.'"

Judge Vredenburgh said, "I take it that was a threat."

"Yes, sir," said Leming. "Well, then Basso says, 'Aw, the hell!' You could hear him. So they went and made the meet, and in about an hour, they are back, and Basso has this package."

"What did the package contain, if you know?"

"Money. It counted to eight thousand dollars. Bailey counted it in the kitchen there."

"And then what happened?"

"Well, after they checked up the money, they seen they were four thousand dollars short—it was agreed this Buck was to give twelve thousand. So they counted it two or three times to make no mistake. Then Bailey took Basso and Howell in the other room, the dining room, and they held a conversation. So Howell came out after a couple of minutes. He says to me,

'You and Dewey go down to the delicatessen and get some beer and sandwiches for later. We are hungry.'"

"Yes?"

"I said, 'How about Zolly?' Howell says, 'I will be frank with you—' He did not look so good and I could see he had been having a drink. He says, 'Frankly, we are going to see Zolly home.' I says to him, 'I hope that you are.' I hoped that they had changed their minds. He begins to laugh and says, 'Yes, Zolly doesn't live here any more'—like in the song. I did not like the sound. So Dewey and I, we go for the sandwiches."

"And how long were you gone?"

"I should say an hour, hour and a half. We didn't hurry none. They were not gone so long; and when we came back, they were there."

"What were they doing?"

"They had out this money, piling it out in piles on the dining room table."

"Did you receive any of this money?"

"Yes, sir."

"How much did you receive?"

"They wanted to give me five hundred dollars. I told them I did not want it."

"But you took it?"

"I didn't want no trouble." From the way Leming looked at him, Abner could see that he was wondering if the admission might, in law, mean something he didn't know, and expose him in some fatal way. It was the answer to any doubts he or Bunting might have felt about Leming's intentions. Far from planning to double-cross the Commonwealth, Leming wilted secretly with a recurrent fear that the Commonwealth had it in mind to double-cross him. To Abner it seemed natural that, looking at Leming, one should not trust him; it might be worth remembering that Leming, returning the look, saw nothing a man would want to trust, either.

"How about the rest of the money?" said Abner. "Was it divided; and do you know how?"

"It was divided. I don't know for sure how. There is three piles, about the same. Oh, yes. Then Bailey sees Dewey look at them; so he reaches and takes this hundred dollar bill off of Howell's, and shoves it to Dewey."

"Now, it is your belief that while you and Dewey Smith were absent, getting the sandwiches, the other three, Bailey, Basso, and Howell, also went out, taking Frederick Zollicoffer with them?"

"I know they did. They are talking about it—"

"And the conversation was in your presence?"

"Yes, sir."

"What, if anything, did you hear them say in reference to Frederick Zollicoffer?"

"Well, one thing I heard them say; after they shot him, they tried to hitch the irons on him in the car; so they said they finally had to take him out of the car and lay him on the ground and tie the irons on him; and then they put him back in the car; and take him up to the bridge, and throw him over."

Harry Wurts stood up. "I object because this witness is testifying to conversations with the ridiculous implication that all three men are all saying the same things all together, all the time. I submit that this witness should be required to answer specifically, and identify the particular individual who made each particular statement."

Judge Vredenburgh shook his head. "No. Not if they were all present and heard it. Who made each particular statement is a matter for cross-examination."

"Continue," said Abner.

"Well, I heard them say—"

George Stacey said, "Now, is this supposed to be a conversation this man heard?"

"Yes, it is," said Bunting from his seat. "His Honor has been over all that, Mr. Stacey."

"Well, I think he ought to name the speaker."

Bunting said, "Where have you been for the last five minutes?"

Judge Vredenburgh said, "He may if he can. He does not have to. It is a matter for cross-examination."

"Well, should I go on?" said Leming.

"Yes," said Abner. "Do you remember who was speaking? If so, name him."

"Basso. Basso said they are there, driving down this road, and Bailey fires a shot. The first shot Bailey fired. And Basso said he fired the second shot."

Abner said slowly, "The defendant, Robert Basso, there—" With a startling simultaneous movement like men drilling, or a ballet, every juror's head turned "—told you that Bailey fired the first shot; and he, Robert Basso, then fired a second shot?"

Basso, looking at the table, lifted a hand and yawned. The simultaneously turned faces of the jury simultaneously quivered with shock and outrage at such calm callousness; but Abner guessed that the calm was assumed. Basso had been hit. The bald truth jarred him, because Basso's defense against truth was every man's defense; a sort of story of his life in which he, the ill-treated hero, understood all, explained all, excused all. It took care of everything—his shooting of Zollicoffer, his trapping by the police, his helplessness here on trial for his life; but it did not take care of that sudden turn of faces. In them, the world suddenly looked him to shame. Given time, that too might be taken care of; but at the moment, in anguish, he lost his grip; he weakly tried to outrage those who had outraged him.

Leming said, "That is right."

Abner said, "And do you recall any further conversation with the defendant, Robert Basso, that night about that time? A conversation about a gun?"

"That is objected to!" George Stacey said in some excitement. "It is decidedly leading!"

Judge Vredenburg said, "Objection overruled."

"Well," said Leming, "not exactly a conversation. Basso give me a gun. He says, 'Chuck it away somewheres.'"

"And did you?"

"Yes, sir."

"Did you throw it out of the car; or—"

"Objected to!" said Harry.

"Correction," Abner said. "Where did you throw it?"

"I threw it in a little creek, like."

"Do you know where the creek was?"

"Well, it was by the road. I think, what is called the Paper Mill Road."

"Do you know where the Black Cat Inn is?"

"Objected to!" said Harry. He got to his feet again. "I submit that the Commonwealth has no right to ask leading questions. Mr. Coates knows better than that; and I think these defendants are entitled to have the questions asked in the proper way. I object to that question."

"Objection sustained," Judge Vredenburgh said. "You must take care of the location, Mr. Coates."

Abner said, "Well, you did throw this gun into a creek?"

"Yes, sir."

"Would you recognize that gun again?"

"Yes, sir."

Abner lifted the paper laid over it on the table before Joe Jackman, and said, "I show you a gun that has been marked for identification as Commonwealth's Exhibit number—" He paused, and Joe, marking the tag, said, "Eight."

"Commonwealth's Exhibit number eight; and ask you to look at it." He picked the gun up and gave it to Leming. "Did you ever see that before?"

"This is the one that Basso had and give me the night Zolly was killed."

"At any time subsequent to the night when you threw a gun into a creek—" (that ought to hold Harry!) "—did you point out to Mr. Costigan, the county detective, the creek into which you had thrown it?"

"Yes, sir."

"And this is that gun?"

"Yes, sir."

With Frederick Zollicoffer disposed of, and the money divided, everyone left the Rock Creek bungalow. It was a fairly workmanlike job, and in engineering it Bailey showed the qualities that make a man a leader. Bailey might not have great intelligence or abilities, but his whole aim, thought and study was that of the born leader—to look out for himself; and he did it with that born-leader's confidence and intensity that draws along the ordinary uncertain man, who soon confuses his own interest and his own safety with that of the leader. The others did all the work—found Bailey a victim, arranged a hideout, collected the money. Bailey simply put a period to it with a revolver shot, and disposed of the body where nobody would ever find it. The bones of Frederick Zollicoffer with the wires and the iron weights could have lain in the bottom of Fosher's Creek until Judgment Day. That they didn't, that they lay there only a day or so over three weeks, was no one's fault but Bailey's. This was where the lack of abilities and lack of intelligence came in. The lack was apparent when Bailey took up crime, for the first test of ability and intelligence is to find a field of endeavor in which profits are large and risks small. A week or so after the murder, Bailey left the others, having got what he could out of them, and went to New York. He left his fairly workmanlike job behind; but he carried his fatal lacks with him; and if not this time, then the next, or the next, they must surely finish him.

Abner said, "How long did you and Basso remain at this house?"

"Around about ten days," Leming said. "I think ten days. Howell wanted we should get rid of this car; and after about a week, they were arguing about that. So finally Basso said he would take care of it—"

"Yes," said Abner. "He was arrested the twenty-sixth, according to our records. That would be a week. Now, during this period, from Sunday, April eighteenth, to Sunday, April twenty-fifth, did you have any conversations with Robert Basso?"

"Yes, sir," said Leming, recognizing what he wanted. "Yes. I had a conversation with him."

Harry Wurts, recognizing it just as well, said, "If this is going to be a particular conversation on some particular subject, I must ask that you distinguish it as to time and place, Mr. Coates, if you will."

"I am about to do that," Abner said. "You mentioned a conversation that you had with Basso," he said to Leming. "Was there something about it that fixed this conversation in your mind?"

"What conversation?" said Harry. "Did he have only one all the time they were there?"

"Yes," said Leming, "this particular one was in the bedroom, I remember—"

"Which particular one?" said Harry. "Mr. Coates asked you if you had any conversations. Did the Commonwealth prepare you carefully on one particular conversation?"

Bunting said, "Your Honor, who is conducting this examination in chief? The assistant district attorney, or Mr. Wurts? I must protest—"

Judge Vredenburgh tightened his lips, his cheeks dimpling with the repressed smile. "The witness says that he remembers a conversation in his bedroom with the defendant Basso. He may repeat this conversation, if Mr. Coates wishes him to. If the substance of it is not material, that will be what you may and should object to, Mr. Wurts."

Abner said, "Now, if you will just describe that conversation."

"Well," said Leming, "we are lying down in the bedroom, and we are talking about different things; so Zolly's name happened to be mentioned; and Basso spoke up and said he hated to have to kill any man in cold blood; so he told me about Bailey fired the first shot, that he fired the second."

"By 'he' you mean?"

"Bob Basso."

"Basso fired the second shot, and Bailey fired the first shot?"

"Yes," said Leming. He spoke with understanding regret. You could see that he thought Basso's expressed sentiment did Basso credit; and though he was obliged by his own interests to testify against Basso, he would not do Basso the injustice of denying him right feeling. "He said he never liked to kill a man that way; especially after he got to know the man so good while he was watching him; and he hated to do it. He watched him, and they played cards, and all; so he got to know him good. He hated to do it. He says if a man puts up a fight with him, he would not have minded it so much."

"Was anybody else there during this conversation?"

"In the house there was; not in the room."

"All right. Now, did you ever have any conversation with the defendant Stanley Howell in reference to Frederick Zollicoffer?"

"Yes, I had one. I was out driving with him, and we happened to come to that bridge."

"That bridge?" said Harry Wurts. Howell, beside Harry, was gazing at Leming with an intensity of mortal malice or fear. What the increased sickness and passion in his face proved—that he feared Leming would now tell some truth about him? That Leming, because he had lied about Basso, would now lie about him?—Abner found it hard to decide. He said to Harry, "The Fosher's Creek bridge, Mr. Wurts."

Leming said, "We are near that bridge. I asked Howell, I says, 'Did you really kill Zolly on the road, or did you kill him in the house?' There had been some talk about killing him in the house. He says, 'No, we killed him on the road.' I says, 'He is in there?' and he says, 'I guess it won't do no harm to tell you now. Yes, he is.' He never knew Basso told me."

"And where did you indicate when you said, 'he is in there'?"

"On the bridge. I pointed like to the deep water."

"The deep water of Fosher's Creek?"

"Yes."

"And that was where Stanley Howell said that he had helped Bailey and Basso put Frederick Zollicoffer's body after the shooting in the car?"

"Yes, sir."

Abner looked at Bunting, and Bunting nodded. To Harry, Abner said, "Cross-examine, Mr. Wurts."

Judge Vredenburgh said, "It is five minutes of twelve. I think it would be convenient to break now. Until one-fifteen."

He and Judge Irwin arose. Nick Dowdy tapped his block. With a shuffle and stir of people standing, stretching, beginning to speak, movement spread over the courtroom; the benches emptying, the jury going out the side door. Rocked back in his chair, Bunting produced and lit a cigarette. Leming, leaving the witness stand, stood motionless a moment and Hugh Erskine crooked a finger at him. Mrs. O'Hara went out the door with Susie Smalley. Adelaide Maurer came up to Abner. "Ab," she said, searching in her folded sheets of copy paper, "how much money was the ransom what's his name paid? I thought I heard someone say ten thousand; but your man said when they counted it, it was eight; and I gathered that what they had been expecting was twelve."

"Eight was what they got," Abner said. "Know what they asked for first? A hundred thousand. If they'd be any use to you, I think Marty would show you the notes. He has them right there. Ask him."

John Clark approached, tucking his glasses, which were attached to a chain that reeled into a little round metal case on his lapel, into his pocket. He shook his long scanty locks of white hair. His noble, large-nosed face was tilted up. His eyelids drooped over his blue eyes. "Abner," he said, "how's the Judge? All right for me to go around and see him? Or had I better not?"

"Why, yes, he'd be glad to see you, Mr. Clark," Abner said. "He's getting on fine." Abner did not know whether his father would thank him for that.

"Good," said Mr. Clark. "I may go up this afternoon, if it's all right. This woman of mine. I think she'd better plead guilty, Ab."

"We think she'd better, too," Abner said. He saw Bonnie and Inez Ormsbee standing up, getting ready to leave. "If she decides to, tell Marty, will you?"

"Well, now, of course, if I advise her to, she'll kind of expect, you know—"

Abner had observed before this, though every time it surprised him, that older men, lawyers like John Clark who had been in practice thirty or forty years, felt a sort of privilege, really, assumed a sort of prerogative, to ignore arbitrary canons of ethics; as though the law were something that applied to the lay public, and rules were for the record. They understood each other; not in a cynical or dishonest way, but just as a matter of common sense. You went through the forms in court, just as you addressed young Horace Irwin or Tom Vredenburgh as your Honor; but, for heaven sakes, John Clark could remember them when—

Abner said, "Mr. Clark, you know all we can tell her is that it's up to the Judge. She mustn't expect anything—"

"Stuff and nonsense, son!" said Mr. Clark. "How many guilty pleas would you get if nobody expected anything? And just where would you be if everyone stood pat and demanded that trial to which he has a constitutional right? I'll tell you. You'd be up the creek without a paddle."

"I guess we would," Abner said, "but I'm not district attorney. You explain it to Marty and see what he says. Would you excuse me a moment, sir? I have to speak to someone—"

The get-away, desperate rather than smooth, carried him to the aisle. Mat Rhea, the clerk of Quarter Sessions, met him there, holding up the printed pamphlet of the Criminal Trial List. "Look, Ab," he said, folding it open, "about number forty-six, here; Commonwealth versus Giuseppe, or however you say it, Bacchilega—God, what a name! First count, assault and battery with intent to kill; second count, aggravated assault and battery; third count, assault and battery. Have you got the papers on that? Judge Irwin wants to see them."

Maynard Longstreet, hurrying on his way back to his office (the *Examiner* went to press at one o'clock), brushed his hand across Abner's shoulder, saying, "What you say, Ab?" and went on.

"Hello, Maynard," Abner said. "No, I haven't," he said to Mat Rhea, "I don't know anything about it. Ask Marty—"

"Hey, well—"

"See you later!" He overtook Bonnie and Inez Ormsbee just past the swinging doors in the hall by the prothonotary's office. Inez said, "My, Ab, you were wonderful. I couldn't hear a thing you said."

"I'll talk to you about that afterwards," Abner said. "I want to make a date with your friend, here."

"See if I care!" Inez said, walking on. Bonnie said, "What do you want?"

"Not like that!" said Abner. "What are you doing tonight?"

"I don't know yet."

"Good," said Abner. "Want to go to the movies?"

"No. Anyway, I said I might go to the Nyces'."

The lofty hall, paved with worn, often cracked, squares of black and white marble, was thronged by the people leaving. Nick Dowdy, who had replaced his blue crier's jacket with a faded gray one of washable material, set on his head a limp, grimy straw hat, and relighted his stub of cigar, paused at Abner's elbow. His big, homely face, rounding in fat amiable curves under his chin, warmed as he looked at Bonnie. He grasped his hat at random and lifted it a little from his head. Around the cigar end clenched in his teeth he said, "Morning, Miss Drummond." He studied her face and arms calmly, with frank satisfaction. "You hear that fellow say when they jumped on him, this Zollicoffer, he thought it was the police? What do you think of that! Being a policeman must be a good business down there. Wish they'd give me a job." He poked Abner's arm with his fore-finger. "Harry Wurts wants to see you, Ab. He's down in the Attorneys Room." He lifted his hat a little higher, smiled, nodded several times at Bonnie, and dropping the hat back on his head, went waddling contentedly toward the door and his dinner.

"As we were saying," Abner said. "Come in here—" He pointed into the prothonotary's office, "before somebody else joins us. You don't want to go to the Nyces', do you? It will just be one of those brawls. Why don't we go out to the quarry and go swimming?"

For a moment Abner, concerned, thought that she was going to refuse. "All right," she said, "maybe Inez and Johnny would like to go."

"If they would, let them go by themselves. I'll take you somewhere and we'll have supper."

"What time?"

"Well, suppose I come around about six, or six-thirty. Do you like our trial?"

"Inez wanted to see it. Who was that awful little man on the stand?"

"He's not awful, he's wonderful," Abner said. "He's the Common-wealth's prize witness—"

In the door, Arlene Starbuck, Abner's secretary, had appeared. She was a small, dark, energetic girl; snub-nosed, cheerful, and intelligent. She had her hands full of papers. "Oh, Mr. Coates!" she said. "Thank goodness! Nobody knew where you were! You didn't come in this morning and—" Stepping in, she saw Bonnie, then. "Oh, hello," she said. "Oh, I'm sorry. I thought—"

"O.K.," said Abner. He smiled. "I had to go over to Mr. Bunting's office. Just couldn't make it."

"Well, there isn't so much, really. Excuse me just a minute, will you," she said to Bonnie. "I didn't know what to do about the praecipe in Overland Mutual. Did you want me to file it? Well, anyway, I guess you don't want to look at it now." Holding the sheaf of papers against her breast, she thumbed over the corners. "In the Steele estate," she said, "there's that petition for citation on the trustee business—there's a note from Mr. Leusden with a copy of the reply the Auditor General's office sent him. He wants to know whether, in view of it—they say no, we can't exempt the interest —you want to answer, to show cause why the tax shouldn't be paid."

"Call him up and say I'm studying it. Anything else?"

"That Mr. Willis, I think his name is, from Warwick, came in with Mr. Van Zant. I told them they'd better see Mr. Bunting."

"I don't place it. What did they want?"

"That was that F and B case last Wednesday." Arlene colored, apparently because of Bonnie's presence. In the office, fornication and bastardy were words in the day's work; but before another woman they offended modesty. "Mr. Van Zant said they were going to move to quash; he just wanted to show you some new evidence."

"Very kind of him," said Abner.

"That's all. I can take care of the rest."

"Thanks," Abner said. "That's fine, Arlene. I know it's hard on you when I don't get in. Look; this is a hot day. Why don't you just shut up this afternoon? Let it all go. I'll try to be there by eight tomorrow for a while."

"Well, I'll just finish typing the Blessington stuff. We have to file that appeal tomorrow, you know. There's the security—that's taken care of; it's entered. And I'm going to have the Register certify the record of proceedings had before him, now. Then we'll be all ready."

"Fine. Do you want another girl in for a few days?"

"Oh, Mr. Coates, I don't need any help! I would have had it done yesterday except the Judge gave me some letters." She nodded to Bonnie and left.

"She's a good kid," Abner said. "You know who her father was? Old Dan Starbuck, who used to drive the ice wagon. Remember the ice wagon? I guess that's before your time. Arlene is smart; and she never had any help, either."

"Well, a girl always likes to be appreciated," Bonnie said. "I'll bet she's very happy working for you."

"Who wouldn't be?" said Abner. "Where are you going?"

"I have to go. I have to get home to lunch. Are you coming this evening?"

"You know I am," said Abner. "Look, Bonnie—"

"Well, all right. I'll see you then."

Gifford Hughes, the prothonotary, came in, his gray mustache drooping. He sighed with the heat. "Marty's looking for you, Ab," he said. "Hello, Bonnie! My, don't you look pretty in all those checks! Nice and cool! Isn't this a scorcher of a day! Wish I were down at the shore!"

"Wish I were, too," said Bonnie.

"There, now," Gifford Hughes said, winking at Abner. "If I were your age, Ab, I'd know what to say to that."

"What you say now is pretty nice," Bonnie said. "Goodby, Mr. Hughes." She went out and passed quickly down the hall to the sunlight in the big door.

Abner turned and went back to the empty courtroom. A burst of muffled laughter sounded from the closed door of the Attorneys Room, and Abner went in. Bunting sat in the corner looking at a copy of a New York paper someone had left there. George Stacey was leaning against the mantel of the disused fireplace. Sitting on the old leather settee near the lavatory door was Jacob Riordan, generally allowed to be the best lawyer in Childerstown; and, to Abner's surprise, Jesse Gearhart.

"Gentlemen," Abner said, bowing. Harry was sitting on the oval table, facing John Clark who occupied the principal armchair. Over his shoulder, Mr. Clark said, "What do you think of a question like that, Jake? Impertinent, I call it."

"All I want to know, Mr. Clark," Harry said, "is whose woman she was. Didn't she confess to you? Didn't you conduct an examination in your office—I mean, verbal, of course? I need hardly say that my interest is purely scientific. And then, besides that, I have a dirty mind."

John Clark was heh-hehing, regarding Harry under his drooping eyelids with that old man's this-boy-isn't-such-a-damned-fool-after-all look. "What a client tells me or doesn't tell me is locked forever in this bosom," he said.

Jacob Riordan said, "What d'you want to mix up in it for, Johnny! It just makes everything longer. Wish they'd get through with these foreigners—going to have Miscellaneous Court next Monday, Marty?"

"We'll have court," Bunting said, throwing the paper aside. "But we won't be through the list."

"Well, when are you going to finish this thing, this murder?"

"Tomorrow, I hope. If Stacey and Wurts don't obstruct matters any better than they're obstructing them now."

"I never saw anybody so damned bloodthirsty as the district attorney," Harry said. "Due process for him is a kind of legal bum's-rush. It isn't decent."

"You want to see me?" Abner said, tapping his knee.

"Not any more. I have arranged matters with Mr. Bunting. Come on. Let's eat! My God, the time wasted around here! Enough to feed a French family for a year—"

"Ab," said Jacob Riordan, "I'm going to represent this Hamilton Mason, the boy in the accident last night. Marty said you talked to Pete Wiener about it. I'm going in to see him now. Anything I ought to know?"

"Not that I can tell you," Abner said. "The state police's charge is manslaughter, I understand. If it's the way Pete seemed to think it was, I guess we'll"—he looked at Bunting inquiringly—"be glad to do what we can to get it through as quickly as possible. I suppose it may develop at the coroner's inquest that there's no reason to hold him, that he can be discharged without returning the case to court."

"Judge Irwin is admitting him to bail," Riordan said. "Well, we'll get him out. I guess the boy'd like to go home."

Jesse Gearhart was looking at him; and Abner supposed that it was a moment to show his good will. He cast about in his mind for something to say; but a stubborn resistance of instinct frustrated him. He found himself shrugging. "That's certainly all right as far as I'm concerned," he said. "Did you want to speak to me, Marty?"

"Just about this," Bunting said, getting up.

Jesse, getting up, too, said, "Ab, are you going to be busy after court?"

"I don't think so," Abner said.

"Had something I wanted to talk to you about. Could you come over to my place when you finish?"

"Sure," said Abner.

It was useless for him to try to like the way Jesse put it. The request was natural, and naturally phrased; but since, for a dozen reasons, it could not be answered no, what was it but a command? Abner couldn't say: No, I haven't anything to see you about; and so he would go, obedient to a practical order; and stand, hat in hand, while Jesse instructed him. A man ought not to want anything in the world enough to do that.

Abner reminded himself that there was only his own guess to make him think that Jesse planned to instruct him, to offer him anything, to sound him out about running for district attorney. "Going to eat, Marty?" he said.

It was embarrassment speaking; but Abner was able to realize that he had acted straight against any good, though half-hearted, intention he might have had to please Jesse. Jesse, if he wanted to be sensitive, too, must read into the short answer and the turning away to speak to Bunting an indifference or contempt that he would have the right to resent far more than anything Abner resented in Jesse.

"Come on, come on," Harry said. "We have to be back here at one-fifteen. Want to eat, Mr. Clark?"

"No, no. Never eat lunch," John Clark said. Getting up, he went and extended himself on the leather couch, laying a handkerchief behind his head. He took the paper Bunting had discarded and set it like a tent over his face. "Let's have a little quiet around here," he said from under it.

They went out the back door, beneath the stone arch of the passage to the jail. In the parking space under the trees, Judge Vredenburgh was just getting into his car, which Annette was driving. "Ah," said Harry, gazing after her. "There's the little siren! Did you hear how Dick Nyce thought he was Ulysses? Dotty had to tie him to the mast."

They came down the diagonal walk and out of the shade to cross the blazing pavement of Court Street by the monument. Bill Ortt, his cap on the back of his head, his badge pinned to his sweat-soaked gray shirt whose sleeves were rolled as far as they would go up his tanned, tattooed arms, stood at the box from which the traffic lights were manually controlled. "Hi, Mr. Bunting," he said. He stopped the traffic two ways to let them go over.

"Thank you, my good man!" said Harry. "You know," he said, "in my subconscious mind, if any, that must be what I'm always hankering for. Traffic should halt when I appear; and then a breathless hush falls, broken perhaps by a few cries of 'Wurts for President!'" Lifting his panama, Harry held it at an angle, and bowed right and left to the halted traffic. They reached the sidewalk in front of the Childerstown House and pushed through the shadowed screen doors.

The dining room was crowded; but the round table in the corner where they usually sat had somehow been saved for them. "Want a drink?" said Harry. "No. You two pillars of public temperance have to sneak your drinks. And not you, George. The district attorney's watching, so they can't serve minors. Well, I will drink alone, and be damned to you! Hello, Marie. Get me a dry martini; and some cold cuts."

When they had ordered, Harry said, "Ab, see the paper, that *Times* up there? Well, remember your friend Paul Bonbright at Cambridge? I happened to see a note in back in the business section. They just made him a partner. Frazier, Graham, and Rogers. Pretty nice, I'd say, at his age."

Abner heard Paul Bonbright's almost forgotten name with surprise. With surprise, too, he saw that Harry, reporting the item, looked disconsolate; as though he were thinking of his own prospects, compared with Paul Bonbright's; or of what a partner in a firm like that made, compared to what he made. Harry stared a moment, his face discontented, down the crowded dining room. He met the eye of someone he knew, nodded mechanically, and looked back.

"Well, Paul can have it," Abner said. "How'd you like to be with Frazier, Graham, and Rogers, Marty?"

"No," said Bunting. "Not on a bet. Life isn't long enough."

"Huh!" said Harry, "a little bird, must have been a buzzard, told me that even you had simple aspirations or ambitions, one of which might be about to be realized. So never mind that exalted tone."

"If you go around talking to birds," Bunting said, "you know what happens to you? They put you in the booby hatch."

"At least I wouldn't have any expenses there," Harry said. "But that

twirp Bonbright! That's what gets you down! Right upon the scaffold,
wrong upon the throne! Why—"

Abner said, "He was no twirp. I think he won the Ames Competition
one year. I know he was on the Board of the *Review*—" Reminded of Paul
Bonbright, Abner could recall him very well—a thin faced, long jawed boy
with wiry black hair, of which he had already lost enough to make his high
forehead higher. He and Abner had never been close friends; but they were
cordial, casual acquaintances, borrowing cigarettes and books from each
other. It was an acquaintanceship begun by accident, a throwing-together
in sections and lecture seatings during the early days of first year, before the
class sorted itself out. Bonbright was one of the people who brought Abner
to realize, with dismay and some chagrin, that there are definite levels of
intelligence, brains of differing strengths and capacities. The innocent
supposition, entertained by most people, that even if they are not brilliant,
they are not dumb, is correct only in a very relative sense.

Abner had never been anything but modest about his own accomplishments. He knew that he didn't know much; and he had at least an inkling
of how much there was to know. At Childerstown High School and at college he had never led his class nor taken prizes; but, without being aware
that he did, he really blamed this on his failure to work hard, or any harder
than he needed to. He knew that he was often inattentive, that he loafed a
good deal, that at college he had been more interested in baseball and in the
debating society than in his courses. What he did not know, what Paul
Bonbright, among others, showed him, was that those abilities of his that
got him, without distinction but also without much exertion, through all
previous lessons and examinations, were not first rate abilities handicapped
by laziness, but second rate, by no degree of effort or assiduity to be made
the equal of abilities like Bonbright's.

The important truth was borne in on Abner, for he started with advantages that made him feel superior, able to help Bonbright. Many young
men, confronted with the case system, have to admit that for their first term
at least they literally do not understand anything. Abner had been born and
bred in a family three generations old in the law. At home, spare rooms
were lined with old reports and piled with back numbers of law journals.
Engravings of Judge Story and Chancellor Kent hung in the hall. At table,
the jargon of the courts, the law Latin, the principles of jurisprudence were
ordinary conversation—what Father, sitting in Common Pleas, had been
doing today. Abner knew the language. Of course, the assignments, the
amount of stuff they expected him to read and memorize, staggered him;
but he worked as hard as he could, harder than he ever had in his life, and he
imagined that he was doing about as well as the rest of them. He found out
that he was mistaken when Bonbright gradually stopped consulting Abner,

the oracle, and began to correct and advise him; and then inevitably they saw less of each other, and Paul took up with his mental peers. Abner said to Harry, "Is it Bonbright's fault that he has more brains than you have?"

"Few if any people have more brains than I have," Harry said. "The Ames Competition! A petty triumph of grinds and pedants! Why, it seems to me you were in that one year. No, no; a Wurts would never sink so low."

"Well, I only sank low enough to come out last," Abner said. "They gave the Scott Club an old *Bouvier* for a booby prize. If you think the man who wins doesn't have to be good—"

George Stacey had been attending closely. He said, "I guess it must be pretty tough up there." He was ready in his diffidence (untinctured, because they were older, not his rivals, with ill-feeling) to admit that his own degree was not quite in the same class.

"Tough!" said Harry, now reminded that after all it was his school. "Why, you come up there with an A.B. from some hick college and they eat you alive. You know what the first thing they say to you is? They say, 'Gentlemen, look well at the man on your right and on your left, because next year one of you will not be here.'"

The classic exhortation was impressive, Abner must admit, when you first heard it. Harry might like it still; but Abner found that he himself definitely didn't. It rang with that unpleasant, really childish, cocky quality which went with the rigor and the exacting standards. It reminded you of certain professors, men of great learning and wisdom; but they none the less sought and enjoyed the poor and mean sport of traducing the stupid. Along with torts or contracts you learned in their lectures a lot of things like that; things you would have to unlearn afterward, or be the worse for all your life.

Bunting, who had prepared for his bar examinations at night school, and in Judge Irwin's office, and who had often found that he knew as much as (and sometimes more than) graduates of the best universities, was listening with the look that answered all these pretensions. He was amused to see Harry (the more fatuously, because it was unconscious) pluming himself to George, not on what he knew, which would be absurd enough, but with an ultimate, almost indescribable absurdity, on where he had learned it. Watching Bunting's face, Abner was jolted to guess that Bunting in the dry and cool privacy of his own mind might very well consider him, Abner, touched with the same ridiculous presumption, ready with the same vauntings and vaporings; so dear to those who had them, so laughable to everyone else.

Mat Rhea, picking his teeth thoughtfully, walked by, headed for the door. Over Harry's head, he said, "Thick as thieves, you look. Who's doing who?" After him came Mr. Wells, who ran a jewelry and watch-repairing shop. "Got that clock fixed for you, Marty," he said. "Any time you want it. Going to cost you a little. I had to replace a lot of bushings. It's a dandy, though. You could get your money out of it, any time you wanted to sell it."

"What's that?" said Abner.

"Old clock I bought at an auction," Bunting said. "I like clocks. If I had some money, I'd collect them."

"Indeed?" said Harry Wurts, arising. "Well, if you gentlemen will now excuse George and me, I have a certain stenographic transcript I wish to pick up—"

"I wouldn't bother, if I were you," Bunting said.

"Of course you wouldn't," Harry said, taking his check. "The secret of my success is that I leave no stone unturned. Do you know what Fisher Ames said of Alexander Hamilton? I often think of it in connection with myself. He said: 'It is rare that a man who owes so much to nature descends to depend on industry as if nature had done nothing for him. His habits of investigation were very remarkable; his mind seemed to cling to his subject until he had exhausted it—' Let it be a lesson to you. Come on, George."

When they were alone, while Bunting was swallowing the last of his coffee, Abner said, "What's Jesse want to see me about?"

Putting down his cup, Bunting said, "You'll have to ask him."

"Don't you know?"

"I might have thought I knew last week," Bunting said. "But for all I know now, he may be going to tell you where to head in."

"And for all he knows," Abner said, "that may be what I'm going to tell him."

"That's right," Bunting said. "I've said my say, Ab. Maybe, like Harry, you think all this is beneath you and you ought to be in New York at Frazier, Graham, and Rogers, or somewhere, getting your twenty-five thousand and your stomach ulcers. I thought you had better sense."

He pushed back his chair, lit a cigarette, and, bending forward, put both elbows on the table. "We didn't mean to tell everyone, because it upsets things; but it seems to be getting out anyway, and you certainly have a right to know, if you care. I'm going into the Attorney General's office in the fall. It's some special trial work I'd like to do. If you want my job here, I'd like you to have it, because you're the best man for the job. You know the ropes now, and you could handle it. Both Judge Irwin and Judge Vredenburgh would like to have you. I always thought it was what you wanted; but I may be wrong. You know about that."

Bunting narrowed his eyes and looked at the smoke rising from his cigarette. "I've done what I could for you, naturally. I've been making you do all I could in this trial, because I wanted it to be as much your work as mine, getting these birds convicted." He shrugged. "I thought your idea was—I mean, that you had it pretty well settled in your head that you'd go on being a hick lawyer, if Harry wants to call it that. I mean, marry and settle down, and maybe in the end get a judgeship—they seem to run in your family. I don't say it amounts to a lot. You won't get rich and you won't get famous; but you have a good life; one that's some use, and makes some sense."

"I agree," Abner said.

"Well, I wonder if you do," Bunting said. "Maybe you just think you do. Look at Harry! That business about your friend was eating him up—"

"Look, Marty," Abner said, "I don't know about Harry, but I know about me. I haven't any use for that kind of a job, and I doubt if it would have any use for me. I'm not good enough. I don't know enough law—"

Bunting said, "I was in a big office for a couple of years after I was admitted to the bar. You know, twelve dollars a week, while you're learning the flourishes. It really isn't law at all. It has nothing to do with justice or equity. What it really is, is the theory and practice of fraud, of finding ways to outsmart people who're trying to outsmart you. Sure, it takes brains! Sure; they'll pay you anything if you can do it for them. But you only have one life."

"I know that," Abner said. Bunting was not much given to speeches; and to hear him making one, and making it so earnestly, not only surprised Abner, but, by the concern or regard it showed, touched him. "And thanks, Marty. I see your point, and I'm going to bear it in mind."

"Bearing it in mind doesn't do any good," Bunting said. "You ought to get yourself organized. Why don't you get married?"

"Well," said Abner, "anyway, I don't see the connection. And if you don't mind my saying so, I don't think I could do it, just on someone else's advice."

"All the same, and I know it's none of my business, there is a connection."

"Gosh," said Abner, "that's a romantic idea!" He stood up. "Say, was that the bell? My watch is wrong."

Coming into the lobby to pay their checks at the cashier's desk, they could hear the heavy tolling from the courthouse tower signaling five minutes to go.

In the shadows and heat of the afternoon Harry Wurts grew warmer as he worked on Leming. Harry's face was red; his cheeks shone with moisture; and little beads of sweat caught in the quarter inch hairs of his sandy mustache; but he worked without distress. Like an athlete warmed to the game, the more he sweated, the better he felt. He tackled his hard problem with all his might, elatedly bucking the odds against him.

The books tell you that the object of cross-examination is to sift the evidence and to try the credibility of the witness. This may be done by showing that the witness has little or no means of knowing what he is talking about, or that his memory for facts is poor anyway, or that his motives are crooked and self-interested or that his character is such that nothing he says should be believed. Harry had no wish to sift strong evidence—a fool's trick, in which you bring out, and with telling effect because you do it, any points in your opponent's favor that he might have overlooked. Harry could hardly hope to show that Leming had no means of knowing the facts, or that his memory was at fault. As for Leming's motive, that was conceded. He was testifying to save his skin. Harry's best hope, and a poor one, was to show that Leming ought not to be believed. There, as in the matter of motive, he was unfortunately anticipated. Harry could not make impressive the point about Leming being a criminal or a drug addict, because the jury already knew. Harry, questioning Leming on his criminal record, only bored the jury. The long series of arrests and trials and short prison terms fell, if anything, short of the mark set by the jurors' imaginations. At this stage they asked themselves not: Can such things be? but: Is that all he did?

When regular approaches, felt out carefully, proved all to be blocked, there remained for the man with the temerity to use them, irregular ones; and Harry was that man. The cardinal principle, never cross-examine at random, posited a working hypothesis that would be good enough to convince a jury if the opposition allowed it to stand. It stood or fell in so far as the facts, or most of them, fitted in. Anybody could see the folly of deliberately asking for more facts on the off-chance that they would prove to be facts for which there was a place. The measure of Harry's resource was the bold admission to himself that the only hypothesis the facts would fit was the Commonwealth's own. The measure of his hardihood was his decision to admit his client's guilt, to abandon the strong position prepared for him by the law in its presumption of his client's innocence. The measure of his acumen was his cool grasp of the fundamentally changed position. The shoe was on the other foot. Bunting would have to find a place for every random fact Harry turned up, so the more the merrier. The only plan Harry had or needed was to go in wherever the Commonwealth paused or backed off, and lug out whatever was there.

Harry said, "Now during this period, you mentioned a trip to New York on which you were gone several days. Was that something you just made up?"

Leming said, "I went to New York."

"And what did you go to New York for?"

"Well," said Leming, "I went over to get something for myself."

"Ah?" said Harry. "What?"

"Some narcotic," Leming said. His manner was deeply distressed. Perhaps he really was ashamed to have to confess his vice; but it was also possible—Leming exhibited curious little flashes of shrewdness—that he knew very well that shamefaced testimony always passed as credible testimony; and a man who confessed what he seemed to want to conceal often gained more from the apparent triumph of honesty over dishonest inclination than he could lose from the substance of the confession.

"Narcotics?" Harry said.

"Yes, sir."

"Opium?"

"Yes."

"Are you a—" Harry hesitated while he selected his term—"a yen hawk?"

"I was," said Leming. He looked apologetically at the jury.

"You smoke opium, do you?"

"I did."

"How long have you been doing that?"

"I did it a couple of years."

"Quite a steady user, eh?"

"Well," said Leming, "I had a habit; yes."

"That means you smoke how often?"

"Twice a day."

"So you went to New York on an opium jag?"

"No, sir. I went to get some."

"You—" Harry stopped. He must have seen or sensed Leming's success with the jury. They felt sorry for him, sitting meek and sad there, while Harry lashed sarcastically at him. Harry said, "Correction. Now, Leming, you testified about a car that came into the street the night you left—"

"No," said Leming. "I never saw that car. It was they told me. Basso says it looks funny, me going, and that car right after. They were sore."

"And what did their soreness signify to you, if anything?"

Leming spread out his hands. "It looked like to me what I told them; they didn't trust me good; like they felt I was selling them out."

"That must have been a shock," Harry said sympathetically, "I mean, to find they had you sized up so well."

"I don't get you, sir."

"You say they thought you were going to sell them out!" Raising his voice harshly, Harry said, "Well, were they right or wrong? That's what you're doing now, aren't you?"

Leming tightened his mouth and color came into his cheeks. He looked at the carpeted floor before the bench and said, "You think so." He nodded several times as though to show that both the question and the lack of understanding that prompted it were what he had expected.

"Yes, I think so," Harry said, watching intently these small maneuvers and plays of expression.

"I don't think so," Leming said. He screwed his mouth up further, wagging his head in silent conference with his conscience. He let it be seen that he had an inner knowledge of one or more circumstances that changed everything.

"Well, you're certainly selling out Howell and Basso, aren't you?"

"No," said Leming.

"No? Why, of course you are! Selling them all out. Trying to save your own skin! Aren't you?"

"No." Leming shook his head. Lifting his eyes, he looked sadly at Harry; but, unable to maintain a gaze to equal Harry's, he looked away.

"What?" said Harry. "How about the promises they made you, if you'd testify for the Commonwealth? You knew they were making a bargain with you, didn't you?"

"Nobody give me promises."

"No promises? Didn't they tell you you'd get off with a short jail term if you sold out Howell and Basso?"

"No."

Seeing Bunting and Abner smiling, Harry was obliged to smile, too. "I am glad to hear it," he said. "Now, you've talked to the district attorney, Mr. Bunting, the man sitting there smiling, haven't you?"

"Never about promises or anything."

"But you've talked to him?"

"Oh, yes."

"Down in your cell in jail here in Childerstown?"

"It was nothing pertaining—"

"I am asking you," said Harry, "haven't you had talks with the district attorney in your cell?"

"Yes."

"And in his office, haven't you?"

"Yes. To him and the other; to Mr. Coates."

"And you have your attorney, Mr. Servadei, watching this case, helping you, haven't you?"

"Yes," said Leming. "My attorney is here." He sat tense in the stand, straining to meet this beating about of questions. He added, "But he don't help me at all."

The strain of Leming's harassment, conveying itself to the court and jury, was broken by laughter. Judge Vredenburgh drew down the corners of his lips, looking at Servadei, who bowed and smiled. "No," said Harry, smiling too, "I didn't really think Mr. Servadei was responsible for these yarns of yours. You just made them up yourself, didn't you?"

"No, sir."

"You didn't make anything up. I see. They told you, then, that all they wanted from you was the truth, that that was all you had to tell to be let off?"

"Yes—no, sir. They never—"

"Well, which? Yes? No? A little of each?"

"No, sir."

"All right. We'll leave that for the moment. Now, who was at this bungalow the night you left to snatch Zolly? Bailey? Basso? Howell?"

"Yes, them."

"And Smalley, of course?"

"Susie? No. She went back to the other house. She wasn't there."

"Sure she wasn't in the bungalow that night?" Harry's deliberate lack of plan made it hard to follow his intention; but Abner supposed that Harry was willing, if he could, to involve as many of them as possible, to show that the defendants had been arbitrarily selected for some sinister reason of the Commonwealth's.

Leming said, "I am positive. Bailey said she was to go. He didn't want she should know about it."

"I see. But some of the time she was there living with you. Why? Why didn't she stay at the other house?"

"Well," said Leming. He spread his hands out again and shifted in his seat. "Well, after we moved up to Rock Creek, she didn't right away know where we went. We would stop and see her, Howell and me; but we did not tell her where the bungalow was. Then Bailey, after a few days,—you see, there was this jail break thing. He did not want to go out."

To Abner, Bunting said, "Get that, will you? Clark said he'd plead her guilty, but you never know until he does."

Leming said, "So Bailey says, after awhile, he would like to see Susie. He asks Howell is Howell sure she is all right? And Howell says, 'She is all right, you don't have to be afraid of her, isn't she, Bob?' he says to Basso. And Basso says, 'Yes, she has proved all right to us.' So Howell and I, we bring her up."

Abner glanced over at Susie Smalley. The seat John Clark had occupied was empty and she sat isolated with Mrs. O'Hara. She was chewing gum slowly, her face sullen and resigned in the afternoon shadows. Whatever her allure was, it had gone out of her. The symbols of it, the dye-spoiled hair and the tight green dress, were set on her like the hair and clothes of a dummy. Perhaps she was thinking of the prison days ahead, which she knew all about, and which she might have promised herself last time she would never risk again. Yet here she was; and she might be mutely arguing why—or, even, seeing why; but what else could she have done? They—the boys—were going to make a lot of money, and she left it to them. She proved all right to them; keeping her mouth shut, doing what she was told, giving Bailey what he wanted; until the whole thing blew up in their hands. What she herself wanted out of it all only she could know; but it was cer-

tain that she never wanted to be here, a prisoner, waiting her turn to hear
what her acquiescence had cost her this time. Of course it was a mistake to
think that Susie deserved sympathy. If she were the victim of misfortune,
it was mostly the misfortune of being herself; but Abner knew from the
records that she was just Bonnie's age; and the circumstance affected him.
It was one of the ordinary horrors of life.

Harry Wurts said, "You brought her up. To do the cooking and light
cleaning, I suppose?"

"Yes. She cooked," Leming said.

"And after she had done enough cooking to hold you all for a while, she
left," Harry nodded. "And didn't come back until the night Zolly was
killed?"

"I never said that," Leming answered.

"Then I am mistaken?"

"Very much."

"When did she come back?"

"She never come back. We went back, after, to where she was."

Harry said, "Now, Dewey Smith was there, too, wasn't he?"

"Well, he come in."

"He heard the discussions there in the bungalow, didn't he?"

"Never at no time."

"Never at no time!" repeated Harry with pleasure. "Quoth the raven;
never at no time!"

"Your Honor," said Bunting, "does the witness have to submit to Mr.
Wurts' feeble witticisms? He is here to be questioned on a serious matter."

Harry said, "Strike out the raven. Now, you know Dewey was there
with you, and he took part in planning the kidnapping, didn't he?"

"I will tell you why not," Leming said. "In the first place, they never
put that much confidence in him."

"It's too bad for them that they didn't feel the same way about you, isn't
it? You mean to say he never came there while Zolly was in the bungalow?"

"He come; but he didn't know about Zolly. I will tell you why he came.
He had been like a steamfitter, an assistant. The pipes there is muddy, and
he went down and cleaned the tank. He used to do something for Susie
when she was there; fix the heater in the cellar, and drained the tank, the
hot water tank. About six or seven times to my knowledge."

"You mean, while he was there he was always doing odd jobs like that,
so he couldn't have heard what was being discussed?"

"He would never put himself in their way when they had any conversation; and they will tell you that themselves."

"But you put yourself in their way?"

"Oh, yes. They discussed with me."

"You were just as much involved in all of it as they were, weren't you?"

Bunting said, "I object to that as a conclusion."

Harry waved his hand. "You knew as much about what went on as Bailey or Basso or Howell did?"

Abner admired Harry. The cards were stacked, and he had not been dealt a single good one, yet Harry held those he had with confidence. Playing them close to his chest, Harry exhausted every resource of bluff or finesse to make them count. Would Leming want to say that there was no difference between himself and the others? He might not. He might think it better to say that he had not shared fully in their wickedness. If he said that, his competence was going to be open to attack.

Leming, however, was no novice. He had been in traps before; and even when he could not see them, he sensed them. He said warily, "I didn't know all that business, no."

"You did not?" said Harry.

"No."

"You've told all of it here on this witness stand, haven't you?"

"What I heard them say, yes."

"As a matter of fact, you're the one who planned this kidnapping of Frederick Zollicoffer, aren't you?"

Leming said, "It is pretty hard to plan something when you don't even know them."

"You knew Zollicoffer?"

"I never knew him."

"You knew Mrs. Zollicoffer well enough to sit on that stand and call her Marguerite."

Under the steady pelting of accusation, Leming had the look of a man caught in a cloudburst. He hunched himself up; he glanced about for shelter. If he had been able to, he would certainly have scurried away as fast as he could. He was not nervous in the desperate, distracted sense that Howell was nervous, full of twitches and fidgetings; he was simply shaken and pulled-about so that he could hardly think. Taking hold of the rail in front of him, Leming said, "If I ever saw his wife before, I hope God never lets me get off this stand!"

"If I were you," Harry said, "I would be careful how I invited divine intervention in my affairs. You knew her well enough to call her Marguerite."

"When the phone call was made, they tell me, ask for Marguerite."

"You used to buy opium from Zollicoffer, didn't you?"

"Never," Leming said.

"You knew he was a dealer in opium?"

"I never knew the man."

"You were a salesman for him yourself, weren't you?"

"You are wrong there. I—"

"You peddled dope all around this part of the country for Zollicoffer, didn't you?"

"I never peddled it. I used it, but I never peddled it."

"You are an addict, an opium user?"

Bunting said, "He has already answered that!"

"If you don't mind, Mr. Bunting," Harry said, "I will cross-examine without your assistance. You were an addict, and to get the stuff, you handled it for Zollicoffer, delivering it to customers, or bringing them around, didn't you?"

"Never."

"And the only explanation you have as to why you so easily and naturally spoke of Mrs. Zollicoffer as Marguerite is that it was a name somebody told you to use in a phone call two months ago?"

"That is right," Leming said.

Shaking his head softly, rolling up his eyes, Harry turned and paced toward the Commonwealth's table; halted; and started back. From the bench, Judge Vredenburgh said, "The Court will now recess for five minutes." He stood up, passed along behind the bench, down the steps, and through the door to his chambers.

George Stacey had signaled Max Eich, who came over to Howell; and Bunting said to Harry, still close to the Commonwealth's table, "Putting on the act again, eh?"

Harry smiled. He shoved aside Bunting's file folders and sat on the table. "Bunting," he said, "let me look at you. You must be pure intellect, mind untrammeled! Your airy dance of ideas bewilders us earth-bound creatures. I don't want to drag you down to our brute level—"

"Mr. Coates," Everitt Weitzel said.

"Yes," said Abner, turning to look at him.

"Mr. Riordan asked me when there was a break to ask you could you see him just one minute. He's in the other room, there."

"Better see him later, hadn't I, Marty?"

"No," said Bunting. "Go ahead. He probably wants to know what to tell the Mason kid about the inquest. Say we'll have it the day after tomorrow. I'll fix it with Doctor Hill."

Abner arose and went over to the door. Moving along with him, Everitt said, "Boy's there too."

"Mr. Gearhart there?"

"I didn't see him."

Like the Attorneys Room, the room next to it was lined with the books of the law library. Jake Riordan, smoking a cigar, was sitting across the table from a young man with short curly hair and a piece of adhesive tape diagonally down his forehead. They both got up, and Jake said, "Ab, this is Mr. Mason. I wanted him to meet you before he went home."

"How do you do?" Abner said, holding out his hand. He had been—for no reason at all, when he thought about it—expecting some snotty little brat with the marks of too much money on him, and the cock-sure, even contemptuous, assurance that his father would take care of him. Mason looked as though he thought nobody would take care of him; and while his clothes were good and expensive, they had necessarily been slept in; and on the sleeve of his coat was a large, partly removed stain—blood. He gave Abner a damp hand. "Have a cigarette," Abner said, offering the package he had taken out. "Were you hurt?"

"No, sir. Just cut my face a little." He took the cigarette and after several tries, got it lit from the match Abner was holding.

"Well, it's a nasty thing to have happen," Abner said. "We hear it wasn't your fault. That true?"

"I don't see how it could have been, sir. It happened pretty quick. But I was on my side. The state police said the tire marks showed that."

"Did they say why they held you?"

"Well, one of them said it was the law. He had to, sir."

"He didn't have to charge you with manslaughter. You hadn't been drinking, had you? I don't mean, were you drunk. I mean, had you had a drink any time that evening?"

"Absolutely not, sir."

Jake Riordan said, "Some of these motor police, Ab, don't show very good sense. The officer should have charged him with being involved in a fatal accident, and the J.P. could have taken bail, and that would be that."

"Yes," said Abner, "that's the only thing." He looked at the boy, and it did not seem likely that Mason was lying; but the first principle in matters like this was not to jump to conclusions. It was true that the police sometimes didn't show good sense; but, in general, the police, particularly the state police, knew and performed their routine business with intelligence and precision—in motor vehicle cases they were almost always right. If the driver disagreed about the speed or circumstances, he might make a case for himself when it was his word against the officer's; but if corroborative evidence appeared, inevitably it showed that the driver was mistaken. As Mason said, those things happened quickly; and alarm, self-interest, and shaken nerves obfuscated the moment's impressions. The crisis past, very few people failed to tamper with their recollections—just a touch here and there to details which, with only a second or fraction of a second to fix them, could easily be altered, or even wiped out, leaving the conscience clear for any practical purpose of meeting a man's eye or swearing a solemn oath.

Abner said, "I don't mean to doubt Mr. Mason; but we haven't had a police report yet. And, of course, we'll want to see the arresting officer. If he has no specific grounds for the charge, we'll have to take that up with his superiors. Well, Jake, Marty's fixing the inquest for the day after tomorrow. Mr. Mason understands what bail means, doesn't he?"

"Yes, sir," Mason said.

"All right, then," said Abner. "See you both Friday." The boy's anxious, uncertain face led him to add, "Don't worry about it. You go home and get a good night's sleep and you'll feel better."

In the courtroom they had already resumed.

Harry, his arms folded, his head tipped up as though he were admiring the shadowed, gold-framed portraits on the high wall behind Judge Vredenburgh, said, "And during that time, were you given any opium?"

"Never."

"No," said Harry. "It was taken away from you down there, wasn't it?"

"I had none on me," Leming said.

"You had to go without it, didn't you?"

"Yes, sir."

"And prior to that you had been smoking regularly?"

"That is right."

"And when they took it away from you, you wanted it, didn't you?"

"Yes, if you got a habit, you want it."

"And to get it, you knew you'd have to testify, didn't you?"

Leming said, "That is a lie."

"You mean, a misapprehension on my part, I hope. It was taken away from you, and you needed it?"

"I needed it," Leming said doggedly, "but I didn't get it."

"They cured you, cold turkey, didn't they?"

"I cured myself. They help me."

"Now," said Harry, "isn't it a fact that since you've been in jail here in Childerstown you've been getting narcotics?"

"Never."

"You weren't given some last night after you got back from this court?"

"No."

"You deny that?"

"I positively deny it. I was given sleeping pills, but no narcotic."

"Oh!" said Harry. "You call it sleeping pills!"

"It isn't opium."

"How often does the doctor come to see you down at jail?"

"Well, he stops sometimes every night or so. He asks me how I am feeling, something like that."

"But he always gives you something, doesn't he?"

"He left a pill for me last night. He says, 'If you cannot sleep, ask the guard for it.' And I didn't take it last night."

"I see," said Harry. "He leaves enough pills for you to go over one night to the next?"

"He leaves pills; but they don't do me no good; so he might just as well not leave me them."

"You'd much rather have it to smoke in a pipe, wouldn't you?"

"Well, not now."

"You wish us to believe you are all cured. How long have you been a doper?"

"How long have I been what?"

"A doper; a user of morphine."

"I never used morphine in my life."

"Just opium, eh? How long have you used that?"

"I told you a couple of years. Around about that."

Abner had been listening abstractedly. He looked at Bunting, who sat relaxed, following the questions and answers with a sort of invisible pointing of the ears, in the habit of court practice that hears, you might almost say, without listening; though paying little outward attention, missing nothing. Bunting held in his hand an inverted pencil, tapping the eraser at measured intervals on the yellow pad before him. He had written: *Doctor Janvier*, the name of the jail physician; so probably he intended a memorandum to answer Harry's insinuations. Next to it he had idly sketched a forlorn, lop-eared dog; with, on second thought, a large bone in its mouth.

Bunting's face, bent down, tipped to the side, caught light from the high windows on the fine textured skin where, around the lips and eyes, the first wrinkles were forming. His flat firm line of cheek and jaw was a good one. Starting, when young, with no claim at all to handsomeness, Bunting's face could be seen to have gained, as the years passed, a fineness of finish. His pointed, convex profile and long neat-lipped mouth took on character. The use of good sense, the habits of control and judgment, informed every feature with strength. Abner was aware of a mild envy, a discontent with his own looser, younger look.

Across the floor at the defense's table Abner could see George Stacey, who was giving good enough examples of what discontented Abner with himself. George's expression showed great but uncertain effort. A look at him told you that George did not know what might happen next, nor what he would do then, if for any reason he were expected to do something. George's fresh, nicely formed face was tense. He was watching Harry closely and calculatingly; he wanted to learn the secret of that assurance. He would like to imitate that ease, that ready command that sent the witness here and there. Knowing his own failings of self-consciousness, the vigor and variety of Harry's attack on Leming probably discouraged George. George had a hand up to his chin, the end of his thumb at his lips, rubbing his teeth with the nail. Beyond George, Basso sat slumped down. He seemed to be asleep. Abner touched Bunting, to point it out to him; but at that moment, Basso moved his eyelids.

On the other side, next to Harry's empty chair, Howell sat huddled, as though, in spite of the oppressive warmth of the shadowed, unmoved air, he felt cold. Howell kept his chin down, half hiding his pale sick face; but his small baleful eyes shifted constantly in furtive arcs. Perhaps in thought he was acting out dramas of escape—perhaps he saw himself starting up, with a blow disposing of one or more of those old men, the tipstaffs; by his speed, making the upper door before the state police at the lower doors woke up. Out the doors and down the hall, he would probably meet no one. Before the courthouse (he was the author of this and could have in it anything that suited him) would be a car at the curb, with the ignition key carelessly left in. Then, with the speed of thought, the engine roaring up, the flashing dart-away down the sun-filled street; off, at seventy miles an hour, while the police whistles died behind him across the summer countryside—only, Howell never made the first move; and he never would. The galvanic fear of death, applied too often and too long, wore out the body's responses. Howell did not stop fearing; but he remained paralyzed, and only his mind hit and ran and got away.

Abner studied him thoughtfully; not himself insensible to that distracting fear; and well enough able to imagine himself in Howell's place. In a month or two Stanley Howell would be dead. They would pronounce him dead, unstrap his body, and carry it out and bury it. Horrible and inconceivable as the idea might be to Howell, that was what was going to happen, not some day, but within a few weeks; as soon as his appeal was turned down with the direction to carry into execution the sentence of the law that you, Stanley Howell, be taken hence by the sheriff—

The words, hard for a man to hear without trembling for himself as well as for Stanley Howell, made Abner recoil. Along with Howell they took hence something in himself—the pleasures of living, the confidence of days to come, the succession of the seasons, the events of the years; and though, of course, in the end it was all one (Beulah cemetery lay there in the moonlight and tree shadows last night)—better later than now! Abner remembered reading in some book, some school book probably, about Greek history or something, of Socrates having been supposed to say, when they told him that the thirty tyrants had condemned him to death: "And Nature, them." The come-back, though noble and even snappy, did not make much sense. Abner shook his head.

Beside him Bunting drew a weary breath. To Abner he murmured,

"Don't know whether this wears down the witness; but it certainly wears me down."

Harry said to Leming, "When you speak of these little cans, little packages of opium, they cost about how much?"

"Oh," said Leming, "there's different sizes. You get small ones; five dollars."

"How long do they last?"

"Well, a small one, about three days."

"Then your use of opium costs you about ten dollars a week. Is that correct?"

This testimony might be wearing to Bunting; but Abner could see that the jury found it full of interest; as good as a conducted tour through opium dens or haunts of vice. In simultaneous movement all eyes went to Harry; and then to Leming, as Leming answered, lingered a moment, fascinated; and then back to Harry; and then quickly back to Leming again. "Now, I think you said you smoked twice a day?" Harry said. "At what hours?"

"Well, generally before I got to bed at night, late at night; and when I first get up."

"First thing in the morning?" (A touch of collective nausea appeared on the jurors' faces. Most men wouldn't even smoke a cigar before breakfast.)

"Whenever I get up first."

"And after you smoke the opium, what happens then?"

"Well, I get up and eat."

"I thought an opium user had no appetite after he smoked."

"Oh, no," Leming smiled and shook his head. "I see you don't understand anything about opium," he said mildly.

"I probably don't know quite as much as you do," Harry said. "That is why I ask."

"You wouldn't ask that question if you understood it."

"Well, can you answer?"

"Yes, I can. Anybody that has the habit can eat after they smoke; but you can't eat before you smoke."

"You smoke; and go right on about your business?"

"That is right."

"I suppose this opium has no effect on your memory?"

"No."

"Well, what effect, if any, does it have?"

"No effect," Leming said, smiling and shaking his head again. "If you was to smoke cigarettes, and I was to ask you what effect they had, what would you say? You have the habit; you keep smoking them. If you see you are out of cigarettes, you have to go get some right away. It is when you don't have them, they have effect. In narcotic, you got to take it to keep yourself from being sick, that is all."

"You mean, as long as you keep taking it, you feel all right?"

"That is correct," Leming said. He smiled encouragingly at Harry. "Now, you are getting it!"

"I should say I am," said Harry. "How long do you stay sick if you don't have your stuff?"

"Oh, well, five or six days. I mean, if you break your habit, after five or six days you don't crave it."

"Now, these pills they gave you in jail; they have the same effect as opium?"

Bunting said, "He has already answered that."

Leming answered, "I should say not!" He was eager, glad to have the advantage of Harry, and aware of the jury's attentiveness. He smiled again; he gave his head a sadder-but-wiser shake.

"You mean they are not a good substitute?"

"They just give them to try to make me get some sleep; but they don't do no good."

"And what keeps you from sleeping?"

"Well, I told you that before," Leming said. "When you get off the stuff, you can't sleep for a couple of months."

"It isn't your conscience that's bothering you?"

Taken by surprise, and plainly wounded or deflated by the jab, Leming said, "Oh, no. Nothing on my conscience bothering me. It should be on the men you are representing!"

Harry said, "I move that be stricken!"

Judge Vredenburgh jerked his chin up and down. "It may be stricken out."

"Now, Leming," Harry said, "if I understand you rightly, you claim that you were not offered any inducements of any kind to testify. But you must have had some reason. What was it?"

"Well," said Leming, "when Howell told his statement, well, then I figured it was time for me to tell the truth; after Howell had opened up himself."

"Who told you to do that?"

"I told myself to do it."

"Had you been advised by your lawyer, Mr. Servadei, or any member of his firm, of any appeal to be made for you if you took the stand for the Commonwealth?"

"Positively not."

"Did the county detective, Mr. Costigan, offer you anything in the way of a promise of leniency?"

Bunting said, "If he did, I would like to know it."

"Never," said Leming.

To Abner, Bunting said, "Mr. Wurts is about washed up, I think." He straightened himself in his seat and began to assemble the papers and file folders on the table. "Ten of five," he said. "I guess his Honor's had enough, too. I was going to put Smalley on and get it over. But she won't take long. We'll have her first, tomorrow. I want Dunglison and Kinsolving; and we'd better read Howell's confession into the record. With luck, we can rest by noon."

Harry said, "Now, Leming, you admitted the police records of your arrests during the last ten years—"

Bunting said, "Do we have to have all that again?"

"The Commonwealth's anxiety to get its witness off the stand is readily understandable," Harry began, but without much spirit.

"I object!" Bunting said. "Mr. Wurts is now testifying himself, your Honor."

"On the contrary, I am trying to conduct a cross-examination, and the district attorney has no business to interrupt it constantly!"

Judge Vredenburgh said, "I must ask both of you to come to order. No more by-play, please! If you have further questions for this witness, Mr. Wurts, put them promptly. The jurors have had a very hot and uncomfortable afternoon, and ought not to be kept here unnecessarily."

Harry said, "My only endeavor is to get through, your Honor. Leming, did you ever conduct any sort of business during these years—I mean, apart from crime; or did crime take all your time?"

"I manufactured dice," Leming, who saw that Harry knew all about it, said.

"Loaded ones, I presume."

"Well, if they wanted loaded ones, and they pay the price for them, I can make them, too."

"You mean you supplied big gambling operators with loaded dice?"

"Big operators don't need no loaded dice," Leming said, smiling indulgently. "They only watch nobody playing with them brings any. With straight dice, by like the law of averages, they got to win."

"I hope we will all bear that in mind," said Harry to the jury. "In short, when not engaged in any definite crime, you made dice."

"I had other jobs," Leming said. "I told you some of them. I was an iron worker, cement finisher—well, numerous things—"

"Yes, numerous things is right," Harry said. "That will be all, thank you."

"Mr. District Attorney," Judge Vredenburgh said, "have you any questions? Or is there anyone else you want to put on whose examination could be disposed of very briefly?"

Bunting shook his head, and Judge Vredenburgh continued: "I think, then, we will suspend at this point. The jury may be withdrawn until to-morrow morning."

While the courtroom emptied, Abner sat watching Bunting pack his brief case. "Want to see me about anything before court tomorrow?" he said. "I told Arlene I'd try to get down."

"I'll ring you there if anything comes up. What did you make of the Mason boy?"

"He's all right, I think. He looked like a decent kid."

"Well, maybe his father's a perfectly decent person, too. If you're seeing Jesse, you might bear that in mind."

"I'm not going to have any row with Jesse."

"If you do, you're a damned fool," Bunting said. "So don't be. Good night." He crossed the empty well of the court and went into the Judge's chambers.

In the Attorneys Room Harry Wurts had taken off his coat and necktie. He lolled on the window ledge in his limp shirt. "And then I said to him," said Harry, "'My son,' I said, 'the world is full of sin and sorrow, of trial and tribulation; and the heart of man is heavy, and we know not what to be-lieve—'"

Joe Jackman said, "This is still you talking?"

Paying no attention, Harry leveled his finger at George Stacey and Nick Dowdy, whose mouth hung open as he watched. "'Receive this truth!'" said Harry, "'Remember it! Mark it! Write it in letters of purest gold! Amid the storms of adversity, in the heyday of triumph, at the hour of decision, in the article of death, say to yourself, as now I say to you: *The wheel that squeaks the loudest gets the grease!*' I thank you!" Carrying his coat and tie, Harry marched out the other door.

"He ought to be on the radio," Joe Jackman said bitterly. The closing door reopened, and Mark Irwin came in. "Hello, toss-pot!" Joe said. "Here it is. That's the whole thing." He lifted one section from a stack of sheets bound in blue paper, glanced at the title page, and handed it over.

"Thanks a lot," Mark said. "Hello, Ab. Going to the Nyces'?"

"No," said Abner. "So long, Joe."

He went out into the hall and down to the back entrance. The windows of Mrs. O'Hara's sitting room in the jail were open and boxes of petunias grew between the bars. There was no breeze, but the sun, declining at last, made everything look cooler. There were shadows across the paving of Court Street. Abner walked down to the gaping Romanesque arch of the door to the three-story, shabbily stone-faced Gearhart Building. He went into the hall, and up the wide, much worn wooden stairs. At the head of them was a window with a drawn yellow shade against which the sun blazed full. Abner passed the open office doors of the Childerstown Building &

Loan Association. Next to them was a closed door marked *Childerstown Water Company*. At the end, giving access to the rooms at the front of the building, were double doors of ground glass with black lettering half faded and flaked off: *Michael Gearhart's Sons. Real Estate & Insurance*; and, lower down, *walk in*.

Abner walked in.

Judge Coates
[from *The Just and the Unjust*]

Abner drove his car into the old stables. The cement floor on which he halted had been laid down more than twenty years ago when Judge Coates decided—an unusual step at the time—to keep two cars. To make room, some disused horse stalls were ripped out, and it was discovered then that the old floor was rotten. When the new cement floor was finished and the workmen gone for the day, Abner put his initials in the still-soft surface with a stick; and for good measure, impressed his bare footprints beside them; and for still better measure, impressed also the bare footprints of Caesar, an Airedale dog they then had.

Time had not obliterated those marks. By the glare of the headlights against the back wall, Abner could still see them, just to the left of the door of what had been the harness room. He remembered all that perfectly; taking off the sneaker he wore; and the cement cool and moist against the sole of his foot; and Caesar, years dead and forgotten, alive and struggling in consternation as Abner pressed down his paw. The exact object, if Abner had any beyond showing interest in a material that could be soft today, yet hard as stone tomorrow, was not clear—perhaps just this; that some day, years after, he might notice the marks and think with satisfaction that he had made them. Snapping off the headlights, Abner got out. He noticed and thought, just as the boy perhaps planned.

Closing the doors, he stood a moment in the broad moonlight looking at the big dark mound of the house. These things, he thought, remained— only for a while, of course; but longer, at any rate, than a man did. His grandfather built the house, and for him it had been new and desirable; a showplace, with its great ornamented bargeboards, its cavernous arched verandas and round shingled tower, in the Childerstown of dirt streets and gas lights in the 'eighties. The Judge, the Old Judge, would not have been surprised—what sentient man could be?—to find that the new became old; and the desirable, undesirable; and the house, once so fine-looking, grotesque. As an exercise in reason this was not hard; but how hard to grasp it, to know that the real today, the seen and felt today, and everything around you, and you, yourself as you stood thinking, would dissolve and pale to a figment of mind, existing, like the future you tried to think of, only in thought!

While Abner stood, the old courthouse clock struck twelve (his grandfather would have noticed that the new courthouse clock carried clearly out here). The faint deep bongs rose over the tree tops and the sleeping hill. Surprised to find that it was so late, Abner walked down the brick path.

Under the moonlit roof of the kitchen wing, in the shadow of the shining slates, a voice said suddenly, "Who's that?"

Starting, Abner looked up. In the window of the bedroom where Lucius and Honey slept, the shape of a head a little darker than the darkness, and the shoulders of a dull white pajama coat, showed. Abner said, "All right, Lucius. Who do you think it is?"

"Mr. Abner? I hear that car. Then, nobody comes down. It might be burglars."

"It's all right. Sorry if I woke you up."

"You didn't wake me, Mr. Abner. I keep an eye on things around here. Judge laid up and you out, somebody's got to. You finish that trial?"

"Yes."

"I guess it's curtains for those gangsters?"

"They'll get twenty years in jail, I think."

There was a silence.

"They not going to electrocute them? They kill that man, and they not going to electrocute them?"

"The jury didn't seem to think they did kill him," Abner said.

"Oh!" said Lucius. "Well, I surely thought it was the chair for them! Well, I guess I'll tell Honey. She thought it was."

"All right," Abner said. "Good night."

"Good night."

There was no light in the lower hall, but a dim glow fell on the head of the stairs, showing that the door of his father's room was open. Abner turned the night latch, found the first step with a practiced foot, and went up quickly and steadily on tiptoe. He was expecting his father to call; but when no call came, he stepped faster, with a tremor of alarm, and stood in the bedroom door. His father rested propped up on pillows, his eyes closed, the paralyzed side of his big face hanging with forlorn helplessness. He breathed roughly, but calm and even; and Abner saw that he was only asleep.

Judge Coates stirred. His face worked a moment; his eyes opened. He brought up his good hand and laid the back of it against his paralyzed cheek, as though to cover while he brought it under what control he could, a spectacle that he knew was distressing. "Well, son," he said with difficulty. "Must have drowsed off! Late?"

"Just struck twelve, sir."

"Jury trouble?"

"And plenty of it," Abner said. "Do you want to go to sleep?"

"No, I don't! Sit down! Sit down!" His voice gained clearness as the muscles limbered. "Tell me about it. Verdict in? Smoke a cigarette." He got one from between the piled books on the table. "Sit down," he said. "Light it myself when I get ready."

"Second degree murder," Abner said, sitting down. "Judge Irwin read the jury a lecture."

"Against the evidence?"

"As square as anything could be. Vredenburgh was fit to be tied."

"Harry make a good speech?"

"That's about the size of it," Abner said. "And plain contrariness. I think Marty may have taken it a little too much for granted—"

Abner broke off. The criticism had been just and judicious when he first formulated it to himself, sitting in chagrin at the Commonwealth's table. There was no disloyalty in the silent recognition of a mistake when Marty made one; and no complacency in noting, warned by the mistake, logical ways to avoid it. When he let himself voice the criticism to someone else, there was a little of both: disloyalty in criticizing when his only object must be the trifling but infamous one of trying to dissociate himself from the failure of an enterprise in which he had shared; complacency, for when he pointed out a mistake, he left it plain that it was not one he himself would have committed. "I mean," he said, "Marty had the case cold. There couldn't be two answers to the facts. He more or less left it at that. Kinsolving, an F.B.I. witness we had, who may be a liar but he is certainly no fool, told me afterward that he thought the jury was jibbing at executing two men for something they argued a third man had really done."

Judge Coates said, "A jury has its uses. That's one of them. It's like a—" he paused. "It's like a cylinder head gasket. Between two things that don't give any, you have to have something that does give a little, something to seal the law to the facts. There isn't any known way to legislate with an allowance for right feeling."

"Well, Vredenburgh told Harry this Court wasn't enforcing the Sixth Commandment."

"From the bench?"

"Oh, no. Afterward, in the Attorneys Room. I guess he thought the jury had given a little more than it needed to. He said he was disgusted with it."

"He won't feel that way tomorrow. Tom's got better sense than that. In his time, he's had trouble with his temper."

"What was that?"

"It was long ago," Judge Coates said. "When he was district attorney,

he used to go off the handle now and then. He got over it. It isn't a matter
of any interest now. Juries didn't always find what he thought they ought to
in those days, either. Justice is an inexact science. As a matter of fact, a
judge is so greatly in a jury's debt, he shouldn't begrudge them the little
things they help themselves to."

"I don't follow," Abner said.

"The ancient conflict between liberty and authority. The jury protects
the Court. It's a question how long any system of courts could last in a free
country if judges found the verdicts. It doesn't matter how wise and experienced the judges may be. Resentment would build up every time the findings didn't go with current notions or prejudices. Pretty soon half the community would want to lynch the judge. There's no focal point with a jury;
the jury is the public itself. That's why a jury can say when a judge couldn't,
'I don't care what the law is, that isn't right and I won't do it.' It's the
greatest prerogative of free men. They have to have a way of saying that and
making it stand. They may be wrong, they may refuse to do the things they
ought to do; but freedom just to be wise and good isn't any freedom. We
pay a price for lay participation in the law; but it's a necessary expense."

"You mean," said Abner, "that in order to show he's free, a man
shouldn't obey the laws."

"A free man always has been and always will be the one to decide what
he'd better do," Judge Coates said. "Entrapment is perfectly legal. The
law lets you arrange an opportunity for a suspected thief to steal so that you
can catch him. I don't think right feeling can ever stoop to it. Compounding a felony is an indictable offense; but a man feels, just the same, that he
has a right to forgive those who injure him, and no talk about his duty to
society will change that feeling. In a case of larceny, it may be no defense in
law that the party from whom the goods were stolen, himself stole them;
but the feeling of the average man does in part defend it by saying it served
him right to lose what didn't belong to him. It is held that drunkenness
does not aggravate a common law offense any more than it excuses it."

He shook his head. "Depending on the circumstances, it may do either.
Most people would feel that committing perjury drunk was not so bad as
committing it cold sober; while committing an involuntary manslaughter
drunk would be worse than committing it sober. Well, I'm rambling on.
I don't know what makes old men like to talk so much. Maybe they're just
talking to themselves, trying to find out what they think. I saw the *Examiner* about the Field thing. That's another case mixed up with what people
feel. Judging by Maynard's editorial, I don't know that it makes for
justice.'"

"What it made for," Abner said, "was the Board giving Rawle a vote
of confidence tonight. Maynard was pretty sore about it."

Judge Coates reached over and took a cigarette lighter from the table. By pressing the top, he made a flame snap up and lit the cigarette.

"Where did you get that?" Abner said.

"Present. Matter of fact, if I have to smoke, I ought to use matches. I was getting pretty handy with them. Mosher is enthusiastic about these wretched little accomplishments. Yes. Cousin Mary gave it to me. She came in this morning."

"What did she want?"

"That's right; she did," Judge Coates said. "She'd heard about the school board business, and she was worried about what was going to happen to Bonnie. I think she thought I might be able to take a hand in it. Of course, there was nothing I could do."

"So you told her not to worry; if Rawle was kicked out and Bonnie lost her job, you'd get her another."

"In substance, yes. When Cousin Mary worries, it shakes the house. You have to stop that at any cost. She has a hard time, really."

"Well," said Abner, "I don't know whether it will make it any easier; but her daughter and I are getting married. Bonnie gave me some supper down there; and we thought we would. I suppose I ought to ask if you mind if we live here awhile."

"When are you going to get married?"

"Some time this month, probably. There are so many forms and certificates and things, you can't say when." He paused. "Don't you like the idea? Last night you were saying I was so damn phlegmatic I hadn't sense enough to get married."

"That was an unfortunate choice of words," Judge Coates said. "I didn't realize you were going to take it so hard. Yes. I like the idea." His face contorted a little, and Abner was stunned to see tears appear in the corner of his eyes. "Are you all right, sir?" he said, starting up.

"Sit down!" said Judge Coates. He plucked at a pile of tissues on the table until he got hold of one. He daubed at his eyes. "You can't tell what I mean by what I do," he said hoarsely. "It would be a favor to me if you wouldn't give things I can't help quite so much attention. Damnation, I'm a sick man!" He dropped the crumpled tissue.

"Well, I didn't mean to upset you," Abner said in distress.

"Phlegmatic wasn't the word; it was obtuse," Judge Coates said. "What did I say that for? I don't mean it. You'd think I wanted to make you mad. I don't want to make anyone mad. I'm not fit to stand up to it. You least of all—"

He brought the cigarette up shakily, cocked it between his lips, and took a puff. "There, that's over," he said. "It just hit me a certain way. If I had to explain it I would only make it sillier. Foolish question, do I mind if you live here. I might ask you, do you mind if you live here. I'll have another stroke and die pretty soon; or if I don't, I'll be a driveling idiot. Don't know whether you want to be in the same house with it. I wouldn't."

Abner said, "I don't think that follows at all. Jesse Gearhart told me his father had a stroke and practically got over it."

"Well," said Judge Coates, "that's true; Mike did. I suppose I might. Just don't want to be such a fool as to count on it. When did Jesse tell you about his father?"

"The other day."

"Oh. I wondered." He crushed out the cigarette awkwardly. "You're probably well out of that. I never liked politics myself. I don't mean I thought I was too good for it. Or if I did, it was when I was very young. Men act through self-interest; and if they do things you wouldn't do, you'd better not assume it's because you have a nobler character. There are noble and disinterested actions done every day; but I think most of them are impulsive. I don't think there's any such thing as a deliberate noble action. Deliberation always has half an eye on how it will look; it wants something, if only admiration, for what it does. Did you ever see a law suit which aimed at disinterested justice?" He took another tissue and wiped his mouth. "Senator Perkins used to say that when a man said he was seeking justice, what he meant, if he was plaintiff, was that he aimed to do someone dirt and the Court ought to help him; and if he was the defendant, that he already had done someone dirt, and the Court ought to protect him."

"That's about it, I guess," Abner said. "I had to get in those Blessington will papers this morning. It's certainly doing the Blessington sisters dirt. Well, I got them in. Intelligent self-interest. I guess what I thought to myself was that I couldn't afford to turn down any business. I don't know."

Judge Coates said heavily, "Woe unto you also, ye lawyers! For ye lade men with burdens grievous to be borne, and ye yourselves touch not the burdens with one of your fingers. Yes. We're vulnerable. A lawyer can't very well do to others as he would be done by. Not in the line of business. I don't know whether you're asking my advice. It's the same conflict we were speaking of before—well, I was speaking of before. You don't get much chance to speak, do you?" He worked himself up a little higher on his pillows.

"Here's your Blessington situation. It's provided by law, primarily by statute, that one of a man's rights which the courts shall protect him in, is the disposal of his property after his death according to his intentions expressed in an attested will. It is a very important right. It is part and parcel of human freedom and dignity. Just as the jury must be free to find against the evidence, we have to hold that a man must be free, if he has the legal capacity to make a will, to make an unequal, unjust, and unreasonable will.

"True, we can't let him make it against public policy. Expediency will set bounds to his freedom. You cannot define exactly and forever what the right bounds of expediency may be; but you can say what they must not be. The intention to realize is not the intention of the Court, nor the intention of Abner Coates, Counselor at Law. In ethics and morals their intentions may be demonstrably better and wiser and fairer than the testator's intention. You've been saying, in effect, that you'd like to devise a better and juster disposal of Blessington's goods. You have no right to do it. The Court has no more right. The point for you is not whether you personally think the will just and good, but whether you can dispassionately and disinterestedly submit to the Court reasons in law and equity that bear out what you feel to be the testator's intention to leave the money to the clients you represent."

Judge Coates coughed, holding up his good hand so that Abner would not interrupt him. "Sorry," he said, gasping. "Now, if you don't feel and believe that such was the testator's intention, you should have nothing to do with it. In your case, I think it is obvious that the testator's intention, or his contingent intention, was that Enoch's college should get the money. If that was his intention, and if it is not an illegal intention, it ought to be realized. Granted that Blessington intended an injustice (and remember, that is an opinion; you and most other people may hold it, but it remains an opinion), would you say to me that the law ought to betray its great first principle and pay off one injustice (a matter of opinion) with another injustice (a matter of indisputable fact)? I think not."

"I think not, too," Abner said. "It isn't what the law should do; it's what I should do." He repressed a yawn. The long day had tired him, not physically in a way to make him sleepy, but in the protracted drain of nervous energy. He could not seem to whip his mind up to the heavy labor of manipulating abstractions. He said, "I'd like to do what was right. Who wouldn't? Maybe that's only one of those deliberate noble actions you don't think much of. It has something to do with how things look, what people think of me." He paused. "Jesse told me your Senator Perkins said you wouldn't worry so much about what people were thinking of you if you remembered that most of the time they weren't. I'm not so good on comebacks. It took me until now to see what was wrong with that."

In spite of himself, Abner did yawn. "What's he mean? Does he mean that most of the time there's nobody looking, so you can do what you want? I don't give a damn whether anybody is looking or not. I'm looking. I care whether I look like a louse. Certainly I care what people think of me. They may only do it for ten seconds once in ten years, but I still care."

Judge Coates said, "Well, we all have our pride. It does a good deal to make us fit for human company. But I don't know how far the world at large, or Jesse in particular, is in duty bound to minister to yours. You made your decision. Don't go on arguing it over."

"Well," said Abner, "today I guess I unmade it. Jesse asked me again, and I told him I'd run."

"You did?" Judge Coates said. "Why did you do that?"

"Because it was what I really wanted to do," Abner said somewhat defiantly. "At least, I suppose that's why."

"Well, that's a good enough reason," Judge Coates said. "Why do you think it isn't?"

"I don't know that I do think it isn't," Abner said. His mind in desperation refused him its services. "I'd like to think there was more to it than just my own advantage. I wish I weren't so sure of that part of it. If it cost me something instead of paying me something—"

"It seems to me it costs you a good deal," Judge Coates said. "For the last few weeks you've been running yourself ragged on this case, this Howell-Basso thing. What do you get out of it? It puts you on edge, all right; I can tell you that."

"I get my salary out of it," Abner said. "Why shouldn't I run myself ragged? It's my job."

"Then just go on doing it, and don't worry. You take care of your job and other things will take care of themselves."

"I don't remember that things ever did. Things don't look as if they would. You can see them cooking up another war for us in Europe; and when they do, I guess all bets are off."

"Don't be cynical," Judge Coates said. "A cynic is just a man who found out when he was about ten that there wasn't any Santa Claus, and he's still upset. Yes, there'll be more war; and soon, I don't doubt. There always has been. There'll be deaths and disappointments and failures. When they come, you meet them. Nobody promises you a good time or an easy time. I don't know who it was who said when we think of the past we regret and when we think of the future we fear. And with reason. But no bets are off. There is the present to think of, and as long as you live there always will be. In the present, every day is a miracle. The world gets up in the morning and is fed and goes to work, and in the evening it comes home and is fed again and perhaps has a little amusement and goes to sleep. To make that possible, so much has to be done by so many people that, on the face of it, it is impossible. Well, every day we do it; and every day, come hell, come high water, we're going to have to go on doing it as well as we can."

"So it seems," said Abner.

"Yes, so it seems," said Judge Coates, "and so it is, and so it will be! And that's where you come in. That's all we want of you."

Abner said, "What do you want of me?"

"We just want you to do the impossible," Judge Coates said.

VI

Style and Techniques
By Frederick Bracher

James Gould Cozzens's major works from *S.S. San Pedro* (1930) to *By Love Possessed* (1957) show a steady growth in psychological richness and moral depth. His baroque style, maturing slowly, reaches its peak in the sinewy eloquence of *Guard of Honor*; here, as in all his later novels, the style is unabashedly rhetorical, in the good sense of that term, and consciously literary. In meditative passages, the sentences tend to be long and complicated, with nests of parenthetical comments within subordinate elements. *By Love Possessed*, especially, abounds in uncommon words like the inkhorn terms of Elizabethan writers, and unmarked quotations from and allusions to earlier writers are frequent.

Cozzens is said to admire Macaulay, and he justifies his own style by implication when Arthur Winner contemplates the florid Victorian inscription in the lobby of the Union League Club:

> That epigraph embodied a seriousness of purpose still respectable. Were people really the better for not talking like that any more? Was there any actual advantage of honesty when high-sounding terms went out? Had facts of life as life is lived been given any more practical recognition? [1]

The plain, bare style recommended by Bishop Sprat for use by the Royal Society in the late seventeenth century is not the only acceptable style, and those who insist on it are apt to fall into the Puritan fallacy of assuming all ornament to be bad.

Even at its most rhetorical, Cozzens's style is rich, sonorous, and masculine. If the decoration is occasionally so literary as to approach the grotesque, at least it is determinate and perspicuous, sharp in the sunlight with no blurred, fuzzy edges. The ornate complications serve to qualify, sharpen, or enrich a meaning already established by the basic structure. By contrast, the rhetorical effect of Faulkner's incremental absolute phrases is cumulative; the meaning is not defined by an articulate structure but emerges as a kind of essence from the tangle of sentence elements, heaped up like

1. *By Love Possessed* (New York: Harcourt, Brace, 1957), p. 201.

branches on a bonfire—a glow that appears now and then dimly through the smoke and occasionally bursts free in bright flame. Though Cozzens's latest style is, occasionally, smokily obscured, the major novels give off a steady, dry light.

Cozzens has a good workman's respect for his tools; characteristically he chooses words with clean precision. But he has also a poet's fondness for embellishing his style with rich language. The main character of *Men and Brethren*, reminded of the phrase "an old style Princeton Seminary supra-lapsarian," comments, "What a marvelous word, by the way!" and he rolls on his tongue its opposite, "infralapsarian," which he equates with "a dreary Arminianism, a mess of Methodist pottage."[2] The orotund terms and the veiled allusion are sharpened by contrast with the Anglo-Saxon earthiness of "Calvin would spit on them," and the whole passage justifies itself completely. Even so uncommon a word as *irruptive* can be effective in context: "the horrid irruptive roar" of airplanes passing close overhead. The complementary adjective, *horrid*, if thought of in its literal Latin sense of "hair-raising," is equally appropriate. Cozzens writes for an audience literate enough to enjoy stylistic virtuosity and able to look at the literary equivalent of late Victorian architecture not with Puritan outrage at its excesses, but with affection and amusement.

The sentences in meditative or descriptive passages show certain distinctive patterns: Cozzens seems to like the complex rhythms produced by interpolated parenthetic elements, and he is fond of a kind of appositival coordination in which one expression (noun, verb, modifier) is followed immediately by another that explains or elaborates the first:

> Though the waking mind clutched at its relief of recognizing the dream as such —not really real, not really happening, not really requiring such an anguished effort to grasp and to explain—the dreaming mind with desperate hypnagogic attachment would not let go, leave off. A running engine of phantasmogenesis, powerfully engaged again, pressed him to dream on; and, little as life, Dunky (could that man be still alive?) angrily, excitedly, confronted him.[3]

Similar devices provide the appropriate rhythms for a meditation by the vicar in *Men and Brethren*:

> The words returned, of themselves, with unforced deliberation, over and over. Soon he was aware, without the distraction or the interruption of taking an interest in it, of the automatically increasing depth of his breathing, the modulation of his heart beat.
>
> Set, by the familiar practice of his will, on the deceptive threshold over which some people stepped to a supposed spiritual apprehension—where the senses, starved of nervous energy, were narcotized, kept no more check on actuality;

2. *Men and Brethren* (New York: Harcourt, Brace, 1935), pp. 44–45.
3. *By Love Possessed*, p. 503.

where reason, deprived of ideas to work with abdicated, impotent; where Grace might very well appear, as Calvin supposed, irresistible—Ernest released himself. (pp. 43–44)

The device of interweaving into one's own sentences fragments from or allusions to earlier writers can easily be overdone, and in *Morning Noon and Night* it becomes tiresome. (On eight pages near the beginning of that novel, one may find twenty quotations, or echoes of quotations, from Shakespeare, the Bible, William Knox, Milton, Marvell, Defoe, Congreve, Pope, Wordsworth, and Longfellow.) Used with discrimination, such buried quotations can enrich key passages or provide ironic contrasts between past and present. Fragments and echoes of the past in the cultivated speech or thought of the Reverend Ernest Cudlipp are pleasantly in character. In *The Just and the Unjust*, unacknowledged quotations are mostly limited to the joking speech of attorneys out of court and often serve to characterize the speakers. Looking out the window on a spring night, Harry Wurts declaims, "'How sweet the moonlight sleeps on yonder bank' . . . Childerstown Bank and Trust Company."

Readers who went to school in the days of Cozzens's youth, if they have even normal literary sensibility, will have retained willy-nilly a stock of poetic lines and tags from Shakespeare (especially *Julius Caesar* and *Macbeth*), Milton, Pope, and the Victorians. To have some of these evoked in new contexts, often ironic, is a minor but real pleasure. The Shakespearean bravura of "They come like sacrifices in their trim / And to the fire-eyed maid of smoky war" is marvelously inappropriate when applied to the newly-drafted nationally famous artist who, in *Guard of Honor*, spends his days drawing diagrams for a field manual no one will ever read.[4]

Standing to review the troops at the end of three hard days, weary in mind, every limb aching, Colonel Ross finds some lines from *Samson Agonistes* running through his head:

> All is best though we oft doubt
> What the unsearchable dispose
> Of highest wisdom brings about.

The random, violent events of the recent past—the crashed night fighter, the near crash of General Beal's AT-7, the snotty young lieutenant posing as a champion of the dignity of man, the suicide of Colonel Woodman, the methodical idiocy of Colonel Mowbray—call up an optimistic passage from Pope:

> All Nature is but art, unknown to thee,
> All chance, direction which thou canst not see;
> All discord, harmony not understood.

4. *Guard of Honor* (New York: Harcourt, Brace, 1948), p. 475.

Wondering about the relevance of recent discords, those harmonies not understood, Colonel Ross seems on the point of announcing a revelation: "From this, we learn——." But he is interrupted by the emergency siren signaling a new disorder: the drowning of seven paratroopers in the lake.

The artifice of these techniques helps to preserve a certain distance between the writer and his material. Speaking through the alert sensibility of Captain Nathaniel Hicks, Cozzens notes that the "wry raillery" and formal sentences of Lieutenant Amanda Turck are part of a "controlled and composed, yet ceaseless struggle" against an "obsessive self-consciousness" (p. 171). He remembers her "in the terrible heat of yesterday's high afternoon pronouncing a little stiltedly: 'The Lybian air adust——' it was defensive, he could see now. It intended the irony, for what that was worth, both ways. Though she reeked, she thought, of sweat, she quoted Milton; and though she quoted Milton, she reeked, she thought, of sweat." The raillery was "aimed at herself: her defense against everything" (p. 600).

Similarly, the "almost rehearsed-sounding" phrases of Julius Penrose, "that mocked themselves with their own affectation," are "a defense against hurts to one's vanity." Though not in the ordinary sense realistic, they are appropriate to the hypersensitivity of a proud, crippled man. Julius's habit of speech, ironic at his own expense, serves to hold strangers at arm's length while partially sharing, with old friends, "the privacy, or even secrecy, which alone, at some points, dignifies a man" (p. 227).

In this respect, Cozzens's own sensibility seems similar to that of Julius Penrose or Amanda Turck. In *Ask Me Tomorrow*, admittedly in part autobiographical, the oversensitive, proud young writer interposes a series of masks between himself and the world. In the later novels, a central consciousness serves a similar protective function and enables Cozzens to attribute to some of his characters a degree of ripened wisdom which an author might hesitate to offer in his own right.

Cozzens's own temperament may also be indicated in the frequency with which certain words are used, especially those connoting a kind of partial disengagement, or shrinking involvement. *Compunction* occurs over and over again throughout the novels, as do the parenthetic tag "I'm afraid" and words like *mortifying, harassed, crestfallen, qualms, chagrin, wounded feelings, quailed, shrank, recoiled*. A suggestion of arrogance and guilt mingled with pity or sympathy seems to define Cozzens's contradictory combination of habitual feelings: protectively detached, oversensitive almost to the point of being finicky, yet worried and involved. Like his ornately involuted sentences, Cozzens's diction reflects his pyrrhonistic temperament, his apoetic intelligence, and his troubled aloofness.

Structurally, the typical Cozzens novel is dramatic; it does not trace the slow development of character as it is molded by environment and experience over a long period of years. Instead, we are confronted at once with fully formed characters involved in some crucial complication of action. The place is limited: a small New England village, an urban parish, or an Army airbase in Florida. The time is characteristically brief—several weeks in *The Last Adam* (the time required for the spread and crisis of a typhoid epidemic), three days in *The Just and the Unjust*, *Guard of Honor*, and *By Love Possessed*; a night and a day in *Men and Brethren*. Into these short periods Cozzens crowds relatively large casts of characters and a variety of crucial incidents.

To bring these together into some kind of unity of action is a difficult technical problem, and Cozzens's awareness of the difficulty is made clear in a letter about *Guard of Honor* to his English publisher:

> I wanted to show . . . the peculiar effects of the inter-action of innumerable individuals functioning in ways at once determined by and determining the functioning of innumerable others—all in the common and in every case nearly helpless involvement in what had ceased to be an "organization" . . . and became if not an organism with life and purpose of its own, at least an entity, like a crowd.[5]

In unifying this material, Cozzens follows the Aristotelian prescription for "the soul of a tragedy," a good plot. "Many events simultaneously transacted" are worked together into an action that is "complete and whole, and of a certain magnitude." He makes heavy use of coincidence and of the dramatic irony implicit in the occurrence of simultaneous events. In *The Last Adam* Dr. Bull, having given only casual attention to the little Devon cow dying of pneumonia—"Devons aren't much use to you anyway"— drinks hard cider with his mistress at her Cold Hill farm and takes her to bed at the moment when Mamie Talbot, the Bannings' slavey, dies of pneumonia while the telephone operator tries frantically to reach the truant doctor. Sitting at dinner at the Brookside restaurant, Arthur Winner reflects that men usually have good cause to worry, but unfortunately they seldom worry about the right things. As it turns out, he should have been worrying not about the erring brother of his secretary, but about the secretary herself. At just the moment when the ladies at the birthday party are sipping, with a "general slight air of devilishness," their one Manhattan, the secretary is drinking poison.

The ironies are not underlined; Cozzens expects his readers to be willing to read closely and to think. In the letter just quoted, he explains:

> I would just have to write off as readers everyone who could not or would not meet heavy demands on his attention and intelligence, or lacked the imagination to grasp a large pattern and the wit to see the relation which I could not stop to spell out between this & that.

5. Richard M. Ludwig, "A Reading of the James Gould Cozzens Manuscripts," *The Princeton University Library Chronicle*, 19 (Autumn 1975). See p. 558.

Unity of place in the Cozzens novels emphasizes the dramatic potentialities of a particularized setting. Perhaps the best example is in *Castaway*;
the dim, deserted department store, crammed with the material wealth of
our society, is useless to the brutish protagonist. The main point of the
novel is an ironic inversion of the Robinson Crusoe story. In the other
novels, sharply etched landscapes and tableaux demonstrate Cozzens's feeling for the picturesque, in the original sense of that term. His pictures
resemble a whole school of landscape painting in their feeling for light and
their use of lighting for dramatic effect.

Scene, weather, and event are carefully harmonized in *Men and Brethren*.
Ernest Cudlipp's *agonia* is set among the dismal buildings, sticky asphalt,
and hot breathless rooms of New York in summer. The sinister, aseptic
coolness of the private hospital in which Mrs. Binney convalesces is an admirable background for the violation of life implicit in an abortion. And it
contrasts strikingly with the fetid heat of the Hawleys' flat on a side street
crowded with vegetable stands and fish dealers, where Mrs. Hawley is dying. Along with the reek of sweat and urine from the locker rooms in the
Chapel House, it is a reminder of the inequalities, injustices, and miseries
that are the contingencies of human life. Place and action in Cozzens's
novels are interdependent, like mathematical functions.

It is in the sad, interminable rain of an Italian winter that the protagonist of *Ask Me Tomorrow* makes his pointless, passionless attempt to seduce
Faith Robertson in Milan. Montreux, a health resort at "the damp lake's
edge" where an occasional rose blooms in December, is filled with semi-
invalids and valetudinarians, absorbed in their symptoms, who take short
walks in the "dank thin sunniness." The appropriate incident here is the
death of Mrs. Cunningham's old dog. Grindelwald, a skiing station in the
Alps where a great wind is blowing white flags of snow off the peaks, has
its human equivalent in the brisk, tough English guests laughing in the
hallways and the elderly British admiral ogling the social director, Miss
Poulter, with "forthright damn-your-eyes adultery going on in his heart
. . . cheerful to see."

A particularly brilliant scene in *By Love Possessed* is the choir procession
entering Christ Church on the serene Sunday morning when Helen Detweiler's body is discovered. Arthur Winner and Judge Lowe are wearing the
unaccustomed morning coats of ushers; Alfred Revere, the black verger,
stands near the bell rope, watch in hand; Elmer Abbott, the organist, blows
jets of music from his pipes. Leading the procession as crucifer is Chet
Polhemus ("arisen from dreams of Ann?"), and behind him come "a dozen
scrubbed, starched-collared small boys piping up, pure and neuter," the
clean soar of their voices "warmed, unmistakably colored with sex" as the
square-capped sopranos pass; then the tenors and baritones, "pulling down
the high chant toward male levels of solidity or strength"; and finally the

basses "heartily roaring together in their barrel chests" (p. 516). The scene serves as a final, almost nostalgic summary of the stable social order of Brocton just before the picture is shattered, for Arthur Winner at least, by the melodramatic events that conclude the novel.

Similar in its culminating crystallization of significance is the *tableau vivant* near the end of *Guard of Honor*. The military personnel, from weeping General to naked black GIs who have been searching for the bodies of the drowned paratroopers, seem to pose for an instant, immobile, at the edge of the lake.

> The hot sun, nearer the horizon, poured a dazzling gold light across the great reach of the air field. . . . The swimmers, who must have been ordered from the lake, . . . emerged with shining limbs, their muscular black bodies brightly dripping. Mounting the low bank, they stole guarded glances at the two generals, then glanced respectfully away. . . . Around the two generals a circle of officers had gathered, posed in concern. In this sad, gold light their grouping made a composition like that found in old-fashioned narrative paintings. . . . The Provost Marshal indicated the lake with a demonstrative gesture; a young Air Force captain faced him, standing tense and stiff. Bulky in his fighting trim, a captain of paratroopers, and Major McIlmoyle, helmeted and dirty, waited in somber attitudes like legates who had brought news of a battle. To one side, a lieutenant colonel, probably the Post Engineer, in stylized haste gave grave tidings to a thin chicken colonel, that instant arrived—Colonel Hildebrand, the Base Commander.
>
> A deferential distance behind these chief figures, touched with the same sunset light, the mustered myrmidons, token groups of the supporting armies, whispered together—the black engineers, the arms-loaded paratroopers; and in the middle background, borne on a stretcher as though symbolically, the wrapped form of the man who had fallen on the runway was passing. (pp. 547–48)

The whole tableau suggests the guard of honor at a formal military funeral, and the likeness is strengthened by one's recollection of a scene occurring a little earlier—the passing in review of five thousand soldiers. Here the color guard, the officers standing at attention, the dropping guidons and formal eyes-right of the troops, the airplanes roaring low overhead, and the volleys of rifle fire from the edge of the field, all correspond to authentic details from an important military funeral. The two scenes constitute a guard of honor on the grand scale—for the drunken suicide, Colonel Woodman, for the drowned paratroopers, for all the soldiers killed and to be killed in the war, for mortal man.

Though Cozzens insists that he does not consciously make use of symbolism in the novels, it is almost impossible not to see connections between some of the things described and the significance of the accompanying action. *S.S. San Pedro* is a lean, stripped-down, objective account of the foundering of a passenger steamer. The progressive disintegration of the ship keeps pace with the slow dissolution of the captain and the demoralization of the crew. While the ship is still at its pier in Hoboken, showing a slight, inconsequential list to port, the Captain gives evidence of illness: he is pale beneath his wind-burned skin, and his hair, "usually a harsh white fur," looks weak and damp. Like the ship, his face droops a little on the left side—because of an early injury to the jaw, it is quickly explained. As the ship's list to port becomes dangerous, his illness becomes increasingly acute; and eventually command must be taken over by the senior second officer, Mr. Bradell.

We have already watched Mr. Bradell at the pier, supervising with crisp competence the loading of cargo, his white and gold uniform sharply outlined against the blue sky. The winch is run by a Jamaican so drunk he can hardly stand. Nevertheless "he remained mechanically precise. . . . Like the boom on its gooseneck, Packy pivoted blindly on the small hard point of habit. Like the boom, he described invariably the same controlled semicircles." [6] Near the end of the story we get another picture of the boom. It has been swung out, while the ship rolls helplessly, in a desperate attempt to jettison cargo and relieve the now terrible list to port. No longer controlled and precise, the boom "tilted, staggered, mounted uncertain toward the perpendicular." Then it "hovered in a broken semicircle, balanced dizzily, went into a drunken side movement," and "like a well-directed club out of the anonymous skies . . . knocked Mr. Bradell's poised figure ten feet into the scuppers" (pp. 126–28).

A similar enrichment of meaning is achieved in the scene in *Men and Brethren* when Carl Willever, a homosexual renegade from the monastery of the Order of the Holy Trinity, is recalled to a kind of limited sainthood. The details, prosaically realistic in themselves, inevitably recall the light from heaven that brought about the conversion of Saul on the road to Damascus. "Breathing out threatenings and slaughter against the disciples of the Lord," Willever has been sneering at Ernest's belief.

> On the clean new back of Holy Innocents' Dispensary one window, high up, without an awning, was catching the afternoon sun in a molten flash, like a mirror. The long shaft of the reflection struck down across the dreary backyards, through the open window, and began to fall on the piano behind Carl. The unexpected light touched him as he rocked back, and, startled, he turned his head. . . . Some intolerable sadness in this false sunshine seemed to unnerve him. The blatant, labored cynicism dissolved visibly away. . . . "Good God, Ernest," he said, "what can I do?" (pp. 258–59)

The question recalls the epigraph of the book, part of a sermon delivered by the Apostle Peter to the Jews on the day of Pentecost, and it is asked by most of the characters in the novel: "Men and brethren, what shall we do?" The

6. *S.S. San Pedro* (New York: Harcourt, Brace, 1931), p. 5.

answer is Repent, and in Willever's case, return to the monastery, the vocation to which he has been called.

Such images are often recurrent: the shaft of light appears at a critical
point in *The Just and the Unjust*, illuminating the marriage license that Abner and Bonnie have, finally, signed. The pocket watch, proud symbol of
efficiency to the Brazilian quartermaster of the *San Pedro*, is smashed as he
gets the wounded Mr. Bradell off the foundering liner; it recalls the watch
in *Castaway* that has stopped mysteriously at quarter past five and only
begins to run again when the corpse in the basement struggles painfully up
the stairway.

The snakes, frequently mentioned or present in the novels, are sometimes merely props; but the rattlesnake hunt in *The Last Adam* manages to
convey a significance beyond the immediate context, and the overtones
recall both classical myth and Biblical story. The serpent was the living
emblem of Aesculapius, god of medicine, who was commonly represented
carrying a club-like staff with a serpent coiled round it. The serpent-
entwined caduceus of Mercury, now the symbol of the medical profession,
was in its oldest form a rod ending in two prongs. Doctor Bull, going rattle-
snake-hunting with a forked stick and an oak bludgeon, is bitten on the
hand that holds the cudgel. His favorite method of killing a rattlesnake—
jumping on the "son of Satan" and crushing its head with his hobnailed
heels—recalls Genesis 3:15 and relates him to the seed of Eve, the last
Adam, who according to St. Paul became "a quickening spirit."

In *Guard of Honor* the coral snake and the moccasin have marked sexual
overtones, but the copperhead in *By Love Possessed* calls up the richest tangle
of associations. "Original sin, man's baser nature, the subconscious" is
described as a crowded snake pit, from which strays occasionally escape,
"creeping above ground, insinuating themselves where nature has fallen"
(p. 397). (Arthur Winner says, "'We don't know where they breed; but
every now and then one turns up in the hollow, here.'" [p. 416]). A stray
from the nest of "unholy gross urges," of "unavowable dark desires," manifests itself in Mrs. Pratt's pleasure at turning the conversation inexorably
from love in general to the details of Arthur Winner's own sexual experience.

Just as she is saying, "You know now who was really responsible," she
sees the copperhead in the garden, a harsh intolerable bit of reality. Her
horror at this "true, tangible (if not very big) hideous serpent in the garden"
forces her to retreat unsteadily from Paradise to the house, where she encounters another bit of rude reality—the angry Mr. Moore, whose "bitter-
looking round small mouth," spitting threats, recalls the tiny, gaping
venomous mouth of the copperhead. Arthur Winner decapitates the snake
with a long-handled hoe, and the "ensuing convulsive thrash of muscular
reflex, the violent castings-about" of the body recall the real subject of
Mrs. Pratt's conversation—the adulterous encounter with Marjorie Pen-

rose, her "paroxysms of pleasure" and her "flings-about in her extremity" (p. 419).

Behind the rich texture and pervading resonance of the Cozzens novels, one feels always the firm hand of a controlling intelligence. The books are novels in the classic sense, and readers looking for exotica or for ingenious innovations in narrative technique will probably be disappointed. Doctor Johnson put it well: "The irregular combinations of fanciful invention may delight awhile . . . but the pleasures of sudden wonder are soon exhausted, and the mind can only repose on the stability of truth." Cozzens' writing demands competent readers, with "the wit to see the relation . . . between this & that," and such readers can trust Cozzens. He will not assault their feelings with false sentiment, nor confuse the sensibility with vain displays of showy virtuosity. His readers can repose with confidence on the stability of his persistent, energetic search for truth.

The Impact of Intolerable Facts
[review]

Oliver La Farge, in his modest preface to this book, explains why he wrote it. Though a history of the Air Transport Command, and not a skimped one, it is no formal history, nor intended to be definitive. It is the story of that course of events by which the old Ferrying Command, shifting a few planes around the country in short hops, was built into the phenomenal ATC.

It was truly phenomenal. Every day in the summer of 1945, ATC had twenty-six Atlantic and thirty-eight Pacific flights each way. Single-handed, it kept China going. In top-secret emergencies, it could produce at a word and in a matter of hours a theatre commander to talk face to face with the Joint Chiefs in Washington, or redress like magic a dangerous balance with anti-tank shell fuses to Egypt or grenades to the Solomons. As a matter of course, it could move here or there divisions of men, the plane, complement of whole air forces, hills of supplies. From this story Colonel La Farge purposes to show "how the emergencies of the war led us to the threshold of the true Air Age, and what that means to us now."

"The Eagle in the Egg" is, then, more than bare history. It is a histori-cal essay of some length, a study of meanings, an interpretation of facts; and this approach to the possibilities of the future by way of the immediate past is effective. Here are facts, many of them at the time little noticed, some that at the time could not be disclosed. Their orderly recital sets out the Air Age with more cogency than all the menacing guesses about World War III or fancy fantasies on the Airport of Tomorrow. Few readers will have known half the story. They will get the food for thought it is intended to give. History so clearly told is indeed a form of prophecy.

With Colonel La Farge as historian, the Air Force, the Air Transport Command and the reader are fortunate. To his job he brings the professional writer's competence, the fullest access to factual information, and the great

Review of *The Eagle in the Egg* by Oliver La Farge, *New York Times Book Review* (as "Those Phenomenal Initials—ATC"), July 24, 1949, pp. 1, 17. Copyright © 1949 by The New York Times Company. Reprinted by permission.

advantage of a military service whose duties allowed or required him to go everywhere and see everything (he was ATC's Historical Officer during the war). The result is a narrative of authority, of often gifted expression, of exact eyewitness reporting, of unobtrusive but copious documentation. That it is pretty clearly also a labor of love is not allowed to be to its disadvantage. The partisan warmth is not doting. The loyal wish to give credit where credit is overdue is not uncritical.

Moreover, Colonel La Farge has another qualification, of the first importance to readers of judgment. Whatever else may have distinguished them, no great number of the many "war books"—whether memoirs, military history or fiction—have been much distinguished by what it is simplest to call adult intelligence. That is, not many have addressed themselves and their material to readers reasonably well acquainted with human beings and human experience, not born yesterday, and not insensible to statements merely self-serving or to sentimental nonsense and bonehead contradictions in terms or facts. Such readers cannot read far in "The Eagle in the Egg" without the grateful awareness that here they are in good hands safe from nonsense on the way to seeing believable aspects of a real war, with no fool for a guide.

Good sense informs the whole book. It is packed into footnotes, pointed, often acerb, often diverting. It gives great merit to incidental descriptions of places and people. It appears at its invaluable best in the explanation of principles and policies, in getting at the truth in mostly misunderstood circumstances and situations. Colonel La Farge has, for instance, the boldness to stand up for the Brass; and only those who never saw the air generals, or did not see many of them, or saw them only from far off, will wonder at him.

Surveying his ATC generals he thinks they were good, not that they were perfect, but that their strengths far outweighed their insignificant weaknesses. With candor, he puts the case to the reader. Robert Olds, a man of the first ability, killed, like Walter Reed Weaver of the Training Command, by the work he made himself do, is shown also as often short-tempered, often a bumptious handful. Edward H. Alexander's gift of leadership and tireless concern for his men (contrary to popular ideas, close or extra-concern of this kind goes with the Academy ring) are noted, and noted, too, is the moody rashness, the less-than-adult taking to heart of that Allergic-To-Combat slur, and the kid's answer of hot or show-off flying. Harold L. George's remarkable capacities, the all-out energy, the unfettered bold imagination get the acknowledgment they deserve. Yet it is not concealed that the imagination could sometimes do with a little fettering, nor that a man of stature is not always above small vanities of place.

Equally perceptive, equally reliable in their informed judgment are the frank accounts of the troubles of high command, of tension, jealousy and conflict existing there, much as the lower echelons always darkly suspected. It is quite true that good men can lose and less-good men win. It is quite untrue that the motives are always or even often venal. There is much reaching and overreaching for power, and ambition plays its part; but the impelling motive is generally a simple, really honorable drive to get additional means to do a bigger job.

When this is on both sides the main interest, collisions are particularly painful, and defeats are bitter and may be bitterly explained. For light on these matters, next best to being there, is such an account as La Farge's of the long, warm staff struggle between HQ/ATC and the director of its women pilots allied with HQ/AAF over who had the say on policy. Many factors will be seen to enter, some not clearly connected with the prosecution of the war. Practical considerations did, and no doubt always will, take a licking when they come up against what was little less than a blonde vision, exquisite in tailored WASP blue, deliciously scented and sometimes close to tears.

The sharp observation and neat reporting extend well beyond these high and interesting levels. Much that the reader may have wondered about will be made plain to him in the concise, aptly placed speculations on the psychology of pilots, the substance of morale, the mechanism of command, or on the ways and means "not covered in the military rules but worked out from habitual American team relationships" by which the essential discipline can be got, when it is essential, in an agreement of reason quite as well as by a drilled-in mechanical reaction.

In this connection La Farge also makes you aware of another means, important when agreement of reason and mechanical reaction may both falter—that recourse which is a call-on the heart, with its reasons and its reactions both unknown to reason, to soften the impact of intolerable facts.

The nature of this process is perhaps illustrated as well as it can be by the author. The easy structure of the book permits him to speak out himself, as himself, when that best serves his purpose; so he can say of a B-29 crew with whom he has just flown the Pacific: "All I could think of was what a grand bunch of young men they were. What a grand bunch, and they were going on to the shooting war, not twelve, but sixteen and eighteen hours of that cramped, fatiguing flight, with, in the middle of it, the run through death, the lottery in which no virtue of skill or courage is protection against final loss. I seemed to ache with wishing them safe passages and a sure return home."

This is a good "war book"; worth the time and worth the money.

Bus Beal
[from *Guard of Honor*]

Twenty years before, when General Beal's youthful look and his eager or active air could not have been less marked than now, fellow classmen at the Military Academy, professing a derision that few of them actually felt, nicknamed him "Buster." Every old Air Corps man still knew him as Bus, and Colonel Ross could not remember hearing any of them speak ill of him.

Yet Colonel Ross knew it would be too much to say that none of them had ever thought ill of Bus. The quality of boyish eagerness, which a man's contemporaries can just stomach if he joins it to a friendly, unassuming nature, is likely to endear him to his superiors, and if it does, it becomes a harder thing to live down.

Colonel Ross, from years of a fairly active reserve-officer's close and sometimes critical acquaintance with the Regular Army, knew what such a boy would be up against. His professional abilities as an officer and a flyer had to stand invidious scrutiny. To stand that scrutiny with complete success, he needed to excel anything yet attained by mortal flyer or mortal officer. Bus was good, all right; but with so little room at the top, and with plums so few and far between, could he possibly be *that* good? Even if the answer had to be yes; even if he stood, by really unthinkable common agreement, well above everyone who shared his date of rank, his superiors would not feel perfectly free, at least in peacetime, to reward his merits quickly. In peacetime, everyone in the Army waits. Singling out a man, merely because of his abilities, and excepting him from the general rule, may give rise to rumors of favoritism. Rather than run such a risk, why not test his character by disappointment and delay? If your man loses patience, resigns his commission, plainly he lacks something; and your wisdom in waiting is established. The Old Man's favorite often takes a hard riding for this good reason.

Of course, Bus Beal made it easier for everyone by never seeming to give a damn for his career. Colonel Ross heard about that in Washington when they told him he was going to Ocanara, and General Beal, when he got back from Europe, would be his CO. If, as time passed, Bus did perhaps get

more, and did get away with more, than other young officers less happily
constituted (though in their own minds not undeserving), no one could say
that Bus worked it by bucking for things, or keeping out of trouble. He
was in trouble often. His Efficiency Rating seldom got beyond *excellent*
(which, in the Army, is pretty bad), because his Efficiency Reports kept
noting undesirable traits of recklessness and impulsiveness. Since he did
nothing about mending his ways, some instinct may have informed Lieutenant, and later Captain, Beal that these censures were mostly for the record, where they would be ready if evidence were needed to show that Bus
got no special favors. His instinct's information was correct. When it became apparent that the Army's long winter between wars was going to end,
nothing was found to prevent jumping him, by two special orders two
months apart, from captain to lieutenant colonel (temporary), and sending
him to the Philippines. He arrived there three days before the Japanese
bombers came over and destroyed on the ground two hundred and twenty-
one of the Air Forces' less than three hundred planes.

Colonel Ross had heard the general mention incidents and circumstances of the bad first months of the war. Behind the locked and guarded
doors of a Council on Reports session, or a meeting of the AFORAD Projects Board, General Beal would suddenly brush aside the proposals of his
Directorate Chiefs, or the contentions of the Orlando, or Eglin Field, or
Wright Field liaison officers, saying: "No. That won't work." Morosely,
then, looking away at the big charts on the wall, or at an unlighted cigarette
which his nervous fingers turned around and around until it broke and
scattered pieces of tobacco over the agenda sheet before him, he would tell
them, in explanation of his view, what he saw at Ido, or what you could
learn from the mistakes at Nichols Field. He meant that until those whose
opinion was different had seen what he had seen, he felt entitled to overrule
them for reasons quite apart from rank.

Indeed, it was not easy for a person who had never been in that situation
to know how a man must feel, and they listened to him, painfully silent,
sternly shamefaced, even when they thought, as some usually did, that the
lessons of 1941 were out of date. Since General Beal knew this as well as
anybody, indeed had helped to make them out of date, the general was
misled by the distortions that pain and emotion gave to facts which were
just facts to people who had been spared his experience.

"Well, the hell with all that now—" General Beal would soon say; for
his accounts never went beyond a half dozen sentences, some incomplete,
some highly ungrammatical in the stress of trying to express what he meant
without talking about it. There would be a profound pause.

Those who were still going to object shrank from objecting at once;
and even those who agreed felt the momentary inappropriateness of getting
right back to business. One of them might clear his throat and say, "Gen-

eral, I wonder if you ran into so-and-so . . ."; or another simply murmur: "Christ!" while he tried on himself the nightmare of everything going down in ruin around you (men wept at Nichols Field when the parked B-17's blew to bits or sank to junk in the flames of oxidized aluminum and running gasoline); your friends killed; your country shamed; disaster heaped on disaster; death at every turn; nothing to fight with; nothing to hope!

Colonel Ross did not think such a picture over-painted. Lieutenant Colonel Beal, putting together again and again the remains of a P-35 (obsolete before the war began), spent January and February flying it off a patch on Bataan to perform limping reconnaissance missions. When he somehow got back, it was often necessary to crash-land the crate. He would then walk away from it and report a few details of Japanese movement which would confirm the completeness of their disaster and the inevitability of their doom. From time to time, General Beal probably still re-lived moments so bad that a man might expect to die of them without assisting cause. In memory perhaps even worse would be the hours and days and weeks of horror rather than terror, when you had to do what you could not do; when you were never not hungry; when you were physically too sick to stand—General Beal had told Colonel Ross that, suffering from dysentery, he solved one problem of those ghastly reconnaissance missions by stuffing the seat of his coveralls with old paper.

If it were suggested to General Beal that Lieutenant Colonel Beal had liked any of these things, which he was not able to speak of without pain and which he winced a little even to think of, he would have stared angrily; but Colonel Ross thought it possible that Lieutenant Colonel Beal did like them better than General Beal now remembered. It was fair to believe that General Beal knew no more about himself than most men; and, out of his self-knowledge, could tell you, no matter how hard and honestly he tried, less than you could learn from what you saw or heard of his behavior.

Considered in this light, Lieutenant Colonel Beal's situation eighteen months ago might have been less than hell. Who but he could have made that P-35 fly at all? Who else could have evaded the Jap patrols? Who else could have brought the plane down without killing himself; and then fixed it to fly again later that week? However harrowing and hopeless looking, everything there was capable of yielding him the gratification of knowing that he had proved himself able to do all or more than any other man in those circumstances could do; that he had not flinched—or, rather, since of course he had, that no one had seen him flinch; and that, come what might, he had stuck it out.

Even on this last point there had been a problem to face and a choice to make, and General Beal could know that he had not fallen down on it. About the second week in March they asked for a volunteer to take one of the last flyable P-40's and try to get to Mindanao with a packet of sealed papers. That man, if he made it, would be out of this; while everyone else was lost. It was not a good chance, God knew, but it was a chance. It was the only chance any of them would ever get. The answer, while not easy, was simple. That a P-40, in the condition of those they had, could ever make Mindanao was hardly possible. If the likelihood of its getting there was greater with one pilot than with another, then that pilot must go. He must take the one chance, he must leave his surviving friends to the Japanese; he must escape, if he could, to life and health, to food and comfort; to honors and promotions. Lieutenant Colonel Beal was fully qualified to name that pilot, and it was necessary for him to name himself.

Colonel Ross did not envy him in this situation. Picking himself meant publicly concurring in the opinion, only decent when others held it, that no one approached him in skill and resource. Moreover, he must privately go on reiterating the unbecoming boast, giving himself specific instances of his clear superiority, since it was the only final answer to the hesitant, sickening query of his own heart. His heart knew how it longed not to die, and how little it regarded any face-saving argument that this escape might be more dangerous than not escaping. Perhaps so; but what pilot there, if the chance were offered him, would refuse it? Lieutenant Colonel Beal knew, too, all that, at that moment, was being bitterly felt and heatedly said about a more illustrious officer, only last week required, by direct orders, and by a sense of the duty that his high estimate of his own abilities imposed on him, to make his getaway. Colonel Beal must accept the certainty that the story of how he gave himself orders to go would pass from contemptuous mouth to contemptuous mouth, not only then and there; but for the rest of his life— or, if tomorrow a flight of Zeros jumped him, or his rickety engine conked out above the Sibuyan Sea, as long as any survivors of Bataan lived. Still, it was simple. Colonel Ross realized that Lieutenant Colonel Beal's temperament and training fitted him to state the problem; and, in this happy case, you could guess that the conscious mind, with its concept of duty, unreservedly replied: I *can*; while the secret image, every man's fond, fantastic idea of himself, whispered low: *Thou must*.

So he left; and he got the Silver Star for reaching Mindanao safely. Very soon afterward Lieutenant Colonel Beal was promoted to full colonel and sent to Australia to organize the fighter defense, such as it was, of Port Darwin. He flew in New Guinea for a month or so, and was credited with two Japanese planes. They then shifted him to the Seventh Air Force; and in May promoted him to Brigadier General. In July they brought him to Washington; and in September or October, he was sent secretly to Colomb Bechar.

Colonel Ross supposed that the game changed and the stakes went up at Colomb Bechar. He did not know what the general went there for. The fact that he did not know, that neither the general nor anyone else had ever told him, indicated the very highest level of policy and secrecy. However, Colonel Ross did know from ordinary sources of information, and by putting various references together, that Colomb Bechar, before it subsided to its present status of a junction point on the Air Transport Command's northwest African routes, had been a French Air Force field. It was three hundred miles south of Oran on the edge of the mountains.

General Beal went there many weeks before the November invasion, so vital preparations for the air part of that invasion might have been involved, and the general must have performed his job satisfactorily, in spite of whatever difficulties Carricker had in mind when he made his reference to the Frogs. There was, of course, the annoyingly complicated political situation in French North Africa. Moreover, Colonel Ross doubted if the general would feel at home with the French; a people who, in one of their aspects probably dismayed him by being so fond of gaiety and light wines; while in others they probably irritated him by their stubborn attachment, even when they were of low degree, to elaborate formalities, or stirred his contempt by their unabashed eagerness, even when they were of high degree, for substantial *pourboires*.

Because of its nature, and the high policy level of the necessary decision, Colonel Ross did not think that Bus Beal had asked for the Colomb Bechar assignment; but it seemed likely that, pleased with him, the high command let him say what he would like to do next. He turned up with the Ninth Air Force, where General Brereton no doubt wanted him. This surely suited Brigadier General Beal down to the ground. The situation was again difficult; but the issue was clear and openly joined, and he was the man to take it on. He was young enough, and himself fighter pilot enough, to uphold, as no one else could, the hand of the air generals against a strong and well-seated opposition.

They, the foot army commanders, controlled all air elements and were benightedly destroying them piecemeal. They must be stopped. The control must be wrested from them. To do this, it was necessary to shake them, or some of them, in their ruinous concepts. To shake them, they must be shown what the right use could do, compared to the wrong use. The person who showed them must be a man able at once to plan the mission, and himself lead it; and, having by rank the unquestionable right to be present at the highest council tables, to report out of his own mouth, so they must listen. Colonel Ross knew that it was believed by the Air Staff that General Beal, more than any other single person, won that fight; and, because of that air victory, they credited air power with winning, by May, Tunis, and Bizerte, too.

This was good; this was fine. Colonel Ross could well imagine it. General Beal, behind him half a skyful of his fighters, his gun hatches open and his magazines shot empty; his hair thick with the African dirt and his eyes dark with it in a face the sun had burned scarlet, must have felt like singing, regardless of more personal knowledge than most generals', that war is hell. He would flash around, four hundred yards off the runway, coming fast, a wing dipped to the tricky crosswind, to put down like an angel on three perfect points. By the dispersal areas beyond the distant edges of the field, all the ground crews jumped from their slit trenches— not long ago, approaching engines were always German. They bowled their helmets on the ground. They yelled and leaped and punched each other, all their daily gripes forgotten in the ecstasy of look the sweet Jesus at the general! Get a load of that aircraft driver! Bus is back from the wars!

General Nichols and Colonel Ross
[from *Guard of Honor*]

General Nichols, in arranging to drive to the Base alone with Colonel Ross, undoubtedly planned either to ask him something, or to tell him something. General Nichols, while he listened to Pop's ill-sorted argument explaining Benny, was looking at Colonel Ross much of the time. General Nichols might easily have read in Colonel Ross's face the question: *Who do we think we're fooling?* At that point the situation became ridiculous. Must they keep up the pretense that I don't know that you know that I know?

Sure of General Nichols's intention when General Baxter was so firmly kept from joining them, Colonel Ross resolved that, while he would not volunteer any information, he would answer a direct question directly: they didn't know where General Beal was. He need not decide what else he would say until he saw how General Nichols took that; but he intended to present, in whatever way seemed best when the time came, an obiter dictum—the learned judge's incidental or collateral opinion, which, while not binding, could be so stated that dissent would be impertinence and ignorance.

He would say that Bus's going-off was natural and sensible. It showed basic good judgment. Bus recognized that he had a problem. He also recognized the effect on himself of the heavy strains and responsibilities of his position. Bus saw that he was in danger of acting precipitately, without due consideration. The way to avoid this, to give himself an uninterrupted chance to think the thing through, was to duck out without telling anyone. Bus had probably gone flying. That would be the easiest way to make sure that nobody could reach him unless he wanted to be reached. There was nothing for anyone, except a chronic worrier like Pop, to worry about.

As this was not Colonel Ross's real or full opinion, he supposed he still had a hope of fooling General Nichols; but his object was not really to deceive. The chance was as good as ever that General Nichols would be glad to accept any plausible line that comported with the facts, as far as the facts now went. To help General Nichols this way, a grave and formal attitude might be useful.

In the hall, Colonel Ross shifted himself, as junior officer, to the general's left and marched silently with him toward the side entrance. He was waiting with reserve for the general's first remark. General Nichols made it as they reached the corner. He put a hand on Colonel Ross's arm, directing them both to a door marked OFFICERS. "Let's go in here a minute," General Nichols said.

Colonel Ross preserved his grave and formal attitude in the lavatory. General Nichols, coming to wash his hands while Colonel Ross sedately washed his own hands beside him, studied his reflection in the long mirror above the basins. The sculpturesque, still face might give a vain man satisfaction; and a vain man's satisfaction is never quite concealed.

Inconspicuously Colonel Ross watched for it; but General Nichols's quick critical glance at the cropped mustache, the clipped hair, the perfectly tied tie, the perfectly fitted battle jacket, was that of the inspecting officer, who shows no interest in what is right. If everything is right, he passes on indifferently. Passing on, General Nichols reached for a paper towel.

The container, as usual, held none.

Colonel Ross turned around, pushed back one of the swinging doors with his elbow and reeled out a mass of toilet paper. He said: "I'm very sorry, General. We're having trouble getting towels."

"Thanks," General Nichols said, accepting a few yards of the flimsy stuff and rubbing it over his hands. "Oh, I know there's a war on." He looked amiably at Colonel Ross. He said: "And you could be still worse off, Judge. You might not even have this. I will tell you an important military secret. Halfway through the Conference sessions at Quebec last month they ran out of toilet paper. Completely. Even in the Governor General's house in the Citadel there wasn't any, and some very important people were tearing up newspaper. Of course we shot a plane off right away and flew in a load. Nobody knows whether it was enemy agents, or whether they just didn't realize how much it takes to keep up with a conference."

By deliberately calling him "Judge," by the joshing tone, and the man-to-man touch of scatalogical humor, General Nichols was deliberately inviting Colonel Ross to lay formality aside. In the whole history of war it was unlikely that a colonel had ever refused such an invitation from a general officer, so Colonel Ross saw that he would have to go along. He laughed appreciatively. "Yes," he said, "that seems to be a concomitant of any human assembly. The end-product does pile up."

As a matter of fact, he would be glad to hear more about Quebec. He did not mean the inside story—what momentous plans had been agreed on, what grand decisions reached. Not enough informed to appraise them properly, in no position to do anything about them, anyway, Colonel Ross would rather not know about those. What he might hear to his profit, what he wanted to hear, was quite different. Encouraged to go on with his experiences at Quebec, General Nichols might tell Colonel Ross a good deal about General Nichols.

Much might be learned, for instance, from his attitude, which would soon be plain, toward the great personages gathered there with him. All unknowingly, General Nichols letting it be seen that this or that interested or impressed him, would show Colonel Ross the way to handle General Nichols. He might, indirectly or incidentally, answer the most important question in Colonel Ross's mind—how General Nichols really rated, what his powers were, what kind of influence he had in high circles.

Colonel Ross got ready a deft, leading remark, which would keep General Nichols on that subject, surely as agreeable to the general as it was to most men, of himself and his exploits. He would incite General Nichols along the way he should go. Before Colonel Ross could speak, General Nichols tapped his arm casually, directing him out the door.

Colonel Ross was disconcerted.

Immersed in his idea, he had been choosing the course, directing things. He had forgotten that he was this young man's junior. Not he, but General Nichols was the one waited-on, the one who always gave the signal. Embarrassed by his own incredulous start, Colonel Ross made haste to obey. He walked into the hall. The original deft, leading remark was lost in this mental shuffle; and before Colonel Ross could find a new one to offer in its place, General Nichols said: "The Old Man had me along to run errands and hand him the papers, mostly."

He let his eyes, grave and candid, rest on Colonel Ross. "He thought I ought to be up on the diplomatic falderal because I'd had some assignments as an air attaché. Then, before we were in the war, they'd sent me to England as an observer in nineteen-forty-one, so I knew personally a good many RAF people and could be useful as a sort of liaison officer. It let me see a lot of what was going on."

He paused, with an air of reminiscent amusement. "They didn't get around to consulting me very much," he said. "One night I was given three minutes to tell the President and Mr. Churchill some grounds we had for our objection to a proposal that was made. The Old Man held a watch on me while I did it and it took me two minutes and fifty-two seconds. When I finished, the President yawned (it *was* pretty late) and said: 'Uh—thanks, General'; and Mr. Churchill said something like 'Harrumph!' I was then excused." The air of amusement grew into a smile.

They had reached the door at the end of the side passage and Colonel Ross opened it and held it for the general. They stepped from the refrigerated hall into the full tropic morning on the steps. The car stood there with the driver in his seat, and at the foot of the steps, holding the car door open, Mr. Botwinick beamed obsequiously. He must have slipped out and run around to make sure everything was all right. General Nichols gave Colonel Ross another casual little tap and Colonel Ross, ducking his big shoulders, scrambled in and took his proper corner.

When General Nichols smiled, Colonel Ross had smiled in return, though weakly. While they came down the steps, while Mr. Botwinick facilitated their entrance into the car, he had the disturbing sense of now seeing, of having certainly felt, what they meant—what made Hal Coulthard say on the verandah last night that he sometimes got the creeps; what threw Pop into that rage of agitation over the idea of General Nichols coming to know too much; what Mrs. Beal—Sal—hysterically apprehended as she tried to learn at the dining room door what "they" were doing to Bus. They must all, from time to time, have been abruptly nonplused as General Nichols finished speaking and smiled.

In the supposed privacy of his mind, Colonel Ross had formed an intention. Before he could even set about acting on it, General Nichols had anticipated him and had offered him at once, still joshing a little, a good part of the specific information, summed up for his convenience, that Colonel Ross had planned to wile out of him.

Did General Nichols, then, for God's sake, read your mind, know everything you were thinking? For slow thinkers like Hal and Pop, for a whimsical and impulsive child like Mrs. Beal, it would be a short jump to that disquieting, even dazing, conclusion. Bewildered, persuaded that he was outclassed by unheard of abilities and up against inhuman attributes, Hal or Pop began warily to study all his old friend Jo-Jo said or did, to find obscure meanings, sinister purposes, hidden dangers. Sal, working up a fright, doubled her fists and hammered them, like a child, on whatever she could reach.

All that was nonsense! When a man knew what you were thinking it was either because you had just told him by your acts or words or appearance, or because he judged you and your situation rightly, and to know what you had in mind, he needed only to ask himself what you would be likely to have in mind. Colonel Ross, restored, thought of other things he would like to know. He said judicially: "Still, the Conference must have been an interesting experience, General. A close-up of the people running things often helps to clarify the situation. I have had some experience in politics. It is very rightly called the art of the possible."

General Nichols gave him a quick, complimentary look. "Yes," he said, "the possible! That engaged them a lot. The problem is always as I see it, to find out what that is; because that's all. You have to work inside that. The top echelon rides in the whirlwind, all right; but sometimes the storm seems to do the directing. That limits your choice, your freedom. Certain things that it might be wise to do can't be done. Of course, it doesn't mean you haven't, at the top, a good deal of choice, a good deal of freedom. You can't order a man to flap his arms and fly; but you can always order as many qualified pilots as you have to take as many planes as you have and fly the wrong way to the wrong place at the wrong time."

Colonel Ross stared at him with attention, pricking up his ears. In that sober, casual observation, if General Nichols would go on and interpret it, might lie some of what Colonel Ross had hoped to learn about General Nichols. It might express disillusionment; and if so, there was a simplicity here, since simplicity is a prerequisite of disillusionment.

General Nichols might be coming late to the realization of the important truism that men are men, whether public or private. A public man had a front, a face; and then, perforce, he had a back, a backside, and in the nature of things it was so ordered that the one was associated with high professions and pronouncements and the other with that euphemistically denoted end-product. They were both always there. Which you saw best would depend on where you stood; but if you let yourself imagine that the one (no matter which) invalidated or made nugatory the other, that was the measure of your simplicity.

General Nichols said: "I've read, I think some Frenchman said, that though you sit on the highest throne in the world, you sit there on your own tail. It is a handicap to you; and it doesn't help much to inspire the people watching you with confidence."

That was helpful. General Nichols's inquisitive, reflective eye did not miss their human plights, their various mental and physical predicaments. He would, perhaps, observe that the Protagonist of the Bull Dog Breed was often grumpy, half a mind on his brandy-soured stomach and throatful of cigar-flavored phlegm. Grimacing, Mr. Churchill must taste, too, the gall of his situation. Fine phrases and selected words might show it almost a virtue that, far call'd our navies melt away; that, on dune and headland sinks the fire; but those circumstances also kept him from the leading position. Except as a piece of politeness, he did not even sit as an equal. His real job was to palter. His field and air marshals, on short commons of men and machines, his admirals of the outclassed fleet, all nerves bared by close to four years of war in the main unfortunate, supported him, courageous and proud, but also at the last word impotent.

Across the table, General Nichols's own side, the Union strong and great, was in a pleasanter position; justifiably cockier. They had the ships, they had the men, they had the money, too! However, the Champion of the Four Freedoms was, in cruel fact, not free to leave his chair; he could not do it unless somebody helped him. His top military chiefs, shown able enough as far as they had gone, were disadvantaged because they had never waged any war to speak of, fortunate or unfortunate. And then, too, though they had so much more of everything else, they faced what they called their opposite numbers with only four, instead of five, stars.

Thus, variously hampered and discontented, these great personages showed General Nichols, the errand boy, the perhaps not-unartful nipper, how to make history. Their proceedings must often be less than sensible unless you understood the object of them. The object could not be simply to concert a wisest and best course. The object was to strike a bargain, a master bargain which was the congeries of a thousand small bargains wherein both high contracting parties had been trying, if possible, to get something for nothing; and if that were not possible, to give a little in order to gain a lot. Since, in each such arrangement, someone must come out on the short end, and since no subordinate could risk being the one, chiefs must meet and agree.

Agreement was ordinarily resisted by mutual misrepresentations, and obtained by a balance of disguised bribes and veiled threats. Plain honest people were often disgusted when they found out that high business was regularly done in these low ways. They were also indignant; because they knew a remedy for the shameful state of affairs. Let every man be just and generous, open and honorable, brave and wise. No higgling or overreaching would then be necessary.

"Yes," Colonel Ross said. "Yes, yes!"

General Nichols said: "I can tell you that the Conference, as well as naming a commander, set the date for the invasion of Europe. There was a certain amount of protest. An invasion plan for this year had already been given up. It was felt that the best use of air power was not being made if we were again prevented from completing projected operations on the scale and on the schedule we planned. The new directive was to do what many people considered the third or fourth best thing, depending on how you looked at it."

General Nichols drew from the inside pocket of his battle jacket a long, flat, silver cigarette case, on which Colonel Ross saw the crowned emblem of the Royal Air Force. Engraved below were several lines, of which he could read the beginning: *Presented to Colonel Joseph Josephson Nichols, USAAF, with the high regard and comradely esteem of—*

General Nichols said: "We are on a tough spot. If the operation is anything short of a complete success, it will be due to our failure to make the best use of air power. We know that. The Old Man knows that. We cannot fail to do what we know must be done merely because we are not to have all the time and all the priorities we thought we had to have. We must do it anyway. The Old Man thinks we can; so at any cost, we will."

By a momentary change of expression, by a movement of muscles that redistributed the lights and shadows on the surface of General Nichols's face, Colonel Ross gained the abrupt impression or illusion of another face suddenly showing through, making a different use of the same marmoreal features. Colonel Ross supposed that he had not quite dismissed those vague, ominous, stated or implied, opinions about General Nichols. Colonel Ross stirred in anxiety, thinking he might be about to discover the mean, plain truth—malice or ambition, coldness of pride, cruelty of self-interest. A human mind and will that saw itself interacting with great events often hid those qualities under the protestation of a higher necessity —*we cannot fail . . . we must do it anyway . . . at any cost we will . . .*

Anxiously poring on this other, underlying face, Colonel Ross concluded with relief that it was fundamentally innocent. It lacked the finish, the artificial guilelessness of the arch-villain or arch-conspirator. Its strength would be in candor, not machination. It was a hollower and an older face. It was severe and pensive, as though thinned and worn by strain or stress or trial. There was a clear mournfulness of eye, suggesting persistent if not deep ponderings, long unlighted vigils, an undeceived apprehension, a stern, wakeful grasp of the nature of things. While so mournful, the eye was at the same time singularly serene, without the slight clouding of subtlety, or the veiling blankness of devious design. General Nichols looked out calmly, in well-earned assurance of rightly estimating the possibilities and limitations of the Here and Now, and so of being ready for what might come.

Though not certain of all that these marks and signs portended, Colonel Ross could recognize their most important meaning. They showed a man past that chief climacteric, the loss of his last early involuntary illusions. A time of choice had come and gone. At least in a limited sense, it had been up to him whether he adopted, as soon as he could learn or invent them, new versions of his boy's-eye views; or whether he tried to go on without them. Colonel Ross was impressed; for if he was right about General Nichols, General Nichols had chosen the hard way, and now went on without them.

People like Bus, people like Pop, people like Colonel Ross himself, might, to this stripped-down, comfortless, plain and simple mind seem superannuated children. Bus and Pop more, he himself (Colonel Ross thought) less, carried over, gave a grown-up handling to, the boy's complicated world of imaginary characters; the boy's long, long, illogical thoughts; the boy's unwarranted entertainment and unfounded terror in a state of things systematically misunderstood.

General Nichols and the never very large number of men like him could watch them with calculating detachment—not underrating these persistent children, nor even despising them. They were boys in mind only. They had the means and resources of man's estate. They were more dextrous and much more dangerous than when they pretended they were robbers or Indians; and now their make-believe was really serious to them. You found it funny or called it silly at your peril. Credulity had been renamed faith. Each childish adult determinedly bet his life and staked his sacred pride on, say, the Marxist's ludicrous substance of things only hoped for, or the Christian casuist's wishful evidence of things not so much as seen. Faiths like these were facts. They must be taken into account; you must do the best you could with them, or in spite of them.

General Nichols said: "I don't mean that the air potential was denied. What we could certainly do—as you may know, Colonel, thanks to the new aids applied in March, the RAF really ruined Essen by July—and what we could probably do were both recognized. It was not denied that our course would be safer, might be cheaper, and could with luck be more quickly and completely successful. I had a little trouble getting the point; but I got it in the end. It wasn't desirable for us to be too completely successful."

Colonel Ross gave him a quick look.

"That's what I thought," General Nichols said. "Some people still think so. Of course, we've got to have a separate air force; and we'll have it. And there may be people who don't want us to look too good—but they aren't people in a position where they can do anything about it. That particular opposition's argument hinged on what we meant by complete success. The Old Man simply figured on beating the hell out of the back areas, blowing up the whole German war potential. That would take care of the German armed forces all right. The opposition felt that the way to take care of the German armed forces was to attack them directly and overpower them. As an operation in itself, they never said it was as safe, as cheap, or as good. They simply said: you want to make the biggest mess in history; and who's going to clean it up? Answer: we are; unless we assume, which we are not assuming, that we won't win the war. The Old Man said: that isn't what you asked us. You asked us how to make Germany quit fighting, and we told you. Say the word and we'll do it for you; we will obliterate them, and obliterate them, and obliterate them again."

General Nichols smiled faintly. "The Old Man's ideas are thorough-going," he said. "He didn't say it was the best thing to do; he just said if that was the thing to do, that was the best way to do it. Naturally, there were compelling reasons why the course we recommended was not adopted. One of them may have been this not-making-too-much-of-a-mess. Then, of course, we weren't starting from scratch, or with a free hand. What we had done already was bound to limit what we could do next; and, of course, we could not do what we *might* not. We have to wait for the word to be said; and if the people who say the word can't see what you see, they won't say it and we don't get to do it. Short of a military coup d'état, which I did not hear anywhere proposed, we would have to make do with what they were able to see. The possibility exists that they are right. It's a matter of different opinions about the same thing. The other thing, the limit put on what we could do next by what we had already done, I heard an RAF fellow state in terms of airborne troops."

General Nichols held out the cigarette case. Colonel Ross did not like cigarettes; but he took one.

General Nichols said: "Once the jump master boots a paratrooper through the hatch, the paratrooper is on his own. How he lands will depend, among other things, on his training, his physical condition, his experience and judgment. He must keep looking to see what's what. He must make the right decisions at the right time. Now, suppose he gets down and it looks bad; the terrain, or enemy dispositions, make it dangerous to land, and he sees he'll probably duff it. What's his right course? Why, unless the man's a bloody fool, he climbs back into the plane and tries somewhere else."

General Nichols struck a match and lit Colonel Ross's cigarette. He said: "What did Bus do, Judge? Duck out?"

Colonel Ross, his eyes on the sheltered match flame, drew a mouthful of insipid-tasting smoke.

"I don't really know, General," he said. "Bus left his office without saying anything. Pop tried to reach him but he wasn't able to; so Bus may have gone flying. He had some things to think over. I could see when we were talking in the dining room there, he hadn't made his mind up about that business. That was why he threw it at me. I could hold it while he thought it over."

General Nichols said: "Did you decide not to have the hearing?"

"I decided not to have it this morning," Colonel Ross said. "I thought it over, too. When you've spent as much time in court as I have, General, you're inclined to keep things out of court if you possibly can. Once you initiate a process, the process takes over—like your friend's paratrooper jumping. Once our MP officer prefers charges, we begin to have a record. Because a record has to show certain things, certain things must follow. While we can still have them, or not have them, I thought we'd just pause for reflection. Bus may think of something. I may think of something. Washington might even think of something, I suppose."

General Nichols said: "Judge, I think you're all making a little too much of this. Bus is, certainly. He has the Washingtoin angle wrong. He really knows that. You must have found out by now that Bus is a little temperamental, Judge. Bus was just feeling sulky this morning. He wanted to have it wrong, so he'd have something to sulk about. Now, no one blames Bus for what happened. Given the situation that exists, it, or something like it, must happen from time to time. Where does Bus come in? He didn't

cause the situation to exist. Is the Old Man, the War Department, or anyone else, going to hold Bus strictly accountable for the facts that Southern
whites feel that Negroes cannot be allowed social or political equality; or
that Negroes don't enjoy being treated like animals? The situation is a
nuisance to us, and we wish it didn't exist; but Bus isn't expected to find
a solution for it."

"Sulk" was a good word for what Bus was, in fact, doing, and General
Nichols used it, not contemptuously, but kindly. Colonel Ross nevertheless bristled in an irritability, already pricked raw by the morning's many
cares and exasperations—too many to keep them all in mind; but while he
concentrated on one, he felt the general soreness of the others waiting on
his leisure for further consideration. Further consideration of some of them
could only mean blaming himself more fully, in greater detail. With others, it could only mean angering himself again over the needless stupidities
of someone else. General Nichols's little dissertation on the "situation that
exists," the easy philosophic detachment, the pooh-poohing of Colonel
Ross's infinitude of troubles by the bland opinion that too much was being
made of this, provoked Colonel Ross. He said: "I'm not sure, General, that
it's clear to me, or to Bus, what Bus *is* expected to do. Is it, by any chance,
also not clear to Washington?"

The rude, railing tone was, Colonel Ross must confess, unbecoming.
At the sound of it, General Nichols gave him a reflective look in which,
while there was no visible displeasure or annoyance, there was undoubtedly
a critical query, an unshown surprise, a naturally menacing speculation.
Was this surly old man being captious? Was he going to be difficult?

In a distress resembling the distress he felt immediately after suggesting to Captain Collins that he was in some rakish relationship with his Miss
Crittenden; the distress of seeing himself put himself wantonly in the
wrong, Colonel Ross felt immediately the hateful consequence—the despite he did his gray hairs; the loss of that precious aplomb of self-respect;
the quailing of mind, no longer intrepid because the knowledge that he
was wrong knocked all its props out, and left his mind with nothing to
give him but the shamed, furtive counsel: *Take care; you don't want to go too
far!*

General Nichols lifted his hand and looked at his fingernails. He said
equably: "A problem in public relations required a statement of policy.
That policy was considered, approved, and announced. Bus, and everyone
else, will keep in line. If circumstances beyond his control, an accident, an
unforeseen contingency, force him out of line, he is expected to get back in
line as quick as he can. That's all there is to it. Bus is not expected to do the
impossible; he is not expected to reverse himself, humiliate himself. He is
expected to act, as far as other duties and responsibilities allow him, to

smooth it over, not stir it up. I don't think there's any difference of opinion between us on that, Judge. From what you say you're doing, I can see we don't differ."

"I don't know that I have a plan," Colonel Ross said. "It isn't complete. It may not work. It doesn't go much further than this. When Pop was talking, I thought I'd have a talk with Willis. Incidentally, Willis's father had word he was injured, and he's expected in this morning. I sent an officer to meet him. I thought I'd have a talk with him, too."

General Nichols said: "After I've given the boy his medal, I'll bow out; and you have your talk. As I see it, he gains a good deal, everything he's worked for, everything he now almost has, if there's no more trouble, if he helps you. I don't think I'd pay a great deal of attention to Pop's notion about what's laying it on thick, and what isn't."

"I won't pretend I like it," Colonel Ross said.

"The boy seems to have a just complaint," General Nichols said; "but I think the question for him is whether he likes his complaint so well he'll trade a medium bomb group—at least three promotions, his name in the papers, all that, for it. That's just a statement of the facts. I don't think it needs to be regarded as a bribe, or as a threat."

"I will try not to so regard it, if he will," Colonel Ross said. He sat somber a moment.

General Nichols said, "There's this about Bus—there always was, Judge. There's you, and there's Pop; and you know him and you work for him and you go to bat for him. And if you will, other people will. They did; they have. The Old Man knows that. A man can't do everything himself— not if what he's doing amounts to much. Up to a point, yes; but then how much other people will do for him is very important." He paused reflectively. He said, "nothing definite is decided yet, as far as I know. The Old Man doesn't project operations around any given individual. Flying is a hazardous occupation; and so is war. You can't be perfectly sure who's going to be here when the time comes. Circumstances may change; so you need a different person. A person may change. Someone else may get to be better. But the Old Man always plans in terms of alternatives, considered possibilities, a long way ahead. I say I don't know anything definite; in fact, I'm sure there isn't anything definite, because it isn't time to decide yet; but I think there might be this in mind for Bus."

General Nichols carefully put out his cigarette in the ash tray under the window. He looked a moment at the passing pine woods soaked in sun. He said: "I think the Old Man has it in mind to give Bus the Tactical Air Force for the invasion of the Japanese home islands; if and when. It would not be inappropriate. The AAF wouldn't mind cutting itself a little piece of that 'I shall return' stuff." He looked back from the passing woods to Colonel Ross. "It wasn't intended originally to bring Bus home this year. Bus pretty well proved in North Africa that he was the best man we had to command large scale fighter operations. A big fighter job was coming up—is coming up. You can guess it. In a few more months, we'll have the planes modified, and we're going to escort the bombers all the way. Of course, Bus wasn't the only one, or even the first one, to see we'd have to do that; but it was really his baby. He went to work. He managed to set up small test missions. From them, he developed some basic tactics and a good operational organization scheme. The Air Staff liked it. That was when the Old Man put him through for major general. I don't know how much of this Bus told you."

"None," Colonel Ross said. "Bus doesn't talk much, about himself, General. Of course everyone knew what he did in Africa. He's said a few things about that, but not much else—to me."

General Nichols said: "Bus got his second star and was pulled out a little before the African business was over and sent to England. Then the Old Man changed his mind. I think I know why. Bus was insisting he be allowed to fly the escort missions himself. He was always flying missions in Africa, you know. Of course, some operations he needed to see first-hand; and leading missions, especially in the early days, was good for morale; only Bus did it all the time. He seems to like it. The Old Man didn't want him doing it all the time over Germany. We can't afford to lose what Bus knows, on the chance that he might get to know a little bit more. It puts too much at stake; it's not a reasonable risk. And, anyway, when the Old Man says something, that's it. Believe me. You don't go on insisting on things."

General Nichols drew a breath. He said: "So it seemed a good idea to have Bus home, stop fighting the whole war with him, give him a chance to cool off. Moreover, he was just what they wanted for AFORAD, Ocanara, here. He certainly knew about operational requirements; so everything fitted in nicely. I know the Old Man had a talk with Bus, and Bus was satisfied. I imagine the idea is for Bus to hold this down until we go ashore in Europe. Then, shoot him over to that Tactical Air Force—not in any command capacity; but to observe how the air-ground co-operation works out. As soon as we get into Germany, Bus would be pulled out and brought right home to start the fighter organization for the Japanese business. That's what I think is in the cards, Judge. Or could be."

"I see," said Colonel Ross.

His mind, tensely following, paused a moment. Might all this be taken, too, as just a statement of facts, no bribe, no threat? He let the puzzle, if one was there, go in favor of another distraction, minor, outside or behind his first line of thought, but urgently relative to another line, to one of those permanent, underlying concerns which, while not often admitted to full consciousness, always waited there, listening for anything it could use. What this constant concern picked up last was General Nichols's matter-of-fact: *As soon as we get into Germany;* and it gave a bound, identifying itself, and revealing by its relief that that was not all it had picked up in the course of this conversation.

The listening concern heard, and it trembled, when General Nichols spoke his doubt that the big brass, the VIP's at Quebec, intended to make the best use of air power. It heard again, and it shrank, when General Nichols proclaimed that, nonetheless, the air effort would proceed *at all costs*. When it learned that fighter planes would soon escort the bombers all the way, it blew hot and cold, considering first the new safeguard, and then the fearful danger which that decision attested. Now, it heard that at Quebec, at Washington, the places where people knew, doubt was not entertained; there was no "if." They ought to know; they felt no serious question; so, thank God, we must be getting somewhere! The identified thought presented itself for an instant in the picture of his son, Jimmy, crouched bundled-up in the bomber's naked, defenseless-looking, transparent nose, the bombsight cup against his eye; neither he, nor the plane whose run he now controlled, able to deviate one jot, evade one inch, while the guns below, with exquisite precision, preternaturally collecting and correcting their own data, laid themselves, and kept themselves, on this creeping, sitting target.

Colonel Ross said: "Then they brought Bus home to have a rest. Do they think he's getting all he needs?"

"They have to think so, Judge," General Nichols said. "I never heard it formulated as policy; but I know, in practice, the only people who get more rest in the Zone of Interior are those who can't be usefully employed. Bus is useful here; and this should be useful to him—a fairly big administrative job. Bus knows he hasn't been sidetracked, or anything like that. It is all to the purpose. I don't believe anyone—not Bus himself—considers Bus an administrative type. They don't want to make him one, either; but he needs the experience that comes from having the problems dumped on him. Picking the right men to handle them for him. You have to have that to manage a unit as large as a whole Air Force. The Old Man doesn't miss much. Bus would be good for AFORAD; and AFORAD would be good for Bus."

Colonel Ross said: "His wife, and my wife, think it would be wonderful if they gave him a few weeks off; just let him go away somewhere and do nothing. They think Washington would do that if you suggested it."

General Nichols said: "Judge, it wouldn't be good to suggest that Bus ought to have some leave, go off for a few weeks. They would want a reason. Keep remembering that Washington has all the troubles it needs—I know nobody in the field ever thinks so—and things could also add up on them, if they let them. They could get in a state, too; except the Old Man won't have it. Nobody can be allowed to make himself a worry. Colonel Woodman was an example of that. He was about to get the ax, you know. I suppose you could say little things had been adding up on him, and he let himself get into a state. Sellers Field was relatively unimportant, and Training Command Headquarters stood between Woodman and Washington, at least until Woodman did some funny business out of channels. In short, they don't like to hear that somebody needs a rest. It's always bad news in their business."

Colonel Ross said: "Isn't it worse news when somebody like Woodman blows his brains out?"

"If he'd been told about Woodman, the Old Man would have had him relieved some time ago," General Nichols said. "He can't be told everything —the day isn't that long. So other people have to take the responsibility of deciding what he must be told, and what he needn't be told, or maybe, mustn't be told."

"I see that," Colonel Ross said.

"Yes; well a couple of people took the responsibility about Woodman. They knew that if the Old Man heard that Woodman was letting things add up on him, that finished Woodman. There is no time for rests. Everyone just has to take it, carry on anyway. It's a little like our pilot-training theory. We don't say too much about it; but you know and I know that it's better, more economical, to push a boy hard, throw it right at him; if it comes to that, let him crack up in a training plane here at home; instead of babying him along so he can crack up a fighter in an overseas theater."

The car was approaching the intersection where the road from the Area joined the highway to Ocanara, beyond the Air Field and the Base. On the highway, in ponderous motion, also approaching the intersection, crawled a tractor-mounted gasoline shovel with a crane boom. Colonel Ross saw it first; but the driver immediately saw it too. He leaned forward and set off the staff car's siren. The tractor halted, the high boom wagging back and forth, and they passed it, turning north ahead of it.

Frowning, Colonel Ross made an instinctive move to push back the glass panel between him and the driver. The great machine with its heavy-lugged tread was hacking up the road surface, and they would assuredly hear about that from the State Highway Department.

"Want to stop?" General Nichols said.

Colonel Ross brought a notebook and pencil from his breast pocket. "No. I won't hold you up, General," he said. He took down the Engineer Corps serial number under the white star on the cabin. "I don't know what makes them do it," he said. "They have definite orders not to move heavy stuff on its own tread over a public highway. They pay no attention. It wouldn't surprise me if that's come a mile or more, all the way down from Gate Number Three—"

"I guess we're going to stop anyway," General Nichols said.

The brakes let out a shriek as the driver stepped hard on them. Around a bend in the scrubby woods a low-bed trailer on multiple sets of wheels stood in the middle of the road. Fallen off the trailer, directly in front of the car, was a great mass of metal, the whole battered fuselage and the torn-off wings of an A-20 attack bomber, painted black as a night fighter. A sergeant and two men, standing idle, started at the sound of the brakes, and turned to look.

The Review
[from *Guard of Honor*]

Colonel Ross pronounced to himself: *All is best though we oft doubt what the unsearchable dispose of Highest Wisdom brings about, and ever best found in the close. Oft He seems to hide His face, but unexpectedly returns, and to His faithful champion . . .*

He was surprised. He did not know why he thought of those lines now; but he doubted if things like that were ever wholly random. His mind, finding him—though his conscious knowledge did not know it—in want of something, determined in its own way what he did not know he wanted, and went off to the past to turn over the litter of memory and see if anything was there. Finding something, if not the very thing, then something that might do, it was back with it, waiting for the first lull of activity on the conscious level to display its finding for what it might be worth.

The finding might, of course, be worth a good deal, if you only knew it. Here you had the answer; but unfortunately you might not yet have received the problem. The answer, moreover, came in the only terms possible for this kind of communication. They were terms of symbol or image, perfectly related to the meaning that was intended to reach you in the flawless logic that things equal to the same thing are equal to each other. It was again unfortunate that the conscious mind was not too bright, and so never could work out the perhaps-worthwhile meaning of most of these messages.

Now old Judge Schlichter, his raised finger oratorically pointing up at Highest Wisdom's home, heaven, boomed majestically on, while the sunlight of mornings years ago fell on the shelves packed with bound reports that lined the musty room where young Ross sat clerking for the Judge and reading for his bar examination. Bemused, old Ross contemplated the enigmatic spectacle.

Regardless of any service the recollection might be meant to do him, Colonel Ross was glad to have it. In recollection, the not-bright conscious mind, all meaning missed, could take it easy. Standing in the first line of the double row of General Beal's staff officers on the bunting-decked platform erected for the reviewing party, and already tired of standing, and of the late afternoon sunlight pouring across his face, Colonel Ross nonetheless rested in most senses.

The ample space, formally left empty, which surrounded the temporary scaffolding of the platform suggested a charmed area which it would be impossible for anybody to cross, bringing him business. He was a full hundred yards from the nearest telephones in the Operations Building. He was a full fifty yards from the convertible coupe with the top down parked with a few other favored cars farther along the ramp. That was the general's; and Cora had driven Sal out in it. Cora and Sal sat there together; and he knew that Cora was watchfully checking up on him from time to time; but she was too far away to advise him about not overdoing things at his age.

While he stood in this security, there were several bands to play for Colonel Ross and since it seemed to be agreed among them that the Air Corps song was most suitable for a march-past the music had an undemanding monotony. No sooner had it gone by, jaunty, passing farther and farther up the ramp to the right, and finally ceasing, than it began again from the left. Far down the hangar line, growing stronger, it came on, making the spine crawl with an ever-louder brave smash of drums, and the fine martial polyphony of mixed brass. Stepping out to it were five thousand marchers, with a good deal of mechanized equipment to come after that.

Colonel Ross noted, quite indifferent, that the marching was better than he would have expected. Fully half these units were made up of men who worked in shops or hangars or offices. The other half were tactical units of various sorts or arms; but tactical units at AFORAD were kept busy acting out field problems that the Directorate of Air-Ground Coöperation was studying and did no more close order drill than the average quartermaster company.

Colonel Ross noted, too, though not so indifferently, since they made a tremendous tiring noise, that Pop's grand aerial display, the contingents of visiting planes, actually were on their complicated schedule—a matter to which Pop at the head of the line called attention by winks and nods toward the south and east horizons. When the fighter groups came in sight exactly as the head of the big bomber flight passed throbbing above, Pop's satisfaction was so great that he lost all control and shattered the decorum of a reviewing party by lifting his hand to show Colonel Ross his thumb and forefinger joined in a triumphant circle.

In front of Colonel Ross, General Beal and General Nichols, with orderlies to right and left, really stood none the worse for all the Air Corps years between them and West Point. Chins up and alert, they put on the reviewing officer's show of ever renewed anticipation and unwearied interest as, through the band music and the noise of planes, new hearty barks and bawls came up, the advancing guidons dropped, the ranked faces in a simultaneous flash of changed color, snapped right.

Colonel Ross supposed that everyone was what passed for happy—the generals, as recipients of all this tradition, form and ceremonious duty, were getting a little of the least palling of human pleasures; the marchers, once they had done their eyes-right and gone by the stand, had the relief, at this point major pleasure, of knowing the unenjoyable exercise was for them nearly over; the spectators had the recreation of participating vicariously in martial, manly goings-on—war in stouthearted terms of the "Soldiers' Chorus" from *Faust*; and a welcome change from their everyday war of ration books, Selective Service classifications, and the low diet of news that many of them would see was doctored by an omission of all happenings not desirable for them to know about, and by the insertion of much semi-fiction it was judged useful for them to believe.

Colonel Ross, too, might pass for happy. He enjoyed his hour or more of being left alone. There was nothing here he need pay any attention to. Shifting at intervals his main weight from one aching leg to the other, Colonel Ross contemplated in peace, with a melancholy no more than slight, the living, speaking image of Judge Schlichter, now twenty-five years in his grave.

At the time that young Ross's good fortune (joined, he might allow, with qualities of determined industry and reasonable intelligence) got him his chance to work in the judge's office, Judge Schlichter had come, now he was along in years, to conduct himself with a stateliness that extended to his smallest actions. Judge Schlichter's discourse—no homelier word described it—must dazzle any young man who had run away from school; and particularly one who regretted running away, and was resolved, at twenty, to recoup the losses he rashly incurred at sixteen. Judge Schlichter's range of vocabulary was so great that he seldom felt at loss for the long word to replace an ordinary man's short one. His learning was not confined in narrow legal bounds. He had familiarized himself with the best that has been thought and said, and quoted it freely. Young Ross wrote down a private list of authors to find out about, and of books to borrow from the public library. He regarded the judge with reverent awe.

This, no doubt, went on some months; but perhaps not very many, for the boy was observant and apt to learn. As he became more at home in legal circles, he would have to notice that the leading members of the local bar, though they listened all right, did not listen with awe to old Schlichter's circumlocutions. They did not hear with pleasure his spoutings of Milton, or twenty lines of Shakespeare declaimed like a ham actor, or verses from Whittier and Longfellow that had been boring everyone for half a century.

A day came, of course, when signs that the judge was going to sound off pricked young Ross with anguish. He foresaw the pompous, struck attitude and the farcically affected boom; he anticipated with shame the eyes of visitors covertly rolled in resignation; the hand-covered asides, impatient, ironic, of counsel in court. How could the judge not know that everyone was laughing at him for a pretentious old windbag?

Here was a baffling question. Judge Schlichter had a mind, in the idiom of the day, like a steel trap. Bending from the bench, or sharply attending in his chambers, he missed nothing and he forgot nothing, and nobody fooled him. He could spot a lie a mile off. In a few minutes' masterly exchange, he was often pleased to demonstrate a slick scoundrel out of that scoundrel's own unwary mouth. When smart young attorneys, busy for several days, had finished crossing up an issue, old Schlichter, coming to charge, glancing at his notes, would strip off in ten minutes every expertly added non-essential. He rescued the lost point; he lucidly restated the evidence; and, in doing that, he made any chicanery on either side as clear as day—most juries had no real need to leave the box at all.

It was too bad that Judge Schlichter could just as readily halt a pleading to bumble: Life is real! Life is earnest! And the grave is not its goal; or to flabbergast everyone by demanding of the prisoner at the bar when shall he think to find a stranger just, when he, himself, himself confounds, betrays, to slanderous tongues and wretched hateful days? What ever became of the steel-trap mind? What had become of the man nobody fooled?

What, indeed? What, indeed?

Colonel Ross, back in the present, caught a slight shifting and stiffening of bodies in the reviewing party. His eyes went left and he saw just in time the approaching break in the marching ranks, a color guard coming on. Colonel Ross, too, stiffened moderately with the line of staff officers. General Beal and General Nichols in perfect unison, with a snap of perfect precision, brought their hands up. Somewhat less perfectly, Colonel Ross brought his up.

It was, he saw, the colors of the WAC detachment; and he was not surprised, a moment later to hear, following a great shift of standing up and uncovering on the stands of spectators, a quick pattering outbreak of applause. In front of him he could see General Nichols, barely moving his lips, faintly smiling, say something to General Beal, who, faintly smiling, barely moving his lips, answered. Coming past now, all by herself at the head of a company, her hand rigidly to her cap brim, was the little snub-nosed lieutenant who stood to make her suggestion in the conference room the other day.

Colonel Ross said: "This is quite a war."

Startled, Major Tietam, next to him, whispered: "Sir?"

Colonel Ross shook his head. He let his mind move off again to find, where he had left him, Old Schlichter being an ass in the cold-eyed younger world which, as the judge himself might have put it, knew not Joseph.

There were, of course, other ways in which Judge Schlichter proved less than perfect. Knowledge of them came more slowly; and to be sure of them needed several years' loyal and discreet service. His discoveries affected neither young Ross's loyalty nor his discretion; but they disturbed his mind. Like Judge Schlichter's mental abilities, which were allowed to outweigh, if barely, his pompous foibles, Judge Schlichter's moral character was held in high regard. In many ways the regard was deserved. Judge Schlichter's professional integrity was absolute. He was incorruptible. In any matter having to do with money he was the soul of honor. The privacy of the judge's private life hid none of those sordid, not uncommon, secrets involving, at best, another woman; but, quite as often, through the modified impulses of senescence, little girls or young boys.

The judge's clerk, because he knew no better than to suppose that every man in high position would naturally have to have them, passed over these virtues and decencies. He expected the judge's character to deserve, not in many ways, but in all ways, the high regard people expressed for it. Young Ross had not liked his growing awareness that he could tell (though he never would) if he wanted to (but he did not want to) what seemed to him "plenty" about Judge Schlichter.

To the strait-laced, carefully respectable community it would also have seemed "plenty." Old Schlichter was a regular churchgoer, a principal pillar of the church; and his severe public stand in issues of piety and right-thinking could be known when he flatly refused on one occasion to admit testimony from a man who declared with scorn that the Bible, brought for him to swear on, was all nonsense, and that he believed in no hereafter, and no God.

But when you heard Judge Schlichter's private opinions, you knew that in general he agreed with this view. Favorite quotations of the judge's came from the Bible, and many others seemed to postulate a Supreme Being and eternal life; but in private Judge Schlichter kept, at most, an open mind about all this. He appeared to consider the basic principles of Christianity consistent with right and reason; but in the doctrines of the Lutheranism he professed on Sundays, or in those of any other church, he certainly did not believe. He just pretended to.

The horrified community, informed of this belief, would probably not have been surprised to hear that the judge went even farther. He also just pretended that he did not drink alcoholic beverages. At the back of his safe were hidden bottles of what the judge, perhaps by way of distinguishing it from liquor or booze, referred to as sound spirits. He regularly enjoyed a nip, either alone, or with one or two safe old cronies. The indulgence was always moderate. The judge never took too many nips, and never took them too often; but tippling in private was a hard thing to square with an uncompromising public stand for teetotalism.

The resulting disturbance in the callow mind of the judge's clerk might seem now something to smile over; but, at that time, young Ross did not suffer from any farm boy's naïve shock that such things as unbelief and whisky-drinking could be. In the Army he observed that most men put no stock in religion, and that most men took a drink whenever they could get it. What he troubled over was, then or now, no smiling matter. It was the indisputable plain truth that Judge Schlichter without the practice of these hypocrisies would be a better man than Judge Schlichter with them.

Judge Schlichter was well aware of this, for he said much too frequently: A wit's a feather, and a chief a rod; an honest man's the noblest work of God. Why then did he choose to live these lies? Young Ross already knew the answer. Old Schlichter weighed what he got from hypocrisy against what he might hope from honesty. He let honesty go. He did not have the nerve to be honest.

Old Ross, Colonel Ross, started from his thoughts. All of them had started, even jumped; General Beal and General Nichols as much as anyone else. They all then realized that it was, of course, the troop carrier planes; the sound of their coming not before noticed in the mutter of the big bombers. The carriers were on schedule. And, by God, they were really down, roaring over the Base! Heads had turned; General Beal did not prevent himself from looking right around. For one second they gave the illusion of barely missing the barrack roofs; it actually looked as though you would be able to reach up and touch them. In another second, you saw that you couldn't; for, on the third second, here they were, right above, breaking your ears with their engines; but a few hundred feet high, at least. Colonel Ross glimpsed the dark hatches open on their flanks. They and their big shadows fled out across the field, dribbling behind them, like an evacuation of their cylindrical steel guts, a string of tumbling paratroopers.

Colonel Ross shifted the tiring load of himself from his left foot, in whose toes he felt a cramp, to his right foot. He worked the cramping toes up and down, hoping to ease them. He heard the pumping of his mistaken heart, now back where it belonged; but still swollen from the bound of terror it took when that horrid irruptive roar of new engines coming too close, coming too fast, stormed his unprepared ears with a savage percussion that told his quailing brain he was surely a dead man. Whether other hearts there bounded as hard, or other brains quailed as much, he could not tell; but he guessed not. He was the oldest man here; and old men have a shameful lack of nerve.

Colonel Ross breathed in his breath and blew it out softly. For himself, for old Schlichter, for mankind, he could feel the same subduing mortifica-tion. There never could be a man so brave that he would not sometime, or in the end, turn part or all coward; or so wise that he was not, from begin-ning to end, part ass if you knew where to look; or so good that nothing at all about him was despicable. This would have to be accepted. This was one of the limits of human endeavor, one of those boundaries of the possible whose precise determining was, as General Nichols with his ascetic air of being rid of those youthful illusions, viewing with no nonsense the Here and the Now, always saw it, the problem. If you did not know where the limits were, how did you know that you weren't working outside them? If you were working outside them you must be working in vain. It was no good acting on a supposition that men would, for your purpose, be what they did not have it in them to be; just as it was unwise to beguile yourself, up there on top of the whirlwind, with the notion that the storm was going to have to do what you said.

General Nichols was indeed wise, young, if he had these points clear in his mind. The not wholly satisfactory idea—that wisdom, though better than rubies, came to so little; that a few of the most-heard platitudes con-tained all there was of it; that its office was to acquaint you not with the abstruse or esoteric, but with the obvious, what any fool can see—might as well be accepted, too.

This was not to say that General Nichols knew all the answers—yet! Now there would normally be a short delay while he passed through the season of tranquillity, the holy calm of the recent revelation which showed him this track was the right one, that the corner of the grand design had been uncovered, that the secret of it all lay this way, not far ahead. With that discard that impressed Colonel Ross, that choice of the hard way, with-out illusions, he had sagaciously bounded the possible on two sides. He would need time to see the side left open, and where that side must be bounded. To the valuable knowledge of how much could be done with other men, and how much could be done with circumstance, he might have to add the knowledge of how much could be done with himself. He was likely to find it less than he thought.

He—General Nichols, Colonel Ross, Judge Schlichter, every man— was so sure to find it less than he thought, because by the time he found it, he was less than he was. The drops of water wore the stone. The increment of fatigue, the featherweight's extra in every day's living, which could not be rested away, collected heaviness in the mind just as it collected acid in the tissues. The experience of seeing, of experiencing, briskly undertaken with the illusion of gain, was, of course, a work of destruction. You saw through lie after lie, you learned better than to believe in fable after fable, and good riddance, surely! Or was it? When you came, as you might if you worked hard, to finish your clean-up job; all trash and rubbish cleared from the underlying nature of things; not one lie and not one fable between you and its face; what would you do? You had what you worked for, all clear, open for inspection; and were you downhearted?

Downheartedness was no man's part. A man must stand up and do the best he can with what there is. If the thing he labored to uncover now seemed in danger of stultifying him, could a rational being find nothing to do? If mind failed you, seeing no pattern; and heart failed you, seeing no point, the stout, stubborn will must be up and doing. A pattern should be found; a point should be imposed. Was that too much?

It was not. This discovery wasn't new. What to do about it exercised the best minds of sixty centuries; and the results of the exercise, their helpful hints, their best advices, their highly recommended procedures, afforded you a good selection; you had only to suit your taste and temperament. Once you knew you needed something to keep you operative, playing the man, you could be of good heart. Your need would find it for you, and adapt it to you; and even support you in it, when those who had different needs, or thought they had none, asked if you were crazy.

Life, Judge Schlichter would agree, seemed mostly a hard-luck story, very complicated, beginning nowhere and never ending, unclear in theme, and confusing in action. Some of it you saw yourself, and while that was at most very little, you could piece out the picture, since it always fitted in with what other people said they saw.

Unhappy victims complained of their unhappy circumstances. The trusting followers of the misjudged easiest way found that way immediately getting hard. Simple-minded aspirants, not having what it took, did not quite make it. Conceited men proudly called their shots and proceeded to miss them, without even the comfort of realizing that few attended long enough to notice, and fewer cared. Any general argument or intention was comically contravened in reported or portrayed dispensations by which the young died and the old married; courageous patience overdid it and missed the boat; good Samaritans, stopping, found it was a trap and lost *their* shirts, too—everyday incidents in the manifold pouring-past of the Gadarene swine, possessed at someone's whim, but demonstrably innocent —for what was a guilty pig, or a wicked one?—to the appointed steep place. Though so sad, the hard luck often moving, it was a repetitious story, and long; and what did it prove? Let somebody else figure that out!

Using the words of a Great, if perhaps not too Good, man, old Schlichter answered with sonorous piety and a noble gesture:

> *All Nature is but art unknown to thee*
> *All chance, direction, which thou canst not see;*
> *All discord, harmony not understood;*
> *All partial evil, universal good—*

Colonel Ross stood, every limb aching, bemused—some trucks or guns or something were passing with men on them sitting absurd and stiff, their folded arms held up—and he began to consider a few recent random contributions to discord, to harmony not understood.

The hulk of *Tarfu Tessie*, stupidly rolled off on the road, spread its stench of rotten blood. Lieutenant What's-her-name—Turck was sick in a paper bag in the plane they just didn't die in; and Sal threw up the rest of the bottle of Scotch and a few things she had eaten on the dining room floor. Nicodemus said: "I hopes I sees you—"; and the Ocanara *Sun* unfolded to *This & That by Art Bullen*. Through the hot night, he heard the drunken voices singing in the lighted hotel and got to his feet. Making impudent speeches, the snotty young lieutenants posed as, and were, the two, obnoxious, only champions of the dignity of man.

Saying: "I don't want you to be glum," Cora kindly pressed him with familiar warmth. The sullen, half-heartedly scheming, black faces, so suited to their old rôle of the abused, the betrayed, mooned up at him in righteous protest; but necessarily in vain. Colonel Woodman breathed whisky fumes across the desk, a palaver of nonsense, with ten hours to go before he put his pistol in his mouth. While Colonel Mowbray gently praised and gently blamed him, Benny, that young Mars of men, averted his hard, thoughtless stare indifferently, and slouched his strong scarred body, eyeing the aerial view of Maxwell Field. Bus, airborne and all well in that fine hefty, though a little heavy at low altitudes, bitch of a so-called Thunderbolt, smiled like the restored Titan who touched his mother earth. Bus marked in the corner of his goggles the encroaching wing tip of the snappily flown P-38, moved his hand; and, Chief again, outsmarted his very best honey of a group commander; scared his nervy little murderer pissless.

Now Captain Collins said equably, of his idiot girl: "Not that special, sir"; and Captain Hicks with a great show of anxious candor said: "It's only that I feel, sir, something pretty good could be done." Arthritic, Luke Howden stooped along, never stopping to fool with disloyalty; and Johnny Sears quickly said: "It's easier to keep people out than to put them out." Poor old Pop, the brainless wonder, halted in distress, getting nowhere fast, up and down his office. General Nichols, so wise so young, let fall from his chiseled lips the calm word: "We must do it anyway."

Wagging his head, Colonel Ross pronounced: "From this, we learn—"; but a sudden sound interrupted him. It was a new noise breaking through the music of the last band, and the drone of plane engines still above the field. It came from a distance; and he was a moment in identifying it as a siren, across there by the lake, piling wail on wail.

When he looked that way last, inattentive in thought, the air had been full of the hosts of falling parachutes, the suspended jumpers from the carrier planes. They seemed to be all down now. Colonel Ross could see nothing at such a distance; but by the lake the siren persisted, far beyond any regular or prearranged air warning signal; and, with sudden attention, he turned his head to look down the line of the staff. He found Major Sears's head turned, too; and their eyes met.

Major Sears's lips moved, saying something. He stepped backward a pace, out of line; stooped, put a hand on the boards of the platform, and dropped lightly to the ground. On the ground, he began to run, heading for the open frame shelter beyond the Operations Building where, in constant readiness, waited the emergency vehicles—a crash truck, a field ambulance, and two fire engines.

Nathaniel Hicks had no time to count the dropping parachutes, but his eye made a sort of calculation for him, an instinctive estimate of the scale of the disaster he might be going to have to see. He guessed that last plane load was thirty or more—three dozen, perhaps.

Meanwhile he was for several seconds engaged in minor but more immediate requirements put on his attention by getting down the lumber pile to the ground. Lieutenant Turck had clutched the hand he held to her; and she needed it, so he paused at each of the higher steps stiffening his muscles to give her a point to steady herself as she jumped. Captain Wiley and Captain Duchemin were down ahead of them.

Lieutenant Anderson, who must have been at his "command post" desk came out from under the fly-top, poised in indecision or dismay; and Captain Wiley put a hand on his arm, jerking his other thumb up. "Look, pal," he said, quickly, but not excited; "some of those are going in the water. I can't see any life vests on them; so maybe you better start making with a boat, if you have one. I don't think they'll swim so far with all that junk—"

Lieutenant Anderson said to a black sergeant who had come out with him: "Double over and let that siren off!" To Captain Wiley, he said: "We have a telephone hookup here. I better ring Operations, if I can—"

"To hell with that!" Captain Wiley said. "What can they do? You got a boat?"

Stepping clear of the corner of the lumber pile, Nathaniel Hicks could see a pattern in the floating parachutes. Though all one drop from one plane, they were in two groups, separated by an interval of altitude, each group strung out, scattered as though by gesture of broadcast sowing. They no longer appeared all hanging together, all headed for the lumber pile. A readjustment of perspective showed that the lower group, or most of it, could not get that far. The first parachutes, sown wide, were almost down, falling toward good ground—the sand and grass reaches within the defense sector, behind those installations on the perimeter which were engaged, not very convincingly, with short bursts of fired blanks, in repelling a "rush" toward them by paratroopers from the other flight who were coming in as skirmishers—not very convincingly, either—from the center of the field.

The defenders reacted to the new development of being taken in the rear with enthusiasm. A paratrooper hit almost on top of an automatic weapons emplacement; and was immediately surrounded by figures scrambling from under the camouflage cover. Two more hit; and then two more. All over the sector, yells were lifted, armed figures arose excitedly from prone shelters and slit trenches, swarming toward the rolling men and collapsing parachutes, plainly intent on "capturing" them.

From somewhere distant, Major McIlmoyle, perfectly recognizable, bellowed like a bull, chiding this mass maneuver, mixing curses and warnings that they were exposed, under fire; they were being attacked; they were exposed; to get down; one or two was enough, goddamn it!

Parachutes still in the air, a last few of the first group, all the second group, were getting lower now; and there could be no more question of hanging motionless, or even of moving slowly. The second group in a dispersed, side-slipping deployment, passed at a good clip, high over the lumber pile on an angle of glide that seemed to stretch as it quickened—not even Nathaniel Hicks could doubt where they would have to land. At the same time, under them, at angles of glide by contrast steadily steepening, the remainder of the first group came fast, landing nearer and nearer the pile; and now one last man was coming right at it. Astounded, Nathaniel Hicks saw that a descent by parachute was nothing like what he thought. It was a barely retarded plummeting; and a parachutist would hit no slower than a man would hit jumping free from, say the high top of the lumber pile.

In shocked alarm, Nathaniel Hicks stood stupid, seeing full in front of him, beyond the pile, and already as low as its top, the swinging solid body in its baggy battle dress, the slightly drawn-up thick knees and big boots held together, the bent helmeted head and upstretched arms holding the risers. The figure fell like a stone; and it fell on stone—the broad, brand-new, never-used imitation stone of the concrete runway.

Since this man was facing downwind, his back was to Nathaniel Hicks as his boots struck. The flexed knees gave. He went over instantly, tilted sideways, rolling, legs slung limply out behind. His clutching fists grabbed in some of the sudden slack in the risers; but the parachute, which had tottered, starting to wilt as its great circumference swayed over and touched the paving ahead of him, felt the breeze and bellied full again. Now the slanting, rolling body landed, an audible smacking thud, on its side and shoulder. Expelled from the man broke a wordless cry, half scream, half groan. His chin strap must have come loose; for the helmet popped off his head and bounded on the concrete with a bright clang of metal. The filled parachute swung like a sail, straining the shroud lines taut, and began determinedly to drag its burden up the runway.

Held by this swiftly developing little horror in the foreground, Nathaniel Hicks's eyes nonetheless distractedly encompassed a background against which the dragged man on the runway moved. This was the sweep of placid blue water beyond the wide white paving, beyond the dun strip of sandy soil at the lake's bank. Into this background—an intolerable elaboration of simultaneous events—arrived the last group of parachutes, well down, well out—a hundred yards or more. The trailed figures rushed near the water; yet for a moment contact was delayed, as though they could not quite reach it.

At that instant three, maybe four, parachutes reversed their motion, rising slightly, puffing away, jostling into others. The phenomenon explained itself; they were freed of the men under them, who must have undone their harness fastenings, and who fell forward, the first down, hitting ahead with high splashes of spray. They were gone before the lifted water fell back. Beyond these plungers, those others still in harness struck with no more delay, plowed trails of foam, foundered under. The bevy of parachutes toppled low; and, quickly sopped, sank awash. There followed, for a gruesome drawn-out minute, a struggling commotion on or near the surface.

From the shed by the lake, the sound of the siren went wailing up. Nathaniel Hicks felt his throat contract to gasp air in, and then contract more, as though to use the air to shout; but nothing came. In his eye sockets, across his eyeballs he felt stabbing twinges like the pain of too much light—perhaps a spraining conflict of muscles caught at cross-purposes attempting to maintain one focus while irresistibly drawn to assume another. This ache of the overpressed eyes merged distractingly with the insufferable demands the eyes made on the mind, the impossible work of anatomizing into instants, enough instants to hold, one instant to one perception, the tumultuous few seconds with their multiple movements above and on the lake's surface, suddenly begun, suddenly all gone.

Meanwhile, the dragged man on the runway made hoarse sounds of anguish, which emerged indistinctly in the ebb of the siren howls spiraling over and over from low to terrible high. He worked with a fast frenzy to stop his rough progress. His clawing hands got the canopy edge, snatched at the wall of silk ahead, and dragged what he could reach down under him. The parachute shuddered, falling suddenly spilled; the lines dropped limp; the great cloth folds, collapsing, sank, and half covered the man, who now lay still.

Captain Wiley said: "Could this be dangerous?"

Captain Wiley was rising from a squat. He must have dropped on his heels, Nathaniel Hicks could not tell when. The realization filled Nathaniel

Hicks with amazement; for he could see in it, dazedly, the work of a wonderful instinct. Economical of action, collectedly denying every vain impulse of confusion and excitement, Captain Wiley calmly crouched, appraising the situation; imperturbably doing nothing, watching for all this to resolve itself and show him something there would be some sense in doing.

While he made his survey, Captain Wiley had scooped up a handful of sand, which he weighed lightly, spilling it through his fingers. Straightening now, he let the remainder fall, brushed the last grains off his palm and walked toward the paratrooper up the runway. Nathaniel Hicks turned and saw Lieutenant Turck sitting on the lowest pile of stacked boards. Her lips were set tightly together and he could see her hands and even her shoulders shaking. Nathaniel Hicks said: "Where's Duchemin?"

Lieutenant Turck got to her feet. She said: "He ran over there—to that landing; whatever it is." She looked after Captain Wiley, and began to move. Frowning, she said: "He must let him lie; not move him. He has at least one leg broken—maybe both—"

Nathaniel Hicks said: "How do you know?"

She drew a breath. "I have all kinds of useless information," she said. "I have a lot of dismal acquirements. Did you know I was going to be a doctor? I happened to get married instead; but he was a doctor, too. I know about anatomy. Legs always bend back; not sideways, or forward." She gave him a distressed smile. "Yes; I was a librarian," she said. "Before and after. I can also operate a switchboard, and milk a cow; if you ever need anyone." She looked past him toward the lake shore. "I am, as usual, a little out of place, I suppose. Should we move on?" She began to walk again, catching her shoes in the loose sand.

Looking that way, too, Nathaniel Hicks could see the thickening crowd, the straggle of figures crossing the runway farther up. The siren had stopped; and there were, he realized, no more sounds of firing behind—all the sham fighting must have been abandoned. Not far away, in rapid movement on the lake bank, a dozen of the Negro engineers were stripping, peeling shirts over their heads, stooping hastily to get their shoes off. Several of them, black bodies now naked, jumped splashing into the water. Out a little way, their heads arose, and they set themselves with varying vigor, to swim—toward what, Nathaniel Hicks did not think they knew. Rather to the left of where they appeared to be heading, he could see, or thought he could, what might or might not be the light-colored cloth of a waterlogged parachute or two. There was no sign of any heads there, any movement.

While Nathaniel Hicks looked, Captain Duchemin detached himself from the staring groups. His big figure came plodding over the sand, gained the runway, and moved toward them, preceded up the concrete by his long shadow. "Not working today, the crash boat," Captain Duchemin said. "Pity, isn't it? I don't think the bathers are going to get anywhere, either. Perhaps somebody ought to tell them to get out before they drown themselves."

"Not me," Nathaniel Hicks said.

"I was thinking of the loot, Anderson. Or our good major, McIlmoyle. I am only an observer, I informed them. A top sergeant, a fine black figure of a buck named Rogers, was the leading spirit. When I gave no orders, he gave some. Have we another casualty here?"

Captain Wiley knelt by the man on the runway, busy with the fasteners of his parachute harness. Lieutenant Turck said: "I wouldn't try to clear those leg straps, Captain—"

Captain Wiley said: "Let me get out that knife he has, there. I'll just hack off the suspension lines. Get him clear of his chute—"

"Yes. Good. Let's cover him with it. They must be sending medical people, don't you think? Would he have a first-aid kit? Could we find it without moving him?"

Around the corner of the lumber pile came trotting now two more paratroopers. One of them cried: "What you got, Shorty?" They came up the concrete with a clatter of steel heels. The other one, a corporal, said: "He hurt?"

"He's out," Captain Wiley said. He had drawn a jungle knife from the fallen man's sheath. Looking at the formidable blade with pleasure, he said: "The things they have!" Catching up the lines, he cut them with quick little slashes.

From Captain Wiley, and Lieutenant Turck bent beside him, the two paratroopers turned their sunburned faces to inspect Captain Duchemin and Nathaniel Hicks, an incurious flash of eyes under the helmet brims. With a direct and simple air of finding themselves alone and getting on with their private business, the corporal said: "Water! Here; my canteen—"

"No, don't!" Lieutenant Turck said. "That's the worst thing you could do. Let him alone!"

They had both crouched; and the corporal looked over at her, amazed. "We got to bring him to!" he said. "You want us just have him lay here?"

"Please do," Lieutenant Turck said. "We want to cover him up. We're getting the parachute clear. He's gone into shock. I think both legs are fractured. They must be splinted; and he mustn't be moved without a stretcher."

"You a nurse?" the corporal said.

"No; but—"

"Better leave us handle it, then, Lieutenant—"

"Uh-uh!" Captain Wiley shook his head. "What the lady says, friend! We cover him up and wait for the ambulance. Much better." Pressing with his thumb, he made a package of cigarettes rise out of his breast pocket and casually proffered it to them. "You got seven in the lake," he said. "This one's doing all right."

"Jesus!" the corporal said carefully. With a mechanical motion, as though involuntarily, they both took cigarettes. The other one said: "Thanks, Captain. We don't have a match." Captain Wiley flipped a paper book of matches at them. The corporal struck one and lit the cigarette in his own mouth. Cupped in his big hand, he then held it for his companion. He said to him: "What crossed? Who was flying you?"

"Lieutenant Tyler."

"Jeez, he's all right! Don't he look where the hell he is?"

With the same simple directness they had again withdrawn themselves, Nathaniel Hicks could see, into their real world, exclusively theirs, talking only to each other. "Didn't your light go?" the corporal said.

"Yeah; but I told you. What happened; number six in our file; his hook-on jammed on the anchor line cable, or something. We couldn't clear any more; maybe a minute. The lieutenant found it out. I guess he was watching to trim his tail up, whatever he does. Anyway, he sees something—I don't know. He bats the door back and yells what the hell. They got the hook-on moving then. I was right behind—next out. I hear our half-ass Powell yell back: 'Line stuck, sir. We're going.' Lieutenant says: 'Jeez, you ham-head, you better go! Think we stand still—'"

"Jeez, you should have held it!" the corporal said.

"Am I jump-master? He gives me the knee, and I went out. He stops counting between, I guess. Anyway, they fed so fast, one hits me—Shorty, here, I think. Say! I thought I had a tail surface across my neck! Then I knew something was buggering my chute up. Shorty's chute, probably." He cut the air with the edge of his hand. "Oh, mama, I said; here's mine! I bet I fell partly open, two hundred, two hundred fifty feet. When we bumped up there, I lost my auxiliary rip ring. Then, the rag snapped, O.K.; but how close it was; right away I landed—what a smack! Only, soft sand—not this."

The corporal looked over to the lake. "Who was after Shorty?"

"I'm not so sure. I'd have to figure. No one in the old platoon, I think. Yeah—that guinea fellow; the one we got right before they moved you, remember? Conti."

"Jeez, they ought to have Powell's stripes!"

"Yeah."

They paused, both open-mouthed, staring at each other in surprise. "Yeah!" the corporal said in turn. "Unless he never jumped, at the end."

"That half-ass would jump, all right. I give him that—"

"Something coming," the corporal said. "They take their time!" He turned his head. "Fire engine!" he said. "They bring a fire engine!"

Nathaniel Hicks, turning too, saw the fire engine succeeded by a heavy truck, and then an ambulance. On the runway paving, a jeep rushed up and halted. In large white letters the words PROVOST MARSHAL were painted on the drab metal below the windshield.

Captain Wiley said: "Better grab that, Nat; tell them this is for the ambulance."

Nathaniel Hicks walked over to the jeep. To the major getting out of it, he said: "We have a man with a broken leg right over there, sir."

"You have a man with a broken leg?" the major said. "Well, you made one hell of a lot of noise about it!" To the lieutenant with him, he said: "Tell them their man's over there!" Giving Nathaniel Hicks an irritable, critical look, he said: "Who are you, Captain? Are you in command here?"

"No, sir," Nathaniel Hicks said. "Major McIlmoyle, I don't know where he is, is in command, I believe. We're observers from the Directorate of Special—"

"Well, for God's sake, if you need an ambulance, someone's hurt, telephone for one! There's a connection right down at the crash-boat berth, there. Use your head, Captain! Don't set off a siren!"

Nathaniel Hicks said: "We had nothing to do with setting it off, Major. It was set off when seven paratroopers came down in the lake. We haven't seen them since—"

"Day!" the Major shouted after his lieutenant. "Get on the phone to Operations! Part of that drop went in the lake!" To Nathaniel Hicks, he said: "You see it?"

"Yes, sir."

"Stick around; I may want you later."

"Yes, sir," said Nathaniel Hicks. "That is Major McIlmoyle coming up to the fly-top, now."

"All right. Any other officers who saw it, tell them to stick around." He turned briskly and marched away.

Left standing, Nathaniel Hicks continued to stand. He supposed, indeed he knew, that the matter-of-factness he found himself feeling, was no more than nature, was no more than sense. The seven men—he would have said six; but he did not doubt that Captain Wiley when he saw anything, made no mistake about it—simply fell in, went down, and well-weighted, never came up.

He remembered disconnectedly someone telling him, as a matter of curious information, that Lake Lalage, though of no great area, was almost everywhere, even within a few feet of the shore, over a hundred feet deep; and that in some parts sounding lines, presumably because those using them had not come prepared for deep soundings, never found any bottom at all—an interesting geological formation. Nathaniel Hicks began to recall, but not accurately, accounts he had read of swimmers recovered after they had been under water—an hour?—a half an hour?—revived by the medal-winning patience of knowledgeable boy scouts, or of police pulmotor squads.

Then he thought of the six, seven, individuals dragged gently down the hundred-foot, or bottomless, gulf of water, choking and bubbling; those without parachutes, perhaps a little faster; but those with parachutes unsupported by them in this element. By now, at any rate—it must be ten or more minutes—though perhaps not all quite dead, there could not be one of them still conscious.

Someone behind him said: "Excuse me, sir—Captain."

Turning, Nathaniel Hicks saw, a yard away, poised hesitant, a thin, dark Negro. He wore much disordered twill work clothes, a helmet liner, but no helmet. Under his arm he pressed the butt of a rifle, hung at an awkward angle from its sling on his shoulder. Faded T/5 chevrons were stamped on his sleeves. He looked out from below the helmet liner with a diffident half-smile.

Nathaniel Hicks said blankly: "Yes. What is it?"

The Negro lowered his eyes. Moving one boot, he gave the sand, on which he stood beyond the runway, a gentle kick. "McIntyre, sir," he said.

"Oh!" Nathaniel Hicks said. "Hello! How are you? I didn't know this was your outfit!"

"Yes, sir," T/5 McIntyre said. "Captain, I only wanted—" he paused in confusion, "well, thank you; getting me that ride back, sir. Well, I bring this—something. I leave it for you, your building there. I don't know did they—"

"Yes," Nathaniel Hicks said, appalled. He found himself reddening.

"Only reason," T/5 McIntyre said. He coughed. "I wanted it for you—if they give it you. We bringing chow over here in the truck—so I have to go; I only leave it—"

"Yes," Nathaniel Hicks said. "I got it. I appreciate very much your wanting to give it to me—"

T/5 McIntyre's diffident smile reappeared. "I get it this morning," he said. "I—"

The sound of a new siren reached Nathaniel Hicks. Looking past T/5 McIntyre, he saw that it came this time from a car, a staff car, whose olive drab was waxed until it gleamed. The car came fast up the truck road, passed behind the lumber pile and wheeled onto the runway beyond. Seeing the small scarlet flag flapping on its bumper staff, Nathaniel Hicks said: "General Beal."

"Yes, sir," T/5 McIntyre said.

Nathaniel Hicks said: "McIntyre; it was very nice of you to want to give me that box; but I had to send it back to you. You see; if you gave me a present for anything I did for you—they could court-martial me for that—"

T/5 McIntyre said: "You don't keep it?"

"I couldn't," Nathaniel Hicks said. "Not in the Army, McIntyre—"

T/5 McIntyre said nothing for an instant. His eyes moved then, going past Nathaniel Hicks; and he shifted his feet quickly. He said: "I was only hoping you have it, Captain." He began suddenly to step backwards. "Well, thank you again, Captain. I got to get back—" he turned quickly away.

Looking where T/5 McIntyre had been looking, Nathaniel Hicks saw the Medical Corps men on the runway by the paratrooper. Coming toward him, almost at hand, was Lieutenant Turck. Still red, Nathaniel Hicks said to her, "That was our friend T/5 McIntyre—the colored kid on the plane. He had me on a spot. He tried to give me a present—"

Lieutenant Turck said: "General Beal's here. Look." She touched his arm; and he faced about.

General Beal had left the car. The general from Washington, Nichols, had come with him; and, moving together toward the lake, they had halted, and stood now not fifty feet away. The tableau, arresting in its grouping and lighting, was what Lieutenant Turck touched Nathaniel Hicks, perhaps involuntarily, to make him look at.

The hot sun, nearer the horizon, poured a dazzling gold light across the great reach of the air field. Under a pure and tender wide sky, empty now of all its planes, the flat light bathed everything; all the men, who appeared for an instant motionless; the lumber pile; the low lake shore; the wide, calm ripple of waters. The swimmers, who must have been ordered from the lake, were in the act of coming out. They emerged with shining limbs, their muscular black bodies brightly dripping. Mounting the low bank, they stole guarded glances at the two generals, then glanced respectfully away, going to the little piles of clothes they had left. They stood swinging their arms, slapping their chests and thighs in the easy exercise of drying themselves in the warm air.

Around the two generals a circle of officers had gathered, posed in concern. In this sad, gold light their grouping made a composition like that found in old-fashioned narrative paintings of classical incidents or historical occasions—the Provost Marshal indicated the lake with a demonstrative gesture; a young Air Force captain faced him, standing tense and stiff. Bulky in his fighting trim, a captain of paratroopers, and Major McIlmoyle, helmeted and dirty, waited in somber attitudes like legates who had brought news of a battle. To one side, a lieutenant colonel, probably the Post Engineer, in stylized haste gave grave tidings to a thin chicken colonel, that instant arrived—Colonel Hildebrand, the Base Commander.

A deferential distance behind these chief figures, touched with the same sunset light, the mustered myrmidons, token groups of the supporting armies, whispered together—the black engineers, the arms-loaded paratroopers; and in the middle background, borne on a stretcher as though symbolically, the wrapped form of the man who had fallen on the runway was passing.

Lieutenant Turck now stirred, in a quiet movement, facing away a little. With a recollection of decorum, a composed delicacy, she had moved so as not to be looking right at the husky naked black men preparing to dress. Nathaniel Hicks looked again at the silent circle of officers, and at General Beal's set face turned toward the water. He could see it clearly; and he was astounded to observe that tears were running down it.

VII

Summa cum Laude
By Brendan Gill

By Love Possessed, the new novel by James Gould Cozzens (Harcourt, Brace), is a masterpiece. It is the author's masterpiece, which in the case of Mr. Cozzens is saying a good deal, yet it would be saying too little not to add at once that *By Love Possessed* would be almost anybody's masterpiece. No American novelist of the twentieth century has attempted more than Mr. Cozzens attempts in the course of this long and bold and delicate book, which, despite its length, one reads through at headlong speed and is then angry with oneself for having reached the end of so precipitately. No other American novelist of this century could bring to such a task the resources of intelligence, literary technique, and knowledge of the intricate, more or less sorry ways of the world that Mr. Cozzens commands. If he had failed, the very ruin of his work might have served as the occasion for grateful thanks and—like that beautiful failure *Tender Is the Night*, which one can scarcely bear to think of Fitzgerald still hopefully tinkering with after publication—perhaps for high praise. But Mr. Cozzens is at every point far from failing. He has been superbly ambitious and has superbly realized his ambitions. Rarely seeming to exert himself, only once showing signs of strain, he has performed the sleight of hand that all writers dream of and that few have the discipline and energy, let alone the talent, to accomplish —that of arresting and rendering the surface of life (oh, yes! this is precisely how it looks) and at the same time revealing in undiminished contrariety the flow of things beneath the surface (but this, alas, is how it is). Like all the supremely satisfying novels, *By Love Possessed* contrives to let us recognize the truth not only of what we have experienced as individuals but of what we have not; it radically alters and enlarges us even as it gives delight. An immense achievement, and if Mr. Cozzens isn't practically beside himself with relief and pride at having brought it off, then life in its incessant pursuit of irony has, as usual, gone too far.

Review of *By Love Possessed* by James Gould Cozzens, *The New Yorker*, Vol. 33 (Aug. 24, 1957), pp. 106ff. Copyright © 1957 by The New Yorker Magazine, Inc. Reprinted by permission.

Not that Mr. Cozzens's achievement is a surprise. The fact is that he has been a formidable writer for a long time now, quietly—indeed, almost stealthily—extending his range and advancing from strength to strength. At Harvard, over thirty years ago, he was writing novels that he has since permitted to drop from sight. (An exceedingly romantic young writer, he recovered quickly, and the cure has been lasting.) Of the canonical works, all are well known and deserve to be: *S.S. San Pedro*, *The Last Adam*, *Castaway*, *Men and Brethren*, *Ask Me Tomorrow*, *The Just and the Unjust*, and *Guard of Honor*. The last of these, though it had nothing to do with combat, has been called the best novel to come out of the Second World War, and won the Pulitzer Prize for 1949. A more surprising distinction is that *By Love Possessed* is the fourth of Mr. Cozzens's novels to be chosen by the Book-of-the-Month Club. In short, Mr. Cozzens is by no means an unrecognized American novelist; nevertheless, he is in some quarters a neglected one. Critics and the kind of readers who start fashionable cults have been markedly cool to him. It may be that his refusal to become a public figure—no TV or P. E. N. appearances, no commencement addresses at Sarah Lawrence, no night-club pronouncements recorded by Leonard Lyons—has put them off. By devoting himself to writing, he has made himself invisible to the world of letters, and even the most agile and perspicacious critics must find it hard to take the measure of an invisible man. It is commonly pretended that any work contains enough to explain its author, as well as itself, but in practice how often is this true? On the contrary, doesn't it happen again and again that the ascertainable facts of a man's life are what prompt large and plausible-sounding conclusions about his work? (For that matter, doesn't it also happen from time to time—though only a cad would call attention to such things—that these same facts turn up a few pages later to prove the validity of the conclusions they prompted?) Mr. Cozzens is an especially awkward case for critics, because he is not merely invisible as a man; he does his best to become invisible in his work. The hints of personality that remain unpurged—a presence reticent to the point of aloofness and even, if approached too closely, of truculence—are of little use to them. Mr. Cozzens simply cannot be dealt with in terms of that mode of criticism, derived from the findings of psychoanalysis, which holds that art is the product of an unhealable wound and that fiction, for example, is some sort of thinly disguised autobiographical howl. (Poor Freud, who worshipped the Muses and has been doomed to spend so many decades as the vulgarly wielded instrument of their degradation!) We have been encouraged to assume that Stephen Dedalus is Joyce, that the "I" of *Remembrance of Things Past* is Proust, that Nick Adams is Hemingway; if we make the same reckless assumption about a Cozzens hero, we are instantly in trouble. For Mr. Cozzens, in a singularly old-fashioned way, invents his books. He chooses a subject and works it up, and the heroes he creates are not in his image but in images appropriate to the subject being treated. Moreover, he is at pains to see that the treatment never dominates the subject. He is a stern creator, and though there are plenty of lively characters in his assorted worlds, there are no runaway ones. The Cozzens intellect, which is of exceptional breadth and toughness, coolly directs the Cozzens heart, with the result that a Cozzens novel is always perfectly under control; to our pleasure, the god of the machine is in the driver's seat.

Hitherto, Mr. Cozzens has seemed to take up subjects as if with the intention of presenting a human comedy of the professions—medicine, the ministry, the law, the military. The authority of every detail of these brilliant raids into the interior of particular categories of life must have cost Mr. Cozzens many months and possibly years of arduous research, yet they are, after all, only formal settings for the moral questions that have always been Mr. Cozzens's main interest and theme. How is a man to act well in a society in which every right action immediately touches on, or is touched by, the invincible corruption of the majority? How is a man to remain good in the presence of evil save by refraining from action? Yet to retreat into paralysis when one is capable of any right action, however small or useless—surely that would be as evil as it would be humiliating. And if one were to find answers to these mere foothills of questions, what of the Everest question that lies beyond? The possibility, not to be flinched by any Cozzens hero, that good and evil, action and paralysis, are equally meaningless and that the hero asking "What does it all add up to?" may hear no better answer than that nothing plus nothing is nothing.

By Love Possessed is, as a story, spellbinding from start to finish; it is also, indivisibly, an eloquent summing up of Mr. Cozzens's moral preoccupations. Tolstoyan in size and seriousness, from its beginning pages it gives the impression that the author has gathered all the feeling, all the knowledge, all the wisdom to be found in his earlier books and has here deliberately pushed them to their limits. It is the work of a man at the top of his powers saying (not without sadness; one has so little time at the top, and the view is stupendous), "Here is where I stand. Here is what I make of what I see." The title contains the key word of the novel, which is love, especially with sexual love. It must have amused him during the years he was writing this book to anticipate the amazement of his accusers on discovering that his finest work was a prolonged scrutiny of love in all its forms—the love of parents for children; the love of children for parents; the love of brothers and sisters for each other; the love of couples courting, engaged, or newly married; the love of couples committing adultery; the love of teen-agers petting and making love; the love of middle-aged couples many years married making love with a passion never known in youth (here is the one sign of strain); homosexual love; onanistical love; the love of the old for the young; the love of the living for the dead; the value of love freely given and taken; the horror of being by love possessed.

The hero of the novel is Arthur Winner, a fifty-four-year-old lawyer in a small town between New York and Washington. As his father had been before him, he is the admired good citizen of the town—the sonhusbandfatherdirectorvestryman on whose shoulders the local honors and responsibilities (in a small town, they are all one) unobtrusively accumulate. Intelligent, successful, tolerant, not without intuition, not without doubts, he is the quintessence of our best qualities; we might not want to be Arthur Winner—who would want to be himself at his best for very long?—but we would dislike a world in which it was impossible to imagine him existing. Little by little, we come to feel that we cannot afford to let him falter, much less fail, and this, of course, is exactly what Mr. Cozzens has it in mind to show happening. The plot of the novel, a marvel of lucid complexity, covers a fraction over two days in Winner's life, and our interest and excitement mount at first hour by hour and then literally minute by minute. Infanticide, possible rape, subornation, suicide, embezzlement—it is a full two days, and the revelations that follow upon the last of these, the discovery of the embezzlement, are like so many blows in the face. Convictions that a man of good will has spent a virtuous lifetime acquiring are put to the test and found . . . not wanting but not useful. The words he has lived by, if never uttered—truth, honor, probity—are suddenly found to be worse than nonsense; they are beside the point. At the moment when they should most apply, they are most irrelevant. In the face of this astonishing development, Arthur Winner, still profoundly good, still sure that it is wrong to tell a lie, can only turn in haste to a new set of irrelevancies: that he is stronger than his enemies (in fact, he has no enemies); that he will endure (in fact, nobody endures). He will get up, he will seem to survive the blows, but life will never be the same for him. Such is the power of Mr. Cozzens's masterpiece that life may never be the same for us. We will be nursing Arthur Winner's hurt, and ours, for a long while to come.

Julius Penrose
[from *By Love Possessed*]

Arthur Winner returned the Orcutt portfolio to the document file. About to push shut the draw and spin the combination lock, he heard, from behind him, a sound of the street door in front opening. Looking over his shoulder, he saw, astonished, a uniformed man step into the lighted reception room, and move the door back with care to stand wide open. From the visored cap and leather puttees, Arthur Winner had first taken this unknown man to be a policeman. He saw now that the uniform was a chauffeur's uniform. The man turned, and stepped out of sight. There was a moment's delay; and the screen door reopened. Holding the uniformed arm in one hand, holding in the other both his canes, while he made with vigor his difficult way up the steps, into the light advanced Julius Penrose. From the door he could see Arthur Winner. In his harsh clear voice, disdainfully made a little mincing, as though Julius intended it to mock its own grating sound, he called: "Ah, Arthur! This is a convenience I hardly expected. I didn't know where you were."

Smiling, Arthur Winner said: "And I thought *you* were still in Washington."

"I don't believe I am," Julius Penrose said. "I think I'm here."

Exertion on a hot night had somewhat reddened Julius's forehead. Under the full light falling from overhead, Julius's nearly square face looked firm and massive, without fat, but heavily muscled—a powerful mouth, a powerful jaw; broad chin and broad brow in a strong, vertical, just-not-concave alignment. He was breathing a trifle fast; but Julius's dark eyes, large; in their quality, limpid; in their expression, calmly critical, regarded Arthur Winner with a detachment and directness that any physical difficulties he might be having were not permitted to disturb. Julius wore no hat; and, under the light, his hair, dense, with a handsome wave, shone vigorously and youthfully black—the hair, you might think, of a man half his age.

Now that he had reached a level surface, Julius Penrose released his hold on the supporting arm. He grasped a cane in each hand. A developed

great strength in his arms and shoulders allowed him, balancing in a practiced way, to straighten his big torso. Propped by the canes, he poised erect
on the braces that stiffened his useless legs. To Arthur Winner, who had
come toward him, Julius said: "This is Pettengill, who's been good enough
to get me here. His kind assistance was provided, along with a motorcar of
great elegance, by Mr. Marple, Bob Ingoldsby's banking friend, of whom
I've spoken to you. We needed some additional papers from the file; so we
arranged that I would drive up, stopping by here to get them. They took a
plane to New York, where I'm going on to meet them—we'd hoped, by
midnight; but we were a little late starting; and Pettengill's had nothing
to eat."

Transferring the cane from his right hand to be held with the cane in his
left, Julius Penrose dipped into a pocket and came out with a folded five-
dollar bill which he must have put there, ready. He said: "Halfway down
the street, where you see a horseshoe in neon tubing, is a fairly clean and
commodious—er—pub, Pettengill. Get yourself some refreshment. And
take your time. This is my partner, Mr. Winner; and I'll be a little while
talking to him."

"Very good, sir. Thank you, sir. If you won't be needing me immediately, I believe I'll first give the dog a walk again."

"Pray, do!" Julius Penrose said.

Alone with Arthur Winner, he said: "As a traveling companion, we
have a cultivated-looking poodle bitch of Marple's named Valentine. She
sits in front and takes turns with the driving. Or, even if she does not, I've
no doubt she easily could. Unfortunately, in spite of her intellectual gifts,
she seems to suffer from the chronic female complaint of constipation. The
state of her bowels causes Pettengill much anxiety. You observe, he would
rather see to that than eat."

Arthur Winner said: "And what about you? You can't have had anything to eat either. Julius, why don't I call the Union League? Alfred's still
there. He'd fix something for you quickly and send a boy over."

"I'm fed," Julius Penrose said. "I ate in transit. I caused the hotel to put
up some sandwiches and a Thermos of tea. So much simpler than stopping
somewhere. The sympathetic interest strangers always take in me when I
make an appearance among them I try to appreciate; yet even after all these
years I can't seem really to relish sympathy, let alone interest. For the same
reason, I prefer not to descend at service stations. My remaining pride is
Montaigne's; I can hold my water eight hours; yet, in Pettengill's sense,
I'll take myself for a walk, here."

He began with efficiency to transport himself toward the lavatory at the
back of the hall. Pulling up near the door, he said: "I won't delay to say that
things have turned out very well. Don't count our chickens until I've finished hatching them all; but after I called you this morning, Beckert called

me. He said he and the commissioner had studied the précis I made for them
of the applicable law as I saw the thing—I left that with them after the
conference. The commissioner's view seemed to be the same as Beckert's;
and he'd been directed to prepare a formal opinion and recommendation—
the gist: that we could proceed along the lines I proposed with fair assurance
of no additional tax liability. Much of the detail was interesting. For one
thing; they were ready to concede that redemption of the bonds was not a
distribution, or the essential equivalent of a distribution, of income. You
remember that point?"

"I do," Arthur Winner said. "I felt sure you were right. Julius, I'm
delighted! I don't see what more the Ingoldsbys could ask. You really must
have done a job."

Julius Penrose said: "Yes, I did. I think I did well. I'll treat myself to
admitting that." He moved; and halted again. "Also, I think I did a job on
Beckert. I told you, didn't I, that I later found out he was Lawrence's boss
—his chief of section? I didn't know that until I had dinner with Lawrence
and his wife—they seem well and happy, incidentally. Yesterday, I got a
chance to mention Lawrence to him; and Beckert spoke of him very highly
—in fact, though he was properly cagey about the matter, I got the impression that if he leaves Internal Revenue he expects Lawrence to go with him.
You may hear more soon." Putting himself in motion, he said: "At any rate,
the plan is, in effect, approved; and for once, at least, the job's a remuner-
able one, not an intellectual exercise for free. Nor are they going to be confused about whose the plan was. To my considerable surprise—and pleasure, be sure!—the idea of incorporating 'thin' seemed never to have
occurred to Marple, and him a banker! I had to spell out the tax advantages
for him—draw him up a couple of contrasting balance sheets." Julius Penrose smiled. "Marple looked what I can only call nonplused. Pretty clearly,
he hadn't expected the country boy even to know what a balance sheet was.
Since they all see how much they're being saved, I reflect with satisfaction
that good stiff fees are going to be in order."

Transferring his cane again, he opened the lavatory door and snapped
the light on. "Yes, I'm very pleased, Arthur," he said. "Perhaps I ought
not to let myself be so far swayed by small triumphs. Still, I feel good. I feel,
if only for a moment, and perhaps mistakenly, that the struggle does avail.
You do learn; you do improve yourself. Ten years ago, though then—and
this is of the essence—I might not have realized it, I wouldn't have known
enough to be able to show those people a thing or two. *Ergo*, I still ripe
and ripe! This, believe me, your father, or Noah when he was really Noah,
wouldn't have been ashamed of." Passing himself in, not without deftness,
he said: "My unbecoming boasting you must lay to my sad disability. Compensatory! Even I realize that. When a man's physically crippled, his character's soon crippled, too. I'm now in fettle fine enough to declare what I've

long known but usually think it unadvisable to say: Never believe that afflictions improve character, enlarge the understanding, or teach you charitable thoughts! The man not afflicted, the easy, open fortunate man is the likable man, the kindly man, the considerate man—in short, the man who may have time and inclination to think of someone besides himself. Be virtuous, and you'll be happy? Nonsense! Be happy and you'll begin to be virtuous."

Julius Penrose shut the door.

Julius Penrose said: "A full day, a full day! I can see that! I'm glad I wasn't here."

Arthur Winner said: "Well, one feels sorry for Helen."

"Yes; one might," Julius Penrose said. "But refusal to face the verities, though not without immediate satisfactions, carries penalties. There's a Fool Killer, personifying the ancient principle; whom the gods would destroy, in this world; and he has a list; and that's a good way to put yourself on it. Then, the question's just one of time, of how soon he'll get around to you. Still, Ralph seems a misfortune that perhaps shouldn't happen to anyone. A simple unaffected lowness about that story engages the misanthropist in me. Boys, off in a corner, will be boys! And girls? Give me an ounce of civet, good apothecary! Have one yourself!"

Sitting erect in the green leather barrel chair by Arthur Winner's desk, Julius Penrose had arranged his wasted legs, outthrust in their braces, at an angle. Since they had been reduced to not much more than stilts of bone, the cloth of his trousers hung from them in loose folds. Taking up the cane that rested against the chair arm near his right hand, he raised it, pointing it, sighting along it reflectively, at the empty fireplace. "So much for moral indignation!" he said. "One practical thought occurs to me. Has the wench's ogress mother taken her to a doctor?"

"I don't know," Arthur Winner said. "Since we're not denying Ralph had connection with her—"

"Nevertheless, I'd investigate that," Julius Penrose said. "Those societies generally offer medical benefits. To provide them as cheaply as possible, they're apt to have a quack or two more or less in their pay. You've seen them yourself in personal injury cases. If I were you, I'd make that my first business tomorrow. If she hasn't been to a doctor; all right. If she has—you could get Garret Hughes to find out for you—I'd make a formal demand on her that she submit, and without delay, to another examination, by somebody like Reggie Shaw."

"Well, there's no way we can compel—"

"No, there isn't—if she refuses. But you'd at least establish the fact of refusal. You should. You might need it. Your theory is she's a loose young woman; and you plan to plead consent. What happens to that plea if J.

Jerome calls a physician, qualifies him in that he says he went to school and it can't be shown he's lost his license yet, and then gets him to put on the record his professional opinion that the state of the prosecutrix's pudenda, seen the day following the alleged assault, was that of the freshly ravished maiden? Not good at all! Unfailingly, thoughts of an intact virgin being deflowered by a brute excite a juror's sympathies—or, could it be, just excite him? In any event, he's more than likely to hold her innocent of consent until she's proved guilty beyond a reasonable doubt. Hard! You've allowed the burden to fall on defendant. I've an instinct in these sordid matters, Arthur."

Lowering his cane, Julius Penrose tapped the floor. He said: "When I was doing criminal trial work, I used to find my instinct invaluable. Something, I cannot say what—a distrustful nature; an unamiable habit of suspicion; perhaps, actually, a nice nose for hanky-panky got from knowing what *I* would be doing if I meant to pull a fast one—had a way of warning me. I soon found I neglected those intimations at my peril. I'm this minute being insistently informed by one of them that, if Brophy indicts the brat and he's put on trial, more will be involved than the mere issue of whether she let him or didn't let him. Instinct says to me: Watch out!"

Smiling, Arthur Winner said: "You couldn't ask instinct to be a little more explicit, could you?"

"No, I could not," Julius Penrose said. "Instinct doesn't like work. Instinct doesn't bother to explain. Instinct just indicates where I ought to look. I'm supposed, then, to use my head. Here, instinct seems to want me to look at this interest J. Jerome is taking."

"I didn't find that very puzzling," Arthur Winner said. "Someone Jerry knows in Mechanicsville must have got in touch with him. Noah didn't like it; but I couldn't see how it mattered. I can't see any reason for Jerry to have a serious interest."

"Well, there's the use of instinct," Julius Penrose said. "Instinct comes in when you need to know, but you can't see. Let us take my instinct's word for it that Brophy *is* interested. Now, we use the head. Why is he? Well, getting a conviction might please people he has a political interest in pleasing. Is that all? I think not. J. Jerome, in case you don't know, though often so practical, has never, or not for some time, been merely practical. The first occasion was indeed a surprise; but on several occasions now I've seen him grasp at intangibles, amazingly disinclined to take cash and let the credit go. Detweiler's a pretty good Brocton name. J. Jerome did not come from Greenwood Avenue. His father kept a low saloon on Water Street. Could this humble origin ever have caused people who did come from Greenwood Avenue to treat him, though of course with all politeness, as not quite one of them? Might there be something not displeasing in getting a son of George Detweiler convicted of an infamous crime and sent to the reformatory? I think so!"

Arthur Winner said: "I see the possibility; but—"

"No," Julius Penrose said, "I don't suggest that he's fabricate evidence himself; but I'd expect him to accept without too-close inspection anything that might help convict. I'd be prepared to see him play to a jury. I'd be careful about that jury. I'd study the panel. In selecting jurors, I'd use my challenges with the general idea of keeping off, as far as I could, anyone with a foreign name and anyone I'd learned was a Roman Catholic. The precaution seems to you extreme?"

"Yes," Arthur Winner said. "I can't feel religion needs to be brought in. To suppose, because Jerry's a Catholic, Catholics would try to find for him, seems to me a view of prejudice."

"I merit the reproof, no doubt," Julius Penrose said. "I can't say instinct is silenced; but I, perhaps, ought to be! Perhaps I should not glance at Mr. Brophy's religion. First; prejudice is in itself held censurable; an evil thing. So I'm anti-Catholic, am I? Still, in passing, I'll confess I wonder, as one of them, why the only people who may be openly criticized, found fault with, and spoken ill of, are those of white, Protestant, and more or less Nordic extraction. I, it seems, am game and fair game for everybody— a kind of *caput lupinum*. Nobody writes the papers threateningly when I'm decried or disparaged. I don't say this is unreasonable. I myself have no wish to abridge any man's right not to like me if he so chooses. Only, in my bewildered way, I keep thinking there ought to be a turnabout. There isn't! Not only may each bumptious Catholic freely rate and abuse me if I reflect in the least on his faith; but each self-pitying Jew, each sulking Negro, need only holler that he's caught me not loving him as much as he loves himself, and a rabble of professional friends of man, social-worker liberals, and practitioners of universal brotherhood—the whole national horde of nuts and queers—will come at a run to hang me by the neck until I learn to love."

A muscular remote smile passed on Julius Penrose's face. "Well, here, *in propria persona*, I stand—or, rather, sit; since I find sitting easier nowadays. And, of course, there's that other very good reason why glancing at Mr. Brophy's religion isn't, for me, quite the thing, right now. What I wished to speak to you about, if you don't mind, is Marjorie. We stopped by Roylan and I saw her for a moment, to say I wouldn't be home until sometime Sunday. Our colloquy was brief; but she told me she'd called you; and that you'd kindly agreed to let her discuss her religious problem with you."

In some embarrassment, Arthur Winner said: "She seemed disturbed, Julius. She seemed to have the idea that I could, I can't think in what way, help her. When I didn't hear any more, I imagined she'd changed her mind."

Resting on Arthur Winner a gaze into which he seemed to put both sympathy and irony, Julius Penrose said: "She might hope you could afford her the help of listening. Anyone can see you are an understanding sort of person. Moreover, there's her subject matter. She observes that you're by way of being a religious man—"

Arthur Winner said: "I don't think I could really claim—"

"Perhaps not, perhaps not," Julius Penrose said. "What a man's religious beliefs really are should never be inquired into. And, of course, still less, why he holds them. On the point of why; belief or professed belief in a supernatural religion speaks for itself. Though believers will give you a good deal of prose on the subject, the subject's always touchy, fruitful of offense and anger; because the awkward truth usually is that they have no reason, they just feel like believing. At any rate, you attend Christ Church. To boot, you're a member of the vestry there. I can imagine Marjorie entertaining, perhaps not aware that she does, some very faint hope that there might be an alternative—"

"In that event, I think she ought to talk to our rector—"

"Do you?" Julius Penrose said. "I somehow doubt if talking to that, I must say personable, young man would meet her need. I don't believe she'd be in her present emotional predicament if good-mannered piety, or gentlemanlike spiritual guidance, or assisting at well-bred devotions were what she wanted. They don't take enough of the responsibility from her. Not able to discipline herself, she craves to be disciplined."

"If that's the problem," Arthur Winner said, "I don't see how she could hope discussing things with me would help her—"

"Who knows?" Julius Penrose said. "There are disciplines and disciplines. More properly, since all disciplines are arrangements of reward and punishment, there are rewards and rewards, and punishments and punishments. She might hope, by talking, to get the reward of your understanding approval. To confide in you, and at length, would be the first step. How, in the classic phrase, does she know what she thinks until she hears what she says? By common consent, I'm a hard man, insensitive to finer shades of feeling, easily put out of patience. Would I be likely to support with understanding that seemingly necessary talking around and around?"

That Julius had such a picture of himself, and that many people who knew Julius Penrose slightly thought of him as a hard man, were both doubtless true; yet an acquaintance of years inclined Arthur Winner to say that both Julius and common consent erred, too easily taken in by harshnesses of manner and sharpnesses of speech which, in fact, manifested that Julius was a sensitive man, not an insensitive. Julius might see himself soured by affliction; by his physical crippling, slowly or quickly crippled in other ways; but what evinced it? Under the first shock, when the cruel misfortune of his paralysis fell on him ten years ago; through the bitter, long (indeed, endless, since he would never be quit of it) job of fair recovery —at least he was not wholly helpless; at least he was able to go on with his work—had Arthur Winner ever found occasion to excuse in Julius, to call explainable, those not-to-be-mistaken strikings-out of someone brought to recompense himself for his hurts by hurting others? Could Arthur Winner pick from his recollection one instance of the self-denominated hard man acting (though he might often seem to speak it) a hard man's regardless, ruthless part?

Julius Penrose said: "As for why you didn't hear any more this week, Marjorie's Polly, this Mrs. Pratt, seems to have been away. Marjorie only had a card today saying she was back. The point, you'll have perceived, is that she and Marjorie have concluded (for some reason!) that I feel an antipathy toward Mrs. Pratt. Meetings must be managed when the field's clear. Thus, Marjorie was dismayed to see me tonight."

"Well, I think Clarissa had told her—"

"Yes. She'd been thinking I'd be back tomorrow, so she couldn't have Polly. Then Clarissa said that you said that I said—so, she supposed tomorrow was clear, and called Polly, who is coming. I soothed her. Tomorrow was still clear. Mr. Marple, as a further kindness, was planning to have Pettengill drive me back here Sunday morning. I offered to extend my absence, if she liked. She appeared moved by my willingness to accommodate her; but she said tomorrow would give her and Polly time enough."

Arthur Winner said: "I don't think I'm quite clear about Mrs. Pratt's part—what Marjorie wanted her down for."

Taking up a cane, pointing again at the fireplace, Julius Penrose said: "I wondered myself. I made free to ask. Marjorie's plan seems to be to talk with you; and then to tell Polly what you said—to see what Polly says to that. It suggested to me Marjorie's possible hope against hope. Something you said by way of advice; or, maybe, something she said by way of explanation, might raise new issues of fact or feeling. She wanted to be able to take them immediately to Polly—who, one gathers, is to hang around in the offing, ready and waiting. The arrangement has an ineptness, an involvement, that, I'm afraid, sufficiently identifies the author."

Julius let the leveled cane drop. He said: "Well! She wanted to get word to you. She called the lake, and they told her you'd had to go down to Brocton. I said I'd find you. Her situation: she assumes, she wishes to assume, that you're willing to see her tomorrow. Her suggestion: would I ask you to let her know if you weren't willing." He made a faint grimace. "Do I flinch a little? Alas, could anyone but Marjorie be speaking? These trifling left-handednesses come naturally to her. She's preordained to fumble; she's fated always to confound confusion. With solemnity, I told her I'd known you for a long time. If you engaged yourself to do a thing, you would do that thing without fail. Will you?"

"Of course I'll see her," Arthur Winner said. "I'm afraid I can't say just when. I don't know how much of the morning our Mr. Woolf means to take; but I'll find time."

"Good," Julius Penrose said. "Or, is it? I'd be deceiving myself if I didn't recognize that this, while more talk, amounts to action. I confess I hoped the matter would never leave the stage of shilly-shally. The hope seemed reasonable—by not deciding, Marjorie protracted the emotional titillations. She must talk and talk again with Polly and with Polly's monsignor. She must even talk, or try to talk, with me. There's a recent sudden change. I fear her hand's being forced. I suspect an ecclesiastical ultimatum has been handed her—in substance: piss or get off the pot! Among the apparent terms or conditions is one that's far from agreeable to me. A contingent or reserve hope of mine had been that, if anything did come to be done, Polly and Polly's pet monsignor would manage the doing in the seclusion of Polly's private chapel. The latest is: that's out! She'll have to go to Father Albright, at Our Lady of Mount Carmel, here. This being sent home has points of interest. I think you've met Polly—Mrs. Pratt?"

"I believe I did, a year or so ago."

"Yes; that was when she made her last open visit to Marjorie. They were college acquaintances. If you remember Mrs. Pratt at all, you'll remember she's a large overdressed woman exuberant in manner, of less than average intelligence and somewhat sheeplike appearance. She and Marjorie had not seen each other for twenty years or more; yet I believe Mrs. Pratt never once failed to send Marjorie a Christmas card. My informing instinct soon told me the story. During their college years, the now Mrs. Pratt had harbored a consuming crush on Marjorie; though Marjorie, my instinct assured me, had not returned the feeling. Did she even know? I feel certain that Marjorie's taste in love was early and uncompromisingly oriented to males. Women's-college affairs, whether short or not short of active tribadism, weren't likely to have hit the spot with her at all. Moreover, at eighteen or nineteen, Marjorie, never of an independent mind, and no leader, would unfailingly have accepted her social attitudes from those around her. At any good woman's college, Polly's faith must have made her something of an outsider—one of that handful of not quite, quite girls who by special arrangement went somewhere for mass Sunday mornings. The others would have no particular reason to get to know any of them."

Raising his eyebrows, Julius Penrose looked at Arthur Winner. "Nasty little snobs!" he said. "However, there's that, warm and uncritical, in Marjorie's nature to give her kindly impulses. Without meaning anything by them, she'd be always, in effect, blundering into kindnesses or civilities. In the weak unwillingness to hurt, she'd say something cordial or do something friendly. A word or smile of the kind, given just because it was easier, probably started Polly dreaming. A few more such accidents, and Polly was probably a goner. I expect she never dared push the matter—something would probably warn her where Marjorie's interests lay; and, so, that any girl-to-girl courtship would be a mistake. I imagine she just dreamed on, feasting silent and from a distance on Marjorie's hair of gold, on Marjorie's adorable face, on the sweet disorder, the pretty confusion of Marjorie's ways. At a venture, one dream had to do with Marjorie somehow turning Catholic; losing all her friends, but not minding, as she twined arms with Polly and they wandered off into the sunset. You follow me?"

"So far," Arthur Winner said. "But time passes, and—"

"I was coming to that," Julius Penrose said. "Twenty years pass. The two of them lead separate lives. There are only the cards at Christmas; yet those, at last, pay off. Year after year, Marjorie, if she should ever want to, knows where to find Polly. Meanwhile, on Marjorie various factors are working. Her life has been mostly a discontented one. Now, to aggravate the accumulated disappointment and regret, come the moods of the menopause; and the rationalist's poor recourse of grin-and-bear-it fails her. Desperate for relief, she remembers, by one of the ordinary ironies of our life, Polly; and how Polly stood apart and aside at college—not, in this retrospect, because nobody invited her in, but because a light of faith, a truth of certainty kept her out. Polly's kingdom was never the pinchbeck one of this world that Marjorie's finding more and more uninhabitable. She writes Polly. Polly instantly comes. Time has worked on them both. Both, I would presume, got some shocks; but one thing hadn't changed. The college crush—I wonder, in passing, what Mr. Pratt, whoever he may have been, found living with her like. He doesn't seem to have lived long—was unabated. Polly was still in love."

By an effort, putting down his elbows on the chair arms, Julius Penrose lifted his hips. With a grunt, he was able to shift his inert legs to a new angle. He said: "And now, bliss of blisses, the advances are Marjorie's. Marjorie doubts, she fears, she asks to be saved. Is she too late? Bursting with joy, Mrs. Pratt cries: 'No, no; there's time yet! You can still get in on the ground floor.' Indeed, I myself recall from Sunday school that you may give the heat of the day a miss; the eleventh hour will do. Every man one cent is the way of the other world."

Breaking off, Julius Penrose shook his head. He said: "I must try to remember that Marjorie is in distress. Making fun of her ill becomes me—and, furthermore, what am I thinking of? The joke, so much on me, is most unfunny. Marjorie is being, or is about to be, converted. Well, I'd, of course, noticed recently an upsurge of primitive religious belief. I give you my word, I've had it from Dave Weintraub that he and his family reverted not long ago to the Jewish dietary law, known, I believe as kashruth. If they divide the hoof, they have to chew the cud. No kids seethed in their mother's milk. Separate sets of utensils—don't get the plates mixed up. Dave reports that, now he's a practicing Jew again, he feels one hundred per cent better."

Arthur Winner said: "I see how that could be."

"Oh, so do I," Julius Penrose said. "I just thought it was an unusual example. Marjorie's project certainly isn't. In the newspapers, conversion to Rome appears to be the fashion, a phenomenon of the day. I confess I hadn't paid much attention—I suppose, because so many of the news-making converts fell in categories to me naturally suspect. A fancy or high-brow author or two. Sentimental newspaper columnists. Inmates of the theater. Figures of flamboyance in politics. Quondam leading Reds or professional atheists. Uneasy Episcopalian ministers. In short, men and women who must long have been ill-balanced."

Arthur Winner smiled.

"Yes," Julius Penrose said, "jokes should be amusing! By hitting them off that way, I clearly mean to make light of them. Still, what I noted, I noted. Not a few of the male converts, for instance, have to me the look of former homosexuals; not a few of the females, the look of former alcoholics. I'm trying to say that what they *were* before their newsworthy conversion strikes me as often suggestive. Doctor Johnson, I believe, once said: To drive out a passion, reason is helpless; you need another passion. The more it changes, the more it's the same thing? I think so! However, this was idle; general reflection on a topic of the times. I only sat up and took real notice when I saw Marjorie might be serious about Romanism. I remembered Lord Macaulay's pronouncement that there is not, and there never was on this earth, a work of human policy so well deserving of examination. High time I examined it!"

Turning his head, he glanced at the bracket clock on the mantel. "The subject's no small one," he said. "I asked a bookstore to inquire. After a little delay—for secular persons to want such books seems unheard-of—I was provided with a standard four-volume study of moral and pastoral theology by a learned Jesuit; an admirably concise treatise on apologetics and doctrine by an Australian—*quod ubique*, I suppose!—archbishop; and the code of the canon law. All, I've perused with much interest and some instruction. I've a better idea of what Marjorie would be comforted to believe than I had before. But I wasn't won over to their way of thinking. I've never asked you. Are you interested in theology, Arthur?"

"I suppose not," Arthur Winner said, "or I'd know more about it than I do."

"Then I won't belabor you with my personal conclusions at any length. My final reflection, I'm afraid, was that if hypocrisy can be said to be the homage vice pays to virtue, theology could be said to be a homage non-

sense tries to pay to sense. The forms are learned and serious. Of the substance, a good idea may be had from an expounding of the now dogma of
the Assumption that I followed with attention. The Saviour, the incarnate
deity, is defined to be without sin. However, his human nature derived
from his human mother—where else could he get any? Now, what does
this tell us? Why, naturally, that the nature of the Blessed Virgin must have
been without sin. More centuries than I would have thought necessary were
given to thinking the thing through; but, in the end, it became of faith that
the Blessed Virgin was immaculately conceived; meaning that, at the instant of her conception, the original sin in all human nature was miraculously removed from her. What now follows? Obvious! Lots less time is
needed here! Death is the wages of sin. No sin, no death. The Blessed Virgin had no sin, so she could not possibly have died. Yet, she is not on earth.
The explanation? In logic, there can be only one. Her human body was
translated to heaven, and is there now. Irrefragable reasoning!"

"I see," Arthur Winner said. "But you are not persuaded?"

"Logicians though they may be," Julius Penrose said, "I question if
they fully grasp the fact that no number of succeeding syllogisms, though
each unassailable in its formal validity, can cure even one unestablished
premise, even one absurd postulate. And, indeed, I'll do them the fairness
of suspecting they feel free to offer argument of this sort only because they
don't actually rely on it. My archepiscopal apologist introduces all his expo-
sitions of the more critical and difficult dogmas with the proem or caveat I
soon got by heart: 'For a Catholic, it is sufficient to know that the infallible
church teaches the above doctrine; the following proofs, therefore, are not
necessary; but they are useful as giving a knowledge of sacred scripture and
ecclesiastical tradition.' Having read that a few times, I couldn't but realize
we had nothing, they and I, to discuss on the rational level, the only one I
can reach. Let us return to Marjorie. Where was I?"

"You said, I think, that she was being pressed to take some action."

"Yes. There seems at long last to have been a cracking-down or getting-
tough policy. Polly's pet monsignor is not proving quite as pet as expected.
Indeed, why should he? He has produced quite a number of more or less
maudlin best-selling books; he is a radio and television performer; he has a
lot to do. Also, he must know a good deal about the use and abuse of emotions, and possible variations on the religious sentiment. His experience
probably said: Let business be got down to! This Mrs. Penrose is married.
She lives in something called Brocton, out in the sticks. Her parish is there.
Polly may be very rich and very pious, but there are limits. Polly can be her
sponsor, yes; but the reception will not take place intimately with happy
mists of tears in that private chapel, probably to have been banked with
lilies. Mrs. Penrose will get her formal instruction from the local priest in
Brocton, and be received there by him. Do you know Father Albright?"

"Not really," Arthur Winner said. "I've met him. I even had one fairly long talk with him last year. He came to me about the board of education's plan to show those so-called sex education films to the high-school children. I couldn't agree with him; but—"

"I'll say it for you," Julius Penrose said. "I've observed him, and heard him speak, on several public occasions. His theme is usually the menace of atheistic communism; and since none of his hearers, whether through ordinary wisdom or plain dumbness, is in the remotest danger of embracing a nonsense too stupid for the intelligent and too complicated for the stupid, he can, not unadroitly, urge the scarcely less nonsensical identification of what he calls 'Americanism' with, of all things, Catholicism. Still, he appears to be a worthy enough fellow, of virtuous, I'm sure, habits; sincere in his peculiar professions; and, as men go, a good man rather than a bad one. You agree?"

"Yes, I do. He seemed earnest and honest."

Julius Penrose said: "Though probably both, the significant, and, so, painful, point to me is that he's also quite common. Of course, when Marjorie's preparing to swallow a camel, to strain at gnats would be silly. It's disagreeable of me, it may be trifling of me; yet I ask myself, with a kind of dismay, how can anyone go, for any sort of 'instruction,' to a person who, when he means 'modern,' says 'modren'; and when he means 'interesting,' says 'inneresting.' I don't, of course, suggest that every Roman cleric is in this case; Polly's Catholic circle I'd judge to be quite a cultural cut above these priests of the people—the least little bit cheap, perhaps (I have monsignor in mind); but I speak as one of his readers only. Meeting him, I daresay you hardly notice, you hardly notice! However, the particular cleric I must consider is Father Albright; and I'm given pause to know that Marjorie's new emotional needs are so imperative that they transcend all fastidiousness as well as all reason. Tell me about your talk with him."

Arthur Winner said: "It didn't end very satisfactorily. He managed to drop a pretty strong hint that one reason I might not care what went on at Brocton High School was that I didn't send my daughter there, I sent her out to Washington Hall. By then, of course, he'd realized nothing he could say would change my attitude—I'd told him at once that I'd seen the films, along with the rest of the board, and considered them in no way objectionable. I daresay he felt that, being an Episcopalian, I wouldn't know any reason why immorality shouldn't be promoted in schools. I could hardly blame him for being put out."

"And just why couldn't you?"

In the tone of blunt inquiry, in the casual pause for answer, Arthur Winner must feel, always glad of it, the force of long-established habit. Over the years, what hours had he and Julius passed in quiet converse, alone together, talking to each other! On evenings when they worked late and the

office was, as now, empty; on afternoons while the law delayed and one or
another of them waited on a jury, or on the court in recess, sitting together
at counsels' table below the bench, or in seats taken at random up near the
door; on winter Sundays with snow on the ground at Roylan, by Julius's
smoldering fire, or his; on forenoons of late spring week ends at the lake,
looking out from the terrace, beneath the great oak beginning finally to
burst its virescent buds of leaves, over the warming water's sunny shimmer
—how many discussions had engaged them! In exchange of unhurried
thought, in give-and-take of comment, they proceeded to how many meetings of mind!

As a rule, these two minds could meet quickly in agreement; but in
disagreement, a conclusion of reticent understanding could be reached,
after so much practice, quite as well. Not by talkative openings of the heart,
but by a silent long-held knowledge of each other, a basic like-mindedness,
they could enjoy a mutual unspoken comprehension. That comprehension
respected the privacy, or even secrecy, which alone, at some points, dignifies a man; yet each, after all, had had a share in shaping the other's thoughts
—amused, Arthur Winner could notice sometimes phrases of his in Julius's
mouth; or, perhaps more often, phrases of Julius's in his. Ceremony between them would be absurd. They were free to differ, if in the end they did,
with no loss of concord.

Arthur Winner said: "Father Albright had a grievance. His argument
seemed to be that since his church wasn't financially able to maintain a high
school in Brocton, parochial-school children *had* to go, through no choice
of his or theirs, to the public high school. I think at first he may have
thought I just hadn't realized, hadn't the moral training to know, that what
I was voting for was gravely wrong. Now that he'd told me, now that I did
know, my duty was plain. I wasn't doing it. I was still set on contributing
to the moral delinquency of Catholic minors. Of course, I told him we
weren't planning to force any child to see the films. Those whose parents
wanted them excused would be excused. I'm afraid I was put out a little
myself when he treated that as more of my ignorance. He said that wouldn't
do at all. That would work a discrimination, make an issue of a child's faith.
Because Catholic parents couldn't, on pain of sin, expose them to what the
church regarded as dangerous to their morals, Catholic children were to be
singled out in an open and invidious way. I think he thought our only right
course was to do as he wanted—not show the films to anyone."

"You may be sure he felt exactly that," Julius Penrose said. "And I've
no doubt his irritation was extreme. What must be the chagrin and frustration of a man, the emolument and solace of whose celibate, hard-working
life is power—*alter Christus*, he can actually say of himself—when he finds
again, except with his own parishioners, he has only the velvet glove?
Where's the iron hand that ought to be in it? Instead of you, a heretic, being

haled before him, and told what to do, and warned on pain of, not just sin, but of fire, to do it, his pitiful only expedient is to come and ask you to please be fair! Yes, I think the bad temper of one who suffers such humiliation is explainable; though I'm not very sympathetic. I know no better than John Locke knew why those who do not, and morally cannot—against truth, error has no rights; and they, and every dogma, doctrine, and practice of theirs is truth; and you, my friend, are error—tolerate should themselves be tolerated."

Shrugging, Julius Penrose breathed wearily. He made a movement of discomfort, reminding Arthur Winner that this, too, differentiated Julius from more fortunate men. To them, pain was passing and occasional; Julius lived with pain—not acute; but never in his waking hours wholly relieved. Julius said: "Yet, of course, the intolerance is a necessity; that exercise— the firm use of power, the rigid requirement of submission—is a true *sine qua non*. Games, to be any good, must have rules. People won't value what doesn't cost them anything. All the slightly troublesome, perpetually recurring, obligations of worship; all the arbitrarily imposed, slightly irksome fasts or abstinences: that, for instance, tails-you-lose-heads-I-win disciplinary stand on contraception, help the players feel this game is real. The same, with the constant exactions of cash; the masses and candles at a price, the tables of the money-changers in their church doors. A wise utilization of great psychological truths, a wise manipulation of the sense of values, enables, if I may repair to Locke again, the priest to offer the more-wanted pennyworth. When all's done and all's paid, the faithful, like Dave Weintraub, feel one hundred per cent better."

Julius's muscular remote smile showed itself an instant. He said: "Yes, I confess to more than a mere temperamental distaste. As a free man, I have to fear that canny practice, that patient know-how, those vibrant God-love-yous—all *that* alarms me. Here, today, Father Albright is still only able to ask you to be fair; you are still free to hold that he's as much entitled to his opinion as you are to yours. But tomorrow? Who may then be beseeching whom to be fair; and who—ho ho! ha ha!—is going to hold that you're as much entitled to your opinion as he is to his? Oh, I know that in Maryland, once their Maryland, a land speculator and political lord of their faith did solemnly declare a resolve, I think sincere, that the weak were never to oppress the strong: so would I could believe I was simply a bigot, merely moved by what the newspapers name bias. Yet does any free man, without grief, without shame, without fear, see names so proud a hundred years ago in their birthright of liberty as New Hampshire, Massachusetts, Rhode Island, Connecticut, little by little in the last fifty years degraded to designate virtual papal states?"

Julius Penrose shook his head. "Yes; there was a trade; messes of pottage were chosen; and stuck with that trade we are! To make a fast buck, our great-grandfathers' grandfathers used their shipping to bring over the black man who could be worked in the South for no wage. Today, hamstrung by our humanitarian principles, what wouldn't we, North or South, happily pay once and for all to be rid of him? To make a later fast buck, the ship-owners' canal-and-railroad-building, their mill-operating, descendants raked, for cheap labor, every area of Europe where, life being wretched, superstition was rife. In consequence, fastened on us—and probably, as Macaulay suspected, forever—we have Rome! Let us now praise famous men! Our God is jealous and visits the sins of fathers on children! Our gods are just, and of our pleasant vices make instruments to plague us." Julius Penrose laughed aloud. "I feel better!" he said.

His expression somber again, Julius sat silent a moment. He said: "I must hurry this up. Pettengill and Valentine will be waiting. I must let them get on. And you. You're going back to the lake tonight?"

Arthur Winner shook his head. "It was just a day's party for the children. Everyone's coming down this evening."

"The children, yes!" Julius Penrose said. "All, today, must be for them. Is this well considered? I hear rumors that my daughter and yours find having an automobile essential. How unkind to deprive them of any pleasure costing only a few hundred dollars! The philoprogenitive instinct, brooding on the brats, is tickled to do them service—the more, the merrier! It's poor Helen again! But, how about the brats? Could we prepare them better for life if we arranged things so that instead of being ministered to all the time, they were soundly cuffed into ministering a little to their elders? Looking at my own offspring, I wonder. Priscilla's been encouraged to play, a gross miscasting, the lass with the delicate air. Indulged, Stewart, no fool, takes a leaf from that young man in Holy Writ who said: 'Sir, I go'; and went not. What's to be done with human beings? What can be done for them? The question puts itself about Marjorie."

Aiming a cane at the left shoe, locked in his leg brace, Julius looked along it, frowning. He said: "I think I should tell you what I believe to be wrong with Marjorie. My instinct identifies the trouble. She's afraid. What frightens her? She is afraid of herself. She feels that she is, and always has been, helpless in the hands of herself. This, an ordinary human situation, is not news to the reflective; but reflective is the last thing Marjorie's fitted to be. She never had any clear grasp of the human situation. Late in time, some sense of that situation intrudes. She can't stand it—and, indeed, the sight's one to shake stouter nerves than hers. She sees a system by which such grasping is made unnecessary. Seek and ye shall find; knock and it shall be opened to you! That means, I learn from the system's loquacious apologists: stop saying; *if* you see, then you'll believe. Believe, and *then* you'll see! There's some smell of charlatanry, to be sure; but charlatans can

show wonderful cures. As it has respect either to the understanding or the
senses, happiness, Jonathan Swift admonishes me, is a perpetual possession
of being well-deceived. Let her be happy. I'd no more argue with her than
I'd take, or try to take, a blindman's coppers. This, assure her, is how I
really feel."

He looked intently at Arthur Winner.

He said: "Of course, Marjorie could have found out by asking me. But,
my forbidding air quite aside, I'm afraid that would have been too easy. She
needs—a requirement of her nature—to do things in roundabout ways. A
paradox: but making things intricate and dramatic is Marjorie's means of
falsifying into simplicity the frightening complications of life. So she'll tell
you her story; and you'll tell me as much as you think I ought to know.
You're to persuade me that, God helping her, she can do no other. What,
she'll ask you, is the best thing? She can't bear to hurt me; and she knows
how I hate the idea of her being a Catholic."

He shrugged patiently. He said: "Dramatic, you see. I *hate* it! The
accurate statement would be that I don't like it. I don't like it, because, to
me, it seems a futile little ignominy, a peace-at-any-price panic. Silliness
in Marjorie isn't new; but this is servile silliness, mean submissiveness. This
has the sheer vulgarity of all frightened acts—the cringe of face, the whine
aloud for mercy."

Julius Penrose shook his head. "Like it, I cannot! But all that actually,
in her term, 'hurts' me is seeing a human being so lowered. Hers isn't the
situation of what I find is called a Cradle Catholic—not, born; babies, you
might say, are all born protestants—who guesses the priest must know
something about religion and leaves all that to him. This is personal. What,
Marjorie hears in terror, doth it profit a man if he gains the whole world and
suffers the loss of his own soul? Of course, not she alone! This type of terror,
though of a womanish cast, is available to men, appears in fact to be true
religion's gist. I seem to recall that one celebrated pietist of the seventeenth
century—a time that was the term, I suppose, of serious attention to such
subjects on the part of any man of really first-rate intelligence—reduced by
his atrocious anxiety over that dear, dear soul of his, proposed gambling as
a figure—belief is the best bet, a wager which a man is mad not to make.
Since, when less than utterly distraught, the mind he records is of often
interesting perceptiveness, he was naturally obliged to own that this feeling
was unreasonable. However, shivering in his shoes, he wanted to be safe,
cost reason what reason might be cost—he couldn't face the dreadful chance
that the mumbo jumbo would work, and he'd miss out; be damned eter-
nally. Not pretty!"

Julius Penrose shook his head again. "No; be it Marjorie, be it Blaise
Pascal, I don't like to think of anyone cowed that way, whimpering on the
knees before some Father Albright: O God, I am heartily sorry that I have

offended thee. I'll do anything, anything, if only you'll let me live forever.
I want it! I want it! Please, please, don't make me just die; grant me eternal
life, and let perpetual light shine upon me! Please, please believe I *am*
heartily sorry—"

He broke off, shrugging once more. "Well, one must remember Marjorie's choice isn't free; to this, she's being driven. Circumstances have combined against her until she breaks—she must quit, give over, cut and run.
Circumstances, I say, combine to drive her; and here *I* come in. This is to
some degree my doing. Here, I'm in *pari delicto*, I'm afraid. Granted that
Marjorie, or Marjorie's nature, was always apt to make her life an unhappy
one. Granted that the self Marjorie fears, she fears with cause. Yet, that's
not the whole story of her unhappiness. By nature, she's unable to do without men; and she has been unfortunate with men. She's found them de-
ceivers ever. She might, of course, be said consistently to have mistaken
their promises to her. At any rate, what she took them to be promising,
they did not perform. And, of course, here, too, she had her sad share in
bringing about whatever happened to her. Even in the case of her first husband, I think there was a complicity. I don't know whether you remember
Carl Osborne?"

"I never met him," Arthur Winner said. "I remember him around,
when they had that place out at Oakdale. What became of him?"

Julius Penrose said: "I wanted to know that myself. My recent studies
in canon law revealed to me that if he was still living, the Roman view, in
which Marjorie must of course acquiesce, was that no marriage ever sub-
sisted between her and me—nor, could one; unless I wished to venture the
considerable sums required to represent before the Curia in Rome that de-
fects in consent had made invalid the union between Mr. Osborne and so-
called Mrs. Osborne under canon ten eighty-three or canon ten eighty-six,
which can plainly be read to void, if grace so directs the court—*stare decisis*
is a principle, I discovered, unknown to their advocates—virtually any
marriage at all; so the Roman rule on divorce is not nearly so oppressive at
least, for the well-to-do, as non-Romanists may suppose. At any rate, I recently had Osborne traced. He's in an institution—which came as no great
surprise to me. When Edmund Lauderdale read the notes of testimony in
Marjorie's divorce, he impounded them in a hurry. Still, of that part—the
remarkable list of duly substantiated indignities to the person—too much
needn't be made. Females have resilient persons; and Marjorie's unpleasant
experiences didn't create in her a revulsion against men."

Julius Penrose looked steadily at Arthur Winner for a moment. "Not
even temporarily," he said. "A month or so after she left Osborne and retained me to start divorce proceedings, she was induced with no great
difficulty to have an affair with me. Though we imagined it to be secret, I
daresay it was known. In a lawyer-client relationship, I must unhesitatingly

pronounce any such proceeding as the height of impropriety and imprudence."

"For one, I didn't know," Arthur Winner said. "This business disturbs
you, I see."

"To a degree," Julius Penrose said. "To a degree! But don't lay that disclosure—not, I admit, in the best of taste—to overwrought feelings. I'm
led by Marjorie's present plight to review as well as I can Marjorie's emotional history. The history's that of one who has been the dupe of designing
persons. What made her so? Manifestly, the fact that her feelings, whether
those known or unknown to her, need only be reached. Reached, they un-
man her. You then take a firm line, and she'll do whatever you want."

A faint wince of pain—the partly wasted muscles in his hips or thighs
must have cramped—passed on Julius's face. Impatiently, he lowered his
elbows and, by a powerful heave, changed again the angle at which his legs
rested. He said: "How, for instance, did Marjorie come to marry Osborne?
Well; she'd probably say she doesn't know; at the time, she just felt she had
to. She'd never think of asking herself why she felt she had to. Knowing her
as I do, I could tell her. She felt she had to because he'd told her she had to.
Indeed, since he often made the threat later, I think he may have said he'd
kill himself if she didn't marry him. Very potent, with a natural-born dupe
of the kindhearted kind! Could she bear to think of him being so unhappy,
when all she had to do was say yes? Then, too; the affecting fact that he was
crazy! Leaving college, Marjorie, determined to be a Career Woman, and
actually imagining she had literary abilities (how typical that she could so
mistake her bent or aptitudes!), went to work for a news magazine. I've
often wondered how she could have got the job. She says she just went in
and asked. Osborne was on the editorial staff. As nearly as I can judge,
everyone who worked there was at least a little crazy; but he was more so."

Julius Penrose moved his head impatiently. "You have to think of the
facts of the case as seen, all of them, through this daze of Marjorie's reached
feelings. Does she observe that he's something of a drunk? Her heart's
touched. She'll cherish him by drinking with him, by becoming something
of a drunk, too. Does she discover—as she quickly did; he, of course, seduced her almost at once—that he's affected from time to time with what
amounts to satyriasis, and that when the fit is on him, his tastes are likely
to be sadistic? Marjorie finds that no impediment to marrying him. She may
wring her hands; but if that's what he wants, she feels she must accommodate him."

Julius was silent, seeming to hesitate. He said: "I'd better be a little
more specific, I think. 'Accommodate' is a vague term; you could form too
tame or normal an idea of what was involved. During the last year of their
life together, Osborne's whim was, on one occasion, to insist that Marjorie

watch while he had intercourse with another woman, a house guest of theirs. Then, in more, perhaps, than fair exchange, he once brought home two men he'd met at a bar, and Marjorie was required to have intercourse with them, while *he* watched. Admittedly these were single episodes, and involved drunkenness. By that time, the Oakdale place had come to be known familiarly in the village as Alcoholic Hill. No doubt, as I say, Marjorie began drinking out of sympathy; but soon enough she was drinking out of what she conceived to be necessity. She early learned to read the signs; so when the signs told her tonight was the night, or this week end was the week end, she'd start getting as tight as she could. She didn't seem to see anything else to do. I'm not sure she'd ever have seen anything else to do if Osborne hadn't, at last, made a serious attempt—there was no doubt about it; he'd have been indicted if Marjorie hadn't refused to testify—to get rid of her by poisoning her."

"That, I never knew," Arthur Winner said. "How really shocking, Julius!"

"Yes, yes," Julius Penrose said. "What, for all we know, or trouble to imagine, any person may have behind him or her is nothing short of amazing. I thought that if you heard some of this, Marjorie, as seen over the years, would be clearer—or more explicable. Remember, to Marjorie, things are a perpetual surprise. She has the childish, almost animal, innocence that hardly connects cause and effect. Deeply discontented, she might feel she was not getting the things she needed; but why she wasn't getting them would always be beyond her. What did she need? Difficult to define; for the good reason that, being a joinder of incompatibles, the needed thing could not, in this life, exist."

Julius Penrose looked at the cane he held. He studied it a moment. He said: "Her need, I believe, was always dual—two needs, or types of needs; and, as I say, in their nature blindly antagonizing together. Most of the time, the need uppermost, the need in charge of the conscious Marjorie, was manifest in Marjorie's little-girl exterior—little-girl needs; pettings; treats; playtime; the story hour. Meeting these, if these were all, would present no problem—except perhaps of patience. But these were far from all. Inside the little girl, not showing most of the time, something quite other, with quite other needs, was implanted—a very part of her, too."

Dispassionate, he looked at Arthur Winner. He said: "We could call this, I think, the principle of passion. At first sight, the idea that such a principle would reside in someone like Marjorie must seem ridiculous. It resides in her notwithstanding. This principle neither trifles, nor is to be trifled with. When its times come, it simply takes over. The little girl's away for a while. Into her place steals, I think, something like a maenad. On a small scale, Marjorie has actually become that Fatal Woman of story and history. What, one asks one's self, is the secret of such disastrous power? The stories neglect to say. They only relate the thing accomplished. One sees Circe; one sees swine. What was in that cup?"

Thrusting his cane at a slant against the brace below his knee, Julius, with an expert twitch, levered his legs a little more to the right. He said: "Personally, I've no doubt that an incidence in these uncommon women of the true classic *furor uterinus*, an oestrual rage, is what does the job. Lying deep, it will usually lie, as well as hidden, quiescent. What discovers it? In some celebrated cases I have a poet to tell me that Anthony comes to supper, and for his ordinary pays his heart; Romeo gate-crashes a ball, and touching Juliet's, makes blessed his rude hand. In Marjorie's humbler case, discovery may be less startling. I conclude that a special, in one way or another, intimate, relationship develops first. The course of the relationship works Marjorie to some pitch of nervous emotion—what emotion, hardly matters; the reaching, penetrating of her feelings is all that counts. Her feelings sufficiently penetrated, the principle of passion, the interior rage—without its hostess's intention; maybe, without even her knowledge—is made to stir. The stir is electrifying. The unsuspecting, very probably astounded, male, in sudden erotic rapport with her, is beside himself. Seizing on him, rage answers rage. I venture to assert that when this gadfly's sting is fairly driven in, when this indefeasible urge of the flesh presses them, few men of normal potency prove able to refrain their foot from that path."

Tightening his fingers on the raised cane, studying the start-out of strong muscle in the back of his hand, Julius Penrose said: "I speak, of course, for and of myself; but I think, also, of Osborne. He being half-mad, his rage, his not-refraining, took half-mad forms. Thinking of those, one thinks first of Marjorie as his victim. If he is to accomplish an act of love, she has to be caused mental or physical anguish. Yet I must wonder if, and in a way quite fatal to him, he was not actually her victim. You see how?"

"You're, perhaps, ironic?" Arthur Winner said.

"No, I'm not," Julius Penrose said. "When I'm ironic you may be sure I mean to say this thing is nonsense. I can't so consider Osborne's plight. Marjorie, by being helpless and hapless, lured him on. He may be guessed to have found her practice of drunken submission insupportably exciting. Such a year-in, year-out round of excitements as Marjorie provided was debilitating to a damaged mind. Osborne, originally half-mad, ended wholly mad. By comparison, Marjorie could, I suppose, be said to have got off unscathed. There, I'm, perhaps, ironic."

Arthur Winner said: "And, if he looks as if he might have money on him, a man becomes guilty of being hit on the head and robbed, if he is?"

"Indeed, I think him guilty, if he takes that look of money where hittings-on-the-head and robbings are accepted means of livelihood," Julius Penrose said. "But I find no parallel, because I think the drinking and submitting deserves a closer look. I feel sure that, as far as Marjorie knew, she didn't like what Osborne made her do, or did to her. How could she like these things? Often, they'd be physically painful; mentally, or if you like, spiritually, they were abominable—revolting debasements; studied outrages; systematic violations of all the sensibilities. Who but the maniac forcing her to them could desire them? My considered answer: Marjorie, though all unknowing, could! She could see such a punishment as condign. She had to submit, because in an anguished way, she craved to have done to her what she was persuaded she deserved to have done to her."

He gazed an instant at Arthur Winner. "You find this farfetched?" he said. "Yes; we who are so normal are reluctant to entertain such ideas; yet that, I believe, was the true why of it. Identifying anything so far removed from consciousness is guesswork. I make the obvious guess—she harbors a consuming sense of guilt. Knowing the principle of passion residing in her, aware of how the maenad could be made to materialize, she gets no rest from that guilt. She must do something in propitiation. For her pleasure, the pleasure that the maenad cannot be denied, she must pay in pain. The situation then becomes this: A madman, as perhaps only a madman could, divines her true state. He perceives her principle of passion, and the potentialities, to him exciting, of Marjorie's guilt about it. At the same time, that guilt of Marjorie's, though Marjorie is quite unconscious of anything but powerful feelings that she 'has' to 'love' the madman, perceives *his* potentialities—by him, every pleasure will be properly punished. She is led to throw herself at Osborne. People, I think, are to be pitied! You consider this too complicated?"

Arthur Winner said: "Perhaps not. But I've often wondered how far anyone can see into what goes on in someone else. I've read somewhere that it would pose the acutest head to draw forth and discover what is lodged in the heart."

Julius Penrose said: "Yes: good! No; I don't insist that these goings on were exactly, in every particular, as stated. Dichotomies of the sort are seldom clear-cut. The parts of a person's mind merge; they change; those once dominant may be superseded; some seem to die; others are born. In Marjorie's case, her final fear for her life served, I think, to relieve her specific guilt. The guilt sense has little use for logic; a last supreme fear may have ended the need that kept her with Osborne. I don't know. At least, at last, she was able to break with him. Next time, she was not to be so lucky."

He looked once more at Arthur Winner. "Yes," he said, "I, too, was a deceiver. For compelling the still-Mrs. Osborne to an affair with me, I'll excuse myself. I don't consider that I wronged or harmed her—the contrary, rather! I think, since she did not know the real reason for her experiences, that secret wish of hers to have them, she imagined there might be something wrong with her as a woman that made normal acts of love impossible. When she found, through me, that this was not the case, I think she regarded me with gratitude. I mean to say, I reached her feelings."

He paused an instant. "No," he said, "I was never the man that I allowed—even, led—her reached feelings to see me as. I was not the man to meet any of her conflicting needs. I had a nature detached and analytical. What Marjorie would take to be my scornfulness and my cynicism were bound to make their appearance, and bound to hurt her. Here was no nice little boy for a little girl to play house with! On the other hand, neither was I a fit instrument for the visiting maenad. The passion I protested was, in a sense, not really mine—not the natural-born sexual athlete's spontaneous expression. It was a temporary response to novelty that the rage in her provoked. Novelty gone, the normally moderate man would too soon lapse into moderation. His analytical mind must, too soon, remind him that this pleasure is, after all, brief; and this position is, after all, ridiculous. Loss of interest may be expected."

Julius Penrose smiled sharply at Arthur Winner. He said: "Of course, the interest's a renewable one. Some regular recurrence could be counted on—quite enough to content most little girls, where a little girl is all there is to content. Here it was different; though I think I could say that Marjorie as maenad was served no worse by me than she would have been by most men. Our known national ordering of habit and convenience that makes, for millions, Saturday night connubial love night—or, not to overornament what must be the fact in more bedrooms than not, the scheduled time for discharge of the seminal vesicle—certifies as much to me."

Raising his hand, Julius Penrose yawned. "The plea's a poor one," he said. "I don't enter it. That defendant's no different from many other men is immaterial. *I* fell down on a job I asked for, I insisted on taking, I engaged to do. Marjorie didn't expect her seduction to lead to marriage. She was, in fact, most reluctant to be made an honest woman of. Though not able to phrase her reluctance, she felt the unwisdom of what I proposed; and, for that moment, I now see, she was far ahead of me in intuitive understanding. But she was also weak; and I'm the man for a firm line. She couldn't bear to wound me with a rejection. So when her decree was made absolute, I directed her to present herself with me before your friend of this evening, Joe Harbison. She, of course, obeyed. We were united. For this, I must answer! I exercised undue influence. For this, I can invent no good excuses. I perpetrated a fraud. Here, I *did* wrong her; here, I harmed her."

Taking the arms of his chair in both hands, Julius Penrose made to rise. Seeing him move, Arthur Winner had risen immediately. "Yes," Julius Penrose said, "if you please! I always like to try. I keep having the fatuous notion that I'll suddenly find I can. All I ever find is that once really well down, I can't. I must get the Ingoldsby folder."

Bending to give Julius a purchase on his arm, Arthur Winner said: "I'll get it for you." Straightening himself, he brought them both erect; and Julius neatly swung his canes in place. "If you please!" he said again. A darkness of anger entered his face. "Hell and death, I tire of this, sometimes! I think I'm reasonable. At my age, I wouldn't ask to run the hundred yards in ten seconds. I'd ask only the privilege of moving around a room like anyone else, of walking with my feet, not my hands."

"And, very little to ask," Arthur Winner said.

Julius Penrose said: "Forgive me, Arthur! Since, yourself, you do nothing stupid and say nothing silly, in my place, I think you'd not waste breath in vain repinings. You are kind to overlook mine. And that, on top of sitting silent while I talk and talk! One perceives you see it's, indeed, compensatory! I can do little; so I say much. I suppose such feats of comprehending are why I love you. Yes; fetch the folder; and be quick, since you're able to be!"

Making his laborious but practiced way after Arthur Winner into the outer office, Julius Penrose said suddenly: "Where did you think of seeing Marjorie?"

Arthur Winner pulled out a drawer of the correspondence file. While he flicked over the index tabs, he said: "I'd thought of calling her in the morning when I got back from the courthouse and asking if she could come down here."

Julius Penrose said: "If by any means you could manage to, I'd just as soon you met her—or them—at Roylan. Mrs. Pratt, the truth is, attracts attention. She has a car quite as large and costly as Mr. Marple's; and the one I saw last was the color of a daffodil. I shrink somewhat to think of Brocton gapers observing her and Marjorie drawing up outside here. Not that I mightn't be wise to accustom myself, as soon as possible, to Marjorie being stared at. She will, I suppose, soon be taking the station wagon, and for the period of a mass, leaving it parked with that dismayingly endless Sunday morning range of cars one sees crowding the curbs around the new Our Lady of Mount Carmel. Well, no help; so, no matter! Yet, meanwhile—" He broke off; and said abruptly: "Clarissa wouldn't like the idea of this talk? She doesn't like the idea?"

Arthur Winner said: "She knows Marjorie wanted to talk to me. She felt, and I must admit I agreed with her, that it wasn't likely anything would be accomplished; and that, in fact, you might not thank me for interfering. She thought I ought, perhaps, to tell Marjorie that I simply couldn't go into it with her."

"Good advice!" Julius Penrose said. "Sound sense! One should be wary when people try to make their business yours. I'd not ask so much of you, Arthur, if it weren't that I feel (I would!) that the situation is a special one

—the sort of thing you might be of help in. Who knows? Your manner of reasonableness might restore a balance. I withdraw the Roylan suggestion. See them here."

Arthur Winner said: "I can see them there. I'd thought, I suppose, of arranging things so I could remark that I'd talked to Marjorie—instead of announcing that I was going to talk to her. But since—"

"Yes; but since!" Julius Penrose said. "I, too, think seeing her and saying nothing would be ill-considered. How very strange that you said nothing! Down that road, there's always trouble. Could you put it to Clarissa that you were seeing Marjorie only because I asked you to? Would that be sufficiently near the truth? I think so. Put it to her."

"I'll do that, if you don't mind," Arthur Winner said.

Carrying the file folder, he came into the hall with Julius and opened the screen door on the front steps. Out in the hot night, in the pale flood of street lighting, he gave Julius his arm; and, supporting his weight, went down the steps with him. From the long black car, the chauffeur started with alacrity, swinging open the rear door. Arthur Winner could see, in the shadowed front seat, the shape of the poodle, head alertly turned.

Preparing himself to make the toilsome transfer from the pavement to the car's interior, Julius Penrose said: "Ah, Pettengill; thank you! Ah, Valentine!"

Hearing her name directed at her, the dog lifted her muzzle. She uttered one clear short bark.

"What enchanting intelligence! What a ravishing creature!" Julius Penrose said. "Were I younger, sound, and a single man, I'd ask her to marry me."

Julius Penrose and Arthur Winner, Jr.
[from *By Love Possessed*]

Make me to know mine end, and the measure of my days, what it is. . . . The simple, inevitable moment, with those counsels of gravity and recollection, better and better known to Arthur Winner as the years went, was again arrived at. It was a moment made sober, made sobering, by the very absence of all ceremony, by the plain-dealing ordinariness of the observances. The double doors of the big wall safe were opened. In a narrow document drawer the right envelope of those numerous open-ended envelopes would be looked for and found. Arthur Winner would remove it. He brought it to his desk. He sat down. He put on his reading glasses. Withdrawing the folded stiff sheet or sheets, he unfolded, flattened on his blotting pad, another last will and testament. Gravely greeting his comprehensive first glance might be this or that flourish of ancient form: *In the name of God, Amen. I—; Be it remembered, that I—; Know all men by these presents—.* At once, he skipped on, passed to the end in automatic professional check—date; proper signature; proper attestation of subscribing witnesses; executor or executors named. Turning back, such points of validity all seen to, a businesslike brisk reading could be begun; an attentive scanning that took in, ticked off, paragraph after paragraph, item after item, this now-corpse's imperious orderings, this now graspless hand's devisings and bequeathings, a scanning that also considered, that critically assessed, the frequent surplusages of fussy direction, the sometimes intricate rewarding or punishing provisions of bestowal. Food for thought, they often suggested that testator, in his Soul-thou-hast-much-goods self-importance, in his plans to continue to rule his heirs and assigns, to bend future time to this will, grasped no better than most men that, in order for his orders to be operative, his will to be done, all scheming and planning of his must first (*huddled in dirt the reasoning engine lies*) have an end, that he was to be dispossessed of all possessions, that the "my death" this instrument so unexcitedly mentioned was to involve actual dying—no more of him.

When the telephone rang Arthur Winner had been at the wall safe. The safe was open by then, but opening it took him a few minutes. Helen always opened the safe. Since he last used the combination, several years had probably passed; he was not sure of the numbers. He had found the envelope quickly enough, and at the buzz of the little switchboard across the office, he was able to carry Helen's will in with him to his desk. The telephone put aside, he took the envelope. To facilitate finding it in the file, *Helen Detweiler* had been penciled—by Helen herself, he saw—at the top. The envelope was without bulk—no self-importance would puff up this testator; a couple of paragraphs could take care of all Helen had and all she might intend. What reason would there be for Noah to think he needed to see it? Of course, there was no reason; Noah had no need to. In stupefaction confounded, Noah said a mechanical something for the sake of saying something. When a person died and you knew a will existed, you always asked to see the will; you always went through the form of reading it before the executors offered it for probate.

No name of God here; no importunings to remember; but, flourishless: *I, Helen Everitt Detweiler* . . . His glasses on, Arthur Winner had given the sheet its comprehensive glance; yet he got no further forward. Executors, he had seen, were Fred Dealey and the First National Bank of Brocton; but there he stuck. Though this was not Noah's incapacitating stupefaction, nor anything near it, a certain thickness or numbness of mind interfered with his efforts to put thought in order—indeed, resisted thought, persisted in what was not thought at all, but only feeling's idiot asseveration, renewed and renewed, that this that was true *couldn't* be true.

From the frame above the mantel, mature face intent and thoughtful, finger forever marking his place in the bound volume of reports held by the competent hand, the competent mind forever pondering its point of law, Arthur Winner Senior, forever unknowing, forever unaware of various later happenings, gazed down at Arthur Winner Junior, father surveying son. Fixed in his moment of time, that year of his life when he sat to the portraitist, Father was, in age, being approached, overtaken; would presently be passed—the man of the portrait quite soon now (how strange the thought) become a younger man than his son. Proceeding to live longer, might the son, being now the senior, sometime come to have learned more, actually (incredible!) know more, than the very paragon of learning, sense, wisdom, whose unpedantic dry instruction for years had gone to teach a young man (in all three relatively lacking) points of learning, points of observing, points of thinking; whose stored sayings were in fact still a bible at the back of the mind, without recourse to which, even today, few days ever passed—for apposite example, what of that favorite half-serious maxim on will-drawing? *Always remember, Son, to provide for the thing you think can't happen; because that's going to be what does happen.* . . .

Yes; exactly! Consider how, here, under his hand, a course of events laughed at the judgment of another day. For Noah to have named himself executor of this will would have been absurd. Already an old man, he couldn't possibly outlive Helen, a girl just come of legal age. Little more likely to survive her were men then past their youth like Arthur Winner Junior and Julius Penrose. The odds, of course, were also against Fred Dealey's surviving her; but disparity of age being less, Fred being young— just entering the office, not yet a partner—they could put his name in for the time being. When Fred came to see himself as too old, he could so advise Helen, help her select someone else. Helen, anyone who knew Helen must feel certain, would still be there, devoted and faithful still to a work and life that suited her so well; white-headed, perhaps, but active and alert, the absolutely dependable, in the field of her duties completely competent, indispensable then as now, manager of the office, as long as he had one, of what would be in her series of aging employers, the last old man. What would he do without Helen? Helen would never leave him!

But tomorrow, Helen, who was always to be here, would not be here. Monday she would not be in. Intruding among the afflictive thoughts of original incredulity, an incredulity of horror that pushed away the idea of Helen, the poor girl, the tormented young woman, dead in despair by her own hand, were now those different thoughts, unconsonant with the decencies of pity, with grief incongruous; yet thoughts pressingly relevant, the thoughts of business that brought along a different incredulity, an incredulous, vexatious foreseeing of a dozen petty practical problems. Why, Helen was always in; she had to be in. Helen opened the office every day. At eight thirty on the dot, she admitted herself with her key. She hung up her hat and coat, perhaps went to the lavatory for a minute, and then, without delay, to her desk. She would have collected the morning mail, fallen through the front-door slot on the floor, and she quickly sorted it. Carefully, so no time would be wasted, she planned, laid out, a day's work for the girls—what, when they came in, she would give Mary, what she would give Gladys. To each of the partner's desks, she brought, with his mail a little list of appointments, of things he must remember to do today. The office now in readiness, in order, waiting for the day to begin, Helen, in her own quiet of readiness and order—the clean tight-drawn shining hair, the unpainted immaculate face, the thin hands whose perfectly manicured nails had never worn polish, the neat, simple, well-fitted, well-cared-for clothes —waited too.

Waiting, Helen kept busy, of course. Those first things done, she would have spun the dial, pushed back the wall safe's doors. There, revealed in the much-compartmented interior, ranged her special charge—those rows of journals and ledgers, Noah's years of fiduciary accounting, Noah's work of a lifetime. Not a few of these records, though never thrown away by Noah, were of accounts long closed, the decree made final, the trust terminated; but many more were live, a formidable continuing task of bookkeep-

ing, almost a whole-time job for anyone. Those endless entries in form of
charge and discharge; the patient postings from journal to ledger; the debit-
ings of inventory and creditings of estate, this to corpus, that to interest;
the often numerous schedules carefully to be kept separate in a single account—for the last five or six years Helen had really been doing it all.
Noah's part, nowadays, was no more than supplying Helen with scratch-
pad memos for this account or that, jumbles of figures with cryptic abbre-
viations well understood between them, but which, you might be sure,
neither Gladys Mills nor Mary Sheen—nor, for that matter, Arthur Winner himself—would be able to make head or tail of. Only Helen, never
wasting a minute, could do it. Tomorrow, the week beginning, eight thirty
would draw near, would come, would go; and no Helen.

But, of course, tomorrow they would close the office. In that vacant but
anxious bemusement, that slightly stunned slowness of mind, even the
obvious could come as a surprise. Arthur Winner hadn't thought of that.
Gladys and Mary must be told. And what else was there tomorrow? Alfred
Revere—well, Alfred, at church when the service was over, would have
heard, would know, would guess that Mr. Winner's Monday appointments
were now canceled, and that Alfred (if wait he could) would have to wait.
The same for any other business. Monday, no one could expect Tuttle,
Winner & Penrose to be open as usual—Noah was unlikely to have any
appointments; with Julius not certain last week that he would be back from
Washington, none would have been made for him. The time, Arthur Winner saw, was twenty minutes past one. He must stop this; he must not just
sit here.

He read: *1. I direct my just debts and funeral expenses to be fully paid and
satisfied. 2. I give and bequeath to Marigold Revere Parsons, if she survive me, the
sum of one thousand dollars. . . .* No more, surely, than an affectionate or
grateful gesture; like those possible executors that age had disqualified,
Marigold, admitting to fifty and probably nearer sixty, could have no real
hope of taking—but, but: *that's going to be what does happen!* Ralph, then,
took the rest, Arthur Winner saw. Actually, he didn't know just what
Helen died seised of. The Greenwood Avenue house; funds to some amount
in trust with Noah—that money to put Ralph through college; oh, yes; and
a secondhand car, now in custody of the police. A small checking account;
perhaps a small savings account. Certainly, safeguarding little Ralph, some
life insurance—with, perhaps, a suicide exception? Arthur Winner
thought (the thought's vain spite surprised him): *Well, I hope so. . . .*

Through his open door, Arthur Winner heard the new buzz at the
switchboard; immediately on his plugged-in line, the green light winked.
Holding his hand a moment—with whom would he have to deal now? Did
he want to?—Arthur Winner then lifted the receiver. He said: "Arthur
Winner."

"Arthur, Arthur—" Noah's stammer was at a pitch of anxiety. "I tried to get you—the line was busy—"

"Everything's all right," Arthur Winner said. "I'll be over presently. I was just looking at the will. It's in order. I'll get out the account file—"

"No," Noah said. "No! Don't bring anything, Arthur. Don't want to see them. Don't feel like seeing them. Leave everything alone. Account file may be in my room. You can't find it—don't touch anything on my desk—just get things out of order. I'll see to it."

Now the old fool would; now the old fool wouldn't! Well, he himself, Arthur Winner must allow, was little better off—he was tired, even though this was only midday or shortly after; he was probably hungry, even if he didn't feel hungry. A moment ago, remember, he was feeling that spiteful hope that Ralph would be paid no insurance money. He said: "All right. Really, I think tomorrow would be better. Today, I think we're all—"

"Yes; don't want anything now. Don't touch anything. Who's executor? Fred? I'll get the will to him. And speak to Willard. He'll have to appoint me that boy's guardian. Don't come back here, Arthur. Don't want to talk about it; don't want people to bother me; not this afternoon—"

Exasperation must subside in compunction. The old man could be seen to have thought things over, testing perhaps his own shaky reactions. He had fallen into worse shakings; the distracted old mind said: No, no—he couldn't face it. The sound was pettish, but the mind's inefficacy could be actual fear—who knew? The weights of grief and dismay might, if increased, stop the laboring old heart. Frightened, he fended off even his serving boy, Arthur—not now, not now!

"Very well," Arthur Winner said. "I'll see you aren't disturbed. If you do happen to want anything, I'll be at Mother's later this afternoon. We'll close the office tomorrow. Julius plans to be back today sometime; so if you feel like it then, we can go over things—"

"Yes; you're a good boy, Arthur. Tomorrow. Tomorrow."

. . . just get things out of order! Conceivably, that was so. In the crowded, the yearly increasing, disorder which Noah, pondering, planning, working, surrounded himself with, order of a sort there might be. Perfectly true that, peering about, padding about, the old man quite soon put his hand on whatever he wanted. Demonstrably, the books and papers that covered in piles every flat surface were not piled at random; they constituted a filing system of Noah's own. Still, Aunt Maud was not far wrong—the place looked like a rat's nest. Going into Noah's room, to lay the will now returned to its envelope, on Noah's desk, Arthur Winner could hardly find a clear place to put it down.

The door had been closed, and on the unventilated air were those traces of mustiness, that ghost of cigar smoke, to intensify the feeling of things past—upholstered furniture in old, old cracked leather; on the paneled walls in need of paint, old, old tarnished gold picture frames containing old, old engravings that nobody would hang today—Sir Edward Coke, in ruff and skullcap; Sir William Blackstone, robed and bewigged. In one thronged large scene, King Charles the First was come before President Bradshaw and the regicides soon-to-be; in another, Webster was risen to reply to Hayne. Above a side table deep under books, displayed on a mahogany mounting, was an enormous stuffed trout caught by Noah in 1909. Above Noah's chair hung the enlarged photograph of a gun dog, a pointer named Boy who had died in the nineteen twenties. Packing the high wide bookcases were undusted sets of legal reference works so outdated—Wait's *Law and Procedure*; Parsons on Contract; Kent's *Commentaries*—that no one would now think of consulting them; and, in runs of ten or even twenty years, bound volumes of law journals or financial periodicals no longer published. In the empty hearth under the fireplace's fine mantel—another part of Noah's filing system—were tottering stacks of newsprint, of what must be roughly the last hundred issues, on the left, of *Barron's Weekly*, on the right, of the *Financial World*. The wide window ledges were deep with accumulated layers of this year's, last year's, and even the year before last's, plain or fancy, interim or annual, reports of dozens of corporations.

In the center of the littered desk, placed on a closed file folder were seven or eight checks—drawn by Helen and put there for Noah to sign. To the one on top a note in pencil had been attached with a paper clip: *Mr. T. this will be an overdraft*—yes, that was the sort of thing you could count on Helen for; the reason for these transactions she might not know, but the result she had always at her finger tips. The checks were lying loose, already a little disturbed, scattered; and bringing them together, Arthur Winner had been about to lay Helen's will on them; yet he hesitated—something too grim about that, too pointed; though pointing to what he could not say. He opened the file folder to lay the checks in there—or would Noah then never find them? In the folder was a long legal-sized sheet headed in Noah's handwriting *Schedule of current indebtedness*—he remembered suddenly the old man moping in the courtroom yesterday—*everybody thinks I'm made of money*. . . .

Arthur Winner smiled. The sheet was covered with what seemed to be notations of money due—dates; what were probably account numbers—yes, he saw: S204 was an account against which one of these checks was drawn. By this confusing record, did Noah, on some system of his own, keep track of his informal, his private transactions—cash advanced, as he glumly said, out of his own pocket? Over the months, constant emendations or corrections had been made—items canceled; items inserted. As nearly as Arthur Winner's casual glance could puzzle them out, the original notations were of amounts in debit, canceled when they were paid. At sight of that long, long array of fussy, grubby figurings, of meticulously kept calculatings, so eloquent of the worried old man's worryings—*I'm a poor man. People don't know how poor*—some brief grief of pity must stir. Closing the folder's cover on the account sheet and the checks to sign, Arthur Winner drew a depressed breath, took a step away. He stopped.

Stopped no less short, even more sharply arrested, the mind held again before its eye the worked and reworked sheet. So seen, did method show in layout of dates and figures, of sums noted as drawn, of sums then paid, or not yet paid? Could a pattern be thought to have appeared? Arthur Winner stood stock still, aware of pricking sensations, a creeping of unease, an increasing coldness as though of a draft on him. *Schedule of current indebtedness* . . . Look again? No, no; no business of his. Private figures, figures not meant for him to see, figures that only by this impossible, this hideous chance—Helen must first die—he ever came to see. *Look again?* Those dates? But *that* was when Christ Church's quarterly money was paid. And from an account numbered S204, and an account numbered S98, Noah withdrew—in an instantaneous fitting-together, a falling into place, the pattern was established. The staggered, the stunned mind must take a meaning. Those accounts uncanceled, left showing money owed (and by token of this continuing, changing record, at any time, at all times, some of Noah's accounts), were short. Which was to say? Which was to say no more nor no less than that Noah Tuttle, this paragon of honesty, this soul of all honor, blameless of life and pure of crime (. . . *a man of complete probity, Mr. Woolf!*) had—for years?—been helping himself to, now repaying, now taking again, money that was not his.

Arthur Winner stood in his continued chill, in a stunned sense of solitariness, as though the early Sunday afternoon world around him had, more than merely stopped, come to a halt, to an end, had dissolved, had withdrawn in space, leaving him on a point of rock, the last living man. He said aloud: "I am a man alone." The silly words, the stilted, sententious sound, jarred him. From the silence no response could be expected; yet, dazedly, he became aware of silence broken—something moving, something moved; a delayed click-closed of a door toward the back; a progress of difficulty—a wounded man dragging himself? A dead man being dragged? His cold was horror's. Slowly, stiffly, Arthur Winner made himself turn, look through the open door. Coming from the back of the reception room into the outer office with a deliberate practiced plying of his canes was Julius Penrose.

Not moving, Arthur Winner said: "Julius!"

"Yes; I've heard," Julius Penrose said. "And though I never thought the day would come when I would need to say it: you must compose yourself, Arthur. Let us go into your room."

"How did you get here?"

"I have transportation," Julius Penrose said. "Marjorie brought me down. She seems in a mood of penitence. I gather she was not herself yesterday; and the subduing aftereffects—I saw you wondering the other night whether I knew that Marjorie's drinking was not absolutely or altogether a thing of the past. I did. I do—conduce to deeds of what I expect she feels is Christian charity. Moreover, Marjorie not being herself, Mrs. Pratt, I understand, was inflicted on you. I agree you're owed an apology; but I find Marjorie is ashamed, would prefer not to see you just now. Having no doubt you'd much prefer not being apologized to, I had her bring the car around the back where I would not need any help with steps. By a little such planning, help is often made something I can take or leave alone. Perhaps I should say that Mrs. Pratt, before she fled my coming, seems to have reported herself more than satisfied with you, your conversation, your courtesy, your kindness—now let us consider this other matter. Sit down, Arthur."

Letting himself carefully into the chair in Arthur Winner's room, Julius Penrose arranged his legs, laying his canes across his lap.

Arthur Winner said: "How did you come to hear?"

Julius Penrose said: "By a set of curious chances. Barely had I been delivered home, when the telephone rang. It was Clarissa. It was about Priscilla, who had, I learned, happened this morning to go to church with her and Ann. Clarissa, getting her news about Helen from Willard Lowe, who got the news, I gather, from you—"

"Yes. I told him. The service wasn't over; but I felt I had to go and see Noah—"

"I concede the necessity. At any rate, Clarissa hadn't been able to find you, and she didn't want to come out to Roylan until she'd talked to you. Therefore, Priscilla would be delayed. Marjorie might worry. Surprised, but also relieved, I think, to find me answering the phone, she told me all she could. Yet—will you believe it?—I knew already."

With steady scrutiny, the dark observant eyes rested on Arthur Winner's face as though they meant to offer him, to carry to him, their calm of preciseness, of impassivity. Julius Penrose said: "More chance: but also, what a commentary on our age! As merrily we rolled along, almost, the good Pettengill and I, arrived at Roylan, he asked my permission to put on what he calls the wireless. The next thing I knew, I was hearing, appended to a news broadcast, an appeal to one Ralph Detweiler, or anyone who knew his whereabouts. Would he come home; there had been a death in the family. A death? In the family? Would Ralph come home? I was indeed taken aback; in part, by the instant intelligence, since I knew Ralph's situation, conveyed. Not very surprisingly, Ralph had lost his nerve, had run; not very surprisingly, Helen, distracted, found this too bad to bear. I grasped all."

"Perhaps not quite all," Arthur Winner said. "She found out that, in order to run away, Ralph had stolen some money."

"Ah, yes. That Fool Killer's touch!" He studied Arthur Winner. "Our actors are all ham—a point not unrelated to the commentary I spoke of— the incident of the—er—wireless. Those things, police doings, I suppose, I'd heard of; but never actually heard—the ear, possibly, of millions taken to ask—solemn moment; death in family—one unsignifying brat to please come home."

With steadiness, with unmoved strength of calm, he studied Arthur Winner again. He said: "Yes; the spirit of the age! We're in an age pre-eminently of capital F Feeling—a century of the gulp, the lump in the throat, the good cry. We can't be said to have invented sentimentality; but in other ages sentimentality seems to have been mostly peripheral, a de-spised pleasure of the underwitted. We've made sentimentality of the re-spected essence. If I believe my eyes and ears, and I do, sentimentality is now nearly everyone's at least private indulgence. The grave and learned are no whit behind the cheap and stupid in their love of it. Snuffling after every trace, eagerly rooting everywhere, the newspapers stop their presses, the broadcasters interrupt their broadcasts, so it may be more immediately available. In professional entertainment, in plays and motion pictures, it is the whole mode. In much of what I'm told is our most seriously regarded contemporary literature, I find it, scarcely disguised, standing in puddles. The houses of congress, the state halls of legislature, drop everything to make and provide it whenever they can. There are judges who even try in their courts to fit the law to it—"

Julius Penrose broke off. He said: "I see my artful indirection does not work. I see this chitchat doesn't divert you. I see you will not be talked out of it, Arthur. Well, we must try other means. Let us be direct. Clarissa is concerned on two counts. Easily enlisting my sympathies, she asked me to find out about them. First: she conceives, because last night Helen seemed to have you worried, that you may be telling yourself this wouldn't have happened if you'd spoken to her." He paused. "Privately, I thought that concern unfounded. I've never seen you act without adequate consideration. One may very well, one may often, wish one had done differently; but when a man has used his best judgment, done his best, the result though disap-pointing, though disastrous even, can't be a reproach to him. He did all any man could do. Regrets of that kind are unreasonable, unrealistic. *It might have been*—not so much the saddest as the silliest words of tongue or pen! Let us face it. What happens to people is simply what was always going to happen to them. To think otherwise is vain visioning. That's not really your trouble now, is it?"

No; not really! Troubles are relative; problems differ in degree, tasks in difficulty. Poor Helen put it well. *Things are funny. Yesterday I was so worried about his not wanting to go to college. . . .* How trifling the troubles, how simple the problems, how easy the tasks of only yesterday! Yesterday morning, the trouble was no more than to determine the best steps to take (which came naturally to him) in a commonplace criminal action where, everything considered, his cause was in good shape, the defense hopeful. His problems were what to answer to a Jerry Brophy's humble petition, and whether he could in conscience (in interest!) go along with a "Whit" Trowbridge's pastoral exhortings, with his rector's good-natured determination to name him senior warden. His tasks were to sustain the embarrassments, the not-undeserved chagrins put on him by an enraptured friendly fool of a Mrs. Pratt; to quell a negligible Mr. Moore; to soothe an alarmed Elmer Abbott; to instruct an agreeably cooperative policeman about that ass Ralph; to accept, in the slight awkwardness of a young Garret Hughes's too-plain apotheosis of him, the gratuities of the district attorney. Indeed; how trifling the troubles, how simple the problems of only an hour ago! Arthur Winner said: "No; that's not my trouble now."

Julius Penrose said: "Second concern: Clarissa conceives you've had nothing to eat. Neither have I. In my cabinet you'll find, as usual, a decanter of sherry and a tin of biscuits. Allow me to offer you some refreshment; though I won't offer to get it. You get it."

Accepting the filled sherry glass, Julius Penrose took a swallow. "This unhappy event has several unhappy aspects," he said. "Well, we owe nature a death, I'm told. By our choosing to be born, we contracted for death. Recision would be inequitable and unjust. Let me hear no more complaining! The terms of payment? Not exorbitant, I think. What could be more generous? If we pay this year, we won't have to pay next year." He took another sip of sherry. "Regarding the dead, our pious rule is nothing if not good. Ralph, let us agree, is a little bastard; and you won't suppose I mean by the term that Alice Detweiler could have ever had the appetite, let alone the imagination, to play George false. Helen is known to have been faithful and true, good and self-sacrificing, and, perhaps not so relevant, but they are qualities in the main admired, chaste and pure. She is, therefore, virtue; Ralph is vice. Because of all this virtue, Helen's sorrows, her sufferings, the last full measure of her rash act, put her publicly, in terms of public opinion, unassailably in the right. Everybody must feel that."

Julius Penrose took a sip of sherry. "Yes; I too feel it; but do I think it? An entrance is won to the heart; but to the head? Passion and reason, self-division's cause! I'm afraid I think that this gentle and unspotted soul was and is, has been and now always will be, very much in the wrong. On people as people, I try never to pass judgment—we can seldom know what the real truth about them is. Yet on acts, acts of theirs, I see no reason to hesitate in passing judgment—this is good; this is bad; this is mean; this is kind. On such points, I'm competent, as every man is. Like the common law, we secular moralists aren't interested in the why; we observe the what. Here, the what that gives me pause is this. Ralph's a little bastard; yes. Something ought to have been done to and about him, I'd think preferably with a horsewhip, if nowadays one could be found. Be good, or I'll beat you! That's in order. That's fair warning and fair play. Could the same be said of a verbal threat to do a thing like this—Ralph must be good, or Helen will kill herself? And how much less, if, for mere threat, performance is substituted? No; there is a want of principle, which is to say, too much feeling. I pronounce this bad. I pronounce this mean. The sentence, of course, is on the act, not the person. I pity the person; I take her to be mad, possessed by love. Her feelings acted. Here is simply more of feeling's comic or tragic, yet, to the feeler, always juicy, fruits. I quote: 'A warmth within the breast would melt the freezing reason's colder part. And like a man in wrath, the heart stood up and answered: I have felt!' Let us pass on. Your refection is spread; take some."

"I'm not hungry," Arthur Winner said. "Julius, how long have you known that Noah's accounts were short?"

"Ah!" Julius Penrose said. "Well, I'm not sorry to have you ask! Yes; that's where I was putting off getting; and I may say that how long *you* could continue *not* to know has been a recurring slight anxiety of mine. Sometimes I even wondered if you *did* know; but each time, I decided no, you didn't. At this juncture—to tell you the truth, it's why I'm here; why I directed Marjorie to get out a car; why I had no lunch—I saw that you'd better know, that there was the possibility of our finding ourselves in a situation of sorts—one of those unhappy aspects of this unhappy event."

"How long have you known?" Arthur Winner said.

"How long?" Julius Penrose said. "Well, let me see. It was, I think, thirteen years ago last July that your father asked me if I'd be interested in joining my practice with Winner, Tuttle and Winner's, coming in as a partner. I would, indeed! Though no longer a boy, nor without experience, I was always one to look to the improvement of my mind. There was his reputation; there was Noah's. My legal acquirements were not too meager; but working with the best minds of our bar would infallibly give them polish. There was the circumstance that you and I had long been friends; and that Noah had no living son. This first-rate heritage we stood to inherit."

His strong teeth bit a biscuit in half. Thoughtfully, Julius Penrose chewed. "Yes; I meant to improve myself by grasping, particularly in fiduciary matters, what I could of the methods of a man of Mr. Tuttle's abilities. My turn of mind, while not I think inquisitive, was and is investigative. Old Mrs. Hunt was still in the office; and Helen, all earnestness, was being, in effect, broken in. To Helen, the figure work had to be explained. I took occasion both to listen, and, the books being out, to look. I am good at figures. Though seemingly satisfactory to her, and to Helen, Mrs. Hunt's explanation of some parts of the accounting process left me perplexed. *This, I kept hearing, is how Mr. Tuttle wants us to do it.* . . . *But why?* I kept asking—myself, not them! *But why?* I needed, if I remember, a number of months—a couple of quarter days would have had to pass before my data became complete enough for me to draw a firm conclusion. So how long have I known? Well, let's say, twelve years, give or take a month or two."

"And you said nothing? Julius, I think that's indefensible."

"Do you? To be able to know and still say nothing often seems to me the most creditable of human accomplishments. King Midas has ass's ears! Whisper it, if only to the reeds, most people must! For overcoming this common weakness, I give myself good marks. What purpose but mischief, and what result but more mischief, could my saying something have? From my standpoint, the business was strictly Noah's; and he was, I soon came to see, handling it ably. I confess that before adopting this disinterested view, I made a careful check of my own legal position. You'll recognize it. Incoming partner. How, then, could saying something be my business?"

"When you know this and say nothing, you're an accessory after the fact. Julius, how could you?"

"I've just explained how I could," Julius Penrose said. "Here was the then situation as I put it together. The greater part of the Orcutt money simply wasn't there—except, you might say, on paper. I don't know whether you ever troubled to read the instrument. Principal is put in Noah's absolute control. The books showed the trust as holding various securities, mortgages, and so on, from which interest was duly entered. Those holdings were imaginary. The so-entered interest was of course real; money has to be. Fortunately, under Noah's almost as absolute control were other trusts, other funds. At bottom, the process is merely robbing Peter to pay Paul. But with improvements, refinements. When the time comes to pay Paul, Peter, unknown to Peter, is caused to lend you some of his money and Paul's paid. And when the time comes to pay Peter; Tom, Dick, or Harry, unknown to him, may be caused to lend you some of *his* money. Of course, you have to look alive, watch your step, exercise foresight and judgment—"

"Julius, I still cannot believe—"

"I fear you're going to have to. Impracticably complicated? Yes; for many people; but to a man of Noah's parts—and also, of course, to a man to whom no least question, no faintest suspicion ever attached—the procedure of lawfully receiving into his possession and unlawfully appropriating money was simplicity itself; even, quite safe. As you very well know, the only circumstance under which the accounts he was tampering with could become subject to audit was if *cestui qui trust*, not getting his money, applied to the court. The circumstance never arises. Income is always paid when due. To keep accounts in any way he wanted them kept, he had, first, Mrs. Hunt; and, then, Helen, both of them practiced with figures, both of them quite incapable of interpreting figures, and both accepting as gospel anything Noah told them—"

"What I can't believe is that you'd knowingly stand by—"

"But I fear you're going to have to," Julius Penrose said. "That's just what I did. I tried to tell you why—"

"As you've said, why, doesn't matter, Julius. What, as you say, is what matters. In this case, it still amounts to compounding a felony."

"I wonder," Julius Penrose said. "A felony is something I must be found guilty of by a jury of my peers. Before that finding, where is the felony? I ask myself how you compound that which does not yet exist. But, yes; *what* is, indeed, what matters. My whole regard was for what. My eye was on the certain results, the fruits. True, that had been done which ought not to be done. I saw that conversion, embezzlement, must have been practiced for some time—and, I confess, the 'some time' seemed to me not unimportant. Who, so far, complained? Nobody. Everyone was perfectly happy. True, the embezzlement was on no small scale. By a fairly easy calculation—given the interest—that is, what I computed to be the sum of Noah's quarterly 'borrowings'—to find the principal. I judged the Orcutt funds short, holding dummy or imaginary securities, to the amount of about two hundred thousand dollars."

Arthur Winner could suppose that the color must have left his face; for, interrupting himself, Julius said: "Yes; when I finished figuring, my wind, too, was rather knocked out. Don't imagine I regarded my discovery as funny. For the younger, rawer man I was then, I cannot but claim my feat in saying nothing and showing nothing was really remarkable. I, let me tell you, was scared. My practice had not happened to turn up anything like this. For the act of one of them, what, if any, limits were there on the liability of other partners? I've seldom applied myself with such intensity of attention to the statutes and to the reported cases. However, as I say, I was soon relieved. There weren't two opinions. The time of the original conversion, which subsequent conversions had been to cover, was what counted. If I had not been a partner when that took place, no action to recover from me personally could lie."

Portentous, despairing, those empty words: *I am a man alone* . . . recurred to Arthur Winner. He said: "So, seeing yourself safe—"

"Yes; just so!" Julius Penrose's voice, though calm as ever, though precise as ever, allowed itself a tone of mild reproach. "Yes; I scare easy;

but recovering from my scare, I found myself rational, able to look at this from all sides. I was free to dismiss self-interest, to do right and fear no man. Whether I'm morally obligated to be my brother's keeper always seemed to me moot. However, my brother's ruiner and destroyer, and for no earthly reason, and for no personal necessity or profit—*that* I surely have no moral obligation to be. If I'd elected to take the upstanding stand you seem consternated to hear I didn't take; if I'd blabbed my not-exactly-stumbled-on yet unintentionally discovered secret; if righteously horrified, I'd pressed for a C.P.A. audit, the beneficiaries of the Orcutt bequests would have been awarded every cent your father had and every cent you had—your innocence of the smallest wrongdoing, as you know, notwithstanding. Seeing myself, in your word, safe, I, no longer scared, naturally did not so much as consider such a dastardly act."

Aware of a sinking in his voice that reflected faithfully a felt sinking of the mind, a vortical faintness, Arthur Winner said: "My father would not have thought that way. He'd have pressed, himself, for an audit—" He put out a hand, took up his glass of sherry and drank it all.

"I'm sure he would have," Julius Penrose said. "Therefore, he had to know nothing. That was not too hard. He had every confidence in Noah, and, happily, a disability of confidence is always that you see what you look for, what you expect to see—"

That sinking of mind was a disturbance so great that no ordering of thoughts was possible—blindly, the mind groped around. Arthur Winner said: "But why would he need to? How could it happen? Yes—I've read the terms of the Orcutt instrument—I know he could do or buy anything he wanted. Yes; bad investments can be made—but not on that scale, not by Noah—"

Julius Penrose said: "I've heard he made a bad investment once. There was the Brocton Rapid Transit Company—"

"No Orcutt money was ever put in that, I know," Arthur Winner said. His responses, labored, seemed to be automatically supplied by some other speaker, aberrant, unconnected with him. "He did put some in before, when they were trying to save the company; but I know where he got that. He borrowed it from my father. You might not remember, but by the time the Orcutt trusts were operative, Brocton Transit was out of business. The creditors chose Noah, and the Federal District Court had appointed him trustee in bankruptcy. There was no more question of investment there—"

"Yes," Julius Penrose said. "That liquidation was interesting. I've tried, without the least success, to learn the particular circumstances. I thought Noah might be willing, by way of giving me a point or two, to tell me what he did. I found that he was not willing."

"I don't think he wanted to think about it," Arthur Winner said heavily. There was that feeling of nothing to hold onto—no, nothing! What did Alfred Revere say? *It's like this funny picture. . . .* "I mean, though he had no legal responsibility, he felt a personal, private responsibility which he took very hard."

"Yes, I've heard that, too," Julius Penrose said. Lifting a cane, he leveled it carefully at the fireplace. "Indeed, I venture to suggest that supposed responsibility might even have deranged him a little. I mean, of course, emotionally. I hear everywhere that his handling of the business was as astute as possible, a masterpiece of management. I, of course, searched out what was of public record. The scrutiny was uninformative; but, forever buried there, I'm irresistibly led to guess, may be something unique in financial history. My guess: the trustee in bankruptcy paid out to the creditors—other than himself—some hundreds of thousands of dollars not received, not realized from assets. I see easily how this could be possible, how it might not be remarked. You've had experience with our Federal referees. You'd look a long way before you found one who knew anything except that good old Senator Joe Blow was a friend of his. He might stir himself if trustee reported in receipts much less than the manifest market value of assets; but, more—well; God bless you, my boy! In short, I think a timely use of Orcutt money saved the financial lives of a number of people like your Mike McCarthy. I say: I think. But the more I think, the surer I am."

"But he'd have to be crazy," Arthur Winner said. "He'd have to see that in the end—"

"Not necessarily, not necessarily!" Julius Penrose said. "Emotionally deranged was my preferred term. He would betray himself, sacrifice himself, before he let down, sacrificed, those who had put faith in him. An emotional idea. Ah, what a mess these possessions by feeling may make of lives! But I think he also hoped, and had some reason to hope, that, given time, he could restore the money. If a man is shrewd—and also lucky, which is usually the same thing—about investments; if a man is frugal and careful —yes; and if a man is brave; not a little may be done. I like to think how trifling, lived with so long, the unending anxiety must by now have come to seem to Noah. But he *has* supported it, lived with it, years and years. Think of that! There's self-command, if you like. There's stoutheartedness; there's prudence; there's a masterpiece of management! I have, as you may imagine, kept what I think I'm justified in calling a quiet eye on this matter. By my latest estimate, he's short now not above a hundred and twenty thousand dollars—maybe less. In July, he made quite a quiet killing with some common stock warrants, you know—or did you? Of course, the debit balance is still not peanuts, not to modestly monied men like you and me; but I do believe the old boy may pull out yet."

Arthur Winner said: "Julius, what you seem to be suggesting just isn't possible. There's an honest course; and a course that isn't honest. If you take the course that isn't honest, you're in trouble immediately—"

"Affirmed as stated," Julius Penrose said. "Honesty's always the easiest policy. Could that be why men so often call it the best? Weaving tangled webs is really work, very demanding."

"No, Julius. It's no good. I cannot be party to doing what's dishonest."

"But you *could* be party to causing to be laid before our Mr. Brophy such evidence of embezzlement as would require him to prosecute Noah? Hm! Specific acts must number hundreds. I see no practicable defense. Offered a plea of guilty—or, as I personally would recommend, since civil action pended, *nolo contendere*—to one indictment, the court, I imagine, would consent to dismiss the others. Five years, and five thousand dollars? In consideration of the plea, we might hope, I think, for two years—with time off for good behavior. I doubt if even Brophy would feel that more of an example than that ought to be made of so old a man, and a man heretofore so generally revered."

Julius Penrose stirred to ease himself. He breathed as though he summoned strength, an extra supply to meet, imposed on the pain in which he lived, this wearying pain of exposition. He said: "And you could also be not only party to, but principal in, taking immediate steps to assign all your property toward restituting and restoring the corpus of the Orcutt bequests? I've a fair idea of your current commitments. I imagine you're doing something for your mother. I know you're helping Lawrence—who, incidentally, is, I came to suspect, on the verge of asking you if you'd be able to advance him what he'll need in the way of capital for this projected venture with his boss. The expense of maintaining a place at Roylan is well known to me. You have a daughter to educate; you have a wife who—again, incidentally—has, I suspect, the indefatigable hope of providing you with more children. You'd be sorry, I'm sure, to see either without proper provision. Yet, by the time you'd made your partner's stealings good, I don't think there'd be a great deal left."

"Julius, I can't understand you—"

Soberly, Julius Penrose said: "Well, perhaps I'm hard to understand. There are times when I myself wonder whether not-as-other-men is what I am. I'm told, for example, that we may forgive those who injure us, but never those we've injured. As far as I go, poppycock! In lines, mostly of business, I've deemed it from time to time necessary or convenient to injure a number of people. I bear none of them the least ill will. Unless they try to retaliate—indeed, unless they succeed in retaliating, my feelings remain entirely cordial; I haven't a thing in the world against them. Then, I'm told that men excuse in themselves what they don't excuse in others. Applied to me, totally untrue! I readily excuse in others what I'd consider inexcusable in myself. What would you? They are only they; but I am I! However, here, in the instant case, on this point, I'd have imagined myself altogether understandable. These are preliminary objections in the nature of a motion to strike. The case for a fine upstanding stand seems to me not made out. Insufficient averment—mere indecisive and unfounded technicalities are being pleaded. Too costly, too."

"The cost needn't worry you," Arthur Winner said. "I agree with your view that you can't be held liable."

"The law is clear. There is no other view," Julius Penrose said. "But I, also, am human, am not without human weaknesses of vanity and self-regard. I have an—er—honor—" he grimaced—"of my own to pet. I wouldn't, I warn you, feel able to dissociate myself, legally liable or not. If you persist in this quixotism, if you're resolved to ruin yourself, I'll have to join you. Yes; I think I can arrange that. I promise you that if you denounce Noah and do not agree to let me share and share alike in the consequences, I'll have to, *nunc pro tunc*, denounce my guilty long knowledge of these peculations. Whether it would be enough to get me prosecuted, I don't know; it would assuredly lose me my means of livelihood by getting me disbarred."

"Julius, that's ridiculous—"

"I think so, too. Neither alternative appeals to me in the least. The first—since I'm sure you'd admit me to the first, rather than force me to the second—would cost me a great deal of money. For this loss, hearing on every hand how nobly we behaved would not really recompense me. I am a cripple; I am getting old. Were I neither, it might be different, of course. The easier way, the easiest policy, could then be a calculated risk—possibly worth taking. Given more life expectancy, I might chance it. Honesty, integrity, honor so well advertised, could pay off. Like Job's, my patience might prove worthwhile. I might end up with more flocks, more herds—and even, were I at that age or stage, more sons and daughters—than I had to start with. But such expectancy isn't mine. I'm on the downgrade. Therefore, I ask you not to do this thing to me, Arthur."

"Julius, after what you said earlier, you can't seriously—"

"Some want of principle, yes," Julius Penrose said. "But I am not joking."

Julius Penrose's look was compassionate. He said: "Yes, yes; think of an octogenarian cast in prison; think of your unfeeling disservice to those near and dear—hard to kick against the pricks, isn't it? So stop! Or, as a wise old man once said to me: Boy, never try to piss up the wind. Principle must sometimes be shelved. Let us face the fact. In this life we cannot do everything we might like to do, nor have for ourselves everything we might like to have. We must recognize what the law calls factual situations. The paradox is that once fact's assented to, accepted, and we stop directing our effort where effort is wasted, we usually *can* do quite a number of things, to a faint heart, impossible." He dropped one cane to the floor and neatly levered his legs a little to the left. "Did I ever tell you how I retaught myself to walk—or, would the juster term be: get around?"

Arthur Winner could feel light creepings of sweat on his forehead; the stand-up collar, the thick folds of formal tie constricted his throat; the slight tightness of the morning coat bound his shoulders.

Julius Penrose, in tone chatty, almost humorous, said: "At the beginning, I must admit I didn't take my, as I hear people say, misfortune, well. I was impressed by the wanton unfairness of this thing, in those days still generally known as infantile paralysis. Exactly! An affliction reserved for children. An adult, a man past his youth, coming down with it was almost unheard of. Then; why, of all men, me? For my sins? They were many, yes; but look at others I could name to whom this didn't happen. Why should I alone get the dirty end of the stick? All those who find themselves out of luck are, I imagine, subject to such thoughts. We feel very hardly used—and, of course, so we are, so we are! Our resentment's reasonable and legitimate, if that's any help to us. A help to us is, however, just what resentment isn't."

To his son, watching wordless beside that bed, that in fact deathbed of many weeks, Arthur Winner Senior, a wasted shape under a blanket, had, on a silent Sunday afternoon, suddenly smiled, had suddenly said: *I've been among the luckiest of men. . . .* Most of the time mindless, massively drugged, the Man of Reason was briefly revisited by mind; comprehending for a moment interrupted uncomprehending. *Maybe one in a thousand has had it happen to him. Close calls, sometimes; sometimes, I saw that in a minute I might not be able to help myself; but I don't remember ever once having to do what I would have preferred not to do. . . .* While the skin-and-bone face, the too-bright eyes were lighted for a minute or more with this vague thankfulness, Arthur Winner Junior, shaken both by the startling announcement, and by his own mind's quick comment: *except this, this?* saw, only mystified, the smile; heard, only mystified, the words, the voice of wonder. Against the sound of Julius Penrose's voice, the measured sentences' light mocking of fate, illumination flared, one more clap of knowledge came: *And now, all these years later, I know at last what he was talking about. The thrusts of fate! Yes; lucky the man . . .*

"Is anything a help?" Julius Penrose said. "Well, Marjorie's coreligionists-to-be have a formula. They say: Offer it, or offer it up. Possibly useful, one perceives. You set yourself to make believe that all misfortune, all pain, has point or purpose, can earn you benefits. The worse the pain, the better—good, if, or as long as, you can believe so! No go, with me, naturally. The underlying idea of a source of merit—the fawning self-recommendation, the humble currying of favor—repelled me. No; vouch-safe me no vouchsafements! If the supernatural is seen as entering, to curse God and die would always, I can't but feel, better become a man. So much for a religious attitude. Among the opposed attitudes of irreligion, that one whose complaint is: unfair, unfair, with its feeble indignation and tire-some self-pity, manifestly doesn't become a man either. The becoming thing, in any given situation, is for a man to try what he can do, not just sprawl there whining. He should get up and walk."

Julius Penrose emptied his sherry glass. "But how are you to walk when you can't even stand? Answer: What makes you think you can't stand, or, at least, do something that will pass for that? With a cheeriness all too un-failing, meant kindly to encourage you yet hard to take, the specialists in these matters heartily cry: Of course you can! They'll see me fitted with what they persist in calling comfortable braces. Then, I'll need crutches—here they are! Now, for it!"

He took another biscuit and chewed thoughtfully for a moment. "Yes; now for it. One try, and you see this is impossible, this can't be done. Tut, tut! they say; a child creeps before he walks! Was it the happiest image? Perhaps! Set your crutch ends a foot ahead of your feet. Now, can't you move your feet toward them? Don't try anything excessive—an inch will do. Fine! Now advance your crutches about an inch; now, move your feet an-other inch. Lo and behold, you're walking! I'm what? Well, you got from your bed to the wall and back, and it didn't take you ten minutes."

Julius Penrose smiled reminiscently. "Of course, even *they* didn't really consider that walking. Just a starter. The walking gaits, so called, are some-thing else; and Rome wasn't built in a day. There's what's known as the four-point. When you're ready to try, you'll need someone behind you and someone in front of you; and you may keep needing them for quite a while. It's important not to fall and shatter your confidence, if nothing else. The technique is: first one foot, then one crutch; then the other foot, then the other crutch. Kindergarten stuff! After a certain number of weeks, or more likely months, the teachable lad may consider mastering the swing-through —what the crutch expert does most of the time when he's in the clear. Of course, you have to remember (no trouble, really) that you have ten pounds of steel on your legs which will affect balancing; so when you swing your pedal extremities forward, you must put your shoulders forward, too, and keep your body straight from the shoulders down—your shoulders swing you, your braces stop you. Amazing how you get over the ground, once you have the hang of it. You feel as though you were flying. And, of course, this—" he lifted a cane—"is ultimate art. You need muscle. Not many of us with both legs out ever graduate from crutches—"

Arthur Winner said: "What, exactly, do you propose?"

"Ah, my old friend," Julius Penrose said, "that's better! I propose that we let matters proceed as far as possible as they've been proceeding. I propose we concert our efforts and our wits on managing this—"

"Julius, the risks are terrible—"

"Agreed, agreed," Julius Penrose said. "But we are not children, nor unable, nor without resource. I think I am a man of judgment. I know you are. Let us put this judgment to use—"

"I don't think you realize just how great some of the risks are."

"If you mean there are some I don't happen to know about, you may be right. But I'm confident I'll be sufficiently sharp to see them as they appear; and I'm not unconfident that, as I see them, I'll see what to do about them."

"Perhaps I should tell you that Doctor Trowbridge is very much set on a move that would make an audit on behalf of Christ Church necessary."

"Indeed, you should! Like two heads, four eyes are better; you will be seeing things and I will be seeing things, and we can counsel together. If your rector is moving that way, you must, of course, yourself move to dissuade him—I assume he entertains ideas of transferring the corpus, otherwise investing the money. He must be advised that he can't, in law; that the donor's intent must be respected."

"I've already done that," Arthur Winner said. "For other reasons—" He broke off. "No, Julius!" he said. "I can't carry out such a plan—pretending to give honest advice. It's impossible."

Julius Penrose said: "Tut, tut! A child creeps before he walks! Think again. What's, here, material? Not, surely, delicacy-of-feeling's comforts or discomforts. Material, is: Can His Reverence be made to do as you say? He can; you can handle him. That risk, then, is already provided for, largely obviated. Yes; and I know there's talk of winding up the Union League, which would mean eventually auditing that account. But only eventually. The talk could take years, particularly if someone like me were helping to see that it did. Anyway, I think that there the deficit is manageable—I mean, Noah would probably be able to borrow enough from other accounts to meet it, if your church wasn't making a demand on him at the same time. What else?"

With bitterness, Arthur Winner said: "You consider that not enough? Just think what you're saying, Julius. The course is desperate from start to finish. We evade; we misrepresent; we use secret influence—"

Julius Penrose said: "Clarissa remarked that the really terrible thing about Helen's business was that arrangements had been made for the charge against Ralph to be dropped—that was what you hadn't told Helen. I gather Garret Hughes let you know yesterday afternoon that the district attorney had been to Mechanicsville, and shortly after, prosecutrix decided not to proceed." He smiled faintly. "May I ask how you worked it, Arthur?"

"I didn't," Arthur Winner said. "I told Jerry, who came in to see me yesterday morning, that I believed the girl was lying, and if she were put on the stand, I had every hope of demonstrating that she was. Later, Garret, who had been to see her, must have told him Miss Kovacs wouldn't submit to a physical examination—"

"May I ask what J. Jerome came in to see you about? Am I to suppose nothing except Ralph's case was discussed?"

"No. He spoke of Ralph's case only in passing. What he came about was how I would stand on the bar association proposing his name to the governor for appointment to this fourth judgeship we're being given. You may not approve; but I told him I would not oppose him. Perhaps you feel he should be opposed."

Julius Penrose said gravely: "On the whole, no. It is true that as district attorney I find him rather offensive; but the thought occurs to me that the attaining of this ambition, this, as it's generally regarded, high honor, would have a salutary effect both on his manners and his—er—morals. I know Fred doesn't like the idea; but Willard and Mac McAllister won't mind. He's not lazy—they could unload a lot of work on him."

"And if you think I offered not to oppose him in an attempt to influence in any way his actions as public prosecutor, you do not know me very well."

"Gently, gently!" Julius Penrose said. "None of us, perhaps, knows any of us very well. Yet; yes, I'm satisfied I know you well enough; and I believe you. Imagine that, Arthur! Do you realize that I'm very likely the only person in the world who could or would believe what you've just told me?"

Arthur Winner said: "I cannot help what people believe or don't believe. I can only tell you that I have never—" (the voice of one dying said: *I've been among the luckiest of men . . .*) "I've never found myself in a position —yes; I can say it; I've never in my professional practice—"

"Nor, I can say, have I," Julius Penrose said. "No; do not look at me that way. Accessory after the fact, if you like, in this matter; but I, too, have never taken nor given a bribe; I, too, have never touched a penny that was not mine; I, too, have never borne false witness, never sworn a man away. Let us congratulate each other; but, also, let us for the moment attend to our grave problem. What else alarms you?"

"Julius, it's everything—" Where, indeed, to begin? Numberless, the general dangers, the uncertainties, the unchartable chances, of this—this wrongdoing, this frantic dice-throwing on which he must wildly stake his —yes, honor; his career; his reputation. (*Good name in man and woman, dear my lord, is the immediate jewel of their souls. . . .*) Ah, yes; how fond the remembrance of yesterday's peace! Arthur Winner said: "Quite apart from whatever outright appropriating there may have been, the accounts, I know now, aren't even in ordinary order. Noah could be tripped up any time. Friday, he almost was. I've no doubt at all that if I hadn't just happened to ask this Mr. Woolf up to the lake for supper, got him—pure accident!—in good humor, when we resumed yesterday morning Woolf wouldn't have been half an hour forcing out what is the fact—that Noah, a couple of months ago, deposited twenty thousand dollars of McCarthy Estate money in his personal account. Helen had checked for me; and from what she said, I had to realize he does that sort of thing all the time, whenever it suits him. To let things just go on, as if we didn't know—there couldn't be a moment's peace of mind. No, Julius; if we do this thing at all, Noah's going to have to be told that we know, that we intend to do what we can to get the money paid back, and that we'll have to take charge of his accounts."

Julius Penrose said: "That, in the end, may be necessary; but I don't think we ought so to determine out of hand. Shun immediate evils is the wise, or at least the smart, man's maxim. Never do today what doesn't have to be done until tomorrow. It is, I imagine, important to Noah to think nobody knows. Told, he'd not impossibly go all to pieces. That would be no service to us; and clearly no kindness to him. There is an unmanly streak in me. I was never able to be a sportsman. Games, when I had the use of all my limbs, yes; but sports, those blood sports of the man's man, no! To hook fishes, to shoot birds or animals, not because I needed them for food, but for fun—well, I could, and can, only ask: What fun? Even as touching food, I've often wondered. If I personally had to slaughter the beasts, would I learn to do without meat to eat? Or, if I had to do without meat to eat, would I learn to slaughter beasts? A nice question."

He looked seriously at Arthur Winner. "No," he said, "I think we should try for a while telling Noah nothing. Humanitarian considerations aren't, let me say candidly, my only ones. As you point out, the risks of what I'm suggesting are far from inconsiderable. We aim to buy time; we hope to see Noah live long enough to get the accounts squared. Intelligent recognition of the risks must include giving thought to what happens if time runs out, if our hope is not realized. If luck should fail us, if the law overtakes Noah, I would like him to be able to testify that we knew nothing of these shortages. The civil liability which must fall on you, and which I shall volunteer to, and will, share is quite sufficient. We do not need to make a criminal liability apparent, too. Since the crime is stealing, and we did no stealing, I can't feel that we cheat justice if we escape indictment in connection with it."

"Meanwhile, what we don't and can't escape is a whole life of lies," Arthur Winner said. "We can't trust Noah—" A seizure of impotent, not-controllable, anger overcame him. "How can a man do this, be this? That case of Sutphin's last week—no, no, not for us! Not perfectly honorable—dishonest intent; and all the time—yes, and Noah, if he only knew, can't trust us. We don't purpose to be open with him. How, when I know you knew this, and yet kept it from me, can I really—"

"No!" Julius Penrose said. "That's not you speaking, Arthur. That's unjust. I don't think you can fairly say I here deceived you. I knew of something that it was my considered judgment you should not, need not, know. I don't think you can fairly believe my motive was any but a hope to spare you while Noah was allowed time to restore, if he could, what he had taken. We have known each other too long for either of us to honestly suppose untruths about the other. If you knew of something that you believed I didn't know, and that you thought it better I should not know, I'm persuaded you'd do as much for me—try every way to keep it from me." He paused. "Let me be more explicit. I'm persuaded, Arthur, that you *have* done as much for me. And, if unknown to you, I've always thanked you for it."

Arthur Winner had felt his surge of changed color—a crisis of consternation outside the control of consciousness; too quick for any summoning up of the mask for the face, the blankness for the eye, the calmness, if he should speak, for the voice. How, Arthur Winner must thunderstruck ask himself, could he have imagined otherwise? Friday night, pointing his cane, Julius said: *Few men of normal potency prove able to refrain their foot from that path!* The well-known habit of the finished phrases, in their level precision almost rehearsed-sounding, the familiar deliberately mincing tones that mocked themselves with their own affectation, that mocked, too, Arthur Winner (but without unkindness, without a wish or a will to hurt— let us consider together human passion and folly; let us smile together!) —could he seriously suppose those phrases had been selected, they had been intended, to tell him nothing, that, because the cane pointed at no one, no one was meant?

In Arthur Winner had succeeded, countersurging against the womanish blush, a coolness of clarity, of shame's sudden remission, a breathing-deep of the amazed, enlightened heart. Yes; thou art the man! Total, the exposure; he stood exposed; yet who condemned him, who scorned him, who triumphed over him? Unsmiling, compassionate still, still steady, Julius's gaze, the speaking clear dark eyes, rested on him, as though without use of words to say: Yes, I know that you have been afraid I would find out. But you had nothing to fear. Don't you see, I've known all along. Our pact is: As I am, you accept me; as you are, I accept you—yes; come, let us smile together!

Julius Penrose said: "We're agreed? I imagine there's no chance of Noah coming in here this afternoon. Lay me out the accounts, then; and I'll study them."

He waited while Arthur Winner stood up. "On my desk, if you will, Arthur. And if you will—"

Arthur Winner presented his arm. "Yes; thanks," Julius Penrose said. Erect, both canes in his left hand advanced skillfully to prop him, Julius smiled seriously. He put his powerful right hand into Arthur Winner's. "Yes; thanks," he said again. As though he, too, had an arm to offer and now offered it, as though Arthur Winner, too, might need an arm to rise, he said: "Be of good cheer, my friend. In this business, we're not licked, not by a long shot. We'll come through this. I have decided that we will. I now get to work. I now see where we stand."

Arthur Winner said: "But isn't Marjorie—"

"I informed her that I might have things to do, that her time for a while was her own. Poor dear, she is capable of amusing herself. Though I believe she was there this morning, in her present frame of mind, I suspect she has taken off for Our Lady of Mount Carmel, always, I understand, open. Amid the twenty-five-cent votive lights and the plaster images, prayer, I think, would be her purpose."

O gentlemen, the time of life is short! To spend that shortness basely . . . Not in context—to recover the context Arthur Winner might have to think at length—the words, known only as a passage that some college course once required him to learn, repeated themselves, perhaps not reasonlessly. They witnessed, it might be, to an age of his innocence, continuing, succeeding, that of the child; more of the rapture of unknowing; more of the doubt-free ignorance; the folly of being wise still uncommitted by that useful football player, the important man in the college yard, the smartly golf-trousered and raccoon-skin-coated part-time student of the plays of Shakespeare. He had been quite a happy fellow; mostly pleasant to people, he had not been such a bad fellow.

Arthur Winner's walk back up the hill had begun. That also I must watch out for, he thought. (Fred Dealey said: *I'd really like to be nicer to more people—the stupid bastards!*) I must not, because I find fault with myself, start finding fault with everyone. (Julius said: *Be happy, and you'll begin to be virtuous.* . . .) Virtuous, could you, like Julius, note no more than in passing, note unprovoked, that this age is cheap, this age is maudlin; that to-day's women must run to religion, that today's men must as well as work, weep—what good was deep feeling when you were quiet about it? How would anyone know you had it?

The stairs from the basement room, from the wrapped body on the stone slab, mounted, Arthur Winner had found there to meet him that tight uniform packed with Bernie Breck, that amiable face packed with flesh, and by consciously creditable feelings again illuminated. *We just got word, I wanted to tell you, Mr. Winner*—as if Arthur Winner had Ralph Detweiler on his mind, cared whether the brat was ever found! The philosophic cop, the tough cop, and so (without fail) the sentimental cop, the cop who slightly turned your stomach, said gruffly, said gently: "I don't think we need to send for him, Mr. Winner; he told them he'd come home. I mean, after giving himself up, I think he will. What it was; he told them he was having breakfast at this soda fountain, and he heard the radio. What I said! No, that boy's not bad; this shows that. Thing to do is, give him a chance to get things straight, give him a helping hand. . . ." Answering, Arthur Winner said: "I would rather talk about it some other time." He went down the police station steps. He began to walk up the street.

Elmer Abbott, only in part a man, said: *I will try to calm myself.* . . . Julius Penrose said: *I never thought the day would come when I would need to say it.* . . . Here were the yellow-brick, collected new buildings of Our Lady of Mount Carmel—church, rectory, sisters' convent, parochial school, impressive and expensive, in their architectural manner modern (modren?), but at all events, advance indeed over the old church on Water Street, the humble edifice that the Pat-and-Mikes, the where-do-you-worka-Johns of another day had yielded their pennies to put up. Suppose, out of one of the church's arched triple doors on which the afternoon sun was falling, Marjorie, comforted by prayer, came suddenly? He strode faster, to get by them.

Federal Street, the shops all closed. On this side, on the whole stretch of sidewalk up to Court Street, to the bank at the corner, not a person was to be seen; though, quiet in the Sunday stillness, one or two cars had passed. Not improbably, those in the cars would know him, might see something strange, something odd—*wasn't that Mr. Winner?*—in his rapid walking all alone along the glass-faced line of closed shops; the straight tall solitary figure, his clothes of a kind which most of those who saw him would have seen in advertisements only, not in life. What phenomenon, what portent, they might ask, was this? Arthur Winner thought: If I'm to be at mother's at four, I haven't time to go out to Roylan and change.

In its wisdom, the law said: *No man shall be judge of his own cause.* Descending Federal Street, two troopers in a state police patrol car slowly drew near. The one not driving, who wore corporal's stripes, gave Arthur Winner a glance, plainly, from appearances in court, identified him; informally respectful, brought his hand to his hat brim, saluting as he passed. To return! *No man shall be judge*—yes, the law; the work of his life. The law, nothing but reason, took judicial notice of man's nature, of how far his conscience could guide him against his interest. For the sake of others, for his own sake, the law would not let him be led into temptation. In its wisdom, the law only aimed at certainty, could not, did not, really hope to get there. This science, as inexact as medicine, must do its justice with the imprecision of wisdom, the pragmatism of a long, a mighty experience. Those balances were to weigh, not what was just in general, but what might be just between these actual adversaries. (Judge Lowe said: *Caroline, you have done something very wrong and very serious.* . . .)

Walking, marching on, Arthur Winner came by the granite bulk of the shut-up First National Bank. Brocton, my Brocton! The courthouse in the trees; the façade of the Union League across the square. Walking, marching on, to his right, now, the building fronts; to his right went by the sober, proper name plate: TUTTLE WINNER & PENROSE ATTORNEYS AT LAW. Over beyond Christ Church's stone-mounded corner opened the vista of Greenwood Avenue, street of his yesterdays. Brocton, my Brocton—yes; and some thousands of other people's Brocton, its ordinary aspects, its well-known sights, owned by each of them—a Jerry Brophy's town, an old Joe Harbison's; the town, now, of the Reverend Whitmore Trowbridge, S.T.D., and, following her nuptials, the town-to-be of a little Miss Cummins; the town, now, of a Lower Makepeace Hughes, Garret, a respecter, looker-up-to of honorable men, who knew a good name is to be chosen before riches, and of Agatha, his wife, who must economize accordingly; the town of a Father Albright in his kingdom, his new yellow brick fortress-city of "Americanism" down there; the town of the tribe whose great name was Revere; the town of some uncertain newcomers called Moore, and Joan, their daughter.

To Helen Detweiler he had said: *Everything you do must be straight. No other way works, and there aren't any exceptions.* . . . Oh, indeed? To Helen, he said: *I can tell you something else; these things pass.* . . . Oh, they do, do they? *None of this will be easy.* . . . (Friend, you can say that again!) He would patch grief with proverbs? Walking, marching on, under the Greenwood Avenue trees, he walked indeed up yesterday. Here a child had passed a thousand times, whistling perhaps, perhaps taking ritual care not to step on the pavement cracks. Brocton, my Brocton! Away at school, somebody, a boy known as Hall II in fact, had said: *You mean Brockton, don't you? That's in Massachusetts. Brocton? There isn't any such place. Nobody ever heard of it.* Winner punched his nose. *Winner and Hall, take two hours' detention!* Yes; these things pass. In the bitter cold, the zero, New England nights, that boy, that Winner, waking in his snug-enough dormitory bed had how many times with passion wished himself home; he would never, never—the adverb, like "always," was inapplicable to this life, to living beings. Before spring came, Winner had forgotten that he once wished such a thing.

Freedom, Fred Dealey knew from reading, *is the knowledge of necessity*. All things pass. Yes; what of all the men who used to be? What of Time's manifold disasters and miseries, of Time's events, eventful or uneventful, that had been, and were no more? When you saw, any summer evening, the hollow of Roylan, how hard to throw off, to know as false, today's picture of seeming permanence—the houses long-standing, today—no expense spared; with all utilities, with all modern comforts—made so soundly new; the tended lawns and fields, the well-groomed roadsides along the smooth paving (once that Queen's, that King's, highway of ruts and mudholes) over which swept gleaming today's cars to take out and bring in those resident there. Yet, you had before your eyes the vine-grown walls of the old mill, the iron-railed plot with the little stone monument to speak to you of other todays—the once-present of the great water wheel going around, the millstones turning; and by the loading porch, the waiting wagons, the patient horses, the sacks of grain and sacks of flour, the knots of farmers gossiping; the once-present of the eighteenth-century night the Royal Anna Tavern was raided, the pound of hoofs, the hastily presented muskets making fire, the yells and roars of butchered and butcherers. The Roylan mill's great water wheel was fallen apart; loyalists and militiamen alike compounded were with clay, and who cared now?

Walking, marching on—here was the house; the boy was home. To Arthur Winner, his mother said: *It's absurd to suggest that you, or Julius Penrose either* . . . The station wagon from Roylan stood in the drive. Good; his mother would know, or would now be hearing. Up the walk! Quietly, Arthur Winner opened the screen door, quietly he entered the high hall. Able to see into the living room he saw that they were all upstairs; and, quietly, he went in—the Canton jar, the potpourri on the air; the *étagère*, the music box; still lying on that table by "her" chair, that faded green silk volume of Browning of his mother's—*For Miss Harriet Carstairs from her sincere friend* . . .

Alone, he stood motionless. To Clarissa, he said: *Whenever you don't tell all the truth you may expect to regret it.* . . . Sagacious words! Indeed, you may! You may look for hard moments, any number of them—very likely, hours together of them. "I'm tired," Arthur Winner said aloud. Speaking the words without intention, almost inadvertently, he felt their truth. He travailed, he was heavy laden. This weight was terrible; yet there was no way to put it off. And so, no knowing how far it would have to be carried, no knowing how long, burdened so, he must daily, hourly, affect to be unburdened. Yes; Julius wasn't wrong. This took courage, this took prudence, this took stoutheartedness. Do I have them? he thought. About that business with Marjorie, I could say: *That* really wasn't I. But this is I. Of this, I am not going to be able to think: I must have been crazy.

Aloud again, he said: "I don't know." (*I don't know, I don't know*, Noah Tuttle mumbled.) In a minute, he thought, in a few minutes, they will face me; I am going to face them. *We are not children* . . . Julius said. Patient, Julius said: *In this life we cannot have everything for ourselves we might like to have* . . . . Yes; life which has so unfairly served so many others, at last unfairly serves me—really, at long last! Have I a complaint? Have I, or have I not, been shown a dozen times those forms of defeat which are the kinds of victory obtainable in life? Givings-up—my good opinion of myself; must I waive that? Compromises—the least little bit of crook? Assents to the second best, to the practical, the possible? Julius Penrose said: *Be of good cheer, my friend.* . . .

Agreed, agreed! Victory is not in reaching certainties or solving mysteries; victory is in making do with uncertainties, in supporting mysteries. Yes, Arthur Winner thought, I must be reasonable. I said how easily to

Helen: *The question is: What's now the reasonable thing to do?* Is that hollow friend, myself, in spite of me to whine: *I would; but I can't, I dare not, I don't know how?* Never; not ever! (Never say never? Well, then; not for now!) This load, this lading, this burden—the need was only strength. Roused, rousing, he thought: I have the strength, the strength to, to—to endure more miseries and greater far, than my weakhearted enemies dare offer! With a start, he heard, down the stairs, a voice—his Aunt Maud's—calling in loud inquiry: "Arthur? Are you there?"

On the mantel, Arthur Winner saw the gilded, the ceaseless ticking clock. In its dead language: *Omnia vincit amor*, the metal ribband unchangeably declared. Timeless, the golden figures—on feeling's forever winning side, the smiling archer, the baby god; below, the peeping Tom, the naked girl—immobile held their pose; and now—the minutes how they run!—sudden, yet slow and melodious, the unseen mechanism was activated, struck a first silvery stroke, a second, a third, a fourth.

Raised to call back, to answer his Aunt Maud, Arthur Winner heard his own grave voice. He said: "I'm here."

VIII

The Job
[from *Morning Noon and Night*]

Lastly, I thought I ought to tell how I make my living. When young I managed to believe a man's means of livelihood need be only that. (I will later set out as well as I can what were my reasons for this silly belief.) I thought of work as something you did for money to support you while you were living, well apart from the job you happened to have, a 'real' life made up of personal interests and private concerns, intelligent enlargements of physical and mental experience, and selective cultivation of fruitful relations with other people. Apparently I was unable to see that money being what you cannot live without, the means by which you get what you cannot live without is never of no moment. Just as you cannot live without the job you hold, you cannot live apart from it—and, indeed, to say a man holds a job is to misstate the fact. The job holds the man. The job. By 'holding' it he gives his time to it, and what a man spends his time doing is what he is, and through what he is he sees things as he sees them.

Of course everyone must have known instances of men wrapped up in their work—the man by his consuming interest in it indubitably held by the job—but the fact perhaps needing to be noted is that if he takes no interest at all in his job, loathes it, neglects it as far as he can, he is just as much held by it. His very lack of interest continually conditions his thinking and feeling. For example: bored with the work or resentful of being obliged to do it, he may think that how bad his work is, so long as bad work doesn't lose him the needed job, can't to him matter. This is grave error. He may not care if the work is bad, but any doing badly constitutes a form of failure, and that must affect his whole frame of mind. Again; if a man does well the work he is doing and it earns him a lot of money, that will have one effect on his view of life. If, though doing the work well, he earns little, that will have one quite different.

These considerations and others like them that come easily to mind may seem a laboring of the obvious, but their possible importance is great and, as my work teaches me, what is obvious may be what is in most danger of being overlooked. To-whom-it-may-concern I am venturing to point out the obvious. Let it be recognized that the who-says-so here, the unidentified 'I' in me speaking now, must think and feel as he does and say much of what he says because his means of livelihood is what it is, because his business affords him position and power, because the profits accruing to him are great. All that will be implicit in conclusions of his, in what you find him telling you about himself and his experiences (and of course he will be telling you only what he feels he wants you to know). I remember a line of Montaigne's: *Amusing notion; many things I would not want to tell anyone, I tell the public*. I see what he means. Droll indeed the reflection that informing against yourself to one person is often imprudent, but not informing against yourself to the whole world. There you can count on a strange but true safety in numbers.

The Profession of Literature
[from *Morning Noon and Night*]

However, thirsting after professorships is not essential to the making of professors, and as my school years ended there was no apparent reason for my not going on and becoming one. While I was of college age, so going on would be encouraged by that entertained notion I spoke of about 'means of livelihood' being one thing and personal 'life' another. At least at first (I will speak later of what came later) it would. Since all my 'living' was to be done apart from my employment, why not be a professor? It was easy work and having watched it being done for years I would know how to do it. And did I know how to do anything else? I did not, presumably because I'd been kept, as I said, from getting around to thinking of anything else. The closest I came to that was when at about fourteen or fifteen I found myself with serious (as I saw them) thoughts of becoming a writer. No doubt such thoughts were permitted me because they were not felt to pose any special threat to inertia's plan. Let me write, if I wanted to (and could). For a professor to write books or magazine articles was very meet and right.

Indeed, this consideration, I judge now, was what led me to do my 'serious' thinking. I must allow that probably working on me here was the urge inciting the physician's son—the wish to get some of what Father gets. Observing the moderate respect my father commanded, I could see many of the marks of respect were formal or perfunctory, meaning nothing, and that would probably have been the whole of it, except for one thing. The thing that won him an attention of genuine respect, definitely distinguished him a little from fellows or colleagues, gave him perceptible small importance, was the writing he did. Like many professors, he wrote articles for learned journals (in which he dealt dryly with Anglo-Saxon or Early English linguistic problems); but, like few of them, he also contributed frequently to general-circulation monthly magazines of then acknowledged literary quality, such as *Scribner's* or the *Century*. These contributions were cultural critical essays, belles-lettres-type popularizations (but quite intellectual) of his Chaucerian studies, to which he gave titles demurely apt: *The Jalous Swan*, or *Epicurus Owne Sone*, or *If Gold Ruste What*

Shal Iren Do. There could be no doubt about a certain distinction conferred on him by his appearance in those pages.

There was also the circumstance that my mother's family had once a published writer in it. By my time he was altogether forgotten and the general public never had heard of him; yet his descendants brought up his name with a complacency which no doubt played a part in my thinking that to be a writer was to be notable. He was my mother's father's father, William Dodd. Though he came by his 'means of livelihood' as a professor of rhetoric at Brown, and later at Trinity College, Hartford, he published volumes of verse on the side. In the engraving after Thomas Hicks's 1866 painting that shows America's celebrated authors gathered (with apparent amity and concord, which anyone who knows writers must recognize as most unrealistic) under what looks like the portico of a vast Ionic-columned temple or palace of the Muses, William Dodd is present, though not among the thirty-odd figures—Miss Sedgwick, Longfellow, Bryant, Irving, Cooper, and so on—who sedately sit or stand meditative or in converse with one another on the tessellated ground floor. He is up on the right descending staircase with Richard Stoddard, Mrs. Amelia Welby, and Frederick Cozzens.

He seems to have been known mostly for a book-length poem called *The Columbiad*, whose heroic couplets celebrated in exalted language the founding and founders of the republic. Issued as a 'gift' volume (containing engraved portrait plates), it was at one time to be found lying on many a parlor table in homes of the cultured. Possibly it was little read then; certainly it is never read now; but he was an author of record, and, plainly, being one brings you extra esteem and out-of-the-ordinary respect. To think that both could be come by so simply and easily excited my boyish mind.

The boy was much mistaken about the simplicity and ease, as he discovered in no time when he actually set himself to write, yet about the esteem and respect, it must be granted him, he wasn't wrong at all. It is difficult to explain why this should be so, but so it assuredly is. No one who sees much of the world can fail to be struck by the amount of notice taken, wherever people many or few are gathered together on social occasions, of individuals who are known authors of books. Adulatory glances keep going to them; those present locate and point them out to each other and with eagerness ask to meet them. They aren't required to be writers of fame. Often their books sell little and their names are seldom heard; they are nonetheless persons of note. To an authoress (she needn't even be young and pretty) of a couple of published volumes of satirical verse, to an 'advanced,' probably loutish novelist of unripe years (that he is also evident bounder and egregious bore won't matter), no industrial magnate of wealth and weight, no financier or business executive of first consequence, no occupier of high elective office, no statesman of more or less international repute can hold a candle.

To be sure, our excited boy wants warning that this agreeable picture isn't the entire picture. This is the beer-and-skittles part. Almost as astonishing as the amount of public notice the writer gets is how little usually comes of it. The lions of an afternoon or evening should not expect adulation to linger on. When the group breaks up they're notable no more. Those who would rather meet them than meet a magnate are, the wish gratified, wholly content. The writer less than famous must not suppose all the attention he got indicates interest of a kind to rocket book sales and bring riches. Having had its way with him, the so-attentive company, dispersing, proceeds indifferent to pass him by altogether. Not a nickel richer or a bit better known, he will find himself obliged to possess his soul in patience until a next, no more profitable, public occasion gives him his chance to put himself on view.

Nor is this the only unsatisfactory part of the picture. Though he may be slow coming to know of them—established literary circles in which writers, critics, and publishers associate informally for business or pleasure are not very receptive to schoolboys—there are other aspects of the game of authors that may disagreeably surprise him. Yet it is true that the boy who by persistence works his way (as I did) to the outer edges of a few such circles and finds himself, if not seeing plain, glimpsing a later Shelley (and his publisher and his critics), will, if he is 'interested in writing,' at first likely think here is heaven.

If I smile it is because, recalling moments of the kind in my own experience, I must recognize that present recollection isn't serving me well. The past is imperfectly recovered. I can re-experience almost nothing of the animation of high interest, the active enthrallment, that once made me hang around the study of some English master at school or instructor at college (they were as likely as not to be 'little magazine' poets or book reviewers themselves, and were friendly with and could occasionally enable me to meet established professional writers whose work was quite well known); and that kept me in close (and rather tiresome, I'm afraid) attendance on such people as Mrs. Van den Arend (I will have more to say of that and of her) whose tastes were literary and who supplied themselves in a profusion eyed greedily by me with the new books, the more arty magazines that printed all the latest in 'experimental' writing, the abstrusely highbrow journals of 'opinion,' and who would submit to my discussings of them. Since I now wince when I think of these pressing attendances, while kindly unrebuffed, never, as I recall, specifically invited, embarrassment colors what I remember. I am not reliving it as it was.

If I was some time pushing to the charmed circle's edges and being able to peer in, I was also—never thinking to see, never wanting to see, a thing amiss there—some time longer in letting myself grasp the fact that the regular inside activities were hardly those of a heaven. The principle of strife, of competition and contest, informs them. The working conditions are such that every would-be writer must find himself pitted against every other would-be writer in an undercover, usually unadmitted, internecine battle royal. The business is a lottery with tickets unlimited—anybody can have one—but with prizes, places in the sun of money and literary fame, limited to a very few.

Competitors at the first step, on that lowest level of getting oneself published, are nearly countless. It is true that if you prevail there, if of the many who consider themselves called you are chosen, you win by appearing in print a preliminary prize—the astonishing attention I spoke of; but, as I also noted, that prize will prove usually a piece of trumpery, its substance shadow, with no market value. The place in the sun, the bag full of gold at the rainbow's end, will remain far, far away, while the crowd, if thinner than the crowd of the as-yet-unpublished, is still thick, and under no circumstances will the distant high seats accommodate even a tenth part.

The natural consequence is a melee which has (except that since it is mental or spiritual rather than physical you may engage in it clandestinely) many features of a rush for the lifeboats. Once you learn to recognize them, the treasons, stratagems, and spoils, the assassination attempts, the furies of partisan bias, the critical dishonesties of sectarian venom, the fetor of envy, hatred, and malice, and all uncharitableness impesting so much of the atmosphere are bound to make the world of letters, of books and writing, seem no nice place to live and work. By the time I was twenty a little of this truth about the literary life had begun to reach me out there on the circle's edges. When added to my early quick discovery that the work of writing can be easy only for those who haven't yet learned to write, not to say the dispiriting effects of failure to get my writing accepted by magazines that paid for contributions (the one editor who ever showed himself really keen to print my verse and short stories was I myself while chairman of my school publications board), it was quite enough to finish off my ideas of being a writer.

I think my giving up may of itself be good evidence that it was never in me to become a writer. I am prepared to believe that the life term at hard labor of serious writing, the disappointments of normal early failure, the discouragements of likewise normal continued unsuccess over months and years, the active large and small nastinesses of the undercover melee, the slings and arrows of enemy criticism's addictive lying, and the poor financial pickings that are the average professional's ordinary lot can none of them, or all of them together, nonplus in the least a person with the true urge to write, the writer born. If you shy away, you aren't that person, you weren't meant to be a writer. (I will have more to say about this.) So believing, I am glad I persisted no longer than I did in what could have amounted to a kicking against the pricks, in foolish refusal to face the inexorable fact that I hadn't the writer's temperament.

Yet sometimes, if only idly, I must wonder whether, though no writer born, not meant to be a writer, I might nevertheless have found myself among that small company of the highly successful—place in the sun, bag of gold, and all. What brings me to so wonder are observations of mine in the course of work we have done on one or two occasions for large publishing houses. In the studies we made we looked at the firm strictly as a business enterprise producing and distributing an article of commerce. Examining the mechanics of book vending and analyzing publishing statistics we found that in a large publisher's school and college textbook departments merchandising will often be conducted along lines consonant with good commercial practice. Specifications to ensure an acceptable standard article are prepared with care, and production is geared almost exactly to a demand that can with accuracy be determined beforehand. Here troubles, if any, would be in a sales staff that didn't know how to do its special selling job.

In the so-called trade department (the general list of fiction and nonfiction; publishing's literary-circle side, which so fascinated me as a youthful would-be writer), studies of the kind we make show us little or none of such tolerably sound business practice obtaining. Here again I must allow that the boy, if only through his innocent ignorance in supposing publishing a cultural rather than a commercial activity, was not mistaken; for practices that *do* obtain are nothing short of shocking to the informed specialist in production methods, or to the experienced analyzer and evaluator of management policies. The general list, if the firm is old and large, may include four or five (rarely more) established best-selling writers of popular fiction whose work can be depended on to approximate a standard article with sales to some degree predictable. That won't hold for most of the rest of the frequently long list. Into drawing the list up may go cultural considerations, but profit motives are seldom absent even in those considerations, and business this *isn't*. It is a guessing game, a hunch-and-hope gamble in which many ventures (the reason why the list tends to be long) are made on the supposition that if you make many the possibility of some paying off is greater than if you make few.

I do not mean to say that well-planned business has to consist solely of sure things—nothing venture, nothing gain is good counsel; or to maintain that trade publishing is unique in unsound practice. We once were called on to do for a client a very comprehensive research analysis of a year's introduction of new products in retail trade by seven hundred and fifty large manufacturers rated highest in their fields in management efficiency. Our final findings showed that four out of five such new items, though aided by sales programs conducted with all experienced competence, get so little public acceptance that they prove unprofitable and are shortly withdrawn. If this is the best that the know-how of experienced and rated-most-efficient business managements can do, the publisher's trade-department performance needn't cause him any special mortification.

Actually, in his offering for sale articles that prove to be not in demand the publisher as purveyor is less fairly than the big manufacturer faulted for business laches. Failure of the manufacturer's article to sell automatically convicts him of negligences not to be excused. The project could never have been given adequate study. He must have allowed to be left undone much that he ought to have done. He can't have assessed his market properly; he must have skipped all or most of the essential preliminary spadework of testing and sampling—any firm like ours could quickly show him the techniques of meaningful testing or significant sampling—which would either give him a reliable go-ahead signal or stop him before he seriously starts.

The publisher's position is different. Nobody can tell just what articles his market is going to want, and neither we nor anyone else could possibly show him how to find out in advance. Nor from his failures can he learn, as the manufacturer may, useful lessons about what will sell and what won't. The publisher who has unprofitably published a book, like the writer who wrote it, is taught nothing. The lesson they learn is only that they are out of luck. I used the word advisedly, for adducible figures from our publishing studies seem to show beyond doubt that neither merit as a piece of writing nor excellence, by literary standards of the moment, as a creative work is the determining factor in making a book a best seller. Indeed, as far as merit goes, so many books of no merit (that is, subsequently conceded to be without any) have had very large sales that, considering these alone, the hypothesis that badness does the trick—you find it proposed by almost every failed-writer-turned-critic in the literary-circle jungle—may seem tenable. It is not tenable because, whatever wishful thinking may wish, there are other figures to show that books of much and evident merit (that is, by subsequent critical consensus held so to be) often sell equally well.

When I am confronted with checked figures disagreeing and shown fact in conflict with shown fact I can only fall back on my long experience in the analyzing of problematic business situations. There, as I've said, given effect, we look for cause. Part of our procedure is to eliminate as we go all that fails to signify, cancels out by showing an inconstancy of sometimes yes sometimes no. In this case we eliminate the factor of intrinsic merit or lack of it in our article's sales success. So, now and then I wonder. Even if no born writer, or naturally equipped to be one, and though writing however badly, I am and always have been outstandingly endowed with luck.

Where advancement is seen to take place with no damned nonsense about merit, what could there have been to keep me if I had gone on writing from getting ahead, finding myself a Famous Author, maybe leading all the rest?

Having here praised again (yes, clearly bowings to Nemesis) that luck of mine, I should perhaps, in closing my introductory apology for myself and my life, particularize a little. My luck's operation is no universal omnipresent beneficence of fortune. I am not destiny's darling, with all my ships coming in, all my wagers winning wagers, and everything I touch turning to gold. My luck's operation may in some respects appear mostly negative —that is, it does a remarkable job of preserving me from perils and dangers. I am the man who, held up by traffic, gets to the airport five minutes too late to catch Flight 118, on which he has a reservation. This is quite annoying, since it's the last flight of the day and now he can't leave until tomorrow morning. Tomorrow morning he will hear that Flight 118, coming in to land at its destination, crashed, caught fire, and everyone on it was burned to a crisp. I am the amateur military officer who takes his leave of the advance command post five minutes before a direct hit utterly demolishes it. (The saving interval, I have had to notice, seems to be always about that, and such constant nice timing does surely look like design, like not being lucky just by chance.) Then there are those incidents I mentioned remembering so uncomfortably. I am the young fool who commits dismal stupidities, and yet as it comes out is not made to pay for them, as most fools are. Anger or appetite often led this fool to do things (if he only knew) hideously dangerous, yet the mortal thrust he invites is deflected; he receives not the least injury.

Even my business success may, rightly seen, be a matter of luck more negative in its actual nature than positive. I am the young man doubtful of what he wants to do, by a little-interested relative thrown with some impatience a crumb in the form of a job assisting a man running a small collection agency. When they regard the present position of HW Associates, many would no doubt be amazed to hear that 'HW' began by helping handle delinquent accounts, writing dunning letters, and tracing 'skips,' but so he did. That crumb, in something like a miracle of loaves and fishes, was by luck expanded into subsistence sufficient for multitudes.

At first sight this might appear luck positive, the luck of getting; but examination of the means by which the miracle was accomplished suggests otherwise. My luck saw to it that I was led safely around most pitfalls awaiting business inexperience, that numerous first mistakes in judgment and practice had no serious consequences. My luck saw to it that I made no unlucky choices when I began taking on subordinates—my servants, agents, and employees. Those I approached or who approached me were, miraculously indeed, always the right ones—I mean men and women who, while intelligent and competent, even gifted, were nevertheless without the independent or ambitious spirit which would be ready to resent finding that I am the one to batten most on the fruits of their talented labor, not they. It is the same kind of luck that provides that nothing if not good about me shall come out, that no truth to my, or my work's, discredit will ever be brought to light.

* *

At the same time, my other idea, of writing, which for a while really had interested me in a way the idea of teaching never did, was interesting me less and less. During my last college years I was kept writing chiefly by Knox Frothingham's precepts and example. Knox simply assumed that his friend Hank, like himself, was and would be a writer. It never seemed to occur to Knox, and it occurred only slowly to me, that necessary aptitude or talent was not come by just through wishing to be a writer or deciding to be one. People with small aptitude and no talent through doggedly writing may now and then make themselves professional writers, but the common experience will usually be that those 'interested in writing' brought by their attempts to write to realize they lack aptitude or talent quickly lose their interest. The interest Knox had been able to keep alive in our Hank went less to the work of writing than to being A Writer, to the charter to give himself Knox's airs of intellectual and aesthetic superiority. The impracticableness of that aspiration, of acting the writer without doing much writing, must grow apparent.

Naturally here, too, 'developments' had been intervening. Without doubt one of them was the termination of Knox Frothingham's influence. Graduated, Knox had been able to find himself, starting in the fall, an editorial job on a New York weekly magazine. The long constant association in college literary circles, the Poetry Club, the *Advocate* board chamber, and, that final year, rooming together in Westmorly was over. Another of the developments can be seen as coming, perhaps comically, from what was Knox's last effective exercise in precept and example. This had been to persuade his friend Hank to attend with him, that summer after graduation, a 'Writers Conference.' Conferences of the kind, today so common, numerous, and often boringly stereotyped, were then a new thing, firing intellectual excitement and conferring intellectual prestige on those attending. Our Hank would have a fine chance to act for a couple of weeks the writer he still retained his interest of sorts in being or trying to be.

The general practice then as now was to have the gathered groups of conferees 'led' by a staff of professional writers, successful in the sense that they were published all right, but not yet, and as a rule never to be (I intend no individual disparagement; as I noted earlier, luck, not merit, is here determining), sufficiently successful to have no need for a little extra money

and no time to waste this way. However, to see that fact of the matter the
eager conferees must be older and more experienced than most of them were
and they present themselves ready to look with awe on people listed in
Who's Who (they don't understand that publishing a couple of books gets
anyone listed, while men of much greater public importance may wait half
a lifetime), whose names were to be seen in literary columns and on bound
volumes for sale in bookstores.

Arriving with Knox to register, our Hank is as impressed as anyone
else. How exhilarating to join so easily an intellectual elite! This is the life!
Yet as business gets under way, as the program of addresses, lectures, sessions of round-table talk proceeds, he is surprised and puzzled to find, a
good deal of the time, the business not what he had been expecting. He had
supposed that how to write was what they would study and discuss. Topics
leaders and their led were choosing to treat often seemed quite unconnected
with writing, whether as trade or as art, or with literature. Surely it's a bit
queer?

I think the question was then a fair one, though presently such non-
writing businesses would become the accepted thing, the whole purpose
of gatherings of writers and would-be writers. Not many years later a pre-
tentiously named American Writers Congress would be centering its whole
attention on how an abstract entity known as 'The Writer' ought to regard
multitudinous intellectual 'issues' with which modern times supposedly
confronted him. No bones were made about a writer being purely hawker
of wares. His writing, whether fiction or nonfiction, is to serve as a weapon
of persuasion, an exercise in tendentious dialectics, an instrument of calculated propaganda. The right use and whole purpose of prose composition
(and indeed also of poetry) is to plug ideologies, to sell partisan dogma, or
inculcate the addlepated line of some latest splinter party. The congress
men and women (self-elected) appear to take their seats already agreed,
most of them, that the convocation's first task is to frame and promulgate
a lengthy Literary Manifesto. Definitive Bill of Rights & Wrongs, this will
declare once and for all what 'position' everyone who writes ought to (must)
take on every world and national social or economic problem of the day.

Such full-blown solemn-asininity lay in the future; yet first winds of it,
perplexing, question-raising, trouble a little the earlier intellectual sym-
posium's calm. A butyric whiff of riper phoninesses to come taints ever so
faintly the rare atmosphere. Time had not been yet for main business to turn
altogether from writing and become 'issues' and 'problems'; yet a number of
the leaders and not a few of the led seemed, that long-ago summer, interested more in sounding off on the innocence of Sacco and Vanzetti than in
the techniques of writing truthfully and exactly about life and people.
(Didn't Doctor Johnson say: *Nothing can please many, and please long, but just*

representations of general nature?) The relevance of the case of dragged-out controversy in the Massachusetts courts to the work of would-be writers wasn't and isn't very clear.

However, I think I would perhaps do well to note in truth's interest that his questioning of this particular unexpected concern of the conference did not mean that our Hank wasn't, like most professional intellectual liberals, or most young and shallow ones, by and large convinced—proving, no doubt, what writers as colporteurs really can accomplish—that those to become the fire-shirted martyrs before summer ended were saintly victims of a monstrous miscarriage of justice, and this I regard as doing credit to his humane feelings, in which I have to see our Hank often deficient. By then the pileup of published liberal protest had so far buried all original facts that even the cruel irony now informing the protracted ordeal went unrecognized. Ingenuously misled by the defendants' unshakable firmness in protesting innocence, an impassioned liberal volunteer defense had itself, with no other help, worked its heroes' ruination.

The engineer hoist with his own petard is sport; yet I think a qualm can be felt when those hoist are, in the law's sense, just his next friends. None of the volunteer engineers seemed able to understand the anarchistic ethic of ends justifying means that made acts in the cause's interest no crime, and could leave the defendants in their own minds honestly innocent of crime. The engineers persuaded themselves that the pleas of innocence meant that what the humble two good men were charged with they hadn't done. Out of nothing but this ingenuous persuasion they contrived, where the Commonwealth's case had every chance of failing, to convince a jury of guilt beyond reasonable doubt and subsequently to bring dismissal of appeals and to lead the extraordinary high commission of review provided by the Commonwealth (yes; Massachusetts, in supererogation of scrupulosity, there she stands) to decide against the defendants.

Much of the prosecution's evidence was flimsy or could easily be made to look so. One solid bit rested on the ballistic tests said to prove the bullet that killed the paymaster came from Sacco's revolver. When you knew that the whole case was a capitalist plot to judicially murder innocent men for their political opinions, you knew those tests *had* to have been rigged. How to show they were? Let's have new tests conducted where they can be checked on. The cartridge that contained the bullet was of an obsolete type and didn't exactly fit the revolver. The thing was plain as day. All the bullet scorings really showed was the misfit. They could have been made by any revolver the cartridge didn't quite fit. Let's get a supply of these cartridges and make other test firings. Those tests, so certain to be conclusive in disproof, the defense was unable to make. Protracted search throughout the country turned up not a cartridge of the type. The engineers had definitely

determined, for the jury's information, that there weren't any anywhere—
none, that is, except the pocketful Sacco had when arrested.

But, as to most people, to our Hank this defense gift to the Commonwealth of what proved with the jury the hanging (or burning) point was
not known, passed overlooked, and he sufficiently sympathized with those
agitating the cause of the moment, even if he wondered why they should be
doing it here. Such random deviations into businesses other than writing
perplex rather than disturb him. What slowly does begin to disturb him are
some of his fellow conferees and some of their leaders. He notices the very
noticeable fact (he would prefer not to descend to personalities; but, here,
how hard to help it!) that a number of those present fall almost generically
into types—the lank and the flat-chested women's-college liberal, looking
rather unwashed and rather debauched; the pompous, obstinately humorless revolutionary young man sprouting his bit of beard, yet in his nervous
giggle less than virile; the craggy-faced, homespun, virile-indeed buck-
fairy on his prowl for boy-does (also sure to be around). Even a few such
look-and-act-alikes viewed grouped together can suggest an imitating, a
copying of each other—which can in turn suggest (maybe not always fairly)
that these are pretenders pretending; fakes, not real writing writers.

My calling attention to generic conference types may, I see, create an
impression of the quality of that years-ago summer gathering and of the
honesty of those attending that would be both unjust and untrue. To be
kept in mind is the newness of the whole concept, the necessarily experimental nature of the agenda, the often extemporized untried and untested
methods. Moreover, while quite noticeably present, the generic types were
really not there in force, were nothing like a majority. Full-scale musterings
of them waited on later-date convocations such as that farcical 'Congress'
of the '30's. There the generic types, the more puzzleheaded 'social activ-
ists,' and all those human oddities once named by Max Beerbohm *adults of
the infantile persuasion* swarmed so numerous that, dominant, they were soon
seized of control, magisterially running the close-to-burlesque show, and
doing all the fatuous talking for what would be the affair's official record.
Indeed, that at our Hank's conference this *wasn't* the case is part of the point
I would wish to make. To disturb him seriously, to give him anxious pause,
the pretended-writer or doctrinaire-critic suspects needn't be numerous.

I must wonder if the fact doesn't show that, while in his own outward
appearance, in what he does and says, he may little resemble the pretenders
present, our Hank is not secure in his difference. The study of even a few of
their stamp may be judged to speak disturbingly to subliminal doubts of
his about his own talent, about whether he, either, has it in him to be a real
writer. Is he finding, through watching these people, himself exposed to
himself? How can he be sure he isn't what so many of them seem to him to
be? Has he a single good reason to believe, if he keeps on writing, he can

make himself anything more than they are? The questions shake him; and, shaken, he may begin to realize that by asking themselves they are answering themselves. The inner doubt gives proof positive that, as well as in all likelihood lacking the talent, he most hopelessly lacks the temperament a writer who is serious about writing has to have.

The temperament is one you must be born with; you can't cultivate or develop it; and if our Hank wonders what signs of being born with it are, he need only look at his friend Knox. At the conference Knox is not failing to see the same things, and he, too, was certainly expecting something else, but his seeing doesn't have the same effect on him. Shaken by no self-distrust, he accepts untroubled, at once perceives as only natural, the straggle of nuts and queers that creative arts must always attract. He is not disturbed by what the pretenders, the half-writers, may do or be like. Sure; the instruction of fools, of the pundits of the little cash-poor magazines, of the radical mouthy doyens of the small-fee sophomore circuit, will be folly —but what the hell else could it be? And what does it have to do with serious writing, with himself as a writer? Egoistically sanguine and confident, he watches them with contempt, sees them as simply good for unkind laughs; and once he is sure that staying in their company offers nothing from which he can profit, nothing to his writing purpose, he drops out. By temperament he is concerned with himself only, and how to express himself. Even if stridulent instruction of the fools turns directly on him and his work (which, should he begin to be successful and celebrated, must be expected; after all, these are self-defense's, self-preservation's envious gashes), his born-writer's temperament is a sevenfold shield. He can be hardly pricked to more than flashes of 'ire'—like my grandfather when his critics heaped their rancorous motivated abuse on him. The truth in one's heart, we are told, does not fear the lie on another's tongue.

Nor is that all the temperament can do for those who possess it. Possessing it will not, of course, mean that you are bound to become a noted writer, successful and celebrated, yet it seems nonetheless to remain faithfully yours. Knox Frothingham has never become a noted writer. Joining his New York magazine and doing, to start, bits of editing and staff writing, he apparently, continuing with it, was able to find in the work adequate means of self-expression, and as time passed and he grew very accomplished, moving up to the editorial top, also adequate means of livelihood. The great novel he had a youthful aim to write remains unwritten, and though finally (he is my age) now made a member of the National Institute of Arts and Letters he enjoys no general literary reputation. Still, he has assured means and authority to write and to cause to be published whatever he wants to write in whatever way he wants to write it. Today I see him touched no more by sense of failure than he would have been by the abusive criticism which at some stage he must almost certainly need to support had he produced his great novel and had luck made it a great success. How very clear that this temperament is not our uncertain Hank's! He is fortunate in so soon realizing it; he is well advised in abandoning hope to write.

Cubby
[from *Morning Noon and Night*]

Francis Bacon writes that death comes to young men but old men go to death. I think of this. Our scene is the library of the big dark time-touched Cuthbertson house on the college's Faculty Row. I sit with my mother's father, Professor Ethelbert Cuthbertson Dodd. He is showing me file folders packed with pages of manuscript that he directed his man Sebastian to bring out after dinner. They are kept in what his maternal grandfather, Caleb Cuthbertson, for whom the house was built, called the strong room —a small vault supposedly fireproof. There must be fifty of these folders resting in two piles on the small stand beside the writing desk. Contained in them are my grandfather's memoirs, entitled by him *My Life and Times*, at which he has been working since he retired from active teaching many years ago.

I have, of course, known about this manuscript and been shown parts of it before. Since I did not believe the old man could ever finish his work I was not too concerned to find with passing years that what he wrote frequently made little sense. In the folders he has handed me I discover him dealing with controversy almost a generation old over the then-new theories of Freudianism. He vigorously attacked them in learned periodicals of the time. Still attacking them, and with bitterness he was brought to feel by personal counterattacks on him, my grandfather had reached a stage of making no sense whatever. And now I *am* concerned, for he has just been telling me the book is almost done. The fifty or so pages I have in my hand he is busy rewriting, but parts that follow it, and the end, like parts that precede it, are finished to his satisfaction, ready for the printer. I have what amounts to a management problem of my own on which I must try to advise myself. The problem is created by an astonishing change that began some years ago to take place in my grandfather's position or status. Back when I believed he would never be able to finish his 'memoirs' I could feel an additional reassurance that even if he finally did they would find no publisher.

Now to feel that is not possible. Now a dozen publishers would jump at a chance to print the stuff, no matter what it was, if he put his name to it.

Really, this must not be allowed to happen to him. He has for years, without the least impatience to publish, been filling his folders. Is the sagacious head of HW Associates lacking the resource to keep him doing so? A little of that practical disingenuousness sometimes essential in our counseling, perhaps? Suppose, grave and judicious, I say that what I have just been reading is material of such importance that a far fuller and more detailed treatment would be desirable, in my opinion. Later, if necessary, the same could be said about other parts of the manuscript. At the rate the old man is able to work today, 'fuller treatment' may require more time than is left him. I must reach a decision. Silent, my grandfather has watched me pretend to read for fifteen minutes. I must say something. I look up, prepared to speak, to offer my adroit suggestion. I do not need to.

The old man sleeps. The desk lamp's radiance shines in mellow reflection across the polished skin of the drooped head's scalp, become altogether hairless. The chin, with its scrabble of white beard, has dropped to the chest. Blankness of lowered eyelids shadowed by still-dense white eyebrows makes the eyes appear even more sunken than when they are open. The long thin sharp nose seems thinner and sharper. The pallid lips have parted. Through them the sleeper breathes with a measured short sighing sound.

Deep in the big chair his figure, relaxed, looks shrunken, emaciated, as though he were a famine victim or one of a concentration camp's survivors. Sleeves of the rumpled light-gray cashmere jacket lie in folds on the inert spindly arms. The too-full trouser legs drape slack from meager bony knees where his hands, disproportionately big with their enlarged joints and blotched with liver spots, rest limply open. I see that count, not of threescore, but of near fourscore years and ten. I look directly at longevity illustrated, at the ways and means of this last of life (for which the first was made?). The little sleep is clear type and shadow of the coming great sleep; the final article of death is here prefigured. Yes; he goes to death.

But he goes slowly. My grandfather has more time left than, that evening, I could conceive possible. Surely the man I see asleep may be expected to die any day now. He is eighty-nine. When he did die he was in his hundredth year, and his death was definitely unexpected. Expecting him to live on had become the natural thing—so much so that the college community could have an aggrieved sense of being unfairly let down by their prize old man. How really *too* bad of him to do this, when if he'd been willing to live a couple of months more he would be one hundred, and plans to commemorate the occasion in a large way were already prepared.

I think the aggrieved had a right to feel aggrieved. They were given no warning at all. Coming up in May for the stated meeting of the college trustees, I myself had seen, quite unsurprised (a few years earlier it always seemed surprising), my grandfather successfully as ever surviving, really triumphing over, one more of those severe winters. Seasonable fine weather, here in the hills not oppressively hot, was arriving again to lift the long siege of snow and ice, relieve the beleaguered position, bring suspension of hostilities. Indeed, in this war there is no discharge; but Professor Dodd, the old campaigner, could be seen, another field won, as safe-returned to summer quarters. Weapons stacked and guards dismounted, he may now rest easy on these his latest laurels, out of danger, out of harm's way while he waits for August thirtieth to bring another birthday around. Why should this year be different?

Conceived possible by me or not, my grandfather had ten years of life left him on the night I so gravely concerned myself over the possibility of his nonsensical memoirs soon appearing in print. As it happened, I needn't have felt concern. The book never came out, though not because of clever contrivings of mine. Factors unforeseen by me were to enter. One of them was that my grandfather, moving on into his nineties, developed an increasing inattentiveness, a general infirmity of purpose. Much of what he was formerly interested in could be seen to interest him no longer—toward the end, not even his book and its publication. I suspect that a good deal of the time he just forgot it—remembered neither what it was about nor that he had written it.

Yet also involved may have been a half-conscious, largely unadmitted recognition of exactly the hazard to the repute he enjoyed that I worried over. I suggest the recognition was never fully conscious or fully admitted because I have come to know the aging mind's commoner habits. Lines of thought are pursued to a certain point, maybe far short, maybe just short, of thinking the thing through and there dropped. The place they were headed for, the logical final conclusions, may remain no more than adumbrated. Never definitely arrived at or accepted, they may still, without being quite reached, be acted on. All around him the old man saw evidence overwhelming that during the past twenty years he had been turned little by little into a legend. Even supposing senility brought him to pretty well credit the legend himself, moments might come when he heard counsels of prudence, glimpsed the great truth that the proper way to preserve legends is to keep hands off, to let them alone.

Could legend now full grown benefit, have anything to gain from, extended rakings up of the past? Not possibly; and in affairs of this kind where you don't stand to gain you stand to lose. My grandfather did seem past realizing the vapidity, the vacuousness in his piles of writing, and so perhaps never understood the real risk to his reputation; yet he might understand perfectly the general chance he would be taking. I'm inclined to doubt that he ever 'decided' publishing would be unwise; but he wouldn't need to. Aware, or half aware, of potential dangers that lay in publication, he could let the whole business slip slowly into the limbo of lost interests, into the keeping of forgetfulness, and, so, happily make any concern of mine uncalled for.

My own life experience has led me to think a good deal about my grandfather and his legend, about legend-making—the breeding of legends, or in the heart or in the head—and their care and cultivation. Here to be thought on are tides in the affairs of men, chance's often unbelievable (yet ordinary) concatenations of surprise and accident, peradventure's intrusive role in the course of events, and that matter of the mind's mistakes in supposing that how things look now is how they used to look. Let me note well that as an individual the old man, my grandfather himself, offers in his almost interminable playing of slipper'd Pantaloon no more than the limited, and to those of riper years surely superfluous, instruction still another *memento mori* may afford them. His later 'life and times' are vegetation. Even his annual returns to summer quarters, his hours of triumph, are tediums of routine, monotonies of petty ritual.

Most summer mornings aged Professor Dodd will be able to have his chair and adjustable writing stand moved out beneath the little colonnade of the old house's secluded shady side verandah and do there such work as he may feel inclined to do. Afternoons (unless rainy or otherwise inclement —perhaps too warm, perhaps too windy) he has his regular twenty-minute walk back and forth through the ample old garden, his man Sebastian in a white coat attending at his elbow to take care he doesn't stumble. Summer sun and air improve his appetite. His energy increases and at night he sleeps sounder. Often he will be in quite good spirits, prepared to talk more and to do it without the vague incoherence he may exhibit when winter shuts him in. Though sun and air constitute no cure for the growth of cataracts, his eyesight seems to strengthen, and with the use of his glass he reads as much as an hour at a time. Halcyon days, indeed! That Professor Dodd is as old as he has lived to be casual observers might find hard to credit.

But few and far between are observers of any kind. The old man lives secluded (doing the legend no harm at all), and coming to see this relic and type without special invitation would be unthinkable. Even the now-famed birthdays pass carefully unmarked by public observance or scheduled ceremony which Professor Dodd might feel it incumbent on him to attend and which might overtax him. For the occasion Sebastian's wife, Alberta, always makes ready a large cake with elaborate icing, but admitted to eat of it are only President Mountjoy and the Dean of the college. Formally dressed, calling formally, these two arrive on the dot half an hour before suppertime. (Not infrequently one or both, away for the summer, will have returned today without other reason than to put in this appearance.)

The expected fall of the knocker is answered and the door opened to them by Sebastian. He goes and announces them. After returning, he ushers them into the library. With apology for having to receive them sitting down, the old man thanks them for this honor done him. Assisted a little by Sebastian he proceeds to cut Alberta's splendid cake. Transferring slices to small silver plates, Sebastian serves the guests. From a gold-inlaid decanter he pours out sherry for them.

Rising with dignity President Mountjoy lifts his glass. To the Dean he pronounces: "Sir, I give you Ethelbert Cuthbertson Dodd, Doctor of Medicine, Doctor of Philosophy, Doctor of Humane Letters, and, of this faculty, Breck Professor of Psychology and Moral and Ethical Culture Emeritus."

Bowing, the Dean lifts his own glass. He responds: "Professor Dodd, sir. His health and long life."

Both drink. After precisely ten minutes of formal conversation, the cake slices consumed and the sherry finished, they bow themselves out to let Professor Dodd get ready for his supper.

While in the years of the full-grown legend this little closed ceremony with its slightly discomfiting note of the mannered or affected (legend's very nature must make for the struck pose, the formal stance, the act put on) came to constitute the whole of the 'birthday party,' it was by no means the whole of the celebrating of Professor Dodd's birthdays. The mail that morning would not be delivered by the postman on the route. There was too much for him to carry; it filled a separate bag dropped off by a post-office truck. By then my grandfather's reputation as seer and sage, as profound scholar and inspired teacher, had been spread, rising as it spread, far indeed beyond a small college's community. Coming to be spoken of everywhere as 'Cubby,' he was generally known and generally revered throughout eastern academic circles, and with customary results. Every year, perhaps every day, new wise, new shrewdly witty, sayings projecting that persona of the good gray professor were ascribed to him. Stories to illustrate his encyclopedic knowledge and intellectual prowess multiplied, all of them pure fiction but getting wider and wider currency as fact.

To stuff the morning mailbag, former pupils, one-time associates, eminent fellow workers in his fields (by now most would never have known him, only this grown reputation of his) were by scores writing to express respect, to convey esteem or affection, to congratulate him and wish him well. With such letters piling higher every year—his ninety-fifth birthday brought Cubby warm congratulations which, if perhaps not personally written by him, were on the President of the United State's official stationery, and personally signed by him—the college and all connected with it could not but find the festive day one for heartier and heartier self-congratulation. On them and all of them and on the institution the Grand Old Man shed ever-greater luster. Other schools might have feathers of a sort in their caps; but had they a Cubby? Not they!

From the legend it might naturally be presumed that Professor Dodd had begun the building of so great a reputation early in his teaching career. His remarkable abilities and rare qualities of mind, you would imagine, always had been his and had always been recognized and acknowledged by what his small-college situation would make the limited little group able to be aware of them. Virtually none of those who paid my grandfather (and themselves) the annual tribute of later years ever knew or could have been brought to believe that the concept of Grand Old Man got its slow uncertain start around the time retired Professor Dodd turned seventy-five. The tide of nearly national renown (witness the White House letter) entered on its impressive rise only as he neared eighty-five.

What made the concept's first taking form slow and uncertain would also be quite unbelievable to Cubby's later venerators. When first they heard it beginning to be rumored around that Cubby was among the great teachers of his time and also a scholar of immense learning, men who had been my grandfather's colleagues while he was actually teaching, to whom he had been known for years, and who were still members of the college faculty probably dismissed it as somebody's little joke. They may be guessed to have thought such a claim so ridiculous (even that appellation, afterward fond, of 'Cubby'—he signed himself *E. Cuthbertson Dodd*—had been used mostly in undergraduate derision and disrespect during his teaching years) that any nipping of the legend in the bud, then probably possible, seemed needless. By the time the legend had, plain to see, become one, and no joke at all, many of those who might have spoken were dead, and of those still alive most would have to consider what motives could be imputed to them if they spoke now; while I think a few, whether merely doddering, whether at an age to see themselves possibly served by any good-gray-professor legend, took to giving a helping hand, to providing purported eyewitness testimony to the truth of it, to remembering nothing more.

Unremembered by them were the circumstances of Professor Dodd's 'retirement.' He had clung to his chair until he was seventy and would have clung longer if means to oust him hadn't been laboriously devised. (Minutes of trustee meetings survive to show that the difficulty of getting rid of him was a principal argument for adoption of a college rule that made retirement mandatory at sixty-five unless the dean of the faculty tendered a specific 'extraordinary' request for temporary longer service.) Nor did that tell all. You needed to know the ouster was engineered notwithstanding definite financial loss the college incurred. On the death of his mother,

daughter of Hosea's son Professor Caleb Cuthbertson, my grandfather came
into control of a much larger share of the Cuthbertson-Alwayne money.
His income, ample already, was so far increased that he felt himself in a
position to, and he did, turn back to the bursar the whole of his endowed
chair's sizable stipend.

The professor able to afford so generous a gesture would be about one in
ten thousand, and even on that uncommonly well-off Faculty Row of the
college's, nobody else made it. Professor Dodd's making it was hardly calculated to endear him to his fellows and associates—neither those well off
who did not see their way to following his example, nor the larger number
who (though some of them full professors) could not live on Faculty Row,
having no money but what the college paid them. Their state of feeling
might be very much the one that is so common in the world of arts and
letters. Few things are more galling than to see a man doing the kind of
work you do yet (just what makes it possible won't matter) living high on
the hog while you pinch and scrape. Our human nature turns a bitter critical eye on him, and such scrutiny is apt to bring feelings that his good fortune is undeserved and to lead to a looking out of faults of his that will show
as much. Examined in this spirit, remarkable indeed if faults manifold and
even monstrous aren't found in him and his work, and more remarkable
still if chances to set them forth are lost. I also can't doubt that it was this
independence of independent means enjoyed by Professor Dodd—the college was his pensioner, not he the college's—that did most to inspire the
virtual hate with which Arthur Abernethy, then the college's president,
came to regard him.

I make the point in fairness to my grandfather. In fairness to those
lookers-out of faults, even if they looked through envy and resentment, or,
like President Abernethy, through enmity of wounded pride of power, I
think it will have to be admitted that the looked-for when found and set
forth, was not made out of whole cloth. Hidden in their eagerness to deni-
grate Professor Dodd might lie motives little to the credit of those hostile
to him, but resulting charges brought by them were not all dishonest or all
unreasonable, given the existing situation.

The situation was that Arthur Abernethy, inducted as the college's
tenth president a year or so after my grandfather accepted the Breck chair,
came to his office highly resolved to revolutionize an institution which if
old and long known—even in a minor way famous—was weak in every
form of scholarship and of low academic repute. The new President was
determined to change things. At the time of his induction he was a big
forceful man of fifty—he used to be known unopprobriously as 'A. A.';
but also as 'The Ape,' which if unkindly not altogether unjustly described
his physical appearance. He bore a string of good degrees, degrees hard to
earn, not hollow, but his real talents were administrative, and the good

degrees served more to let him know what genuine learning was than to make him learned. Knowing what learning was, he meant to turn the college into an institution of learning of the first order, with standards recognized everywhere as those of excellence and everywhere respected.

Starting out, A. A., big and forceful though he might be, lay under the handicap of lacking largely the autocratic power that goes with some college presidencies. Then there were several of the trustees (the new president found getting them replaced slow work, since periodic election for stated terms was not at that time in the ruling *Laws of Order*) who could only conceive of a college as social and sporting club. Its proper studies were athletic contests, fraternity life, and alumni reunions. Since all three were in a flourishing state they saw no need for any kind of change. Then there were those many among the reunioning alumni who, never greasy grinds themselves, did not want their sons to have to be greasy grinds. Then there were their High Mightinesses, the Faculty Row professors, every one of them naturally long and well satisfied with the courses of instruction he gave given as he gave them, and with the quality of his own teaching.

That the college little by little did definitely begin to change testified to President Abernethy's abilities in manipulation, in getting around difficult people, as well as to a truly dogged tenacity of purpose. Working on his side he had the fact, becoming evident even before the First World War, that the Bright-College-Years brief era of the '90's was done; the tables down at Mory's, and fight, fight for every yard, and stands our noble Alma Mater, and all that, things of the past; and the irreversible tide of change full set against the kinds of opposition A. A. faced. However, time had still to run before they were wholly swept away, and as first changes in the college began, each small success won by the new President alerted opposers again, alarmed them more, made them more stubborn in recalcitrance. As years went by, President Abernethy was also, I think, suffering from the effect of his successes on him personally. They provided proof that wanted change was not impossible, and, so, could increase his impatience to bring change about in shorter order. He redoubled his great exertions, and symptoms of overstrain resulting were soon to be seen in an impairing of the judgment and discernment through which he had gained the ground gained. The judgment kept in precise sight actual objectives. The discernment let him pick tactics and minutiae of persuasion—telling him, for example, just when a conceding of what wasn't very important could be means to win what was. Unimpaired, I think they would have told him that if the good of the changed college seemed to him to require Professor Dodd's resignation, feuding with Professor Dodd was not the way to get it.

Of course in stand of opposition to my grandfather the new President could count on the kind of underground faculty support whose motivations I have suggested. As his project proceeded, as inch by inch (man by man) he got the faculty about a quarter made over in the image he proposed, he was gathering more support. Without doubt a consensus of abler new members would be that Professor Dodd amounted to no great shakes either as teacher or as scholar. Indeed, what on earth was he professor of? What was 'Psychology and Moral and Ethical Culture'? Professor Dodd, accepting an established chair (you might answer), was not to be held responsible for peculiar ideas entertained by Mr. Breck, a devoted early alumnus and wealthy manufacturer of paints and varnishes who set up and munificently endowed a chair he chose so to name near the turn of the century; but this did not prevent my grandfather's enemies from declaring that no man of real intellectual parts or genuine learning could ever have let himself be named professor of stuff and nonsense.

Similarly, if you wanted to run down Professor Dodd, the propriety of his listing a medical degree after his name could be questioned. That he held the degree was not to be denied; but it was not to be denied either that the degree came from a dubious institution which went out of business (the right word) even before 'medical schools' of the sort were finished off by the Flexner Report. Moreover, 'Doctor' Dodd never had been licensed to practice, and his detractors, rightly or wrongly, insisted that where acceptable standards prevailed he never could have got himself licensed. If objection was made that the license was irrelevant, or, if it showed anything, showed that he had undertaken medical studies only as an adjunct to his studies in psychology—and, however substandard the school's courses, he could hardly help gaining a knowledge of anatomy and physiology greater than the average psychologist's—the detractors could and did hotly answer that what remained as relevant as ever was the (to their minds) disingenuousness, if not outright dishonesty, of hitching an M.D. to your name when you couldn't show you were qualified to practice medicine.

Let me parenthetically admit the fascination that such small puzzles of lost past facts have for me. Some of them I can't quite get out of my head. They are trifling, the answers if learned of no possible moment, yet the tantalizing why, why, why of them keeps nagging me. That semispurious medical degree of my grandfather's is, of course, one. The scanty facts of record present enigmas or oddities I am not able to put in order. For a young man who planned to teach psychology (in those days looked on as a division of philosophy) to see the taking of a medical degree as a proper or necessary first step might be intellectually possible—indeed even an indication of unusual intelligence—but it cannot be made to seem probable. However, the improbable allowed, what in reason can explain the picking of the kind of medical school he picked? The general public could perhaps have trouble in distinguishing a mere diploma mill from medical colleges that offered instruction, by the best standards of the day, sound; but my grandfather, born and brought up in academic circles, even if not those of the larger universities, could have had no trouble finding out which the good schools were. My perplexed questionings are vain. I note them only because most of us may from time to time want reminding that to have our conclusions correct we will often need to know what, now known to no one living, can never be known.

I am left to wonder whether his situation could not have been a little like my own when young. While growing up, my grandfather, too, might have found himself, whatever the reasons, prevented from settling on anything he particularly wanted to do and, like me, he was under no pressure of poverty to decide. His father had personal means as small as a professor (and minor poet) would usually have, but his mother, Caleb Cuthbertson's daughter Dorcas, was richly provided for, so a child of theirs could take his time about choosing an occupation. My notion is that his choice when he made it amounted to one of protest or defiance—he chose *not* to follow in Professor William Dodd's footsteps. Perhaps he resented that pressure of doing what comes naturally, a paternal taking-too-much-for-granted of what he was going to do; but possibly, also, a circumstance in his parents' life which I will speak of later made him emotionally hostile, had him bearing his father a grudge. Feelings of the kind could explain very well a declaration of independence in the abrupt announcement that he would be a physician, and a deliberate making of his arrangements without asking anyone's advice—in turn, accounting for the selection of the inferior school.

My further notion is that by the time his medical studies ended he had come to find medicine not at all to his taste. With no wish to practice it, he never sought a physician's license. The doing what came naturally could now take over; since through tradition's compulsion he had to do something, he might as well teach, and I must suspect what he taught was determined not by what interested him but by what was the best opening among those the college had at the moment available to a young man with the family influence to get one offered to him. It just happened to be in the Philosophy Department, which was then small, 'Natural Philosophy'—botany and geology, chemistry and physics—having been not many years earlier separated from it. The teaching staff consisted of a single full professor—the Breck chair had yet to be established—an assistant professor, and two 'lecturers.' My grandfather became one of the lecturers.

I find difficulty in picturing him as he would have looked then. He lived so many years as an old man that childhood impressions I might have of 'Grandfather' when he was not yet really old are overlaid by later ones. When I try to visualize him at thirty or forty I have to help me no more than a little packet of old photographs. I have seen only one that shows the young lecturer. This is a group picture of the college faculty taken what would have been the first year he was a member of it. Many of the seventy-odd individual faces, though in a twelve-by-fifteen print necessarily small, come quite clear under a magnifying glass. Unfortunately my grandfather chose the moment of exposure to move his head.

A few later snapshots were preserved, most of them made at the shore at Old Harbor. They are undated—one shows him wearing a bathing suit whose cut suggests the middle 1890's—but in all except the bathing-suit picture, where a floppy hat deeply shades his eyes and nose, he is in a group of people—Old Harbor summer neighbors, or family connections (his wife, Ishbel, my maternal grandmother and also a Pierce—making my mother and father third cousins—a niece of President Seth Pierce of the college, President Abernethy's predecessor; his children—my mother, Nancy, and her brother, my Uncle Timothy—and older relatives now not possible for me to place or identify). They picnic on the bluffs, they play battledore and shuttlecock or croquet, they walk in a line on the beach, and my grandfather seems always to be caught looking away, turned around, or half concealed by some of the others. The earliest perfectly clear picture I have found was leafed in as frontispiece to an article of his in a 1907 number of the *American Psychologist*, and obviously the almost cataleptic staring stiffness common in commercial studio portraits of the time is much distorting it.

You are shown a high forehead, a high starched collar, and a curved thick roll of short mustache. While definition is sharp, an ill-chosen camera angle results in what I can feel sure is a loss of actual likeness, since the face remains still instantly identifiable as the Cuthbertson face—that is, a face distinguished by certain features descending in a family, as sometimes they do, generation after generation. His mother's father had them, though in the college library portrait of Caleb Cuthbertson they are half hidden by a voluminous chestnut beard. My mother had them. They bypassed me, Worthington genes, or perhaps, more probably, compounded Pierce ones, prevailing, but a strong suggestion of them reappears in my daughter, Elaine. With the women, no doubt because of normally slighter, more delicate feminine bone structure behind them, they are usually features of winning attractiveness. Only as rendered in that magazine photograph of Professor Dodd do they have a faintly foxy look—just a hint of the shallowly inquisitive, the craftily devious.

Whether or not the picture tells you anything true about my grandfather's temperament or nature, the frontispiece picture's presence in a learned periodical does tell you that he had not been backward in making himself a contributor to such periodicals, or in engaging in projects of research—activities President Abernethy, with his anxiety to start improving the college's academic 'image,' might be expected to applaud, but Professor Dodd's detractors had opinions there, too. Both his writings and his projects, they insisted, brought the college not repute but ridicule. One of his projects I clearly remember. I would then have been little more than a child, and though I could not now say why, I felt, I recall, the liveliest interest.

This particular project had to do with sleep, or, more exactly, possible effects of prolonged sleeplessness on mental and physical processes. My grandfather assembled a group of undergraduate volunteers (if the term applies to young men who were to receive for their services one hundred dollars each, a large sum in those days and paid, of course, out of the Professor's own funds). They agreed to allow themselves to be prevented from sleeping for as long as possible. They were to undergo a series of tests first administered after a normal night's sleep and then repeated when they had been awake for eighteen, for twenty-four, for thirty hours, and so on as long as any of them could be kept awake.

Predictably, through its 'human guinea pig' aspects, the project when announced got the college and Professor Dodd newspaper space, but serious scientists seemed agreed in making little of the experiment's possible value even if (as they said was not the case) proper controls and monitoring had been provided to assure findings of specific significance. As it was to happen, there were no findings of any kind, because the college Medical Director intervened. Since some of the tests involved use of gymnastic apparatus, the volunteers were quartered in the college gymnasium's wrestling room. (That no one felt able to refuse Professor Dodd the use of college facilities sheds, I think, interesting light on powers of a Faculty Row professor.) Into this room shortly before the twenty-four-hour tests were scheduled marched the Medical Director—his M.D. was impeccable—escorting a deputy sheriff. The sheriff produced a court order, issuing on the Medical Director's representation that it was not known, and certainly not by 'Doctor' Dodd, that damage to brain cells as grave as that resulting from a restricted oxygen supply might not be caused by sleeplessness designedly protracted, and enjoining him from proceeding with his project. The result was even more newspaper publicity for the college, but not of a kind to please President Abernethy.

In the matter of 'publication' Professor Dodd, a rapid and, also according to his detractors, unclear and dully prolix writer, was early turning out learned articles with all the frequency and regularity anyone could ask. (Since his contributions seem to have met with ready acceptance, it is possible they had more merit of one kind or another than his enemies cared to admit.) A psychologist in those days was generally a philosopher, too, or perhaps first a philosopher, and it was my grandfather's philosophical papers that were the preferred target of the detractors. They charged him with being a positivist one moment and a phenomenalist the next. His views were said (and proved) to be now monistic and now dualistic. They assailed him for writing as an associationist some of the time and as a non-associationist some of the time. They reproached him for seeming either unaware of or undisturbed by any paradoxical contradictions a system of pluralism plus pragmatism plus radical empiricism necessarily produced.

If most of this could also be said, and I am assured by men of learning more than mine that it can, of my grandfather's so highly distinguished philosopher-psychologist contemporary William James, what was offered in defense of James—he was dedicated to 'heuristic' principles; his was the Socratic aim of inciting pupils to think things out for themselves—might, I suppose, be offered in defense of my grandfather. If I seem doubtful, I'm afraid it's because in reading some of those long-ago published pieces of his—my work has trained or accustomed me to read with patience where most people wouldn't—I see in them, while not a qualified judge of their content, signs of what I *am* qualified to judge, since equivalents of it turn up in our business research. My grandfather's inconsistencies have to me a look of being due more to his forgetting what he said elsewhere than to any considered conviction that thesis and antithesis should be kept confronting each other.

Though regular acceptance for publication of my grandfather's work might be proof that it wasn't as stupid and empty as those hostile to him held it to be, they were not wrong in pointing out, as they constantly did, that there was no evidence of his making through his writings his professional mark as pace-setting thinker or accepted authority. Publishers didn't compete to commission him to do definitive books for them. Learned societies of which he was a member exhibited anything but eagerness to bestow on him that recognition whose solid form is office, honors, and awards. Clearly Professor Dodd hadn't arrived, and, moreover, he didn't even look like a rising or coming man.

This was the state of my grandfather's professional fortunes and reputation at mid-career, and chances of a change at that, it would then seem, late date looked poor. The attention he was about to attract must have been the last thing anyone, himself included, would foresee or expect. The way it happened illustrates, I think nicely, what chance may do in our affairs to change without notice that which at any given moment we see as 'the chances.' The mid-career estimate of the chances of a change rested evidently on the assumption that only new, original, preferably massive work of Professor Dodd's own could bring change. Overlooked are possibilities that might lie in developments analogous to what the stock market knows as Special Situations. Here the special situation was the controversy then commencing over theories of Sigmund Freud—what I spoke of when I told of my looking uneasily at his 'memoirs' the night my grandfather fell asleep.

Few workers in the field of psychology were inclined to be receptive to theories so startling and often so altogether inconsonant with received dogma of the day. Nevertheless, by their work's very nature their minds were generally kept open. To most of them, rather than flat rejection, the right course would normally seem one of judgment reserved until the presented propositions were gone into further and evidence that might support them more fully examined. Just because this was the course generally taken at the time, there were those to suggest that Professor Dodd in acting otherwise acted as an opportunist, cannily and from some standpoints a trifle unscrupulously, speeding to turn reserved judgment's juncture to his own account. I feel reasonably certain that there was in fact nothing canny about it. My grandfather blundered, speedily, to be sure, but blindly, into his unanticipated prominence.

Be that as it may, while others hesitated—many perhaps with the creditable wish to give new doctrines a fair hearing, to wait before judging until something closer to the whole corpus of the work became available; some perhaps just playing it safe, waiting to see which way the cat jumped —my grandfather didn't hesitate. He seems to have had a fair amount of German, and in his manuscript memoirs you gather (though he doesn't say so outright) that already read 'in the original' was a great amount of material before first articles—short, introductory in character, hardly more than progress reports on European acceptance or non-acceptance in the past decade of the sketchily summarized theories—appeared in English here.

I must doubt that he knew when he entered on his quick rebuttal quite as much as he later implies he knew about the quarrels and schisms (indeed, not all of them had yet occurred) involving Jung, Adler, Stekel, Rank, Reich, or Lou Andreas-Salome's idolatrous practices, or Georg Groddeck's dubious projections on the psychosomatic origin of organic disease. I think he may quite innocently have later confused what he knew at first with what was dug up at following stages of the controversy when he needed to defend his position. Still, in his first article he comments on Freud's relationship with Wilhelm Fliess, the eccentric numerologist, and a footnote seems to prove that he had seen Fliess's 1897 monograph on (the note takes care to leave it untranslated) *Die Beziehungen zwischen Nase und Weibliche Geschlechtorganen*. This certainly does suggest that Professor Dodd actually had read some of the German material and so when he took his pen in hand was better prepared than many of his fellow pundits to deal with the palpable errors of a system alien and in the eyes of those days often flagrantly obscene. (My grandfather's first paper speaks of 'false emphases of fact and non sequiturs in logic.' It is full of phrases like: 'He misconceives the role and underrates the importance of . . .' and '. . . not much critical force is found in these conclusions. . . .')

The sensation, at least in that self-contained little specialists' world for which he wrote, was immediate. I think one may safely guess that a good many of his readers, though not themselves ready to venture pronouncements on theories still undigested and evidence far from all in, had anxious hopes that Dodd was right. Digested or undigested, the new theories threatened what for many men was work of a lifetime. Freud's coming to prevail, even if only in principle, must force a general discard of earlier ideas and consequent discrediting to some degree of those who held and taught them.

(I have reflected with interest that an upset of this kind would be seen in physics when the theory of quantum mechanics was given its presently accepted form and Max Planck's earlier uncertainty relation—no connection with my own uncertainty principle—was developed by Heisenberg and Niels Bohr in dispute with Einstein, who remained dubious of anything not 'deterministic.' The difference in their differing was that no one had vested interest in established error. So-called 'classical physics' rested classically, impersonally, on proofs agreed by all, in the state of knowledge of the times, to be conclusive. New proposals were subject to challenge when proposed, but only until the truth of them came to be adequately established, and there could be no serious dispute, since free and open scientific demonstration was required, about what constituted adequate establishment.)

Such hope, such anxiety-ridden concern, of the possibly-to-be-discredited in a 'science' so uncertain and inexact as psychology guaranteed my grandfather's rapidly turned-out statements of objection to novel theory eager readings, readings more sympathetic and far more respectful than any past work of his had ever been given. Professor Dodd was the faithful champion of the *status quo*. At first alarm, he snatched weapons from the wall. Intrepid, he sallied forth to mount and maintain on behalf of conservatives just that all-out attack which is a threatened position's best defense. The wishful glad word was repeatedly given and quickly passed along: *Don't miss Dodd in . . .* (whatever learned journal was printing him that month). *He utterly demolishes . . .* (whoever had in some previous number ventured a defense of the theories). *He doesn't leave Freud a leg to stand on. . . .*

For a while those who took care not to miss Dodd might warm with the comfortable feeling the question was settled once and for all and so hold high the man who did the settling. It was, I'm sure, a trying time for President Abernethy and the others whose serious consensus had been that for the good of the college, of the college's academic good name, my grandfather ought to be got rid of. The attention now given him was different indeed from the occasional notice, mostly in the form of confutations and charges of muddleheadedness, brought him by his philosophical papers, or from newspaper publicity gained by 'research' like that sleep project—not to mention later animal experimentation, in some of which, using a device of striking resemblance to the later notorious Noble-Collip drum, he set about inducing nervous breakdowns in laboratory cats and dogs; and of course soon had 'animal-welfare leagues' putting out press releases to denounce the college. Here he was making his name (and academic affiliation) known, and as yet almost nowhere unfavorably known, to every university psychology department and to practically every individual psychologist of standing in the country. The plight of Professor Dodd's habitual detractors will be apparent. I think it may have been a little like that of those laboratory animals when my grandfather was busy with his experiments aimed at determining scientifically how best to drive them crazy.

One immediate result seems to have been a truce. President Abernethy's plans to oust Professor Dodd were shelved in short order. There was no real peacemaking and no evidence that A. A. liked him any better than before. True, Dodd was doing for the college's 'image' just the kind of thing the President wanted done, and he wouldn't cut off his nose to spite his face, yet it was surely a sore trial to have Dodd the one to be doing it. When winds of change in psychology's intellectual climate, bringing signs that anti-Freudians had stopped having things all their way, began to rise, I suspect President Abernethy, cost though it might the college's brief gain in reputation, was joyful. What, with passage of time, the signs were showing was that despite hopings, despite anxiety-ridden wishings, the issue hadn't been once and for all settled, that what Freudianism took from Dodd hadn't been its quietus, that Freud, though the future would find out serious errors and lapses in his theory, retained plenty of legs to stand on.

Material for which the equitable (or cautious) reservers of judgment were waiting had come to be in good supply. The extensive study of principle and practice that translation made possible was soon posing grave questions of whether the side on which Professor Dodd had so unhesitatingly put himself, and even done something like direct and head, was not going to prove the wrong, the losing, side. Another year or so and this became not possibility but certainty. My grandfather's positions were being rendered untenable and must presently look ridiculous.

He seemed undisturbed. He gave not an inch. The id-ego-superego topography of the mind was nonsense. The theory of libido development, with its oral, anal, urethral, or phallic levels, was scatological claptrap. The proposed interpretation of dreams was pornographic idiocy. Unfortunately those who at first applauded and supported such typical contentions of his were more and more of them defecting. More and more of them felt compelled to join in a mass capitulation, to concede the probable basic truth of the upsetting propositions, dissenting only on detail. A few more years and Professor Dodd stood virtually alone. Moving ahead, psychology as a science was leaving him behind, and his consistency in rejecting all new principles must come to mean a steadily increasing ignorance, by accepted standards, of his subject. The learned periodicals started finding his contributions unacceptable. In the learned societies he was disregarded or dismissed as a preposterous old numskull.

As I've said, I think President Abernethy found the fairly quick decline and fall most gratifying, while at the same time his earlier animosity may have been aggravated by his own mistake in ever letting himself be, as it now seemed, deceived into the truce, and by his current finding that what he took, if against his will, for service Professor Dodd was doing the college had turned into grievous, intolerable disservice. He renewed his efforts to pluck the thorn from his side. President Abernethy was by then a dying man and known to be. Without doubt it was their so knowing that brought a necessary number of trustees, compunctious, to grant what they could see as close to a dying wish. Since Professor Dodd still flatly refused to resign, they took steps in their corporate power to superannuate him. Their deed of grace may have helped President Abernethy, dying soon after, to die happier.

When these concluding unhandsome episodes in my grandfather's active professional career are passed in review, to feel at least a little sorry for him seems reasonable, natural. Here surely are hard lines; and surely they would be made no less so by the cutting off of relative prominence's short hour—at long last a table prepared in the presence of his enemies; but hardly has he seated himself when it disintegrates and is whisked away. He is back down again while the enemies, more contumelious than ever, are up—prepared, eager, and before long able to finish him off. It is a relief to me to feel as sure as I do that sorrowings for him would be superfluous.

I see now that my grandfather lived the life—and the fact's instruction about our human condition is what leads me to treat of him at length—of that rare happy man who can't see error in himself. The state must be distinguished from the deceiving of yourself by saying you have no sin, or from any regarding of yourself as morally or ethically superior. My grandfather would have owned at once to numerous daily-life faults of omission or commission—but in what he *did*, not in what he *thought*. This made him proof, as well as against criticism of his work, against slights, rebuffs, and blows to self-esteem. Like another man, he might be angered by them, but, unlike most men, he was not hurt by them. To be hurt I judge you must (like most men) harbor in your breast a traitor-doubt, a live and present secret fear that the affronts offered you or the injuries done you *could* be condign, only your all too just deserts.

But, one may ask, can hide and heart of such proof actually be in human nature? Is it ever in human nature not to notice that other names are sounded more than yours, that honors awards and offices shower on others, but not on you? And can it be ever in human nature not, sore tried, to mind? Considering myself, I would say it cannot—that is, not in my human nature—but considering my grandfather, I believe it could be—was—in his. The disposition or temperament that prevented him from seeing error in him-

self, that kept him satisfied with his own perfect rightness (not righteousness), could also prevent him from ever seeing himself as someone else
might see him. Unless you know degrees of self-dissatisfaction, wishing
you like to one more rich in hope, featured like him, like him with friends
possessed, desiring this man's art or that man's scope, how can you feel
mortified or humiliated? You may take a moment's umbrage at success of
others, resent their having it, but you do so with no wasting anguish of envy
or consuming pang of jealousy. Though you may crave such success for
yourself, at bottom you would prefer being yourself as you are and unsuccessful to being successful and not yourself as you are.

Such a special variant in my grandfather's human nature is the sort of
thing I find, growing older, so instructive, and it was well displayed when,
having been opened, the Freudian controversy quite soon grew ugly. On
bare cause-and-effect grounds Professor Dodd may fairly be held instru-
mental in making one of the meaner uglinesses an issue and therefore fairly
charged with disgraceful conduct. I am inclined to exonerate him. Just as
I think he never perceived and so couldn't have moved to grasp at possible
personal opportunity in the impending dispute, he never, I think, intended
to make the ugly issue an issue, never had the faintest idea he was going to
raise an issue—again, planless and imperceptive, he simply blundered into
something, something it seems to me also usefully instructive in the ways
of our human nature.

What he blundered into was this. Though professing no religion, the
early Freudians, like Freud himself, were almost to a man of Jewish extraction. In the course of his first paper on the subject my grandfather made
mention of the fact. His mention was no more than passing and, disinterestedly read, seems difficult to take for an expression of anti-Semitism.
I'm sure he intended none, and the possibility of its being so taken never,
I imagine, crossed his mind. His comment was to the effect that though this
man Freud affected to regard religious belief as a father-image delusion, it
might perhaps be of some interest to observe how distinctively Jewish, how
much in keeping with the historical genius of Jewish religious thought—
rapt, prophetic, poetically visionary—a great deal of the teaching really
was. *Or,* my grandfather then appended (he was too fond of banal tags in
other tongues), *plus ça change, plus c'est la même chose?*

In the phrasing sounds a clear note of condescension, and that of course
would be intentional. The faint-smile-of-superiority approach is the most
used gambit in learned disagreement, so much a part of standard operating
procedure that one doesn't expect it to provoke anything more than a coun-
tering in kind. When, the article having come out, my grandfather was
shown a first little spate of letters to the editor excitedly and venomously
attacking him, he was doubtless taken aback. As is customary in such snip-
ing, the letter writers took every care not to reveal (and thus vitiate charges

brought by making clear the real motive in bringing them) what the actual provocation was, and so, to begin with, the very evident *Hass* would be all the more bewildering, confined as you found it to angry general assertions that in his piece Professor Dodd was a witless disgrace to the profession; he was a knave, an idiot, a liar, an execrable prose stylist, and totally unqualified to have an opinion about anything.

Maybe because my own line of work can involve certain disingenuous practices, I find, I confess, diatribes like these of special interest. Their methodology is by and large one of misrepresentation, and for this purpose a good deal of recourse is had to quotings out of context—often most ingenious; for while rancor may weaken general judgment, it frequently sharpens craft, gives deviousness inspiration. Wonderful to observe are the twists of sense and even total reversals of meaning to be effected in many written lines simply through deleting some that precede and some that follow; or through artful ellipses indicated by a set of points to suggest, all innocence, that phrases or sentences omitted hadn't been relevant. When excerpts from pieces published by my grandfather were subjected to nice work of this kind I think no one reading the results would deny that as a writer he comes out sounding less than literate, and as a thinker a perfect fool.

Few of us are imaginative enough to recognize and allow for the power or the prevalence of feelings with which we ourselves never had personal experience, and this might be particularly true of my grandfather. Temperamentally proof against the criticism, the slights, the rebuffs by which the run of men are hurt, he could not know what being hurt that way was like. It followed that he would not, by looking in himself, be able to anticipate how those who were hurt might act. Specifically he could know nothing about the feelings of people against whom forms of 'bias' are or have been shown. If he observed, as soon he must have, that Freudians so virulently assailing him mostly bore Jewish names, I think he might (at least at first) in his obtuseness of unknowing still not see it as signifying anything in particular—after all, just as he noted, Freudians of the time were generally Jewish.

Quite unconscious of having written anything derogatory about their 'religion,' or of Jews as a race, he could miss the meaning of venom that said so clearly here was no technical argument over disputed psychological hypotheses. Even after he had finally been stung into turning on 'those Jews' I'm sure he remained baffled, unable as ever to understand that while he might have said nothing intended to be, or by any common consent likely to be held to be, offensive he had assigned them by implication at least a difference, indicated that he thought of them as another breed, not like himself and his fellow gentiles. He touches a very sore spot—touching there, the mildest ironic turn of phrase becomes a vicious sneer. He does a cruel despite, and because not to be replied to, one that may gall more than any amount of outright abuse or direct traducement.

That temperament that made my grandfather invulnerable to the hurts other men may feel left him slower to anger than some men, and his anger when belatedly stirred would be always a sort of ire of indignation, not the spitting rage, the furibund anger of the injured, exhibited by those attacking him. Unfortunately the one is no prettier than the other, even though the 'ire' may take somewhat more account of reason. Asking himself if he did right to be angry, my grandfather easily made himself a demonstration that yes, he did. Regard the written, the printed record! Hating him without a cause, most evident villains were unprovokedly slandering, abusing, and wantonly misrepresenting him.

Very well, he would pay them back in their own coin. He, too, distilled his decoction of spleen. His attackers, their science fake, their doctrine filthy rubbish, were themselves most palpable knaves, idiots, liars, wretchedly bad writers, and now, be it noted, also all *Jews*. In short, as the attackers saw it he had been forced by them into the open, driven to disclose his animating bias, and (leaving aside the fact of possible relevance that their own rancor and venom had been to blame for his eventual returning of it) I can't doubt they were here quite right. Given my grandfather's upbringing, at least a degree of anti-Semitism would almost have to be bred into him. When he was a boy such gentile bons mots as *How odd of God to choose the Jews* bespoke a settled social attitude by which he could scarcely go unaffected. Soon after he became a professor not a few college communities were beginning to stir apprehensively—*look what's happening at Columbia; look what's happened at Pennsylvania*; or, as one educator of the day, pettish, summed it up: *Are we to sit still and have our campus overrun with Ikeys and Jakeys?*

In the question one may find a touch of wry humor. With that sort of objector to his presence the luckless Jewish youth seemingly couldn't win. When, as the case came to be, he was more often than not Sidney, or Stanley, or Irving, or Norman, why what vulgar cheek for him to take names to which his people had no historical title. Retaining concepts early and naturally given a cast of prejudice by such environmental constant pressure of suggestion, Professor Dodd, though most of the time without occasion for antipathetic feeling, and honestly unconscious of it, must nevertheless have 'bias' lying latent in him, ready for rousing. Vilely (he thinks) abused, personally provoked, he will find himself well prepared, really preconditioned, to regard the intemperate attacks on him as ample demonstration that 'those Jews' richly deserved to have said against them everything that their persecutors had in malice been long saying against them.

One needs to remember that this engagement of anger and injury never came to more than a spiteful fracas in a very small teapot. The general public heard nothing. The learned world was little interested (solid scholarship did and does look askance at such stuff), and even among psychologists hardly a dozen became directly involved. The rest, if not all indifferent, remained just spectators and hadn't in fact much to see, because the learned periodicals involved were not yet prepared to help heat up the controversy to the point where subscriptions might be canceled. A few of the first vituperative letters of protest (higher notes of teeth gnashing and chattering with rage by gingerly abridgement left out) were printed, and so were some short disagreeing articles in language fairly moderate (*Apparently untrained in scientific method Professor Dodd shows himself altogether incapable of grasping fundamental principles or comprehending the importance of* . . .).

Only in the little liberal subsidized 'journals of opinion' (where such projects as exposing a benighted, backward, narrow-minded, ignorant, and, here for the first time openly so called, anti-Semitic reactionary of a college professor would always be undertaken with eagerness) did my grandfather's iniquities get treatment at real length. In the two pieces that I have seen, the writers took the same line of gravest alarm. Make no mistake, here was a crisis in higher education. If any Professor Dodd were to be allowed the status of responsible teacher, the integrity of all learning stood to collapse. Fatal lowering of every critical and intellectual standard must follow. These attacks, with their avowed aim and open hope of destroying his reputation, perhaps excusably heightened that ire of my grandfather's; but in fact such journals had then as now insignificant paid circulation and, outside their own editors and contributors, very few readers. In law Professor Dodd would have been hard put (he thought of bringing suit) to demonstrate the smallest actionable damage done him.

With the airing of these 'liberal' views, in manner so sententious, in matter so crooked, the little altercation attained its piffling apogee and promptly petered out. Since Professor Dodd would very soon start looking like the loser, supporters who might have kept his side alive slipped away, while the other side, looking, festive, like the winner, could unwind a little, return to regular work and let the issue resolve itself. Perhaps because he was no longer winning, because he hadn't success's incentives, my grandfather, once his brief final burst of annoyance over the 'journal of opinion' pieces passed, visibly lost interest altogether. He was beginning to occupy himself with questions of extrasensory perception (his detractors, I am sure, must have said: *He* would!) and had presently turned his whole attention to the laborious devising of complicated tests by which he expected to prove powers of the kind existed. With what I'm afraid seems like intellectual frivolity, he forgot about Freudianism. For him the war was ended.

That his forgetting about the matter didn't end the war for everyone will be no surprise to students of human nature. Anger my grandfather showed was surface anger that flash-burned, an ingenuous indignation at 'unjust' misrepresentations (could he in common sense imagine attackers moved as the Freudians and liberals have been moved were going to be 'just'?). Such angers can quickly spend. The festering deep-down anger of the wounded, of people hit where they live, spends slowly—or maybe never. Several of his enemies are found over a surprisingly long period working into almost everything they wrote, no matter what the subject, some sneer or denigration to carry on a sort of *Dodd-delendus-est* vendetta.

Presumably they relieved their feelings, but they wasted their time. They had no chance of disturbing or distressing my grandfather. He had ceased to read the periodicals for which they wrote, and I only know of the persevered-in references bcause the college librarian showed, as curiosities, a few of them to my father, by then the college's president. He would say nothing to his father-in-law. My grandfather's much later reverting to the controversy when composing his proposed memoirs might suggest that he, too, was unforgiving, nursed an ancient grudge. I don't think so. Off (at the time) in pastures new of ESP, busy with his lively and, I'm afraid, lightweight work, he wouldn't be giving the stale quarrel a moment's thought.

In those notes on my grandfather and his 'life and times' I will be seen to have assembled for the most part my own thoughts about him and them. I did not intend to attempt a biographical sketch. What I make of my memories of him and of what at one time or another happened to him I have been at pains to set down as possibly pertinent to what I am undertaking to tell about my own life and times. When the a priori forms imposed by my particular mind on data supplied to it have processed such memories, here is how he looks. My hope of not missing useful hints afforded by an example so striking of the vicissitudes of as-luck-would-have-it will be plain, and slantings of such interest must make what I select to note down say quite as much about me, about the who-says-so of my recount, as about E. Cuthbertson Dodd, the late renowned Cubby. Though at first glance he and I may look unlike, I must see the look could be misleading.

We are unlike in that where his *tempera* never fails to keep him equipped with assurance's armor of proof, my own leaves me open to doubt, to that principle of uncertainty's penetrations, to carpings of self-criticism. He was a remarkably impractical professor, of judgment unsound more often than not, unacquainted with business; while I am notable for practicality, of soundest business judgment, and the well-known sagacious head of HW Associates. He was cloistered in a college all his life; in my work I range far and wide in a wide world if anything too much with me. Cloistered or not, my grandfather was for years involved in or made the subject of continual quarreling. My business situation allows me to seek peace and ensue it. In my work I am not called upon to be for or against things. I need neither challenge nor contend with anyone. Disinterestedness and impartiality are natural part and parcel of service my people and I offer.

It is when I ponder some of the known-only-to-me devices and desires of my heart that I can't but see a little of my grandfather in me. Reviewing certain things (again, known only to me) that at one time or another have happened to me I perceive certain parallels. We neither of us ever suffered real want. Nothing can be more critical or perhaps crucial in the conditioning of a man's mind than whether or not he has known sick anxiety about where the money's coming from. Here is a fence and I am with my grandfather on one side of it, all poor people on the other (even if they were only on it as boys, poor boys, and later perhaps became far richer than those on our side of the fence had been or ever could be). Closely tied are the mind-conditioning effects of never having been in any social sense what is today called 'underprivileged.' At many junctures both he and I will want understanding. Subjected to something like the Freudian attack on him (I never was), I would be apt to see no better than he saw what I had 'done' to make the attackers so devoutly hope I would drop dead, and would not find any more explicable the honest belief of the haters (like Goethe they can promise to be sincere, but not impartial) that all dishonesties they published about him were honest, their criticism of name-calling sound, just, and reasonable. Both of us exhibit this same grave defect in comprehension.

Both of us—though he only in his old age and I quite young—came to enjoy essentially unmerited high reputation and regard. We were not born with them; we did not achieve them as clear consequence of our own efforts; we had them thrust upon us. The matter of unlike temperament may now re-enter. My grandfather, I am certain, felt no qualm or question, accepted the unmerited with easy mind—and would I were like him there! Come now to be known well to me, my character is not one I can admire; yet a man of piety has written that we should ever strive to be in charity with ourselves as well as with our neighbors.

On Narrative
[from *Morning Noon and Night*]

That question of causal materiality (or immateriality) presses on me as I come to conclude, much dissatisfied with it, my attempt to put together a meaningful account of my life—how I have drawn breath and walked the earth. Reviewing my passages of writing I am obliged to see I offer little more than a disordered compilation of rough notes, exhibiting frustration rather than accomplished purpose. Perhaps my mistake was in choosing to avoid consecutive narration. I made the choice because I for long have felt that setting out courses of events in the natural, seemingly straightforward way can, oddly enough, distort truth and obscure meaning, at least in the sense of limiting or lessening for a reader his possible new acquist of true experience, since he will not have been told beforehand what he has to know if he is to grasp the real significance in many reported happenings. By imposing an arbitrary order on experience's actual disorder and inconsecutiveness, the consecutive narrative too often sounds that note of falsity, of unpersuasiveness, found in statements or confessions recorded by police stenographers. Even if clearly true transcripts, read or heard they are apt to disturb you with a doubt that it could have been as simple as all that, with a question whether a calculated arrangement, a design of intention (and for what conceivable end but to make a worse appear a better reason?), isn't being imposed on the until now unarranged or designless. Some *post-hoc-propter-hoc* positing, or at least an appearance of it, is hard to exclude—that is, the progressive disclosure of happenings by its mechanical regularity inclines you to presuppose what is not necessarily so, to prevent your seeing where one thing, though it may have followed another, in truth by no means followed as a result.

If the state of today's letters is any indication, I must judge that what to do about such problems of telling the truth are of sorest perplexity to every writer whose serious aim is a just representation of life and people (as contrasted with those who do not have this aim, but, as I was so naïvely disturbed to find when young, use 'creative writing' as a stalking-horse to hide the hard sell of ideas or theories they are out to tout, and who have no truth problem because truth is for them irrelevant). The writers for whom truth has relevance, who feel a need in their writing for what an early novelist called "very minute fidelity," must, I imagine, often confront in themselves today that predicament described in *Tamburlaine the Great*. No matter how hard or ingeniously they work, no matter how (partly) successful their achievement in employing words, they will have still hovering in their restless heads that one thought, one grace, one wonder at the least which into words no virtue can digest.

We may see with sympathy the different mind-taxing (to reader usually as well as writer) experimental efforts undertaken by heads thus troubled to accomplish a digestion, to compel words to convey an extra wished-for *something*; but when you examine with any care their toil's final fruit I think you can't but conclude, and in every case, that means aren't to be found to do what isn't to be done; and furthermore, what may have been a compositional labor of Hercules (. . . *in the childman weary, the manchild in the womb*) will, the sad fact is, simply come out conveying less (perhaps because never having much) meaning, not more; prove poorer, not richer, means of communicating. Ought we to learn from this that the one best form a relation of events can take begins at a plain beginning and, dogged and simple, plainly pushes on (*I was born in the year 1632, in the city of York, of a good family though not of that country, my father being a foreigner of Bremen . . .*), and this is the way we write our books; and that is that; and that will be all? Unfortunately for the cause of reasonableness, writers of forceful imagination, generally perverse and foolish, are seldom willing to settle for it.

Thus, I apologize for my apology's method (though not meaning to count myself a creative writer or among the imaginatively forceful) as well as for the incompleteness of its content. I see incompleteness as more than likely connected with the problem of causal materiality that I spoke of as pressing me. Though on the record I find much of my attention turned to large affairs in which the part I take is important, even leading, I must observe that I have been usually caused more and deeper concern by trivialities. Watching my stage plays of memory I must note that measured by the minute or hour the greater part of my mind's time is again and again given to nothing of more consequence than businesses like the marital misadventures of that (as she might put it) incorrigible divorcée my daughter.

In telling of my life I note that what I find myself most inclined to recount are undistinguished events, some puerile experience like my scared seduction by a married woman vexed with her unfaithful husband, or shabby later adult ones like my mere vagrant looseness of appetite making me exact from my secretary the carnal connection I know she will let me have with her (and so leading me to the more serious mischief of the remorseful reparation—it amounted to that—of insisting on marrying her when I became free to, and the bad end this would have). I seem to have felt a need (exculpatory?) to report musings on longevity and reputation occasioned by the career of Cubby, my senior-citizen grandfather, the All-American (almost) good gray professor. I seem to have wanted to say a lot (again exculpatory?) on my moments of discomfort in the presence of phoniness, whether that of liberal intellectual pretenders, the social-activist fake or half-writers of my youth, or that of aspects of my later business which if not plain fraud or sham are certainly legerdemain and pretty much of a piece with liberal intellectual deceit and hocus-pocus. It is a discomfort, I have to suspect, that can only be caused by secret knowledge of potential phoniness of one's own.

What I have been at, plain to see, is a work of unburdening myself, and those who patiently attend aren't going to learn much except what my burdens are or have been. (When Henry Thoreau declares most men lead lives of quiet desperation, you learn no more than what the life of Henry Thoreau was like.) My creative effort is hardly one to serve the high end that has been defined as enriching the reader's soul and enlarging his personality; I can hope to work no catharsis of pity and terror. I will try to excuse and console myself with the so-evident common truth that bowels unbound by such catharsis seem very apt to be those that reason and good sense were binding, and a diarrhea of factitious feeling, a frequency and looseness of maudlin sentiment (*acervatim*), can all too regularly result. Horrid truths and violent images may jolt you into 'awareness'? But what awareness? Usually, I think, an awareness of, a momentary belief in, the *thing that is not*. In gained awarenesses of the *thing that is*, I point out to myself the significance of the trivial. Of necessity the useful truths of this life are trivial; they are helpful hints when met with quandaries of ordinary existence. Any truth that purports to be great by so purporting must make itself an untruth, will have only the stopgap usefulness the earnestly told lie may sometimes have. (I think of that cryptoskepticism of my father's.) Nothing, I read, can exceed the vanity of our existence but the folly of our pursuits. I don't know about that. I believe the other way around is better.

So morning has been, noon has been, and, if not quite night, it is now evening. I see some twilight scenes. In my HW Associates' generous-sized gracious room selected business is deferentially brought to the old man (he does not feel as old as they show him he looks to them when they come bearing the business in), every care taken not to excite or overtire him. I find a boyish-faced Carl Mabon—yes, Mark Mabon's son—with all respect but also with great patience explaining to me a long company prospectus he feels I might have trouble understanding. In the so-called Meeting Room of Old College Hall the trustees' clerk pronounces: *Henry Dodd Worthington?* I answer in ancient prescribed form: *Adsum;* and presently I am turning my sagacious mind to such business as whether parietal rules ought to allow girls to be entertained in dormitory rooms until 1:00 A.M. instead of merely until twelve midnight. (Like, I'm sure, a number of the graying or balding men around our polished oval table, I am privately, at bottom, dumbfounded. Why should girls ever be there at all at any time? In my day in Cambridge—and naturally here, too—the undergraduates themselves wouldn't have stood for it. A few might chase tail around town, but to take it to your college room—well, where the hell were you brought up, anyway?) True, I and most of the others weighing with me this grave twelve-or-one point are probably viewing the matter under discussion with a touch of that inappetency I discussed earlier. While none of those present is seventy, I know not one of us is less than fifty.

So things go, and time's processes aren't stopped. Last year they told me, Heraclitus, they told me you were dead—and it was the truth. Apparently Jon LeCato had been working on a brief in his firm's law library. A volume of *Corpus Juris Secundum* and half a dozen bound reports with places marked lay open around him where he sat at a table. Halfway down the sheet of a legal-size pad his unique, very nearly copperplate, script stopped, and the pen was fallen from his fingers. Nothing was disturbed or in disorder, and his secretary at first thought he was asleep. I must suppose that like Mr. Garesche he had a 'condition' which he never mentioned to anyone. He was quite dead.

Bitter news to hear? Bitter tears to shed? I spoke of my having certain thoughts of death while I once waited in the Woodfield Center graveyard. I was not young then, and when I hear this news I am older still, and aging has one perhaps melancholy-to-think-of, yet merciful, easement. The news is not bitter, not shocking, to hear; just sorrowful, saddening—that is the way things are. No, I do not cry. How good, I've grown to see, if everyone you cared for, if he or she is going to predecease you, would have the kindness to wait to die until you are quite old. You'll then hardly mind at all. The sense of loss seems lost; you pass into impersonality, a state of mind queerly (or naturally? *Sans* everything?) like that of an unknowing young child. I keep from my boyhood a figure or image of going to the grave, inexactly remembered, not quite placed. Could it have been the Grand Army funeral of that veteran, my forebear, Henry Worthington? Perched, I believe, on my father's shoulder, I see the marching blue-coated men. I hear the band, a many-pieced military one, precision-paced, rendering in deadmarch time slow, stern, hammered-out strains of the "Battle Hymn of the Republic," steadily proceeding nearer (. . . *His truth is marching on*). And now called down on that last note is the crescendo of drums crashing, a moment of tympanic thunder, before the full brass soars suddenly, thrilling, piercing (*Glory, glory* . . .), and they go by. Popeyed, the child on his perch may take death to be only fine loud ceremony.

I look around at the twilight, and I look back on my life. I see how it consists of a succession of acts or happenings related in that they were done by or happened to me and were little governed by logic or demonstrable cause and effect—not that there can be effects without causes; still, in the order, may be something of the Queen of Hearts' sentence first, verdict afterward. If I have feelings perhaps not consciously known to me of resentment, I have no complaint that I can formulate. Yet I don't doubt, deep down, I harbor a kind of contumacious stubborn persuasion that, given a free hand and almighty means, even with intelligence as limited as mine I could hardly fail to order the order of things better. I can show no reasonable ground for the persuasion. Has that A-1 management consultant I am supposed to be shown himself ever in the management of life competent to make a master plan, to lay out schedules of perspicacious, respect-commanding, brave, and decent measures to shoot life's trouble, fix it, put the business on a sound productive basis? In fact, here at my end I am at my business beginning. In wisdom (I know my old man's lurking principle of uncertainty insinuates the thought; but how to doubt my doubt?) I am no different than when Parker Ilsley took me to his father's Mr. Crane, and I could only pretend that I had some idea of what ought to be done.

When in certain moods I look back I seem to watch myself wandering directionless down these many years in a kind of game or exercise of blind-man's buff—now sightlessly bumping into things, now surprised by sportive unreturnable blows. When in certain moods I look around me, I seem to see current experience as resembling progress of a tourist who revisits relics of the past. I pick with subdued curiosity an aimless way through memory's remains. I investigate fragmentary scattered ruins, eons old, of a lost city of antiquity whose traces extend over a campagna otherwise empty under a clear level vacancy of sunset light.

Like that childishly remembered pound of band music cemetery-bound, the picture can be guessed to take shape from a forgotten actual incident of long ago, a childhood occasion in the course of foreign travel with my parents when on an unidentified day at an unidentified place the little boy finds himself wandering out beneath evening skies to gaze at scattered classical ruins which are the local sights—temple columns in twos or threes still loftily upright, damaged capitals held high, while marble drums of others fallen apart lie around them sunk in earth, half concealed by bush and grass. He looks down curving wide ranges of shattered stone steps while he is informed that here had once been a theater. At a distance he can see the tall line of a dozen or more aqueduct arches, commencing suddenly, suddenly ending; coming now from nowhere, now going nowhere. Thin final sunlight of a sort sometimes seen in Canaletto paintings gilds gently enigmatic ancient stone, sere swards of coarse modern grass, and occasional broken hunched old trees. A calling or twittering of skylarks or other birds has ceased; the immense twilight silence settles, and the child must soon be taken away to bed. Yes; good night, good night. Good night, any surviving dear old Carian guests. Good night, ladies. Good night, all.

IX

Foreword to
Roses of Yesterday

Nanae Ito's water colors, so handsomely presented here, must have, I should think, an abashing effect on anyone setting himself to write about old roses. Those illustrated (and a great many others) seem all to possess peculiar qualities of charm that a piece of writing doesn't properly communicate. This is seen in a moment when you look from the lucidity and precision of Dorothy Stemler's descriptive notes (she and the late Will Tillotson worked out phrasings that do as much as careful phrasing can do) to the artist's rendition of the rose described. A writer simply hasn't means adequate to make you see them. Here, to say a picture is worth a thousand words, understates it.

To some degree this may even be true of new roses, though a lot of these seem to me well enough served by any ordinary catalog treatment. In *Modern Roses V*, along with 333 species, 7562 named varieties appear. This is up from 2511 in the original 1930 *Modern Roses I*, and would suggest that during the last 35 years about 500 "new" roses have been introduced. Nobody can have seen them all, and I can have seen no more than a few hundred; but risking the wrath of their doubtless doting originators, and perhaps of the Rose Society, I venture to asseverate (yes; sight unseen) that at least 4900 of them aren't much good (except of course in the sense that any rose is better than no rose).

Zeal of hybridizers working with skill and patience is usually evident and I am all for them. May they work on! Yet I can't but suspect their delicate task often becomes a thing in itself. What absorbs them is manipulating genes to produce "sports" of a kind that the botanist studies with respectful interest. Sometimes such a mutation can indeed amount to an "improvement," but my observation is that rather more often the resulting difference makes for an inferior, not a superior, strain, and so will be at its happiest when measureable only by experts.

I tip my hand. I am not the impartial judge and what biases me must be apparent. Whether or not I can quite make myself believe it, I have become old-time too, of yesterday. Of course I don't see "new" roses as what roses used to be. Let us face it. Long long ago is when, as a child, I was brought up in a garden. The garden included perennial borders with customary plantings and there were many spring bulbs, but roses were my mother's deepest interest. She grew as many as she could. This was no great number for her whole garden had to be contained in a hedged plot about 150 by 50 feet.

The plot was on Staten Island, where development into Staten Island of today was then barely beginning. True, it had already been denominated the Borough of Richmond of "Greater New York," but you saw nothing city-like. Trolleys and the little trains of the Staten Island Rapid Transit Company connected up a dozen or so of what amounted to straggling villages, or at biggest, towns of a few built-up short streets. Around and between them spread wide second-growth woodlands (and, west, great expanses of the flat marshy, empty, "Kills"). Many functioning farms, as they had for a hundred and fifty years, grew vegetables, harvested hay, raised chickens, and maintained small dairy herds.

Not long before, George William Curtis, a resident (his widow still lived not far from us when I was a child) and once regarded as a distinguished man of letters, had been moved to pronounce (I think I have the wording right): "God could have made a more beautiful place than Staten Island, but He never did." Let us allow for a touch of there's-no-place-like-home but many prospects that pleased him were still pleasing, though I must realize now the writing had come to be on the wall.

Our house and garden were in fact proof of this. They occupied acreage of the Henderson Estate. Immediately south of the old stone "manor house" some of it had been subdivided to lay out what was called Saint Austin's Place. Provided was a short double street with succesive narrow oval turf strips in the center. Along flagged sidewalks on either side had been planted Carolina poplars—trashy, messy, short-lived trees, but growing fast to give a good shade. By the time I saw them they were, to a child like me, big—perhaps eight inches in diameter and forty feet high.

The houses erected were from designs by Stanford White. I think he must have had the idea of showing what he could do for the modestly monied (the men of the families who came to live in them were generally, like my father, Manhattan executives but young—rising, in no case top). That ruled out anything grand or big, but I suspect White took it as a challenge. He could have wanted to show lesser architects that even when there was no million dollars to spend *he* could provide houses neither mean nor shoddy, neither ill-planned nor ill-built. When I came to live there, only six had been put up—three east, three west. From their placing I judge the surveyor's plan had twelve lots on each side. This meant that making up the frontages were small open fields growing Indian grass. They were fine places for the children to play.

As nearly as I can calculate, my mother's garden would have been brought into being about 1908. The roses she then planted were mostly hybrid perpetuals (though I distinctly remember a group of the Hybrid Tea Kaiserin Auguste Viktoria. I grow it in my garden today. I can see it may have much to do with my thinking so little of some later hybrid teas). It was my mother's practice to plant together at least three of a kind. This ought of course to be everyone's practice. Dealers should refuse to sell less than three. A single bush, unless in time it can grow very big (and mean-while you wait and wait) will not show off its blooms to best advantage. I know no good reasons why this should be so, but so it is. Of the roses to plant my mother's choice was naturally limited to what nurseries were then offering. One or two—they were not far off, over in New Jersey—had fairly long lists, but few included the truly historic roses Mrs. Stemler speaks of.

I think my mother would have been inclined to buy a number of such roses (if anyone had had them) because, going to a good deal of trouble, she early supplied herself with that Alba, Koenigin von Daenemarck you will admire on page 33. What she put in was either a division or a rooted cutting coming from a bush that grew in a garden in Wolfville, Nova Scotia, when she was a child. The climate there makes for bleakness, and anything that can survive it is no doubt more cherished. Her transplant was most success-ful. Mrs. Stemler describes exactly the way this one (if only one) came to behave in June in our garden. Another such transplant my mother at-tempted proved, to my lasting regret, a failure. Like the Koenigin von Daenemarck it seems to have been from a bush got in England by either her father, or probably, her grandfather. Both were sea captains, and through the 19th century Nova Scotian vessels were sailing to Europe and the West Indies in astonishingly large numbers.

The one that failed was what my mother, with the convincing positive-ness of a child remembering, insisted always had been the true "York and Lancaster"—not any streaked or striped Variegata now often given the name. A profusion of Alba-type blossoms covered it. Some were all white; some a deep shade of red; and some, among mostly white petals threw a number of whole red ones, or among mostly red petals, a number of whole white ones. I wish I could say I had actually seen it.

One item mother picked from her nursery lists were Frau Karl Druschki which (hard to believe now) was really a "new" rose. There was also Gruss an Teplitz, quite "new" too. The books date it 1897. Mrs. Stemler, sharp-eyed in her devoted rose interest, discovered reference to it in a novel of mine, and quotes it in one of her catalogs. If you wonder how such refer-ences may come about, this is how. Other choices of my mother's were La Reine Victoria (page 49), American Beauty (page 51) and Paul Neyron. I may as well admit I long considered this the best rose because there was such a lot of rose in each blossom. We also had Mrs. John Laing which I remember as my mother's favorite. Certainly her half dozen grew for her in a way that produced more blossoms more often than anything else in the garden.

And we had Eglantine bushes, though not in the rose plantings. They were what I have now come to know was the Lord Penzance hybrid, a cross with Harison's Yellow. I suppose the nursery had it because it was "new"— developed in the '90s. Its flatter, nearly beige or tan-colored flowers strike me as a good deal less attractive than those of the natural Eglantine brier that page 23 shows you.

But naturally this wasn't the point. The planting had been planned to go under a side porch. It was surmounted by a screened sleeping porch my mother used. (Indeed a period touch. She was supposed to be of delicate constitution—she many years outlived my hardy and athletic father to die at 78—and physicians then had a notion that outdoor air was strengthening). If rain or even heavy dew wet the dense, crinkled sweetbrier foliage, profusely wafted up was the delicious penetrating fragrance usually described as of apples. That's not quite it; but try calling to mind anything closer.

Of course I realize now that it cannot have been June in those days as much of the time as it seems to have been, and my impression that a tea tray was brought down to the bottom of the garden among the roses every afternoon is mistaken. Still I think it must have been there most nice days, and about quarter past four my mother regularly poured tea for herself and one or two women, neighbors' wives with whom there had come to be no standing, she or they, on formalities of invitation.

I was allowed to be present briefly, and I see no reason to doubt that charms I now find in roses may have an admixture of the charms of small hot-buttered muffins and petits fours. (The plural is inexact. I was given one of each. I was not supposed to do any serious eating between meals).

Long shafts of declining warm sun, the stir of shady air under the little pergola and trellises, the enclosing thickets of well-grown roses in bloom (those like Mrs. John Laing, American Beauty and Paul Neyron were as tall as I then was), the gleam of silver tea things and the rose patterned (of course) Spode cups and muffin plates, the two or three women in their light dresses chatting and resting in ease of friendly familiarity (yet in those days sure to be sitting quite straight) make the picture in my mind. I think then I may very well have imagined that everything was going to be like that all the time always.

My father, I'm afraid, felt no lively interest in gardening. For exercise he liked to go down and play tennis at the old Staten Island Cricket Club, and we had a regular part-time "gardener" (he took care of furnaces in the winter) who did any harder jobs my father might have felt he must help my mother with. However, I do remember my father showed enough interest to prepare a garden plan (he had a gifted amateur's knack for drawing) of some elaborateness. He laid it out on a long piece of parchment thumb-tacked to a strip of heavy matchboard (scale one-half inch to one foot). He sketched on it signs of the zodiac and compass points with cherub heads blowing out wind. Periodically he painstakingly, and I think with enjoyment, lettered in my mother's plantings and replantings.

My one retained picture of my father among the roses shows him on a Sunday morning when he was to usher at church (members of the vestry in pairs took turns). For the purpose he puts on a morning coat and striped trousers. He places on his head a shiny top hat taken from a leather box lined with red silk. Ready to go over to church, he walks down to the end of the garden. Mrs. Stemler notes that his eminent contemporary, Theodore Roosevelt, favored a Duchesse de Brabant for his buttonhole. I think that charming rose (page 47) was too nearly all Tea to grow for my mother. Mr. Roosevelt probably had it from the White House gardens, but not at Oyster Bay. In any event, I don't think my father could ever have allowed himself to choose it. He was of old Rhode Island extraction and I have cause to know this can make for austerities of practice, especially in small matters. Using a gold-cased penknife attached to his watchchain, he cuts himself a gravely selected Frau Karl Druschki bud. As we all know, this rose, opening to the most splendid white there is, has, alas, no fragrance. Austerity gets its sop.

It will be seen that predilections of mine for the old roses praised by Mrs. Stemler (and so most properly, works added to good words, by her purveyed) may have reasons that reason knows not of. Be it so I am prejudiced in these roses' favor. I'm prejudiced in Nanae Ito's paintings' favor. I'm prejudiced in favor of Dorothy Stemler, who is, by those having long rose-growing dealings with her, apt to be regarded as something of a rose herself. I like, I love my prejudices.

FHS: A Faith that Did not Fail
[essay]

When Pater died, after supporting so courageously his cruel illness of years, not a few Kent men of the early classes must have said to themselves: there's the end of Kent School. Grounds for the sad surmise were not far to find. With the hand that shaped Kent no longer able to guide, or active to care for Kent, signs of change began very soon to appear; and those who knew the earlier school had watched for some time with uneasiness—an uneasiness all the greater because one could not really say what was happening; one could only ask. The difference, the change, had been not so much seen as felt.

Seen changes, changes of form, are those that time unfailingly exacts; they are part of any continuing life; and they are often requisite. Doing things differently may be a lasting institution's very means of remaining what it was. The change unseen, the change only felt, is usually another matter. That kind of change goes to spirit, or at least, attitude; and here what may be true of changed form cannot be true. Change here is no saving adjustment to new days and different conditions. Change here is a lethal change of alteration by abandonment. If it proceeded, such a change must mean a different school—no longer Kent.

There had been, then, the disturbing perceptible fact of changes felt, the signs of slow changing. If this could have happened with Pater living still, still present at Kent, must not these signs be portents? What could they mean but that Kent had been the projection of one man's vital personality? One resolute mind conceived Kent. Overcoming every obstacle, one man's unique vigor created it. One strong heart warmed it with life. That vigor gone, the school was showing a want of sustenance. Though appearances were left, though a school of sorts that bore the name and used the buildings could profess for awhile to be the same school, when that heart stilled, must not the already shortening day of the real Kent be done?

To affirm just that, recollection and reflection joined quickly. Kent had been Kent because Pater had been Pater. The interdependence was impressive. What was meant by Kent could not be found in any assemblage of

Father Sill's Birthday, March 10, 1956, pp. 7–10. Reprinted by permission.

buildings, in any faculty and student body. Kent meant that carriage of the head, majestic and leonine; the sharp-eyed turn of the forceful face, softening to smile or alert to frown; the vigorous movement of the sloping but strong shoulders from which the coarse white habit, majestic, too, took its energetic swing. Kent also meant, the majestic being put off, that different affectionately-to-be-remembered costume, for convenience in coaching sports put on in its various variations—those deplorable knickerbockers; that sweater; that used baseball cap, or the winter thing of wool that could be pulled down! Did ever another headmaster walk with dignity so indefeasible that no fear for dignity, no thought for mere appearance, need enter his head—or, on the same point, was there ever another headmaster whose sufficient setting was of so little state as the old study—hardly more than a made-over attic? Kent meant also that unfashionable apartment; sloped walls covered with shabby matchboard, each vertical wall, before, behind, and out to the dormer windows, jammed frame to frame with photographs in no order or arrangement; carpeted with that very wreck of a rug; oversupplied with any-old furniture battered and scuffed by many school generations of sixth-formers taking tea and other formers taking sacred studies; and, for the proprietor's own relaxation, that sagged easychair beside the desk to which he could move when not at work, settling with formidable lack of grace and a magisterial but good-natured glancing through his horn-rimmed glasses while he filled from the pound tin of Prince Albert tobacco his wholly utilitarian bulldog pipe.

Such affecting reminiscence can and did easily lead—we shall not look upon his like again!—to conclusions of seeming moral certainty. To a same conclusion tended arguments perhaps more logical; drier facts. Why was the concept of Kent proving, as slowly but surely it appeared to be, incommunicable? On the face, neither obscure, nor complicated, nor even highly individual, the concept looked easy to grasp. No definition could have been plainer: this was a school which would especially encourage simplicity of life, self-reliance, and directness of purpose. In so plain a statement of ends, an equally plain statement of means, a rule or measure, seemed implicit. Anything that offered this encouragement belonged at Kent; anything that didn't, didn't.

In Pater's Kent the concept was always grasped easily. There, as well as implicit, the enabling means were explicit. Questions to perplex—exactly what do we mean by simplicity of life, by self-reliance, by directness of purpose? Exactly how do you encourage them?—had not been anticipated because in Pater's day they never could have arisen. They did not arise because Pater's Kent knew without question what was meant by those terms. Simplicity of life was Pater's everyday way of living. Self-reliance was Pater's competent and capable practice of doing things for himself. When a man could dig if he tried; to beg, he should indeed be ashamed!

Directness of purpose was Pater's own honesty of intention, an integrity of
unskimped effort that had no truck with vain show or false pretense. As for
what encouragement consisted in, what else but the obvious measures by
which doing things they ought to do in realization of Kent's objectives was
made easy for boys, while doing things they ought not to do was made hard?
That these measures were to him never anything but obvious was Pater's
gift—approaching, in fact, genius. Where the Kent he meant to make, and
made, was concerned, he was given to know with intuitive certainty, with
instant unreflecting sureness, what was, whatever the situation, the required measure, the one right thing to do next.

This kind of knowledge, the intuition that is genius, is never to be
gained by taking thought. Study and experience may get a man information; by themselves, they do not get him understanding. Where the rare
insight called understanding comes from isn't easily said. That loving is
involved seems probable; yet the evidences of life suggest that loving is a
consequence, not a cause. The real source often seems to be in a power of
imagination by which the man who is inspired to understand not only
transposes himself, puts himself in another's place; but, momentarily, for
the purposes of the enlightening moment, virtually *becomes* the other. Looking back, one guesses this to have been Pater's gift. Not losing nor impairing the man's judgment, and with none of the unnaturalness of most grown-
ups who, ill-advised, (fooling no boy) offer to act the boy, he could at will
and need become the boy. He felt the feelings of a boy. He could accept as
real the values of a boy. A boy's wants were obvious to him; a boy's intentions were readily foreseeable.

The result was that when the undeliberated magical transposition took
place in Pater, the boy in any boy, whether he was able to realize (he probably wouldn't be) what was happening or not, recognized the real thing.
The mature man still confronted him; but present in the man had come to
be someone who thought understandable thoughts and talked comprehensible language. On the one hand, an alliance of interest became perfectly
feasible. If a boy needed help in doing those things that he ought to do, an
uncondescending auxiliary, a trusty comrade, stood reassuringly ready to
go, with a grown man's dazzling resources, with patience and kindness, to
all trouble to help him help himself. On the other hand—and quite as
important—that mysterious familiar who spoke as a boy, understood as a
boy, thought as a boy, was (for that very reason) not easy for a boy to hood-
wink. You would be unwise to tell him the sort of lie adults usually swallowed. Knowing what to look for, he readily found out wrongdoing, easily
identified mischief, and moved, often memorably, to discourage them. In
themselves, as abstractions, patience and long-suffering may always be
good; in practice, and particularly in this practice, whose subject is the
unlicked cub, the callow youth, in his half-learning still mainly oaf and

fool, mildness may be no kindness. Measures too temperate do the boys the disservice of misleading them about a life in which you reap what you sow, and of misleading them—by letting them think they deserve to be indulged when they don't—about themselves. How wholesome the qualms of consternation, how salutary the examinings of conscience, with which many of us once started when we heard that anxious word passed: *the Old Man's on a rampage!* Whether in disciplining one contumacious brat, or rating the whole school for some momentary idleness or refractoriness, the wisdom of instinct made how few mistakes, failed how seldom justly to determine, each in due season, the time for helping, the time for chastising, the time for forgiving!

The argument of despond had been, of course, that these remembered things, all meaning Kent, and so many of them highly personal, so many of them quite inimitable, must add up to Kent. Yet, did they? In the count of arresting qualities, in the recollection of that particular genius, was something overlooked, something left out? The effective approving kindnesses, the effective measures of disapproval, were, in essence, works; what of faith? What had been Pater's life and work—they were really one—but a long act of faith? His faith had been that he would find ways, that means would discover themselves, to accomplish every purpose of good. Practice of this faith, with the experience of faith so often rewarded, could be observed to have formed in Pater, as years passed, a sustaining confidence, a clear conviction. If he, with the love that was easy, with the patience that sometimes came hard, did his part, his best, bread cast upon the waters would be found. The conviction was not the satisfied pride of a man who sees rightly that he has done what many men couldn't have done. That part of the conclusion of despond that proved personal regard, that told him how much he was missed, would no doubt have touched him; but one can guess the almost irate objection he surely would have offered—what? Could there be, among those he had taught to know better, so blank a misunderstanding of what he aimed at; what he worked for; what, by grace, he had in fact accomplished?

In words of another noted headmaster, to which Pater recurred often enough to show how full of meaning he found them: he strove for success, without ever thinking himself successful. The humility of an instructed mind—one well aware of how much must always be left to do—would not rest on what was already done, nor bother to sum up preliminary gains. Not in Pater would it be to figure Kent School as a personal triumph—Kent, as his. Rather, with humble confidence, with religious certainty, he was Kent's—the concept's instrument, its implement. His own whole life of hard glad service, the ceaseless demanding use Kent had made of him, assured him of that concept's power. Would he ever have desponded over temporary difficulties or little delays?

Nothing, we may be sure, shook his faith. His faith was that the spirit of that purpose which had found and used him so well would, in its own time and way find others fit to use. Others would grasp it, cherish it; and so, with an aroused resource, with devotion like his own, gladly serve. They would serve as he had served—not in mechanical rehearsings of any past; but in creative renewing, the free recreating which on each new day and each new tomorrow could provide (as he had always provided) the means and forms to keep Kent, Kent. Its author and its instrument, could Pater ever have doubted—should anyone have doubted?—that the superintendent spirit lived, which, living, informing, guiding, only waiting to draw to it its own, would take care that what was Kent's would know Kent's face?

Foreword to
A Flower in Her Hair

I accept with particular pleasure the opportunity offered me by the Bruccoli Clark Collector's Edition series through its plan to present hitherto unpublished pieces of a writer's work to see in print a writing of mine I liked— that is, felt content to publish, and expected to publish; and yet through chance and mischance of events oddly falling out came a first time, and then a second time, not to publish; came to take as lost and gone for good any hope it ever would be published. Speaking in writing man's part of fond begettor I must feel a little like the Prodigal Son's father. Astonishment over the never foreseen recovery, the coming to light by sheerest accident, must for me touch it with qualities both of a rarity and of a relic. Both impel me to tax the reader with a couple of notes, both perhaps excusable if he takes them for caveats.

(1) Matter of relic. When, by a kind but unwise publisher's bringing out a schoolboy novel of mine I, in Doctor Johnson's agreeably apt phrase, commenced Author all of half a century ago the Literary Establishment of the time was in aims, values, critical standards little like today's. That non-representational mode, coming through this century to take over all creative arts, had yet to make much headway in writing. The old mode, by precept and example taught me (and never unlearned) was what today may see as hidebound by Shakesperean banalities of mirror-holdings up to nature, by hackneyed Miltonic handouts of purported acquist of true experience made to fit metered verse; by pedantic insistence on telling it as it is, not, free-spirited, telling it like it is. The short story, perhaps most of all, suffered from set-form bondage; it must be self-contained; it must be self-explanatory. In whatever conforms to that mode the modern reader must be warned against brain-wracking to see systems of symbols. They aren't there. For Deeper Insight, there can be no prize of recognition that here, retold to relate to modernity's social, economic, ecological, political or ethnic issues, or for some good propaganda purpose, is, say, the great fable of Leda and the swan. Here, what he gets is what he sees—story only.

(2) Matter of rarity. Commenced as Author, I had of course written,

while years passed, a great deal (reams would be no overstatement) that
never saw print. Very little I did on first writing, read over, contented me.
False starts, irrelevant middles, poor conclusions were destroyed by the
wastebasketful. I can recall only three pieces to which this didn't happen—
that is: pieces finished, contenting me to some degree at least, and so not
destroyed, even when not in the usual course presently published. When
my publisher suggested (no common happening for novelists; now Barabbas
was—well, more endeared to me than ever) a story collection (*Children &
Others;* 1964) these three were to be included. Duly two of them were, and
so may be passed over. There remained "A Flower in Her Hair," left unique
in its intricate history of piffling misadventure, mischance, misplacement.

Being work in the old mode, a job that must be self-contained, self-
explanatory, the story does not, I trust, fail in itself to make clear that the
mirror is held up to the long-ago; that the characters, their dialogue sometimes in phrasings not current now and even occasional details of different
behaviour, were with every care for versimilitude, of that time. So is their
semi-colonial Cuba—by no means to be taken for Castro's brave, new, by
most sad accounts near-ruined Cuba now. Dating the scene is not however
to date the writing. That came years later when my mother's estate turned
over to me a packet of letters and snapshots I sent her from Cuba in the winter of 1925–26. Result was a past recalled with startling force and clarity,
and the results' result (how common with writers) an urge to write about
what, missed at the time, now brought new understanding. I wrote, I wish
I could say with speed and ease of inspiration but in fact with usual hard
writing and rewriting. Done, and close to my content as I can expect, it
went to my agents.

Now began that run of little mischances. A large women's magazine
had urgently asked to be shown a story of mine when one next became available. (I didn't write them often.) The urgence, I can't doubt, came from a
novel of mine that year receiving a Pulitzer prize—by then become very
much like mischance, unwanted by writers who in conceit very common to
them took their work seriously; yet still by the trade seen as of moment,
thought valuable. At any rate, that magazine got the story; and awkward
indeed was this to prove. By the line of their editorial policy it was "unpleasant," not for a readership like theirs.

I saw their concern—the flirtatious girl, the ugly outcome. That was
that; it would go to my usual market; but chance, if not mischance wasn't
finished. At about the moment of the return of the ms. I got a letter. A lady
I never heard of wrote me to say she had been told, and was it true as she
hoped since the picture was so good, so realistic, that the character of a
banker in an early Cuban novel of mine had her late husband as its original.
Indeed it had; he was manager of the Royal Bank of Canada branch in
Sancti Spiritus, so I felt free to tell her so. However, about "A Flower in Her

Hair" real pause was given me. That had been done, too, with the old representational mode's care for exact detail, and I was being advised that people depicted were still around, still likely to read anything I wrote. Personally I thought the "unpleasant" point nonsense; and since, while all else was fact, the disagreeable end was not—that was mine; my story, what I had retrospectively and with a start seen, could have happened, had been on the verge of happening, but never did, just in reality fading out. I betrayed no secret. Still, I liked those people, and had to know, too, they were really those the magazine's editorial policy had concern for. Did I want to hurt them? I did not. I withdrew the story. Later, maybe.

With the putting together of *Children & Others* later duly came; only with it, mischance once more. Sent along with the other stories to be set up, in that so well-known way that seems peculiar to manuscripts (keep a carbon is first professional advice to every new writer) "A Flower in Her Hair" proceeded to disappear. Why, where, how—no clue or hint. *Children & Others* must go without it. Just where that particular copy, the one withdrawn got to must be forever unanswered. What I did not know, had forgotten, was that the carbon of providence, professionally made of course by me, remained. So-called 'top copy' withdrawn, it stayed in my agents' files. On a last year cleaning out of old folders there its faded pages proved to be. Here it is.

Laborious Explanatory Note for
A Rope for Dr. Webster

A century and a half after his murder trial the shade of hapless Doctor Webster should surely rest in peace. Indecency may be the word for a digging of his dust here set out. Yet I risk it; I must protest, since patient readers have rights, that when my hanging story was, as planned, in regular place of a publishing scheme the retelling is neither idle, purposeless, nor even aimed at mere gain. I feel freer to say this of the scheme because I didn't shape it. I can go further; call it original in concept, of intrinsic interest in its material of a sort not before seen where selected American last century trials have been treated; with, moreover, all to be drawn together in discovery of what contemporary critics like to call (repellently) Relevance; of custom and especially law that touch, in ways needing clearer realization, ourselves now, our lives now.

Deponent can say no further; for this is all, sole remnant of that far more ambitious scheme. The essence was issuing of a volume in which perhaps twelve published novelists of at least some note told of the one or another last century criminal case that most engaged him, and why. The 'why' was important. How these various presumably creative minds saw what they saw and described it as they did would be analyzed in an epilogue of some detail by, prudence was seen to demand: *Amicus Curiae*—though actually done by me. Here I meant to offer a short treatment of the Common Law under evident present insidious change; what it had earlier been accepted as being; what little signs were starting to show it could, left unwatched, drop to become.

Evidently the person capable of arranging to make such a collection and of getting a publisher for it had to be a rarest of individuals, truly a modern-times endangered species whose chief qualification was (perhaps despite of a high taste and judgment) he in simple fact *Knew Everybody*. As here used, the phrase is to denote one well acquainted with most of those, amateur or top professional, deep in devotion to creative arts, any or all of them; and who himself was of a temperament or disposition to so charm or cajole those selectively wanted for his purpose as to make each under uncommon powers of persuasion go along, taking new ideas eagerly as his own ideas. One must see the charmer as partly at least what Hamlet meant to designate when, the skull in hand, he remembered Yorick as a fellow of infinite jest, of most excellent fancy—only in this case bettered by no chance of alas poor Yorick's sycophancy, or alas poor Hamlet's plain over-relishings of despair. So far, so good. There *was* this person. Yet the hitch in that most excellent fancy—facile, he could open out schemes by the score—is guessable, quite foreseeable. How many creative writers would take interest that exceeded everyday detective story tastes in the Common Law; let alone be willing and able to give the damn I thought important—the sort Henry Adams felt—in the degradation of that law's underpinning dogma? In short, not a dozen existed. The project had to fall through.

Though that was the finally proved fact of the matter; I mean the way I would, sorry for his sake, have then seen it and told it, I am certain now, these years later, this view—a supposed blow of sorts to him—was happily mistaken. Looking back, slightly wiser, much older, I must doubt (those always-coming potential new ventures by the score?) he felt no more than traces of chagrin over one loss where usually he won. My fellow of infinite jest, not much disappointed, nor, with such worldly knowledge, even surprised would eye its amusing side. By this I don't suggest Puckish spite, real root of much infinite jesting, but never his. Being that rarity, that endangered species of witty man, entertainments he got were very clearly warm-hearted, indulgent; come of a kind-mindedness which, perfectly perceiving what fools these mortals be, watched them in something between pity and paternalism. Unlike, say, Fulke Greville stultified by humanity's condition my infinite jester's serene temperament, nothing human alien to it, made funny to him life's prank of mirth in being vainly begot and yet forbidden vanity. In the flat fact of a Matthew Arnold's Darkling Plain as precise term of truth for this world that seems to lie before us like a land of dreams he could find, laughing, nature's comic play, the old mistaken identity hoax—cruel, outright fell, a bastard's job—yet isn't fun here for excellent fancy, isn't, here, along with the tears, the pratfall of things? A smile will go a long long way, won't it? (Well; I just asked.)

That I was late in knowing this particular person of unique parts is a regret to me; yet my own fault. In what was nothing but callowness, half snobbish, half conceited, I early in my writing life took to regarding the literary set with distaste, even disdain—their cliques of self-admiration, their log-rolling, their critical hates of envy and deceits of partisan malice! Well, I would and did have nothing to do with them (now, what could I have been expecting where many think they are called, while few indeed, mostly through luck, are chosen?). I'm afraid I actually preened myself over *not* Knowing Everybody; and to cure that silliness took nothing less than a World War. We, the Knower of Everybody and I, encountered as Army

Air Force majors, arbitrarily transferred late in 1943 to Pentagon head-
quarters staff, fantastically multifarious, and, in record, nowhere through
all its strange work and workings explicitly so named, of what by the mil.
ser. (as orders have it) termed CG/AAF. This diverse, sharply compart-
mented (in fact, aides; but never called that or wearing that insignia) group
did what is most simply and accurately described as just about Anything—
work, paper or flying mission, of true TOP SECRET gravity now; now
turgid mouse-out-of-mountain speech or article farces for favored Chiefs,
or Deputy Chiefs, or the Old Man—never anything but 'Mr. A.' in our
security use; now periods, whole days, of idleness when we sat feet on desk
in our small enclosed (token of our importance) room around the corner
from Mr. A's E-ring fastnesses.

During those feet-on-desk days long hours for reading and talking
abounded and our fellow of excellent jest could make them delightful both
with what he wished to say and what he wished to hear. I found I could use
close to a drawerful of picked-up second hand Everyman's Library editions
—one; Sir William Blackstone's *Commentaries*, the original text without
the later voluminous trash of annotation. It was from that of course that our
excellent fancier with nice tastes and universal interests in next to no time
conceived our project. I don't mean he had to consume the whole work
(admittedly a task) but he read charmed (as in fact some years before *I* had
read, all amazement: thinking: *where has this* (the Common Law) *been all my
life?*). And with reason. One understands in a moment why such a juris-
tically hostile critic as Bentham felt forced to confess Blackstone "first to
have taught jurisprudence to speak the language of the scholar and the
gentleman." For excellent fancy here was one more enrichment, and I can't
doubt source of private jest of his kindly kind. I was easily brought to talk
with convertlike overplusage of zeal (Catholics or communists often tire-
somely show it) about parlous states of law I saw today—our ugly, ironic
alteration of Grand Jury whose forseeing brought the prescient British law
lords to abolish it, and so should we; the termite tunnelings in *stare decisis*
that ate away the meaning of Justice Holmes' dictum: *Law is not of logic but
of experience*; the yearly larger and larger legislative tomfooleries of power-
grabbing to play Judge. He would not crack a smile, but how wonderful
all my twaddle of solemn didacticism, my never possibly availing much
ado about the matters of course.

Moreover when the no-go was certain, when all recourse of experienced
search proved unable to turn up the wanted separate piece material, or as
my elegant fancier might say: *But it was not to be* (his brief, deft settings-out
of speech mannerisms was peerless) the never-cracked smile doubtless in-
wardly grew as I worried over so minuscule interest in Law clearly existing
among today's equivalent of those for whom Sir William's perfect wording
ought to be fit. The war was over; and, there, my odd staff job showed well

worthwhile in that I could pull strings that soon had me resuming my country solitude. Still, while the book project was dying, when I was in New York we met for long lunches from time to time at the Men's Bar in the old Ritz on Madison Avenue, he busy with his ever fresh fancies; writing —short stories when he felt like it, gracefully whimsical though in a sharp-minded and witted concise prose to which that unappetizing word can't often apply; frequent articles on food and drink and cooking (arts too, both in his thoughts and in his hands; criticism of music and ballet, theatre and painting, architecture and even 'mobiles.' Presently, the old Ritz stupidly torn down, I was reduced to the Harvard Club for New York accommodation, and I think that false 'togetherness' of clubs and clubmen was never to his fastidious taste in relationships. Anyway, time passing, our meetings grew farther between—no falling apart; simply he lived in a crowd of chosen friends; I, naturally solitary, needed none—only people to watch and study, preferably always unaware of me.

Of necessity that meant, since I never got my Serious Call into print, he must miss promised entertainments of my I fear irrepressible *I told you so* when successive years came to take the course they have—when that Grand Jury system did exactly what the wise English ending averted, free men's once-shield against the Crown horridly twisted into the very Star Chamber it was meant to quash forever; when the evils flourished, directly or indirectly derived, of anti-Administration legislature (second horrid historic irony) turned Rump Parliament (*There, take it away* . . .) complete with inquisition committees, forceless subpeona, shameless citations for—yes; *contempt*! And so by natural consequence (shades of Dr. Webster's innovative trial) the swell of the idiot, false-witness bearing, unabashedly (as needed) treasonable 'media' of our times, some baseless Right-of-the-People-to-Know providing color of that patriotism, long last refuge of scoundrels. And why not; when on the high bench could sit long, too long, the legal coxcomb who never blushed to say: *I come here not to follow precedents but to set them*; when the judicature of whole Federal Districts stood sullied by some Maximum John's smiling menace of plea-dealing, intricately 'lawful' yet with its sickish *Code Napoleon* whiff of end justifying means, to break that time-tried honor by practical necessity among political thieves, by losers' sleight of hate the tacit consents of custom made 'felonies'—as though any kid won't spit on squealers, the sneaks who don't cover up for friends; as though any Dante can't tell you hell's bottom holds the faithless, the trust-breakers. (I can hear that excellent fancy saying: *Watergate; yes, odious crime! I speak of its architecture, of course.*)

The separation had to mean also that, last year, only by thirdhand hearsay (and the media, if only on obituary fact quite credible) that one night taxi borne returning with friends from a theatre party to prepare them a fondue, more art of his, in his apartment he, of a sudden, tossed them a quip, smiled as they laughed, and appeared to doze off. The taxi home and halted, the door opened, he was found to be dead. No; I have not named him. To that 'Everybody' he knew this would be needless. For all others, I feel he would love, last private jest, his enigmatic rich life signed only: ANON.

Letter to *Fact*

Yes, I do have first-hand knowledge of inaccuracies in *Time*; but I doubt if it can be of use to *Fact*. A 'cover story' *Time* ran on me a number of years ago was so full of inaccuracies, of nonsense evident to anyone who knew me, that it would have amounted to a joke if much of the misinformation hadn't been phrased in ways that seemed to make me deride and despise, individually or collectively, quite a lot of people. Put into my mouth was a series of pronouncements some asinine, some gratuitously unkind, that I'd be about the last writer in the world to make.

Of course I thought this was outrageous; and I was good and sore; yet even then I had to realize I was very much more to blame for it than *Time*. I've spent most of my writing life fending off (not hard, if you really mean it) all kinds of publicity. As a result, cornered at last by *Time*, I had little idea of the usual, normal things I might be up against. I didn't allow for an obtuse and humorless, though certainly skilled, research man; nor for a writer working, careless and imperceptive, from probably unclear notes. I must hope such inexperience explains, if it doesn't by any means excuse, an attitude which I've learned this hard way could be nothing less than irresponsible. I never once thought of bothering to do what any experienced person would be bound to do—that is: before publication, require that he be shown whatever he was going to be said to have said; and insist that it be agreed he had said it.

In short, my own negligence, not any 'slanting' or distorting of facts by *Time* accounts for all or most of what was ridiculous and untrue in the story. *Time* has been, and under the conditions of journalism is apt to have to go on being, now misinformed, now seriously mistaken, now foolish in degrees of emphasis and extent of coverage. But, sore about my personal experience or not, I have to remind myself that no one ever found in *Time* anything to approach the conscienceless partisan distorting and misrepresent-

James Gould Cozzens: A Checklist by James B. Meriwether, Bruccoli Clark/Gale Research, 1972. Copyright © 1972 by Matthew J. Bruccoli and C. E. Frazer Clark, Jr. Reprinted by permission.

ing done as a matter of course, and indeed, as their very reason for being, in periodicals of the liberal or sectarian 'little review' type. I'm driven to say that, all considered, you go a long way before you find editing with consistent basic regard for truth and respect for fact *Time* can generally be counted on to show. I'm sure the publisher has 'biases'; but who doesn't? Not I? Not you?

X

A Reading of the
James Gould Cozzens Manuscripts
By Richard M. Ludwig

September, 1957, may come to be remembered in literary annals as the Cozzens month. Only the author, his publishers, his friends, and that loyal band of readers who long ago formed one-man evangelist societies were prepared for the explosion—there is no other word for it—that followed the appearance of *By Love Possessed* on August 26. Within five weeks the bookstore sales of Cozzens's twelfth novel exceeded the regular hardcover distribution of all his other novels combined. The Book-of-the-Month Club, *Reader's Digest*, and Hollywood paid him handsomely for secondary rights.

But gratifying as this financial success must be to a man who published his first novel thirty-three years ago, the current critical acclaim must also warm his heart, no matter how he feels about critics. Brendan Gill, in the *New Yorker*, was among the first to declare this novel Cozzens's masterpiece. Malcolm Cowley, Jessamyn West, Orville Prescott, John Fischer, and every other major reviewer welcomed the book as a distinguished novel, even though some of them, notably Richard Ellmann in the *Reporter*, raised relevant objections, at the same time admitting that *"By Love Possessed* is so pleasant to read that it is almost savage to seize upon its flaws."* Cozzens has had popular recognition in the past: *Guard of Honor* won the Pulitzer Prize for 1948, and four of his novels were Book-of-the-Month Club choices. But the critics, both professional and academic, have been slow to acknowledge his achievements and his growth, to give him the unqualified recognition that his twelfth novel has now earned. In 1949 Bernard De Voto, writing from *Harper's* "Easy Chair," chastised "the exalted caste who are called literary critics," who were loath to recognize "one of the finest talents and one of the most expert skills at work in American fiction" because "his novels are written. The word has to be italicized: they are *written*. So they leave criticism practically nothing to do." De Voto was not wholly correct; the novelists Brendan Gill and Mark Schorer had in their reviews of *Guard of Honor* raised the Cozzens banner high for the best novel to come out of

The Princeton University Library Chronicle, Vol. 19 (Autumn 1957), pp. 1–12. Copyright © 1957 by The Princeton University Library Chronicle. Reprinted by permission.

World War II. Other reviewers had warmly praised *The Just and the Unjust* six years before. But the serious recognition—in the literary sense—of a serious novelist has been slow in coming. Cozzens has waited long for the deeply satisfying kind of critical study which the poet Louis O. Coxe published as "The Complex World of James Gould Cozzens" in *American Literature* (1955). Doubtless we shall now have an epidemic of Cozzens studies. We can only assume that the author knows they are long overdue, just as his faithful readers know that the very qualities which have been everywhere proclaimed in reviews of *By Love Possessed*, the enormous scope, the narrative power, the explorations of moral responsibility, were all present in varying degrees in his earlier novels.

Some of these studies, particularly the longer ones, will want to take cognizance of the large body of material which Cozzens has given to the Princeton University Library. His papers and manuscripts fill fifteen file boxes;[1] Books from his library number well over eight hundred. They are a scholar's gold mine. And exactly as one would expect of so comprehensive an intelligence as Cozzens's, they reflect wide reading, painstaking craftsmanship, and an absolute devotion to his art. The book titles indicate the kind of reading which has been Cozzens's vocation and avocation, his source books and his hobbies. Quite possibly they intermingled. A random list clearly reflects Cozzens's work: *A History of the Cuban Republic*, Lecky's *Wrinkles in Practical Navigation* (could the author's name have served Cozzens years later in *Castaway*?), Gay's *Typhoid Fever*, MacCallum's *Text-Book of Pathology, Notes on Pennsylvania Criminal Law and Procedure*, Wellman's *The Art of Cross-Examination, Airmen and Aircraft*, Benét's *Military Law and the Practice of Courts-Martial, The Army Air Forces in World War II*. Here would be proof enough of Cozzens's professional competence if we did not already know that to write *The Just and the Unjust* he visited the near-by Doylestown Court House and filled himself with lawyers' shoptalk, to write *The Last Adam* he read medicine and checked his manuscript with several doctors, and that he did the same for the theology of *Men and Brethren*, the

---

1. Since this article was written (Sept. 1957), Mr. Cozzens has enlarged his archive by numerous gifts to Princeton University Library over the past twenty years, including the corrected setting typescript and galley proofs of *By Love Possessed* and of *Children and Others*; the corrected typescript, galley proofs, and page proofs of *Morning Noon and Night*; his original typed wartime diary (1942–45) and memoranda prepared for the headquarters of the Army Airforce (1944–45); ten bound volumes of a holograph journal (1960–65); over 200 letters; and first editions of his books, in English and other languages. In 1977, Mr. Cozzens also placed on deposit two important gatherings of personal papers: hundreds of family letters to and from the author (1920–69), diaries, photographs, clippings, and memorabilia, as well as correspondence with publishers and critics, Air Force papers, working manuscripts, and notebooks. All of this material, both gifts and deposits, is unavailable to scholars until Mr. Cozzens's restrictions are lifted.

ship mechanics of *S.S. San Pedro*. But Cozzens would be the first to deny that he only "researched" his best books. *Guard of Honor* proves him right; he lived much of this one. And *By Love Possessed* is so crowded with profound observations, so ideally a mirror held up to nature, that his older readers see it as an accumulation of years of astute introspection, the natural outcropping of this one man's honest curiosity about the human condition.

The Cozzens manuscripts tell us far more about the man and his methods of composition than any bookshelf can. Included in the gift are two boxes of personal correspondence (much of it concerning his published work) and two boxes of papers relating to his World War II service. They give us an intimate look at a man who dislikes personal interviews and public appearances, who refuses to comment on his own work. "I have never known a writer," he said, "speaking about his own work who would not have been wiser and more estimable if he had just shut up." Cozzens so distrusts the subjective observation that he even tries to discipline himself out of his own work (*Ask Me Tomorrow* being the exception). But in the letters we read Cozzens clearly. They are dated from the early thirties to the present. Most of them are from his American and English publishers, from his readers (inquiries and compliments abound), from his friends (especially Air Force officers), and from students and a few critics. The carbons of his replies are preserved as well, and they reveal without exception an immensely patient, generous, sober-minded man, a professional writer in love with his profession, an alert, acquisitive mind humble before knowledge. In 1949, for example, he wrote his Harcourt, Brace editor:

> I was conscientiously making my way through Mons Sheen's new work when the rude thought struck me that I had never seen a fuller and richer use of the classic fallacies and this soon set me to collecting them and that soon set me to realizing my meagre college logic was far behind me and I was rusty about analyzing them. So when I could (this is a long story) I stopped in at the university library at Princeton where Mr. Young is always obliging. This time he obliged me with a shy youngster, an instructor in philosophy writing his thesis, and directed him to go through the stacks with me. He was so bright and respectful that though it could not have taken him two minutes to realize I was a dope and an ignoramus it took me a couple of hours to learn from him what I daresay you and other educated men well know; that what Mons Sheen and Aristotle and I quaintly thought of as 'logic' was a childish little game or exercise in quibbling by which it was absurd to think of demonstrating anything—except perhaps the user's ingenuousness in making false assumptions and his weakminded inability to hold to any point. The youngster thought it might be a good idea, if I was interested, for me to acquaint myself a little with such elementary matters as the propositional calculus and the functional calculus of first order because without them there was nothing much he could do for me; you just had to have a technique for exact expression because without it you could not see what was wrong with traditional logic and until you saw that you would just go

on thinking you thought. It consoled me to find that with the books before me
I was not too long in getting his point—not that I expect to learn to think.

There are few American novelists more modest about their intellect, or with
less cause to be. From the year Cozzens left Harvard (1924, at the end of his
sophomore year), he commenced rather than ceased learning. Kent School
and Harvard never challenged his mind in the way his own desire to record
life challenged it. He had to see in order to know. He wrote to one of his
readers in 1934:

> I simply put down, when I write, what the things I have seen and known look
> like to me. I try not to intrude what I think. It is my idea that an author's talent
> for writing, if he is lucky enough to have one, is the only thing of any interest or
> importance about him. To attempt to instruct his readers is a piece of imper-
> tinence since they are either too stupid for instruction, or quite intelligent
> enough to instruct themselves on the basis of any true things the writer may have
> called convincingly to their attention.

What Cozzens has called to our attention, in more than thirty years of writing, is a distillation of his observations *minus* his own personality. This
detachment has led more than one critic to call him aloof, cerebral, superior. Or as *Time* put it (perhaps with little awareness of their own *double-
entendre*), "Cozzens is really alien grain in the American corn." He aims to
be; he has spent his life avoiding sentimentality. He wrote a fellow novelist
in 1949 that too often in American fiction

> hogwash . . . [is] mistaken for Deep Feeling. I am well aware that the public
> likes it. I am well aware that the line is a fine one and my intense aversion to
> what seems to me false and maudlin . . . unfits me as a dispassionate judge; but
> there's nothing I can do. I could not write with pleasure and certainly not with
> conviction what did not seem to me real or true. Much that is both may be out-
> side my perception; but of course I don't believe it, and couldn't be brought to.

Writing to still another novelist, who in 1944 was enjoying the success of
a best seller, he was even more certain of his own dicta:

> When I read it in ms. it was a matter of concern to me that it was so painfully
> true. I mean, not just true about the writer, but also in a disturbing way true
> about any reader with enough perception to take in those personal truths. Of
> course they (we) all compliment ourselves on our dear love of truth, but I think
> it is eyewash and that the public (we) never really enjoyed the classic process of
> catharsis unless it was good and remote in the persons of kings or gods. I thought
> that there might not be enough people who would submit to read what they
> were bound to find so disturbing. The normal remedy would be to call it a dis-
> torted or partial picture and so dismiss it. The counter-remedy is to apply the
> simple compulsion that makes the reader, whether he likes it or not, have to
> find out what happens next. In print—whether it ought to or not, that does
> make a difference—that compulsion seems to me to come out strong. This is

really art, often so much more important than mere truth. When you have, as you have, both, you have something and I hope you're enjoying the general acknowledgment of it.

Between the publication of *S.S. San Pedro* (1931, his fifth novel) and *The Just and the Unjust* (1942, his tenth) Cozzens worked diligently at achieving this combination of truth and art, balanced so as to turn his reader to self-contemplation at the same moment it gripped him with a compelling narrative. His heroes—Dr. George Bull, the Rev. Ernest Cudlipp, the young writer Francis Ellery, the small-town lawyer Abner Coates—are indestructible characters, so "right" as to be uncanny, considering the variety of professions they represent. But Cozzens never captured a large audience, in spite of book-club distribution. His letters during these years give every indication that he would not be deterred from writing as he had to write, more in the nineteenth-century mode than in the contemporary. Jane Austen and George Eliot were his models: a clearly stated "subject" developed by a well-articulated plot, often low-pressure characters, always a serious digging into the roots of human behavior and the thoroughly understood motivations behind this behavior. When *Guard of Honor* arrived in 1948 we knew we were in the presence of a writer who by dogged practice had prepared himself to write a great novel. Cozzens told his English publisher soon after the American edition was in print, in a time of paper shortage in England:

I was disconcerted on my own account to find myself running over 600 pages. I had often contended that there was no excuse for a novel of more than 400 pages. Anything over that was just proof of incompetence . . . but when I came to write Guard of Honor I found myself in a difficult situation. What I wanted to write about here, the essence of the thing to be said, the point of it all, what I felt to be the important meaning of this particular human experience, was its immensity and its immense complexity.

This feeling had grown on me as my so-called military service drew on and I began slowly to realize that through no fault (or indeed merit) of my own I was being shown the Army Air Forces on a scale and in a way that was really incredible. I was coming to know about, I had to know about, more of its innumerable phases than anyone with real command duties would ever have time to know. Not many officers, and I would guess not any, had reason or opportunity to fly into and look over such a number of airfields and installations of a variety quite unbelievable. With the exception of the CG himself, in whose office I was at the end working, I don't think anyone had occasion to sit down with and listen to so many of the air generals. . . .

With my head full of all this, I could see I faced a tough technical problem. I wanted to show that real (as I now saw it) meaning of the whole business, the peculiar effects of the inter-action of innumerable individuals functioning in ways at once determined by and determining the functioning of innumerable others—all in the common and in every case nearly helpless involvement in what had ceased to be just an "organization" (I think it ceased to be that when it grew past the point where one directing head could keep the whole in mind) and became if not an organism with life and purposes of its own, at least an entity, like a crowd. . . .

I saw that I would have to show it, with all that that meant in many scenes, many words, many characters. I would just have to write off as readers everyone who could not or would not meet heavy demands on his attention and intelligence, or lacked the imagination to grasp a large pattern and the wit to see the relation which I could not stop to spell out between this & that.

Cozzens was not only prepared but willing to take these risks. A lesser talent would have balked at the scope or quailed at the potential loss of audience. The point is this: the intellectual detachment is here a virtue, the aloofness toward his public almost a necessity; and Cozzens was able to couple these attitudes with his skill at drawing three-dimensional human beings. From General "Bus" Beal down to T/5 Mortimer McIntyre, the people in this novel are alive. They are alive because they are contradictory. Back in 1936 Cozzens had written one of his readers: "I think a person can be at the same time officious and devoted, self-important and self-sacrificing, insensitive and sympathetic. Indeed, I think that is exactly what most people are most of the time. I regard it with indulgence." Twelve years later he was demonstrating more clearly than ever before that this indulgence could suggest to him a splendid observing intelligence (the patient, tolerant Colonel Ross) and this view of personality (the insoluble, the contradictory) could create a cast of characters wholly credible, individually compelling. The highest accomplishment of this novel may be its "immense complexity," in that a whole "world" (here Ocanara Air Base, Florida) is so neatly articulated. But it is also possible that without Cozzens's knowledge of and concern with man as individual it would never have come alive. He suggests this dual concern in a letter to an ex-Air Force general who, he hoped, would read his manuscript for errors:

> As in my trade we use everything, the AAF and the war effort are used as occasion or excuse to go on about Life. Though long and hard, it is fun. You will certainly find sad though I hope short slips in the incidental attempt a writer always makes to show the reader that a writer knows everything—in this case, all about (a) the Army (b) the higher echelon (c) military aviation (d) life. I hope you will be willing to strike out for me whatever you think is wrong.

A year later, in one of his rare critical statements, Cozzens unconsciously described his own achievement when he reviewed Oliver La Farge's history of the Air Transport Command, *The Eagle in the Egg* (*New York Times Book Review*, July 24, 1949):

> Whatever else may have distinguished them, no great number of the many "war books"—whether memoirs, military history or fiction—have been much

distinguished by what it is simplest to call adult intelligence. That is, not many have addressed themselves and their material to readers reasonably well acquainted with human beings and human experience, not born yesterday, and not insensible to statements merely self-serving or to sentimental nonsense and bonehead contradictions in terms or facts. Such readers cannot read far in "The Eagle in the Egg" without the grateful awareness that here they are in good hands, safe from nonsense, on the way to seeing believable aspects of a real war, with no fool for a guide. Good sense informs the whole book.

Guard of Honor shows good sense *and* adult intelligence *and* scope. Cozzens's readers expected no less of him in his latest novel.

The eleven boxes of typescript are further documentation of Cozzens's perfectionism, his will to learn by doing, by canceling out the insufficient action or the inadequate word. The manuscripts of his three youthful novels are not here. The collection begins with *The Son of Perdition* (printer's copy), continues through *Castaway* (in four versions), *Men and Brethren* and *Ask Me Tomorrow* (printer's copies), *The Just and the Unjust* (a final draft), *Guard of Honor* (printer's copy), and *By Love Possessed* (printer's copy, corrected galleys, and hundreds of sheets of early versions). *S.S. San Pedro* and *The Last Adam* are missing. Apart from the published work there is a group of six completed and ten incomplete short stories, four fragments, and two unpublished novels: *Ignorant Armies* (undated) and *The Careless Livery* (ostensibly a rewriting, dated Villa Igiea, Palermo; East Marion, L. I. 1927). Lynn Riggs's play based on *The Son of Perdition* (in typescript) completes the collection.

Inspecting these manuscripts is sheer pleasure, like looking into Cozzens's mind. Here are visions and revisions. Titles were particularly troublesome. *The Son of Perdition* was at one time called *Foreign Strand*. Cozzens preferred *Bodies Terrestrial* or *A Cure of Flesh* to *The Last Adam*; Alfred Harcourt did not. *Ask Me Tomorrow* had two earlier titles: *Young Fortunatus*, the first choice, was changed to *It Was the Nightingale* (until someone, more than likely, discovered the Ford Madox Ford memoir by that name published seven years before). *The Summer Soldier* was changed to *The Just and the Unjust*, in spite of a 1912 novel written by Vaughan Kester under that title. *Guard of Honor* and *By Love Possessed* were Cozzens's choices; he would not alter them.

Page one of the manuscript version of *Ask Me Tomorrow* confirms the suspicion that Cozzens was consciously eliminating the first-person observation from his work. In 1955 he wrote an inquiring student that

Ask Me Tomorrow is autobiographical to the extent that . . . in 1925 and 1926 I was living in Europe. Under the circumstances described (though much detail is fictitious) I spent some months tutoring a nice kid who suffered from infantile paralysis while I also tried to act the published author which I then was . . . and to manage an affair of the heart. I think the only thing I did even fairly well was teach the kid some Latin.

The opening of this novel is a joltingly melancholy description of Florence. Doubtless it is how Cozzens felt about the city at twenty-two. His typed manuscript reads, "I am writing of ten or more years ago, but it seems unlikely that anything I have mentioned has changed." In print the sentence is altered to: "This was ten or more years ago, but it seems unlikely that any of the things mentioned have changed." And later in the same paragraph whole sentences are removed before printing, notably this observation: "I suppose this patronizing attitude, into which I see that I have slipped, is what makes Americans so hated."

All seven of these manuscripts deserve close study for exactly this kind of stylistic revision, but none is as rewarding as *By Love Possessed*. Cozzens has preserved a first and a second text (so labeled in his own hand), the final printer's copy, the corrected galleys, and hundreds of assorted sheets of versions abandoned or altered during the novel's eight years of incubation. He wrote his editor in 1950:

> The book is called as of now: By Love Possessed. It has to do, I'm afraid at length, with a lawyer no longer young who finds his personal life in crisis (but you know me; I'll have it so hedged and qualified that the salesmen, poor willing brutes, won't hardly know it's a crisis and will just have to say as usual it's Significant) arising out of a conflict between the works of human thinking and the works of human feeling. It has long been my opinion that in the affairs of life the Law's rational design to have the facts and to prevent more from being made of them than unassisted reason makes is in flat opposition to the usually triumphant emotional wish (sometimes merely sentimental; sometimes gravely religious) to down mere 'facts' and to rise over them by a different logic where feeling counts as Higher Knowing.
>
> I have to acknowledge that I work under a limitation here in that such Knowing is utterly beyond me; yet I think it is true when I say I have no hostile feelings and no wish to deride what I do not understand; on the contrary, seeing it as I see it, I find it affecting—an example of the general wistful human persistence in make-believe. Naturally I will deal only with what I am able to know, which is the cold dismay or unhappy amazement which those whose minds can get no higher than the Law's level of common sense must find themselves experiencing when they come up against the goings-on whose origin is spiritual—specifically, my lawyer's difficulty in imagining what can possess his wife in slowly going Catholic. I don't see this as a matter to handle with theological arguments or expository conversations on doctrine or discipline, which puts me to the slightly awkward technical necessity of having his wife away when the book opens and still away when it ends. I mean to make what points I can in action—not, I hope I needn't say, the acting-out of tracts of theses, but in my man's relation to a young lawyer son, to another who died in the war, and to a considerably younger daughter, which I will try to illuminate as well as I

can by selected developments in the legal cases in which he is at the moment professionally engaged.

The history of the growth of this novel is only hinted at here; the evidence is prolific in the preserved sheets. In the course of the work's revision, Arthur Winner "lost" his Catholic wife and "gained" two others: Hope, who died in childbirth, and Clarissa, his second wife. The Catholic wife became Marjorie Penrose, and with her creation new complications began, Julius Penrose being one of them. The law offices of Orcutt & Winner became Winner, Tuttle & Winner as, probably, Noah Tuttle came into being. An especially fascinating sheet lists "Ralph's Case" followed by seven alternatives for the placing of this pivotal character, Ralph Detweiler: "a) R is Helen D's brother; b) R is the banker's son; c) R is the son of Mrs. X, NT's secretary; d) R is NT's nephew"; and so on. When, one wonders, did Cozzens make his final choice? And when did he discard this opening page of the novel?

> All Tuesday morning, in a gloom more like evening than morning, the November rain continued. It came down so hard that a low spray was raised over the pavement of Court Street and the fast run-off of cold water nearly filled the gutters. Across Court Street, behind veil on veil of rain, the white marble shape of the Brocton County Court House loomed dull in its stand of big trees. . . . Arthur Winner, at his desk in his private room in the law offices of Orcutt & Winner, looked back from this mournful morning beyond the windows.

The manuscript marked "first text" has a radically altered first page:

> When he came into the unadorned room with bright lights that Joe Harbison used for his office Arthur Winner's first care was to give Helen Detweiler a look of encouragement or reassurance. From Helen's grateful answering look, he immediately saw that she needed neither; and though he was glad of this in one way, in another that candid perfect confidence in Helen's eyes increased Arthur Winner's disquiet. On the telephone Helen's voice had been unsteady and high, full of fear; but that was half an hour ago. Now—perhaps, indeed, on the very word that Mr. Winner was coming—Helen feared no more. Faith cast fear out.

Within another five thousand words Arthur Winner is deep in the examination of Ralph Detweiler's denial of the rape charges. The "second text" has a new epigraph (from *Cymbeline*), new section titles (I. Halloween; II. All Saints' Day; III. November Second), and a substantially altered tone in the opening page though the ensuing action remains the same:

> Love, Arthur Winner thought, might come to this. By means of it the heart defeated the head. Love was the heart's freedom from the bonds of thought. Love set aside the bitter findings of true experience. Love could know for a fact what was not a fact; love untroubled believed the unbelievable; love wished, and made it so. In this, its seeming weakness, was love's strength. Love's unrealities,

realities assailed in vain. They might as well wound the loud winds, kill the still closing waters—

    Was this too much to say? No, Arthur Winner thought, it was not too much to say! Arthur Winner's first concern, when he entered the bare room with bright lights that Joe Harbison used for his office as Justice of the Peace, had been to give Helen Detweiler a look of encouragement or reassurance. He had now Helen's look in answer. It was thankful enough; but it showed him that Helen had already willed herself her own encouragement, wished her way to her own hectic reassurance. The vehemence of her feelings gave her means to believe what she needed to believe.

Is it too much to say that the steps from this text to the splendidly conceived opening paragraph of the printed version may have been legion? When did Arthur Winner's mother "grow" into the narrative, so that we might see at once, in the first paragraph, her French gilt clock with its unsettling motto: *omnia vincit amor?* In these three words we have the title; and the verb is the master. Cupid *vincit*. When, indeed, did Cozzens decide to transfer Arthur Winner's thought on love (not "too much" at all) to Arthur Winner, Sr., in still another context, on still another page, and leave us with the devastating question: "Would someone, sometime, read the motto; ponder this figured triumph of unreason, see the joke?"

    By Love Possessed is now ours to read. We have only begun to study it.

Plates

1.

i.

Arthur Winner, awakening, heard the sound of wind and
rain. A chilly raw wind blew ~~from~~ in the open window into the
bedroom whose darkness seemed no different than that of the
middle of the night. Confused, an instant, Arthur Winner regarded the darkness doubtfully, ~~an instant~~. In another instant, Repossessed of his faculties, ~~that~~
he remembered that he was going to get up early, that he wanted
to be at his office by eight. He ~~had~~ told Mrs Duffy that he
would like breakfast at half past seven. Then, before he fell
asleep, he ~~had~~ told himself to wake up at quarter to seven.
Turning his head, ~~he~~ Arthur Winner saw the luminous dial of the clock on the
small table between the beds. It ~~said~~ was exactly quarter to seven ~~exactly~~.
The dark would be the natural dark of an early morning in Novem-
ber and of a rainy day.

That he could do this --tell himself when to wake
~~up~~ and be obyed without fail, literally to the minute, was a matter
of private satisfaction to Arthur Winner. The interesting capacity ~~had~~
he had the capacity in himself
~~discovered~~ ~~itself to him~~ more than thirty years ago when he first went to
was at
It was a detail in the of learning
Law School, ~~a part of those~~ austere, really punishing regimen that
he along with ~~every~~ almost everyone else submitted themselves to.
~~struck neither him nor anyone else as excessive~~. As often as not

he would work until the library closed at midnight, go to his room,
exhausted, but still able to put himself whichever that would consequent duly
~~give himself his instructions,~~ and ~~wake~~ at five or even four to
Such a procedure struck no one as excessive or unusual
work again. It was certainly tough; it was hard, it was even painful; but of course it was also, in its austere way, very satisfying.
There was a definite exhiliration in the atmosphere; the mind,
essaying its prodigies of application and concentration felt fine.
taut, efficient, well managed, most firivlous matters disciplined

PLATE I. *By Love Possessed*, Part Three, Chapter One Opening. "B" Version

(G)   1.

i.

      Shaken ~~partly~~ awake Arthur Winner reached
mechanically for the alarm clock whose dial glowed on the
table between the beds and ended its ringing. He identified
the sound of steady rain outside the open window. The clock
meanwhile glowed in a darkness no different from that of the
middle of the night. It seemed impossible that it could be
morning and in thick confusion he could not be sure whether
the alarm clock actually had rung and had been shut off by
him an~~d~~ instant ago, or whether ~~it~~ was ~~all~~ dreaming. ~~This~~
doubt was too much for that part of his mind which, brought
to consciousness, perceived that he dreamed and that the
dream was bad. Another part, ~~which was~~ working to hold the
~~dream~~ phantasmagoria together, to continue him in it, now submerged him in
sleep, ~~so that~~ he was still attempting, or attempting again,
to reason; in impotent dismay putting it to himself: Now,
just keep calm. Go slow. Think it out...

      This difficulty, the sense of exhausting involve-
ment ~~in which he could not think~~, was what he wanted to conceal
his difficulty. It was essential.
from Dunky. While he worked to remember where this was, how he
came to be here, he looked fixedly at Dunky, saying nothing. In
fact, he must not speak until he remembered what they were talking
about. Coldly staring, he saw that Dunky could not have been to bed,
for he was fully dressed. Dunky, of course ~~wore~~ one or the other
of ~~what everyone had decided were~~ two suits, practically indistinguishable -- both black, both threadbare, both, in their mean-

PLATE 2. "G" Version

THE DREAM-MRS PRATT[1]

i.

The night had been disturbed by ~~his~~ dreams, and
Arthur Winner now struggled to leave them. He was confusedly
of the alarm clock ringing;
aware ~~that the alarm clock had rung~~ and that he had shut it
continuous
off. He had identified the sound of ~~hard~~ rain and felt the
raw
~~chill~~ breath of wind from the open window; but in the bedroom
the deep darkness of early morning in November, the delayed dawn
seemed to him to if the it
of a rainy day, ~~was no different from~~ that of the middle of the
As
night, ~~and he~~ lay in doubt, wishing to awake, to have done with
last painful sense of grief, the anxieties
~~some acute grieving~~ that was part of the dream; and yet the dream
again
would not release him. The half-awakened mind sank, submerged ~~again~~
He heard himself say
in it, ~~and he said~~ with a sarcasm of annoyance: "As it happens,
Dunklemann, the lady you saw is my wife. There's nothing wrong
about it."
neither of bad taste
In ~~irritable~~ contempt, he found himself studying Dunky
--the pale pasty face, the prominent Adam's apple working in the
scraggly, dirty-looking throat, the air of uncertain, vainly
attempted authority. Dunky wore of course one or the other of
what everyone had decided must be two suits. They were hardly
to be distinguished --both black, both threadbare, both in their
meanness of cut and material, European, ~~years ago bought cheap~~
in a poor shop in a poor quarter of some German university town.
so
Arthur Winner felt anger; the fact that Dunklemann was ~~such a poor~~
a
defenceless, wretch made it hard to answer him as he ought to be
His wounded look
answered. The resulting cruel wounds would disgust you with yourself
with   *Arthur Winner*
as well as him. "Oh, go away!" ~~he~~ said. He gave Dunky a light push;

PLATE 3. ["H"] Version

645.

1

From the peace of sleep, Arthur Winner (he could
understand) must just have stirred; even, started. To himself, MW
with deep inquietude, with tense anxiety, he was actively repeating: I must keep calm; I must reason this out.... The admonition
clearly had to do with the progress of a dream which this coming
to consciousness now suspended, ~~you~~ left, ~~viable~~ ᵖᵉⁿᵈⁱⁿᵍ ᵐ -broᵏᵉn into only;
not broken up. Though the waking mind clutched at its relief of
recognizing the dream as such ᵐ--not really real, not really happening, not really requiring such an anguished effort to grasp and to
explain ᵐ-- the dreaming mind with desperate hypnagogic attachment
would not let go, leave off. A running engine of phantasmogenesis,
powerfully engaged again, pressed him to dream on; and, little as
life, Dunky (could that man be still alive ?) aᵣgrily, excitedly,
confronted him.

        Dunky was, of course, wearing one of his two funny-
looking, European-made suits. He was as cadaverous as ever; his extraordinarily prominent adam's apple moving up and down in his skinny throat. Dunky was saying: This is unheard of, Winner; this
is impossible.... His voice was reduced to a hissing whisper. He
kept rolling his eyes apprehensively as though to see behind him
in case someone was coming up the ill-lit bare brick hall (this
place was known perfectly to Arthur Winner; but where, but when ?);
in case any ₚf the long range of doors opened. He hissed on: I am

PLATE 4. Final Version

A Note on the Texts

The texts of James Gould Cozzens's writings in this volume are from the latest corrected or revised printings of his books.

Ask Me Tomorrow. [1940]. Uniform Edition. New York: Harcourt, Brace & World, 1968.

The Last Adam. [1933]. Harvest Book. New York: Harcourt, Brace & World, 1956.

Dr. Bull, pp. 24–49.

Henry Harris, pp. 119–27.

Town Meeting, pp. 291–314.

"The Way to Go Home" [*Saturday Evening Post*, 204 (26 December 1931)]. *Children and Others*. New York: Harcourt, Brace & World, 1964, pp. 249–63.

"Every Day's a Holiday" [*Scribner's*, 94 (December 1933)]. *Children and Others*. New York: Harcourt, Brace & World, 1964, pp. 264–78.

"One Hundred Ladies" [*Saturday Evening Post*, 237 (11 July 1964)]. *Children and Others*. New York: Harcourt, Brace & World, 1964, pp. 213–32.

Men and Brethren. [1936]. Uniform Edition. New York: Harcourt Brace Jovanovich, 1970.

Ernest Cudlipp, pp. 28–44, 179–85.

"Notes on a Difficulty of Law by One Unlearned in It," *Bucks County Law Reporter*, 1 (15 November 1961), 3–7.

The Just and the Unjust. [1942]. Harvest Book. New York: Harcourt, Brace & World, 1965.

The Courtroom, pp. 110–88.

Judge Coates, pp. 423–34.

"The Impact of Intolerable Facts," published as "Those Phenomenal Initials—ATC" in the *New York Times Book Review* (24 July 1949), 1, 17.

Guard of Honor. [1948]. Harvest Book. New York: Harcourt, Brace & World, 1964.

Bus Beal, pp. 17–24.

General Nichols and Colonel Ross, pp. 388–407.

The Review, pp. 524–48.

By Love Possessed. [1957]. Harvest Book. New York: Harcourt, Brace & World, 1967.

Julius Penrose, pp. 210–42.

Julius Penrose and Arthur Winner, Jr., pp. 534–70.

Morning Noon and Night, [1968]. New York: Harcourt, Brace & World, 1968.

The Job, pp. 37–39.

The Profession of Literature, pp. 53–66, 241–50.

Cubby, pp. 96–137.

On Narrative, pp. 400–408.

"Foreword," *Roses of Yesterday* by Dorothy Stemler and Nanae Ito. Kansas City: Hallmark Cards, 1967, pp. 5–12.

"FHS: A Faith that Did Not Fail," *Father Sill's Birthday, March 10, 1956; Kent School's Fiftieth Year*. Kent, Conn.: Kent School, 1956, pp. 7–10.

"Foreword," *A Flower in Her Hair*. Bloomfield Hills, Mich. & Columbia, S. C.: Bruccoli Clark, 1974, pp. 7–10.

"Laborious Explanatory Note," *A Rope for Dr. Webster*. Bloomfield Hills, Mich. & Columbia, S. C.: Bruccoli Clark, 1976, pp. 5–72.

Letter to *Fact, James Gould Cozzens: A Checklist* by James B. Meriwether. Detroit: Bruccoli Clark/Gale, 1972, p. 86.